D1338659

DATE OF RETURN

Do Not Remove the Date Slip

F

7523203

29. JUL. 1978

LONDON BOROUGH OF RICHMOND UPON THAMES
CENTRAL LIBRARY

This book must be returned on or before the date on the slip above otherwise fines will be charged in accordance with the current rate.

You can renew your book by telephone or in person unless the book has been reserved by another reader. Please quote the NUMBER and the DATE due back.

0 571 10545 9 0110

PL.26.

JHB.

THE REVOLT OF
APHRODITE

THE REVOLT OF APHRODITE

Tunc and *Nunquam*

by

LAWRENCE DURRELL

FABER AND FABER
3 Queen Square
London

Tunc first published in 1968
Printed in Great Britain by
Latimer Trend & Co Ltd Plymouth
Nunquam first published in 1970
Printed in Great Britain by
Ebenezer Baylis & Son Ltd,
The Trinity Press, Worcester, and London
Both published in one volume 1974
as The Revolt of Aphrodite
All rights reserved

ISBN 0 571 10545 9   0110

TUNC

For

CLAUDE-MARIE VINCENDON

deux fois deux quatre, c'est un mur

Dostoievsky. *Voix Souterraine*

I

Of the three men at the table, all dressed in black business suits, two must have been stone drunk. Not Nash, the reproachful, of course not. But Vibart the publisher (of late all too frequently): and then Your Humble, Charlock, the thinking weed: on the run again. Felix Charlock, at your service. Your humble, Ma'am.

A pheasant stuffed with nominal chestnuts, a fatty wine disbursed among fake barrels in a London cellar—Poggio's, where people go to watch each other watch each other. I had been trying to explain the workings of Abel—no, you cannot have a computer with balls: but the illusion of a proximate intuition is startling. Like a buggerish astrology only more real, more concrete; better than crystal ball or divining rod. "Here we have lying about us in our infancy" (they clear their throats loudly) "a whole culture tied to a stake, whipped blind, torn apart by mastiffs. Grrr! And here we are, three men in black overcoats, ravens of ill-omen in an oak-tree." I gave a couple of tremendous growls. Heads turned towards us in meek but startled fashion. "You are still drunk Felix" (This is Nash). "No, but people as destinies are by now almost mathematically predictable. Ask Abel."

"Almost"

"Almost"

"You interest me strangely" said Vibart dozing off for a second. Emboldened Charlock continued: "I call it pogonometry. It is deduction based on the pogon (πόγον) a word which does not exist. It is the smallest conceivable unit of meaning in speech; a million pogons make up the millionth part of a phoneme. Give Abel a sigh or the birthcry of a baby and he can tell you everything."

Vibart dropped his fork on the floor, I my napkin. Leaning down simultaneously we banged our heads smartly together. (Reality is what is most conspicuous by its absence.) But it hurt, we were dazed.

"I could explain what is wrong with you" said Nash all pious, all sententious "but in psychology an explanation does not constitute a cure."

* * * * *

I was brought up by women—two old aunts in lax unmanning Eastbourne. My parents I hardly remember. They hid themselves in foreign continents behind lovely coloured stamps. Most holidays I spent silently in hotels (when the aunts went to Baden). I brought introspection to a fine art. A cid I fell into milk; a ribonuclear cid. Where was she? How would she look if she came? Abel could have told me, but he wasn't born then. Eheu!

"And what" says Nash, all perk and arrogance "could Abel tell *me*, eh?"

"A lot, Nash, quite a lot. I had you in frame not a fortnight ago. I've recorded you frequently on the telephone. Something about a woman who lay on your horsehair couch, eyes shut, exciting you so much by a recital of her sins that you found you were masturbating. A real psi experience. Like religious confessors knee deep in sperm leaning forward in the confessional so as not to miss the smallest excuse for absolution. I didn't bother to find out her name. But Abel knows. Now where is your Hippocratic oath? You let her smash up the transference because she wanted to do it with you there and then. Daddy! I have your squeaks and gasps; afterwards to do you justice you swore and shed tears and walked up and down."

Nash lets off a screech like a parrot; he is on his feet, scarlet, his mouth fallen open on its hinges. "Lies" he shouts.

"Very well, lies; but Abel cannot lie. You must try and imagine it this way—as Abel sees it, with that infallible inner photoelectric eye of his. He X-rays time itself, photographing a personality upon the gelatine surface of flux. Look, I press a button, and your name and voice rise together like toast in a toast-rack. The fascia blaze blue, topaz, green, white. I spin the needles and they pass through the fixed

12

points of a sort of curriculum vitae. The basic three points are birth-love-death."

Vibart gives a burst of hysterical laughter; tears crowd his eyes. We are going to be asked to leave at any moment now.

"Now if you take a simple geometrical progression, a scale, you can elaborate your graph until the needle passes through an infinity of points: whatever you choose to set up—say, jobs, skills, size, pigmentation, I.Q., temperament repressions, beliefs. . . . You see the game? No, there's nothing wrong with cogito or with sum; it's poor bloody ergo that's been such a curse. The serial world of Tunc whose God is Mobego. But come, we mustn't be cry-babies, mustn't pout."

I suddenly felt the need to vomit. Leaning my cold head against the colder glass wall of the urinal I continued. "As for me, scientifically speaking the full terror of death has not informed my loving. Ah Nash, my boy. I was a gland short." Ah Benedicta, I might have added under my breath. He holds my head while I am sick: but he is still trembling with rage at this astonishing exposure of his professional shortcomings.

I am forced to laugh. This carefully prepared hoax, I mean, about Abel. Actually I got the facts from the girl herself. At last my stomach comes to rest again. "The firm has given and the firm has taken away, blessed be the name of the firm" I intoned.

"Listen" says Nash urgently. "For godsake don't develop a delusional system like so many have. I implore you."

"Pish! Abel has coordinated all the psi-factors. A computer which can see round corners, think of it! On the prospectus it says distinctly 'All delusional systems resolved'; now what is our civilisation but a . . . ribonucleic hangover, eh? Why, Abel could even give you a valency notion for literature. Jerk, jerk, jerk, you in your swivel chair, she on her couch."

"I've told you it's a lie" he shouts.

"Very well."

Myself I much needed to be loved—and look what happens. At full moon in Polis, when cats conjugate the verb "to be", I held the thousandth and second night in incompetent arms watching the silver climb the cold thermometers of the minarets. Ach! I yark all this gibberish up for little dactyl my famulus; faithfully the little machine compiles it. To what end? I want the firm to have it, I want Julian to have to wade through it. When I am dead, of course, not before.

Iolanthe, in this very room, once removed the spectacles from my nose—like one lifts the lid from a jar of olives—in order to kiss me. Years later she starts to have a shadowy meaning for me, years later. While I had her, possession of her, I was quite unaware that she loved me. I had eyes for nobody but Benedicta. With her things were different, floating between rauwolfia-induced calms. Something had jumbled up her inner economy, she had never had a period: would the brain poisoning have started from this? I don't know. But I started things off. "Now" she says "I am bleeding at last, profusely bleeding: thanks to you, my darling Felix, thanks to you. Now I know I shall have a child." Well, and what came of all that? Answer me that, gentlemen of the jury. Rolling back to the alcove table to join Vibart my mind oscillates between the two women once more. Iolanthe talking of her film husband: "Always accusing me of not loving him, of not *trying*; but just when you're trying your best to come off an irrational thought crosses your mind and freezes you: if I forgot to turn off the stove those pigeons will be cinders."

Nash trots along beside me holding my sleeve. "I have an awful feeling you are going to try and break away, make a run for it. Tell me Felix? For goodness sake don't. The firm would always find you, you know." I gave him an owlish glance. "I have been granted leave by the firm" said firmly. "Up to two years' sick leave."

"Ah well. That's better." Nash was vastly relieved.

"I am going to the South Seas on legitimate leave."

"Why there?"

"Because it's like everywhere else nowadays. Why not?"

Is that why I am in Athens? Yes, just to make things a little difficult for them. Vindictive Felix. Partly that, but also partly because I had a sudden desire to come back to the point from which all the lines sprang out—the point of convergence being little Number Seven in this flyblown hotel. One candle and by God, the little wooden pattens which recently turned up in a suitcase full of junk—the very pattens of Iolanthe. The survival value of objects never ceases to puzzle and enthral me. People, yes, they turn up again and again, but for a limited time. But things can go on for centuries, quietly changing their owners when they tire of them: or quietly changing their owners *tout court*. I am terribly tired. Most of the pre-recorded and digested stuff I have fed into Abel—for the computer is simply a huge lending library of the mind—most of it has passed through these little dactyls, as I call them. Do you think it would be possible to resume a whole life in terms of predestination? I have imagined my own so thoroughly that you can switch it on like an obituary. The two women, one dark and one graven fair; two brothers, one darkness one light. Then the rest of the playing cards, catalogues of events, humble contingencies. A sable history! Well I've brought it up to this point. Abel must be carrying it on. Just pull the lever on the sign manual and traverse across the fascia marked "contingent data". Every sensible man should make a will. . . . But only after a long, wasteful and harmful detour across the parching watersheds of celebrity, financial success. I, Felix Charlock, being sound in mind and body ha ha do hereby etc etc. Not that I have anything much to leave; the firm has got its hands upon everything except for a few small private treasures like the dactyls here, my latest invention. I found a way to get the prototypes built without them finding out. Hardly larger than a lady's dressing case, she is a masterpiece of compression, as light as a feather. What is it?

Come closer, I will tell you. The dactyl was designed for those who talk endlessly to themselves, for Everyman that is. Also for a lazy man, such a one as myself who has an abhorrence for ink and paper. You speak and she records: more than that, she transcribes. The low feminine voice (the frequency dictated my choice) encodes the words and a tiny phonetic alphabet, no larger than a lama's prayer wheel, begins to purr. From the snout marked A the tip of the foolscap protrudes, and goes on slowly extending until with a sniff the whole page is evacuated, faultlessly typed. How is that done? Ah, that is what any firm would like to know. Nor is there any limit to the amount of dactyl's work, save lack of paper or a failing torch battery. But it is easy to see why the toy is so valuable—it could put all the stenographers in the world out of business in a matter of weeks. Moreover the machine will sensitise to an individual voice to such a degree that she accepts a code-tone instead of a switch. This is arbitrary, of

15

course. But in my case "*Konx*" will set her off, while "*Om*" will cut her out. She has made a joke of the laborious anachronism of typing. Yet I did not dare to try and take out a patent in my name, for the firm keeps a watchful eye on the Patents Office. They are at once informed when something new is in the wind . . . Julian anyway.

The reasons I have for wanting to get away are various and complex; the more superficial being self-evident, but the more profoundly buried inexpressibly difficult to expose, despite my relative experience with words. After all, the books are decently written, even though they deal with mechanics, electronics and that sort of thing. But if I were to apply a little archaeology to my case I would come upon the buried cultures of deeper predispositions I suppose which determined what I was to become? On the one hand, purely superficially, I could date my existence from the moment when, with a ball of thin twine and two empty cigarette tins, I managed to make an imitation of the telephone. Ting a ling! Nothing very strange about that, you will say; the old Bell system was clear as daylight even to a schoolboy. But then let me take a plunge in another direction. I gradually came to equate invention with creation—perhaps too presumptuously? Yet the symptoms are much the same, are they not? Anxiety, fever, migraine, anorexia nervosa, cyclothymia, (The Mother!) . . . yes, all the happy heralds of the epileptic fit. An intense strain, sense of dispersal. Then, quite suddenly the new idea breaking free from the tangle of dreams and fevers—Bang! That's how it is with me. The pain was in allowing the damned thing to ferment, to form in the imagination. In my youth I had not learned to recognise the signs. When my teeth began to chatter I suspected an attack of malaria. I had not learned to luxuriate in the convenience of a nervous breakdown. What rubbish!

Well, I have been off the map for some days now, alone in Athens with my famulus, doing a little occupational therapy every day in the form of these autobiographical notes! I have been delayed in my quest for Koepgen; the one man who could tell me where he is is out of Athens and nobody knows for how long. *Om.*

* * * * *

16

I went to see Nash in a purely formal way: I have always got on with him. He can rise to a joke on occasions, plonk! Like all analysts he is highly neurotic, leashing his hysteria with little grins and yawns and airs of omniscience. Take off glasses, cough, tap thumb, adjust paper flower in button-hole. I make him, I think, feel a little uncomfortable; he wonders no doubt how much I know about everything, for is not Benedicta his patient? We sparred gracefully in the fashion of well-educated Englishmen overcompensating. He was not surprised to   I was going away for a rest. I did not mention the firm but I   see the thought flicker across his mind. Did the firm know wher   es, the firm knew where—I took care to tell all my friends where: Already no doubt a message had flashed out to our agent the   find a large pink blotchy man in a Panama hat waiting shyly   for me. Quietly, tactfully, unobtrusively my arrival would b   reported upon. "I suppose you are just tired" he said. "Yet   ause for it. You've done nothing for months now, locked up do   tshire. You are a lucky man Charlock. Except for Benedicta's   have everything." I watched him quizzically and he had the   blush. Then he burst out laughing with a false heartiness. We un   ood each other only too well, Nash and I. Wait till I tell him a   Abel, just wait.

"Shall we talk syllogistically, Nash, or just talk? Causa   y is an attempt to mesmerise the world into some sort of significan   We cannot bear its indifference." Tears came into his eyes, con   o-pathetic tears, left over from laughter turned sour. "I know you a   sick of your job, and just about as ill as I am, if I *am* ill." He blew out a windy lip and gave me a cunning sidelong glance. "You sound as if you have been playing with R.N.A. It's dangerous, Charlock. You will miss a step and go sprawling among the archetypal symbols.

We'll have to reserve you a room in Paulhaus." That was the firm's private mental asylum. "It is true" I said "that I wake up with tears pouring down my face, sometimes of laughter, sometimes of plain tears."

"There, you see?" he said triumphantly. He crossed and uncrossed his legs. "You had better take some action smartly, go on a rest cure, write another scientific book."

"I am off to Tahiti. Gauguin was here."

"Good."

"Inventors are a happy laughing breed." I stifled a sob and yawned instead. "Nash, is your laughter a cry for help?"

"Everyone's is. When do you go?"

"Tonight. Let me give you lunch."

"Very well."

"The glands all down one side are swollen—the sense of humour is grossly inflamed. Let us go to Poggio's."

He was pouring out Chianti when Vibart put in an appearance—my publisher, purple with good living: a kind of tentative affability about him whenever he spoke about the book he wanted me to write for him. "The age of autobiography." He solicited Nash's good offices in the matter. He knew too that over all these years I had been dribbling into recorders of one sort or another. A friend of twenty years' standing I first encountered here, yes, in Athens: dear old slowcoach of a horse-tramway buried in some minor proconsular role with his cabinets of birds' eggs. And here was Vibart persuading poor Felix to quit quasars and debouch into memoirs. I drank deeply of the wine and smiled upon my two friends in clownish gag. What was to be done with them?

"Please Charlock" he was fearfully drunk.

"Let those who have a good bedside manner with a work of art throw the first stone."

"Nash, can't you convince him?"

"Flippancy is a form of alienation" said Nash rather to my surprise; nevertheless I could not resist making dear Vibart sing once more "The Publisher's Boating Song". We were always asked to leave when he did this. I beat time with my fork.

Lord, you may cancel all my gifts,
I feel they can be spared
So long as one thing still remains,
My pompe à merde

My books will stand the test of slime
My fame be unimpaired
So long as you will leave me, Lord,
My pompe à merde.

To my surprise, despite angry glances, we survive this outburst.
Vibart has just been acclaimed Publisher of the Year by the Arts
Guild; he owes his celebrity to an idea of breathtaking simplicity.
Who else would have thought of getting Bradshaw translated into
French? The effect on the French novel has been instantaneous. As
one man they have rallied to this neglected English genius. Vibart
bangs the table and says in a sort of ecstasy: "It's wonderful! They
have reduced *events to incidents*. It's truthful to your bloody science,
Felix. Non-deterministic. In Nash's terms it would be pure catatonia.
Hurrah. We don't want to get well. No more novels of the castration
complex. Do you like the idea of the God of Abraham advancing on
you with his golden sickle to cut off your little—your all too little bit
of mistletoe?" He points a ghastly finger at Nash, who recoils with a
shudder. "Nevermore" continues my friend thickly. "No more
goulash-prone Hungarian writers for me, no more *vieux jew*, I spit
on all your frightened freckled little minds. I'm rich! Hurrah.
Bookstalls display me which heretofore were loaded with nothing
but blood-coooling sex-trash. No more about sex, it's too boring.
Everyone's got one. Nastiness is a real stimulant though—but poor
honest sex, like dying, should be a private matter."

His voice failed and faltered; I noticed the huge circles under his
eyes. His wife committed suicide last month; it must do something
to a man's pride. One says one is not to blame and one isn't. Still.
Quickly change the subject.

We could see that he was rippling with anxiety, like wet washing
on the line. Said Nash unkindly, "He needs a rest, does Felix, O
yes."

Yes, this was true.

Yes, this was true.

I remember Koepgen talking of what he called the direct vision, the Autopsia. In a poem called "The relevance of thunder". In the Russian lingo. "Futility may well be axiomatic: but to surprise oneself in the act of dying might be one way to come thoroughly awake, no?" I let out another savage growl. The waiters jumped. Ah! They are converging on us at last.

Later, leaning out of the taxi window I say in a deep impressive voice. "I have left you a message written on the wall of the Gents at Claridges. Please go there and read it." My two friends exchange a glance. Some hours earlier, a bag-fox drunk on aniseed, I had written in my careful cursive, "I think the control of human memory is essential for any kind of future advance of the species. The refining of false time is the issue." I did not leave any instructions about how to deal with the piggybank. It was enough to go on with for people like Nash. I waved them goodbye in a fever of health.

In the southbound train I read (aloud) the Market Report in *The Times*, intoning it like a psalm, my breast filled with patriotism for Merlins.

MILAN

The bourse opened quiet yesterday but increased buying interest spread to a number of sectors including quicksilvers, properties, textiles, and insurances, giving way to a generally firmer trend. Towards the close there was brisk buying of leaders with Viscosa and Merlin prominent.

AMSTERDAM

Philips, Unilever and Royal Dutch opened lower but later met some demand on some local and Swiss demand.

BRUSSELS

The forward market was quiet and prices showed little change.

FRANKFURT

Reversed the recent weaker trend in initial dealings and showed a majority of gains later: the close was friendly with gains generally up to seven points.

PARIS

Sentiment improved slightly under the lead of metallurgical shares, notably Merlin, which were firm.

20

Quiet but easier.

Prices moved higher. All major industrial groups, along with rails, participated in the upturn. Market quarters looking for a significant summer rally found much to bolster their hopes. Among companies reporting improved net income were: Bethlehem Steel, Phelps Dodge, Standard Oil, Merlin Group.

On the blackboard in the senior boardroom of Merlin House I had left them some cryptic memoranda for their maturer deliberations like

> motor cars made from compressed paper
> paper made from compressed motor cars
> flesh made from compressed ideals
> ideas made from compressed impulses.

They will take it all seriously. So it is. So it is. Really it is.

Watching the trees go by and the poles leap and fall, leap and fall, I reflected on Merlin and on the F. of F. The Fund of Funds, the Holy Grail of all we stood for. Nash had said so often recently: "I hope you are not thinking about trying to escape from the firm, Charlock. It wouldn't work, you know?" Why? Because I had married into it? *Vagina Vinctrix!* At what point does a man decide that life must be lived *unhesitatingly*? Presumably after exhausting every other field—in my case the scientific modes: science, its tail comes off in your hand like a scared lizard. ("The response to shadow in the common flat-worm is still a puzzle to biologists. Then again, in the laboratory, inside a sealed test-tube the gravitational pull of the tides still obtains, together with the appropriate responses.")

Yes, he was right, I was going to try and free myself. "*Start*" Koepgen used to say wryly, sharply, lifting his glass, little drops of ouzo spilling on to the cheap exercise book which houses the loose nerve ends of poems which later, at dead of night, he would articulate. "Tap Tap, the chick raps on the outer shell in order to free itself—literature! Memory and identity. *Om.*"

★   ★   ★   ★   ★

But before leaving I did what I have so frequently done in the past—paid a visit to Victoria Station, to stand for a while under the clock. A sentimental indulgence this—for the only human fact that I know about my parents was that they met here for the first time. Each had been waiting for someone quite different. The clock decided my fate. It is the axis, so to speak, of my own beginning. (The first clocks and watches were made in the shape of an egg.) Seriously, I have often done this, to spend a moment or two of quiet reflection here: an attempt perhaps to reidentify them among the flux and reflux of pallid faces which seethes eternally about this mnemotopic spot. Here one can eat a dampish Wimpy and excogitate on the nature of birth. Well, nothing much comes of this thought, these moments of despairing enquiry. The crowd is still here, but I cannot identify their lugubrious Victorian faces. Yet they belonged I suppose to this amorphous pale collection, essence of the floating face and vote, epitome of the "90 per cent don't know" in every poll. I had the notion once of inventing something to catch them up, a machine which solidified echoes retrospectively. After all one can still see the light from technically dead stars. . . . But this was too ambitious.

Perhaps (here comes Nash) I might even trace my obsession with the construction of memory-tools to this incoherent desire to make contact? Of course now they are a commonplace; but when I began to make them the first recording-tools were as much a novelty, as the gramophone appears to have been for primitive African tribes in the 'eighties. So Hippolyta found them, my clumsy old black boxes with their primitive wires and magnets. The development of memory! It led me into strange domains like stenography, for example. It absorbed me utterly and led me to do weird things like learning the whole of *Paradise Lost* by heart. In the great summer sweats of this broken-down capital I used to sit at these tasks all night, only pausing to play my fiddle softly for a while, or make elaborate notes in those yellow exercise books. Memory in birds, in mammals, in violinists. Memory and the instincts, so-called. Well, but this leads nowhere I now think; I equipped myself somewhat before my time as a sound engineer. Savoy Hill and later the BBC paid me small sums to supply library stock—Balkan folk-songs for example; a Scots University collected Balkan accents in dialect in order to push forward studies in phonetics. Then while messing about with the structure of the human ear as a sound bank I collided with the firm. Bang. *Om.*

Victoria, yes: and thence to the bank to transfer funds to Tahiti. Then to my club to pick up mail and make sure that all the false trails were well and truly laid: paper trails followed by vapour trails traced upon the leafskin of the Italian sky. Then to drift softer than thistledown through the violet-chalky night, skimming over the Saronic Gulf. Charlock on a planned leave-of-absence from the consumer's world. Second passport in the name of Smith.

> *"Hail, O Consumer's Age" the voices boomed,*
> *But which consumer is, and which consumed?*

As might have been expected I caught a glimpse of one of the firm's agents hanging about the airport, but he was not interested in the night-passengers, or was waiting for someone else, and I was able without difficulty to sneak into the badly lit apron where the creaking little bus waited to carry me north to the capital.

The taste of this qualified freedom is somewhat strange still; I feel vaguely at a loss, like a man must who hears the prison doors close on his release after serving a long sentence. (If time had a watermark like paper one could perhaps hold it up to the light?) I quote.

Yet the little hotel, it is still here. So is the room—but absolutely unchanged. Look, here are the ink stains I made on the soiled marble mantelpiece. The bed with its dusty covers is still hammock-shaped. The dents suggest that Iolanthe has risen to go to the bathroom. In the chipped coffin of the enamel bath she will sit soaping her bright breasts. I am delighted to find this point of vantage from which to conduct my survey of the past, plan the future, mark time.

23

Iolanthe, Hippolyta, Caradoc . . . the light of remote stars still giving off light without heat. How relative it seems from Number Seven, the little matter of the living and the dead. Death is a matter of complete irrelevance so long as the memory umbilicus holds. In the case of Iolanthe not even a characteristic nostalgia would be permissible; her face, blown to wide screen size, has crossed the continents; a symbol as potent as Helen of Troy. Why here on this bed, in the dark ages of youth. . . . Now she has become the 18-foot smile.

Junior victims of the Mediterranean *gri gri* were we; learning how to smelt down the crude slag of life. Yes, some memories of her come swaying in sideways as if searching deliberately for "the impacted line which will illumine the broad sway of statement".

The grooves of the backbone were drilled in a tender white skin which reminded one of the whiteness of Easter candles. On the back of the neck the hair came down to a point, a small tuft of curl. The colouring of Pontus and Thrace are often much lighter than those of metropolitan Greece—vide Hippolyta with her ravenswing darkness and olive eye. No, Io had the greyish green eye and the hair tending towards ash-blonde which were both gifts from Circassia. The sultans used to stock their harems with toys such as these; the choicest colourings were such, lime-green eyes and fine fair curls. Well, anyway, these tricklings through the great dam of the past cannot touch her now—the legendary Iolanthe; she may have forgotten them even, left them to litter the cutting rooms of gaunt studios in the new world. For example, I had trouble to get her to shave under the arms; in common with all girls of her class, the prostitutes of Athens, she believed that men were aroused by an ape-swatch under each arm. Perhaps they were. Now however when she raises her slender arms on the screen like some bewigged almond tree the pits beneath them are smooth as an auk's egg.

The young man that I was then cannot escape the charge of exercising a certain duplicity towards her; he condescended, letting his narcissism have full sway. Well, I don't know, many factors were involved. This little angel had dirty toes and was something of a thief I believe. I found some notes from this period whose irrelevance proves that even then Charlock had an obstinate vein of introspection running along parallel, so to speak, with his mundane life of action. The second, the yellow exercise book—the one with the drawings of the cochlea and the outline for my model deafness-aid—had other kinds of data thrown about in it.

Walking about Athens at night he might note: "The formication, the shuddering-sweet melting almost to faintness. . . . Why, the structure of the genitals is particularly adapted to such phenomena, Bolsover. (Bolsover was my tutor at Kings. I still converse with him mentally in prose and worse.) The slightest friction of a white hand will alert the dense nerve ganglia with their great vascularity. The affect disperses itself through the receiving centres of the autonomic nervous system, solar plexus, hypogastric plexus, and lumbosacral or pelvic. . . . Hum. The kiss breaks surface here. The autobiography of a single kiss from Iolanthe. Note also, Bolsover, that in embryology the final organ is progressively differentiated from an anlage—which may be defined as the first accumulation of cells recognisable as the commencement of the final organ. This is about as far as one can go; but even this is not far enough back for me. Surely once in the testes of my old man, in the ape-gland once, *I was*?"

These problems brought sadness and perplexity to my loving. I would light a candle and examine the sleeping figure with concern for its mysterious history; it seemed to me that it might be possible to trace back the undermeanings of pleasure and pain, an unreasonable wish I now recognise. Ass. Ape. Worm.

Her teeth were rather fine and small with just a trace of irregularity in their setting—enough to make her smile at once rueful and ravenous. She was too self-indulgent to husband her efforts in the professional sense—or perhaps too honest not to wish to give service? She could be blotted out sexually and retire into an exhaustion so extreme as to resemble death. Poor Iolanthe never got enough to eat so it was easy for a well-fed man to impose orgasm after orgasm on her until she reached the point of collapse. In our case the thing worked perfectly—indeed so perfectly that it puzzled her; we ignited each other like engines tuned to perfect pitch. Of course this is purely a technical question—one of perfect psychic and physical fit—queer there is not a science of it, nor a school in which one can try it out experimentally. If we could apply as much exactitude to sexual habits as, say, a machine turner to his toys, much unhappiness in love could be avoided. In an age of advanced technology it is surprising that no attention is given to such problems. Yes, even with her eyes closed, piously trying to think about something else in order to avoid exhaustion: even then, the surf carried her irresistibly to the other beach, rolled her up into the blessed anonymity of the fading second. Sometimes he shook her awake simply to stare into her eyes. But if at such moments she had asked him what he was thinking he would probably have replied: "The true cancer cell, in the final analysis, an oxygen-deficiency cell, a poorly breathing cell, according to Schmidt. When you coughed I suddenly saw in the field of my instrument a patch of tubercule bacilli stained with eosin to a pretty red—anemones in some Attic field." People deprived of a properly constituted childhood will always find something hollow in their responses to the world, something unfruitful. You could accuse both of us of that, in order to explain the central lack. The weakness of the marrow. A racing heart. Of course other factors help, like environment, language, age. But the central determinant of situations like this is that buried hunger which is only aggravated by the sense of emotional impotence. *Om*.

II

The Parthen[on]
in some poor w[...]
real science." We[...]
of female pudenda.[...]
—hardly a corner of [...]
its proportions gave i[...]
enamel air the human v[...]
and wave to her from th[...]
below. "I-O-lanthe!" Not[...]
syllable not the third, and tha[...] w she
is known to the world in a hid[...] n with the
stress on the third syllable. Act[...], as it makes her
real name private property. She [...], to Number Seven,
and to the Nube, to the eternal Ath[...] ich miraculously still sur-
vives outside memory. In that mirror over there she wrestled with
her eyebrows which had a tendency to grow too thickly. You should
see them now—single soft lines of the purest jet. Though the room
squints out on the marbles we dared not open a shutter until dusk;
we lived all day in brown shadow like carp in a cool pool. Until sunset.

Sunset! Wake suddenly against the lighted wall and you have the
momentary impression that the whole marble spook has taken fire
and is curling up like burning cardboard. You put your hand to the
hideous wallpaper and feel the actual heat of the mere reflection—or
so you imagine. Up there outside the honey-coloured marbles, after
a full day's exposure to the sun, echo on the heat long after nightfall,
temperature of mammals' blood. Gradually the light sweats dried ...
stomachs gummed together like wet leaves. Yawning and smoking
they lay about in whispers. She has a toy vocabulary and an island
accent.

29

whiteness of
..., veers, founders.
...nettus and into the sea
...islands to glow like embers
...eillumine. (They lie beside each
...s but would break the curvature of the
...radually leaks up from Salamis the smell
...ions, tar, borne on the breath of the evening
...will soothe wet armpits and breasts.

...d been refugees from Pontus, and had trekked down with
...cing bear to settle in Crete. When the bear died (their only
means of livelihood) they had a last tearful meal of the paws in oil. A
smallholding barely sustained her parents. To lighten the burden
she had come to Athens in search of work—with the inevitable result,
for work there was none. When she described these days she stood
up and acted the bear, the padding and jingling of paw and bell, the
harsh panting. The froth gathered at its snout where the iron ring
ran through. It was half blind, the whip had struck out an eye.

The sheet had lipstick-marks on it, also the tooth-mug; our shoes
lay side by side like fish. But she was gay, friendly, almost mannish in
her directness and simplicity. A gaily coloured little parrot from an
island. In those days for a whole summer black fingernails were *de
rigueur* among her friends and workmates. This beastly shellac stuff
used to peel off on to the sheet. Her one brother had "gone to the
bad"; her lip shut on the phrase, framing it instantly in the harsh
rectangle of peasant judgement. Had she, then, "gone to the good"?
It was an attempt at a pleasantry which miscarried; her long underlip shot out, she was in tears. During the microfield tests on Abel I
sifted a good deal of this stuff about her through the field, and the
king of computers came back in oracular fashion with some chunks
taken from another field—Koepgen I think. It was all about love, its
scales. (After Io leaves I can watch her from the window. She takes
the crooked path up the side of the Acropolis, swaying a little, as if
she were a trifle tipsy, hand to heart.)

Thus Abel: "If we could only make all time proximate to reality
we could see a little more deeply into the heart of our perplexities;
the syzygy with its promise of a double silence is equally within the

grasp of man or woman. If ever they combine forces in their field you might speak of loving as something more than a term for an unclassifiable animal. It is unmistakable when it does happen for it feels as if the earth had subtly shifted its epicentre. How sad it seems that we, images of insipid spoonmeat, spend our time in projecting such strange figures of ourselves—delegated images of a desire perfected. The mystical gryphus, the 'perfect body' of the Alexandrian psychology, is an attempt on a telenoetic field. (What space is to matter, soul is to mind.) Some saints were 'dry-visioned'. (Jerk, jerk, but nothing comes; taking the 'distressful path' towards after-images of desire.) They were hunting, poor buggers, for a renovated meaning or an infantile adoption by a God. Unhappily words won't carry the charge in these matters, hence the deficit of truth in all verbal fields. This is where your artist might help. "A craft is a tongue, a tongue is a key, a key is a lock." On the other hand a system is merely the shy embrace by which the poor mathematician hopes to persuade his bride to open up." Koepgen never met her, I think, yet at his best he seems to be talking about her.

* * * * *

My frail old black recorders with their clumsy equipment were a source of the greatest concern; jolting about as they did with me on country buses, on caiques, even on mules. My livelihood depended on their accurate functioning, and this is where Said came in. The little watchmaker was a friend of Io. One-eyed, mission school, Christian Arab, he had his little workshop in a rotting hut in the Plaka, more fitting for rabbits than for a workman capable of craftsmanship of such extraordinary delicacy. Mud floor, fleas jumping in the straw and nibbling our ankles; we spent hours together, sometimes half the night, at his little workbench. He copied from any drawing. One-eyed Said with his watery optic pressed to a butter-coloured barrel, among the litter of fusees and escapements and hairs. Eager and modest in discussion of trade topics such as the use of invar etc. He made my echo amplifiers in a couple of weeks. Small as a garden pea, and beautifully done in mother of pearl. Graphos now! But I will be coming to that.

It was the recorders that brought me to the notice of Hippolyta. Vivid in a baroque hat like a watering can she dispensed tea and éclairs in the best hotel, coiling and uncoiling her slender legs as she questioned me about the mysteries of the black box, wondering if I could record a speech which was to be made by some visiting dignitary. My impression squared with all I heard afterwards of her public reputation. It was typical of back-biting Athens that she sounded so unsavoury a figure; the truth was that she was a mixture of naivety and wrong-headedness punctuated with strange generosities. The hard voice with its deeper tones and the fashionable boldness of the dark eyes were overcompensating for qualities like shyness which even her social practice had not enabled her entirely to throw off. The green scarf and the blood-red fingernails gave her a pleasantly old-fashioned vampire's air. "O please could you do that for me?" She named a figure in drachmae so high that my heart leapt, it would keep me for a month; and held my hand a trifle longer than formality permits. She was a warm, pleasantly troubling personage. Despite the impressive jewellery and the orchids she seemed more like a youth than a girl. Of course I accepted, and taking an advance made my way back to the Plaka delighted by such good fortune. She promised to let me know when the person in question—the speech-maker—arrived. "I can't help liking slightly hysterical women" I confided to the Parthenon.

At Spiro's tavern, under the vine-trellis, I paused for a drink and caught sight of a familiar object at an empty table; the little yellow exercise book which Koepgen used for theology and musing alike. It lay there with his pen and a daily paper. He must have gone to the lavatory. At this time Koepgen was a theological student embarking on the grim path of monkhood. A typical product of white Russia, he spoke and wrote with equal ease in any of four languages. He taught me Greek, and was invaluable on out-of-the-way factors like the phonetics of this hirsute tongue; things like the Tsaconian dialect, still half anc. Doric. Well I sat and riffled while I waited.

"The *hubris*, the overweening, is always there; but it is a matter of scale. The Greeks traced its path with withering accuracy, watching it lead on to *ate*—the point at which evil is mistakenly believed to be good. Here we are then at the end of the long road—races dehumanised by the sorceries of false politics." Koepgen weeping for Russia again. I always want to shout "stop it!" At last he stood before me, full of a devout nonchalance. He was a small dapper man, contriving to look clean despite the threadbare soutane and grotesque smelly boots. His long hair, captured in a bun, was always clean. He seldom wore his stovepipe hat. He reproached me for my inquisitiveness and sat down smiling to hear my tale of good fortune. Of Hippolyta he said: "She is adorable, but she is connected with all sorts of other things. I came across her recently when I did some paid translation —O just business letters—for an organisation, a firm I suppose, in Salonika. She organised it. But something about it gave me an uncomfortable feeling. They offered me very large sums to keep on with the work, but I let it drop. I don't know quite why. I wanted to keep myself free in a way. I need less and less money, more and more time."

C

There are other data, floating about like motes in a sunbeam, waiting to find their place: the equipment in the abortioner's leather bag. The needle-necked appurtenances which mock the spunk-scattering troubadours of a courtly love. The foetus of a love-song. ("One way" wrote Koepgen "might be to take up Plutarch's idea of the Melisponda. This should be within the grasp of anyone.") Mara the hag with a pair of tongs worked off a car-battery. I am not so sure whether in the brothels of Piraeus he did not achieve the *mare pigrum* of the philosophers and alchemists. Here one bares one's sex to a whole landscape—internal landscapes of empty sea, nigger-head coral, bleached tree-trunks, olive-pits burnt by lye. Islands (each one a heart and mind) where the soft spirals of waves shoulder and sheathe floors awash with the disquiet of palaces submerged in folded ferns. Symbol of the search is the diver with the heavy stone tied to his belt. Sponges!

Then lying about among my own records I come upon some stone memoranda like altars and tombs; stuck in among them some moments of alarming happiness. If the portly Pausanias had seen the city's body through that of a young street-walker his catalogues would have had more life. Names and stones would have become the real fictions and we the realities. After dark we often sneak through the broken fence and climb to the cave below the Propylea. Her toes are fearfully dirty in her dusty sandals, as are mine, but her hair is freshly washed and scentless. We are never quite alone up here. A few scattered cigarette-points mark the places where other lovers wander, or lie star-gazing. Up on these ledges in winter you will find that the southern gales carry up the faint crying of sea-mews, sacred to Aphrodite; while in the spring the brown-taffeta nightingales send out their quiet call-sign in the very voice of Itys. "Itú, Itú, Itú" they cry in pretty iteration. Then by moonlight come the little

34

owls. They are tame. (No more!) Turning their necks in strange rhythms—clearest origin for ancient Greek masked dancing.

Down below in the later sequences of the play the tombs face east with their pathetic promise of resurrection. The modern town rolls over it all like surf. Prismatic gleams of oil-patches on macadam; coffee-grounds and the glitter of refuse (fish-scales) outside the smelly taverns with their climbing trellises and shelves of brown barrels. Once a golden apple was a passport to the underworld, but today I am only able to buy her a toffee-apple on a stick which she dips in sherbet, licking it like a tame deer.

A true Athenian, free from all this antiquarian twaddle, she knows and cares nothing for her city; but yes, some of the stories alert a fugitive delight as she sits, sugaring her kisses with her apple. It is pleasant to babble thus, floundering among the telescopic verb-schemes of demotic; telling her how Styx water was so holy as to be poisonous, only to be safely drunk from a horse's hoof. They poisoned Alexander this way. Also how Antony once set up his boozing shop in the Parthenon, though his was a different sort of poisoning, a chronic narcissism. (She crosses herself superstitiously as a good Orthodox should, and snuggles superstitiously up to me.) Then . . . about embalming bodies in honey—human toffee-apples: or curing sick children by making them swallow mice coated in honey. Ugh! But excited by this she responds by telling me of witches and spells which cause nausea and impotence and can only be fought with talismans blessed by a priest. All this with such earnestness that out of polite belief I also make the sign of the Byzantine cross, back to front, to ward off the harms of public utterance from us both. ("There is no difference between truth and reality—ask any poet." Thus Koepgen sternly, eyes blazing, a little drunk on ouzo.) The quiet wind blew dustily uphill among the moon-keepers. To make love in this warm curdled air seemed an act of unpremeditated simplicity that placed them back once more in the picture-book world sacred to the animal kingdom where the biological curve of the affect is free from the buggerish itch of mentation. Warm torpid mouth, strong arms, keen body—this seems all the spiritual instruction the human creature needs. It is only afterwards that one will be thrown back sprawling among the introspections and doubts. How many people before Iolanthe? Throats parched in the dry air we drink thirstily from the sacred spring. She washes the sugar from her lips, washes her privates in the icy water, drying them on my old silk scarf. No, Athens was not like other places; and the complicated language, with its archaic thought-forms, shielded its strangeness from foreign eyes. Afterwards to sit at a tin table in a tavern, utterly replete and silent, staring at each other, fingers touching, before two glasses of colourless raki and a plate of olives. Everything should have ended there, among the tombs, by the light of a paraffin lamp. Perhaps it did?

*   *   *   *   *

The news of Caradoc's coming was conveyed to me by Hippolyta one fine Sunday afternoon; once more bidden to tea, I found her in a corner of the Bretagne where she kept a suite permanently available, playing patience among the palms. She looked a little less forbidding this time I thought, though she was fashionably turned out in the styles of the day. Bejewelled, yes, but this time without much warpaint. Moreover she was short-sighted I noticed; raising a lorgnon briefly towards me as I advanced, she smiled. The optic changed her clever aquiline face, giving it a juvenile and somewhat innocent expression. The eyes were noble, despite their arrogance of slant. She was immediately likeable, though less beautiful this time than last. I compared her mentally to her reputation for extravagant gesture and detected something which seemed at variance with the public portraits, so to speak. Somewhere inside she was a naif—always a bad sign in a woman connected with politics and public life.

"You remember we spoke? He is coming—you may have heard of Caradoc, the architect? No? Well. . . ." She suddenly burst out laughing, as if the very mention of his name had touched off an absurd memory. She laughed as far back as a tiny gold stopping on a

36

molar and then became serious, conspiratorial. "The lecture will be on the Acropolis—will your machine be able . . .?" I was doubtful. "If there is wind it won't be very clear. But I can make some tests in the open air? Sometimes very small things like dentures clicking, for example, ruin the quality of the sound and make the text difficult to recover on playback. I'll do what I can, naturally."

"If you come to Naos, my country house, in the garden. . . . You could practise with your instrument. He will come there. I'll send you the car next Friday." I reached for a pencil to give her my address, but she laughed and waved away my intention. "I know where you live. You see, I have been making enquiries about you. I did not know what your work was or I would have offered my help. Folk-songs I can get you two a penny." She snapped white fingers as one does to summon a waiter in the Orient. "On my country properties I have singers and musicians among the villagers. . . . Perhaps this would interest you later?"

"Of course."

"Then first make this speech for us." She laughed once more. "I would ask you to stay and dine but I have to go to the palace this evening. So goodbye."

That evening the fleet came in and Iolanthe was summoned back to the naval brothel in Piraeus leaving me alone to pursue my studies with Said. Three of my little orient pearls had been manufactured now, and I was mad keen to find a deaf man to try them out on. Koepgen had said that he knew a deaf deacon who would be glad of a mechanical cure so that he would not flounder among the responses! But where was Koepgen? I left messages for him at the theological school and at the tavern he frequented.

*   *   *   *   *

Naos, the country house of Hippolyta in Attica, was large enough to suggest at first sight a small monastery skilfully sited within an oasis of green. By contrast, that is, to the razed and bony hills which frame the Attic plain. Here were luxuriant gardens rich with trees and shrubs within a quarter of a mile of the sea. Its secret was that it had been set down, woven round a double spring—a rarity in these parched plains: oleander, cypress and palm stood in picturesque contrast to the violet-grey stubbled hills, their fine soils long since eroded by weather and human negligence. The dangling rosegardens, the unplanned puffs of greenery made full amends for what was, at close sight, a series of architectural afterthoughts, the stutterings of several generations. Barns climbed into bed together, chapels had cemented themselves one to another in the manner of swallow-nests to unfinished features like half-built turrets. One huge unfinished flying buttress poked out nature's eye, hanging in mid air. One step through the door marked W.C. on the second floor and one could fall twenty feet into a fishpond below.

A series of gaunt and yet dignified rooms had been thrown down pell mell about a central cruciform shape, rambling up two floors and petering out in precarious balconies which looked out on the ravishing mauve slopes of the foothills. On reflection one established the origins of the whole place. Clearly Hesiod had started it as a grange for his cattle; Turks, Venetians, French, Greeks had carried on the work without once looking over their shoulders, enlarging the whole place and confusing its atmospheres. In the reign of Otho utterly nonsensical elaborations had tried to render it stylish. While one corner was being built up, another was crumbling to ruins. Finally those members of the family lucky enough to have been educated in France had added the ugly cast-iron features and awkward fenestration which would, one presumes, always make them nostalgic for St.

Remo in the 'twenties—Marseille tile, Second Empire furniture, plaster cherubim, mangy plump mouldings. Yet since every feature was the worst of its epoch and kind the whole barrack had a homogeneity, indeed a rustic dignity which endeared it to all who came, either to visit or inhabit it. It was here that Hippolyta held court, here that her old friend, sheepish Count Banubula, worked in his spare time cataloguing the huge library hurled together rather than collected by several generations of improvident noblemen more famous for their eccentricities than their learning. Woodrot, silverfish, death-watch beetles—all were active and industrious though nobody cared except the poor Count, tip-toeing along creaking balconies or shinning up precarious ladders to rescue a rotting Ariosto or Petrarch.

Here Hippolyta (the Countess Hippolyta, "Hippo" to us) lived when she came home—which was rarely; for the most part she preferred Paris or New York. Other members of the family (with whom she was not on speaking terms) also came from time to time, unheralded, to take up residence in various dusty wings. (There was one ancient and completely unexplained old lady, half blind, who might be seen crossing a corridor or scuttling off a balcony.) Two younger cousins were ladies-in-waiting at court, and also occasionally put in an appearance attended by beaky husbands or lovers. Hippo made a point of not letting her own visits coincide with theirs; it was we, the members of her little court, who usually ran into them—for there was always someone staying at Naos; permission was freely given for any of us to spend a summer or winter there.

Here then in Naos, of a spanking summer evening, I was carried to the lady with my devil machines. (Tapes A70 to 84 labelled G for Greece have been fed back into Abel.) Well, she was clad in Chinese trousers of fine Shantung, inlaid Byzantine belt, and an impossible Russian shirt with split sleeves; she lounged in a deck chair by the lily pond while a hirsute peasant clumsily assuaged our thirst with whisky and gin. She was smoking a slender cheroot, and was surrounded by a litter of fashion papers and memoranda gathered in coloured folders—esoteric Greek pothooks which I feared might be the beginnings of a book. Two huge pet tortoises clicked across the paths and came bumping into the legs of our chairs, asking to be fed;

and this Banubula undertook with an air of grave and scrupulous kindness shredding lettuce from a plate. My little toy was greeted with rapture and some amusement; Hippolyta clapped her hands and laughed aloud like a child when I reproduced a strip of conversation harshly but clearly for her consideration, while old Banubula cleared his throat in some surprise and asked whether it wasn't rather dangerous, such a machine? "I mean one could take copies of private conversations, could one not?" Indeed one could; Hippo's eye shone with a reflective gleam. The Count said in his slow bronze-gong voice: "Won't Caradoc mind?" She snorted. "He knows these machines; besides if he is too lazy to write it all out, if he prefers to extemporise . . . why, it's his affair."

There was silence. "I saw Graphos today" she said, a sudden expression of sadness clouding her face. Presumably she was referring to the politician? I said nothing, nor did they. In the moment of embarrassment that followed we heard the noise of the car drawing up, and the figure of Caradoc emerged among the oleanders—the stubby frame hunched up with a defiant and slightly tipsy-looking mien; he carried a much-darned Scotch plaid over his arm, and in his hand a leather-covered flask from which he drew encouragement as he advanced. No greetings followed, much to my surprise; Hippolyta just lay, the Count just stared. Staring keenly, menacingly under shaggy white eyebrows, the architectural mage advanced, his deep voice munching out segments of air with a kind of half-coherent zeal. At first blush he seemed far too sure of himself, and then as he came closer the impression changed to one of almost infantile shyness. He spread his arms and uttered a single phrase in the accents of a Welsh bard: "What it is to work for these beneficed Pharisees!" Giving a harsh bark of a laugh full of ruefulness he sat down by the pond, turning the bottle over thoughtfully in his fingers before pushing it into the pocket of his cape. A heavy air of constraint fell over the company and I realised that it was caused by my presence; they could not speak freely before me. I unshackled my machine and excused myself. But through the window of the ramshackle lavatory on the ground floor I heard, or seemed to hear, Hippolyta give a low cry and exclaim: "O Caradoc, the Parthenon! Only Graphos can fight it." Caradoc gave an incredulous roar in the accents of the Grand Cham. "They told me nothing, they never do. Simply to come at once and bring Pulley for costings. I was hoping to build Jocas a seraglio. But this. . . . No, I won't believe it."

"Yes. Yes." Like the cry of a sea-bird. That was all. By the time I returned the whole picture had changed; the constraint had vanished. They had exchanged whatever they had needed to, and though there were still tears in the eyes of Hippolyta she was laughing heartily at something the Cham had said. Moreover his assistant Pulley had now joined the company—a lank north-country youth of yellowish cast, with huge hands and teeth. He said little. But he yawned from time to time like an eclipse of the sun.

A dinner table had been set out among the oleanders on a nearby terrace; the still air hardly trembled the candles in their silver sockets. Wine soon oiled the hinges of the talk. The Cham, after a short period of reservation, frankly gave me his hand.

"Charlton, you said?"

"Charlock."

"Well, Charlton, here's my hand."

Then he turned in business-like fashion and began to mash up his food with vigour, talking in loud and confident tones as he did so. No reference was made to my function, and I made none, treading warily; but towards the middle of the meal Hippolyta made a gesture inviting me to record, and I obeyed unobtrusively, while Caradoc continued with a grumbling one-cylinder monologue. He was in a curious mood it seemed, uncertain whether to allow the wine to make him gay or whether to become testy and morose; presumably he was still troubled by whatever she had told him, for he suddenly said, in an aside: "Of course I shall never cease to be grateful to the firm—how could one not be? It has allowed me to build all its cathedrals, so to speak. But one can build cathedrals without being a religious man? Anyway I don't propose to be upset until I know for certain what is in Jocas' mind." Then, as if to pursue the metaphor he turned to me and said: "I'm talking about Merlins, my boy. Easy to join but hard to leave. Nevertheless there comes a day. . . ." He sighed heavily and took Hippolyta's hand. "Now" he said "we must make a real effort to enjoy ourselves tonight. No good can come of worrying. I propose to lead an expedition to the Nube, and I invite

41

the lot of you as my guests. By the navel-string of the Risen Lord we shall have a marvellous time. Eh? Do you know the Nube, Charlton?"

"The Blue Danube? By repute."

"It is a home from home for us, eh Pulley?"

He consulted the circle of candle-lit faces as he barked out the phrase. There seemed little enough response aroused by this proposition. He was pained. As for the Blue Danube, it enjoyed a mild repute among frequenters of houses of ill fame. Its name, in frosted bulbs, had been changed for it by wind and weather; the letters had either fallen out of their frames or gone dead. All that remained for the wayfarer to read against the night sky now was the legend The Nube, ancing, aberet. "I should like to come" said I, and received a friendly thump from the Cham. He was delighted to receive support from some quarter. His good humour returned. "It is run by an adorable personage, daughter of a Russian Grand Duke, and sometime wife to a British Vice-Consul, most aptly so entitled, and she calls herself Mrs. Henniker." Hippolyta smiled and said: "All Athens knows her." Caradoc nodded. "And with justice; she has the cleanest girls in Attica; moreover there is one Turk called Fatma." He embraced a large segment of air to suggest her dimensions. "A heroine is Fatma."

All this was becoming less and less esoteric. Caradoc dished us all a stoup of red Nemean and cajoled us with prophecy. "You will see," he said "Graphos will get in and save our bacon." She smiled, yes, but sadly; shaking her head doubtfully. "I'll give you the big car" she said. "But I won't come. In case he phones or comes to see me. But I expect you'll find all your friends at the Nube, including Sipple. He knows you are arriving today." Caradoc registered approval, commended the cheese he was cutting up ("This Camembert has lain a long time, not in Abraham's bosom but in the hairy armpit of the Grand Turk himself") and added, with his mouth full: "Give me Sipple the clown any day." Pulley explained that Sipple was an "undesirable".

"But irresistible, my favourite *numéro*" insisted the Cham. "A man of parts."

"Second-hand parts" said Pulley. He seemed from his facial expressions to live in a state of furious though repressed disapproval. Caradoc, by now distinctly mellow, turned aside in disgust and confided some thoughts of the first magnitude, so to speak, to the mild and tentative Count, who had registered an expression of pained alarm at the mention of a house of ill fame. It was clear that he would not be joining us in this bacchanal. Caradoc, feeling perhaps an unexpressed reservation, tried to cajole him with high thinking to concede some virtue to low living. This sort of stuff. "The Nube is the perfect place for self-examination, better than a church. Why not, after all? The nearest vicarious approach to death is by the orgasm which produces its temporary simulacrum." ("Ow!" exclaimed Hippolyta with superstitious disgust.) The Cham warmed to the pulpit, his tone now tinged distinctly with Welsh tabernacle. "That is why it has been surrounded with prayer, poetry, propitiation, tabu. The Greeks saw a clear relationship and in their wisdom compounded temple and brothel. We haven't the imagination. Fools! The priest has tried to harness its power, dynamo fashion, to make more braindust. A foul repression is written all over our mugs. Look at him, him, her. *Look at me!* In the East we are told he has managed to crack the mould and liberate the statue of the silver man. But in the West our methods have failed—the silly reticule of the human brain can only generate a sterile flight of symbols and concepts which have given us certain insecure powers over matter but none over ourselves."

Pulley began to express his disapproval of all this bardic verbosity by beating himself about the chest and biceps and making animal noises and monkey faces. This delighted the Cham, who now stood up and in the pleading accents of a Welsh preacher admonished and cajoled him. "Now which is wiser, Pulley my dear fellow: to wear all nature like a suit of clothes, or to rape and tame it?"

Pulley gave a thin yowl and said: "Pack it up Carry, like a good fellow. I've had nothing but this all day in the plane." He turned to us for support. "Can you bear it when the bloody Druid comes out in him?"

"Of course they can" said Caradoc majestically, still poised for flight. "Only just" said Hippolyta.

"It gives me the bloody shivers" said Pulley.

"Very well." Caradoc sat down unsteadily. "Very well you Philistine. Very well." He took my hand and began to recite.

> If a monumental mason
> Carved a monumental turd
> As a symbol of humanity at prayer,
> We could cast it as a bronze
> And distribute it to dons
> As an article of college table-ware

He was sufficiently pleased with the response to threaten us with a ballad beginning:

> How nugatory and how glum
> The endomorphs of scholarship
> Like hippos on a sinking ship
> Stay bum to silly bum.

But he could push the matter no further, and submitted to Hippolyta's amused disapproval with mock contrition. She had kicked off her sandals and was smoking a Turkish cigarette in a black bone holder. Caradoc helped himself to a rose from the bowl on the table. "The moon is late tonight" he observed with petulance. He had been watching the little dab of whiteness on the horizon which marked its point of emergence. He had been here before, then? Supposedly.

The night had been still down in this garden with its unhovering candles, its slow-moving warm currents of scent. Now came a small gust which blew out the light and left us in half-darkness.

"A fitting end to our dinner" said Caradoc. "And a sign that we should be about our business. How shall we arrange matters?"

Hippolyta was staying; Banubula elected to be dropped off in Athens, "if we could face the detour". That left the three of us. I left my sacred boxes in a safe place against a future return and joined them. Pulley had taken the wheel of the car, sitting beside the chauffeur whose air of misgiving showed that he knew he was in for a long night's work. "Drive carefully" cried our hostess from the gate.

Caradoc sang softly to himself, beating time with a finger.

> Drinking, dicing and drabbing
> Drabbing, drinking and dice,

44

You can say what you like they are nice
You can say what you like they are nice

Faces with nothing behind them
Or behinds with nothing before. . . .

Pulley nearly ran into an unlighted cart and threw us all about widdershins. Banubula made turkey-noises. He was obviously a timorous man and was relieved to be deposited on the outskirts of the capital, pausing only to retrieve a silver-knobbed walking stick and to bow a ceremonious good-night. Then down towards the sea we turned, and now the young tardy moon was rising; it rode with us along the whole circuit of the long walls, past the rabble of dingy villas nestling in sterile palms, the beer factory, the refuse-encumbered Ilyssos. Below the Acropolis the olive groves melted away downhill towards the little railway. No horizon was ruled as yet, only a point at which stars began to prickle up out of the darkness. The last curve of the coast road sprang out like a branch in full blossom and elated by the moonlight and the silver spangles of the mild sea Pulley increased speed until we were whirling down towards Sunion —stars cool now as cress and shining waternibbled rock. Caradoc's rose was black. The night was placid and reassuring. Caradoc had decided for the time being to stop acting the rhetorical mountebank; the lightly varnished night-sky was a narcotic. In an absent-minded fashion he tried to catch a moonbeam in his cupped hand.

Nor was it long before we swerved off the pitted macadam of the main road on to hard dune: thence on to flaky sand dunes, to bump and skitter and slide into the rotting garden of the Nube and come to rest hull down under a single balcony where the one and only Mrs. Henniker awaited us in the attitude of a gaunt Juliet in retirement. The electric sign throbbed weakly: though for reasons of economy or aesthetics the current had never been taken inside where the lighting was by paraffin lamp or candle. Caradoc announced our arrival and at once Mrs. Henniker bobbed out of sight, only to reappear a minute later at the front door, arms extended in welcome. The long horse face with its patchy pink skin inspired confidence. She exhaled rectitude and forthrightness like the best sort of seaside

45

landlady. Her tones were tart and martial, her back as straight as a ramrod. She was at once fearful and endearing. Behind her one could sense the long and thankless lifetime spent in putting up with the lopped-off capacities of her typical clients. ("The Goddess of Sex, who, like the multiplication table, repeats her demands, always trying to raise herself to a higher power, perhaps in order to precipitate a true self?" Who the devil was that? Yes, Koepgen.)

At any rate it was to the Nube that humanity shuffled, lugging its heavy baggage—the interior pains and massive depressions. Among Mrs. Henniker's girls they were exorcised. Not us, mind you, for we were heartwhole and in sportive mood—to judge by the tone set by Caradoc. He introduced me as Mr. Chilton and added agreeably "He is a man of the world like us." Mrs. Henniker, who took everything with deadly seriousness, fluffed out her feathers like a bird and said, with intense feeling, "My poy. My poy"; taking as she did so, my right hand between scaly palms. It was all very formal, very graceful, very relaxed. Pulley gave a German professor's bow.

We entered the Nube with well-bred enthusiasm to go through the statutory ritual with the big wooden statue of the Curé d'Ars—a cordelier with an unhealthy leer. This came as rather a surprise to me. Caradoc embraced the statue warmly, addressing it as Saint Foutain. Then he indicated a slot in its shoulder large enough to admit a drachma. "Initiate yourself" he cried jovially, tendering me the coin. It tinkled into the body of the Curé and there was a whirr followed by a click. All at once a hatch in his robe flew open and he thrust out a beautifully hand-painted penis the length of a sermon. "Don't reel, don't recoil that way" said Caradoc reproachfully. "Put your hand on it and wish." I obeyed, offering up a shadowy half-formulated wish, fragile yet iridescent as a soap bubble, in the general direction of the absent Io. Pulley followed suit. "He's an infallible fellow. You only have to ask him and it comes true. He was bequeathed to the Nube by a commercial traveller in French wine, as mark of his esteem and entire satisfaction." So, feeling suitably shriven, we advanced upon the candle-lit interior through a succession of dusty curtains; here the girls waited, yawning—about half a dozen dressed in baggy Turkish trousers and no tops. They looked nice and tame, if rugged; and dying of boredom.

Time hung heavy, one gathered, when there were no clients in the Nube. A gramophone, yes, but the discs were few and scratched. Film magazines in plenty, but ancient. So it was that our majestic appearance on the scene evoked a burst of energy and merriment that was spontaneous and unfeigned.

But wait, we were not completely alone. In one corner of the room, on a table, lay a red-headed man apparently dead, and clad in nothing but his underpants. A large and heartless-looking fellow of Celtic cast, he was still sentient for he breathed stertorously through his nose. Not dead, then. The girls giggled as they examined him like some entomological specimen, lifting an arm to let it drop plump, peering into a glazed eyeball, up his nose. "I don't know who he is" said Mrs. Henniker in dismay. "We will have to wait until he comes round." One of the girls explained how the eyeballs of the corpse had suddenly rolled upwards into his skull like a doll; she mimed this horribly. Caradoc approached the figure with an air of medical knowledgeableness and said: "Aha! Cheyne-Stokes respiration. My diagnosis is Merchant Navy. Have you looked in his clothes?"

"He has none. He arrived on a bicycle with some money in his hand. Nothing but his underpants."

Caradoc tutted sympathetically. "You see" said Mrs. Henniker piteously "what we are up against all the time? How to run a respectable house what I mean? Tomorrow I will ring the Consul."

They submitted the corpse to a further series of tests, tickling its privates with a quill, smacking its cheeks, rubbing it with Cologne—but all to no purpose. Finally with a sigh they drew a bead curtain over the figure and Mrs. Henniker led us away among the further alcoves where, among the dusty divans, siphons and bottles awaited us together with plates of various comestibles. Here Caradoc was very much *en pacha*; Fatma had already discovered her lost love in him. I pitied and admired him, for she was a fearsome golliwog of negroid cast, though amiable in a pockmarked way. A shelf of gold and tin teeth adorned a cheerful and matronly grin.

The girls closed in now with chatter and laughter, piling themselves around us on the cushions like stray cats. It was all very domesticated and soothing. In the far corner Miki played a tune on a tinny piano which evoked dim and far-off things. There was no disposition to hurry, except in the case of the playful Fatma who made many a playful grab at the Cham's cods to see, as she said, "if there was any fruit on the branches as yet". Pulley said with an unmerited acerbity, "She's got a hope she has"; and in truth Caradoc seemed to derive more satisfaction from conversation than anything else. The sound of his own voice filled him with a vivid auto-intoxication. "They always ask me" he said somewhat sadly "if I am not married and why and how many children and so on. I try and explain that I was never convinced about the state. But at long last I got so fed up that I began to carry around a wallet-full of children just to humour them. Look." He tipped out of a wallet a series of grotesque pictures of nude children of various ages. "This is my youngest" he explained, holding up the most hideous. "He must be a man of forty by now; but this poor damsel won't know any better." Fatma crooned over the pictures. They were passed round the eager circle of baby fanciers. They had the effect of increasing enthusiasm. Eager to entertain, someone started to scratch a mandolin and croon. Others in a burst of baby-worship produced their knitting and fell to work in aid of an imaginary seventh-month foetus. Tina dabbed us all with scent from a bottle labelled *Phul* and exhorted us to have *kephi*—joy. Somewhat to my surprise Mrs. Henniker also relaxed and laid down with her head in Demetra's lap, allowing the girl to brush her harsh hair and massage her temples. She kicked off her shoes and extending thin arms in rapturous abandonment allowed two other girls to knead and palp them slowly. A fine fat peasant girl closed in on me, polite and nonchalant. Of course in those fine free pre-salvarsan days nobody could help being slightly nagged by syphilophobia. I thought of Schopenhauer's "*Obit anus Abit onus*" and sighed into my flowing bowl. As if she read my mind Mrs. Henniker opened one eye like a chameleon and said: "She is all right; we take no chances here; the safety of the client is our guarantee." I tried to look as if I needed no such reassurance, allowing myself to be fed like a pet bird with aromatic scraps of entrail on toothpicks. "I want to see Sipple," said Caradoc "that velvet prick in an iron mitt, that specialist in all the unwashed desires." "Later" said Mrs. Henniker, "he always comes later"; and then as if the word had reminded her of something she consulted her watch and rose to excuse herself. "I am hiring some

48

new girls" she explained. "The doctor is coming to examine them."
So saying she filtered through a wall of curtains and disappeared.
Dispersing slowly upon our various trajectories I heard, as if in a
dream, Caradoc admonishing me with: "I hope Charlton that you
are not one of those Englishmen who forever dream of some sodomy-
prone principality with a fringe of palms where the Arabs wear
nothing under their nightgowns."

Silence, dispossession, plenitude. The little rooms on the first
floor of the villa were spotlessly clean and bare of all ornament.
Scoured wooden floors and enormous old-fashioned beds squatting
like sumpter camels, with mattresses too tough to be dented by our
bodies. Outside the sea sighed along the strand. "Some magi among
the barbarians seeing Harpalus despondent persuaded him that he
could lure the spirit of Pythonice back from the Underworld. In
vain, despite the voice which issued from the bronze bay-tree." She
came from no island but from the mulberry-starred plateaus where
the Vardar flows, and where the women have voices of steel wire. The
fish-markets of Salonika had been her only school. Pitiful black eyes
of a mooncalf adorned this kindly personage. Her freshly washed
hair, though coarse, was delicious as mint. But then ideas turn sideways in their sleep, seduced by the lush combing of waves upon sand,
and one turns with them, sliding towards the self possession of sleep
and dreaming. Once more I saw Harpalus among the tombs. "Harpalus the Macedonian, who plundered large sums from Alexander's
funds, fled to Athens; there he fell madly in love with Pythonice the
courtesan and squandered everything on her. Nothing like her
funeral had ever been seen, choirs, artists, displays, massed instruments. And her tomb! As you approach Athens along the Sacred
Way from Eleusis, at the point where the citadel is first seen, on the
right you will see a monument which outdoes in size every other.
You halt and ask yourself whose it is—Miltiades, Cimon, Pericles?
No. It is Pythonice's, triple slave and triple harlot."

On my way downstairs—I took a wrong turning and lost myself,
blundering down at last into a sort of cellar which must once have
served as a kitchen when the villa had been a normal habitation.
Here a strange scene was taking place, illustrated, so to speak by the
shadows which whirled and loomed upon the dirty ceiling. A group

of starkly silhouetted figures stood grouped about a deal table on which lay the figure of a girl. It was their shadows which lobbed about up above like daddy long-legs: fascinating cartoons, travesties of ordinary gestures magnified to enormous size. Mrs. Henniker occupied the foreground of the animated Goya. Her friend the doctor was bent intently over the girl on the table whose parted legs suggested a fruit tree in espalier. To one side, seated along a bench, fading yellowly away from the centre of lamp light sat half a dozen candidates with cheap handbags. They looked contrite and hopeful, like extras at an audition.

Abashed and curious I hestitated in the open door. Mrs. Henniker, who stood holding a bull's eye lamp, turned with nonchalance and beckoned me in with: "Come in my poy, we are just finishing." The doctor grunted as he inserted some kind of oldfashioned catheter with a bulb—or a swab. His bent head obscured for me the face of Iolanthe as she lay there like some taken sparrow-hawk. I was handed the torch while Mrs. Henniker busied herself with some documents, reciting the name and state of the subject. "Samiou Iolanthe, maid-servant in Megara." The doctor wound up his gear and threw a towel over the exposed parts. "This one is also clean" he said and sitting up abruptly the girl gazed into my startled face. Her features sketched a mute imploring expression—almost she put her fingers to her lips. The doctor seized her thumb and stuck a syringe into the ball. She gasped and bit her lips as she saw him draw off a teaspoonful of venous blood to fill a tiny phial. Mrs. Henniker explained her pre-occupations to me in a series of thorny asides. "I have to be careful they don't come from other places, dirty places, what I mean. Specially the sailor's brothel in Piraeus. So I take every precaution, what I mean." I did see what she meant—for that is precisely where Iolanthe came from; nor did she, nor had she ever hidden the fact from me, for there was no promise of exclusiveness between us. On the contrary it was thanks to her that I had visited the place when the Fleet was away.

We clattered down one summer dusk in the ill-lit and musty little metro; it was not a long run to Piraeus—a ragged and echoing town-ship aboom with sirens and factories and the whimpering of seagulls. The place lay some way outside in a crepuscular and unsavoury quarter picked out in old bluish street-lamps obviously left over from the Paris exhibitions of '88. It was traversed by a squeaky tram-line so sinuous that the occasional tram bucketed and swayed about as if stricken by palsy. The establishment had more than repaid my curiosity. It was built like a barrack around three sides of a wide flagged courtyard with a fountain in the centre, suggesting nothing so much as a khan at the desert's edge. The flamboyant fountain, choked and dribbling, trickled down into a basin full of green slime and moss. On all three sides of the long low blocks stood the cubicles of the girls, somewhat like a row of bathing cabins; now of course, the place was empty, all doors lying open. One or two of the cells had been left still lit by cotton wicks afloat in saucers of olive oil —as if their tenants had just slipped out on an errand and would soon be back. But the only inhabitant of the place seemed to be the janitor —an old half-crazy crone who talked cheerfully to herself. "Soft in the head" said a gesture of Io's.

Outside every door stood a pair of wooden clogs, or pattens. It was extraordinarily beautiful in a story-book way—the dense shadow, the elfish yellow light, the dark velvety sky above. All the doors had the traditional Judas cut in them, but this time heart-shaped, which enabled the clients to peer in on the lighted girl before making their choice. Moreover on each of the doors was painted, in crude lettering, the name of the girl—all the names of the Greek anthology, the very perfection of anonymity! The furniture of each cubicle was identical, consisting of a clumsy iron bed, small dressing-table and chair. The only decoration was personal—tortoise-shell mirror, tinsel strips from biscuit tins, postcards of far-away ports, an ikon with a bottle of fresh olive-oil beside it. The oil performed a double service both religious and laic—for the only instrument of contraception was a slip of Kalymnos sponge dipped in it. Thus the sacred juice celebrated its historic ancestry by a double burning, igniting up man and saint alike. On the back wall, innocent as a diploma on a seminary wall, was the medical certificate of health with the date of last inspection. On this figured the girl's real name.

Her cell now (Antigone) was occupied by someone called Euridice Bakos according to the chart. But she too was away on some mysterious errand, though the wick burned in the alcove before a misty

51

St. Barbara. This ikon was however Iolanthe's—for she blew out the wick and reclaimed it. In the drawer of the rotting dressing-table with its gaudy oilcloth cover she rummaged purposefully to disinter a comb and brush of doubtful cleanliness and a few shabby articles of wear. Lastly in a corner, under the bed with its tin chamber-pot, she picked over a bundle of cheap magazines—*Bouquetto, Romanzo*, and the like—to trace a serial she wanted to continue; also a French grammar and an English phrase-book.

The pattens she had not wanted to take, although they were hers; but I was loath to surrender the clumsy things and slipped one into each pocket. Later the ikon stood upon the mantelpiece in Number Seven. They lighted an expensive candle before it and turned off the harsh electric light. The clogs served later as book-ends. Then disappeared. Here they are again. The persistence of objects and the impermanence of people—he never ceased to reflect upon the matter, as he lay there listening to the distant music of the Plaka taverns and the nearer heartbeats of his watch. She slept so lightly, with such a shallow respiration, that at times she looked dead, as though her heart had stopped. Then to lie back under that shadowing ceiling and yonder into introspection once more, allowing his mind to fill up with all the detritus of thought—things far removed from fornication's rubber pedal; and yet with the idle side of his mind he could go over her points like a mare or a hare. Reflecting I should suppose upon the unconscious alchemist he might one day become, the lion-man. But no, this is a perverse attempt to read back from memories which have faded. About sex? No. About death? Never. This young man never thought of making a will. No he thought in fields, fields which he hoped that one day Abel would arrange in valencies. Some document! It would ideally record how one day he, like everyone else, began to face the disruption of the ordinary appetites, the changing electric fields of the impulses, so hard to place, to tame, to convert into practical usage like, say, the orgasm of electric light in a bulb, or a wheel moving under a lever.

Koepgen used to say that human life is an anthology of states; chronological progression is an illusion. And that to be punished for what one does not remember except in dreams is our version of the tragedy the Greeks invented. The poetry is in the putty, as Caradoc used to say!

Patterns of fading music from the south; early cocks compose their infernal paternoster. Clytemnestra lopped off the heavy limbs and carefully wiped her fingers in the thing's hair. Delicate white fingers with their enormous vocabulary of gestures. The shadows on the cave of Plato lobbed and bounced now upon the walls of Mrs. Henniker's dungeon. The performance was at an end. My smile of friendly complicity had reassured Iolanthe. But to my surprise I suddenly felt the pricking of a puzzling jealousy. The scientist does not like to see his algebra get up, shake itself, and walk away. I promised myself another banquet of Greek twilight soon, though it hardly allayed the absurd sensation. On the dirty wall I thought I descried moving ideograms of other love-objects living in their Platonic form—"man" "rose" "fire" "star". All the furniture of Koepgen's poems, which he claimed were really "acts, the outer skin of thought". All this had passed over the head of the recumbent Charlock; now he had come back to take up the dropped stitch, so to speak, to recapitulate it all for Abel. All this vulgar data when "screened out" by the sign-manuals of the computer, or "panned out" (as if for gold), would be sifted down through the spectrum of language itself, punctuated and valued, to yield at last the vatic tissue which owes little to ordinary looms. Now I know that everything is remediable, that finally somehow somewhere memory is fully recoverable. These thoughts then bursting on the surface of the mind in little bubbles of pure consciousness would provide red meat for the Lion—Abel's raw aliment.

Life is an image (Koepgen) of which everything is the reflection. All objects are slowly changing into each other—dead man to dead tree, to dead rock, to vine, to marl, to tan sand, to water, cloud, air, fire . . . a movement, not of dissolution but of fulfilment. (To fulfil is to fill full.)

Chemical reincarnations by the terms of which we all become spare parts of one another—excuse the biblical echo. Abel roars and roars. Our modern oracle like the ancient is this steel animal: bronze bull, steel lion. His diagnosis is as follows: "This young man should read Empedocles again. Complexity, which is sometimes necessary,

53

is not always beautiful; simplicity is. Yes, but after the last question has been asked and answered there will always remain something enigmatic about a work of art or of nature. You cannot drain *la dive bouteille* however much you try."

The object of Abel's operation you see was never the manufacture of a factitious literature, no; but a way of remodelling sensation in order to place one in a position of "self-seizing". Such words then become merely a novel form of heartbeat as they do for the poet. In "real" life. Has not Koepgen always called his poems "my little prayer-siphons"? Gradually I find my blundering way back through the stale curtains. . . .

Caradoc was there, musing over a drink, and looking somewhat gibbous after his exertions; Fatma had produced a manicure set and was touching up his square fingernails. He indicated a siphon and said: "Drink, boy, until you detonate the idea within you." He was I thought a trifle detonated himself already. Inconsequential ideas trailed through his mind. He stroked the golliwog and extolled her "great bubbles of plenty". Ugh! He enjoined her to give us a tune on her zither, and then without waiting for accompaniment sang softly, wearily:

> Ah take me back once more to find
> That pure oasis of neurosis called
> The Common Mind
> To foster and to further if I can
> The universal udderhood of man.

Obscure associations led him to speak of Sipple. "Sipple was a clown once, a professional clown. Aye! I have seen him at Olympia come on with boots like soap-dishes and a nose like a lingam. His trousers furled like a sail and the whole man was held together by a celluloid dickey which rolled up like a blind and knocked him down. His greatest moment was when the second clown set fire to his privates with a torch. Talk about Latimer's ordeal: you should have heard the ladies screech. But his proclivities were not those of the refined. His habits were rebarbative. There was a scandal and he had to retire. Now he lives in honourable retirement in Athens— don't ask me on what. Even the firm can't tell me that."

He broke off and gave a surprised roar, for in the furthest alcove in the room a figure which had been lying completely buried in cushions suddenly sat up and gave a yellow yawn. It was a dramatic enough entry on cue to satisfy Sipple's sense of theatre—for it was he. His pale lugubrious face was creased with sleep; his small blood-shot eyes, full of a kind of street-arab meanness, travelled round the room in dazed fashion. Only when he saw Caradoc advance upon him with outstretched arms did a vague smile wander into his coun-tenance. "So you got here" he piped, without much relish, hitching his tubular trousers on to sagging braces, and laughed *chick chick*. His face was alive with little twitches, tics and grimaces—as if it did not know into what expression to settle. No, it was as if he needed to stretch out the sleep-creased skin. He submitted to some massive thumps of welcome from his friend, and yawning hugely accepted to come and sit in our corner of the room. A tame sloth I would have said: with a queer pear-shaped furry head.

The Cham pushed and pulled him about as one might a pet. I was introduced and shook a damp octopoid hand; bizarre was Sipple, and rather disturbing. "I was telling the boy here" said Caradoc "about why you had to leave the motherland." Sipple shot me a doubtful and cunning look, unable to decide for a moment whether or not to pick up this gambit, an obvious comedian's "feed". His eyes were far too close together; "made to see through keyholes" a Greek would have said. Then he decided to comply. "It was all Mrs. Sipple's fault, sir" he whimpered with just the suspicion of a trem-bling underlip. "Yes" he went on slyly, moistening his lips and gazing sideways at me with a furtive and timorous air. "She didn't hold with my exhibitions. We had to part."

Caradoc, who appeared to hang on his lips, struck his knee with massive sympathy. "Wives never do. To the ducking stool with them all" he cried in jovian fashion. Sipple nodded and brooded further on his wrongs.

"It was the lodger" Sipple explained to me in a painstaking under-tone. "I can only do it in exceptional circumstances, and then it all goes off in spray." He looked woebegone, his underlip swelled with self-commiseration. Yet his ferret's eye still watched me, trying to size me up. I could see it was a relief when I decided to find him

55

funny, and laughed—more out of obedience to Caradoc than from my own personal inclination. However he took courage and launched himself into his act—a recital obviously much-rehearsed and canonised by repetition. Caradoc added rhetorical flourishes of his own, obviously keenly appreciative of his friend's gifts. "You were right" he cried. "Right to leave her, Sippy, with dignity intact. Everything you tell me about her fills me with dismay. God's ruins! Covered in clumps of toc. Ah God to see her haunches stir across the moon at Grantchester. No, you were right, dead right. A woman who refuses to tie up a Sipple and thrash him with leg-irons is not worth the name."

Sipple gave the stonehenge of a smile exposing huge discoloured teeth with some extensive gaps. "It wouldn't fadge, Carry" he admitted. "But here in Athens you can do as you would be done by, as the scripture has it." I suppose you could call it extra-suspensory perception.

"Tell me again" said the Cham eager for further felicities of this kind, and the little pear droned on. "It came over me very gradual" said Sipple, raising his arms to pat the air. "Very gradual indeed it did. At first I was normal as any curate, ask my mates. Give me an inch and I took a mile. And I was never one for the boys, Carry, not then I wasn't. But suddenly the theatrical side in me came to the fore. I was like a late-blooming flahr, Carry, a retarded flowering. Perhaps it was being a clown that did it, the magic of the footlights, I dunno."

It was funny all right, but also vaguely disquieting. He put his head on one side and winked with his right eye. He stood up and joined his fingers to say, with a seraphic sadness: "One day I had to face reality. It was quite unexpected. I pulled out me squiffer when all of a sudden it abrogated by a simple reticulation of the tickler. I was aghast! I went to see the doctor and he says to me: 'Look here Sipple, I must be frank with you. As man to man your sperm count is low and the motility of your product *nil*.' I reeled. There I had been, so young, so gay, so misinformed. 'Sipple' went on the doc 'it's all in your childhood. I bet you never noozled the nipple properly. You never had seconds I'll avow.' And he was right; but then what little nipper knows how to tease the tit properly and avoid abrogation in later life when he needs all the reticulation he can get, just tell me that?" He wiped away an invisible tear and stood all comico-pathetico before an invisible medico. "You have all my sympathy" said Caradoc, drunk and indeed a little moved. He swallowed heavily. Sipple went on, his voice rising to higher more plaintive register: "But that was not all, Carry. The doctor had drained away my self-confidence with his blasted medical diagmatic. Yet there was a crueller blow to come, 'Sipple' he said to me 'there is no way out of your dilemma. You are utterly lacking in PELVIC THRUST.' "

"How unfair" cried Caradoc with burning sympathy.

"And thank God untrue" squawked Sipple. "Under the proper stage management it is a wanton lie."

"Good."

"I have shown you haven't I?"

"Yes."

"And I'll show you again tonight. Where is Henniker?"

"I'll take your word for it, Sippy."

Sipple poured himself out a massive drink and warmed to his tale, secure now in his hold over his audience. He must have been a very great clown once, for he combined the farcical and the sinister within one range of expression. "Some day I shall write the story of my love-life from my own point of view. Starting with the dawn of realisation. One day the scales dropped from my eyes. I saw love as only a clown could: what struck me was this: the *position*, first of all, is *ridiculous*. No-one with a sense of the absurd could look at it frankly without wanting to laugh. Who invented it? If you had seen Mrs. Arthur Sipple lying there, all reliability, and fingering her ringlets impatiently, you'd have felt your risibility rise I bet. It was too much for me, I couldn't master myself, I laughed in her face. Well, not exactly her face. She was too heavy to turn over, you'd need a spade. It was only when her night-dress took fire that she realised that all was over. I couldn't help laughing, and that made her cry. 'Farewell forever Beatrice' I said turning on my heel. I sailed away and for many a month I wallowed in the dark night of the soul. I reflected. Gradually my ideas clarified, became more theatrical. I had found a way through.

57

"So I went back to the doctor, all fulfilment, to tell him about my new methods. He jumped and said I was a caution. A caution! 'It's very very unBritish, you know' he said. I hadn't thought of that. I thought he'd be so pleased with me. He said I was a traitor to the unborn race. He said he wanted to write a paper on me, me Sipple. I grew a trifle preremptory with him, I'll allow. But I hadn't come all the way back to Cockfosters to be insulted. He called me an anomaly and it was the last straw. I struck him and broke his spectacles." Sipple gave a brief sketch of this blow and sank back on to the sofa. "And so" he went on slowly "I came here to Athens to try and find peace of mind; and I won't say I didn't. I'm assuaged now, thanks to Mrs. Henniker's girls and their broomsticks. No more abrogation of the tickler."

Caradoc was having one of his brief attacks of buoyancy; drink seemed to have a curious intermittent effect upon him, making him tipsy in little patches. But these were passing clouds of fancy merely from which he appeared to be able to recover by an act of will. "Once," he was saying dreamily "once the firm sent me to build a king a palace in Burma and there I found the menfolk had little bells sewn into their season tickets—believe me bells. Every movement accompanied by a soft and silver tinkle. Suggestive, melodious and poetical it was to hear them chiming along the dark jungle roads. I almost went out and ordered a carillon for myself. . . .

> *Come join the wanton music where it swells,*
> *Order yourself a whopping set of bells.*

But nothing came of it. I was withdrawn too soon."

A large scale diversionary activity was now taking place somewhere among the curtains; Pulley appeared looking sheepish and incoherent, followed by Mrs. Henniker who was greeted with a cry from Sipple. "What about it, Mrs. H?" he cried. "I told you I wanted to be tortured tonight in front of my friends here." Mrs. Henniker clucked and responded imperturbably that there had been a little delay, but that the "torture-room" was being prepared and the girls dressed up. The clown then excused himself with aplomb, saying that he had to get ready for his act but that he would not be long.

"Don't let him fall asleep" he added pointing to the yawning Pulley. "I need an audience or it falls flat."

Nor did it take very long to set the theatrical scene. Mrs. Henniker reappeared with clasped hands and bade us follow her once more down into the same gaunt kitchen where the shadows still bobbed and slithered—but a different set of them; moreover the dungeon now was full of the melancholy clanking of chains. More lights had been introduced—and there in the middle of things was Sipple naked. They had just finished chaining him to a truckle bed of medieval ugliness. He paid no attention to anyone. He appeared deeply preoccupied. He was wearing the awkward oldfashioned leg-irons of the cripple. But most bizarre of all were the party whips, so to speak. The three girls who had been delegated to "torture" him wore mortar-boards and university gowns with dingy fur tippets. The contrast with their baggy Turkish trousers was delightful. They each held a long broom switch—the sort one could buy for a few drachmae and which tavern keepers use for sweeping out the mud-floored taverns. As we entered they all advanced purposefully upon Sipple with their weapons at the ready while he, appearing to catch sight of them for the first time, gave a start and sank kneeling to the floor.

He began to tremble and sweat, his eyeballs hung out as he gazed around him for some method of escape. He shrank back with dismal clankings. I had to remind myself that he was acting—but indeed *was* he acting? It was impossible to say how true or false this traumatic behaviour was. Mrs. Henniker folded her arms and looked on with a proud smile. The three doctors of divinity now proclaimed in very broken English, "Arthur, you have been naughty again. You must be punish!" Sipple cringed. "Nao!" he cried in anguish. "Don't 'urt me. I swear I never."

The girls, too, acted their parts very well, frowning, knitting black brows, gritting white teeth. Their English was full of charm—such broken crockery, and so various as to accent—craggy Cretan, singsong Ionian. "Confess" they cried, and Sipple began to sob. "Forward!" said Mrs. Henniker now, under her breath in Greek, adding the further adornment of a thick Russian intonation. "Forward my children, my partridges."

59

They bowed implacably over Sipple now and shouted in ragged unison, "You have again wetted your bed." And before he could protest any further they fell upon him roundly with their broom switches and began to fustigate the fool unmercifully crying "Dirty. Dirty."

"Ah" cried Sipple at the stinging pleasure of the first assault. "Ah." He writhed, twisted and pleaded to be sure; he even made a few desultory movements which suggested that he was going to fight back. But this was only to provoke a harsher attack. Anyway he would have stood little chance against this band of peasant Amazons. He clanked, scraped and squeaked. The noise grew somewhat loud, and Mrs. Henniker slipped into the corner to put on a disc of the Blue Danube in order to mitigate it. Bits of broom flew off in every direction. Caradoc watched this scene with the reflective gravity of one watching a bullfight. I felt astonishment mixed with misgiving. But meanwhile Sipple, oblivious to us all, was taking his medicine like a clown—nay, lapping it up.

He had sunk under the sharpened onslaught, begun to disintegrate, deliquesce. His pale arms and legs looked like those of a small octopus writhing in the throes of death. In between his cries and sobs for mercy his breath came faster and faster, he gasped and gulped with a perverted pleasure. At last he gave a final squeak and lay spread-eagled on the stone flags. They went on beating him until they saw no further sign of life and then, panting, desisted and burst into peals of hysterical laughter. The corpse of Sipple was unchained, disentangled and hoisted lovingly on to the truckle bed. "Well done" said Mrs. Henniker. "Now he will sleep." Indeed Sipple had already fallen into a deep infantile slumber. He had his thumb in his mouth and sucked softly and rhythmically on it.

They surrounded his bed filled with a kind of commiserating admiration and wonder. On slept Sipple, oblivious. I noticed the markings on his arms and legs—no larger than blackheads in a greasy skin: but unmistakably the punctures of a syringe. The shadows swayed about us. One of the lamps had begun to smoke. And now, in the middle of everything, there came a sharp hammering on a door somewhere and Mrs. Henniker jumped as if stung by a wasp and dashed away down the corridor. Everyone waited in tableau grouped about the truckle bed until she should reappear—which she did a moment later at full gallop crying: "Quick, the police."

An indescribable confusion now reigned. In pure panic the girls scattered like rabbits to a gunshot. Windows were thrown open, doors unbolted, sleepers were warned to hurry up. The house disgorged its inhabitants in ragged fashion. I found myself running along the dunes with Pulley and Caradoc in the frail starshine. Our car had disappeared, though there seemed to be another on the road with only its dim sidelights on. Having put a good distance between ourselves and the house we lay in a ditch panting to await developments. Later the whole thing turned out to have been a misunderstanding; it was simply two sailors who had come to claim their recumbent friend. But now we felt like frightened schoolboys. Concern for the sleeping clown played some part in Caradoc's meditations as we lay among the squills, listening to the sighing sea. Then the tension ebbed, and turning on his back the Cham's thoughts changed direction. Presumably Hippolyta's chauffeur had beaten a retreat in order not to compromise her reputation by any brush with the law. He would be back, of that my companions were sure. I chewed grass, yawning. Caradoc's meditations turned upon other subjects, though only he and Pulley were *au courant*. Out of this only vague sketches swam before me. Something about Hippolyta having ruined her life by a long-standing attachment, a lifelong infatuation with Graphos. "And what the devil can she think we will achieve by my giving a Sermon on the Mount on the blasted Acropolis?" Nobody cared what savants thought. Graphos might save the day, but his career was at its lowest ebb. He had had several nervous breakdowns and was virtually unable to lead his party even if the government fell, as they thought it would this winter. And all because he was going *deaf*.

I perked up. "Can you imagine a worse fate for a politician raised in a tradition of public rhetoric? No wonder he's finished."

"Did you say *deaf*?" I said.

"Deaf!" I had become very fond of the word and repeated it softly to myself. It had become a very beautiful word to me.

"And I have to sermonise on the Mount" repeated Caradoc with

61

disgust. "Something to give ears to the deaf, something full of arse-felt greetings and blubberly love. I ask you. As if it could avert the worst."

"What worst?" I asked; it seemed to me that for days now I had done nothing but ask questions to which nobody could or would provide an answer. Caradoc shook himself and said: "How should I know? I am only an architect."

Lights were coming down the road. It was Hippolyta's car. We signalled and galloped towards it.

*　　*　　*　　*　　*

Somewhere here the continuity becomes impacted again, or dispersed. "I was the fruit of a mixed mirage" said Caradoc, dining Chez Vivi with a group of money-loving boors with polish. Laughing until his buttonhole tumbled into his wineglass. "We must work for the greatest happiness of the highest few." I had by then confided my orient pearls to the care of Hippolyta for Graphos. A queer sort of prosopography reigns over this section of time. Arriving too early, for example, I waited in the rosegarden while she saw Graphos to his car. I had only seen his picture in the paper, or seen him sitting in the back of a silver car, waving to crowds. I had missed the club foot; now as they came down the path arm in arm I heard the shuffling syncopated walk, and I realised that he had greater burdens to carry than merely his increasing deafness. His silver hair and narrow wood-beetle's head with those melancholy incurious eyes—they were set off by the silver ties he wore, imported from Germany. Somewhere in spite of the cunning he gave off all the lethargy of riches. I came upon exactly the quality of the infatuation he had engendered in an ancient Greek poem about a male lover.

> *He reeks with many charms,*
> *His walk is a whole hip dance,*

62

His excrement is sesame seed-cake
His very spittle is apples.

Insight is definitely a handicap when it comes to loving. (His rival shot him stone dead with a longbow.) On the lavatory wall someone had marked the three stages of man after the classical formula.

satiety
hubris
ate

"The danger for Graphos is that he has begun to think of himself in the third person singular" she said sadly, but much later. All this data vibrates on now across the screens of the ordering condensers in Abel, to emerge at the requisite angle of inclination.

Nor was my experiment with Caradoc's voice less successful; amongst the confusion and general blurr of conversation there was a brief passage extolling the charms of Fatma to which she listened with considerable amusement, and which I found centuries later among my baggage and fed to A. "She may not be a goddess to everyone" he begins a trifle defensively "though her lineaments reveal an ancient heritage. An early victim of ritual infibulation was she. Later Albanian doctors sewed up the hymen with number twelve pack thread so that she might contract an honourable union. No wonder her husband jumped off a cliff after so long and arduous a honeymoon. In their professional excitement the doctors had by mistake used the strings of a guitar. She gave out whole arpeggios like a musical box when she opened her legs. Her husband, once recovered, sent her back to her parents with a hole bored in her frock to show that she was no virgin. Litigation over the affair is doubtless still going on. But meanwhile what was Fatma to do? She took the priapic road like so many others. She walked in peace and brightness holding the leather phallus, the sacred *olisbos* in the processions of Mrs. Henniker. Nor must we forget that these parts were *aidoion* to the Greeks, 'inspiring holy awe'. There is no special word for chastity in ancient Greek. It was the Church Fathers who, being troubled and a trifle perverted, invented *agneia*. But bless you, Fatma does not know that, to this very day. When she dies her likeness will be in

63

all the taverns, her tomb at the Nube covered with votive laurels; she will have earned the *noblissima meretrix* of future ages. Biology will have to be nudged to make room for Fatma."

But the rest scattered with the talk as gun-shy birds will at a clapping of hands. Something vague remains which might be guessed to concern the Piraeus brothel where many of the names live on from the catalogues of Athenaeus—like Damasandra which means, "the man-crusher": and the little thin ones, all skin and bone and saucer eyes, are still "anchovies". Superimposed somewhere in all this Iolanthe's just-as-ancient moral world out of Greek time. Skins plastered with white lead to hide the chancres, jowls stained with mulberry juice, blown hair powdering to grey, underside of olives in wind but not half as venerable. The Lydians spayed their women and did their flogging to the sound of a flute. Depilatories of pitch-plaster battling desperately against the approach of old age. . . . The appropriate sounds of the fountain whispering and of a leather-covered bottle being decanted. Then amidst yawns C's declamation of a poem called The Origen of Species

> One god-distorted neophyte
> Cut off his cods to see the light,
> Now though the impulse does not die
> He greets erections with a sigh.

Somewhere, too, room must be made for the scattered utterances of Koepgen—his notebooks were always to hand, not a drop was spilt. Records from some Plaka evening under a vine-tent, mewed at by mandolines. "First pick your wine: then bleed into it preciously, drop by drop, the living semen of the resin. Then pour out and drink to complete the ikonography of a mind at odds with itself here below the lid of sky. The differences can be reconciled for a while by these humble tin jars." Singing has blurred the rest of it, but here and there, like the glint of mica in stone, the ear catches a solidified echo. "Have you noticed that at the moment of death a man breathes in through both nostrils?"

These simple indices of acute anxiety, racing pulse, incontinence, motor incoordination (wine jar spilt, flowers scattered, vase broken) involve the loss of reflexes acquired within the first year of infant life.

Iolanthe cannot be to blame. She sleeps like a mouse-widow with her hair in her mouth, black fingernails extended on the pillow like grotesque fingerprints. Bodies smelling hot and rank.

Somewhere here also, among the shattered fragments recovered from old recordings, Abel has the germ plasm of Hippolyta's voice, vivacious and halting, running on like a brook in a dry river-bed. The black of that perfumed hair when set seems to be charcoal, carved and buffed—or a Chinese ink which holds its sheen even in darkness. She walks naked, unselfconscious, to the balcony to find the car keys, and when he has driven off without a backward glance she goes barefoot down the garden path to the small Byzantine chapel at the end to consult the hovering Draconian eyes of the ikons, the reproachful smile of St. Barbara. Here to light the lamps and mutter the traditional prayers.

It never ceases to amaze me that throughout all this period, unknown to me, Benedicta was approaching; she was sliding down the mighty Danube whose feeble headspring crawls out of a small opening in the courtyard of some German castle. Lulled by the voices of the Nibelungs she sees great castles in ruins brooding on their own reflections in the running water. Trees arch over Durnstein: then Vienna, Budapest, Belgrade and down through the Iron Gates to scout the Black Sea coast of Bulgaria in a Rumanian packet slim as a cigarette; and so down the Bosphorus to where the crooked calligraphy of mosques and spires waited for her in Polis. And for Charlock.

The journey had been arranged for her by the firm; young widows must do their forgetting somehow.

Little eddies of thyme and rosemary lay about in parcels among the columns; one walked into them. There was no breeze. The sun had completed its impressive weight-lifting act and plunged into the darkness. Violet the Saronic Gulf, topaz Hymettus, lilac bronze the marbles. The oncoming night was freshening towards the dews of midnight and after. Here we were assembled, some two hundred people, at the northern end of the Parthenon. *Tenue de ville,* dark suits, cocktail dresses. It seemed a fairly representative lecture audience—members of the Academy and the Temple of Science, professors and other riff-raff of this order. In this cool stable air everyone was relaxed and informal, indeed mildly gay. Except Hippolyta, who was in a high state of nerves, eating valerian cachets one after another to calm herself. On the top plinth, among the columns, stood a lectern with a lamp. It was from here that Caradoc was supposed to be lecturing. The general disposition of the chairs for the audience was pleasantly informal. They were dotted about in groups among the shattered rubble. Everything promised—or so I thought. Doubtless the site itself was responsible for these feelings for who can see the blasted Parthenon at dusk without wanting to put his arms round it? Moreover in this honeyed oncoming of night with its promise of a late moonrise, an occasional firefly triggering on the slopes below, the owls calling?

Below the battlements glowed the magic display of precious stones which is Athens at night: a spilled jewel-casket. The shaven hills like penitents bowed around us and domed the whole in watchful silence. Yes, but what of the lecturer?

"I haven't been able to reach him all day. He's been out with Sipple, drinking very heavily. They were seen on bicycles at Phaleron this afternoon, very unsteady. I've hunted everywhere. If he doesn't come in another five minutes I shall have to call the whole thing off. Imagine how delighted the women will be to see me humiliated like this." I took her arm and tried to calm her. But she was trembling with anxiety and fury combined. It was true that a slight restlessness had begun to make itself felt in the audience. Conversation had begun to dwindle, become more desultory. The women had taken stock of each other's clothes and were becoming bored. "Give him time" I said for the fourth time. People had started to cough and cross their legs.

At this moment a vague shape emerged from among the distant columns and began to move towards us with a slow, curmudgeonly tread. At first it was a mere shadowy sketch of a man but gradually it began to take on shape as it approached. It held what appeared to be a bottle in its left hand. Head bent, it appeared to be sunk in the deepest meditation as it advanced with this lagging unsteady gait. "It's Caradoc" she hissed with a mixture of elation, terror and doubt. The figure stopped short and gazed at us all with amazement, as if seeing us all for the first time, and quite unexpectedly. "He's drunk" she added with disgust gripping my arm. "O God! And he has forgotten all about the lecture."

Indeed it was easy to read all this into the expressions which played about those noble if somewhat dispersed features. It was the face of a man who asks himself desperately what the devil he is supposed to be doing in such a place, at such a time. He gazed at the lectern with a slowly maturing astonishment, and then at the assembly grouped before him. "Well I'm damned" he said audibly. At this moment the despairing Hippolyta saved the day by starting to applaud. Everyone took up and echoed the clapping and the ripple of sound seemed to stir some deep chord in the remoter recesses of the lecturer's memory. He frowned and sucked his teeth as he explored these fugitive memories, sorting them hazily into groups. The quixotic clapping swelled, and its implications began slowly to dawn on him. It was for him, all this! Yes, after all there was some little matter of a lecture. A broad smile illumined those heroic features. "The lecture, of course" he said, with evident relief, and set his bottle down on the plinth beside him—slowly, but without an over-elaborate display of unsteadiness. It was impossible to judge whether he looked as drunk to the rest of the audience as he did to us. They did not perhaps know him well enough to detect more than a desirable flamboyance of attitude —the nonchalance of a great foreign savant. Moreover his tangled mane of hair and his rumpled clothes seemed oddly in keeping with the place. He had appeared like some sage or prophet from among the columns—bearing perhaps an oracle? A ripple of interest went through us all. The Greeks, with their highly tuned sense of dramatic oratory, must have believed this to be a calculated entry suitable to a man about to discourse on this most enigmatic of ancient monuments. But it was all very well for him to remember the lecture at this late date—it must have been gnawing at the fringes of his subconscious all day: but if he had prepared nothing? Hippolyta trembled like a leaf. Our hands locked in sympathetic alarm we watched him take a few steps forward and grip the lectern forcibly, like a dentist about to pluck out a molar. He gazed around in leonine fashion under frowning eyebrows. Then he curtly raised his hand and the clapping ebbed away into silence.

"All day," he said on a hoarse and delphic note "I have been locked in meditation, wondering what I was going to tell you tonight about this." He waved an arm towards the columns behind. Hippo sighed with growing relief. "At least he is not completely out." Quite the contrary. His speech was thick but audible and unslurred. He was making a rapid recovery, hand over fist. "Wondering" he went on in the same rasping tone "how much I would *dare* to reveal of what I know."

He had unwittingly fallen upon a splendid opening gambit. The hint of mysteries, of the occult, was most appropriate to the place as well as to the gathering. There was a stir of interest. Caradoc shook his head and sank his chin upon his breast for a long moment of meditation. We, his friends, were afraid that he might indeed doze off in this attitude—but we did him an injustice. In due course he raised his leonine head once more, and with the faintest trace of a hiccough, went on in oracular fashion. "Time must inspirit us with all the magniloquence of the memories which hover here. Who were they, first of all, these ancestors of ours? Who? And how did they manage to actualise the potential in man's notions of beauty, side-step history, abbreviate eternity? Perhaps by prayer—but if so to whom, to what?" He licked his lips with relish and raked his audience with flashing eye. Hippolyta nudged me. "This is good stuff" she whispered. "But most of them don't know English and they won't realise that it means nothing. But the tone is perfect, isn't it?" It was; he was clearly beginning to surmount his infirmity rather successfully. If only he could keep up the oracular note it wouldn't matter much what he actually said. Hope dawned in our hearts.

"Anyone can build, place one stone on another, but who can achieve the gigantic impersonality of such art? The cool thrift of that classical indifference which only comes when one has stopped caring? In our age the problem has not changed, only our responses are different. We have tried to purify insight with the aid of reason and its fruit in technics: and failed—our buildings show it. Yet we are still here, still full of sap, still trying, grafted on to these ancient marble roots. They have not disowned us yet. They are still lying in wait for us, the selfish and indifferent nurselings of matter, yes; and their architecture is the fruit by which ye shall know them. It is the hero of every epoch. Into it can be read the destiny, doctrines and predispositions of a time, a being, a place, a material. But in an age of fragments, an age without a true cosmological notion of affect and its powers, what can we do but flounder, improvise, hesitate? A building is a language which tells us all. It cannot cheat."

"The only trouble" whispered Hippolyta again "is that all this is useless for my purposes. It's all gibberish, damn him."

"Never mind. At least he's here."

Caradoc's self-possession was gaining ground. He had retrieved his bottle by a stealthy sideways movement, and placed it on the lectern before him. He seemed to draw courage from an occasional affectionate glance at it. He pursued his way, adding judicious and expressive gestures.

"What can I tell you about him, this man, these men, who realised and built this trophy? Everything, in fact. Moreover everything which you also know full well, though perhaps without actually realising it. For we have all done our spell in the womb, have we not? We were all inhabitants of prehistory once, we all squirmed out into the so-called world. If I can give you the autobiography of this monument it is only because it starts with my own birth; I will give you its pedigree in giving you my own.

"In the first twenty-four hours after birth we must recognise a total reorganisation of the creature in question from a water to a land animal. No transformation from chrysalis to butterfly could be more radical, more complete, more drastic. The skin, for example, changes from an internal organ, encapsulated, to an external one, exposed to the free and abrasive airs. This little martyr's body must cope with a terrific drop in external temperature. Light and sound pierce eye and ear like gimlets. No wonder I screeched." (At this point Caradoc gave a brief but blood-curdling screech.)

"Then, to pursue the matter further, the infant like an explorer must supply his own oxygen requirements. Is *this* freedom? Nor could the stimulants of his puny machine be less irksome to come to terms with—small whiffs of deadly carbon monoxide, with its inevitable slight hypoxia. *Aiee!* Can you wonder that my only wish was to retreat, not only into the sheltering maternal pouch, but right back into the testes of the primeval ape for whom my father merely acted as agent, as representative? I can tell you that Caradoc found this no fun at all. My respiratory centre was labouring heavily. I lay on the slab, the mortuary slab of my immortal life—twitching like a skate in a frying-pan. But even this would have been too much if it had not been enough. Within a few hours an even more drastic reorganisation was to be forced upon me. My whole cardio-vascular system, so cosily established and equilibrated in the socialist state of the womb, had to change from the dull but munificent throbbing of the placental intake to a new order of things—a whole new system. From now on my own lungs were to be the primary, indeed the only source of my oxygen supply. Think of it, and pity the shuddering child." Here the lecturer provided a few illustrative shudders and took a brief pull at the bottle, as if to seek warmth and consolation against these memories.

"At birth the heat-regulating centres are sadly immature. It takes weeks of running-in for the motors to improve. At birth, as I said, there is the calamitous temperature-fall, but as yet no teeth to chatter with. It takes overcoming, and somehow I did it. I achieved the state known as poikilothermic—a shifting of temperatures to respond to the degree outside. The doctor was in raptures at the very word. Poikilothermic! He pushed a dynamometer up my behind and began to read off the impulses, beating time with his finger. But already I was dying to retire from this unequal struggle, to draw my pension and relinquish the good fight. But I must not deny that I had already had a little practice in swallowing during my period *in utero*. There had also been a few languid movements of the gastro-intestinal tract —a mere dummy practice. But I knew no more about its meaning than a conscript knows about the intentions behind intensive arms-drill; less, even, I should say, much less. He may guess—but how should I guess my own future?

"Of course some sucking motions had been present before there was anything to suck on, so to speak. Ah the teat, when it came— what an inexpressible relief! What a consolation prize for the sur-render I had made!

"All this is essential to realise if we are to think seriously about the Parthenon, my friends. The inside of a baby is sterile at birth; but a few hours afterwards . . . why, it has apparently taken in all the germs

70

that make human life so well worth unliving among our mortal contemporaries. As you can imagine I found all this most distasteful, and made it plain with whatever vocal chords I possessed. In the meantime however the skin had started to influence fluid balance by evaporation. But the whole thing felt so damn precarious—the capillary system is so liable to dilatation and contraction. Yet I went on—not consciously, by my own volition—but propelled by my biological shadow. Slowly the respiration began to stabilise. But how slowly the systolic blood-pressure comes up during childhood. The pulse-rate, so high at birth, slowly comes down to the average adult beat of 72 to the minute. But meanwhile I was also developing an enzyme system for digesting the various chemical entities I should be required to ingest in order to keep body and snail together. How slow! I mean the evolution of the body membrane in order to filter proteins adequately. At birth the lining of the intestinal tract is a hopelessly inadequate barrier which allows the more complex of the proteins to be absorbed in the blood-stream undigested. The key to later allergies may well be here; to this day I cannot face crab unless it is marinated in whisky. Then, too, the filtering and concentrating powers of the kidney are woefully immature at birth.

"Up to twenty-six weeks after the fatal event I was struggling with the shift-over to an entirely different chemical type of haemoglobin. You see, my respiration was far more diaphragmatic than intercostal. I had to be patient, to let it settle into intercostal. I did. I have never had any thanks for this. Of course *some* muscle-tone had been present *in utero*. I am not boasting. This is normal. At birth the infant presents itself with a hypertonicity of muscle which gradually levels off. Mine did. I will not dilate on all the other skills which had to be mastered if I was ever to hope to live on to build cities or temples: bowel-control, feeding, self-feeding. I passed through all these phases until by the end of late infancy the homeostasis of my physiology had become more or less established. Biting and chewing had replaced sucking—but with great reluctance. Teeth, which begin to appear after six months, gradually reach the normal size of the first deciduous set at about two years. By then, of course, I had already marked my mother with my personality by biting her breasts to cause more than one attack of nipple inflammation.

"I should add here that by the time I could utter one word I had passed through the university of a human mother's care and absorbed from her—from her voice, taste, smell, silences—a complete, overwhelmingly complete, cultural attitude which has cost me half a century or more to modify, to objectify. A cultural stance derived from every scintilla of her own anxieties, disgusts, predilections, moral and mental prejudices. All this was conveyed to me as if by massage, by radio-wave—in a fashion quite independent of the reasoning forebrain. Mould-made, then, and with the classical penis in a state of erection I capered upon the scene to play my part—a remarkable and distinguished one—in the charade of people who believe themselves to be free. 'Woman,' I cried in parody 'what have I to do with thee?' She did not need to answer. In the confessional intimacy of these first few months of absolute dependence I had received an impress, a mould-mark, a sigil which will perhaps never be effaced. My very body-image I owe to her—my slovenliness, lubberliness, my awkward gait, propensity for strong drink—responses she bred in me by leaving me alone too long to cry: by going out of the house and leaving me alone. . . . How can I thank her? For all my cities have been built in her image. They have no more than the four gates necessary to symbolise integration. The quaternary of resolved conflicts—even though it is harder to construct creatively upon a rectangle than upon the free flow of a curve or ellipse.

"And yet, even here, after so much struggle, can I say that I have succeeded? What is the education of the adolescent, the adult even, compared in power to this primary school of the affect which leaves its pug-marks alike in human minds and the marble they quarry? The notion of education, used in its ordinary sense, is surely nonsense. O perhaps it once might have connoted some sort of psychic training towards freedom from this chain, this biological prison within which all mothers want their sons to be sexual bayonets and encourage them to be such, while all fathers want their daughters to be merely fruitful extensions of their wives. Yet bayonets end in battles and deep graves—look about you: and women in order to mask their satisfactions end up in lustful widows' weeds, tailored for beauty.

"How soaring an act of insolence, then, was a construct of this

72

order, and my god, how fragile an act of affirmation! with all the dice loaded against him this man one day stood upright in his mother's shadow and evolved this terrifying stone dream. He dared not yet conceive of the existence of another shadow, an unfettered one, the soul. A meaningless but fruitful placebo. Aye! For this early conception of a soul of the dead presupposed at first a subterranean continuation of life on earth, and led inevitably to tomb-building ... the stone-age binding up of corpses symbolising their tethering to one dwelling place. The first house, the tomb, became the outer casing for the dead soul, just as the first house proper (its windows breathing like lungs) was a case for man—as indeed his mother's body had been a case to house the water-rocked embryo. But from all this to the temple—what an imaginative jump! It takes him soaring beyond the chthonian tie; for here at last is a bus-shelter, and an ark for the immortal and the divine.

"Somehow he managed, for one brief flash, to get a glimpse of the genetics of the idea and to break the incestuous tie. Hurrah, you might well say; well, but to escape chthonos is one thing and to face your own disappearance (without mummy there to help) is quite another. His tomb becomes a boat to sail him over the dark waters of the underworld. Poor little embryo, poor mock-giant. This recurring flash of vision is eternally lost and found, lost and found. His cenotaphs are battered into ruins as this has been.

"But if you can't take it with you, you can't entirely leave it behind either—the inheritance. Now comes the big historic dilemma. His sense of plastic had to cling to the morphology of what he now, tactually as well as factually, knew. The scale of his vision, however much it might include past, present and future, had to remain human. The fruit of this struggle, and this dilemma, you can see partly resolved here in this stone cartoon. Vitruvius has told us the story—how when Ion started to found the 13 colonies in Icaria he found that the memories of the immigrants had begun to fail them, to turn hazy. The workmen entrusted with the task of setting up the new temples found that they had forgotten the measurements of the old ones they wished to imitate. While they were debating how to make columns at once graceful and trustworthy it occurred to them to measure a human foot and compare it to a man's height. Finding

73

that an average foot measured one sixth part of a man's height they applied this to their column by laying off its lowest diameter six times along the overall length, the capital included. Thus did the Doric column begin to mimic and represent the proportions and compressed beauty of the male body in temple-building. And the female? You cannot have one without the other. Our author tells us that when they came to the problems raised by Diana's temple they thought of something which might symbolise the greater slenderness of the female form. The diameter would be one-eighth of the length in this case. At the bottom, then, a foot representing the slender sole. Into the capital they introduced snails which hung down to right and left like artificially curled locks; on the forehead they graved rolls and bunches of fruit for hair, and then down the shaft they made slim grooves to resemble the folds in female attire. Thus in the two styles of column one symbolised the naked male figure, the other the fully dressed female. Of course this measure did not remain, for those who came later, with finer critical taste, preferred less massiveness (or taller women?) and so fixed the height of the Doric column at seven, and the Ionian at nine, times the mean diameter.

"How to forbid oneself to elucidate reality—that is the problem, the difficulty. How to restore the wonder to human geometry—that is the crux of the matter. I do not feel that this marble reproaches us for a finer science, a truer engineering, but for a poorer spirit. That is the rub. It is not our instruments which fault us, but the flaccid vision. And yet . . . to what degree were they conscious of what they were doing? Perhaps like us they felt the fatal flaw, saw ruin seeping into the foundations as they built? We shall never know the answer to this—it is too late. But we, like them, were presumably sent here to try and enlarge infinity. Otherwise why should we read all this into this bundle of battered marble? Our science is the barren midwife of matter—can we make her fruitful?

"But what, you will ask, of the diurnal man? What of his housing? We can of course see that the individual house bears the shadowy narcissistic image of himself embedded even in its most utilitarian forms. The head, the stomach, the breast. The drawing room, bedroom, the kitchen. I will not enlarge on this. All the vents are there. I would rather consider the town, the small town, whose shape can embody both trade and worship. Now Vitruvius, in common with the whole of classical opinion, describes the navel as the central point of the human body. For my part the argument that the genital organ forms the *real* centre has more appeal to one who has always kept a stiff prick in an east wind. But I have only once met with it, and then in a somewhat corrupt text—Varro! But perhaps this was mere Roman politics, an attempt to oust the Delphic omphalos as the true centre of the world? That would be very Roman, very subtle, to try and oust the deep-rooted matriarchal principle and set up father-rule in order to promote the power of the state. This is as may be. Let us deliberate for a moment on the little town itself.

"Do you remember the rite practised specially by the Mediterranean nations in town-building? It was established around a previously marked-out centre, the so-called *mundus*. This centre was a circular pit into which they poured the first fruits and the gifts of consecration. After this the limits of the town were set by a circular boundary line drawn round the *mundus* as a centre of ritual ploughing. The simple pit or *fossa*, the lower part of which was sacred *dis manibus* to the spirits of the dead and the underworld Gods—was filled up and closed in with a round stone, the *lapis manalis*. Do you see the connection establishing itself between the two ideas—*urbs* and *mundus*?

"Then came other factors, deriving perhaps from old half-forgotten complexes—like the propitiatory building sacrifice, for example, which has hung on until today. On your way home look at the skeleton of the new gymnasium in Pancrati. Today the workmen killed a cock and smeared its blood over the pillars. But even closer at hand—do not the caryatids over there speak clearly of such a sacrifice? If ever they should be opened or fall down will we not find the traces of a woman's body in one of them? A common and deeply rooted practice. In your great narrative poem on the bridge of Arta the same ceremony is mentioned—the girl bricked into the piers. It has hung on and on in the most obstinate fashion. Stupidity is infectious and society always tries to maintain the illness in its endemic state.

"Now comes the important question of orientation to be considered so that the inhabitants or worshippers might find themselves within the magnetic field (as we should say today) of the cosmic influences pouring down on them from the stars. Astrology also had a say in the founding of temples and towns. Spika was the marking star for the ancients—people far earlier than the sophisticates who built this sanctuary. In those times it was accurately done by the responsible agent, the king, with the aid of two pegs joined by a cord, and a golden mallet. The priestess having driven one peg into the ground at a previously consecrated spot, the king then directed his gaze to the constellation of the Bull's Foreleg. Having aligned the cord to the hoof thereof and to Spika, as seen through the visor of the strange head-dress of the priestess, he drove home the second peg to mark the axis of the temple to be. Boom!

"Mobego, the god of today, does not require any such efforts on our part. Yet perhaps defeat and decline are also part of an unconscious intention? After all, we form our heroes in our own likeness. A Caligula or a Napoleon leaves a great raw birth-mark on the fatty degenerate tissue of our history. Are we not satisfied? Have we not earned them? As for the scientific view—it is one which drags up provisional validities and pretends they are universal truths. But ideas, like women's clothes and rich men's illnesses, change according to *fashion*. Man, like the chimpanzee, cannot concentrate for very long; he yawns, he needs a sea-change. Well then, a Descartes or a Leibniz is born to divert him. A film starlet might have been enough, but no, poor nature is forced to over-compensate. We are all supposed to be pilgrims, all supposed to be in search; but in fact very few among us are. The majority are mere vegetables, malingerers, fallers by the wayside. All the great cosmologies have been stripped of their validity by human sloth. They have become hospitals for the maimed, casualty clearing stations."

Hippolyta, understanding little of all this, was in a state of deep depression though tinged with relief. But Caradoc swept on, hair flying, voice booming. My only concern was for my devil box. I was anxious lest the faint wind in the mike should give me boom as well as rasp.

"There is no doubt in my mind that the geometries we use in our buildings are biological projections, and we can see the same sort of patterning in the work of other animals or insects, birds, spiders,

76

snails and so on. Matter does not dictate the form but only modifies it in order to make sure that a spider's web really holds the fly, the bird's nest really cherishes the egg. And how much the whole matter is dependent on sexual factors is really a dark question. Among squids and octopods, for example, the males have a special arm with which to transfer the semen to the female, inserting the spermatophore into the cloak or mantle of the lady. In the chambered nautilus the female clutches and retains the arm which breaks off. Spiders are differently catered for; the end of the pedipalp is used as a syringe to suck up and transfer the sperm; but before this can be done the male must discharge this into a special web which he weaves for the purpose. In fact the female does not have to be present. In the axolotl however the female picks up the sperm case with her hind feet and inserts it—a labour-saving device which Mrs. Henniker's young ladies would be prepared to perform for elderly clients. In birds sometimes, by fault an egg can produce weird gynandromorph forms, half male and half female. Aye! In the smallest thing we build is buried the lore of centuries.

"All this and much more occurred to me in my youth as a prentice architect playing about among the foundations of Canberra with Griffin, one of Sullivan's lads. It has occurred to me all over again here in Athens among the girdling shanty towns like New Ionia which your refugees from Turkey have run up, almost overnight. In these provisional and sometimes haphazard constructs you will find many a trace left of the basic predispositions we have been discussing. They have woven them up spider-wise out of old kerosene tins, driftwood, scraps of bamboo and fern, rush matting, cloth and clay. The variety and inventiveness of their constructions are beyond praise. Though they are unplanned in our sense of the word these settlements are completely homogeneous and appropriate to their sites and I shall be sorry to see them vanish. They have the perfection of organism, not of system. The streets grow up naturally like vines to meet the needs of the inhabitants, their water-points and sanitation groupings intersecting economically and without fuss. All the essential distances have been preserved, needs sorted and linked, yet everything done unprofessionally, by the eye. A micro-climate had been established where a city could take root. Streets of soft baked earth into which has soaked urine and wine and the blood of the Easter lambs—every casual libation. Flowers bloom everywhere from old petrol cans coaxed into loops and trellises, bringing shade to the hot gleaming walls of shanties. On a balcony of reed mats a cage of singing birds whistling the tunes of Pontus. A goat. A man in a red nightcap. There is even a little tavern where the blue cans go back and forth to the butts. There is shade where bargainers can fall asleep over their arguments and card players chaffer. You must compare this heroic effort with the other one we are contemplating tonight. They have much in common. A city, you see, is an animal, and always on the move. We forget this. Any and every human settlement for example spreads to West and North in the absence of natural obstacles. Is there an obscure gravitational law responsible for this? We do not know. Some law of the ant-heap? I cannot answer this question. Then reflect how quarters tend to flock together—birds of a feather. Buildings are like the people who wear them. One brothel, two, three, and soon you have a quarter. Banks, museums, income groups, tend to cling together for protection. Any new intrusion modifies the whole. A new industry displaces function, can poison a whole quarter. Or the disappearance of a tannery, say, can leave a whole suburb to decay like a tooth. Think of all this when you read of the shrine of Idean Zeus, floored with bull's blood red and polished—as in South Africa today.

"And now that we have spoken at length about womb-building and tomb-building it is time to consider tool-building and perhaps even fool-building."

Here the transcript became blurred and faulty for as he spoke an extraordinary interruption had begun to take place, a completely unexpected diversion.

A large white hand, with grotesquely painted fingernails, appeared around the column directly behind Caradoc's back. It advanced in hesitant snail-like fashion, feeling the grooves in the stone. The speaker, noticing the thrill which had rippled through his audience at this sight, and following the direction of everyone's gaze, turned his own upon this strange object. "So there you are, Mobego" he muttered under his breath. "Good."

We all watched with intense concentration as the hand became an

78

arm clothed in a sleeve of baggy black with a preposterous celluloid cuff attached to the wrist. Hippolyta drew several sharp breaths of horror. "It's Sipple" she whispered with dismay; and indeed it was, but a Sipple that none of us had ever seen, for the creature was wearing the long since discarded equipment of his first profession. Slowly the apparition dawned among the columns of the temple, and the singularity of his appearance was dumbfounding in its wild appropriateness to the place—like some painted wooden grotesque from an ancient Greek bacchanalia which had suddenly stirred into life at the rumble of Caradoc's words. First the face, with its rhinoceroid proboscis of putty, the flaring nostrils painted on to it as if on to a child's rocking-horse: the bashed-in gibus with the coarse tufts of hair sprouting from it: a tie like a cricket-bat; huge penguin-feet in bursting shoes: ginger hair pouring out of rent armpits. . . .

A shiver of apprehension ran through us all as this semi-comatose little figure stepped shyly blinking into the soft lamplight. Hippolyta's shiver was naturally one of social apprehension; but the audience stayed mumchance, unable to decide whether to laugh or cry out. Here and there one heard a few giggles, quickly repressed, but these were purely hysterical reactions. We were riveted to our seats.

Still blinking, this grotesque advanced slyly on Caradoc, who for his part seemed also to be immobilised by surprise and indecision. Then, while we were all in this state of suspended animation, hardly daring to breathe, Sipple made a sudden rush in the direction of the bottle. Caradoc, awakened from his trance, tried to counter this somewhat ineffectually by grabbing at the clown's wrists. But with a dexterity one would hardly have expected from this strange batrachian, Sipple secured the heavy bottle, and with a single wild leap jumped into the audience and began to run like a hare towards the north battlements, scattering deck-chairs and the ladies in them on either side of his passage.

The spell was broken. There were some shrieks now from the tumbled womenfolk. Everyone else was on his feet gaping. Some began to laugh, but not many. Caradoc had lost his balance and fallen forwards off the plinth, still holding on to his lectern. Knocked almost insensible he lay motionless among the historic stones. His oil-lamp exploded and set fire to a chair; fortunately this was rapidly extinguished. But while a few concerned professors moved forward, impelled by compassion, to pick up the body of the lecturer, the greater part of the audience, still screaming, watching the dramatic trajectory of the figure with the bottle held high above his head as if it were an umbrella. The speed of his flight was astonishing; one wondered how he would manage to brake it by the time he reached the outer wall.

But Sipple had other ideas. With one wild cry, like a demented sea-bird, he gave a leap clear into the sky and ... crashed down into the lighted city far below him. It was a tremendous acrobatic leap, his knees drawn up almost to his chin, his coat-tails spread upon the night sky like bats' wings. He seemed to hang up there for one long moment, outlined upon the shimmering opalescence of the capital below: and then plummeted down and vanished, his terrible yell fading behind him. More ragged screams went up and half the audience rushed to this high corner of the battlements to look down in the expectation of seeing the crumpled body lying far below. But just under the crowning wall there was a decent-sized ledge; relief and doubt began to mix, for surely this is where he would have fallen, out of sight of his audience? Or had he overshot it and actually fallen into Athens? They hung here pondering, hearing the deep burr of the traffic below and the soft honking of klaxons. From the ledge itself, too, there seemed to be no way down the cliff. Where the devil was he, then? The watchers craned, and turned perplexed faces to each other. The whole episode had been so strange and so sudden that some must have wondered if the whole thing was not an illusion. Had we dreamed up Sipple? His disappearance was so sudden and so complete. One could see nothing very clearly.

But by now the keepers had been summoned, and a number of chauffeurs as well, to examine the slopes of the Acropolis for the supposed body of the clown. Torches were pressed into service. A line of glow worms appeared along the fringes of the cliff. It was all to be in vain, however, for the clown had clambered down a steep goat-track and made good his escape.

Attention turned to Caradoc who had cut his forehead slightly and had the wind banged out of him. He was too incoherent still to answer questions about the episode and showed signs of being still a trifle drunk as well. Hippolyta herself was almost weeping with vexation. But with great presence of mind she delegated some of the local savants to conduct him lovingly down the staircases and ramps to her car. He went out like a hero, to ragged applause. Meanwhile Hippolyta bade her guests goodnight, fighting back her tears. But in fact, she found to her surprise, the whole evening had been—for all its strangeness: or perhaps because of it—a great success. People still stood about in excited thunderstruck groups, discussing what they had seen and trying to evaluate it. Accounts differed also, and arguments followed. I collected my boxes which had unaccountably escaped damage and followed her down the long staircases. She walked at a furious pace and I feared she would sprain an ankle.

In the bushes below the winged victory a figure approached her and muttered something in an undertone. I took it, from its ragged clothing to be a beggar soliciting alms. But no, it handed her a letter. She seemed filled now with a sudden new concern. She tore open the envelope and read the message in the light of the car, and it seemed to me that she turned pale, though this may have been an illusion caused by the beam of light. I loaded my gear into the boot. Caradoc was asleep in the front seat now. We climbed in and she laid trembling fingers upon my arm. "Will you do something for me tonight, please? It is very urgent. I will explain later."

The car swirled us away towards the country house. I smoked and dozed, listening to the rumble of Caradoc's voice; he was apparently continuing the lecture in his sleep. Hippolyta sat stiff and upright in her corner, lost in thought.

At Naos all the lights were on, and she stalked rapidly through the rosegardens into the house where we found the sleepy-looking figure of the Count half dozing by the telephone. She handed him the slip of paper, but it seemed that he was already *au courant*. "Yes, they phoned here" he said, and added "What is to be done?"

"Is your passport visa'd for Turkey?"

"Yes."

"Then take the car to the Salonika border; it will be easy to get him over if we lose no time."

The Count yawned heavily and pressed his ringed hands together. "Very well" he said mildly. "Very well."

Hippolyta turned to me and said: "Will you find Sipple for him? You know where he lives."

"Sipple?"

"We must get him out of Athens as swiftly as possible. The Count will drive him to Salonika if you can find him and persuade him to pack in a hurry."

"What has Sipple been doing?"

"I'll explain everything later." But she never did.

Banubula took the wheel of the big car after having stowed away a small dressing case, containing I presumed a change of clothing; he would be away a night at least. Somewhat to my surprise he proved a powerful and fastish driver, and it was not very long before we were back in the streets of the capital. We proposed to divide the labour; he would go to Kandili and draw oil and petrol, while I crossed the Plaka and alerted Sipple. We should meet at the Tower of the Winds as soon as may be. It could not be too soon for me, I reflected, for I was very tired and the hour was late. A faint grey pallor on the sea-horizons of the east suggested that the dawn—which breaks very early in summer—was not far off. In the meantime . . . Sipple. I crossed the Plaka rapidly, using my pocket torch whenever necessary in the unlighted corners.

I had never been inside Sipple's quarters; but I had had them pointed out to me during one of my walks about Athens at night. He occupied the whole of the first floor of a pretty ramshackle building of a faintly Byzantine provenance. Long narrow wooden balconies looked out towards the Observatory and the Theseum—a pleasant orientation. Two long wooden staircases mounted to the first floor from the street level—and these were a mass of flowers and ferns sprouting from petrol tins. There was hardly a passage to be pressed between them. As I made my way up, however, I noticed that the glass door at the end of the balcony was ajar, and that a faint light shone from somewhere inside the cluster of gaunt rooms. This would offer some encouragement—I should not have to knock and wake up all his neighbours.

The first room was dark and empty of everything except some rickety bamboo furniture. The walls were decorated with esoteric objects like pennons, flags of many nations, and photographs of

Sipple in various poses. Two large bird cages, muffled against the light by a green shawl, hung in the window. All this my pocket torch picked up with its vivid white beam. I half whispered and half called his name, but no answer came out of the inner room, and I made my way towards it after a decent interval, pushing open the door with my hand.

The light—dimmer than I had supposed—came from a fanlight which marked, no doubt, a lavatory. In the far corner of the room stood a rumpled and disordered bed. I did not at first look at it carefully, deeming that Sipple himself was to be found beyond the lighted door attending to the calls of nature. Indeed I could hear him breathing. More to mark time than anything I swept the cheap deal table with my lamp. On it stood a half-packed suitcase and a British passport made out in the name of Alfred Mosby Sipple. So he was already packing! I advanced to look at a framed photograph on the chest of drawers, and then something impelled me to take a closer look at the bed. I was not prepared for the shock that followed. I suddenly became aware that there was a figure in the bed lying with its face turned away towards the wall and the bedclothes drawn up to its chin. It was Iolanthe! Or at first sight it seemed to be her—so remarkable was the facial resemblance between her and the sleeping figure. One would have said her twin brother—for it was a youth, his style of haircut showed it. Intrigued, I advanced closer, feeling my curiosity turning to a vague alarm at the silence and pallor of the face—this face of Iolanthe. A glimpse of white teeth showed between bloodless lips. Then, as I touched the sheet, drawing it back, my blood began to curdle for the youth had had his throat cut like a calf. The pallor and the silence had been those of death, not sleep. There was no immediate trace of blood for it had all drained downwards into the bed. The deed then had been carried out in this same position while the youth lay sleeping. I recoiled in horror and as I did so I heard the clumsy bang of the home-made watercloset. A bar of sallow light entered the room through the open door frame in which stood Sipple, doing up his trousers. We stared at one another for a long moment, and I suppose he must have seen from my expression that I knew what had taken place in that soiled and rumpled bed. His face seemed to float in the yellow light like a great yolk. Traces of greasepaint still clung to it, grotesquely outlining one eye and his chin. His fingers depended from his wrists like cubist bananas. He gave something between a sob and a giggle; then taking a step towards me he held out a pleading hand and whispered: "I swear I didn't do it. He's mine, but I swear I didn't do it." We stayed fixed in this tableau for what seemed an age. Somewhere a clock ticked. The dawn was advancing. Then I heard the first sleepy chirping of Sipple's birds under their covers. My throat was parched and aching. Moreover something else had begun to play about the corners of my mind in disquieting fashion. In lifting the sheet I had noticed traces of something, just a few grains here and there, scattered on the sheet and pillow; I thought at first of powdered graphite which can give off a sheen. And then I was reminded of the black nail varnish of Iolanthe, the dark shellac mixture which set hard and glossy, but also chipped easily. It was not a thought or observation I pushed very far—my mind was like that of a startled rabbit. But it stayed, it nagged. Meanwhile here before my eyes was Sipple, apologetically shortening his braces and pouting at me, like a man who has been wronged and feels upon the point of tears. Behind him the sky was whitening over the sleeping city. Far off came the buzzing tang of a semantron from the Theological Seminary, calling the students to early prayers. The birds stirred, half asleep. Sipple said brokenly, but under his breath, talking purely to himself, "It's leaving the birds that really hurts." Now I heard the whimper of the big car climbing the steep slope by the temple, and reversing into position.

The tiredness which had been overwhelming me had been banished at a stroke. I walked about the city for more than an hour, drinking a raki or an ouzo in the few taverns which opened at dawn in preparation for the market carts rolling into the city with their produce. I could not get the picture of Sipple's empty bedroom with its silent recumbent figure in the corner, out of my mind. I even returned and circled the quarter like a criminal returning to the scene of his crime, gazing up at the silent windows, wondering what I should do, if anything. Finally I fell asleep on a park bench and woke when the sun was up, stiff with rheumatism from the heavy dew which had soaked my clothes.

I limped back to the hotel, relieved to find the clumsy front door already open; the porter Nik, still in his underclothes, was brewing coffee in a little Turkish coffee spoon. He jerked his head sleepily—a gesture which had become formalised both as a greeting and as an indication that Iolanthe was at present upstairs in Number Seven. Yawning with fatigue I shuffled my way up. The door of the room was ajar, and so was the door of the bathroom. Her handbag and clothes were on the bed, but I could hear her stirring next door. She had not heard me come in. I walked to the half-open door and once more my heart turned a complete somersault. She was lying in the dry tin bath covered from head to foot in fresh blood—for all the world as if she had been brutally murdered and cut to ribbons. I almost cried out but abruptly caught sight of her rapt and happy face. She was crooning to herself in a soft nasal tone, and I could just catch the words of an island song which was very much in vogue at that time: "My father is among his olive-trees." As she sang she was dabbing the vivid menstrual blood on her cheeks, her forehead, her breasts—literally painting herself in it. I recoiled before she caught a glimpse of me, and retreated on tiptoe into the corridor whence I re-entered Number Seven, this time making a characteristic noisy entrance. I heard her call my name. The bathroom door was abruptly closed, and with a swish the bath-taps went on.

I took off my shoes and lay half drowsing on the bed until she had finished. She emerged wearing my old green dressing-gown, her face radiant with a kind of defiant elation. "I have news" she said breathlessly. "Look!" She took up a key from the mantelshelf and held it up, tapping the air with it. "The key of a villa!" She sat down by my feet, bubbling over with joy. In the absurd phrasing of newspaper demotic she added: "At last! I have been solicited by a great personality! Think, Charlock! A salary, clothes, a little villa in the Plaka." For the girls of her persuasion this was the ultimate dream realised—to find oneself the mistress of a rich man. My congratulations seemed to her somewhat tepid—though in truth they were heartfelt enough; it was simply that I was dazed, half asleep, and with my mind swimming with the events of that evening. She put a sympathetic paw on my thigh, misinterpreting my lukewarmness, and went on: "Mind you, I would have stayed with you if you had really wanted. If you had spat in my mouth and said you owned

85

me. . . . But it is better that we should be good friends like we are, is it not?"

Her sincerity was so disarming that I almost began actively to regret the intrusion of this "great personality" upon the blameless youthful life we had enjoyed in Number Seven. I saw, so to speak, rapidly thrown down upon one another—or fanned out like a pack of gaily coloured cards—the thousand and one glimpses I had obtained of Athens entirely through her kind offices. I saw her buying fish, or Easter ribbons, or coloured chapbooks containing the shadowplay texts, or swimming in a cove with towed hair fanned out behind. "It's really excellent news." She crinkled her laughing eyes up, relieved. "And it may lead to other things. This man has great influence." I could not then imagine what other things such an assignment might lead to.

"Who is he? Do you know?"

"Not yet." This was a lie, of course.

The trouble with memory, and its prolix self-seeding process, is that it can always by-pass the points of intersection at which we recognise, or seem to recognise, the action of a temporal casuality. Is it a self-indulgence to want to comb it out like a head of hair? Reminded of the severed heads of Turkish traitors prepared so scrupulously for exhibition—the hair washed and curled, the beard pomaded, the eyesockets massaged with cream by terrified Greek barbers. Or the shrunken heads in bottles of spirit which still fetch great sums as talismans in the High Taurus. Well, and among these fugitive snapshots I found a faded one of Io on her island, helping her old father with his small crop of maize. At one blow she could shed the city with all its spurious sophistications and revert to the healthy peasant. Once on holiday I had seen her barefoot walking the deep dust of the road, bronze-powdered from head to foot, with a poppy between her teeth. Given the means this would have been her idea of advancement—to help the little man with his walnut-wrinkled face on some burning hillside, among the banded vipers. The key to the stuffy villa in Pancrati was the sesame which might lead her homewards, though not before she had endured all the vicissitudes and privations which come from exclusive ownership. Months later appearing, dressed like a typical adulteress in a volu-

minous scarf and dark glasses, to announce that she was going away
—traded presumably to some wealthy client on the Nile. But no,
something better, far better. Then in a tone appropriate to the comic
side of Athenian life—its Aristophanic simplicities. "Ouf, I can
hardly sit down; he has a taste for the whip, this one."

I did not go back to Naos until I was summoned, a week or two
later; nor, by some curious chemistry of the unconscious, did I
mention anything at all about Sipple, or about my visit to his rooms.
Neither did Hippolyta. Nor, most perplexing of all, could I find any
reference to the matter in the newspapers which I so diligently
perused in the Reading Rooms of the local library. Not a word, not
a breath. It was to be presumed then that the whole thing had been a
bad dream? Hippolyta was alone in the rambling house, lying almost
waist-deep in newsprint, her cheeks pink, her voice crackling at the
edges with triumph. She embraced me with a curious reverential, a
devotional tenderness—the precise way that the Orthodox peasants
salute an ikon. "Graphos" she cried, the tears rose to her blackbird's
eye. "O do look. Have you read it?" I had not. The press was plastered with it. "It is the greatest speech he has ever made—all Athens
is thrilled. He has found himself again."

These esoteric matters concerning the vicissitudes of Athenian
political life were of no concern to me; or so it then seemed. "But
you don't understand. His party is reformed at a single blow. He is
certain now to carry the autumn election and that will save the day."

"For whom? For what?"

"For us all, silly."

She poured me a drink with shaking hand, wading through the
bundles of newsprint with their vivid many-coloured letterpress, all
bannering the name of Graphos, all carrying cartoons of him, photographs of him. "He wants to see you, to thank you. He will receive
you whenever you wish."

And receive me he did, in one of those high-ceilinged rooms in the
Ministry with polished parquet floors and beautiful Baluchistan
carpets—receive me moreover at a magnificent rosewood desk containing nothing but an empty blotter and his own silver cigarette
lighter. It was the sort of desk which is only used to initial an occasional treaty. He was paler, thinner and a good deal sadder at close

quarters than I had imagined him to be—but the thin man gave off a sort of excited candence. It was gratitude partly, but also mixed with curiosity. Touching his ear with a tapering finger he asked if anyone knew of my inventions, and whether I had taken any steps to profit by them. I had only thought vaguely of the matter—the first thing was to perfect the idea. . . . "No. No" he said emphatically, standing up in his excitement. "My dear friend, do not lose your chance. There may be a great fortune in this for you; you must protect yourself somehow." His rapid and fluent French conveyed better than English could have done the temper of his excitement; I suppose I must have presented myself badly, vaguely, for my apparent indifference piqued him. "Please," he said "I implore you to let me express my gratitude by putting you in touch with my associates who would be glad to help you put the whole thing on a proper basis. I am determined that you must not lose by this thing. Or must I plead with Hippolyta to convince you? Reflect." I confess I thought he exaggerated somewhat, but what was there to lose? "You could at least examine their proposals; if you agreed with them you would find yourself well protected. There could be a great fortune in this device."

I thanked him and agreed. "Let me take it upon myself to send you to Polis for a few days to meet them and discuss with them. No harm can come of it; but at least my conscience will be at rest. I owe you a debt, sir."

I was indeed a little puzzled by my own hesitation in the matter. Certes, I had vaguely thought of patenting the device one day and licensing it perhaps; but several reasons came into play here. First, it seemed to spoil all the fun, second I could not be sure that other devices of the same order had not been thought of—the principle was spade-simple. But these considerations seemed to carry little weight with Graphos who brushed them aside with the remark that within a week he could find out and have the matter put upon a professional basis. Well, I let it go at that, but before leaving congratulated him somewhat sychophantically upon the speech which I had not read. He winced and became shy, and I suddenly saw what an effort it must have cost this shy, reticent and orderly mind to launch itself into public affairs. He had the soul of a grammarian, not a

88

demagogue. When I spoke, for example, of the poetry I pretended to discover in it he held up thin hands to his ears and protested. "Rhetoric, not poetry. You could not convince with mere poetry. Indeed there has always been something a little suspect about the latter for me since I read that Rimbaud insisted on wearing a top-hat in London. No, our objectives are limited ones. If we get in again it will be to try and prove only that the key to the political animal is magnanimity. A frail hope I agree." And he smiled his pale sad smile, moistening his lips with his snaky tongue. His fine small teeth were turned inwards, like the spokes of a lobster-pot. "So you will agree to let me send you?" I nodded and he sighed with unfeigned relief and rose to shake my hands with a surprising gratitude. "You don't know how much pleasure it will give me to send you to see my associates; even if nothing should come of it I shall feel I have discharged my obligation to you. Certainly you will have nothing to complain of from the firm."

The blue sunlight of Athens seemed so firm and stable a backcloth to my restless ideas that I was not conscious of having made any kind of decision, far less a momentous one. Hippolyta slept in her cane chair under a fallen triumphant newspaper, showing a tip of tongue, smiling like a javelin-thrower who has scored a hit. Caradoc, beside her, put a finger to his lips and smiled. It was still early, the bees dew-capped from the flowers they visited. "An olive-branch nailed to the inn-door of the world." Far away in the harbour the sirens went bim and their echoes bim bim to slap the buttocky waters of the sound, scattering from one steel surface to the next. "I am going to Turkey." Caradoc gestured. "Shh!"

So we sat, hushed in sunlight, until I felt a drowsiness creeping over me—compact with fragments seeded from recent memories of conversations jumbled and jostled—switching points like express trains as they roared through deserted junctions. Hippo, for example, in a reported speech: "I cannot sleep alone, yet no-one pleases me. It is a real dilemma." The turntable spinning away into sleep, lips parted. Then with equal suddenness some articles from Sipple's rooms which I was not conscious of having noticed at the time: cold prunes and custard in a chipped soup-plate, a blue enamel teapot, and a large pair of dressmaker's scissors. Then some un-

89

identified naked woman from the Anthology, "of delicate address and lovely insinuation". Dead notes on a classical keyboard—or might it have been already Benedicta? Here is a love-letter. "Benedicta, I love you. The collection of delta spacings for several radiations permits the identification of spurious peaks resulting either from target contamination or incomplete filtration of K alpha radiation. Your Felix". Yes, on some mutinous machine like Abel, will dawn one day the cabyric smile. Idly drifting, thistledownwise came Koepgen with his "promissory notes drawn upon reality". Monks with impetigo, their heads shaved, arousing his pithy sarcasm with their great leather-bound octavo farts. "Must one, then, negotiate with God?" he exclaims oddly; hunting as if for a thorn one can't quite locate—this is not in my line. Some tiny tufts of north wind rise now and shuffle the roses. Caradoc is trying to keep awake by writing a Mnemon, as he calls it. We have promised to collaborate on a macabre pantomime to be called "The Babes in the Food". As sudden but less distinct comes the scorching rain of white roses in *Faust*—whole epochs of redemption or desire. Caradoc saying with much severity about K: "He has been slumming among the Gnostics, selling his birthright for a pot of message. He will end by becoming an Orthodox Proust or a monarcho-trappist. All monks are grotesque lay figures—figures of funk."

Then away beyond Cape Sunion towards those distant lighthouses of sorrow across the waters, memories of Leander, where the Moslem dead await us with an elaborate indifference. Sweet, aquiline and crucial rise the stalks of the women's tombs, the soulless women of the Islamic canon. In marble one can see the pointed conciseness of a death which promises no afterlife—without the placebo of soul or resurrection. My own faint snoring matches that of C's and the soft even breathing of Hippolyta in that Athenian sunlight.

III

Well, and so it was that the little Polybus alternately leeched and strode across the mountainous yet sunny Aegean, buffeted by a fresh north wind—a sea rolled into episodes, into long spitcurls of sea-sodium. The dirty little steamer was used to this and worse—the shrapnel bursts of spray along her grimy spars. On we went bounding like a celluloid duck. Mountains of excrement and vomit accompanied the dazed passengers, and the sea held until the straits were reached and we turned down the long brown sinus with its darned shrub—its hint of an alimentary canal leading to the inland sea. Here we gathered a hard-earned knot or two of speed. So upwards at last into a misty gulf and thence, wheeling now in a long arc to the left, to paddle into Kebir Kavak for *pratique*. Here, while they were hauling the yellow flag up and down and exchanging the windy garble of mariners' talk, I first set eyes on Mr. Sacrapant who had been detailed to meet me. He sat in the stern sheets of the quarantine cutter gazing with a kind of sweet holiness up into my face, watching my expression as I fingered the engraved visiting card. It had been sent aboard by a sailor and it read

Elias Sacrapant
B.Sc. Economics London (external)

I ducked and he ducked back; a faint smile illumined that pale clerkish countenance. The infernal noise of engines precluded more intimate exchanges. But presently he was allowed aboard. He negotiated the gangway with an erratic and somewhat elderly spriteliness. His hands were warm and tender, his eyes moist with emotion. "We have been waiting for you" he said almost reproachfully "with such impatience. And now Mr. Pehlevi is in the islands for the weekend. He asked me to look after you until he comes. I cannot express my pleasure, Mr. Charlock." It seemed a bit overdone but he was charming in his white drill suit, elastic-sided boots, and white straw hat. A very large tie-pin gathered the wings of his collar over his scraggy neck. His eyes were very pale blue. Once they may have been very beautiful, almost plumbago. He spoke English as it is learned in the commercial schools of the Levant, a sort of anglo-tradesman; but very accurately and with a pretty accent. "You may relax, Mr. Charlock, for you are in my hands. I will answer any questions you put. I am the firm's senior adviser."

And so it was with Sacrapant as a companion that I came upwater at last to dangle in view of the Golden Horn where the immense inertia—the marasmus of Turkey—drifted out with sea-damps to finger my soul. Cryptogram, yes, these huge walls of liquid dung baked by the sun into tumefied shapes. It all had a fine deliquescent charm—the coaxing palms, the penis-turreted domes, the lax and faded colouring of a dream turning to nightmare. Mr. Sacrapant pointed out all the sights and explained them carefully, with the exactitude of a book-keeper, but in kindly fashion, chuckling from time to time as he did so. Moreover he was splendidly efficient, darting here and there with tickets and passports, buttonholing officials, exhorting sailors and porters. "For tonight the Pera hotel" he explained "will enable you to rest. There is every luxe. Tomorrow I will come and take you to the Pehlevi *danglion*—a water pavilion. It is prepared for you. It will be very comfortable. You will be just fine, fine." He repeated the word with his characteristic pious effervescence, joining his hands together and squeezing them. Very well.

It was the least I could do to offer him dinner when at last we arrived, and he accepted the invitation with alacrity. I confess that with the sinking sun on that gaunt but beautiful terrace I was glad of company for I felt the death-grip of the Turkish night settling upon me—a sort of nameless panic wafted up with the smell of jasmine from the gardens below, from the chain-mail ramparts of forts and ravelins which enclose Polis like the scar tissue of old wounds upon which the blood has dried black. Sacrapant was someone to talk to— but not until our meal was well on its way. He addressed himself to the menu with the same fervour—indeed he removed his wrist-watch and placed it in a safe corner before picking up his knife and fork. Also he put upon his nose a pair of pince-nez the better to instruct me in the intricacies of the local cuisine. A small vermouth had brought a flush to his cheek. But at last, somewhat assuaged by the fare, he leaned back and undid his coat buttons. "I cannot tell you what pleasure it gives me" he said "to think of you joining the firm—O I know that you have only come to discuss with Mr. Pehlevi." Here he pointed his long forefinger at his own earhole to show that he knew the subject of our discussion. "But if you agree with him, you will never never repent, Mr. Charlock. Merlin's is a marvellous firm to work for—or to let it work for you." He chuckled and rolled his eye. "Marvellous" he said. "Whether one is its slave or its master." I stared at him, eager to know more.

Mr. Sacrapant continued: "Excuse me if you think my feelings are excessive, but when I look at you I can't help the thought that if I had a son he would be about your age. With what joy I would have seen him enter Merlin's." He spoke about the organisation as if it were a religious order. "That is why." And he gave my hand a shy pat, adding ruefully "But Mrs. Sacrapant can only make girls with me, five girls. And here in Stamboul for girls ..." He rubbed finger and thumb together expressively and hissed on a lower note the word "Dowries". Then he once more lay back in a sort of infantile rapture and went on. "But there again, the firm, thank God for the jolly old firm. They will look after all. No detail is too small, and no organisation offers comparable status and benefits in the Levant. We are a hundred years ahead of our time." He poured himself a thimbleful of wine and drank it off like a hero.

It was puzzling, this string of homilies—as if he had been sent to soften me up before my negotiations with Pehlevi began. And yet ... Sacrapant was so guileless and so likeable. He dropped his napkin, and in retrieving it inadvertently revealed a strip of sock and calf. I was intrigued to see, strapped to his thin ankle, a small scout-knife such as a girl-cub might use to pierce the tinfoil on a jampot. He followed the direction of my glance. "Shh" said Mr. Sacrapant. "Say nothing. In Stamboul, Mr. Charlock, one never knows. But if attacked by a Moslem I would give a good account of myself—you may be sure." He blushed and tittered and then all at once became grave, plunged in reverie. "Tell me more about the firm" I said, since it seemed his only topic. He sighed. "Ah the firm!" he said. "When will I ever cease to be grateful to it? But I will do better, I will show it to you. I have instructions to do so. At least as much of it as we manage from here—for we are only the Levant end. The firm is world-wide, you know, in London Berlin New York. Mr. Pehlevi's brother Julian runs the London end. Yes, you shall see it for yourself. It will take up the time until Mr. Jocas comes back from the islands on Monday." It sounded an interesting way of passing the time and seeing something of the city. As I walked him through the damp garden with its throbbing crickets he went on sincerely, rather touchingly. "You know—perhaps you don't—how hard it is in the Levant to have any sort of security, Mr. Charlock. It is hard to earn good money if you have children. That is why I am so happy. The firm has meant to me serenity for wife and loved ones. Yes, and insurance too, we are all covered. Believe me, outside the firm it can be ... very hard cheese I think you say in English? Very hard cheese."

Before taking the one dilapidated taxi he lingered for some further chatter, unwilling to end the evening; and I was glad, thinking of the ghastly bedroom that awaited me. I had forgotten to bring something to read. For his part Sacrapant behaved like a man who had been deprived of any social life, who was hungry for company. Yet he had only this one topic, the firm. "You see it is very wide. Old Mr. Merlin the founder did not believe in building up and cornering one market; he preferred to build horizontally." He drew his hand along his body with a stroking gesture. "We are very wide rather than very tall. There is great variety of holdings, but few are exclusive to ourselves. That is why the firm is so wide, why there is room for everyone in it—well, almost everyone." Here he stopped and frowned. "There are some exceptions. I forgot to tell you that Count Banubula is staying in your hotel. Now he is one. He has tried for years to join the firm but with no hope. It is nothing to do with his behaviour, though when he is in Stamboul he behaves ... well, very strangely. You know him I think."

"Yes, of course. But what has he done?"

"I don't know" said Mr. Sacrapant compressing his lips and shooting me a furtive glance. "But I expect the firm does. Anyway, they will not let him in; he has exhausted his nerves in pleading but Mr. Jocas is adamant. There are one or two like him. The firm makes an example of them, and they are blocked. It is a huge pity for him for he is a gentleman, though his behaviour in Stamboul would not let you think so."

"But he is a very mild and quiet man."

"Ah" said Mr. Sacrapant on a reproving note.

"And is Merlin still alive?"

"No" said Mr. Sacrapant, but he spoke in a whisper this time, and in a fashion that somehow carried little conviction. I had the impression that he was not at all certain. "Of course not" he added, trying to bolster the simple affirmative; but all of a sudden he looked startled and somewhat discountenanced, like a frightened rabbit. He took my hand and squeezed it saying: "I will come tomorrow and take you down to the offices for a look. Now I must go." On this somewhat ambiguous note we parted. I turned back into the hotel relieved to see that there were still a few lights on—notably in the bar. And here I was overjoyed to come upon Count Banubula, the only occupant of the place, gloomily consulting his own reflections in the tarnished mirrors.

His appearance had undergone a subtle change which had not been apparent when I entered the room. How to say it? He looked flushed, snouty, and somehow concupiscent. He swayed ever so slightly, almost imperceptibly, as very tall buildings do. "Ah" he said as he caught sight of me, in a new and rather insolent fashion. "Ah Charlock!" I echoed his "Ah" on the same note, my curiosity aroused, for this was certainly not the Count Banubula I knew. "What about a little drink?" he went on sternly. It was virtually an order and I obeyed gladly. His waistcoat was undone and his monocle tinkled loosely against the buttons. The light was too bad to enable me to be sure, but it seemed to me that his lips and eyebrows had been discreetly touched up. This is, of course, a service which any barber will perform in the Orient on request. Banubula raised the sad plumes of his heavy eyebrows and closed his eyes, breathing slowly through his nose. Yes, he was drunk.

The barman produced two whiskies and disappeared through a hatch. Still with eyes shut the Count said: "I knew you were coming. I have been here some time. Ah, my goodness, if you only knew. I can't leave till Thursday now." He started an involuntary spin like a top, and just managed to find his way to a chair. "Sit" he said, in the same authoritative way. "It is better so." I obeyed, and sat opposite him, staring at him. There was a very long silence, so long indeed that I thought he would drop off to sleep but no, he had been setting his mind to the problem of conversation. "Do you know what Caradoc said about me?" asked the Count with slow sad tones. "He said I looked like a globe artichoke, and that I would die, a whisky-stiffened mummy in some Turkish bagnio." He gave a sudden squawk of laughter and then sank back into this oozing gloom, eyeing me narrowly. "Cruel man" he said. "They are all cruel men. For years I have done their dirty work. There have never been the small rewards I asked for. Nothing. No hope. I go on and on. But I have reached the end of my tether. I am in despair, Charlock. At my age one can't go on and on and on and on. . . ." his voice sank into a mumble. "But who are these people?" I said.

"It isn't anybody special, it's just the firm."

"Merlin's?"

He nodded sadly. "O Lord" I said "does no one talk about anything else in this city?"

The Count had taken a leap into autobiography and did not heed my remark. "I love my dear wife" he said "and I esteem her. But now she sits all day with her hair done up in a scarf and curl papers writing long letters about God to Theosophists. And I have become abnormal, you see Charlock? Without wishing it. In these hot climates one cannot be deprived of one's rights without something happening. Since she became religious all is ended; yet I could never divorce her because of the scandal. My name is an ancient one." He blew his nose violently in a silk handkerchief and dibbled a finger in his right ear to clear it. Then he shook his head with equal violence, as if to clear his brain. "And then all these negotiations, all this pleading. It has made me a very superstitious man, Charlock. I feel I must try and avert a horrible fate—unless they relent. Look!" He threw open his waistcoat to reveal a plump white chest to which was attached an iodine locket. He waited for my comment, but it was somewhat difficult to find words; the iodine locket was the talisman of the day, much advertised in the vulgar press. It promised health to the wearer for a very small outlay. "But health is no good" said Banubula sadly "if one's fate is wrong. I have been a student of Abraxas

98

for several years now, and I know my fate is wrong. Do you know how I defend myself?" I shook my head. He detached from his key ring a small Chaldean bronze leaf inscribed after the fashion of amulets thus:

```
S A T O R
A R E P O
T E N E T
O P E R A
R O T A S
```

Banubula nodded like a mandarin. "It is only to prove to you that I have tried everything. I even tried love potions on my spouse, but they made her violently ill. I meant well. That much you will grant me." I nodded, granting him that much.

"O God" said Banubula, drinking deeply, thirstily. "My sorrow seems bottomless, bottomless." The choice of phrase seemed to me bizarre, but I did not comment. "Just how would things change if... if all these negotiations were successful?" I asked. At once his large hairless face changed its expression, became animated with a fiery enthusiasm. "Ah then everything would be different, don't you see? I should be *in*!"

The officious barman started to bang shutter and door and indicate brusquely that the bar was closing; he refused us another drink. "You see?" said the Count. "My whole life is like that—one refusal follows another, everywhere, in everything." His lower lip dipped steeply towards a self-commiserating burst of tears, but he restrained them manfully. "To bed I think" I said, with as much cheerfulness as I could muster. And I did what I could to steer the yawing bulk of the Count upstairs to bed. "I won't bother to undress" he said cheerfully, falling upon his bed. "Goodnight."

I turned at the door to find that he was regarding me with one eye open with the air of a highly speculative jackdaw. "I know" he said "you are dying to question me about him. But I know so little."

"Could Sipple be working for Merlin's?"

"Certainly. At any rate it was they who cabled and telephoned to Hippolyta asking her, us, to get him over to Polis as swiftly as was humanly possible."

"What on earth could Sipple do? Spy?"

Banubula yawned and stretched. "As for the boy you said you . . . found; that has nothing to do with the case. I mean it's a quite independent fact which has nothing to do with the firm. It's Sipple's own business."

"But how do you know about it?"

"Sipple told me. He denied having anything to do with it."

"There was no mention in the newspapers; somebody *must* have found the body. Who hushed the whole matter up?"

"In the Middle East" said Banubula sighing "a London detective would go out of business; there are so many people with such unusual motives. . . . I mean, look, suppose Sipple's landlord thought that the discovery of a corpse would prejudice him letting the room to someone else. What would he do? He would put it in a sack and slip it into one of the sewers, or take it to the top of Hymettus and fling it into a crevasse—there are some hundreds of feet deep, sheer falls, never been explored." Banubula cleared his throat and went on in a shyer tone of voice. "Once I was forced to get rid of a rival for my wife's hand in somewhat the same fashion; though in my case it was complicated by blackmail and menaces."

"You killed a man?" I said admiringly.

"Yes . . . well . . . rather" said the Count with modesty.

He lay back, closing his eyes and breathing coolly through his nose. Then he said in somewhat oracular fashion: "Haven't you noticed Charlock that most things in life happen just outside one's range of vision? One has to see them out of the corner of one's eye. And any one thing could be the effect of any number of others? I mean there seem to be always a dozen perfectly appropriate explanations to every phenomenon. That is what makes our reasoning minds so unsatisfactory; and yet, they are all we've got, this shabby piece of equipment." He would doubtless have had more to say, but sleep gained on him steadily and in a while his mouth fell open and he began to snore. I slipped off the light and closed the door softly.

*   *   *   *   *

Sacrapant was as good as his word and appeared next morning on the dot—but this time with a big American car driven by a Turk dressed in a sort of bloodstained butcher's smock. He was all frail animation and charm as we bumped and careered down towards the waterside sectors of the town, through souks rendered colourless now by the dreadful European reach-me-downs worn by the inhabitants of this artificially modernised land. At the best the Turks of the capital looked opium-ridden, or as if clubbed half insensible; the clothes set off their mental disarray to perfection. Of course I did not voice my sentiments as strongly as this, but my hints were enough to convey the general drift of my thoughts to Mr. Sacrapant. To my surprise he expressed stern disapproval. "They may be ugly" he said. "But thanks to them we brought off one of our biggest *coups*. The firm was in touch with Mustafa's party when it was still a secret society. It knew his plans, and that when it came to power it would abolish the fez and the Arabic script. It waited. By skilful bribing we made an agreement, and the very day the *firman* was launched, we had six ships full of cloth caps standing by in the roads! We swamped the market. We had also collared the contracts for printing of stamps and the national stationery—we had been importing presses for months. You see what I mean? Doing business in the Levant is rather a special thing." He bridled, flushed with pride. I could see that all right, O yes.

The oldfashioned counting-house, down among the stinking tanneries of the yards, was rather impressive; the interior walls of three large factories had been taken out and replaced by a huge acreage of tile floor. Here, cheek by jowl, worked the Merlin employees, their desks brow to brow, practically touching one another. A deep susurrous of noise rose as if from a wasp's nest, deepened by the throaty echo of electric fans. Here there seemed to be no sleep— I could hardly see one face that did not signal itself as belonging to a Greek, Jew, Armenian, Copt, Italian. A sort of dramatic electrical current seemed to have generated itself. Sacrapant walked between the desks, bursting with a kind of hallowed civic pride, nodding to right and left. I could see from the way he was greeted that he was much beloved. He walked as a man might show off a garden, stopping here and there to pluck a flower. I was introduced to a few people, a swift sample, so to speak; they all spoke good English and we exchanged pleasantries. Also, in one corner—the only screened section —I was presented to three elderly men of Swiss accent and mien: they looked both authoritative and determined. They were dressed in formal oldfashioned tail-coats which must have been stifling to wear in summer. "They speak all our languages" said Mr. Sacrapant, adding: "You see here each man is very much head of his own section. We have decentralised as much as humanely possible. The great variety of our work permits it." He picked a bundle of ladings and C.I.F. telegrams off a desk and rapidly clipped out the words "Beirut, Mozambique, Aleppo, Cairo, Antananarivo, Lagos."

I accepted a traditional black coffee of the oriental variety and expressed my approval of all this creditable activity; afterwards we stepped out blinking into the sunlight. Sacrapant had taken the day off in order to show me something of the town and together we walked laterally across it, making clever detours to visit the choicer monuments. In the honeyed gloom of the covered bazaars I bought a few coins and some beaten silver wire of Yemeni origin, with the vague intention of presenting them to Hippolyta on my return. We sauntered through the courtyards of sunbaked mosques, pausing to feed the pigeons from a paper bag full of Indian *gram*. Thence to Al Quat for a really excellent lunch of pigeon and rice. It was late afternoon by the time we started to saunter back to the hotel, and by now I had come to see what an immense graveyard Stamboul is, or seems to be. The tombs are sown broadcast, not gathered together in formalised squares and rectangles. Graveyards were spread wherever humanity had scratched up a tombstone behind it, as in a cat-box; here death seemed to be broadcast wholesale in quite arbitrary fashion. A heavy melancholy, a heavy depression seemed to hang over these beautiful empty monuments. Turkey takes time to know.

Truth to tell, I was rather anxious to leave it and get back to the noisy but freer air of Athens. "You have brought your box, of course?" said Mr. Sacrapant. "I know that Mr. Pehlevi is most anxious to see it." But of course he would not be available for another twenty-four hours; yes, I had brought my box. Mr. Sacrapant accepted tea and toast and reminisced awhile about the business community of Smyrna where he had learned his English. In parenthesis he added: "By the way, Mr. Pehlevi told me to tell you that there is a commercial counsellor here and he will insist that any contracts we offer you should be seen by him. Just in case you have no business head. He wants everything to be above board and clear. It is part of our policy. I have told Mr. Vibart and he agrees to advise you. So all is in order." I have no idea why this remark should have seemed slightly ominous to me but it did. He sighed, and with great reluctance excused himself, saying that he had a dinner engagement. For my part, after so long and exhausting a walk, I was glad to go to my room and siesta—which I did to such good effect that it was after dark when I awoke and groped my way distractedly down to dinner. There was no sign of Banubula in the dining room, and there were few other guests whose appearance offered hope of time-killing conversation. But later I ran him down in the sunken billiard room playing mournful Persian airs on a very tinny cottage piano. Several large whiskies stood before him—a precaution against the barman with his capricious habits of shutting up the bar when drinks were most needed. He was, I should say, a little less drunk than he had been the evening before, though the number of the whiskies boded little good; he allowed me to take one and sit beside him. He was in a morose, cantakerous mood, and was hitting a lot of false notes. At last he desisted, banged the piano shut. "Well," he said, sucking his teeth "tonight I will be handing over Sipple, and then byebye to Polis."

"Handing over? Is he in irons?"

"He should be" said Banubula savagely. "They all should be."

He growled awhile into his waistcoat and then went on. "I suppose you have seen Pehlevi, eh? That swine!" Such an outburst from this mild, courteous and bookish man was astonishing.

"Tomorrow." Banubula sighed and shook his head with a gloomy star-crossed expression.

"Tomorrow you will be *in*, over my head."

It was my turn to get annoyed by this repetitive and meaningless reiteration—this eternal *mélopée*. "Listen to me" I said poking his waistcoat. "I am not in, not out, and will not be. This might be a commercial agreement over a small toy which may make me some money, that is all. Do you hear?"

"You will see" he grunted.

"Moreover any contracts will be vetted by the commercial consul" I added primly.

"Ha ha."

"Why ha ha?"

"Over whose dead body?" said Banubula inconsequentially. "Over mine, my boy. In you go and out I shall stay." He drained a tumbler and set it down with exaggerated care. Then all of a sudden the cloud seemed to lift a little. He smiled complacently and stroked his chin for awhile, looking at me sideways. "Caradoc does not spare our infirmities" he said.

"Is *he* in?"

Banubula looked at me incredulously. "Of course" he said with disgust. "Has always *been* in; but he wants to get *out*!"

"It's like a bloody girls' school" said I.

"Yes" he said with resignation. "You are right. But let us talk about something pleasanter. If I had not been on duty here I might have shown you some of the sights of the capital. Things that most people don't see. In one of the kiosks of the Seraglio, for example, is Abdul Hamid's collection of dildoes, brought together from all over the world; all carefully labelled and dusted. He was impotent, they say, and this was one of his few pleasures."

"Is old Merlin still alive?" I asked suddenly. Banubula shot me a glance and sat up straight for a moment. Ignoring my remark he went on: "They were kept in a long row of pipe-racks presented by the British Government in a vain attempt to curry favour with him. The names were so beautiful—*passiatempo* in Italian, *godemiche* or *bientateur* in French. No? They illustrate national attitudes better than anything else, the names. The German one was called the *phallus phantom*—a ghostly metaphysical machine covered with death-dew. Alas, my boy, I have not the time to show you this and other treasures."

"It's a great pity."

Banubula consulted his watch with pursed lips. "In another half hour they will take over and I shall be free. But I think I should just make sure that Sipple is all right. Do you want to come with me?"

"No."

"It won't involve us in anything, you know."

I looked and felt somewhat doubtful; depressed as I was at the thought of spending another evening here alone I did not want to become involved in any of the Count's escapades. On the other hand I was a bit anxious for his own safety. It seemed unwise to leave him alone. I must have looked as confused as I felt for he said, cajolingly, "Come on. It will take me a quarter of an hour. I will just peep through the curtain at the Seamen's Relief Club, and then we can return happy in the thought of duty well and faithfully done."

"Very well" I said. "First let me see that you can walk straight." Banubula looked wounded in his self-esteem. He rose heavily to his feet and took a very creditable turn or two up and down the room. His own steadiness rather surprised him. He looked somewhat incredulous to find himself navigating with such ease. "You see?" he said. "I'm perfectly all right. Anyway we will take a cab. I'll send these remaining whiskies up to my room for safety and we can go. Eh?"

He pressed the bell for the waiter, and gave his instructions in faultless Turkish which I envied him.

Once more we slanted down the ill-lit streets where the occasional tram squealed like a stuck pig. Banubula consulted a pocket notebook which appeared to have a rough plan pencilled into it. Why not a compass? I wondered. So like an explorer did he behave. We left the taxi on a street corner and set off in an easterly direction, skirting the bazaars. The Count walked in what I can only describe as a precautionary way, stopping from time to time, and looking behind, as if to see whether we were being trailed or not. Perhaps he was showing off? The town smelt heavily of tannin and garbage. We crossed a series of small squares and skirted the walled exterior of mosques. The city seemed to become more and more deserted and somewhat sinister. Finally however we reached a corner where light and noise abounded, where spits hissed and bagpipes skirled. A section of the sky had been cut out by the flares. There can be no mistake about the

Greek quarter of any town. An infernal industry and gaiety reigns. Here we entered a large café the interior of which was full of mirrors and birdcages, and domino players, and crossing it reached a court-yard where, in the dimness, a notice could just be discerned which read "Seamen's Relief Club". Banubula grunted as he addressed himself to a flight of creaky stairs. "How does one relieve a sea-man?" I asked, but the Count did not reply.

On the first floor there was a sort of large drill hall full of smoke and the noise of feet and chairs scraping; there was also a good deal of laughter and clapping, as if at some performance or other. Banubula stopped outside a dirty door sealed by a bead curtain. "I'm not going in," he hissed "but we'll just see. I think he's acting the fool for them now." And with sinking feelings I heard the flat nasal whine of Sipple, punctuated by the roars of laughter of the merry tars. "Yes, you may laugh, my sirs, you may laugh—but you are laughing at tragedy. Once I was like you all, I wore me busby at an angle. Then came that fatal day when I found myself abrogated. I found myself all slanting-dicular to the world. Up till then my timbrel was normal, my pressure quite serene. I lived with Mrs. Sipple in a bijou suburban house with bakelite elves on the front lawn. Not far from Cockfosters it was. (Cheers!) Every day I rose, purified by sleep, to bathe and curl my hair, and put on a clean artichoke. I travelled to Olympia in a Green Line bus like the public hangman with my clothes in a bag. It wasn't exacting, to act the clown—a pore fart-buffeted blorque. But when me whiffler abrogated I lost all my confidence. (Clapping.) Ah you may laugh, but when your whiffler becomes a soft lampoon what's to be done? I found my reason foundering, gentlemen. I started drinking tiger-drench. I had become alembicated. I had begun to exflunctify. Then when I went to see the doctor all he said was: 'Sipple you are weak in Marmite.'"

All this must have been accompanied by some fitting stage busi-ness of an obscene kind for it was greeted with roars of laughter. From where we stood we could not see Sipple; the balcony overhung him. He was immediately beneath us; all we could see was, so to speak, his reflection in the semicircle of barbarous faces, expressing a huge coarse gratification. Banubula consulted his watch. "Four more minutes" he said. "And then he's off. Phew, what a relief!" He stretched in the gloom and yawned. "Now let's go and have a drink, what?" We went downstairs again and crossed the courtyard; as we reached the lighted café a large black car drew up in the street outside and two men climbed out, yawning, and made their way directly past us, looking neither to right nor left. Banubula watched them pass with a smile. "That's the committee" he whispered. "Now we are free." And in a heavy jolting way he started to hurry along the street towards the corner of the square where the taxis were, coiling and uncoiling long legs.

"I can't tell you the relief" he said sinking back at last on the back seat cushions and mopping his brow. Indeed his face had become almost juvenile and unlined. "Now you can come and watch me pack, and I will share my whisky with you." I was puzzled by my own equanimity, by the ease with which I seemed to be accepting this succession of puzzling (even a little disquieting) events. "I've stopped asking questions" I said aloud to myself. Banubula overheard me and gave a soft chuckle. "Just as well to save your breath" he said.

I sat on the bed and watched this infernally clumsy bear-like man trying to fold a pair of trousers and squeeze them into his suitcase. He was a trifle tipsy again, and his little performance would have almost done credit to the clown Sipple. "Here," I said "let me help you." And gratefully Banubula slumped into a chair and mopped his white brow. "I don't know what it is about clothes" he said. "They have always eluded me. They seem to have a life of their own, and it doesn't touch my life at any point. Nevertheless I wear them very gracefully, and pride myself on being quite smartly turned out. These shoes come from Firpo in Bond Street." He stared at them complacently.

I had shaken a batch of notepaper out of his coat pocket; it fell on the floor. "O dear O dear," said the Count "how forgetful I am." He took the papers, set them alight in the ashtray and sat watching the flame like a child, poking at it with a matchstick until the paper was consumed and the ash broken up. Then he sighed and said: "Tomorrow I shall return to Athens and my dear. To resume my old life again."

"And Sipple?" I asked, curiosity getting the better of me. "What will become of him?" Banubula played with his lucky charm and reflected. "Nothing very special" he said. "No need for dramatic imaginings. Hippolyta says she was told that he was an expert on precious stones; that would give him a connection with Merlin all right. Then someone else said he was retained by the Government to supply political intelligence. There again . . . much can be learned in the brothels of Athens. Politicians build up dossiers about each other's weaknesses and there is hardly one who hasn't some pretty little perversion up his sleeve which could lay him open to political pressure, or even blackmail. Graphos makes them dress up and whips them mildly, so they say; others have more elaborate needs. Pangarides insists on the 'chariot'. . . ."

"What is the chariot?"

"It's really a Turkish invention I suppose. A sort of *en brochette* effect. I've never tried. It's having a small boy while the small boy himself is having a girl. With clever timing it is supposed to. . . . But heavens, why am I telling you all this? I am usually so discreet."

He sighed heavily. I could see that he was possessed by a heavy sense of regret that he should soon be called upon to resume the trappings of respectability in Athens. "Why don't you stay here, and live in a bagnio?" I asked and he sighed. Then his expression changed: "And the Countess, my wife? How could I?" Affection for her flooded into him; tears came to his eyes. "She is devoted to me" he said under his breath. "And I have nobody else in the world." His tone touched me.

"Well. Goodnight, then" I said, and he shook my hand warmly.

Next morning I slept late, and when at last I came downstairs I found that the Count had left for Galata; he had favoured me with a last communication in the form of a visiting card with a crown below the name Count Horatio Banubula and a few words pencilled on it. "Above all be discreet" he had written. But what the devil had I to reveal—and to whom?

Sacrapant was not due to appear before dusk so I lazed away the heat of the day in the garden under the shining limes watching the shifting hazes of the skyline condense and recondense as the sun reached its meridian. As it overpassed and began to decline the army of domes and steeples began to clarify once more, to set like jelly.

Light sea airs from the Bosphorus were invading the Horn now, driving the damp atmosphere upwards into the town. It must have been some sort of festival day, too, for the sky was alive with long-tailed kaleidoscopic box-kites—and by the time we reached the water under the Galata Bridge to pick up the steam pinnace which had been sent for me, I could look back and upwards at a skyline prepared as if for some mad children's carnival. In such light, and at such a time of day, the darkness hides the squalor and ugliness of the capital, leaving exposed only the pencilled shapes of its domes and walls against the approaching night; and moreover if one embarks on water at such an hour one instantly experiences a lift of the senses. The sea-damp vanishes. God, how beautiful it is. Light winds pucker the gold-green waters of Bosphorus; the gorgeous melancholy of the Seraglio glows like a rotting fish among its arbours and severe groves. Edging away from the land and turning in a slow half-arc towards Bosphorus I allowed Mr. Sacrapant to point out for me features like the seamark known as Leander's tower, and a skilfully sited belvedere in a palace wall whence one of the late Sultans enjoyed picking off his subjects with a crossbow as they entered his field of vision. Such were the amenities of palace life in far-off times. But now our wake had thickened and spread like butter under a knife, and Sacrapant had to hold on to his panama hat as we sped along, curving under the great placid foreheads and wide eyes of two American liners which were idling up the sound. It grew mildly choppy too as we rounded the cliffheads and turned into the Bosphorus. The light was fading, and one of the typical sunsets of Stamboul was in full conflagration; the city looked as if it were burning up the night, using the approaching darkness as fuel. Sacrapant waved his arm at it and gave a small incoherent cry of pleasure—as if he had momentarily forgotten the text of the caption which should go with such a picture. But we were near in to the nether shore now and travelling fast; stone quays and villages of painted wooden houses rolled up in scroll-fashion and slipped away behind us. Here, rising out of a dense greenery, one caught glimpses of walled gardens, profiles of kiosks smothered in amazed passion flowers, marble balconies, gardens starred with white lilies. Then higher up again small meadows shaded by giant plane-trees, leading to softly contoured hilltops marked with umbrella pine or the slim pin of a cypress, eye-alerting as a cedilla in some forgotten tongue. Thickets of small shipping passed us, plodding industriously into the eye of the sunset, heading for Galata. Somewhere hereabouts, in one of the small sandy coves with high cliffs, would be the wooden landing stage which marked the entry to that kingdom Merlin had called "Avalon". Sacrapant explained that it was a ruin when Merlin bought it—part Byzantine fortress and part ruined Seraglio which had belonged to a rich Ottoman family that had fallen into disgrace. "The sultan expunged them all" said Sacrapant with a kind of sad relish. "It was named thus by Mr. Merlin himself." He made a motion with his slender hand.

It was still light when we came into the landing stage where the small group of servants awaited us, two of them with lanterns already lighted against the approaching night. They were supervised by a fat bald-headed capon of a man whom I had no hesitation in identifying as a eunuch. It was partly because of the unhealthy lard-coloured pallor of his skin: partly because of the querulous spinster's voice which inhabited the fat body. He bowed in deeply submissive manner. Mr. Sacrapant waved him away with my suitcase as together we walked up a steep path into the garden of a small villa, with charming vine-trellises on three sides, and a fine balcony overlooking the sound. This was apparently where I was to stay, and here I found my case already lying on the bed open; two servants under the supervision of the bald majordomo were hanging up my clothes. Sacrapant had a good look round and satisfied himself that all was well with me before taking his leave. "I am going back with the boat" he said. "Now in half an hour a man with a lantern will come to lead you to the villa where Mr. Jocas will be waiting for you—both of them in fact."

"Both brothers?"

"No. Miss Benedicta arrived last night. She is staying for a few days here in the other villa. You will meet her also."

"I see. How long do I stay?"

Mr. Sacrapant looked startled. "As long as ... I don't know sir ... as is necessary to conclude your business with Mr. Jocas. As soon as you see him all will become clear."

"Have you ever heard the name Sipple?" I asked.

Sacrapant thought gravely and then shook his head. "Never to my knowledge" he said at last.

"I thought perhaps as you knew Count Banubula you might also know Sipple, an aquaintance of his."

Sacrapant looked desolated, and then his face cleared. "Unless you mean Archdeacon Sipple. Of course! The Anglican clergyman."

It did not seem a fruitful line of enquiry to pursue, and I let it slide out of the picture. I strolled back with him towards the landing stage, along the winding paths which smelt of some powerful scent—was it verbena? "One more thing" I said, in spite of myself. "Who was the young woman watching us as the launch pulled in? Up there among the trees. She turned back and slipped into that little copse there."

"I saw no one" said Sacrapant. "But that is where Miss Benedicta's villa is; but you know, Mr. Charlock, it might have been anyone from the harem. There are still quite a lot of old aunts and governesses living there. Mr. Merlin was very generous to both relations and servants. Why, it could have been her English or French teacher— both live there still."

"She was youngish, handsome, dark."

"Well it was not Miss Benedicta, then."

He said goodbye with a shade of effusive reluctance; I felt that he would very much have liked to accept an invitation himself to the Pehlevi table. But it was not to be; he sighed twice, heavily, and once more took his place in the pinnace. The crew was Turkish, but the captain was Greek, for he spoke to Sacrapant in his mother tongue, saying something about the wind freshening. My friend answered impatiently, placing his hat safely beside him. He gave me a small genteel wave as the distance lengthened between us.

I stood for a moment or two watching the light dying out along the mauve hills and combs of the Asiatic shore. Then I walked back to the little villa. Someone had already lighted the petrol lamps and their white fizzing flame carved black shadows out of the rooms around them. I shaved my jumping reflection in the bathroom mirror and put on the only summer suit I had brought with me. I was sitting, at peace with the world, on the side terrace when I saw a lantern coming slowly down through the trees towards me. It was held by the fat majordomo who had been present at the landing stage. He bowed, and without further words spoken I followed him slowly upwards through the gardens and copses towards where in some room (which I could not readily imagine) my host Jocas Pehlevi awaited to offer me dinner.

(If it gives me vague pleasure to recount all this, dactyl dear, it's because it seems about 100 years ago.)

It was eerie as well as rather beautiful to pass in this fashion up the hill, guided only by the single cone of light which threw up silhouettes of buildings without substance or detail. Owls cried among the bushes, and in the heavy night air, the perfumes hung on, insisted. We crossed a ruined quadrangle of some sort, followed by a series of warrens which suggested kennels; ducked through an arch and walked along the side of a ruined turret on a broad flagged staircase. Now lights began and the bulk of the main house came into view. It suggested to me a huge Turkish khan built as such caravanserais were, around a central courtyard with a central fountain; I heard, or seemed to hear, the champing of mules or camels and the whine of mastiffs. Up through a central massive door and along a corridor lighted with rather splendid frail gas-mantles. Jocas was sitting at a long oak table, half turned sideways towards the door which admitted me, staring into my eyes.

In those disproportionately huge hands he held a piece of string with which he had constructed a cat's cradle. As we looked seriously at each other I received a sudden flock of different impressions—almost like a shower of arrows. I felt at once a feeling of being in the presence of someone of great virtue, of psychic goodness, if you like; simultaneously, like an electric current passing in me, I felt as if the contents of my mind had been examined and sifted, and as if all my pockets had been turned out. It is a disquieting effect that one sometimes runs into with a medium. Side by side with this however I had an impression of a naive and almost foolish man, half crippled by nervousness. He was wearing, goodness only knows why, the traditional three-quarter frock coat and the Angora bonnet of wool—articles of attire which, on such a night, must have been a torture to support. Perhaps it was his desire to show some little formality towards a stranger? I don't know. I stared at that strange face with its swirling peruke of hair, and the tiny piratical rings in the ear lobes, and felt unaccountably reassured. When he stood up one saw that, though thick set, he was on the short side; but he had extremely long arms and huge hands. The hand that grasped mine was moist with anxiety—or perhaps just heat generated by the absurd clothes? He wore a couple of ribbons—a Légion d'Honneur and something else I could not identify. He said nothing; we just shook hands. He motioned me to an empty chair. Then he threw back his head and gave a laugh which might have seemed sinister had I not already taken such a liking to him. His canines were tipped with gold points which gave his smile a somewhat bloodthirsty effect. But his teeth were beautiful and regular and his lips were red. He was of a swarthy cast of countenance—a "smoked" complexion: and while he seemed a hale middle-aged man there was quite a touch of grey in his hair. "Well" he said. "So at last you have come to us." I excused myself for my dilatory habits and the delay I had caused. "I know, but you have other things to do, and are not interested in making money." I assured him that he was in error. "So Graphos says" he said, dropping the string into the wastepaper basket and moodily cracking a knuckle. He seemed plunged in thought for a moment; then his face changed expression. He became benign. "You see he was right, Charlock; there was no time to be lost, there never is in matters of this kind. You were distributing these things free, were you not? Well, I had one copied, and took our drawings and articles on it for a patent. In your name, of course. That means that whatever happens —you may not want to let us handle it—the invention is yours and can't be stolen." He waited a long time, staring sorrowfully at me. "My brother Chewlian did it for you. He runs the European side of the firm in London. He is an Oxford man, Chewlian." A haunted, wistful look came into his eye. "I have never been further than Smyrna, you see. Though one day. . . ." I thanked him most warmly for this kindly intervention on my behalf; he knew full well that I would not know how to go about patenting such an object. He got up to adjust a wavering gas-jet, saying as he did so: "I am very glad you are pleased. Now at the same time Chewlian drew up a contract offer for you to study. Benedicta brought it with her, you will have it tonight. Myself I think it errs on the side of over-generosity, but that is Chewlian all over!" He sighed in admiration at his brother. An expression almost maudlin in its affection crossed his face. "He behaves like a Prince not a businessman." Then all at once he grew tense and serious and said: "That remark has made you suspicious. Why?" It was perfectly true; and he had read my mind most accurately. I said lamely: "I was thinking how incompetent I am to understand business documents, and hoping you would give me time to think them out." He laughed again and slapped his knee as if at an excellent joke. "But of course you shall. Anyway you have already taken your precautions haven't you?" I saw from this that he knew I had decided to take Vibart's advice before signing anything.

I nodded. "Come, we will have a drink on it" he said cheerfully, going to the corner of the room where decanters and plates glimmered. He poured me a glass of fiery mastika and placed a cheese pie beside me on the arm of the chair. "But there is something much bigger than this one small thing. Chewlian says we should try and enter into association with you to handle all your inventions. You have others in mind, have you not?" He got up impatiently and strode up and down the room again, this time in a fit of vexation, saying: "There! once again I have made you suspicious. I am going too fast as always." He spoke a curious English with a strong Smyrna intonation, slurring the words as if he had picked them up by ear and had never seen them written. "No" I said. "It is just that the idea is completely novel to me."

He snorted and said, "My brother would have put it to you much more . . . gentlemanly I suppose. He says I am always like a carpet seller." He looked rueful and absurd in his black curate's tail coat. "Anyway he has sent us a draft paper—articles of association—for you to look at." He fingered the dimple in his chin for a moment and stared at me narrowly. "No" he said at last. "It is not suspicion so much. You are slow. To understand."

"I admit it."

"Never mind. When you understand you can see if you want to join us or not. The terms are generous, and nobody yet has been dissatisfied with the firm."

I tried my hardest not to think of Caradoc and his strictures lest my thoughts be read by this disarming yet determined little man. I nodded, attempting an air of sageness. He crossed to the door and called "Benedicta" once, on a sharp hawk-like note which was at once humble and imperious. Then he came back and stood in the centre of the room staring down at his own shoes. I looked about me studying the jumble of furniture and decoration which gave it the air of a store-room. An expensive chronometer on one wall. A case of chased silver duelling pistols. Then I identified the slightly sickly smell of rotting meat. In one corner on a tall perch slept a falcon in its soft velvet snood. From time to time it stirred and very faintly tinkled the small bells it wore. While we were waiting thus the door opened and a dark girl appeared, holding a briefcase which she placed in an armchair. I thought she bore a resemblance to the girl who had watched the launch come in to shore from the grove of trees up the hill. She stopped just outside the radius of the lamplight and said, in somewhat insolent fashion: "Why are you dressed up like that?" The note of icy contempt withered Jocas Pehlevi; he shrivelled to almost half his size, ducking and joining his hands almost in a gesture of supplication. "For him" he said. "For Mr. Charlock." She turned a glance of indifferent appraisal upon me, echoing my bow with a curt nod. It was a cold, handsome face, framed in a sheeny mass of dark hair twisted up loosely into a chignon. A high white forehead conferred a sort of serenity upon it; but when she closed her eyes, which she did in turning her head from one person to another, one could see at once how her death-mask would look. The lips were full and fine, but most of their expressions hovered between disdain and contempt. She was, then, as imperious as only a rich man's daughter dares to be: and noting this I conceived a sort of instant dislike for her which rendered her interesting.

Her entry had reduced Jocas to the dimensions of a small medieval playing-card figure; he scratched his head through the woollen bonnet. "Go and change at once" she said sternly reducing his self-esteem still further; he slipped away with an ingratiating bow in my direction, leaving us face to face. If she had moved forward a pace I would have been able to identify the peculiar blue of her eyes. But half in shadow like this they glowed with a sullen blue magnetism. She looked at me as if she had the greatest difficulty in mustering any interest in me or my doings. Then in a low voice she excused herself and turned aside to the dark corner of the room where the great falcon sat in the manner of a lectern-eagle. She was wearing a long, stained garment of some sort of leather or velveteen. Now she pulled on an extra sleeve and worked her hand into a gauntlet. Somewhere in the shadows there came the dying fluttering of some small bird, a quail perhaps, and I saw with disgust that she was busy breaking up the body with her fingers into small tid-bits. She suddenly began uttering a curious bubbling, crooning sound, uttering it over and over again as she drew a long plume softly over the legs of the peregrine; then the gloved hand teased the great scissor beak with the bleeding meat and the bird snapped and gorged. As it ate she reiterated the single word in the same crooning bubbling fashion. Slowly, with the greatest circumspection, she coaxed the falcon on to her wrist and turned to face me, smiling now. "He is the latest to be taken" she said. "I don't know as yet whether I shall succeed in bringing him to the lure. We shall see. Do you hunt? My father was a great falconer. But it takes an age to break them in."

At this moment the tall doors at the end of the room opened and I saw a long dinner table laid upon a wide balcony. Jocas had already arrived upon the scene after a change of clothes. He wore now a comfortable Russian shirt of some soft silky material. His mane of hair was brushed back above his ears. "Lights" called Benedicta sharply, and at once the servants diminished the amount of light by blowing out half the candles. This left a small lighted area at one end, with two places set. "Don't move please." Still softly crooning the girl advanced to the balcony and crossed it towards the shadowy end of the table where she was to sit throughout the meal, eating nothing herself, but from time to time feeding the falcon. Jocas and I sat at the other end of the table, served by the expressionless eunuch. Out of the corner of his eye the little man kept glancing at the girl with a professional curiosity. For her part she now removed the easy fitting rufter-hood for brief intervals, and then slipped it back into place. "It needs the patience of the devil" said Jocas. "But Benedicta is good. If you like we can take you for a day's sport—francolin and woodcock. Eh Benedicta?" But the girl sat absorbed before her plateful of bleeding odds and ends and did not deign to look up or answer. Presently she rose—it was part of the routine it seemed—and announced that she must "walk" the falcon; bidding us good-night she walked softly down the marble staircase into the garden and disappeared. It seemed to me that Jocas addressed himself to his dinner with a sort of relief after this—and he also became more voluble.

"Merlin was a great one for peregrines" he said. "And we have all taken after him—even down to small things. By the way, have you got the papers? In that briefcase Benedicta brought." He jumped up and fetched the article. "Here they are, you see, the two schemes set out separately. One is for the hearing device only; the other is a more detailed scheme—to manage all your work. You would become part of the firm, on a fixed retainer, with royalties etc." He replaced the documents carefully in the briefcase and patted it. "At your leisure: the patent is safe—only your signature is needed. But first you must see your advisers. Tomorrow I will send you back to Polis for the day, yes?"

"Tell me about the firm" I said, and Jocas twinkled with pride and pleasure, in a manner which reminded me a little of Sacrapant. "Well," he said "where to begin? Let me see."

"Begin with Merlin."

"Very well. Merlin was what you would call a merchant prince, a self-made prince. He arrived in Stamboul perhaps in the eighties of the last century on board a British yacht. He was a cabin boy. He deserted his ship, settled in the capital and began business. Much later when it had grown almost too big to handle he found myself and my brother and offered to let us become associates. How I bless the day." He joined his huge hands together and, laughing out loud, squeezed them until the knuckle joints cracked. "He was really a genius—you know all through the period of Abdul Hamid he never failed in his negotiations, he always got his firmans through. You know of course that Abdul Hamid was mad—mad with a fear of assassination. He lived up in the Yildiz palace in absolute terror. Loaded pistols lay in every corner, on every table. If startled by a sudden move he would open fire. Once his little niece ran into the room while he was dozing and he shot her. Merlin used to take special precautions when he went to see this madman—to walk slowly, talk slowly, sit quietly. He also worked out elaborate flatteries. Sent him a life-size sculpture of himself in butter, in ice-cream. Sent him clocks of extraordinary workmanship specially designed in Zürich. It was he too who achieved other objectives for the firm by skilfully planted rumours. Abdul Hamid was very superstitious and had his horoscope made afresh each day. The firm suborned the court astrologer. In this way Merlin became in a sense the most important man in Turkey. But he was as wise as he was foreseeing. All the time he was giving money to the revolutionaries, to the Young Turks. And then the fleet—it was allowed to lie there and rot in harbour because Merlin told Hamid a pack of rumours about the use the allies would make of it—playing on his fear and credulity. Why, I have seen those battleships rusting there all my life. They grow flowers on the decks. So gradually, even during the bad period, the firm grew and grew. Now of course times have changed, it is easier for us. Then when Merlin . . . left us, we two brothers took over the responsibility for Benedicta. We became her uncles." He laughed very heartily, wiping his eye in his sleeve. "And his wife?" I asked. All of a sudden Jocas looked nonplussed. His face grew serious. He thrust out his bearded chin and spread his hands in a gesture of inadequacy—as if he were powerless to answer the question satisfactorily. "There were many compromises made" he said, a trifle defensively. "There had to be. Merlin, for example, adopted the Muslim faith when he was in his fifties. Inevitably there were rumours of his wives and . . . ladies; but there was nothing very concise, very clear. This place was like a little walled city, and when you live à la turque the secrets of the harem are guarded from strangers. Benedicta was brought up in the harem, with foreign governesses first: then Switzerland for some years, that is why all her languages are so perfect." "But she is English?" Jocas nodded his head rapidly. "Yes. Yes. But I have never discussed with her, nor has Chewlian. Merlin never spoke with us about his private things. He was a very secretive man. I know that Chewlian also knows nothing because once he asked me."

Coffee, cigars and brandy found us removed to the further end of the terrace where a sort of belvedere had been improvised out of carpets and cushions, and here the conversation turned to the recording machine which I had put at the service of Hippolyta in Athens. "I heard about it from Graphos," admitted Jocas "and I could easily ask Chewlian to get me one and send it; but I understand that they are very hard to *drive*, no? And very delicate. So I waited to speak to you, to ask you about the matter."

"What would you use it for?" I asked, thinking of board-room meetings and the like. Jocas plucked his lips and looked sideways at me, with an air of exaggerated cunning. He considered. "I will tell you. We do not meddle in politics, as you know, but so often politics meddles with us that we really have to be up to date, to know what is afoot. At the moment there is a secret branch of the Young Turk officers having secret meetings. I do not want to spy on what they actually have to say; but I am on the look-out for one voice I know very well. If he has joined them, then I know all the rest. I would like a box to make a short talking of such a meeting. Would you do that for me? This has no connection with any of the other matters?" I agreed, but with every professional reservation. My little mikes were not powerful enough to record through thick walls or at a hundred metres. He shook his head. "There is a fireplace in their room; beneath one of the big cisterns. I will have a brick removed for you to put your instrument."

"In that case very well."

"I will tell Sacrapant to take you, then" he said, with considerable unfeigned relief, touching my hand. "So very good."

He rose now and gazed out across the dark garden. A heavy sea fog had been rolling up as we talked and settling over the waters of the sound below; we could hear the muffled horns and bells of the sea traffic as it moved cautiously down towards the city. It had turned a trifle cold and damp. I thought it time to take my leave of my host, but he would not let me go without a visit to the old dark barn which had been turned into a "mews" for his hunting birds. I fell in with the suggestion out of politeness: indeed there was nothing to see for the place was kept in almost total darkness. Vaguely I saw the shapes of the birds stirring on their wooden cross-bars. Jocas went among them with the assurance of long familiarity. He made a low hissing noise with tongue and teeth as he went from one to the next, checking the jesses which bound them to their perches. The smell of rotting meat was almost unbearable; and I could feel the fleas jumping from the dirty flagstones on to my ankles. "This week end we shall have some sport with them" he cried cheerfully. "If you are interested."

I agreed, for despite my personal indifference to the sport I found myself recalling to mind the image of the dark girl with the falcon on her wrist. It stirred me in some way—perhaps it was only curiosity taking fire. Nevertheless it would be interesting to go out with them, if only for the ride, and I said so. "Fine" he cried. "Fine."

We had a last whisky on the terrace, and then the majordomo appeared with the light to conduct me back to the guest house. I found that I was quite unsteady on my legs, though my head was clear enough. We had agreed that I should spend next day in Polis consulting my advisers and return once more at nightfall by launch. The old eunuch led me slowly and steadily downhill, suiting his pace to mine, until at last I stood once more upon the little terrace. He entered the house to light the lamps. I stood, breathing the damp fog-bound night air. There was no sky, no water, no stars. I floated in the swirling mist on my little balcony as if on a raft. His task completed the servant bowed and made his way up the hill. He was swallowed with the suddenness of a shutter falling. Then it was I heard the voice of the girl in the copse above the house. I could not see her in the darkness; but I could hear the low crooning of her voice as she addressed the bird on her wrist "Geldik gel ulalum", over and over again, varying the monotony of the phrase by small changes of intonation. The disembodied voice moved across the hill and faded on the ear. I was tempted to call her name once—and the thought surprised me very much indeed. Instead I went to bed and lay in a tangle of damp sheets dreaming fitful and discontinuous dreams in which the voice came from a great bird not a woman. A strange bubbling croon, like rose water agitated in its bowl by the drawing narghile; a sound at once tender and obscene. On the one hand as sweet as the calling of turtledoves, on the other as incisive as the hiss of a snake. Great wings hovered over me in a dark sky; huge talons of iron entered my shoulders and I cried out. Then the long staggering fall earthward. But I fell into one of the kiosks of the Seraglio and was chased down dark corridors and into deserted ballrooms by three blind men. They operated by sound; when I made no move they halted, nonplussed, scimitars in hand. Then my breathing would alert them and they would rush towards me once more. I woke in a fever of perspiration and anxiety. The fog had lifted somewhat and there was a frail horned moon afloat in the water. Once more to bed where I wrestled awhile with insomnia before sinking once more into the grim quagmire of the dream.

I was awoken by the sun in my eyes. It was pouring across the terrace and into the windows of the little room. Moreover, to my surprise and confusion, Benedicta Merlin was there, sitting on the stone balustrade of the verandah, staring in at me as I slept. Beside her stood the briefcase which I had forgotten the evening before. Her face was serious, almost intense, almost as if she had been deeply concentrating as she watched me asleep. I uttered an incoherent good-morning as I ran my hands through my hair, and she nodded. Her expression was still serious, almost a little puzzled. "You've been watching me asleep" said I with some vexation. "Why didn't you wake me?" She sighed and said: "I was counting up to a hundred. Then I was going to." She stood up and brushed some pollen or leaf mould from her hands. "I brought you this" she said, pointing to the briefcase. "The boat has arrived already and is waiting."

"Are you coming to Polis with us?"

She shook her head. "No. Not today. Why?"

"I don't know: we could talk."

"Talk?" she said in a higher register, and with a look of genuine suprise—as though the idea of someone wishing to talk to her was a novelty of the first magnitude.

"Why not?"

She turned on her heel almost shyly now and whispered "I must go." She crossed the path and went slowly up the hill. I stood in my pyjamas and watched her. At the edge of the copse she turned and looked back at me. I raised my hand in a greeting and she responded, but in a curious way—abbreviating the gesture, breaking it in half. Then she turned and vanished out of sight among the trees.

I retrieved the briefcase, and dressed in a hurry, knowing that the patient Sacrapant would be waiting for me in the stern-sheets of the *Imogen*, elegant yet stiff like some praying mantis or a tall crane in the docks.

121

I was suitably apologetic for having kept them all waiting and was heartily forgiven on all hands; soon we were skirling along the Bosphorus coast, scoring deeply into a marble sea and throwing out a wake of white chips as we went. Everything—the great drop-curtain of the city coming up before us—was hesitant, milky, tentative, mirage-edged. It was beautiful to sit within inches of the water, intently passive, so to speak: watching the glossy surface slide by under us. At such moments idle thoughts drift in star clusters, in cloud formations, across the nodding mind. I thought of Jocas' capacity for mind-reading and compared it to my own: neither was very esoteric. If one concentrates on a human being, really concentrates, one can see his astral shape, so to speak, unfolding and progressing forward into his future: can divine the shape of what he might become. Well, I thought to myself wryly: aren't we being the little Faustus, now? And tell me cher maître, what would you divine in the smooth pious visage of Mr. Sacrapant who sits beside you holding the sacred briefcase which is to have such a strange effect on my life? "Sacrapant?" I replied to myself. "Hum. Let me see." All this was long before he fell out of the sky. The phrases came unbidden. "Case 225 Elias Sacrapant. He has listened all his life to Turkish music— music of a transcendental monotony. His wife loves with such piety that she has driven him steadily towards a nervous breakdown." But Mr. Sacrapant was talking, pointing out places of tourist interest. (How travel narrows the mind!) I nodded and took refuge in the steady hum of the engines. Then, still engaged with my Faustian self, I presented another figure for analysis for an X-ray, so to speak: Benedicta! Here my self-possession quite deserted me. I saw a succession of snapshots of that cold face—the unselfconsciousness of beauty of its lines and planes and expressions. Case 226, so to speak. "She is living in absolute terror—and there is no reason for it. She has not realised that just as art is not for everyone so other subjects like lovemaking or mathematics can only come to fruition in the hands of their adepts. Her case is so hopeless that one must, absolutely must, love her." These ideas frightened me so much that my hair almost stood on end.

Vibart occupied a modest but comfortable little villa in a palm-filled garden beyond Pera whence he conducted a good deal of his business which concerned business men for the most part. The front room had been converted into an office with a few files and a hospitable sideboard full of bottles. He scanned through the documents from the briefcase with care but at speed, his mouth open with astonishment. Then he pushed his horn-rimmed glasses up on to the top of his head and said: "Jesus Christ, man—have you read them?" I nodded, adding: "But I'm no lawyer and wouldn't spot any catches."

"Catches!" he laughed in exasperated amazement, and took an agitated turn up and down the room. "My dear sir! Have you seen the sliding royalty scale, the size of the retainer? You should have signed the articles of association *at once*, do you hear? They not only offer to pay you royally for what you do, but to market it; and as if that weren't enough to provide ways and means for you to experiment to your heart's content." He sat down and held his ears briefly. "I don't know what to say. I'll look at them in more detail if you like but really, on the face of it. . . ."

"I felt it was almost too good to be true: as if there were something fishy behind it all."

"Merlin? Fishy? You must be mad, Charlock. The firm is as sound as a rock and highly respectable. You are damned lucky to have got into it at your age and in your line of business. I wouldn't hesitate if I were in your shoes. As a matter of fact I know quite a lot about Merlin because I was once asked to do an article for *The Times* on our Levant merchants, and I started to research on him. But somehow or other I got sidetracked, couldn't get enough material; Pehlevi raised some trivial objections—not this one, Julian, who runs the London end. I was sorry because the story was a most romantic rags-to-riches one. It started very modestly with this naval cadet deserting his battleship, and going to ground in Polis. Then, bit by bit, with his headquarters in a wine-shop he started dealing with true Scots judgement: hides, coal, corn, poppy from Lebanon, qat from the Yemen, tobacco, perhaps a touch of slaving on the Red Sea. . . . It grew up slowly but steadily into a giant he couldn't handle alone. Hence the two Pehlevi brothers, God knows where Merlin found them; they couldn't be more unlike each other in temperament and background. Jocas . . . well you've seen him. Julian I have never seen but only heard about. A tremendous career at Oxford, a spell in the Bank of England, and then he took over London for Merlin. With the disappearance of Merlin from the scene the firm divided by a sort of binary fission—rather like the division of the Eastern and Western churches: only of course they work hand in glove the two brothers. Julian is all banking, investment schemes, manufacturing, stocks and shares and so on: while this end you have chiefly trade based on marketable raw materials. Istanbul is still a conventionally strategic entrepôt for whatever comes down the Black Sea into the Med. Don't look so gloomy Charlock. With one scratch of a pen you can secure more than financial independence, man, but *riches* as well as the security to go on doing your work in peace. It makes me feel hysterical to think of your luck."

"What of Benedicta Merlin, the brunette daughter?"

"Brunette? She's blonde—or one of us is colour blind. No, I remember now that she is given to wearing wigs of various colours. But she is blonde I swear, and very handsome. There, my boy, is another prize worth carrying off. I should say she's one of the richest women in the world."

"But she's a widow. Yet they never use her married name."

"Yes, so it seems. I never saw her husband."

I stood up and finished my sherry thoughtfully. "Well," I said "I'll leave the papers with you for the time being, for a closer look into them. Then, if you still think ... I don't know." I had an obscure but obstinate feeling against tying myself down with such finality—though I could bring no reasoning to bear on it. I could not elucidate it.

"Righto" said Vibart, disappointed. "Only in a world where almost everyone has compromised and is doing a job he doesn't like or want in order to eat—one can't help envying a chap an offer like this."

"What would you do if you could?"

"Get out of diplomacy, where everything is so much smaller than life and ... no, I won't say the word, Charlock, I won't say it."

I sighed for him, having heard all this bleat before. "I know" I said. "You want to write." Vibart groaned and ran his hand through his blond hair; he smiled that attractive smile of his and agreed shyly. "My dear Charlock," he said "I have always been big with book, but it will never get written unless I WAKE UP." He shouted the last three words and banged on his desk so loudly that I was startled. "Sorry" he said. His wife called from the other room to ask if he was all right. "Of course I'm all right" he cried indignantly. "That is the whole trouble." Under the foolery I could sense a very real anger and frustration. Vibart was a charming and highly articulate victim of his education. "I must escape before I contract the diplomatic pruritus" he went on. "Better anything than to live forever in terror of committing a mere imprudence." I laughed and invited him to walk off his ill humour and he readily agreed to accompany me back to my point of rendezvous with Sacrapant. In the course of his long rambling self-decortication he threw in small scraps of hearsay, tid-bits of information which sometimes struck me as false—or if not false, then on the face of it at variance with what I would have myself surmised as true. For instance, that Sacrapant was a crack pistol-shot and had won a number of cups thereby; that Julian had ordered some Corinthian columns for the Merlin estate and had them broken up and scattered about in order to imitate a Greek temple. "But let me talk about myself" said Vibart, still seething with the desire of self-castigation. "It is my only real subject. I come, Char-lock, from an interesting family with a record for profligacy, de-generacy, philistinism and selfishness which stretches back to Tudor times. But where are all these qualities? The strain has gone thin and sour, for I am wise and good. I can show you nothing worse than sloth, shoddiness, self-delusion and sanctimoniousness. Bad enough, you may say: but all negative things. What, shall I stay on forever, and lobby myself a dwarfdom by dancing the Boaconstrictor with a Councillor's wife?"

"Well why not begin?" I asked.

"That's the whole point" he said sadly. "I would not be content with anything less than perfect. And you cannot, it seems to me, do it simply by being nice and well conducted and full of notions— though why the hell not? It's as if my parents had bought me an ex-pensive wheelbarrow when they sent me to Winchester—and here I am too lazy to garden. It's despicable." He struck his calf with his cane and uttered an oath. "On the other hand how can one believe in literature? Nor is the contemporary scene very reassuring for the newcomer. Crowns of rhubarb 1st Class, parsley, sage, rue. Tinsel for the new boys. Then the allocation of honorary titles like 'The Thrush of Finchingfield'. This is more than a little dispiriting."

"Well I don't know what to suggest."

"Of course you don't: nor do I. And here is time flying by and I'm putting on weight. Soon I shall be only fit to write the history of Adipose Rex—sorry!"

We arrived at last at the intersection of streets where Sacrapant had promised to meet me; Vibart hung on, talking, unwilling to relinquish a listener.

"I have mislaid myself" he announced with a grandiose gesture of his stick in the direction of the Grand Bazaar. "E quindi uscimmo a riverder le stelle—but where do I fit in, please tell me? Shall I carve myself a niche among the waterbabies of socialism—the songsters of the back passage? Or contract criticism, that superior form of blood poisoning? Shall I present as a Protestant Radical—one who will not take yes for an answer? Or is reticence the better part of valour? Shall I focus my 200 rabbit power eyes on the future and stay mum?"

I persuaded him to allay his vexation somewhat by entering a café with me to have a mastika; here he continued with this unwearying self-examination for my benefit. "I have mapped out my whole career more than once. I have even written my own press book. 'Full of characteristic felicities and written at gale force. Who is this Vibart? We must know.' (*Sheffield Clarion*): or 'Subtle, thought-provoking and full of lovely mince' (*The Times*): or 'Ecstasy to riffle and give away' (*Vogue*). I am already at the height of my career. How did I achieve this transcendent position? I became so thin they gave me the Nobelly Prize and a whole page in the Literary Sacrament. . . ."

"It won't do, Vibart."

"I know it won't. Comely of form was he, but with the temperament of a field-mouse. Damn. Damn."

All this of course masked a very real dilemma; I saw that to accuse himself of vainglory, narcissism, selfishness and so on was something more than just a defence; on the one hand it earned him kudos for honesty and insight—on the other it absolved him from *doing* anything about it. But then, on the other hand, why should he? I liked him the way he was. Besides one day he might shake the drops off and address himself honestly to life. "Well keep trying" I said. "And I'll get in touch with you in a day or two about the contracts." He took his leave with many a sad cautionary head-shaking, and I watched the tall athletic figure slipping away through the warrens of the souk. And here, as if by magic, Mr. Sacrapant appeared at my elbow with his characteristic air of piety. He gazed moistly at me and clasped his hands together. "Have you joined us, Mr. Charlock? Have you signed?" For some reason this incessant harping had begun to get on my nerves. "No I have not" said stoutly with a mulish expression. "I have left them to be carefully examined. It will take a day or two."

He gave a disappointed sigh, and then shrugged his shoulders. He looked inexpressibly saddened and pained—I suppose by my suspicious hesitations over joining the firm. I saw him suddenly—a grey-haired, winged and ithyphallic little man off some shattered Phrygian marbles, standing there eternally with that look of sadness, but silent now, silent as rain on fleece. Elias Sacrapant Esq. He stood upon the axis drawn by intersecting arcades, silent and friendly. "Let us talk of other things" I said. "What about this political meeting you want monitored?"

Sacrapant came down to earth at once and took on the aspect of a conspirator; he leaned forward, after a glance around him, and said: "I was going to bring that up today. I knew you had been approached. It would be just a minute or two. They meet every evening, about six, all this week. So you could choose your time." I reflected. "You know," I said "I have left one of my boxes in my room at the Pera. If you like we could get it and do the job this very evening. What do you say?"

Sacrapant's eyes kindled. "Good. Excellent. The sooner Mr. Pehlevi knows the truth the better for the firm. I will go down and tell the launch to wait for us, and then taxi up to join you at the hotel. You will walk I presume? Well, we have time, we have time."

I fell in with his wishes, and woolgathered my way back to the hotel where I tested my machine and the spare microphone. Then I lay on my bed and dozed off incontinently—to dream a confused dream of childless blue-stockings lecturing to Vibart on the novel.

Little bas bleu
Come blow up my horn
And sanction a tumble
Amid the green corn,
My pretty blue stocking
My supercherie
With prune and with prism
Fandangle with me.

I awoke with a start to find myself looking down the barrel of a pistol. I cried out incoherently and Mr. Sacrapant burst into a thin peal of delighted laughter. "It isn't loaded of course" he said. "But how was I to know that?" He became all contrition. "I am sorry. But I have been told to take some weapon with me. In case."

"In case what?"

"You never know."

I began to feel indignant. "Look here, I wasn't told that there was any danger about this performance."

"There isn't theoretically. None at all."

He slipped the weapon shyly into an inner breast pocket and pulled his coat down. "In a while we can start" he said.

It was my first introduction to the fantastic honeycomb of ancient cisterns upon which the city appears to have been built. Afterwards I returned to explore them in some detail, but on this occasion we found our way to the Yeri Batan Serai—the Underground Palace built by Justinian under the portico of the Basilica itself. Its entry was an obscure hole—like a shaft dug into a tumulus. A leather and wooden door, fastened with wire, marked the entry to the long flight of steps which led downwards at a steep angle to the water's edge. Here Mr. Sacrapant, true to form, produced a couple of pocket torches. It was awe-inspiring to plunge down all of a sudden into this watery cathedral. The symmetrical rows of columns stretched away on all sides in extraordinary perspectives, picking up the light and shadow simultaneously. The depth, the gloom, the reverberation of our footsteps on the staircase swelled the sense of mystery; moreover from one of the darker corners—across the long lanes of dark water which threw wobbling shadows into the heavy vaulting overhead—I saw a light. Mr. Sacrapant whistled, but very softly; and he was answered after a pause by a replica of the sound, soft and mellifluous. The light approached us now, and I saw that it was on the prow of a small skiff, being rowed by a single old Turk who wore a fez. "Come" breathed Mr. Sacrapant, and held the nose of the boat steady for me to climb in with my gear. Then lithe as a lizard he leaped in after me, and we set off down these long dark galleries of water. The rower propelled his boat noiselessly with a simple twisting motion of the oars, standing upright and never letting the blades rise to the water-surface. It was fearfully damp; the least sound—crepitation of water in the caverns, peppering of sand falling from the roof—became blown up, magnified, hazy. None of us spoke. The rower seemed to know his destination. Mr. Sacrapant sat forward flashing his torch upon the darkness ahead. His lips moved. He was it seemed counting the columns, for presently he muttered a figure under his breath and tapped a signal on the back of the Turk, who turned the boat at a sharp angle, and set off down a side-gallery. We came at last to a shallow flight of stairs—a sort of water-gate—which led upwards into the throat of the cistern, so to speak; it pierced the ceiling with a rotten trap of wood. This was our objective, or so it seemed. Here Sacrapant began to behave with a good deal of muffled circumspection, using gestures and mime wherever they might replace spoken words. The staircase was solid enough, but the heavy recorder was a clumsy thing to man haul, particularly in the dancing uncertain light of the little torches. However we managed the operation without mishap; and now I followed the lanyard-like figure upwards into the gloom, along a cob-webbed corridor, and then upwards again. He was hunting along the wall of a particular place. The white light jumped and flicked along the gloomy stone facings—the ground floor of a deserted subterranean Venice I thought to myself as I followed him, by this time feeling more than a touch of apprehension. Blind man's fingers. I had not visualised this sort of exploit when Pehlevi spoke to me about my recorders. But it was now too late to withdraw and show a white flag. Sacrapant skidded along the corridors in lizard fashion until at last he came to a marked stone in the wall. He produced a pocket knife and, beckoning me to preserve an absolute silence, inserted it in the interstices of the stone

I

to exercise leverage on it. It came away with relative ease and on his invitation I took a look into a sort of flue which I was soon to realise was that of a vast fireplace. The hole, admirably camouflaged, stood about six feet above ground level.

As far as the room was concerned there seemed to be a meeting already going on; chairs scraped, the hum of voices swelled and subsided. It was all barks and glottal stops to me. For my part all I had to do was to let a microphone dangle as low as possible above the hearth and start printing this medley of sound. Pertinacious Mr. Sacrapant seemed now to be in an agony of apprehension; he stood on one leg and then on the other. Why? The operation was a simple one and it was not very long before I saw my blue pilot nodding away at me in the gloom, and heard the soft whirr of the machine "taking". Down below in the board room or officers' mess or whatever the place might be, new voices came up. Some sort of speech of welcome was made; measured and sententious sentences without subsidiary clauses, following one another in dactylic progression. I had copied for about ten minutes when Sacrapant signalled me to cut out. It was quite enough, he contorted; and so I began to pull in my line like some benighted fisherman and swash up my equipment. And here all at once there was a hitch. My line must somehow have dislodged a small stone or pebble from the interior of the flue—for something fell into the fireplace with a clatter, bouncing on the iron firedogs. At once I was aware that the inhabitants of the room below had been alerted by this sound. Voices came up the flue now—they were trying to look up the chimney. I hauled in like mad; it was not a moment to hang about. Sacrapant hopped and cajoled me to hurry up. For my part I did not even wait to replace the stone, so infectious was the little man's anxiety. I hulked the stuff down and jumped into the boat; Sacrapant followed, but as he did so his little pistol slid out of his pocket and into the dark water with a splash. The Charon-like Turk was now urged to carry us away from the place at all speed; but he was typical of his leaden unhurried race, and so we set off at the same funeral pace, moving at right angles to one set of pillars. We had extinguished the light of the boat, and depended for direction on an occasional torch-blink from Sacrapant. So we scored our slow way across the inky water of the cavern. Suddenly, far away to the right, there came a gleam of yellow light—as if from a door which had been thrown open—and one heard the nibble of voices. After a moment's delay—perhaps for deliberation—we heard the snickering of pistol-shots ricocheting from the vaults and falling in the water. It was not clear whether they were aiming at us or not but the sound was ominous. Mr. Sacrapant with great prudence lay down in the bottom of the boat and complained about feeling sea-sick. The Turk was completely unmoved and plodded on towards our own landing-stage. I tried as far as possible to sit in a position which would have shielded me from our aggressors, though their exact whereabouts as well as the direction of their fire was somewhat in doubt. It seemed to take an age before we grazed the landing-stage and bumped to a halt. By now we were far away from the scene of our imprudence and it seemed possible to use the torches again; we paid off the old man and clambered out into a surprise—for darkness had already fallen upon the city. Nor did it seem possible even at this early hour to find a taxi so we were forced to content ourselves with a horse-drawn cab which jogged us, juddering and swaying, down to the Galata bridge where the launch waited, its captain smoking patiently on the bridge.

We dined late that night, but on the same balcony overlooking the darkened garden, and this time my host was in high spirits at the success of our operation of the evening; Sacrapant was invited to dinner throughout which he sat in a daze of self-congratulation. "We were shot at" he repeated wonderingly more than once. "Mr. Charlock and I were shot at." I said nothing about him lying in the sheets, or about my heroic attempt to shield myself behind the rower. We were heroes. Bravo, Felix! I was only sorry that the mysterious Benedicta was not there to share in all this grandeur; but she had crossed over to the Asiatic side, and was to meet us next morning for a day's falconry. "You know, don't you, that she has been very ill?" said Jocas Pehlevi in what seemed on the face of it an inconsequential aside. It had nothing to do with the preceding conversation. I could not quite decide whether his tone implied a warning or the registration of a simple piece of information. But the phrase cracked open a new area of comprehension. Pausing for thought, I understood now the secret source of that striking and distracted gaze—the source of what I called her beauty. It was not simply the happy disposition of features, it was the sadness and withdrawnness of her illness—the fragmentation of neurasthenia—which gave her the air of someone distractedly listening to an interior monologue, a private musical score. The total solipsism of . . . but I won't say it: why offend the doctors? But if she had not had this she might have seemed as commonplace as half a hundred good-looking blonde girls; with it she achieved a kind of legendary quality—a sick muse embedded in a statue of flesh and bone. This realisation so kindled my sympathy that I hardly heard Jocas saying: "Now can we hear your records please?" I came to myself with a start. "Yes, of course."

I had been somewhat doubtful about the quality of my recording, but here again luck held. It was pronounced clear. Jocas listened with intense concentration, smoking a cigar, head down; but after the fourth repetition he said with a sigh of relief: "It was not Mahmud was it?" Sacrapant shook his head joyfully. "Then we will not have to act for the time being" said Jocas. "Good. Good."

The conversation shifted crabwise to other and more impersonal matters which did not concern me, and I turned my attention adrift, not surprised that it wandered off in the direction of Benedicta, recalling all the minutae of her behaviour and appearance as if to find in each fragment a specimen of the sick beauty which had once become her master. I excused myself early that night, as we were due to set off before dawn, and made my way back to my waterside bungalow. I took off all my clothes and went over my body point by point, holding up the light in the mirror the better to study it. I did not know why I was doing this—nor did I ask myself any questions. But afterwards I sat down in despair on the bed and said aloud: "Is this what it is like?" What was I talking about? I don't know. I found my beauty unconvincing I suppose! Moreover to add to this feeling of horrible dispersion and inadequacy there came its twin—the conviction that I had made a choice that was as bad as it was irrevocable! But, O dear, how clearly I saw that face! Nevertheless the realisation must have cleared the air, so to speak, for that night I slept the dreamless sleep of early childhood. Iolanthe must have been dreaming about me.

As for Benedicta herself I must confess that I had seen her before, in a manner of speaking. The gesture with which Iolanthe sank down upon the carpet and drew forth the greasy little pack of playing-cards always heralded a prolonged scrutiny of the auspices, an evaluation of her future and mine; she kept them separate even then, out of who knows what sad tact? And, youthful and self-sufficient boor that I was, I hardly noticed the crestfallen tones in which she might say: "Our story is coming to an end for many years. Soon I shall go from you, and the other will come, the widow. She will be sadder than I, much sadder. I see many doors around her, and all of them closed." I yawn, of course, in the manner of one who has known (as Caradoc would say) *"des femmes de toutes les caté-gorilles"*. We scientific chaps cannot countenance divination by aces and spades. "My story is one of riches, riches, but much dissatis-faction, much unhappiness. Then look, we meet again in another country—but it will be too late to start again. Meanwhile the widow will hold you. She is fair. You will recognise her by her right foot—something is wrong with it."

"A cripple? Does she limp?"

"No. I see her dancing with you, beautifully."

Regarding with distaste the hot and crumpled sheets upon which Iolanthe gazed with such tenderness. Now when I think of it I go all-overish. All this for me was mere pleasure which never exploded into insight, couldn't disturb the egocentric flow of my hugged imaginings. The arts of introspection nourished on a junior loneliness and too much bloody education. Sentient beings for me were still almost convincing dummies, that was all. Am I typical then? A thousand little acts of attachment passed over me unnoticed. Well, later memory takes them and turns them into spears. One cries out in one's sleep, one curses. Like, I mean, taking the spectacles off my sunburnt nose as one lifts the lid from a jar of olives—to kiss me. Made foolish by too much knowledge I did not see her then as she was, namely in her natural state; I only began to "see" her when she had created her artificial self, the actress. Then she hit me between the eyes. But then one can't start loving retroactively—or can one? Too little, Felix, and then too late. Matter of fact or fact of matter? With Benedicta I chewed off my own tail in a cloud of unknowing. For better or for hearse. But wait. It was not all so vague, for she had deep and pitiful experiences to chew upon, and was gifted with a strange aberrant insight, as when she was describing early sexual experiences once and came out with: "If you push passion to extremes you are bound to tumble into mere mysticism." What a strange use of the word "mere"! But wait a minute.

It was well before dawn when I woke with a jolt to find Jocas standing over me, jack-booted and spurred, holding a lighted candle and grinning like a dog. "Sea fog" he said oracularly, and I heard the engines of the pinnace warming up, ticking over, in the obscurity below. Over his arm he carried a miscellaneous collection of clothes and boots—gear more suitable for a day of riding than the suit I had brought with me. I foraged about amongst it all and equipped myself with a good pair of boots, ill-fitting riding-breeches, an empty bandolier and such other sundries as seemed to me to be to the purpose. Then before climbing down the hill to the boat he poured us each a small cup of scalding sage-tea backed by a sip of gasping mastika. So we careened out of harbour into an olive drab mist which coiled around us, condensing upon hair and eyebrows. The dispirited dogs drowsed and yawned among the tarpaulins. "She went over early with the old falconers," said Jocas "and we'll meet later today. Hullo! What's that?"

The channel even at this early hour was full of ships labouring cautiously down towards the Horn, their bells clanging out warnings, soft wet lips of fog-horns, etc. In smaller craft the lookout banged upon a saucepan and shouted from time to time to mark position. As we had to cut directly through the middle of this traffic to reach the Asiatic side the operations of the pinnace were delicate in the extreme, although we were equipped with engines of great power and a fog-horn whose melancholy resonance was enough to set the dogs ululating. Jocas smoked a short pipe and waited patiently as his pilot trod cautiously among the indistinct shapes and sounds on this dark waterway. This funeral pace was imposed on us for nearly an hour and then, in the most dramatic fashion, the fog was peeled aside by a scurry of wind and we were in the full light of an early sunrise riding down along the low purple headlands of the nether shore where our drumming wake rippled down upon sleeping villages to set the coloured boats bobbing at deserted landing-stages. Everything was still sticky with fogdamp and Jocas would not let the guns out of their cases until the sun was fully up. The dogs were rubbed down with straw. We drank black coffee in tin mugs and watched the chromatic scale of yellow Byzantine light loop up the eastern end of the sky—until it ran over and raced everywhere, spilling among the shady blue valleys, and touching in the vague outlines of the foothills. Sunrise. Carob, sweet chestnut, oak—and plaintive small owls calling.

We were running along the low toothy headlands of the coast now, in view of the country which we were to hunt. Clumps of swaying bamboos marked the points where shallow streams had nosed their way down into the bight. The land soothed itself away to the girdle of foothills, the shallow intervening valleys wearing their scrub and green screes bravely, pin-pointing here and there a cypress plume or a regiment of olives; but for the most part dwarf oak, juniper, myrtle and arbutus—the classical combination so easily negotiable (so it seems) until one tries to follow a gun-dog into the impenetrable jungle of interlocking roots and thorns. Jocas swept the land with a powerful glass, grunting with satisfaction; then he handed it to me, pointing out here and there a shattered fragment of an abandoned temple, or a cluster of pruned stone where a seamark had been allowed to dribble into a heap of rubble under the rubbing water. But away to the north his blunt finger directed me to a small landing-stage, a tiny harbour carved in shale, where the horses awaited us. Then, moving away to the right over the green land he indicated a tall hillock, with a fine tall stand of oak-trees where, in the shadow, one saw the movement and glitter of what seemed to be an encampment. "Benedicta is up there" he said. "She will have the birds. We won't use the guns today unless . . . I suppose a boar might be tempting. But they are not very numerous now."

We were met by a little group of horsemen whose repellent ugliness and strange attire suggested to the mind the inhabitants of remotest Tartary. They were clad in greasy duffle, with jackboots of soft leather crudely sewn. Their rifles were antiques, muzzleloaders. Their little round hats with the shallow brim emphasised the almond-shaped eyes. They greeted Jocas with an awkward curtness which suggested not so much discourtesy as the shy manners of remote mountaineers. There wasn't a smile between the lot of them.

We mounted and set off across the fields feeling the sun hot upon our backs. I had not ridden for a long time—not indeed since a bit of mild hacking at university—and felt very much of a novice. Jocas rode sturdily but without elegance: indeed he sat like a sack of meal. But his huge hands and his grip on the reins suggested that a troublesome horse would receive no quarter from him.

We crossed a half-dry marsh and began to climb the hill. Here the sun had started to make the wet land steam, and the rising mist swept upwards into the trees. It was through this abrupt dimming of our vision that Benedicta appeared, mounted dramatically on a bronze stallion, her yellow hair flying loose. She was a different woman from the dark girl with the heart-shaped face; this was someone imperative, assured, even perhaps cruel when one thought of the dense blue eyes under frowning brows: periwinkle-blue, large, fierce, finely formed. "You're damned late" she said to Jocas, reining in and turning into a slow-plunging, arse-banging reorientation in order to come alongside us. Then still unsmiling she reached out and pressed my wrist in a gesture of greeting which was, to say the very least of it, puzzling: I could not decide if it were descended from some oriental form of greeting—or was an expression of personal intimacy. I was tempted to raise my wrist to my lips but refrained. The gesture itself may also have meant nothing; but it illuminated something for me in a flash. I understood what the meaning of my strange behaviour on the night before could be: I mean examining myself so carefully in the mirror, measuring so to speak the degree of my own narcissism in the face of this reflected man, I had been thinking of something like this: "Yes, but then we are modified effectively by the contents of our skulls, by what we think. This science nonsense has reduced your ability to affirm yourself. You would, faced by a challenge like this— I mean a girl who sets herself down in front of the target—turn the whole thing into hollow propositions which you would lodge in the conscious mind. You couldn't just bite into her like a fresh apple. Yum, Yum. And if you did try to warm up your feelings in a more generous direction why you'd go soft, you'd go sentimental. Too much scientific thinking has poisoned feeling, has reduced your pulse-rate so to speak. What will you do if she embraces you?" Fall off my horse I suppose.

This is where the extraordinary melancholy came over me. (At this moment my heart was simmering, my blood had turned to quicksilver. I saw her then in some almost legendary form—this slender woman riding down upon us like some drunken queen of the Iceni.) It was the melancholy subject of the night before which reflected and told himself that perhaps we are forced to choose as lovemates, shipmates, playmates those that best match our inward ugliness—the sum of our own shortcomings. No, I did not know that as yet. Not then.

There was sweat upon her upper lips and temples; her cheek was red, little blonde hairs twinkled. The eyes didn't have any particular expression—perhaps a touch of disdain. But when they turned upon mine a whole new world of feeling darkened them. Incredibly enough, I could have sworn she was in love with me. Riding like that through the mist I had a sudden feeling that I was about to faint, to fall out of my saddle into a bush. It did not last long, this vertiginous feeling, but it altered the whole scale of my sentiment. All of a sudden I was sure of something, I knew where I was; I longed to escape as a fish longs to escape from the hook. If one could apply some rational system to subjects like these how nice it would be: instead one must always talk as provisionally as possible and in terms of poetry. But damn it Charlock is a scientist—and scientists, moved by pure reason, never let themselves get into such awkward positions. Was it Koepgen who said that science was built upon defensive measurement and art upon propitiation?

"I knew you would have to come to me" she said in a low voice. A minatory note, a little too intense: I did not like it one little bit. This again did not need saying now: at the touch of her fingers on my wrist I had realised that she had been willing me to return once more in a slow curve to that point of reference in time at which our natures had ignited each other. Heavens, what a way to express it! But we *are* modified effectively by what we think. (Charlock, cool your mind with the calculus.) Benedicta waited for me to answer her—but what was I to tell her about the whole deathscapade of lovemaking? The soul of modern man is made of galvanised iron. She turned away, biting her lips. I felt sad to have to wound her by a silence and an awkwardness at a time when our feelings had defined themselves, grouped themselves, were waiting only to be honourably avowed and recognised. Thoughts incoherent and dispersed floated through my skull as the horses undulated up the slope. I heard for example (why?) the disembodied voice of Sipple say: "Blowed if I see any culture in the Parthenon. To me it's just a marble birdcage. They say it's old but how is one to tell? There are no maggots in marble." But if I could see her so clearly as she was that day I could also see, by simple extension of her look, her manner, the Benedicta who could sit for hours before a mirror with a finger to her lips, her eyes wide with fright; I could see those cupboards full of fancy-dress costumes, the masks. Puppetry! Among the cartoons of monks and demons there hung whips with knotted thongs. Yes, I saw Benedicta always elaborately gowned and cloaked, always wearing some fabulously expensive bracelet over a left-hand glove: Benedicta dressed like an Infanta to welcome me to the white walls and glassy balconies of the Sanatorium in Zürich which her father had once endowed. If I had dared then to say simply: "Benedicta I love you" it would have been like the report of a gun, the discharge of a firearm that blows the top of your skull off. The hero of the New Comedy will be the scientist in love, grappling with the androgynous shapes of his own desire. Wouldn't you say?

But we had come now to a shady clearing among the trees on the nether side of the hill which dipped down towards flat green country of simple brush, iodine coloured. Here the old falconers were gathered about the awkward wooden cages which held their choicest birds. They looked like all specialists look—all members of bowling clubs, artisans, artists, tend to look. Old wrinkled specialists who spent their whole time hanging about the falcon market in Istanbul waiting to pick up a bargain—an eyas tiercel or a peregrine or a jack Merlin (strange that should have been the name of Benedicta's father). Did he look rather like the bird? The little group talked in low moping tones, they had all of them grave bedside manners, walking among the unfidgeting birds. A single cigarette passed from hand to hand. The gunbearers stood about in dispirited fashion, but with our arrival all was animation; the horses were trimmed, girths checked. Jocas elected to fly the largest of the falcons, his favourite, while the girl chose a smaller short-winged bird—one that could be discharged from the wrist at the first sight of prey almost in the manner of a shotgun. We wound down the hill in single file before fanning out the beaters and the dogs, trained skilfully not to overrun. Once down the hill Jocas looked over our dispositions and released his hawk with a shrill musical cry, slipping the hood from its eyes. After a swift look about the great bird rose magnetically, its wings crushing down the air as it rustled upwards in a slow arc, to take up its position in the sky. This one would "wait on" in the higher air to have the advantage over far-flying quarry. But as yet we had hardly begun the beat, moving with the sun at our backs; a couple of woodcock rose with a rattle and began their crashing trajectory across the lower sky. At once the shrill ululations of the falconers broke out, encouraging the great falcon: sometimes these sounds reminded one of the muezzin's call to prayer from a minaret in the old city. So the battle began. One of the woodcocks went to earth in the bracken and refused to be flushed, but the second put up a struggle characterised by tremendous speed and finish. It seemed to be able to judge the moment when the falcon had positioned itself for the stoop; instantly it would dive for cover, only to be flushed once more by the ever advancing line of beaters. After the third or fourth repetition of this tactic it began to tire; its flights became shorter and more erratic, its plunges for cover more desperate. The hunt had now broken into several parties, interest being divided by other quarry, by new birds taking the air. I saw Benedicta discharge the short-winged hawk from her wrist at the sight of something rising among the holm-oaks. It flew at incredible speed—fired like sling-shot.

But the battle between Jocas' falcon and the woodcock had drawn us on ahead of the rest. It was exciting, the gallop across the flat plain after the failing woodcock. It was after about a mile and a half that one saw the falcon shortening its gyres, closing the space between it and its quarry. It was winding it in almost, as a fisherman winds in a fish. The woodcock despite its fatigue was game and rose again and yet again, but falteringly now. It was becoming clear that the end was not far off. The falcon once more positioned itself, helped now by a slight change of the wind's direction. It took careful aim and suddenly came plummeting down at incredible speed, adding impetus to its own great weight. Too late the woodcock tried to evade it by a feint, sliding sideways as it fell. The falcon struck it a devastating blow with its hind talons—must have struck it stone dead in fact. Down they both went now in a tangle of wings, leaving a trail of slow feathers in the amazed sky. At once the horsemen shrilled and ululating broke into a ragged gallop to retrieve. Jocas, red faced and sweating, was radiant now. "It was that shift of wind" he said. "Game won't fly upwind under a hawk. What elegance eh?"

So the day wore on; the quarry was rich and various, and the incidents of the kill quite absorbing. I quite forgot my saddle-soreness. The longest and dourest battle Jocas fought was, strangely enough, with one of the slowest birds of all, a marsh-heron. One would not have believed that this slowcoach of a bird could outwit a trained hunting falcon, but this was very nearly the case. Indeed the heron proved so cunning that it had Jocas swearing with admiration. Though in lateral flight it is slow, the big concave wings give it the power of rising rapidly in the perpendicular, almost in balloon-fashion: meanwhile the falcon has the task of trying to gain sufficient height for her swoop by circling. The old heron used this advantage so skilfully that the battle ranged over several miles. Twice the hunter misjudged its distance, or the heron sidestepped it in the sky: for the falcon, missing it, lost the superiority of altitude and was forced laboriously to circle once again until it could take up the required position. But at last—and both birds were tiring—it found its site and with a swoop "bound to" the heron and both came tumbling out of the sky together with a crash and scream.

The sun was well past meridian when we broke off the sport, all parties converging once more on the hillside where, on the eastern side, there was an old abandoned marble fountain in the denser part of the wood. Here a spring boomed and swished among the rocks and the air was sweet and dense with moisture. Here we lounged and ate the food which had been sent up from the boat in a wicker hamper. The cool shade was luxurious and sleep-inducing—and indeed Jocas had dozed off for a few moments when a messenger rode into the camp from the boat and summoned him back on urgent business to the town. He left at once, with a resigned good humour, promising to send the pinnace back to collect us that night. I was left alone with

Benedicta. Watching her move among the falconers, smoking a cigarette, I felt the same tightening of the heart-strings as I had when she rode out of the mist towards me. That, and also an awkward sense of premonition: the sense of having embarked upon a course of action which would reward me perhaps by the very damage it might do to my self-reliance, or my self-esteem. Rubbish. And yet at the heart of it all there was a magical content—for there seemed to me to be absolutely no alternative to make me hesitate. Apart from the greed of the eyes and the mind which contemplated her bright abstract beauty there was a kind of inner imperative about the matter —as if this was what I had been foreordained to execute. Yes, I had been born to get myself into this extraordinary, this bewitching mess. So that it was with a complete calm assurance of happiness that I merely nodded and agreed when she said: "I am sending them all down to the boat this evening, but I shall stay here tonight with you. Yes?" The "yes" was quite unnecessarily wistful, and now I repaid the debt of my earlier negligence by taking up the slender fingers and pressing them back to life. So we sat side by side on the grass eating a pomegranate, surrounded by all the bustle of the encampment breaking up. They were to leave us sleeping bags, wine and food; torches, cigarettes, and horses. It took them hours to pack up. We stood side by side in the green evening light to watch the cavalcade straggle down the valley towards the sea. Then, thoughtfully stripping off her clothes, she turned slowly towards the broken marble cistern where the water drummed, she walked into it, seizing the foaming jets with her hands, crying out with joy at its intense cold. So we lay rolled about and were massaged by the icy spring, to climb out cold and panting at last, and lie down as wet as fish in each other's arms. But before making love or attempting any kind of intimacy, lying mesmerised like this, still trembling from the cold water, she uttered a cautionary phrase which to my bemused mind sounded as normal, as natural, as the bustle and boom of the water in the marble dish below us. "Never ask me anything about myself, will you? You must ask Jocas, if you want to know anything. There's a great deal I do not know. I mustn't be frightened, you see."

It seemed to me perfectly logical and I accepted the proposition, sealing the pact there and then with kisses that grew ever more breathless, refining themselves, exploding like oxygen bubbles in the blood. It was like that, the sun shone, the water drummed: everything had become explicit. We sank, deeper than pain, into this profound nescience. And here again (as always when we made physical love) her teeth were drawn back in a kind of agony under her lips, and she said: "O help me, please help me, you must help me." An awkward Galahad was born. I vowed to help her—how I did not know. And mentally I replied—as I have continued to reply ever since—"Of course, my darling, of course: but against what, against whom?" There was never any answer to my question, only the pain swelling up between us; she pressed ever harder upon me as if to blot it out, as if to still the ache of some great bruise. Thus our sensuality was touched by a kind of unconscious cruelty—kisses inflicting pain, I mean, rather than pleasure. It was all very well the "Help me": but afterwards she lay like the ghost of rigor mortis itself, her lips blue, her heart beating so that she could hardly breathe. But at last her eyes unclouded by the invading terror. Sex cleared the brain, if only for an instant. She ached in my mind like a choice abstraction.

A flock of ignorant chattering birds, perhaps starlings, crossed our middle vision and settled in a cloud in a nearby tree. Benedicta foraged for the little carbine which they had left behind with the horses and began shooting at them. She shot in a brilliant unpremeditated way, like a woman making up her face, and with an unerring exactitude. The birds began to fall on the ground like overripe fruit. She emptied the magazine before throwing the hot gun down on the sleeping bag. How easily she could fill me with disgust. It was beautiful, the polarity. Then she went and lay face down by the spring, almost touching the foaming tumbling cataract with her lips. It seemed to me then, smoking and watching her, that she was something the heart must desire and I grew afraid of the depth of my feelings. I had never before actually feared to be parted from a woman; the novelty was overwhelming. Tomorrow I must leave for Pera, I decided; if only to get away from this suffocating network of ambiguities. After all, with her wealth etc. etc. I could hardly keep her as a mistress. ... The ideas rose in clouds like sparrows to a gunshot. But even before they had fallen back into place she was saying:

"I feel this is decisive—that you'll never leave me. I have never felt that before." She always said this: she felt men expected it. All introspection now seemed little more than a fruitless mental debauchery. I closed up my mind and searched ever more frantically for that tame and now touchingly tremulous mouth. We fitted into each other like Japanese razors.

I had collected a couple of huge leeches which had settled on the back of my thigh; by the time I felt the slight discomfort their bites caused, they were already gorged with my blood and fit to burst. Benedicta found a salt cellar in the basket and dosed them until they spewed out the blood they had sucked and fell writhing into the dust. She seemed to like this. I went to wash in the spring. It was her turn now to sit and watch me which she did with a discomforting intentness.

Then she nodded to herself and came to sit beside me to dangle her long legs over the marble parapet. With a long stealthy look about her—as if to make sure that there were no interlopers about in the wood to oversee her—she bent down towards her right foot. I had already noticed that the small toe was bound up with a piece of surgical tape, perhaps to protect a scratch. It was this tape that she now stripped with a small slick gesture, holding out the foot for my inspection. The last toe was double! They were both perfectly formed in their twinship, but joined together. She watched me watching her with her head on one side. "Does it disgust you?" she said. It did, but I said that it did not; I bent to kiss it. Moreover I understood why she kept it bound away, out of sight of the super-stitious inhabitants of the place—for it was a clear mark of witch-craft in popular oriental belief. The vestigial toe, known to the medievals as "the devil's teat". She flexed her feet, stretched, and then wandered away to sit under a tree with an air of morose intent-ness. "What are you thinking, Benedicta?" Her grave, unwavering abstraction melted; she put a stalk of grass between her teeth and said: "I was wondering what they will think when they know. But what can they do, after all?"

"Who?"

"Julian, Jocas, the firm; when they know what I have decided. About you, I mean."

"Has this anything to do with them?" She looked surprised at the question and turned her head away to frown at the darkening sealine. "Besides," I went on "just what have you decided?"

But to this her only answer was to beckon me down among the blankets where we lay luxuriously cradled between snore and wake. For much of the night we talked quietly between snatches of sleep. She spoke about a youth spent in Polis—but haphazardly, at a venture. And from these imprecise snatches of dialogue a sort of picture emerged of a childhood full of loneliness like my own, but spent in the sunken gardens of the Seraglio, in the glittering emptiness of the harem with its shallow female sensualities. In the summer heats of the old capital she had learned everything there was to be known about the sexual appetites before she reached puberty. Learned and forgotten. Perhaps this was why for her there clung about the act of lovemaking a hollow, disabused quality? I don't know. She behaved as if her feelings, her private mind, were enclosed in the frailest of eggshells easily smashed by an indiscreet question. I asked her, for example, if her father was still alive; the idle question made her stiff with anxiety. She sat upright like a frightened hare and admonished me savagely for breaking the rule she had made. I must ask Jocas, she said. I had quite a task in calming her.

At dawn, or just after, we heard the purring of the ship and saw the long white furrow lengthening towards the harbour. She bound up her toe in haste. It was time to gather up our gear and leave. Benedicta was sunk in deep thought as the horses negotiated the shallow slopes of the hill. At last she said: "When are you going to sign those contracts?" I had completely forgotten their existence, and the question startled me. "I hadn't really decided to in my own mind. Why, do you want me to?" She considered me gravely from under frowning brows. "It is strange that you should doubt us" she said. "But I don't," I protested "my hesitation hasn't been due to doubts about the validity of the contracts, no. They are overgenerous if it comes to that. No, it was something else. You see, it isn't easy because I am in love with you." She raised her quirt and struck me across the wrist. "Reflect," she said "reflect."

"I'll see" I said. She looked at me curiously but said no more. The ride back was smooth and uneventful. Jocas was waiting for me with a hospitably decorated table; but Benedicta disappeared, after saying that she would lunch in the harem. I tried to visualise it—a sort of glass and pink satin *bonbonnière* looking out over the calm straits, the light filtered by the intricately carved wooden screens; to this I added some cage birds singing away in melancholy fashion and a few old deaf women, all clad in black, and a few wearing clumsy and ill-chosen frocks from Paris and London. Lots of gold-leaf and mirrors. There would be a horn gramophone with a pile of outdated waltzes and other jazz, and bundles of old picture papers. . . . I wondered how near the mark this was. There did not, for example, appear to be a book anywhere. "You are wrong" said Jocas sharply. "She has a very smartly decorated suite of rooms, satin and gold mouldings; brilliant chandeliers, and electric pianola, two black cats, and a bookcase full of beautifully bound books by Loti and company."

"Thank you" I said ironically, and he made a mock bow.

"At your service" he said. "We are not all equally gifted alas. I should have been a fortune teller in the bazaars I suppose. That's what my brother Chewlian says. I was very backward as a boy; even now, do you know, I read and write with difficulty. I have to pretend that I have mislaid my glasses. It has hampered me very much. It kept me a trader whereas Chewlian is truly a merchant prince. I stayed here, but he went on to brilliant studies. He found a patron, one of the monks who ran the orphanage found him a rich man to stake his education. But I was always ill, always wet my bed until my twentieth year. Had no head and no taste for paper. Only in middle age did I calm down, when Merlin found us."

"But you were orphans?"

"Yes."

"And *brothers*—how would you know?"

"It's only presumption, partly a joke; we shared the same door-step on the same evening. What more is a brother? I love Chewlian and he loves me."

"I think I shall go back to Pera this evening."

"Yes, why not?" he said equably, pressing my arm. He was a most lovable man. "You will see nothing of Benedicta for at least two days now. She has a treatment. But she will get in touch with you if she wants. I think she has to go back to Zürich this coming week."

I found the idea curiously chilling. "She didn't say anything?" I asked, in spite of myself.

"I am not Benedicta's keeper" he said frowning, in a chewing way.

This line of conversation seemed to come up against a brick wall; I felt that perhaps I had unwittingly offended him and strove to be a trifle more conciliatory as I went on. "Tomorrow I'll have a last session with Vibart and decide about the contracts. I will certainly sign for the little ear device—which I call a 'dolly'. About the more general terms of association I'll have to see."

"I know the cause of your hesitation" he said, and burst suddenly into a peal of clear laughter. "It is perfectly justified. Once when I mentioned something I saw from your expression that you were surprised: because it meant that someone had been through the papers you had left behind in Athens. The new device for electric Braille remember?"

He was dead right. I looked at his jutting nose and laughing eyes. "You thought it was us, didn't you? Well, it wasn't. It was Graphos, one of his hirelings who went through your stuff; what they expected to find I don't know. But they photographed everything—all the parts in shorthand and the mathematical materials. Now, when I asked Graphos for details about you after this first idea came along, he was able to supply quite a number of them—things you are working on. I saw at once that we needed you as much as you need us. We can shorten your labours by years if we give you the right equipment, by years. How, for example, can you work on the firefly and the glowworm without a chemist, indeed a big laboratory to help? We have such a place—Lunn Pharmaceuticals belongs to us. Do you see?"

"The firefly produces light without heat" I had written once, unwisely. "Note. If we could find just *how* chemically we would be on to a new light source perhaps." But of course he was right, one could hardly conduct this kind of experiment from Number Seven. Jocas was watching me intently, still smiling. He said "The trembler fuse, the iodine and sodium bath experiment—how will you ever do it?" All of a sudden the lust for this vocation—of tampering with the universe and trying to short-circuit its behaviour—grew up in me and seized me by the throat. I drank my wine off at a thrust and sat bemused, staring through him. O God! There was also the danger

146

that they might sow these idle speculations broadcast behind my back, that other talents with bigger means might scoop me. I was ashamed of the idea, but there it was! Pure science! Where does the animal come in? "Also a passage where you ask why bats can navigate in the dark and not blind men in the light, eh?"

"Hush," I said "I'm thinking." I was, I was furiously thinking of Benedicta, sitting here trapped between conflicting hesitations.

Jocas said softly: "I do not see that the matter of Benedicta alters anything." He was doing his mental lip-reading act again. Here he was wrong; she hung above all these abstractions and ambiguities, like a wraith, an *ignis fatuus*. That long cobra face seemed to symbolise everything that this vast organisation of talents stood for. I was looking fame and fortune in the eyes, and the eyes were adding the promise of love to these other riches. "Yes" I said at last, surprised to find how very hoarse my voice sounded. "Yes, I am a fool. I *must* sign on."

In retrospect this epoch, these scenes, astonished me very much when I recalled them; I mean after everything went to wrack, the period of illnesses and confusion, the period of intemperate recriminations, quarrels, fugues. Once, when she was hovering on the outside edges of logic I even heard her say: "I only really loved you when I thought you were determined to be free from the firm. It seemed to promise me my own freedom. But afterwards I saw that you were just like everyone else." Then in my fury I shouted back. "But you made me sign on, Benedicta. It was you who insisted, remember?" She nodded her furious head and answered: "Yes. I had to. But you could have stuck to your guns and that would have altered everything. For us both."

"Then why, knowing this, did you insist on having the child? There was no need, was there?"

"There were several reasons. Partly because Julian said so, Nash said so, it was a question of cure as well. Then also the question of succession, inheritance. Then me. All those miscarriages were a challenge I had to face. Above all I wanted a Merlin of my own, of my very own." She paused and gazed about her as if to identify a small sound, audible only to her inner ear. "You see," she added tonelessly "hardly anyone saw my father in the flesh—though everyone saw Julian at some time or another. Then the firm—O Felix, Benedicta is only a woman, she has always tried to be just." Nearly sobbing.

"You talk about yourself as if you were a *product*."

"I am. I am." That was the *tu quoque*!

Then later when I was speaking to her about love she could say with burning indignation: "But love is a reality not a recipe." As if in offering her mine under any other guise I had tricked her. Woman!

But all this lay far in the future on that day when Jocas walked down to the landing stage beside me with his choppy deliberate tread. "You will go back to Athens and wait" he said and his tone was one of delighted relief. He embraced me warmly and added "Benedicta will come to you very soon. You may find her the key to everything. Sacrapant will deal with all the contractual details. I myself am going to the islands for a week. Felix!"

"Yes, Jocas?"

"You are going to be very happy."

But I felt bemused still and shaken by my own decision. Sacrapant gazed at me with lachrymose tenderness; it seemed that he too knew, without being told, that I had agreed to sign, but tact held him silent. We roared away across the opalescent water towards the dim horizon where the city lay half asleep, embedded in time as in a quagmire—the Orient Venice snoring its life away.

Vibart was at his habitual desk, only today he was blowing an egg to add to his collection. He had pierced the blue crown with a needle and was blowing with soft absorption into the tiny hole; from the opposite hole the yolk was being gradually expelled to fall with a plop into his waste-paper basket. "There" he said with relief, placing the tiny object in a velvet hollow among others like it. He closed the casket reverently and joined his fingers together as he gazed at me. The contracts lay on the corner of the desk among his papers. Without saying anything I picked up the pen from its slab of marble and signed in all the required places. "Well" he said in great good humour "I should bloody well think so. Fame and fortune, my boy, and all for the price of a signature. The luck some people have." I sat, staring into the middle distance, still confused and somehow fearfully sad. Somehow he must have felt it (he was a discerning young man under his flippant exterior) for his tone changed to one of quickening sympathy; the drink he poured out with which to celebrate the event was a stiff one, and I needed it, or felt I did. Though why?

I seemed to hear the voice of Sacrapant saying: "The firm is wonderful, Mr. Charlock, sir. When I could not find anyone for my wife's womb the firm found me someone."

The telephone rang squeakily. "It's for you" said Vibart. I recognised the voice of Jocas, distant and crackly. "Felix I forgot. I have a message for you to give your friend Koepgen in Athens. He is your friend, isn't he?"

"Yes. I didn't know you knew him."

"I don't personally. But when you see him will you tell him that we have located the ikon he has been hunting for?"

"The ikon?"

"Yes. We know the monastery now."

"I'll make a note of it."

"Thank you very much Felix."

I drew a deep breath and said: "Jocas, I have just signed the articles of association."

"I knew it" he said. "I felt it. I was sure."

Vibart sat sipping his drink and staring at me. "I think" he said "you need cheering up. I shall invite you to dine with me and hear all the details of my literary career. It's really moving forward. And by the way, I have found a good *French* tavern. You know the French will eat anything and everything? If the sky rained corpses' legs they would become cannibals without a second thought. Moreover it would be doubly enjoyable because it was all free. Will you?"

"Very well. But I must first take these down to the firm and draw some money."

This I duly did, walking through the crowded and insanitary streets among the snarling bands of dogs. Mr. Sacrapant was waiting for me: but oh, he looked so grave and tender, like an undertaker's mute on his best behaviour. He took the documents and cashed me a voucher for what seemed to me an immense sum of money which I stuffed into my slender wallet with cold fingers.

"You'll be going back to Athens I have no doubt" he said. "I shall treasure the memory of our association. Mr. Charlock."

"Thank you. In a day or two I expect." The truth of the matter was that I was reluctant to leave the city before I had seen Benedicta once more—and yet, there seemed to be no chance of that. Should I perhaps send her a message? Perhaps the mere information that I was still in Polis might.... "I think I shall be here another full week if you should need me" I told him. "At the Pera as usual."

The malignant tumour of a passive love! All of a sudden the gloomy steamy city seemed peopled with ghosts. I was still numb from the astonishment of finding myself freed at a stroke from all the smaller preoccupations that beset ordinary men—financial dependence, occupation, etc. It was puzzling too because anyone in my place would have felt exultant, bouyant. I felt absolutely nothing. I took a cab back to the detestable hotel, confirmed my reservation, and ordered lunch in the garden. There were no familiar faces there, much to my regret. I would be grateful for Vibart's company while I was waiting. Waiting! But suppose Benedicta did not come? There was Zürich of course.

At dusk Vibart called for me and together we wandered through the city towards his newly discovered eating-house. His wife would join us there later. As usual he was preoccupied with the building of this imaginary career upon which he was too hesitant to embark; the self-rebukes multiplied in all directions. He had decided to reverse the usual order of things and start by writing his own reviews. "Why not the obits?" I suggested. "They are always the warmest reviews. The one consolation about death is that everyone will be forced to be nice to you behind your back."

"I never thought of that" said Vibart settling his napkin round his neck with the air of a man putting on a cummerbund. "And I think it's too late. My novel *The Asparagus Tree* comes out this week. ('A novel of surpassing tameness'.) The press will be very mixed. I console myself by saying that the jealousy of opinionated dunces is the finest of literary compliments. I have arranged a good sales picture however. What do you think of thirty thousand in the first week? On a sliding scale that should be a clear thousand, no?"

"Too good by half" said his wife with the resignation of one who has been forced to live with an obsession. She was a handsome brunette with shy green eyes. Her name was Pia.

The food was excellent. "I should give it up" I said "and go for criticism. Grudge yourself off in the weeklies. Loll your way to fame. Tell yourself that you are not really a bad man, just unprincipled."

"Can I" said Vibart in envious tones "tell my wife about your terrific coup—the new job?"

"Of course." He did so at once and at some length. She watched me curiously, surprised by my lack of animation. I suppose I looked guilty. I tried to explain. "You see, Vibart, in a sort of way I am in the same boat as you. I didn't want to be just an artificer, I wanted to go for abstractions: use the calculus as a springboard. Like you, I have not got the talent. I shall be forced to confine myself to tinkering with nuts and bolts instead of dealing with poetic abstractions, new universes. And I did *so* want to be the age's little Copernicus. Hence the apathy you criticise. I am the wrong kind of scientist. I shall have to be content to try and do something about the faulty five senses in this smaller way."

He reeled off, in quotation: "An eagle for sight, a hart for hearing, a spider for touch, an ape for taste, and a dog for smell."

"I would have liked to achieve in my line whatever would correspond to a work of art—which my friend Koepgen has defined as an act of disciplined insubordination. But if one isn't up to it?" My God, we were getting drunk.

"Oh dear," said his wife "here I am surrounded by failures." But she was grateful for this self-identification with her husband's private myth.

Vibart was put into a very good humour now, and decided that all further self-recrimination should cease until he had reached the coffee. The food, he said, was too good to poison, and besides the only metaphysical problem for the gourmet was: is there a life beyond the gravy?

A freak thunderstorm had sprung up and rain was needling the tragic arcades; we sat long over our brandies, waiting for it to stop, and once more the consuming restlessness beset me. My wrist-watch purred on in tireless itching iteration and I found myself wondering about Benedicta and the new equivocal pattern of relationships which she alone could disentangle and sort out. Time is the only thing that doesn't wear out. "I think I shall probably leave for

Athens tomorrow" I said, since Vibart was planning a picnic for the week-end and I had suddenly tired of him. The rain was thinning off now, and a fresh wind was flapping at the awnings of the cafés. By luck we found a cab to take us back to Pera, where I dropped off at my hotel. Here all my doubts were resolved for on the mantelpiece of my room I found a single joss stick burning in a vase and a visiting card of Jocas' with a few words written on it in that curiously shapeless and hesitant hand which I was to come to know so well—Benedicta's. She was coming to visit me on the morrow at noon. All at once—like the wind dispersing storm cloud at a single puff—I felt the whole weight of my preoccupations lift and disperse. I fell asleep almost at once, but it was to dream elaborate and intricate dreams, worthy of Vibart, about the long life-lines of the firm which channelled all the riches of the Orient into the huge granaries over which Jocas presided—furs and skins and poppy, caviar and salt and wax, amber, precious stones, porcelain and glass: dreams of such fervent inaccuracy that even while I dreamed them I was forced to correct the picture, to bring it up to date with less romantic commodities like pit-props from Slovenia, oil and wheat from Russia, bauxite and tin and coal. And somewhere in the middle of this meretricious romancing I saw the pale face of Benedicta staring down at me as if from a lofty window: and I woke with a start with a question on my lips, namely, "You must be sure that her riches play no part in any decision you make." But riches cannot be side-stepped; they mark one like a hare-lip. I studied her handwriting with misgiving. A graphologist would have hinted at glandular imbalances. But I loved her, I loved her, I loved her.

Then in the morning, following out in some obscure fashion the train of thought which had dribbled through my sleep, I went out to the fashionable Pera shopping area with the scientific intention of spending a very large sum of money: in order to see exactly how it felt. I thought I might buy a sporting gun or a wrist-watch or a fountain pen of abhorrent splendour. Accustomed to live meagrely if decently, to find myself frequently short, not of necessities, but of luxuries, I wanted to taste the sensation of pouring out some of my own fairly earned gold over some merchant's counter. But my desire for these unnecessary objects ebbed away as soon as I sighted them. What the devil would I do with a gun? Hippolyta would always lend me one. A wrist-watch? I should forget to take it off when I swam. A pen? No sooner bought than lost. In desultory fashion I mooned about the souk, allowing myself to be plucked and cajoled and lectured by the swarthies. I did not know enough then about precious stones. (Now of course my artificial diamonds flourish all over the globe.) Nor perfumes. But finally, with Benedicta in mind I allowed myself to be tempted by a small and lovely carpet—an authentic Shiraz according to the label. With this rolled up under my arm I walked back to the hotel in time to see a flock of hamalis—the grotesque cow-like public porters of the capital—carrying a string of black suitcases and hat-boxes all marked with the gold monogram I was to come to know so well. But she was already there, dressed like a fashion-plate, sitting upon the terrace with her gloved hands in her lap. Gloves! Her large fine straw hat cast dancing freckles of amber light over her features.

She was staring at her gloves and her lips were moving as if in prayer or in a secret conversation with her own mind. Everything seemed to warn me, but I walked up to take her hands—remove them from her field of vision, claim them and with them her attention. She responded, when I uttered her name with a glance full of abstraction—as if she were seeing me for the first time. "Everyone is agreed" she said softly—the most desolating words that a man in love can hear. "But everyone, without exception, even Julian. They are all on our side." She trembled a little when we embraced; slender and pliant, and fragrant with a scent I could not identify. "I want you to say my name; to hear how it sounds: I haven't paid attention before." I repeated her name twice. She sighed and said "Yes, it is just as I thought." It was as if something had been put to the proof. I sat beside her and unrolled my gift. "I brought you a small Shiraz" I said proud of my acquisition, only to be dashed by her smile as she said: "It's Afghan. You've been cheated." She laughed and clapped her hands as if at an excellent jest.

All my gear had been moved from my room into a very large suite on the second floor; it mingled oddly with her collection of shining suitcases. A Turkish maid was busy hanging up her dresses. A lunch table had been laid upon the balcony. She stood with her probationary eyes narrowed critically as she surveyed the room with its huge four-poster and velvet baldaquin. Then she turned suddenly to me and said: "I can only stay three days this time. Then I must go north. But I will come to you in Athens or in London later. Yes?"

"Very well."

Three nights, three days of calendar time; to the bemused (and it *was* reciprocal) it could have been three centuries, so marvellously did the spilled seconds transform my view both of her and her melancholy city of historic afterthoughts: it had become a sort of extension of her childhood and its memories, a coherent demesne. All the stagnant beauties, its repellent corners of dirt and disease, the marsh gas thrown off by the rotting corpse of Byzantium—they all coalesced into a significant shape. She walked about it with the un-conscious assurance of long familiarity. It was a wicked place to fall in love with a woman, an unmanning place: or was this simply Benedicta, and the obstinate alarm bell sounding in the back of my mind, muffled by the sweet minaret-calls, the sage boom of sirens from the Horn? Let us say that I saw her reflections in it—imprint of the imago which underlay the kisses which were not blithe and free, as they should have been, but concentrated, perverse, bewitching. The central enigma hasn't changed from that day to this; I could have seen her even then, if I had tried, as someone born to be loved yet doomed to die, in solitude like a masterless animal. Yet how lucky I was myself—for I was able to surrender—and this gave me the illusion that I could however briefly cross the distance that she put between us. The victories of applied science! I gave her everything that I had learned from Iolanthe! For one moment had the convic-tion that I had stopped the great moving staircase of the heart! I stubbornly averted my face from the notion that in all this first en-counter what I really saw was the first sketch, so to speak, of a more massive alienation. Did I? I don't know. Anyway, making love with a sort of breathless resignation—or else desperately, like someone trying to pull an arrow from the flesh before the poison has time to spread. And she knew ways to excite, the praying mantis, like "tie up my wrists" or less judiciously "O it is too big, I shall split." Incitements to the furies let loose in men when they love an aggressive woman. To couple so perfectly and yet be denied any sort of initiation! Kisses were warnings I did not recognise; but the feeling of finality was delicious, vertiginous—things could not have fallen out otherwise could they? Gentlemen of the jury, we should tackle reality in a slightly joky way, otherwise we miss its point. It isn't solemn at all, it's *playing*! It's all very well telling poor Felix that now; he too is wise after the event. Suppose we could make the electric chair into a romantic symbol? If you section the olfactory gland of the rabbit you condemn it to impotence; snick off the salamander's head while it is coupling, and it feels nothing; caught in the divine rhythm it continues as if nothing had happened. Perhaps nothing has? Benedicta! Rapidly cooling worlds, we lie asleep in each other's arms. The mysteries do not matter. I come upon her sitting on the balcony in flood of tears. "Why, Benedicta?" She doesn't know, staring up at me with tear-laden lashes, tears running down her long subtle nose. "I don't know." Yet ten minutes later laughing heartily at the antics of a monkey on a barrel-organ.

Well then, as I say, her city began to borrow some of her colours; our excursions and promenades became the unfamiliar delight, and she knew corners and nooks which escaped the industry or perhaps taste of other guides like Sacrapant or Vibart. It is not possible for me now to think of Polis again without seeing Benedicta's face super-posed upon whatever it is—mosque, graveyard, tilting forest of shipping in the Golden Horn. She owns it as Io owns Athens. There were puzzles, of course, and singularities: I remember that wher-ever we went we found someone to receive us—someone waiting outside a mosque with the keys for example. The difficulty of gaining entry to the smaller mosques, the difficulty of tracing the guardian with the keys, is too famous an aspect of Polis to need elaboration; every visitor has complained of it. Yet wherever this fateful couple went—and so often on foot—the guardian was there waiting. Had she warned him, or caused him to be warned, I asked? "No, it is just that we are lucky, simply that."

Then again, with the same equivocal air—an expression of pride and sorrow almost—she led me through the beautiful cemetery at Eyub, among the marble incantations with their tell-tale-turbans and flower-knots. We came to one grave set in a small grilled en-closure of its own. I could not read the flowing Arabic inscription, of course; but below it, in small Roman letters, I saw the name Benedicta Merlin. There was no date. "Who is it—your mother?" I asked; but she only turned away abruptly, picking a stalk of green with which to tease her lips as she walked down the hill. "Benedicta, please tell me." She stared at me intently, and then once more turned away and resumed her slow progress among the graves. It was useless to press her. At the edge of the cemetery she turned and embraced me, pressing me to her with a strange sort of fury, as if to extirpate some unhallowed memory of the past. But no words, do you see? And then with a soft kind intensity she took out her handkerchief to rub the lipstick marks from my mouth. Never, it seemed, had anyone looked at me with so much overflowing love, vulnerable tenderness; what did it matter that she should have her secrets? The stern mask of the priestess had slipped. Briefly I saw a woman.

So the time passed, dense with the special fulfilments of physical possession; I averted my mind from the prospect of her vanishing back into Europe—dragged by the slow Orient Express through the great walls of the city towards Zürich. Then in the middle of everything—or rather at the end, for it was the last evening—came the most singular event of all: the death of Sacrapant. It was so sudden and so unexpected that it deafened the mind—though afterwards of course it was explained satisfactorily. Events of this kind are always clothed in a factitious causality when we see them in retrospect. Was it, though?

Sunset is the finest hour; with the city nimbling softly away towards darkness while the sun fights its lion-battle against the skyline driving the dense mists higher and higher into brief priceless colours and shapes. To sit in the darkening garden of the hotel quietly drinking an aperitif and waiting for the blind muezzin to climb into his perch among the buildings and send out his owl-cry to the faithful— this was the best way to spend this hour, watching the lights beginning to twinkle over by Taxim, and the shipping rustle and moo on the darkening water.

This particular eloquent evening we were very silent; the express left just before midnight, her packing was done. We sat there between two worlds, neither cast down nor elated: existing in a curious abstraction of certainty about the future. One side of the mind turned towards that quiet call which must soon come from the mosque—the old blind face of a bird uttering the quiet nasal cawing of the Ebed. And I saw in the gathering dusk a slim figure in white limping among the distant trees; it walked with just a trace of unsteadiness but with resolution as if towards a predetermined destination. I recognised my friend, though I did not comment on the fact; so, I think, did she, following the direction of my gaze. There would have been nothing unusual about that; but then to my surprise I saw him pause, squint upwards into the sky, and enter the circular staircase of the mosque. But now his pace had changed; he walked slowly, wearily, as if bowed under a great weight. I saw him appear at the little window-slit half way up and could not resist a puzzled gasp. "What the devil, it's old Sacrapant. . . ." She looked at her watch and at the sky.

It was still early for the muezzin. The frail figure appeared at last at the balustrade, raising small fern-like hands as in an invocation to the darkening world about the tower. It was indeed an invocation, but a frail and incoherent one; the sense of the words hardly penetrated the heavy layers of the damp night air. I thought I heard something like "will find fulfilment in the firm. Give it your best and it will be returned an hundredfold." One could not be absolutely sure, of course, but among the wavering incantations I thought I heard so much. Then I jumped to my feet for the frail figure had started to lean forward and topple. Mr. Sacrapant started to fall out of the night sky in a slow swoop towards the dark ground. A crash of a palm tree, and then a thud of unmistakable finality, followed by the splintering jingle of broken glass and small change. I was transfixed by the suddenness of it all. I stood there speechless. But already there were running feet everywhere and voices; a crowd gathered in no time, as flies will do about an open artery. "My God" I said. Benedicta sat quite still with bowed head. I turned to her and whispered her name; but she did not move.

I shook her gently by the shoulders as one might shake a clock that had stopped and she looked up at me with an intense unwavering sadness. "Come away quick" she said, and grabbed my hand. Away among the trees the sounds had become more purposeful—they were gathering up the loaves and fishes. Blood on marble. I shuddered. Crossing the dark garden hand in hand we moved towards the lighted terraces and public rooms of the hotel. Benedicta said: "Jocas must have given him the sack. O why must people go to extremes?" Why, indeed! I thought of the pale humble face of Sacrapant shining up there in the evening sky. Of course such an explanation would meet the case, yet. . . . The evening lay in ruins about us. The silent dinner, the packing away of the luggage into the office car which had appeared—these operations we performed automatically, numbed by the sadness of this sudden death. My mind reverted continually to the memory of that pale face leaning down from the tower; Sacrapant had looked like someone who had been carefully deprived of an individual psychology by some experiment with knife or drug. For one brief moment his coat tails had flattened out with the wind of his fall giving him the shape of a dart—like a falling mallard. But he had fallen, so to speak, slap into the middle of our emotions; the widening rings of his death spread through our minds now, alienating us from each other.

We embraced, we parted, almost with disgust. The hideous station with its milling tortoise-faced mob of Turks mercifully precluded speeches of farewell. I stood holding her hands while the carriage was found and the luggage stored in it by the chauffeur. "Or else" she said gravely, in the tones of one continuing an inner monologue "he suddenly learned that he had cancer, or that his wife had a lover, or that his favourite child. . . ." I realised that any explanation would do, and that all would forever remain merely provisional. Was this perhaps true for all of us, for all our actions? Yes, yes. I studied her face again with care, with an almost panic-stricken intentness, realising at last how useless it was to be loving her; she had climbed into the carriage and stood looking down at me from the open window with a hesitant sorrowfulness. We could not have been further apart at this instant; a cloud of anxiety had overshadowed all emotion. I felt my heavy despairs dragging at their moorings. Tomorrow I should return to Athens—I should be free from everyone, free even from Benedicta. My God, the only four letter word that matters! The train had begun to move. I walked beside it for a few paces. She too was looking almost relieved, elated. Or so it seemed to me. Perhaps because she felt sure of me—of her hold over me? She wound up the glass window and then, with a sudden impulse, breathed upon it in order to write the word "Soon" on the little patch of condensation. At once the pain of separation came back.

I turned away to let my thoughts disperse among those sullen crowds of featureless faces. The car waited to take me back to the hotel. That night I slept alone and for the first time experienced the suffocating sense of loneliness which came over me with the conviction that I should never see Benedicta again. This whole episode would remain in my memory, carefully framed and hung, quite self-subsisting: and quite without relevance or continuity to anything else I had ever done or experienced. An anecdote of Istanbul!

Nor did this feeling completely leave me even when, from the windy deck-head, I saw the white spars of Sunion come up over the waters. The season had turned, autumn was here, the marbles looked blue with cold: and I had turned a corner in my supposed life. It was baffling, the sense of indecision which beset me; I supposed that the novelty of this new life was what had numbed me—simply that. Simply that.

Hippolyta met me at the dock with her car, bursting with excitement and jubilation. "We're saved" she cried as I clambered down the gangway with my suitcase. "O come along do, Charlock; we must celebrate, and it's all due to you. Graphos! He has swept all the provinces. My darling, he's changed completely. He is certain to get back into power." Apparently something had been averted by the resuscitation of the great man's party and its electoral successes. Well, I sat by her side, letting her babble on to her heart's content. We headed for the country directly because they were all "waiting to congratulate" me. I was returning like a conquering hero to the hospitable country house. "Moreover" she said, taking my hand and pressing it to her cheek "you have joined the firm. You are one of us now." In the back of my mind I had a sudden snapshot of Benedicta walking alone in some remote corner of an untended garden, among rare shrubs and flowers which discharged their pollen on her clothes at every step, like silent pistol-shots. In the house great fires blazed and champagne-glasses winked. Caradoc was there and Pulley; and the immaculate spatted form of Banubula. Everyone burst into a torrent of congratulatory rhetoric. I drank away the feelings of the past weeks, lapped around by all this human glow. It was only when,

as an afterthought, I said: "By the way, I am going to marry Benedicta Merlin" that the great silence fell. It was the half second of
silence at the end of some marvellously executed symphony, the
mesmerised rapture which precedes the thunder of applause. Yes.
That sort of silence, and lasting only half a second; then the applause,
or rather the storm of congratulation in which, to my surprise, I
strove suspiciously to detect a false note. But no. It rang out in the
most genuine manner; Caradoc indeed seemed rather moved by the
news, his bear-hugs hurt. I surrendered myself to my self-congratulation invaded by a new sense of confidence. It was late when at last I
gathered my kit and borrowed the car to return to Athens; I was
curious to see Number Seven again, to riffle my notebooks. Yet I
noted with some curiosity that all of a sudden the absence, not of
Benedicta but of Iolanthe, weighed. Some obscure law of association
must be at work; I had not give her a thought in Istanbul, she was not
appropriate to the place. Nor would Benedicta ever be to Athens. I
looked up from under the shaded light and imagined her entering
the room as she always did, punctual as a heartbeat. These sentimental polarities of feeling were new to me; I disapproved of them
thoroughly. Frowning I returned to my scribbles. I roughed out a
schema as a basis for my work for the firm when at last I should be
summoned. Then I noticed a letter on the mantelpiece, a letter
addressed to me. It was from Julian, written in an exquisite italic
hand; it congratulated me most gracefully on the excellent news and
told me that I need not move from Athens for the time being; but I
should map out a work-scheme and submit it. Did I wish to start
with the mechanical end of my research? A limited company called
Merlin Devices would be set up as part of a light-engineering subsidiary of the firm. I would find the technicians and the tools ready
to hand for whatever I dreamed up. It was a marvellous prospect, and
I fell asleep happily that night in the stuffy little room, with my
counterpane littered with notes and formulae and diagrams.

At seven, when the porter brought me my coffee I found that
dapper Koepgen had followed hard on his heels and had taken up
his usual watchful position in the armchair. Koepgen of the elf-lock
and the lustrous eye. For the time of day he looked unnaturally
spruce and self-possessed. "Go on" he said with ill-concealed ex-

citement. "Tell me what it is." For a moment I had forgotten. "Jocas cabled me that he would give you a message for me." Then I remembered. Sleepily I repeated the message to him. He drew a long hissing breath, his face at once rueful and amused. "What a cunning old dog, what a swine" he said admiringly, and struck his knee. "I only worked a few weeks for them but it was enough for the firm to find my weak point. They are incredible." He chirped his loudest laugh.

"What's it all about?" I asked; there was a small bottle of ouzo on the mantelpiece; Koepgen made a by-your-leave, drew the cork and tilted a dose into a toothmug. He drank it off quite slim and said: "He's holding me to ransom, the old devil. He wants me to go back to Moscow and deal with some contracts for the firm; I refused, it doesn't interest me. Now I see I will have to go if I'm ever to get my hands on the bloody thing."

"What bloody thing?"

"The ikon."

"What next?" It sounded to me as if the firm were busy doing some elaborate trade in antiques; but no, said Koepgen, no such thing. What they were after were some contracts from the Communist Government for wheat and oil in exchange for machinery. Nothing could be more prosaic. And the ikon—where did that come in? Ah. He burst out laughing again and said with exasperation, "My dear Charlock, that is a piece of Russian folklore which will sound to you quite silly; but nevertheless it has cost me several years and hundreds of miles on foot." He sat down suddenly with a bump in the chair.

"But wouldn't it be dangerous, I mean Communists and all that?"

"No. One of my uncles is Minister of Trade. No, it isn't that. I just didn't want to work for the firm; but I made the mistake of telling them my fairy tale, and of course this is the result. You see, when I started this theological jag I chose one of the great mystics, a big bonze of Russia as a guide. As you know, absolute obedience is required, even if one is set a task that seems an idiocy. I was set a task which turned unwittingly into a pilgrimage on my poor flat feet. There was an ikon once in the private chapel of my mother; when the estate was confiscated it had vanished. I was told to find it or else."

"Or else what?"

Koepgen grinned. "Or else no progress, see? I should be stuck in the lower ranks. Never get my stripes. Don't laugh."

"What fantasy."

"Of course you'd think that; but there is more than one kind of truth, Charlock."

"O crikey," I said "don't do the theological on me."

"Well, anyway, hence this bloody long walk across Russia into Athos. I traced it there. After that I drew a blank for a while. It was a Saint Catherine of a rather special kind. And of course the woods are full of them—Saint Catherines. It might be somewhere in a wayside shrine on Olympus or stuck in some great monastery in Meteora. In spite of all the help I got I drew blank after blank. The Orthodox Church is an odd organisation or perhaps I should say disorganisation; what is the good for example of an encyclical when half the minor clergy are illiterates?"

"Offer a reward."

"We did all that. I sorted through hundreds of them big and small; but I couldn't get the one belonging to my mother. You see? Now the firm has stepped in found it and will tell me where it is on condition. . . ."

"I have never heard such rubbish in my life" I said. Koepgen nearly burst into tears. "Nor have I," he said "nor have I."

"I should damn well refuse to go."

"Perhaps I shall. I must see. On the other hand I suppose it isn't such an arduous undertaking; it might cost me a month or two in Moscow, and then at least I would have found it and satisfied my *staretz* old Demetrius. O dear." He took another swig from the bottle and fell into a heavy melancholy silence, turning over these weird contingencies in his mind. I drew a bath and lay in it awhile, leaving him to brood in the armchair. I had decided, on the strength of my new-found fortune, to move all my belongings today to the best hotel in the town—to take a comfortable suite. I did not need more space but I was most anxious to experiment with the notion of spending a lot of money. Yes, of course the grub would be much better. I was drying myself slowly when Koepgen appeared in the doorway. He was still sunk in a kind of abstraction, and gazed at me

162

with unfocused eye. "You know" he said slowly at last "I have a feeling that I shall have to obey Julian. After all sacrifices have to be made if one's going to get anywhere in life, eh?"

"Hum" I said, feeling very sage and judicial, yet indifferent.

"You will see," he said "you will see, my boy. Your turn will come. Have you ever met Julian?"

"No." I dressed slowly; it was a lovely sunny day, and we walked across Athens on foot, stopping here and there in the shadow of a vine arbour to have a drink and a mézé. Koepgen made no further reference to his ikon and I was glad; the whole thing seemed to me to be a burdensome fairy tale. After all if a man of such sharp intelligence in his forties allowed the firm to play upon these infantile superstitions, well good luck to it. But such reflections filled me with shame when I glanced at his sorrowful and now rather haggard features. I had come to like him very much. As we parted, I to reserve my new quarters and organise the move, he to return to his seminary, he said under his breath: "I fear there is no help for it. I shall have to go. I'll cable Jocas today."

He started to walk down the winding street and then, on a sudden impulse, ran after me and caught my sleeve. He said in a humble, beseeching tone "Charlock, can I leave my notebooks with you if I decide to go?" His manner touched me. "Of course." And that evening when I got back to my new hotel, rather aware that my shabby wardrobe would have to be replaced if I were ever to match the splendour of such surroundings, I saw the familiar pile of school exercise books on the mantelpiece. A rubber band held them together. But there was no word with them; I must presume that Koepgen had fallen in with the wishes of the firm, perhaps he was already on his way north. I rather envied him the journey in a queer sort of way. My dinner had been left in the alcove to await me. I could not help touching the smooth expensive napery which enveloped it. In Athens such costly and beautiful ironed covers and napkins were quite a rarity. I had decided to work that evening on my crystals, and had set out my white china trays in the bathroom. But the telephone rang and when I picked it up Benedicta stood before me, so to speak; her voice was so clear that I thought she must be calling me from the floor below. But no, she was in Switzerland.

"Darling", the endearment made my heart suddenly turn over in its grave. Every doubt, every hesitation, was puffed away on the instant and I realised with a reviving pang how much I wanted her here, right here. The enormous inadequacy of words belaboured me. "Never have I missed anyone so much. It confirms everything." So it seemed to me also as I sat, gripping the black telephone, grimacing into it. "We will be married in April. Julian has arranged everything. In London. Do you agree?"

"Why wait so long, Benedicta?"

"I have to. I am under orders. I won't be free to move until then. O how much I miss you, miss you." The clear magnetic voice took on a note of familiar despair. "Julian is arranging the terms of the settlement, the marriage contract."

"What settlement?" I said in perplexity.

"Well, about my share in the firm. We must have perfect equality in love, my darling." All of a sudden the line went dead and a thousand other voices came up, trying to restore the broken communication. "Benedicta" I cried, and I could still hear her voice, though what she was saying was indistinct. An operator squashed her out and promised to call me back. I went and lay on my bed in a confused frame of mind—a mixture of rage and euphoria.

Gentlemen of the jury, now I can tell you that I have loved a woman who sat on numberless committees for the emancipation of other women, never speaking, and with the bitten nails of her left hand sheathed in a glove. Actually what women need is to be beaten almost to death, enslaved, raped, and forced to cook meals when they are heavy with child. Bite through the nape of the neck, Wilkinson, stick her with a bayonet, and she's yours forever. A bottomless masochism is all they seek to indulge; the penis is too kind a weapon by far. No, the emancipation of this creature is a joke. (Benedicta, look into my eyes.) They are waveborn, slaveborn; and yet somewhere among them may be one, just *one*, who is different, who fills the bill. But what bill, Felix? Love! We never had before nor never since, seen it, I mean. Burp! Pardon my parahelion.

Perfect equality in love, I thought. God! Tomorrow I would go out and buy the most expensive microscope in the world and a Stradivarius and some strawberries and a car. . . . But in love there is never enough equality to go round. We will have to settle for equity among men and women—a humbler target. Benedicta ached on. After half an hour of futile suspense I tried to restore the broken communication from my own end, but this proved impossible. They could not trace the number from which she had called me. The hall porter brought me a bottle of whisky and a siphon. I tried to resume the precious train of thought about crystals—the fragile line of reasoning which, after so many years, has given Merlin's a near monopoly in the field of lasers. Benedicta kept intruding among my scribbles. ("The ordering of their atoms is never quite perfect or they would not be able to form, to grow.")

Then the phone did ring again and I leaped at it. But it was only Caradoc, rather drunk and indistinct, calling me from the Nube, his gruff voice framed in a background of mandolin music. "Charlock," he said in his usual growling vein "we are waiting for you down here. Why don't you come?" But Benedicta had covered me in a sheath, a caul of discontent. I could not think of the sweaty Nube, the dust-filled curtains, without distaste. "I am waiting for a phone-call, and doing some work" I said, fearful lest our own conversation might be holding up a long-distance contact. Caradoc growled on reproachfully. "Ah you scientists in love! Soon you will be accusing nature of a moral order. Push!"

"Push to you" I said. "Now for godsake hang up and leave me alone will you?"

He did so, but with evident reluctance. "Well, hard cheese" he said as a parting shot, and I had the sudden vivid image of Mr. Sacrapant leaning over a desk looking gravely at me and saying "You are right to be precautionate, Mr. Charlock." And what was the other expression? Yes, "I have inaccurised the document, sir." Presumably he meant that he had been through it for inaccuracies. Ah, pale Sacrapant, falling out of the air like these autumn leaves tumbling into the parks. Again the phone rang and this time Hippolyta's clear youthful voice sprang from the mouthpiece as if from the ear of a goddess. "Charlock, I heard you'd moved. How does it feel to be really loved?"

"O leave me alone" I cried in anguish, much to her surprise. "Hang up. I'm waiting for a call."

But Benedicta did not ring again.

Indeed I had no word from her throughout the months which lay ahead. However, filled with the *gai savoir* I buckled down to my plans for the little Merlin subsidiary which I should virtually run single handed from London. Or so I thought. Two members of its hypothetical board flew out to meet me, Denison and Broad, and I was glad to find them both accomplished and experienced men. Needless to say I knew nothing about company law, patent claims, and similar esoteric subjects, and was glad to delegate this side of things to them; when everything was ready I should transfer myself to London with a basketful of preliminary ideas. This little respite was useful; it enabled me to map out my own objectives more clearly and to get them down on paper. Moreover I had nothing to fear from the Athens winter while I was lodged in such warm and comfortable quarters.

I sorted not only my papers but also the vast collection of tapes, fragments, dialects, etc. and transcribed them on to matrices; many were the felicities I had culled from the conversations of my friends. (The voice of Sipple saying, gravely: "You might say that I belong to the Purple People. In the case of Mrs. Sipple now—although I didn't know this till later—she used to come up every Wednesday from Broadstairs where she had been playing with the mighty organ of a DSO with Bar.")

I saw a good deal of Caradoc who was marking time before being sent off on a new assignment. As I've said, he had invented what he called the mnemon which he insisted was a literary form—"an art-form in which free Freud and solipsism marry and make merry. You might say it was a soft cotton pun dressed up in the form of a *Times* personal." They were indeed *Times* Personals of a slightly surrealist tinge, and I had the pleasure of helping him father a few. To my surprise he actually had them printed in the newspaper where they doubtless passed completely unnoticed or were supposed to be an obscure code, a love-call for some religious sect.

> Jewish gentleman in Romford, expert on
> vibraphone, urgently seeks father figure.

> Small pegamoid man, fond of soft clinics,
> seeks tangible rubber acme. Own plug.

No poet ever derived greater pleasure from seeing his work printed, and Caradoc spent a good deal of money on these confections. Then came his sixtieth birthday and he woke up to find himself knee deep in telegrams of congratulations and press cuttings. There were long articles on his work everywhere, photographs of the Hoarah Bridge, the University of Tobago, and other masterpieces of his implausible genius. To my surprise all this backslapping made him sad and plaintive, and once more he began to talk about leaving the firm. "About twice in your life you get a chance to change everything, to jump over the side; but a moment's hesitation and the chance slips away. It's late in the day for me but who knows? I might get another yet. I'm keeping my eyes skinned." Meanwhile the firm had found him a new assignment with which he could hardly quarrel: a new university and senate in the Cook Islands. He would be entirely his own master. Already his fingers itched when they were near a pencil and he spent much of his time, absorbed as any child, modelling in plasticine. "The game of volumes, my boy, the most intoxicating of them all. They've promised me aerial pictures of the site, I can't wait to get my hands on them. And think of new settings, palms, volcanoes, surf."

"When will you leave?"

"As soon as I can. There's nothing more to be done here."

The season was shifting, our little group was dispersing slowly; Hippo moved back into Paris with her sails spread and only occasionally sent us a postcard. Banubula went to the New Year's Eve ball dressed up in a quaint oldfashioned stock of Edwardian provenance with a twinkling pin, looking very much like a vampire on his evening off. "He is dark umber, the bloody Count" said Caradoc who enjoyed parodying his friend's exquisite and lapidary English. "I'm sure he would subscribe himself as 'Your Umber Servant'." The poor Count made no allusion to his Turkish excesses, and nor did I. He had resumed his Athenian persona. The Countess still sat alone for the greater part of the day in a dressing-gown and slippers, her hair caught up in a purple scarf: playing patience, and writing letters to Gurdjieff. "Horatio has been so strange this winter" she might say stretching out long phthisical fingers towards her coffee cup. "So strange." Did she see him as we did who were not

167

privy to his innermost secrets? I mean dark brown voice, cotton gloves, silver-capped stick with heavy rubber ferrule, one ring-seal, iodine-locket, rebus. . . . It was hard to say. Benedicta wrote disturbingly "I have been ill, I have had a small absence": in French this time.

Then Caradoc was summoned to London to establish his team of draughtsmen for the new project, and I realised that I was going to be very lonely without him. Worse, I did not realise that we should never meet again—though in retrospect I cannot see the logic of such a sentiment. We had a farewell party in the Nube where I successfully masqueraded as sufficiently unwell to spare myself the culminating pleasures of the bed. An idiocy, I suppose—but what is one among so many? Here Sipple intervened, or rather the memory of him for Caradoc entertained a fantastically high opinion of his friend's gifts and much regretted not to see him before he left. I questioned him about the incident of the dead boy, but found that he knew little more than I did. It may have been something to do with blackmail. "I think Sipple must have been working for someone, perhaps Graphos, who knows?" "The Purple People no doubt" I said.

"On the other hand Banubula thinks it was purely and simply a family affair—an affair of honour. The boy's father had said he would punish him for soiling the family honour. This *is* the Balkans after all."

"What does Hippo think?"

Caradoc drained his glass and said oracularly "It's like everything else in life—those who know can't tell."

And at this moment Mrs. Henniker came into the room whinnying like a polo pony and waving a tattered magazine which the girls had been reading; it was a magazine devoted to film. "Look" cried Mrs. Henniker with a triumphant flourish, waving it under my nose. "One of my girls." To my surprise there she was, Iolanthe, all sepia and deckle edged, staring out at the world with a kind of forlorn lascivious grin. She was tricked out as some sort of Eastern houri and appeared to be bearing the head of the Baptist upon a trencher. The letterpress concerned a new film made by a Frenchman in Egypt. Apparently she had lobbied herself a small part in it. I was delighted and amused,

168

unaware that we were witnessing the beginnings of so formidable a career. Mrs. Henniker was beside herself with pleasure. "One of my girls" she kept repeating in a dazed sort of way. I was obscurely touched as I looked at the gruesome inexperienced face of young Samiou. Why "inexperienced" though? Caradoc set the paper aside with a grunt of surprise. "Well, may they all prosper" he said at last. "The little dumplings."

Pulley came in with a huge watch dangling. It was time to be going home. It was freezing in the car, the Attic plain was all glittering under hoarfrost; the sewers steamed up through the manholes all the way along Stadium Street like so many geysers. Caradoc pressed my hand and declined a parting drink, showing unwonted resolution. "Just time to pack my traps" he said "and then hey for the Virgin Isles. Think of me basking out there, eh? And remember that all perfected cultures have depended upon a high infant mortality." No, he wasn't drunk: he was full of the sadness of farewell. "As for you, Charlock, everything is moving in your direction now. You have only to spread your sails a bit. You are going to be very happy. O yes. Very happy indeed. A future full of sperm my boy."

I could see nothing illogical in the proposition, and yet I was filled with a sudden nagging nostalgia for the days of solitary poverty, the days before the firm took me up. But then the memory of Benedicta swept over me like a landslide; she was worth everything. I did not feel as if I had a separate existence any more.

"Caradoc bless you."

"Goodbye."

Om

IV

Konx. Ah! the brave new chrysadiamantine world of Charlock's nuptial London! O world of delegated sympathies, of mysteries, of great achievements. The expensive cars that soothed away the roads moving like ointments; the clothes that fitted like second skins. And in the midst of it all the white wand, the blind man's dowsing-rod, Benedicta. It is not I who speak, Lord: it is my culture speaking through me. It is hard to disentangle this first time from the others—for she was always going away, always coming back. In the Paulhaus everything has been catered for—chapels for six denominations. People are never too ill to pray. Either she appeared at airports clad in mourning; or else delivered in a white ambulance, laughing, cured, joking with the driver: to run up the steep steps into my arms. Try as you will, there is no explanation for madness, happiness or death. At first it would have been silly to speak of souls darkened by troubling presentiments, of dialogues bathed in strange lights. Later of course, one has all the time in the world to study the fatal metastases of the idea of love.

I counted upon her for very much, I discovered, sorting through my emotions with a new, a rather disgusting humility bordering on self-abasement. She would develop me like some backyard province perhaps, promulgate a charter. I did not even know her husband's name: whom could I ask? And then, where should we meet at last but under the backward clock at Victoria. Yet at once the Turkish image, brilliant as a postage stamp, gave place to another; she had become very thin now, very tense. She vibrated in my arms like a high-tension wire; her eyes were over made-up which increased her pallor, deeped the dimple in her cheek. But with such relief, such passion, after so long an absence. "And all this time you never wrote, Benedicta." "I know." (But afterwards she would write every day for weeks on end in her mirror hand: things like "It is snowing again. They have tied me to the same chair.") But here she only gave a small sweet groan as we broke apart to plunge our eyes into one another. "Felix!" She had managed to capture my very name and make it her own; it emerged newly printed. I had never liked it very much: now I hoped she might go on repeating it. "At last it is over." At last it had begun.

I had already been here alone for nearly a month, living at the beautiful house in Mount Street among the sumptuous impersonal furniture. There had been no signal of her arrival. I contemplated with superstitious awe the huge wardrobe which filled the glass cupboards in our room—my own new wardrobe. The devil! I recalled that one day long ago Jocas had asked me, as a personal favour, to allow his tailor to take my measurements: and though puzzled, I had complied. As one among so many ambiguous happenings this small trifle had hardly seemed worth troubling about. Now I understood. I stood, biting my lip, and contemplating myself in the mirror both ashamed and delighted at my own splendour. The silver-backed brushes were good to the scalp; the bathroom was crowded with expensive toilet waters and monumental soaps. It was perfectly understandable, I told myself, that I should dress appropriately, to match my new, my enormous new salary, and in general my new role in affairs. For Benedicta's sake, as well as the firm's . . . nevertheless. Nor was it too soon, for I had already taken possession of my new suite of offices at Merlin House in the City; I had already met everyone—except of course Julian who was away. Things had begun to move forward with irresistible momentum. Yes, I had even seen the fangled Shadbolt and initialled the preposterous marriage settlement. And now all these scattered elements were knitted together and resolved by her phone-call from Victoria. "I'm here at last. Please come to me at once." It was a familiar creature of course, her perfume was the same. All the signals of recognition the same. Yet a difference lay perhaps in the fact that so much time had passed and circumstances had subtly altered—this foggy soot-bellowing grime-tank of a station. And then her tremendous assortment of luggage which followed in a second taxi with her maids and manservant. Some lines of Koepgen drifted idly across the back of my mind like these mushrooming winter clouds. Something like "the human face upon its stalk perpetuates only the type of a determined response; there are so few elations and so few dismays to wrinkle between a laughing or a crying death, between a truthful or a lying breath." Benedicta sat gripping my manicured hand and staring unseeingly out of the window watching London lumber by, keeping its viscous slow coil. "You have seen Shadbolt, haven't you?"

"Yes."

"He explained and you agreed. Now we are really one." It was only the context that made the phrase sound extraordinary.

"I signed the document, though really I remained unconvinced inside. It's too generous, my dear. Why should I share everything so completely?"

"O God" she cried vehemently "I was afraid you wouldn't see."

"It was too generous; after all I'm earning my own way now. Why shouldn't you keep your fortune? We could have had a *separation des biens* arrangement."

"No. Never. Besides didn't he tell you that I have no personal fortune outside the firm? It's all I have, the firm. Darling, I want to possess you utterly, without reserves of any kind. I can't believe in myself in any other way." Well, so did I, so did I. "But I also wanted you to feel a little independent. Room to breathe."

She began to mutter under her breath, as if she were swearing *sotto voce*. Her knuckles grew white as she gripped my hand. A strange, rather ominous sense of impending misunderstanding cast its shadow over us. It might be possible to embrace it away, to exorcise it. As I kissed her I thought of Shadbolt. He was one of the five solicitors who dealt with the firm's affairs; he had presented for my perusal a thick handbook listing all the firm's holdings and all its subsidiaries. A heavy-breathing slothful little man with plum-coloured countenance, whose spectacles were attached to his lapel by a heavy black ribbon. When he put them on he did so reverently, as if he were in mourning. Voice of an old bugle full of spit. The marriage contract was an elaborate document couched in the sort of phraseology which made the trained mind swim. I was too intimidated by his air of being a papal emissary to prevail upon him to explain in too great detail. His grinding humourless voice grated upon me. "Everyone in

Merlin's seems to be obsessed by contractual obligations" I said somewhat peevishly. Shadbolt removed his spectacles and stared at me reproachfully. "How else shall one do business?" he asked with surprise, almost tenderly.

"But this isn't business" I said.

"Frankly," said the little man rising with infinite slowness to gaze out of the window "I would have hesitated had I been in Miss Benedicta's place. You will allow me to be frank? But she insisted. From your point of view Mr. Charlock, you have everything to gain and nothing to lose by it. It's a most generous gesture, a gesture of faith and trust and if I may use the word without immodesty, love. It fully incorporates you in all her fortunes. But if you wish we can tear the document up."

He crossed the room cumbrously with his penguin-like gait. I hesitated for a long moment, feeling very much out of my depth. "I somehow don't like to think about relationships, our marriage, in these terms." Yes, that was really the full extent of my reservations. The lawyer gave a bleak smile. "The sentiment does you much credit. I understand your feeling as you do. On the other hand there is nothing so very strange about making a marriage contract. Many people do. I was rather more concerned about her position than yours. All this" he tapped the white papers against his knee "would not be easily revoked if ever there were need. She is, in a sense, putting herself entirely at your mercy and the firm as well."

"That is what worries me; there isn't any need."

But, after all, since the whole thing was merely a whim on her part . . . I took up my new gold fountain pen and signed the document. Shadbolt sighed slowly as he pressed the blotter down upon the wet ink. "You are a lucky man," he said "a very lucky young man."

Now it seemed to me, as I sat beside her with her slender arm through mine, that the phrase might qualify as the nadir of understatement. Those nervous, tender blue eyes turning to grey in this pallid cloudlight met mine with such burning candour that I felt ashamed ever to have felt doubts or reservations about these paper conventions.

"What is it, Benedicta?" But still staring at me she only shook her head as she continued to explore her own inmost feelings—pre-occupied, like someone trying to locate a hollow in a tooth. It was in this euphoric trance that we drew up at last in Mount Street. Baynes opened for us and ran down the steps to greet her; but she hardly acknowledged his presence, stalking past him into the hall with what might have seemed an insolent air, had her preoccupation not been so evident.

She threw her gloves on to the table and consulted her appearance in the tall mirror with a careful disdainful air. There was a big bowl of flowers on the side table by the wall, near the silver salver which held some engraved visiting cards and tradesmen's bills. "I told you I did not like the smell of flowers in the house" she said icily to the butler. "Take them out at once." As a matter of fact it was I who had ordered the flowers; but the kindly Baynes, after a glance at me, simply swallowed and decided to take the blame. "Yes, Madam."

Benedicta turned with a dazzling smile and said: "Now let's go through the house shall we? I love coming back here." And so we went from room to room in order to greet the more choice of her possessions—the little statue of Niobe, for example, and the wonderful gallery of golden heads of Greek gods and Roman, modern work by *cire perdue*. It was only when we were climbing the staircase that she said: "There's no one else here is there?"

"Of course not. I'm quite alone."

But now she walked with an air of quaint precaution, letting me enter each room ahead of her to draw the curtains. Nodded smiling, as if satisfied; so we perambulated the densely carpeted floors to come at last to the fine bedrooms where I had been sleeping. Here, at last, she experienced a sort of relief, clapped hands softly before my face and laughed as I trapped them. Well, then, whatever it was we had outwitted it. She walked about, opening cupboards, bed-bouncing, opening cupboards full of my gloatworthy clothing. Then abruptly she paused and said: "My God, I'm tired and dirty. I must have a bath."

I locked the door and drew her one in my scarlet bathroom, tossing in bunches of salts; simple and swift she undressed and stepped into it, and all of a sudden I was carried back in a flash to the Benedicta who had once walked into the foaming cistern of "The Copious Waters" in distant Turkey; her preoccupations were gone. I sat beside her, touching the pale shoulders with my fingers. Afterwards she rolled herself in the great towelling kaftan and lay on the bed, flushed rosy from the heat. "Tell me now." And so I told her all about the thrilling activities of Charlock in London, unable to disguise the triumph and excitement in my voice. She listened nodding from time to time, but the nods were only part approval—she was like to doze off at any moment. Well, about the two small factories which had been set up near Slough to start production on two of my "devices"; about a study group which had been convened to test the more nebulous experimental stuff. Intoxicating stuff. I really could not blame her if her eyelids fluttered and drooped. "And as soon as Julian gets back I shall make contact and. . . ." But she was suddenly snapped sharp awake. She looked at me curiously for a moment and then, yawning, ran her fingers through my hair with a queer little gesture—that of a mother, ever so faintly commiserating, who hears her small son boasting about matters he could not as yet understand. "Ah Julian" she said, and I thought of the empty chair in the board room faced by the little marble plaque and the virgin blotter. "He's amazing really," I said, "despite his absence in New York; you know, he gets the minutes of all our meetings, annotates them and bangs them back within twenty-four hours sometimes. He must be a glutton for work. One feels his presence very strongly despite the empty chair."

Yawning, she went to the telephone, unlocking the door en route; Baynes answered hoarsely from the kitchen. She ordered him to bring some champagne in a bucket and to tell the office that she would use her box at the opera. "Do you agree?" over her shoulder. "It's my first night in London for so long? And Baynes bring us *The Times*. We must see what's on; and a car, please." A patrician simplicity, both authoritative and endearing. I consulted my watch. There was lots of time. She began her lingering toilet, slipping through the secret panel into her own mirrored rooms. Soon Baynes came, bringing all these trophies of a fashionable life, and I scanned the paper absently. "Ah!" I said. "An obvious mnemon by Caradoc! I wonder where he is now." And I read out: "Continental type orgy

178

sought by plain living British family, Hornchurch area. No agents."

"Ask the office; they'll tell you" she said, and then in the same breath "You know they want to send us round the world for our honeymoon? Think, round the world."

"Who do?"

"The firm. Julian. Everyone." I reflected on this a moment. "Isn't it a marvellous idea?" She eyed me.

"Yes" I said, but rather doubtfully, and my tone seemed to puzzle her, for she stopped in front of me as she combed out her hair. "Well, isn't it?" she insisted. I lit a cigarette and said: "Yes, enormously kind of them. But, you know, I was rather hoping we'd sneak off all alone, by ourselves, like a couple of students. I know a dozen little places in Italy and Greece where we could be quite alone, quite out of touch—even with the firm. Besides, why put them to the expense? Think of the cost!"

"Cost?" she said on a chilling note of interrogation, and with a singular expression on her face. "How do you mean—'cost'?" I would perhaps have laughed had her strange expression not struck me so forcibly. All this became clearer later on when, after the marriage, I made the intoxicating discovery that we had no real income whatsoever against which to calculate our costs. I mean that there was no ceiling, no budget, no margin. She simply drew money as one draws breath. Any one of the four banks owned by the firm honoured her cheques; notes of hand—the merest scribbles on the back of a postcard or on a page torn from an address book—were honoured by Nathan, the administrative secretary. She never saw a bill in connection with any of the houses she owned. This contributed a vertiginous singularity to her dealings with money. And now that our fortunes were merged by the Shadbolt document I woke up to find that I too was in the same situation. I had no money of "my own"—yet what the devil does the phrase mean? At first it was intoxicating, yes, of course, not to have to reflect on costs; but later (I am talking of the period of the crack-up) I began to feel this as a major factor which contributed to her general confusion of mind. She was capable of buying a bracelet for ten thousand pounds and of leaving it in a taxi. When I grew alarmed about her general state of health, and found myself unable to see the elusive Julian face to face,

I remember writing a long eloquent memorandum to him which finally wound up on Nash's desk. I emphasised that even the Queen had a budgetry ceiling voted by Parliament, yet Benedicta had none. The confusion and waste were simply due to her total lack of knowledge as to what money might conceivably mean. Julian merely replied to my memo with another, neatly typed and signed in that inimitable hand: "Her doctors have been consulted, and also the principals of the firm. No change need be contemplated for the present." But at this moment I only saw the childish, endearing expression of puzzlement on her face and longed to kiss her. What is more endearing than the capriciousness of a rich woman? O, it is lovely. I might answer the rhetorical question very differently today I suppose. And heavens, I have had eight years or more in which to ponder the matter, along with more recondite subjects—Charlock sitting at his massive desk in Merlin House, drawing on his blotter with the golden pen which lived in a fat agate slab. Scribbling on a blackboard in coloured chalks.

She turned her white shoulders to me with a sigh. "Do me up at the back, would you please?" And for better or for worse, in sickness and in health, I did, stooping to touch the white skin with my lips. So hand in hand we sauntered downstairs casting admiring glances at ourselves on every landing. Baynes had made up a brown paper parcel of my prehistoric clothes, baggy grey trousers and tweed coats with leather elbow-patches and so on: the uniform of the poor sage! He asked me reverently what he should do with them. I was about to tell him to offer them to the nearest jumble sale when Benedicta intervened with an air of crisp decision and said: "Burn them in the furnace, Baynes." Baynes bowed to the heavenly will, and so did I, though I opened my mouth as if to speak. What did it matter? He had found an old French briar in one of my pockets, and this he had set aside. I was glad to see it again, though it was pretty much burned out; yet under the cool glance of Benedicta I found myself strangely incapable of reclaiming possession of it. I thought of the sweet-smelling box of cigars in the drawing room. From now on nothing but the choicest Juliets would touch the lips of Charlock. There was a conveniently placed leather case, already filled, upon the mantelpiece. "I think it had better go—it's pretty used up" I said treacherously to Baynes. He bowed again. "The boots and shoes I have given to the gardener" he said. "They fit him."

So we equipped ourselves with coats and wraps and floated through the front door to find the office Rolls—flatus symbol of the new Charlock—lying at anchor, waiting for us.

Memory refuses to recover the rest of that evening in any detail—behind the stripes and bars of Busoni's music; only towards dawn, lying exhausted beside each other, I awoke with a jerk to find her talking Turkish in her sleep—the strange crooning bubbling tongue which I had once heard her use to her hawk. She was feverish, tossing and turning in bed like someone trying to throw off, in her sleep, the imaginary bonds of some painful dream. But by morning the shadow had fled with the fever, and she was in sparkling spirits again. I walked half the way to the office across the spring-fermenting city with its frail sunlight, revelling in the green of the parks, the light rime of hoarfrost on the grass. Well, I was dense with happiness—the poor scientist could have trumpeted his joy like an elephant. Jevons the commissionaire was on duty as usual, stamping and chomping with the fresh cold, clad in his green coat with polished brass buttons, his billycock hat; his huge umbrella lay beside the directors' lift. He lavished his customary hearty pleasantries upon me, and even went so far as to tip me a conspiratorial wink as I passed him with my own black umbrella. It is amazing how quickly one can develop the condescending wave of an umbrella which somehow goes with city clothes. And a bowler! In stately fashion the lift bore me up to the third floor, to the silent and comfortable office from which one could glimpse a corner of St. Paul's far away to the left of the invisible river line. My despatch-box had already been brought up by Miss Tee, its contents neatly arranged in the metal tray for my perusal. The memorandum of the latest meeting upon the subject of the new light bulb project was already here, duly annotated by the absent Julian and signed by his secretary in his absence. How did he do it, I wondered? I supposed that the minutes were sent to him by Telex. "I am extremely eager to see this project realised," he wrote heart-warmingly "as it seems one of the most imaginative we have ever undertaken. Please keep it upon the secret list until production department is ready to market. Only one consideration comes to mind. We must remember the prohibitive price of mercury at £150 per 75 lb flask when costing. In this context however I hope shortly to have good news of negotiations going forward in Moscow for supplies of mercury. If we can capture this new market and thus sidetrack the chlorine plants which are responsible for the shortage and high price of this element we should be well on our way towards a signal success. Please press ahead with the first five hundred prototype bulbs."

I rang the manservant in the buttery and told him that for the eleven o'clock break I would very much like a bowl of strawberries and cream with a glass of the finest sherry. Corbin was perfectly used to requests of this kind; he would despatch an office boy at once in search of the strawberries. I put in a call to Slough to find out how the engineering department was dealing with the new filament and what the first tests had demonstrated. All was well; there was no deterioration in spite of the tremendous load. It was almost too good to be true, things were moving with such speed and smoothness. There was no meeting today and hardly any paperwork, so I opened the newspaper and sank into a pleasant daydream about Benedicta and the future—a daydream compounded of such various elements that it would not have been possible to sort them all out into a coherent pattern. At any rate not then.

Later she rang up and said she missed me. *She missed me!* I was overcome. And as far as Benedicta was concerned I found that I liked her all the better for knowing so little about her; this factor contributed something enigmatic to her—to her strangely withdrawn personality which flourished in privacy like some heavy-perfumed magnolia. Everything therefore was a surprise. Had I felt that she was deliberately keeping secret things she might have shared it would doubtless have been different; but her prohibitions and retreats into panic did not suggest this at all. She had thrown up simply the defences which over-sensitive, perhaps even rather neurotic, people throw up consciously against experiences too deeply felt to be the subject of open discussion. Of course at first the tabus were a little bewildering—but then why should someone not wish not to discuss their fathers or past husbands and so on? It was perfectly defensible; doubtless as we got to know each other better these defences would melt and give way to new understandings. (The strawberries were watery, the sherry indifferent, but I did not care. I was tied to a comet's tail.) And when I arrived back at Mount Street in the evenings there was no shadow of doubt about the warmth and eagerness with which she threw open the door, forestalling Baynes, to run down the steps and embrace me, almost ravenous for my embrace. Thus arm in arm to the warm fire crackling on the hearth, the winking bottles and decanters, and the prospect of a whole evening spent alone together. "Julian telephoned today and told me to send you his warmest greetings." Everybody loved me.

I had noticed that even in the first few days a flock of white envelopes addressed to her had landed like doves upon the hall table. In the morning the office sent her a social secretary to deal with such correspondence, so that when I arrived back I found an equally massive bunch of envelopes stamped and addressed for despatch. I sifted somewhat ruefully through them. "Heavens, you seem to know everybody worthwhile in London."

"Those are all refusals" she said. "Besides, I don't see people any more. I want you to myself. I haven't for ages. Besides you don't want to go out and about do you?"

"Good Lord no."

"And then after April I shall be in the country where nobody ever comes. Do you see? And you will drive down for week ends or whenever you get a chance. We'll be married there, too, if you agree. Julian has arranged it. Just the two of us I mean, with nobody."

"So you didn't want to escape with me?"

"It wasn't that, Felix. It's just that I can't just disappear like that. I have to stay in touch, you know."

"With whom, with what?"

She looked at me curiously, as though the question were an unexpectedly foolish one: as if she had not expected it from me. "I mean" I went on "you are not working for anyone; you don't have any real obligations, have you?"

"None at all." She gave a small sharp laugh, a sad laugh as she sat down on the hearthrug before the fire to rest her chin upon her drawn up knees and stare into the burning coals. Then it occurred to me that it might be something to do with her doctors, and I kicked myself for a prying fool, kneeling down beside her to put my arms about her shoulders. "I'm sorry Benedicta" I said. She had a trace of a tear in the corner of her eye, but she was still smiling. "It's of no importance. Come, sit beside me and tell me what you have been doing for the firm. Will you? I want to share everything."

This was more easy to do, and most congenial to my mood; and yet, as I started talking about the three first devices which Merlin was to put into immediate production, I could not but feel a sort of helpless despair that they were not more interesting and revolutionary than they were. They were only mechanical contrivances which, however useful, provided crutches for people in need. In the back of my mind I was thinking along more abstract vectors, groping towards something of which Abel is still only a shallow prototype. A behaviouristic abacus of patterned responses which might respond to the very oscillations of the nervous system—something which might both prophesy and retroprophesy. . . . Nothing was clear as yet; there was so much as yet to be done on the theory of mathematical probability. It made me dizzy thinking about it. But meanwhile my *alter felix* continued his lucid exposition of the toys for which the firm were to be responsible, and all the time Benedicta listened avidly, as if to music, her head thrown slightly back, eyes closed. And when I had finished—when I had even shown her one of the tiny filaments as some people will show the relics of an operation, a calculus in a bottle—she sighed deeply and put her arms round me, pressing herself to me as if all this prosaic recital had been almost sexually rousing.

"It's going to be marvellous" she said. "You will see."

There was no doubt of it in my mind; nor anything but overwhelming gratitude to this extraordinary golden creature whose head had sunk now to my knees, half fire-tranced. "I'm determined you are going to be happy" I said. "Happy and not scared." Put down that goblet, Felix!

She jumped up at once, startled, and said: "Who said I was scared?" She made as if to walk towards the door but I captured her hands and drew her gently back to the fireplace. "Did Julian say anything?" she said sharply and I answered in the same tone: "Nobody said it; besides I have never met Julian. I thought some-

184

times you seemed worried, that was all. But it's over now for good. You have got me to rely on." I caught sight of my face in the mirror and suddenly felt foolish.

For good! My clumsy advocacy worked at last; she seated herself beside me once more, relaxed and calm again. Beside the bed that evening I found a couple of books of essays, beautifully bound in green morocco. "I borrowed them from Julian's flat" she explained. She didn't say when. Each bore a pretty bookplate with the owner's initials entwined and a rebus—an ape climbing a pomegranate tree. Here and there passages of the books had been underscored, presumably by the owner. "Out of the present we manufacture the future; what we dream today becomes tomorrow's reality. All our ills come from incautious dreaming. Trivial or impure dreaming literally rots the fabric of the future. But the dreams of a rarefied psyche help to resolve tensions and build up good sources." I yawned, she was already asleep, curled up beside me with her head under her wing. Drifting now in her direction with half-shut eyes I dreamed I was addressing the politely subservient members of my board on topics of the greatest moment. "The sails of fancy, gentlemen, swell with the following wind of good fortune." I was learning how to raise my voice, to suit gestures to the words, to perorate. . . .

So the brightly etched days rolled by. Julian had apparently returned from his trip abroad, but still put in no appearance at the boards, though his comments upon our lucubrations were as prompt and cogent as ever. I gathered that he did much of his work at home and was hardly ever in his office. It seemed to me strange that he did not make personal contact, if only to shake my hand. In fact I rather looked forward to meeting him. I even suggested to Benedicta that she might ask him to dine with us, but she shook her head doubtfully and said: "You don't know Julian. He is tremendously shy. He hides himself away. I'm sure he wouldn't come. He'd just send a huge shelf of flowers with a last minute excuse. You know, Felix, hardly anyone in the office has so much as seen him. He prefers to speak to them on the phone." It was intriguing to say the least, and at first I was inclined to think that she was exaggerating; but not so. Then one day he phoned me to discuss some point or other—but from the country. His voice had a thrilling icy sauvity. He spoke slowly, gently, in a dreamy way which suggested more than a hint of world weariness—one imagined Disraeli dictating a state paper in just such a disenchanted tone. I expressed my eagerness to meet him and he thanked me, but added: "Yes, all in good time, Charlock. We certainly must meet, but at the moment I am simply worked off my feet; and you have so much other fish to fry—I refer to your marriage to Benedicta. I can't tell you how happy that makes us all."

There seemed nothing for it but to bow to his whim for the time being. But one morning my own phone rang at the office and I could tell from the timbre of his voice that the call was coming from somewhere inside the building. It was Julian all right—by now I was quite familiar with his voice, we had already spoken to each other frequently; moreover I knew that he had an office at the end of the corridor where Nathan, the general admin. sec. presided over his papers. Why, I had even recorded him once or twice for my collection. I thought in playful fashion that I might surprise him, meet him in the flesh. So while he still spoke I put down the receiver on my blotter and stalked down the long corridor to throw open the door of the office in question. But there at his desk sat Nathan only; a small dictaphone, attached to the telephone, was still playing. "Ah you've hung up, Mr. Charlock" said Nathan with mild reproach, cutting off. I felt something of a fool. Nathan switched over and said. "He was in very early this morning and recorded half a dozen conversations. He often does so."

I recounted this incident somewhat ruefully to Benedicta; but she only smiled and shook her head. "You'll never catch Julian on the hop" she said. "Until he decides."

"What does he look like, Benedicta?" I asked. She gazed at me thoughtfully for a moment and then said, "There isn't anything special about him. He's just like anyone else I think."

On a sudden impulse I asked: "Have you ever seen him?" The question was quite involuntary, and the moment it was out I knew it to be absurd. But Benedicta swallowed and answered: "Of course, quite definitely." But the tone in which she said it struck me as curious. If I had had to "interpret" it in the manner of the inimitable Nash I should have taken it to mean: "I think that the person I have seen is Julian, but I am not absolutely sure." The thought as it

186

crossed my mind however seemed to be ever so slightly disloyal, so I stifled it and changed the subject. "Ah well" I said "I expect we shall see him for the wedding at any rate." But once again I was to find myself in error, for neither Julian nor anyone else came to the wedding though the house was bursting with presents and telegrams of congratulations.

The wedding! What could have been more singular? I had asked no questions, of course; but then on the other hand I had been asked none. The arrangements were not of my making, but it was to be presumed that Benedicta (if she were not herself responsible for them) had at least been consulted. I supposed that she had decided to get married in the strictest privacy, that was all. Only that and nothing more. Nor had I anyone that I wished to invite. No family. An uncle in America, some cousins in India, that was all.

But it was my first visit to "Cathay", that preposterous, gloomy country house which was to be our home; moreover by night, for the marriage was arranged for midnight. "Cathay" forsooth! With its turrets and fishponds, great park, cloth-of-gold chamber, huge organ by Basset. At the end of a normal office day my fellow directors came in one by one to wish me luck and a happy honeymoon—cracking the usual awkward jokes about visiting the condemned man in his cell etc. After these so amiable pleasantries I took a taxi home to an early dinner, to find the hall full of luggage and the office car already outside the door. It was piquant, mysterious, rather exciting to be motored down into the depths of the country like this. It smelt of orange-blossom and elopements in the dark of the year. I visualised some great house-party with Julian and some of his collaborators, perhaps with a wife or two present to balance the forces of good and evil. Indeed I thought that Julian could hardly do less than witness for us. We did not speak much as the car nosed its way slowly through the slippery gromboolian suburbs towards Hampshire. Benedicta sat close beside me with her gloved hand in mine, looking pale and somewhat contrite. After the ceremony we were to drive on directly to Southampton to board the *Polaris*—a Merlin Line cruiser. But the wedding itself was of course to be a civil one. No church-bells for Charlock.

It was a long coldish drive with fine rain glittering in the white beam of the headlights, prickling through the greenery of forest land and heath. My initial elation had given way to a certain tender solemnity. "Benedicta" I whispered, but she only pressed my hand tightly and said: "Sh! I'm thinking." I wondered what her thoughts might be as she stared out across the darkling light. Of a past she had confided to nobody?

At last we crackled down the long avenues towards the bowl of golden light which gleamed at the end of the long green tunnels. The house was ablaze with light, and crammed with people all right. A telephone was insisting somewhere. But to my surprise "the people" were all servants. In the rococo musicians' gallery with its mouldy Burne-Jones flavour a quintet played ghastly subdued music as if afraid to overhear itself. Butlers and maids moved everywhere with a kind of clinical deliberation—yet for all the world as if they were making preparations for a great ball. A staff like this could have mounted a wedding reception for four hundred people. But I could see no trace of any guests. But a mountain of telegrams lay unopened on the marble tables in the hall, and the preposterous Edwardian rooms leading with an air of ever greater futility into each other were bursting with presents—everything from a concert grand to silver crocks and gew-gaws of all sorts and sizes. The mixture of portentous emptiness and reckless prodigality staggered me.

But Benedicta moved about it all with a kind of fiery elation, moth-light of step, her face glowing with pleasure and pride. She held her head high against the forest of candle-branches and spectral Venetian lustres. It struck me then how foreign she was. I divined that this old house with its musty gawkish features offered a sort of mental association with Stamboul—those rotting palaces in *style pompier* copied and recopied, criss-crossed with mirrors set in tarnished mouldings. Shades of Baden and Pau—yes, that is what made her feel so at home, so at one with it all. "But is there nobody except the servants?" I asked, and she turned her dancing eyes upon me for a second before shaking her blonde head. "I told you, silly. Only us." Only us! But we had just passed an enormously long buffet prepared for a midnight supper: apparently the baked meats (I thought in muddled quotation) were destined to grace the servants' hall. It was marvellous, it was macabre. I felt quite a wave of affection for poor Baynes who now advanced towards us with a sheaf of telegrams—congratulations from Jocas, Julian, Caradoc, Hippolyta: his was a familiar face. These brief messages from the lost world of Athens and Stamboul gave me a little pang—they seemed almost brutally gay. Baynes said: "They are waiting for you in the library, madam." Benedicta nodded regally and led the way. The noise of the quintet followed us apologetically. Everywhere there were flowers—but big banks of flowers professionally arranged: their heavy scent swung about in pools among the candle-shining shadows. And yet . . . it was all somehow like a cinema, I found myself thinking. Baynes marched before us and opened yet another door.

The library! Of course I did not discover the fact until later, but this huge and beautifully arranged room with its galleries and moulded squinches, its sea-green dome, its furnishings of globes, atlases, astrolabes, gazetteers, was a fake: all the books in it were empty dummies! Yet to browse among the titles one would have imagined the room to contain virtually the sum total of European culture. But the books were all playful make-believe, empty buckram and gilt. Descartes, Nietzsche, Leibniz. . . . Here, however, all was candlelight and firelight, discreet and perhaps a trifle funereal? No, not really. A large desk, covered with a green baize cloth, conveyed the mute suggestion of an altar, with its flowers, candles and open registers. Here sunning his shovel-shaped backside stood the Shadbolt, beside the registrar for the district; their clerks stood by to act as witnesses if need be—mouldy and dispossessed-looking figures. We greeted each other formally and with much false cordiality. Benedicta gave the signal while I groped in my pockets for the ring.

To my surprise she seemed quite moved by the grim routine of the civil ceremony. It did not last long. At a signal the tremulous Baynes appeared with champagne on a tray and we relaxed into a more comprehensive mood of relief. Shadbolt toasted us heartily; and Benedicta made her slow way through the house to touch glasses with the servants who had also been provided with a little spray with which to respond. It all seemed to happen in a flash. Within an hour we were on our way again, down the long roads to Southampton. It was raining. It was raining. I thought of the blue gourd of the Mediterranean sky with longing. Benedicta had fallen asleep, her long aquiline nose pointing downwards along my sleeve. I cradled her preciously. She looked so sly. From time to time a tiny snore escaped her lips.

Dawn's left hand was in the sky by the time we negotiated the sticky dockland with its palpitating yellow lights and climbed the long gangplank of the sleeping ship to seek out the bridal suite on A deck. Benedicta was speechless with fatigue and so was I; too tired to supervise the stacking of the luggage, too tired to think. We fell into our bunks and slept; and by the time I woke I felt the heart-lifting sensation of a ship sliding smoothly through water—the soft clear drub of powerful engines driving us steadily seaward. There was too the occasional lift, and hiss of spray on the deck around us. I had a bath and went on deck—a wind-snatched deck with a light grizzle of rain falling upon it. The land lay far behind now in the mists of morning, a grey smudge of cloud-capped nothingness. We were on our way round the world. England hull down in the sea-mist of dawn. It was so good to be alive.

Just time to return to my cabin and finish the study of the mantis which Marchant had lent me. "Another theory was constructed on the physiological experiments of Rabaud and others; in these it was found that the superior nerve-centres restrain or inhibit the reflexive system. The control is weakened by decapitation. The visible result is that the reflexive-genital activity of the headless male is made more vigorous and therefore biologically more effective." Benedicta sighed in her sleep and turned to snuggle deeper into the soft pillows. The same goes for decapitated frogs, while any hangman will tell you that a broken spinal cord will produce an instant ejaculation. I put my book aside and smoked, lulled by the lilt of the ship as she manned the green sea. Then slept again to awake and find my breakfast beside me and Benedicta sitting opposite in a chair, naked and smiling. We were sliding back towards Polis, that was why perhaps—towards those first intimacies which seemed now to lie far back in the past. Did she suit her lovemaking to the country she found herself in? Now as she came to sit cross-legged on the end of my bed I thought back to those ancient kisses and little punishments—the water torture, the wax torture, the frenetic zealous kisses with their word-

190

less pieties—all of them making a part of the bright fabric of the past which must be carried forward into a future bright with promise. And here I was with the creature within arm's reach. Moreover what could well be more delightful than the life of shipboard with its defined routines, its lack of demands upon one's personal initiative? And with it isolation, being surrounded by water on every side. It seemed so soon when we found ourselves sliding past Gibraltar into calmer seas, cradled by light racing cloud and water far bluer than we deserved. She had flowered into a kinetic laziness which suited itself marvellously to the holiday mood. The only interruption was an occasional long cable from Julian about the minor details of some industrial operation; but even these dwindled away into silence.

Three months! But they passed in a slow-motion dream; already the lazy life of the ship had bemused us, sunk us into a tranced nescience. Talk of Calypso's island—I forgot even to make notes, forgot to figure. I read like a convalescent. I was even able to find relief from those half-unconscious trains of reasoning which had always formed a sort of *leitmotiv* to my quotidian life—so much so that I could honestly say that there had not been a single moment until now when I was not fully occupied with my private thoughts. An invisible censor clad in gumboots strode up and down before Charlock's subliminal threshold—O a far more competent fellow than the greybearded Freudian one. A primordial biological censor this, rather like a beefeater in the Tower of London.

Of course there were interludes in all this uxorious sloth when my alter Charlock reproached me bitterly and pushed me into involuntary attempts to show a leg. At Monte, for example, I rallied sufficiently to consider playing the tables. I collected a mass of those long printed sheaves of paper which record the numbers thrown out by the wheels. They are of great interest to those unwary souls who wish to study form with a view to establishing a system and so breaking the bank. I was hardly less unwary and thought that a brief analysis might—I had been playing about with mathematical probability— ah wretched artificer! But when I suggested this Benedicta came back with a very decisive "Ah dear no. Have you forgotten that the firm owns nearly all the shares in the Casino? Do you think they would let me lose on my honeymoon? We'd win a fortune Felix—

what would be the point of it?" Indeed! I let the long sheaves float away in the wind and settle in the pale waters.

The firm was omnipresent, though in a queer tactful sort of way; nor do I mean simply that the captain and crew of the vessel knew who we were, and had received instructions to take specially good care of us. It went a bit deeper than that. At every point of disembarkation we were discreetly met by the resident agent and taken on a conducted tour of the place, much in the manner of visiting minor royalty. This was most welcome in countries where we did not know the language and habits of the natives—Cambodia, India for example. Nevertheless I could well understand this unobtrusive tutelage becoming oppressive in the long run. There were a number of state occasions to be observed as well which made me sigh for the anonymity of a hotel-room in Florence; a Governor here and there bade us to his table: those huge mournful Government houses full of sighing chintz and mammoth billiard tables, full of bad pictures and unpalatable cooking. Well, I sighed—we both sighed—but there was nothing to be done but accept and attend. This of course was more marked east of Suez: we were familiars of the Mediterranean, needing no help in Athens or in Jocasland of the tumbled minarets. But Athens was strangely hushed—everyone was away it seemed, either abroad or in the islands. Nor could I get any news of Banubula or Koepgen, try as I would. I had a small fugitive inclination to visit the Plaka and perhaps Number Seven as well, but I dismissed it, telling myself that time was short. But at Stamboul it was no surprise to see a little white pinnace scuttling across the sea to meet us with Jocas steering her—this long before the mists divided to reveal the ancient city trembling among the tulip-topped bastions. I saw the great confiding hand of Jocas come sliding up the gangplank rope like a deepsea squid; then he was before us, with his shy dancing eye. There was nothing equivocal in the tenderness with which he greeted us, pressed us to his heart. He had brought some small presents like newspapers, Black Sea caviar, Turkish cigarettes and some rare pieces of jewellery for B. So we spent the day a-gossip under a white awning, watching the city swim up from the deeps. Our lunch was served on deck and Jocas drank his champagne to us, uttering the familiar druidic toasts to bless our union. Benedicta looked ravishing in her new brown skin; the fine hairs shading from temple to cheek had already turned silkworm golden. "I have never seen her look so calm, so well" said Jocas softly in an aside, and indeed it seemed to me to be so. He was full of news of the property and of course the birds and their form. Benedicta questioned him eagerly. Indeed at one point she wanted to stay a week, but the itinerary was already so charged. . . . Omar the master falconer was dead, but Said had taken over and was doing very well. He had invented a new kind of lure. And so on. But mixed also in this animated exchange of fact were scraps of news about other friends and acquaintances—Caradoc in New York, for example, preparing to fly out to his new venture. Graphos was going from strength to strength, after having nearly ruined his career because of an infatuation with a streetwalker. And Koepgen? "He is doing well in Moscow; he will have a year or two yet. I know you have his notebooks." As a matter of fact I had one with me on the voyage. "And then what?" Jocas twinkled the gold smile and rubbed his hands. "He will get a large bonus and be free to pursue his studies."

"And that ikon?"

"Yes, we have found the one he wants; it is quite safe, waiting for him. But the firm comes first." Jocas giggled. "It's a lure, eh?"

The liner was scheduled to stay only a few hours; it was hardly worth going ashore for such a brief period; a gaggle of sightseers were rushed ashore, crammed into buses and given a swift glimpse of the great walls of smoking dung. But we sat on deck, talking drowsily, until they returned and the warning siren sent its herds of echoes thundering across the sky. Benedicta was leaning at the rail now, staring down into the water. "In the old days" Jocas was saying dreamily "they had bird-fairs all over Central Europe—singing birds I mean. Her father was a renowned breeder of songbirds, and won prizes everywhere with his exhibits. They say he was the first to think of blinding birds in order to improve their singing—you know, red-hot copper wire. It's easily and painlessly done they say. He built up quite a trade in cage-birds at one time, but the business outgrew it. Now only a few specialists are interested; the fairs have all lapsed. There is no room for them in the modern world, I suppose."

"Did it improve their singing?"

"It would improve anyone's singing; one sense develops to compensate for the loss of another—you know that. Why do they try to find a blind man always for muezzin? It needn't be eyes necessarily. The voice of the castrato, for example." He yawned heartily, by now half asleep. "Benedicta," he called "I must leave you, my dear. I wish I could come too but I can't."

The sightseeing passengers were panting aboard again led by two steatopygous priests—soutanes stuffed with blood-sausage. Benedicta came thoughtfully back to us and said, without any preliminary gambit: "Jocas, did you give Mr. Sacrapant the sack?" Jocas was surprised into a smile as he answered. "Of course not."

"Then why?" she said with a puzzled frown.

"His suicide? But he left a letter listing a number of reasons—mostly trivial ones you would say, even insignificant reasons. Yet taken all together I suppose they weighed something. Good Lord, the firm had no part in the matter." He looked shocked. She drew a sigh of relief and sat down. "Then?" Jocas went on, frowning, as if trying to puzzle out the matter for himself. "We look at things from the wrong point of view. I mean, how many reasons could you give for wanting to go on living? The list would be endless. So there is never one reason, but scores. You know in a funny sort of way he could never get used to the idea of security—it was almost as if he couldn't wait for his wife to get her pension." He burst out laughing in a strange half-rueful way and struck his thigh. "Ah! old Sacrapant!" he said and shook his head. "He will be impossible to replace." I saw the little figure falling.

A bell rang urgently and someone signalled from the deck house by the bridge. Reluctantly Jocas took himself off, to stand in the sheets of the little pinnace looking up at us with a curious expression on his face—a mixture of affection and sadness. "Be happy" he called across the separating water, as if perhaps he had scented some fugitive disharmony in us after all: and the little craft suddenly reared up and began its glib motion as it raced away towards the land.

"Come," said Benedicta, taking my arm "let's go down for a spell." She wanted to go down to the cabin, to lie about and talk or read—most probably to make love: until the first bell went for dinner. Well, but by dark we were crawling through the Straits again bound for the furthest corners of the world. Columbus Char-lock! I do not believe that one can love without analysing—though I know that too much analysis can spoil loving: but here at least nothing but contentment found a place, a luxurious self-surrender which made death seem very far away. That was it, death!

Somewhere there is an album full of photographs of this royal progress—photographs taken, not by us, but by the captain and crew who shepherded us through all the adventures of travel with such docile assiduity. Later a handsome bound volume, with the record duly mounted and in the right order, arrived on the hall table with the compliments of the shipping line. Well then, on the back of bloody elephants bucketing up the holy mountain in Ceylon, wearing weird pith helmets against the sun. Then some tiger shoots in India —Benedicta lavender-pale and slender, with her triumphant little boot upon the head of the beast: the rigor had stiffened its snarl into a silent travesty of the last defensive gesture. Smack! Hong Kong, Sydney, Tahiti—the long ritual led us on, offering no demands upon us.

But these superficial records could not deal with everything, take account of everything. For example, unknown to either of us, Iolanthe was also aboard—or rather her image was, the public one, printed on celluloid. Among the films we were shown as we crossed the Indian Ocean was one made in Egypt, trivial and melodramatic, in which to my surprise Iolanthe had a small part. She swam up out of the screen without warning, moving into close-up which projected her enlarged face with its heavily doctored eyeshapes almost into my lap. My surprise made me sit up with an exclamation and grip Benedicta's hand.

"Good Lord."

"You know her?"

"It's Iolanthe of all people."

It was not much of a part, it lasted barely half a minute. But it was enough to glimpse an entirely new person grafted upon the one I had known. After all, the smallest gesture gives a clue to the inner disposition—a way of walking, position of hands, cant of the head. All right. Here she had to cut up food and put it on a plate; then to walk with the plate across a strip of sand, to bow, to serve. In this very brief repertoire of acts and gestures—some so familiar from which I recalled the old being—I saw a new one. "It's a common little face" said Benedicta with distaste and a contempt that extended itself with justice to the whole ridiculous film, with its sheiks and dancing girls. "Yes. Yes." Of course she was right; but how much less coarse, less common, than the original Iolanthe I had known. On the contrary these photographs suggested a new kind of maturity; her gestures had become studied, graceful, no longer impulsive and uncoordinated, fluent. Some of this I tried to express to Benedicta but she did not follow; she turned her cryptic smile upon me and pressed my hand confidingly. "But she is being directed and rehearsed by the *metteur-en-scène*, my dear: and he probably sleeps with her as well to get her to do things his way." Of course this was true and yet . . . entirely factitious? The change seemed to hold a whole range of significance for me. I was puzzled; more mysterious still, I felt wounded in an obscure sort of way—almost as if I had been tricked. Could I perhaps have missed the most interesting part of my little mistress by the merest inattention? I was nudged into surprise by that short insignificant scene. Moreover, in order the better to analyse my own response to it, I asked for it to be played over again the following afternoon while Benedicta was taking her siesta. No, the astonishment remained. The coarseness, the street-arab knowingness, had found a point of repose where it could manifest itself calmly as naked human experience. This gave point to a new angle of the head, to the resurrection of a smile which I knew on lips which I knew—but which I had never noticed. Or had they not then been there? Iolanthe! Heavens! I saw the rust-stained marbles rising against the keen skies of Attica. I rummaged, so to speak, among my stock of memories, to find correspondences to match this new personage—in vain. The screen-figure corresponded so little to the original that I felt as if she had somehow hoaxed me. My mood of puzzled abstraction lasted until dinner time, when Benedicta noticed it—for she missed nothing. "I hear you have been visiting your girl friend while I was asleep" she said with a rather cruel smile, her lips curving mischievously up at the corners. "Isn't it rather early in the day to start being unfaithful to me?" It was a joke, and should have been taken as such.

But I wanted to be serious, to explain how confused and puzzled I had been by this parody of nature. O yes I did. Benedicta would have none of it. "You can have all the women you want provided you tell me about it in detail" she said, and a sudden new light, a little grim this time, came into her eye. It was rather annoying for this was hardly the point. Besides nothing could be more distasteful than to provoke the sort of middle-class tiff common to middle-class couples in the suburbs of loathsome capitals. I was outraged by her vulgarity. "It was only a joke" she said.

"How idiotic to quarrel over a strip of film."

"I am not quarrelling. Felix, look at me."

"Nor am I." I obeyed. We kissed but with constraint. What the devil was wrong? But we finished the meal in silence and after it stalked up on deck to sit side by side in deck-chairs, smoking and musing. "How much do you know about this girl?" she asked at last; somewhat peevishly I replied. "Certainly more than I know about you, even after all this time." Benedicta's eye narrowed with anger, and when she was in this mood she set her ears back like a scared cat.

"I will answer any question you put to me."

"I have never insisted on you answering questions."

"How could you *insist*?"

"Or even ask. I want you as you are, exactly as you are at this moment; I don't care if you are still a bit of an enigma."

She turned her hard blue eye upon me with a new expression which I had not seen before and which I might describe as an amused contempt, and yawned behind her brown fingers. "My poor Felix" she said in a tone which made me long to strike her.

I took myself off to bed with an improving book, but when the clock struck midnight and she had not put in an appearance I dressed again and went on deck to find her. She was sitting alone in the deserted bar, leaning heavily upon it, dozing. "Thank God you've come," she said incoherently "I can't stand up." She was in fact dead drunk. It was all the more surprising because she was ordinarily a very modest drinker. I helped her laboriously along the deck to the cabin where she sat on her bunk, swaying slightly, holding her head in her hands. "On Thursday we touch at Macao" she said. "That is where Max died of typhoid fever. I do not want to go ashore." I said nothing. She went on: "He was a musician, but not a good one. But he had invented something which didn't exist until then—a copying machine for scores, for parts. It wasn't complete, and it took some of the best brains in the firm to develop and market it. Anything else you want to know?"

"Did you have a marriage settlement with him?"

Her eye lit with a sulphurous gleam, the embers of a queer triumph shining through the whisky daze.

"No" she said; but the tone in which she said it permitted me to construe the words "There was no need." (I jumped with guilt at so treacherous a thought.)

Then she held up her cupped hands pleadingly and said: "But even if he had been alive I'd have left him for you."

It was not possible to resist her when she was in this mood—sitting like some forlorn collapsing edifice, foundering among its own distresses. I felt crushed under the weight of my self-reproaches. I soaked her patiently in hot water, helped her to be sick, and towelled her back to some semblance of sobriety; afterwards she lay, pallid and exhausted, in my arms until daybreak when she was able once more to whisper the little phrase which had become almost a slogan for us. Always after making love she would say: "Let's always, Felix."

So Macao passed, and with it some of the weight of her private preoccupations; her mood lightened and made room for a new gaiety, a new responsiveness. We had become used to the ship by now and familiar with the habit of life. It was almost as if we had never lived land-life. And as we neared our final port of disembarkation we even started to take part in the absurd dinners and fancy-dress dances which we had found so distasteful during the first weeks of the voyage. In fact the night before we reached Southampton we went the whole hog and borrowed fancy dresses and masks from the extensive wardrobe of the vessel. I was Mephisto I think, with eyebrows of jet; she was a nun in a great white coif of starched linen. It was while she was making up her face in the mirror that she said, in an almost terror-stricken tone: "You know Felix I may be pregnant —have you thought about it? What shall I do?"

"How do you mean?"

About the blood and all that. It was not very consistent.

She was sitting there in front of the mirror staring into her own wide eyes with an expression of silent panic. Then she gave a long trembling sigh and shook herself awake from the momentary trance, turning away towards the door of the cabin with the air of someone leaving the condemned cell. And all that evening she hardly spoke; from time to time I caught her looking at me with an expression of inexpressible sadness. "What is it, Benedicta?" But she only shook her head and gave me a tremulous smile; and after the dance, when we reached the cabin, she tore off her coif and shook out her golden hair, turning upon me with a sudden air of agonised reproach, to cry: "O can't you see? It will change everything, everything."

That last night we lay side by side unsleeping, staring up into the darkness, our strange voyage almost over.

We stepped ashore in a mist of grey watered silk, to find the car waiting on the dockside. Someone had already been aboard to take charge of the luggage; we had nothing to do except to negotiate the gangplank and take refuge under the black umbrella the chauffeur held for us. "Welcome back!" We sat in the back of the car, hand in sympathetic hand, but quite silent, watching the ghostly countryside whirl away around us. Gusts of wind stirred the tall trees; heath moulded itself away into heath, dotted here and there by statuary of soaked forest ponies. At last we came to the big house, which seemed no longer full of people; but there were fires going everywhere, and the muzzy smell of oldfashioned central heating filled the air. A lunch table had been laid for us. It was a queer sensation to be on land again; I still felt the sea rocking in my semicircular canals. Baynes was there to greet us with his air of lugubrious kindness; he had mixed one of his excellent cocktails, Benedicta took hers upstairs for a while. I heard the telephone ring, and saw Baynes switch the extension lever sideways so that it would sound on the first-floor landing. I heard Benedicta speaking, her voice sharp and animated. When she came down she was all smiles. "It was Julian. He sends his love to us. He says that you'll have a pleasant surprise when you next visit the office. We've had a big success with your first two devices."

That afternoon I motored up to London to my by now unfamiliar desk, to be greeted with good news that Julian had promised me. Congreve and Nathan brought me the whole dossier, including all the advertising and promotion. "It's a landslide, Charlock" said Congreve happily, washing his hands with invisible soap. "You sit tight and watch your royalty scale; there seems to be no ceiling—the German and American figures aren't even complete and look at sales."

All this was extremely gratifying. But at the back of the dossier was another folder somewhat cryptically labelled "Dr. Marchant's adaptation of the filament to gunsighting". Neither Congreve nor Nathan could enlighten me as the meaning of it. When they left me I picked up the phone and asked the switchboard to try and unearth Julian for me; this took some time, and when at last I did locate him his voice sounded a good way off, as if he were speaking from the depths of the country. I cut short his conventional greetings and congratulations and at once broached the subject of the dossier. Julian said: "Yes, I was meaning to talk to you about it. Marchant runs our electrical side down at Slough. You may have met him, I don't know. But when we were going into production he at once seized upon your device and applied it to something he himself was working on—a vastly improved gunsighting system. It looks very promising indeed; the Services are most excited by it. We have not moved properly into prototype as yet, but in a month or two we'll have a trial shoot with the Army and see what we've got. I don't need to emphasise the importance of the contracts we might get; and of course your patent is fully protected. It would mean a terrific jump in your royalties. I hope you are pleased."

My silence must have disabused him of the idea, because he repeated the last phrase somewhat more anxiously and went on: "Of course I should perhaps have consulted you—but then you were somewhere on the high seas and Marchant was eager to get going with this infra-red electrical device...." His voice tailed lethargically away. "I feel" I said "as though my invention has been wrenched out of my hands." It was marvellous the way he managed to convey the notion of a sympathetic smile over the phone, the kindly touch upon the elbow. "O don't take it like that, Charlock. It isn't the case. It's your device differently applied, that is all."

"Nevertheless" I said stubbornly, spectacles on nose. "Nevertheless, Julian." He clicked his tongue sympathetically and went on with redoubled suavity. "Please accept my humblest apologies; I should have asked. But now the damage is done, so please forgive me won't you?"

There was in fact nothing to be done but bow to it. "Where is Marchant?" I said. "He is on his way up to you now" said Julian, his voice suddenly fading into a thicket of scratchy interruptions. There was a click and we were cut off. I looked up to find Marchant standing before my desk with the air of an aggrieved collie, tousle-haired and shortsighted behind steel-rimmed spectacles of a powerful magnification, basted with insulation tape. He held out a long limp hand with fingers heavily stained by nicotine and acid. "It's me" he said in his whining disagreeable voice, without removing the wet fag end from his lower lip. "Of course we've met." "Sit down" I said with as much cordiality as I could muster. His whole appearance spoke of the stinks labs of some provincial university—much-patched tweed coat and grey bags: extremely dirty and crumpled shirt with missing stud. He threw a bundle of drawings on to the desk and drew up a chair in order to explain them, pointing cautiously with a silver-hilted pencil. His tweed smelt of wet. I was disposed to adopt an attitude of somewhat boorish resentment towards him, but one glance at his papers showed me the marvellous elegance of his application; he had made full use of the new sodium-tipped contrivance and applied it, with slightly modified mountings, to the conventional sighting screen of a weapon. I listened to his lucid explanation with unwilling admiration. "But then weapons!" I could not help saying at last. "How disappointing. I was hoping my toys would help the human race, not . . . well, contribute to its quarrels." He looked me over, coolly, critically, and with some contempt. Then he lit a cigarette and said: "It's quite the opposite with me. I hate it. Anything I can do to make things harder for it I will, so help me." He exposed a row of uneven yellowish teeth in a ferine grin.

"Anyway" I said with unconcealed distaste "I must congratulate you I suppose."

"It's too early" he said. "Wait till we have our first shoot and see

201

if this blindsighting device works out. Nor need you repine too much, Charlock; compared to some of the things the firm is working on, this is . . . why, virtually harmless." The little intercom panel below my desk lit up and buzzed. Nathan's quiet voice said: "Mr. Charlock, more good news. Mr. Pehlevi says to tell you that the mercury contract is secure; we can substantially reduce our price on the new costings."

Marchant was quietly wrapping up his plans and preparing to slide them back into the cardboard tube. His cigarette dangled from his lip. "Marchant have you ever seen Julian Pehlevi?" I asked curiously; I found I was addressing this question to more and more people these days. Very few could say yes—Nathan was one of the rare ones to have had the privilege. Marchant depressed his cheek in a grin and shook his head. "Can't say I have" he said. "He keeps in touch by phone."

He hovered for a moment, standing on one leg, as if everything had not been said on this particular topic. "I must say," I said with a laugh "his damned elusiveness is getting me down—he's like some blasted ghost." Marchant scratched his nose. "Yet" he said, surprisingly "he must exist somewhere—look at your paper today." There was a daily paper lying unopened in my in-tray. Marchant took it up and hunted for a moment before doubling it back at the financial page and handing it to me to read. Julian had made a speech to the Institute of Directors which was reported in full. "You see?" said Marchant. "Several hundred of those bloody directors must have listened to him for an hour yesterday."

Despite the long tally of successes on every front it was with a kind of subdued melancholy that I drove down to the country that evening. Benedicta had already gone to bed when I arrived. I went up and watched her sleeping by the rosy glow of the night-light, her breast rising and falling, her features relaxed by sleep into an expression of forlorn simplicity. It seemed to me that there were several thousand things I had to tell her, to ask her: yet they were locked up somewhere below the threshold of consciousness. I could not bring them out, rationalise them. What were they? I did not really know—but they swarmed and pullulated inside me like bees from some overturned hive. I watched her thus for a long moment, before turning away and moving silently towards the door. I had my hand upon the panel when I heard her voice say: "Felix." I turned, but she was still lying with her eyes shut fast. "You were watching me" she said.

"Yes."

"I have seen Nash and Wild. They think it is true, I am."

"Open your eyes."

"No."

Two tears welled slowly out from under the closed lids and ran down her aquiline nose. "Benedicta!" I said sharply. She sighed deeply. "But *you* said you wanted a child."

"I do. But I did not know it would be like this."

I dabbed her nose with my handkerchief and stopped to kiss her lips, but she writhed away on the pillow. "I can't bear to be touched, don't you see? Please don't touch me."

I realised in a confused sort of way that a whole new pattern of our relationship had come into being, ushered in by these words. "Go away. I must sleep now." Her tone might well have signified "I find everything about you repellent, disgusting." Her eyes were open now, and they said much that lips could not. In the hall I sat down in a chair and stared hard at the opposite wall, completely bemused and discountenaced. "It will pass I suppose."

I had just finished dining that evening when I heard the sound of a car upon the gravel drive outside the house. It was Nash, whom I had seen only once or twice before—small, pursy and pink: he stood before the fire somewhat self-importantly, rocking slightly on his heels, and drank a whisky. We spoke about Benedicta. "She often gets into states of mild confusion or hysteria—but this you probably know. There is nothing to be done, and as yet nothing to get unduly alarmed about. I've brought her a sleeping tablet or two; if you don't mind I'll go up and have a word with her in a minute. By the way, terrible thing about Caradoc."

"What about Caradoc?"

"Haven't you seen the *Evening Standard*? Killed in an air crash. I couldn't believe my eyes." Caradoc killed! It was like a hammer-blow in the centre of the mind. Nash extracted a paper from his briefcase and made his way up the long staircase, shaking his head and muttering to himself.

Sydney

An Australian airliner reported a very close miss with an Eastern Over-ways DC 7 which crashed into the sea off Sydney yesterday afternoon. The Federal Aviation Press has issued the transcript of an exchange between the plane and the control tower. The DC 7 was at 3,700 feet soon after take-off while the airliner was coming in at 3,500 feet, although not quite at the same time. The transcript reading was as follows: "We had a close miss here. We are turning now to three six zero. Did you have another target in this same spot? About the time you turned over?"

"That's right, Southbound, affirmative. However not on my scope at the present time."

"Is he still on scope?" "No, sir."

"It looked like he's in the bay, then, because we saw him. He looked like he winged over to miss us and we tried to avoid him and we saw a bright flash about a minute later. He was well over the top of us, and it looked like he went into an absolute vertical turn and kept on rolling."

"Air Japan reports a big fire going out on the water. Route traffic control keeps asking where is Eastern six thirty-three. I don't scan him any more."

There were 40 passengers in the crashed aircraft but only four survivors, one seriously injured. So far twelve bodies have been recovered. Units of the Australian Navy are on the scene to lend aid. Among those listed as missing . . . *Professor Noel Caradoc"*

The name swam out of the text with paralysing force, holding me to my chair with my untouched drink beside me.

Nash came downstairs once more to reclaim his drink and to stand beside me in sympathetic silence for a long moment. "Wretched bad luck for us all" he said at last. "I shall miss the old bastard." Then he replenished his glass and turned back to the topic of the moment. "You know, Charlock, on reflection I think I did right; I told her as long as she felt like this she should go away quietly for a while; re-cover her good spirits in Zürich, say. Get away from you—what do you say? I'm not unduly alarmed, but she has after all a bit of a medical history—and as you know women often get strange and hysterical when they are going to have a child."

"But it isn't even absolutely certain is it?"

"No."

"And besides she doesn't need to keep the damned child if it's going to unbalance her, need she? I don't want to be responsible for her cracking up."

"She wouldn't dream of losing it."

"Are you sure?"

Nash sat down and smiled his sad and wrinkled little smile which was always so unexpected, and gave him a sudden simian expression.

"Yes."

"I am not so sure."

"Anyway, humour her for a while."

"Of course."

No alternative line of action seemed to commend itself; listless and apathetic I walked the little man to his car and watched the head-lights wander away down the long leaf tunnel. I walked back slowly into the house, still preoccupied by the image of Caradoc's sudden disappearance from the land of the living. Suddenly the huge house seemed stuffy, confining. I took the paper and started upstairs to bed. On the turn of the second landing a sudden impulse made me look up. Benedicta was standing staring down at me with a queer feverish expression which made her pointed features look almost wolfish. She moistened her lips and said: "Has Nash gone?" I nodded. "And you don't mind if I go away for a bit?" I shook my head. "Thank God" she said with relief. She turned away and disappeared on the instant and I heard the rattle of the key turning in the lock of her door.

By the time I returned the next evening she was already gone, though she had left me a few tender words on a postcard, ending with the phrase: "Believe me, it won't be for long. And then happiness again."

★   ★   ★   ★   ★

V

The new life, which displaced the old with such abruptness, had a somewhat hollow flavour coloured as it was by apprehension about Benedicta's fate with its sudden reversal of values. But Nash was kind and kept me in touch; she was well, it seemed, and living in a small chalet in the grounds of the Paulhaus near Zürich. She was always most composed when she inhabited a snowscape—clouds, pines, snow—and by now she had made up her mind about having the child, indeed seemed to welcome the idea. I wrote to her every week, giving her an account of our doings, but the letters sounded ominously hollow to my ear; the old scaffolding of such common intimacies and confidences as we had been able to build was summarily removed. Subconsciously too I suppose I must have felt that the raw new building exposed, like an aborted piece of architecture, the slack and insubstantial nature of my loving. Yes, something of that order. Also it was somehow humiliating to feel myself replaced by a series of couriers who brought me news of her without ever having a direct message to retail. Julian too was kindness itself and phoned me regularly to demonstrate how close he was keeping in touch with events. The weeks deepened into months, and yet time appeared to have slowed up, to be almost standing still. I had left the country and moved back to the town house in order to be nearer to my work, but I went out very little. I knew hardly anyone in London; and during this period I saw most of Pulley, perhaps, for whom I had developed a great friendship—due in a queer sort of way to our joint misfortune in the loss of Caradoc. The Cham, far from being absent, seemed to go on growing as we sorted out his effects and grouped his papers into some sort of order against the forthcoming publication of whatever might be publishable in all this diverse mass. A great deal of scabrous verse, limericks and the like, were scattered about in his notebooks, and these we supposed would

O   209

hardly be found suitable—though they afforded us great amusement and pleasure: almost as if he himself were present. Strangely enough, too, the putative publisher of the essays on the history of architecture turned out to be—I would never have guessed it—Vibart of all people. One day he strolled into my office, fit and brown and smiling, to grip my hand and, sinking into an armchair, announced that he was "saved". "Saved?" I echoed; the word had all the flavour of religious conversion. "And all due to you, Charlock Holmes" he said, waving his hat and lighting himself, sumptuously, a cigar. This was surprising indeed. "As they say in stories written for housemaids, I have *found* myself; I have left the F.O. thus avoiding a posting to Sofia and I am now—why here, let me give you my card."

"A publisher!" I said, peering at it. "How is this?"

"Jocas Pehlevi" he said with his shy grin-frown. "Some while after you left he came to see me and said he knew all about my ambitions from you."

"But I never mentioned you to him."

"My dear chap, he could quote some of my conversations verbatim." Perhaps, then, I had recorded Vibart at some stage? My memory held no record of the event, but it is true that I usually made samples of everyone for my voice library—the five vowels etc. (More of that anon.) Perhaps Jocas had helped himself? "Well I'll be damned."

"But he went further; he said that in his view I was no writer but that I would probably make a good publisher. Now as the firm owned half the Norwegian paper stock. . . "

"Does it? I didn't know, but nothing surprises me nowadays."

"It does. It does. He offered to set me up in business with a young Frenchman here in London. Presto! The first fifteen titles are on the stocks already—among them the stuff you are digging out by your friend whatsisname, Caradoc. Do you see?"

"With no strings attached?"

"The firm never attaches strings" said Vibart in a vibrant histrionic register. "Why should it?"

"You really surprise me. But I am glad."

He became very serious now, putting on his most humble and endearing expression as he puffed his cigar. "So am I. Glad? O Lord, it goes deeper than that. I really feel I am going to fulfil myself. It's really saved everything—you know my marriage was going steadily on the rocks because of my incessant whining? And I was getting more and more costive instead of less. My life was terribly abortive; and now look at me! Aren't I a wonderful figure of a man, a publisher? Large cigar, slight *embonpoint*?" He rose and spread the wings of his coat, rotating slowly before me like a mannequin showing off a dress. We both laughed, and I ordered up some sherry to celebrate this surprising resurrection from the dead. "So you see" he said "I only dropped in to thank you, and to ask you in my official capacity when the manuscript will be ready for us."

"But I have all the material at home and we are still working on it; listen, you must dine with Pulley and myself and help us sort it—after all, it's your responsibility really, and there are decisions to be taken. Some of the stuff is characteristically comic, too."

A change. This meeting led to at least one or two delightfully congenial evenings in the Mount Street house, reading, sorting and reminiscing over this huge bundle of papers and notebooks. Moreover I was able to supplement much of this material by a series of recordings made at different times—yes, many of indifferent quality, but sufficiently clear for transcript. It was Caradoc alive who lumbered into the circle of firelight before our very eyes, growling and grumbling and perorating. Pulley at times had tears in his eyes, as much from laughter as from tears. "Pulley standing there like a cow, with his udders swollen out, needing to be milked of this abstract transcendental love of humanity—his religion of service. Eh Pulley, damn you? Ethics not based on metaphysics—that's what it is." "Whee" answered the static.

> Deaf as a piecrust
> Smooth as a sage
> This old man is anyone's age.
> Younger than a schoolchild
> Older than a Norn
> This old man was to the manna born.

This must have been the Nube at some point; criss-crossed with mandolin whirrs and tonic sol-fa and snicking of St. Foutain's painted penis. Then a sudden shift of venue, the noise of a tavern with its clanging cans against butts and the whistle of wind in the trees. Here, rather surprisingly, Koepgen's voice raised angrily—one can well guess against whom. "But you become what you hate too much, you attract what you fear too much." A series of piercing whistles drowned an altercation.

So we listened while the Cham roared on, and Vibart made notes on a pad; we would obviously need to have most of this set down on paper, but the only problem was to find a blushproof secretary capable of undertaking the task.

It was getting on for eleven when the doorbell rang; Baynes had gone to bed. On the doorstep stood the junior office messenger with a letter. It had come in that evening. I could recognise at once the handwriting of Benedicta—but it was mirror-writing; another hand had drawn a line through it and readdressed the envelope to me at the office. I tipped the boy, and excusing myself went upstairs to the bathroom where I opened the letter and unearthed a shaving mirror in which to decipher it. "My son" it opened shakily, with the words thrice repeated. "It is so dark here, down here. The darkest of the three nights and the train has not come in. It goes very slowly when you are waiting but the eyes will always be the same, watching. We will compare notes later, unless I am too bored to exist. In that case goodbye. Julian knows how I feel."

I returned to the firelight, to the room from which all the gaiety seemed to have disappeared. "What is it?" said Pulley. "You look pale." "Bad omens" I said. "Let's have a drink."

It was late when we parted—but for me all the pleasure had gone out of the evening; a massive anxiety had replaced it, anchored in frustration—for there was clearly nothing to be done, to be said, to be acted upon. I grabbed at the chance to walk Vibart across London to his new flat in Red Lion Square for the sake of his company; and when finally we parted I pursued my own walk, erratic and un-studied and frequently turning back upon itself. Vague notions of finding somewhere open which might provide a coffee to drink; but it was either too late, or not early enough. On a hoarding in Oxford Street the post-stickers had already begun to glue up the announce-ments of next week's film. On one hoarding there was half a poster already up, waiting for its twin to complete it, like the missing piece of a jigsaw puzzle; on it there was a girl dressed in black, but split neatly down the middle—half a face, one breast, one leg. It was Iolanthe—or rather so it seemed to me. I peered among the titles to see if her name was there among the credit lines. Yes, there it was, though it too was split in half; but its size indicated that she was a star of some consequence already. The dawn was swarming up now; wind-triggered, opalescent. A few people were out, walking with ghostly step and wearing cadaverous early-morning faces. A policeman eyed me speculatively as I stood, gaping at the poster; he was almost minded to move me on, but I saved him the trouble. I woke a sleeping taxi at the corner of Bond Street and made my torpid way home. The morning papers would bring the world the knowledge of her runaway marriage to the greatest box-office star in Hollywood. Reno. There was no such thing as a private life for her any more. In *The Times* she looked radiant. but in the evening paper she was more suitably crying with emotion.

$$\ast \quad \ast \quad \ast \quad \ast \quad \ast$$

Somedays later I received a phone-call from Marchant to tell me that his new gunsight was ready to be proven. "All things being equal day after tomorrow, early, Salisbury Plain. Can I ride down with you? We'd better take a thermos and something to chew. Oh, and you know what? Julian says he is coming, so at last you'll see him in the flesh." In the flesh! At last the promise of something to relieve the monotony of the passing days, something to pique my curiosity.

We set off together accordingly in the middle of the night—we were supposed to reach the proving grounds at seven. But as we neared our destination a thick fog began to settle over the world, and soon we were travelling at a snail's pace inside a frosty bowl of yellow light from the dashboard panel. Here and there a corner would lift and the chauffeur broke away and made a dash along the highway to gain ground before the thick white curtain closed again, submerging our powerful headlights in pools of whirling snowflakes. It was lucky there was no traffic at all to intensify our difficulty. Nevertheless we nearly ran into the little cluster of jeeps and staff cars which were waiting at the point of rendezvous. It was eerie to see the bustle of shapes and figures moving about upon this damp screen; the head-lights yawned in the obscurity. The chauffeur was anxious about the plain, fearing he would get stuck in the mud; but Marchant was delighted. "What could be blinder than this?" he repeated. "The conditions are perfect." A tall figure emerged with startling sudden-ness from the veil around us; it was like a swimmer surfacing. "Brigadier Tanner?" called Marchant, and was relieved when the tall personage answered to the name. "I'm glad you've got here" he said. "I've detailed a staff car to guide. We're all set up on the side of that hill. . . ." He laughed in an exasperated way to find himself pointing into blankness. "The Minister is coming down I believe; God knows if he'll ever get here with this muck. How far along did you hit it?" We exchanged fog-information in a listless way. It had turned quite cold of a sudden. Marchant had unearthed an old sheepskin coat which gave him more than ever the air of an unbrushed collie dog. We did not dare to wander too far from our car in case we lost it altogether. "Julian is with the Minister" said Marchant. "But I don't propose to hang about; we'll get our shooting over and bugger off back to town after we've eaten, what do you say? They can come along any time and talk to the Army."

At first the Brigadier seemed rather reluctant to comply with this view but, when Marchant pointed out that the fog might hold them a prisoner indefinitely and that they might never arrive, he took the point; he would leave a picket on the main road to guide them if they turned up. We were to follow his string of glow-worms across the plain; there was no danger of mud, it was perfectly dry and safe.

We moved off in formation, our engines whimpering in bottom gear; the journey seemed endless at this pace. The scout-cars had to stop frequently to reassure themselves that they were on the right path; the light carrier behind us was working on a compass bearing which did not square with that of the leading picket car. A conclave of shrouded figures exchanged grim pleasantries and grimmer oaths. "The bloody thing's demagnetised" suggested a cockney voice. Shrouded up like this against the dawn-airs they looked like a group of Stone Age figures moving about in the whiteness, engaged on obscure tasks. Now and then a patch of curtain would lift, and the whole convoy would break into a canter, so to speak, for a hundred yards or so. It was getting lighter though; a kind of salmony tinge was beginning to run along the higher reaches of the whiteness—as if something were slowly bleeding to death in the upper sky. The variations in visibility gave human movements some of the quality to be seen in underwater swimming, or else in slow-motion film; the shifting depth of focus teased the eye and dazzled the mind. People seemed far away at one moment; the next they swam up in front of the car as if they had been fired by a cannon. The gradient had sharpened now and we were moving through patches of scrub; earth had changed to gravel on which our tyres sizzled agreeably. The chauffeur grunted with relief. He did not believe the Brigadier's tales about there being no mud. "You can never trust the Army, sir" he said to Marchant. "I was in it. I know." Marchant giggled and stumped out his nauseating cigarette, filling the car with acrid smoke. "So was I" he said.

At last they were there; suddenly and quite mysteriously materialised upon a lightly sloping hillock—the three tall weapons looking more like combine-harvesters with snouts cocked at the sky. The gnomes that tended appeared first in a sort of tableau, leaning forward to identify us—in fear, I suppose, of being run down. Hoarse voices barked orders, answered one another; the Brigadier re-emerged from the nothingness and opened the door of the car. We followed him across the field to where soldiers in blankets now moved—but with the immortal listlessness of a typical apathy. The ground-glass tones of a sergeant major tried to stir them up with quaint oaths and elephantine jokes. But they moved like somnambu-lists. Marchant's toy was a clumsy great barrel-organ of an instrument whose panels glowed with a whole spectrum of coloured switches.

He lurched across to it with a welcoming gesture, arms open, almost as if it had been a girl; then he crouched over it with an over-elaborated delicacy, touching now this part now that, manipulating switches, patting it and peering about him shortsightedly as if seek-ing some sort of reassurance from the sky. Watching him thus so vulnerably exposing the whole range of his naive gestures, his anxiety, his frail hopes, I had a sudden pang of sympathy for him; and at the very same moment I was swept by a conviction that here was not simply a scientist, but a sort of genius. His whole waking mind moved among abstractions now, like a fish in its element. And I made an involuntary comparison with my own gifts—the mere tinkering with string and wire, the superficial meddlesomeness of the second-rate gift: and I realised that I would have given anything to be Marchant, to belong to his tribe. How trivial my string of elementary devices seemed to me as I took in the feverish engrossed state of my fellow inventor; the very skeletal posture seemed to have the pulse of a different sort of fever running through it—an electrical charge. "We'll have to modify the whole armature, of course" he said. "She's far too heavy. But first let's see if she works eh?"

We were surrounded by more figures leaning down to tend these metal engines with the air of men carefully watering plants in a high window-box. These were the flint arrowheads of our wretched culture!

I could watch all this activity with a certain bemused detachment, since I could not interpret all these diverse movements; I was like an amateur at a ballet or a bullfight. All I knew was that these stubby snouts raised in sinister elevation against the lightening sky would spit out a momentary stab of flame. The Brigadier was counting; he held something in his right hand attached to a long landline. His air was that of a doctor taking the pulse-beat of a patient. A plane drowsed languidly overhead, established radio contact, and moved off. More orders came harshly out of the mist and a thick snicking of oiled steel. Marchant produced a little box, such as airlines issue to their passengers, containing ear-plugs, and urged a couple on me. Then came another interminable wait before the shoot began.

When it came I was quite unprepared for it; a tremendous pulse-beat ran through the ground under our feet and ran swiftly away to the horizon in an accumulating wave. The snouts recoiled slowly, with great elegance, hissing; only to return and flame again briefly. Fire and recoil, fire and recoil. The nearest part of the mist had been blown to bleeding patches; there were tears everywhere in the fabric now, it hung down and swirled slowly about. Marchant knelt down staring at his barrel-organ, hands over his ears, chattering to himself. A smear of sharp light illuminated a large-scale map over which hovered some disembodied moustaches. Then followed a silence during which a devout signaller communicated with the unseen through earphones, his box of tricks spluttering and crackling. I divested myself of my plugs and turned up my coat collar. Marchant was in a state of high elation. "It's going to be all right; the modifications are nothing" he repeated; he had grabbed the sleeve of the soldier who disengaged himself politely, his attention turned on his signallers. Again. There seemed to be a long moment of suspense now followed by a lot of jabbering in military argot. The Brigadier shook hands with Marchant, and as he did so an equestrian figure emerged slowly out of the mist on our left with a high degree of improbability and walked his tall horse over to the battery. "It's the General" said Tanner, and went over to give an account of his stewardship. "Well done" said the mounted figure in sepulchral tones. "You can wind it all up now. The Minister has got stuck somewhere along the road, waiting for this fog to lift. We'll have to wait and see what he says. I expect he'll put it off until next week."

"Well, that's the lot" said Marchant. We climbed back into the car; he sat beside the chauffeur to take advantage of the light from the dashboard, for he had already resumed notebook and pencil in order to cover the pages with hieroglyphics and drawings. "Sorry" he said apologetically over his shoulder. "But unless I get things down they have a habit of disappearing."

The fog was thinning out quite perceptibly and once upon the gravel road the chauffeur professed to know his way; we were able to dismiss the single jeep which had been delegated to shepherd us back to the main road. It turned aside with a roar and bounced back into the obscurity, leaving us to our own devices. We pressed on slowly with the headlights ablaze; from time to time the chauffeur sounded his melancholy horn—a desolating croak like that of some solitary marsh-bird. And then we found ourselves lost again; the gravel gave out and we were rolling softly along grass inclines. Marchant used a great deal of bad language, but added: "Thank God we brought some grub. This can't last for ever. Let's press on a bit eh? After all what is the worst that can happen? We might end up in Cornwall that's all."

"There's no mud yet, sir."

"Well, it's your fault for sending the Army back."

"I'm sorry, sir."

But even as we spoke a miracle started to take place; a wind started to flap from nowhere, lifting huge panels of fog almost bodily, rolling them back upon one another like so many strips of sodden newspaper. Huge rents and whorls and eddies began to appear all round us. In corners the white screen had begun to pour away like suds down a sink, to shiver and swirl like the dust devils of the desert. Huge slices of visibility were thrust upon us, and the sun started to shimmer through the opaqueness. It was like watching the scrambling retreat of an army. Even the terrain looked firm and promising; elated we moved into second gear and gave chase, squeezing down the soft inclines, further and further. "A compass damn it; we should have borrowed one" said Marchant, but I was breathlessly watching the bewitching phosphorescence of the mist retreating from us. Larger and larger grew the spaces, until with a last sudden flick of the wrist a whole valley burst open to the view, radiant with sun and green grass on which glittered a million diamonds of condensing fog. The theatrical effect was vastly heightened by the fact that there, right before us, glowed the melancholy and enigmatic pillars of Stonehenge. Involuntarily we all three exclaimed. We were alone, surrounded by a good square mile of radiant sunlight. "Marvellous" shouted Marchant. "We'll eat our grub here. Abandon ship, my lads." It was doubly lucky as the chauffeur could now reorient himself in relationship to the stone monuments—we had been travelling at right angles to the correct bearing. The fog was now vanishing with greater speed, restoring the whole landscape to us, stretch by stretch. So it was that in a state of high elation we took our provisions and devoured them among these mysterious blocks.

It was not unduly cold in this frail sunlight. Marchant fell upon the chicken and ham with ardour, speaking volubly as he chewed. "Well, it went off all right, Charlock, didn't it? The only fly in the ointment is that we didn't see Julian." He chuckled mischievously. "But I didn't expect to. I don't. I say, you are not much of a chemist are you? I'm not being rude, I'm asking." I shook my head ruefully. Alas. "All the better stroke of genius that guess of yours—but I'm not sure that sodium is your answer; I'll see what I can do to improve on it. It's marvellous that you are not a jealous person."

"Alas, I am."

He gazed at me wide-eyed, his mouth full of cress.

"O Lord" he said in dismay. "I did hope not."

We sparred good-humouredly for a while as we ate and gulped the scalding coffee; the chauffeur maundered off among the ruins, still wounded in his *amour propre* by having mistaken his road. "As for Julian . . . well damn him. I don't *want* to meet him any more." He chuckled. "As a matter of fact I once had the impression that I *had* met him—and I'm not given to fond fancies. But once he asked me to take some drawings up to his flat and leave them. When I arrived there was a singular-looking bird in the lift, very striking in a queer way. Deeply lined face, eyes like dead snails, medium to tall, dressed rather well in a stockbrokerish way, with a spotted bow tie. A brown signet ring. He was waiting for me in the lift. I tried to get him to speak, because then I would have recognised the voice, but he wouldn't. So I simply said: 'Second floor' and let him press the button. I addressed a question to him but he shook his head without speaking and gave me a sort of sad smile—a lost world of a smile. On the second I stepped out and up he went to the top floor. Well, I rang the bell, but the manservant was a hell of a while coming to open the door to me. All this time I could hear this chap just above me in the liftshaft—hear his breathing I mean and smell his cigar. He hadn't got out of the lift, he was just standing there waiting. Well, when my door opened and I was let in—while I was still standing in the hall having the front door closed behind me—I heard the lift coming down again. The servant said: 'You've missed Mr. Pehlevi by a few moments, sir. He's just gone out.' Well now, had I missed him? I wondered."

He laughed again with schoolboyish elation. "I say, you aren't depressed are you?"

"No." But really I was, depressed and confused. "As for Julian," he went on "I've given him up, as I say. But it's curious how a little thing like his obstinate Trappist-like refusal to manifest himself gives rise to rumours. You can never trace the source, of course, it's always at second hand. But someone had heard that he was disfigured by lupus and was too ashamed to show up; another chap in the office had heard that Julian was going through a long and complicated piece of facial surgery. There may be something in that one. The Institute of Directors were addressed by a man who had a huge dressing across his forehead, and wore dark glasses. It's rum, I suppose, but I've got used to it. Strangest of all was Bolivar, a weird painter fellow; Julian bought some of his things for the firm. You may have seen them. Well, he claimed to have done a sort of composite portrait of him based on the evidence of those who said they had seen him—what they call an Identikit nowadays I suppose. On the sly, of course. Bolivar was an awful drunk and lived on some repulsive cat-food in a basement room in Campden Hill. He's dead now, poor chap; but during his last illness he rang me up and said that he was going to leave this portrait to me, and that I should find it in the drawer of the bureau in his room. I went round, but he was already delirious and the drawer was empty. I say Charlock, cheer up. When a civilisation has decided to bury its head in the sand what can we do but tickle its arse with a feather?" Marchant raised his pale and grubby finger and apostrophised the sages of antiquity. "O Aristotle, your civilisation too was based on slavery and the debauching of minors."

It was almost noon before we piled back into the car to start the homeward journey, and by now almost the whole landscape had come back into sheer focus. The fog had banked up to the north and west but in our immediate vicinity visibility was virtually total. It was pleasant to feel the car at last able to slide up the scale into top gear, and to see the hedgerows sliding by. In the remote distance among the dangling coils of remaining mist moved an ant-line chain of Army cars crooning across the plains; but we had gathered momentum now, and our tyres whirred upon the fine macadam. I settled myself in the back, wrapped my coat collar around my ears and fell into a doze. I do not know how long I was asleep, but when at last I woke it was with a start of surprise. We were in the middle of a forest moving in almost total darkness through a fog much heavier than the one we had experienced; moving, moreover, in a long slow string of main-road traffic, tail-light to tail-light, in a slow forlorn processional. "It's come back" said Marchant angrily. "It'll take us weeks to get back to London at this pace." So it would seem.

We were advancing slowly and circumspectly in measured distances; at some of the cross-roads ghostly policemen walked up and down the lines with torches keeping the files as free for movement as possible. There were long inexplicable halts, followed by short advances, and then new halts. It was on one of these halts that I suddenly saw, in the whiteness of our headlights, the number of the car in front of us; it was Julian's Rolls! We had drawn up almost touching his rear number-plate. "My God, it's Julian" I cried to Marchant. "He must have turned back." And before the matter could be discussed—indeed in quite spontaneous fashion—I opened our car-door and lurched into the road. I ran up alongside the Rolls, calling out "Julian" and rapping with my knuckles on the glass of the side windows. But the whole car, like our own, was virtually misted up. Only the windscreen wipers kept a triangle of visibility open in front of the chauffeur. I tried to draw his attention, but he was watching the road ahead and did not appear to see me. I tried the rear glass again, shouting once more, and from inside a hand lowered it about an inch. A voice, not Julian's, said: "Who is it?" I wiped a circle of mist from the outside and said: "Is Mr. Pehlevi in there?"; and from the misty interior the voice—probably that of the Minister—answered testily. "Yes, who wants him?" The glass was lowered slowly and I said, somewhat foolishly: "Julian, it's Charlock." There were two figures sunk in the dark depths of the limousine, and I could see the face of neither clearly. Just an etching of two black Homburg hats. "I was looking forward to meeting you at last" I went on naively. One hat turned to the other, as if waiting for it to take the cue and answer me; but Julian did not speak. I was still hanging there anxiously when there came a hooting of horns and the confused sound of traffic police shouting: "Move along there smartly please." A torch flashed moth-like from somewhere near. "Julian" I cried, I wailed. But the Rolls was moving forward now—the whole line sagged forward and peeled itself off softly into the obscurity. The window went up with a slap; I was forced to rejoin Marchant in our car, furious and disappointed. "It's his car all right" I said. "And he's in it. Next time we stop. . . ." But we had reached a double cross-roads with an island now, with slightly better visibility; the cars ahead were moving to left and right now, the file had thickened and started to disperse down the various lanes. By the time we came up to the faintly glowing beacons Julian's car had disappeared, and we were hard behind a charter bus, hemmed in on either side by small cars. A mournful hooting filled the air. Marchant laughed and slapped his knee. "I suppose you can't catch them" he said to the chauffeur; but the rejoinder was an obvious one. They could have slid away down any of four roads. Once again he had given us the slip.

Characteristically enough within the space of an hour the fog had dispersed again and we were racing away towards London in a fine clear rain. The chauffeur put on a turn of high speed in order to try and catch the Rolls if indeed it were travelling along the same road—

the main London road. But strive as we might we overtook nothing that looked like it. Marchant found my disappointment rather comical, and once or twice I found him glancing at me with his cruel sidelong smile. When we arrived back at Mount Street he invited himself in for a bath and a drink; a flock of messages waited for us. Congratulations from the office, presumably on the strength of Marchant's success with the Army; a note from Pulley to say he would come in after dinner—some of Caradoc's drawings had been washed ashore. But most surprising and heartening, there was a short note from Benedicta which was both coherent and very tender, promising that everything would soon be over and that she would rejoin me. I rang up to tell Nash the news, only to find that he was very much *au courant*. "Yes, she's had a splendid period now, a complete change, and the outlook is excellent. By the way, she is convinced it will be a boy. Women usually get what they want, have you noticed?"

Marchant had his bath, though except for damp hair awkwardly combed back towards his ears one would hardly have guessed it. We joined each other for a drink by the fire; and he asked if he might play the piano for a moment before taking himself off. He attacked several of the more complicated preludes and fugues of "the 48" with great assurance, but with a total lack of sensibility, working at them like a woodpecker or a cobbler at his last. "Poor Bach!" I said. "I know," he said cheerfully "I know." But he seemed to derive great enjoyment from this somewhat awkward operation; he wagged his head about as he played. When he stopped to light a cigarette I said: "You have never been married, have you, Marchant?" He looked at me slyly, his hands poised to resume playing. "Good Lord, what a question. No. Why?" I refilled his glass. "An idle question" I said. "I was wondering why not." "Why not?" he repeated, as if trying the question, so full of novelty, upon himself for the first time. "I've never felt the need. I doubt if real scientists ever do—the need for these charming articulated mummies. At least, I think we belong to a dispossessed tribe, all our affective life is passed in the head; and then, again, after forty you begin to feel out of date and out of sympathy. Do you care for this age particularly? I mean, once our hero was a St. George doing in a Dragon to free a damsel; but now our hero seems to be a spy doing in a damsel in order to escape the dragon. The genius of suspicion has entered the world, my boy. And then, what do you make of the faces of the young? As if they had smashed the lock on the great tuck-box of sex only to find the contents had gone mouldy. Sex should be like King's drinking, not piglets at teat."

"My goodness" I said, delighted. "You are an oldfashioned romantic, Marchant. I would never have guessed."

"I was once in love with a little female butcher, a pretty widow. But you know with all the handling of the meat her little paws had got the fat worked into them. White little plump mortuary fingers. When she touched me I could feel her handling those swinging carcasses. I was cured, but not before I had made some very valuable scientific observations on her. You know the pharmaceutical boys down at Lund's working on the firm's perfumes. I was able to turn out a cream for old Robinson which is second to none for rough or chapped skin. But I had to leave her all the same, the girl in question."

"A sad story."

"Perhaps; but it illustrates another extraordinary fact about this game. Your best discoveries are always accidental by-products of a search for something you never find; you set out to hunt something and presto, along comes something else, something quite unexpected. Did I tell you about our bottled sweat project—we call it that for a joke? It's still experimental which means non-existent. It's interesting in a farcical sort of way. Toller works on perfumes, as you know; well, Nash came up with some Czech psychiatrist's notion that all perfumes contained a kind of built-in echo of human sweat, and that some types of sweat, male sweat, contained a sort of paralyser which women could not resist—like cats with valerian. It was a complicated and wordy essay this, but it advanced the idea that the irresistibility of Don Juan was not due to looks or charm, but due to his smell. All Don Juan types are ugly and stunted, says this chap, who had run over a few psychoanalytically. But they all had a smell which spelt out danger. It sounded silly of course, and the team busy making things for women's armpits got a hell of a laugh out of it. But Toller and I ruminated a bit; we started to do a leisurely survey of sweats, every kind of sweat: a woman with her period, an athlete after a race, sun

224

sweat, fear sweat. You will hardly believe how much smell changes according to circumstance, temperature and so on. For years we played about this notion; I can't say we were entirely serious. It was a by-product of the scent-business. It was a rest and a change from worrying about what smell makes women irresistible; what, we asked ourselves, makes a man irresistible?

"The actual chemistry, the analysis, was fearfully complicated, a real challenge; we had to devise a sort of scent-log. And for a long time we were at sea. We used what we knew of the rest of the scent range—from garlic to magnolia blossom. Then one day I had a glimmer; fundamentally women want to be raped I think, taken by force; things haven't changed much since the Stone Age. On the other hand, as the biological left hand of the partnership responsible to the tribe for childbearing, they had developed a heavy load of conscience about it. In order to really give in it had to be in a fashion which unequivocally excused the lapse. In other words they had to be *frightened* almost to the point of insensibility before they could clear themselves with their own consciences. Our hypothetical Don Juan, then, had this paralysing gift. He could scare them into surrender by his scent. All right, laugh; but sometimes these crazy ideas have a point. It was a sort of rape-mixture we were after. Where to find a laboratory of smell? It suddenly occurred to me (do you know the smell of schizophrenes, of epileptics?) that all of the kingdom's top rapists are locked up in Broadmoor! Nash arranged for us to send in a small team to hunt around among them, and see what we could find. Well, after four years' work we have, very tentatively, isolated something which might break down into this vital secretion. Women beware! From the sweats of paranoiacs we have husbanded something which will permit your lasciviousness full play and your consciences rest! It has no name at the moment and the quantity is small; but we have put it out on test for a try-out."

"Do you mean you have a lot of London bobbies walking around smelling like goats and making women drivers turn dizzy at the wheel?" Marchant gave his characteristic giggle. "Of course not. They would never get near enough to do the damage; what I *have* got is a willing experimental team of fifteen provincial hairdressers, women, who have agreed to wear nothing but this stuff for six months. Now they are always bending over their clients. Moreover there is always fug to help things along. We shall see what effect if any that has. Might start a wave of Lesbianism in the blameless purlieus of Norwood or Finchley. Then we should feel our little extract was the real thing."

He banged down the piano lid and stood up, groping for his briefcase in order to produce a dirty handkerchief wherein to blow his nose. "I'd offer you some," he said "but you wouldn't need it, being a married man of consequence and place." There was no hint of bitterness in his tone—it was simply a light-hearted sally: but to my surprise it stung me. Taken unawares by an overwhelming sense of futility and inadequacy I heard myself saying: "Yes. I am Mr. Benedicta Merlin, no less" in tones of savage irony. Marchant looked at me keenly and with a new sympathy. "I didn't mean anything by what I said," he told me apologetically "truthfully."

"I know you didn't."

"Good."

I poured him a stirrup-cup to show that there were no hard feelings. "Listen," I said "I wonder if later on you would let me pick your brains a bit; indeed you might help me build it. When I've sorted out my library of voices—it will take ages. I wanted to build a sort of sound-bank based on phonetics. I can already build up voices from a sort of sound-bank—based on the vowel-sounds. A sort of embryology of language. Just like Cuvier deducing his whole animal from one bone; some time I'll get around to developing it, but I'd need help on the practical side—the electrical wave-mechanics side. For the moment I'm snowed under with other projects."

"So am I. But of course I will."

"But this is something of my own, outside the firm. I wouldn't, for example, tell Julian about it."

He walked slowly towards the door, brooding. "I wonder Charlock" he said "if you aren't under the same misapprehension as I was; I mean in imagining that he runs the firm. He doesn't you know. He has to fight tooth and nail sometimes for his own ideas about how things should be done, and very often he is overruled by his own boards. No, nobody runs the firm, strictly speaking; it's a sort of snowball with its own momentum now, the bloody organisation. I

226

pity Julian, in fact; to be so powerful and at the same time so power-less."

"Truthfully I am beginning to dislike him" said I.

"Ah! the father-figure" he said cryptically. "I think that's a waste of energy. You are in it now, you are part of it, rowing with the rest of us. Myself I would have got nowhere without the firm; they picked me out of a provincial university. I would have spent my life in a senior common room babbling about Rutherford forever had it not been for them. As it is I am marvellously free to give of my best; once they even gave me three years off to travel. No, Merlin's is a godsend—at least for me."

So might it have been for me, I thought, had I not made the mis-take of marrying into it. Or was that really the reason? The whole problem of Benedicta rose like an overtoppling wave and engulfed me. I shook my head doubtfully. "Well," said Marchant shaking my hand "thanks for being decent; and count on me when you want anything."

I watched his slight figure disappearing down the street, with its queer slanting stride. The telephone was ringing. The telephone was ringing.

*   *   *   *   *

We always think that we are thinking one thought at a time because we have to put them down one under the other, in a linguistic order; this is an illusion I suppose. Here I was talking to the office while my hands riffled the coloured pages of a weekly magazine which dealt with Iolanthe's new conjugal life in a turreted Hollywood mansion bearing a fair resemblance to parts of "Cathay". Her swimming pool, her bedroom, the expensive scents, the loaded racks of clothes, the press-cuttings, the emptiness of the mirror-world. She herself looked pale and tired, clad in riding boots. Expression of a frail oldfashioned devotion which no longer had any place in our world, but which the screen still perpetuated as a herd-echo. Her husband looked palatable and superficial. I wished her luck. O yes, I did.

Summer passes, autumn comes; and with it the news that Benedicta had produced the intentional man-child, who was to be called Mark. (I was not consulted on this point among others.) Shoals of telegrams like flying-fish, cases of champagne. Moreover she was planning to return for Christmas. Nash pronounced her in excellent health, but advised me to make no move, to let her do things at her own rhythm. "It is maddening and worrying for you, I know that" he added with sympathy. "But it will come right, I am sure, with time." In the meantime there was only one thing to do—to become absorbed in my work, the classical response. My list of trophies mounted gradually, one success following another, but with an ease and rapidity which somehow had the hollowness of an illusion. Entangled in its coils I felt a sort of heartbreak as I found myself harking back nostalgically to the promises which the past had once sanctioned —Istanbul huddled among her veils of mist. All the more poignant because distance in time had cast all these events in the brilliant colours (memory-induced) of half-fictions. Small fragments broken from the bright screen of days passed with a different sort of Benedicta, a woman who might seem forever unreal to me now; naturally with fear comes misunderstanding, with anxiety the sense of separation, of drifting apart. Unless. Unless what? An outside chance of reversing the immortal process.

Hippolyta came to London somewhen about now to nurse a broken ankle. Sitting before the fire, crutches beside her, she was staring bitterly at the face of Iolanthe which adorned the cover of a glossy magazine. It was startling how much she had aged—perhaps the crutches by association made it seem so? No, there were great meshes of white at her temples. Crow's foot, reading glasses and so on. Nor was she the only one for "Charlock, you've changed" she cried: and breaking out, as if from a mask of witch-hazel, her face flowered once more into that of the impetuous inquisitive Athenian. Yes, of course. I had been putting on weight, my hair was badly cut, lustreless and dandruffy, my suit unpressed. "Longer cigars, shorter wind." But we embraced until she winced from the pain of her leg. "Wiser! Sadder? Have you seen this new face?" She pointed ruefully at the star. ("The body dries up, the mind becomes toneless, the soul reverts to chrysalis; the only providing power lives on and on, independent of a dogmatic theology. The only thing that does not wear out is time." Thus Koepgen.) She smiled up at us like a mummy, and tapping her face with her glasses Hippo said, with the same downcast expression, "I get more and more jealous of less; she gets better and better, Felix. She is a real personage now. Have you seen her new film? I've come over for it specially. I shall choke with rage, but I must see it, I must see them all. It's become an obsession. I hunt among her expressions for the traces of Graphos."

"Graphos!"

"Yes. And to think that all that time I didn't know that this common little fiend enjoyed the real thing."

She lit a cigarette with steady hands and blew a great plume of smoke like a denunciation. "And now he's dying slowly, out of reach of everybody. Nobody knows as yet, he is still active. But he knows." She poked up the fire with one of her crutches. I said "Graphos" on a sort of grace-note. She smiled. "He explained it to me. You might say it was hate at first sight—the only form of love they could know; they had the same values, were both frustrated in the same affective field. But they did not have to *pretend* to each other. It lasted like that, for ages and ages. And, to my humiliation, I did not know. Does one ever? I rebuilt his career, poor moonstruck me." She used some very bad language in Greek; brief tears came into her eyes. "And now I am obsessed with her because of it. But never mind, she has made her mistakes, even though she now wears her sex like an expensive perfume. Aha, but the man *she* married creaks, *creaks*. I am glad. There is no joy to be got from *him*. It's malicious, but I can't help being pleased."

"No. That's not you, Hippo."

"It is. It is. And what galls me worse is that she is *articulate* now; I stole some of her letters to Graphos. You see how low one can sink? I can remember parts by heart, like where she says: 'As for me, having been in a sort of clinic of love, a captive when young, and forced by circumstance to take on everyone, young or old, I missed the whole point. My understanding remained unkindled. The sex act misses fire if there is no psychic click: a membrane has to be broken of which the hymen is only a parody, a mental hymen. Otherwise one can't understand, can't receive. So very few men can do this for a woman. You, Graphos, did this for me. Though I never could love you I'm grateful.' "

She banged her crutch on the floor and turned the journal over on its face, her face.

Well we dined there, by the fire, plate on knee; and there was a kind of luxury to talk about the past which for me had become pre-history—yellowing snapshots of the Acropolis or Byzantine Polis. After dinner Pulley and Vibart put in a short appearance, and though our talk gathered a superficial animation we could still feel the hang-dog death of Caradoc looming over us. It was a deeply felt physical presence—not only because all his papers were stacked up there on the sideboard. It would only have increased the sense of constraint to have played out his voice upon my machines, so I did not try to. But there was news of Banubula who might be coming soon to London to have his prostate looked at. "In the morning he still retires to the lavatory for an hour with a churchwarden clay pipe and a bowl of soapy water. There he sits in silent rapture blowing huge iridescent bubbles and watching them float out over Athens. In harmony with himself. Only he still moans a good deal about not getting into Merlin's. Otherwise no change."

Vibart had just returned from a visit to Jocas who was also recuperating from a fall and a fractured hip. Picture of him bedridden before a huge fire taking castor-oil out of an oldfashioned soupspoon; having his toenails trimmed for him by the eunuch. Almost mad with boredom, and unable to read, he had hit upon a solution— a model railway. His little trains ran all round the house, and around half the garden. Carried from point to point in a sedan, he passed his time agreeably in this fashion.

But at last talk lagged; Caradoc ached on like a bad tooth. The decanter was empty. They took their leave, reluctant to leave the evening unachieved, yet realising they could not revive it. Hippo stayed on to gossip and meditate. "Will you come with me? I have located four other films in the provinces in which she plays. I am here for a week—all too short for London." I agreed, feeling curiously stirred by the idea; apart from the brief glimpse on board the vessel of love I had seen nothing of Iolanthe. She pressed my hand; we spoke of other things, and I mentioned the dead boy in Sipple's bed. Who was finally responsible, both for the deed and for hushing the matter up? She did not know; and I could sense that she was telling the truth. "Sipple had threatened to do it because the boy was going to blackmail him. Fifteen all. But later he said it was done while he was out. Thirty fifteen. Yes, it was a brother of Iolanthe, and her father, who was in Athens that week end, had also threatened to punish the boy. Thirty all." She gave a little groan and patted her head. "There seem to be a hundred reasons to account for every act. Finally one hesitates to ascribe any one of them to the act. Life gets more and more mysterious, not less."

"I must say I thought that she herself might have. . . ." I gazed in abstracted fashion at the doe-like face of the world star. "I wonder if the firm knows."

"You must ask Julian."

Later, of course, I did. He said something like: "You know most questions become more macro or micro, more Copernican or Ptolemaic: they don't stay still, the pendulum is always on the move. They change as you watch. And always the answer proposed, particularly by an organisation like the firm, is provisional, short-term. We have to accept that." There was an overwhelming sadness in his voice. I was so touched by his sadness that I almost had a lump in my throat.

"Questions and answers" said she with bitterness. "How should I explain you loving Benedicta Merlin?"

"Easy. It was like breathing in."

"And now?"

"Exactly. I am all confused."

She gave a cruel little laugh. "Ah wait" I said reproachfully. "It still goes, on my side."

"No woman can stand her" she said. "You know that."

Of course I knew that. It wasn't easy to explain the sort of mesmeric influence Benedicta exercised over her witless scientist. "A form of hysteria I suppose; in the Middle Ages it would have been classified as possession."

"They say that the firm has her regularly burgled in order to offset her tremendous expenditure against insurance!"

"Malice" I said.

"Very well, malice."

There was a ring at the door; I had ordered her a taxi, and now slowly and reluctantly I helped her hobble to it. She turned in the street and said: "Shall we tomorrow afternoon? Please."

"Of course we shall." She meant the film of Iolanthe. Away she rolled with a wave of a white glove and a tremulous smile.

All at once the house seemed very old and damnably musty, like some abandoned tomb which the grave-robbers had not spared. I got out one of the firm's calendars—huge meretricious pictures of colonial landscapes—and marked off the days to Xmas. I supposed I should have to make some preparations to receive her. Or should I just leave it to chance, let her walk back naturally into the circle of our common life if you could call it that like one who had only left the room for a few moments? I wondered. I wondered.

But the pilgrimage to the shrines of the love goddess intervened among these preoccupations—poor Hippolyta's week of self-torture and admiration; riding to suburban cinemas in Finchley and Willesden where the sacred mask was being exhibited in a series of hieratic roles which, superposed at such speed one upon the other, and with such variety of age, situation, landscape, hypnotised me hardly less absolutely. Sitting in musty seats, inhaling dusty floors whose peanut shells crackled under foot: in afternoon flea-pits, holding the white glove of Hippo and watching, heart in mouth—well no, I couldn't any longer use the prop of her name as a memory-aid. Iolanthe had slipped away, far beyond me now, out of sight of Number Seven, of Athens, the Nube. She brought to this new silver life a gravity, authority, distinction, even a tender mischievousness which bewitched; she had refined her potential for gesture and expression in some radical fashion. No. No. This creature I did not know at all. I whispered her name once or twice, but it raised no echo. And yet it was with real concern for her true self that I watched this mammoth distortion of Iolanthe into a world-fetich. (Hippo gasping after some great scene, saying "marvellous", touched to the quick.) But my goodness, the responsibility she had taken upon herself was frightening. She lived by the terms of this mock-art, lived a travesty of a life passed in public: as much a prisoner of her image as any of us to the firm. She couldn't walk down a street to post a letter unless she was disguised. I saw in the flash the sad trajectory of her new life, the life of a priestess, with a clarity that no further information could ever qualify. It was all there, so to speak. Even what she told me herself afterwards added only detail—even the worst things, like having to dress up and "really act" when she wanted to be alone, out of the glare of the following pressmen. For example, even to visit their securities in the bank vaults twice a year—a ritual the husband insisted upon: it lulled his sense of insecurity. Then about how one day the child gets locked in a safe, suffocated, brought out dead—all that stuff; and running down the street from the hospital in tears there comes a snap from a street-photographer and a tendered card. "Your picture, lady?" He did not notice the tears under the dark glasses. Well and then pacing a long low-ceilinged room with her new camera-shy walk, so painfully learned from a ballerina, she says piteously: "Why should I not love this life, Felix? It's the only real life I have known."

Indeed. And then Hippo saying savagely: "If it were an art-form she would be really great. Thank God it isn't. I should be even more angry."

"How can we know?"

"Why it's aimed at the mob."

"And?"

"And!"

Then later over repulsive tea and buttered toast in some small café she explained in more detail. "You see, the majority must always be denied the higher pleasures like art etc. which in our age it feels entitled to. It's not a matter of privilege, my dear. Just as literacy doesn't confer the ability to really read—so biologically the many are unfitted for the rarest pleasures which are travestied by Iolanthe; love-making, art, theology, science—they each contain whole lives, silver lives, encapsulated in a form. They exist for the maker and his few subjects. She exists for everyone. When we speak of the destruction of an ethos or a civilisation we are describing the effect on it of the mob-discovery of it. The mob wants it, but it must be made palatable. Naturally the efficacy becomes diluted. There you have Iolanthe."

I was not sure at all about this. I had spilt butter on my tie. But inside I simply ached with vexation at never having met Iolanthe.

But there was no news until the day before Christmas when Nash rang up very chirpy. "Well, here she is at last" he said with his false-sounding heartiness. "All safe and sound."

Flowers! In my benign way I had always thought of her returning to Mount Street; but Nash dispelled the illusion. "No, she's in the country. She wants you to bring Baynes down to her if you will—you will go down this evening won't you?" I said I would, though I had to disguise a distinct pique that Benedicta had neither bothered to inform me of her arrival before the event—nor telephoned me to tell me of her whereabouts. However I swallowed the toad-like thought as best I could, and went out to buy such presents as might be deemed suitable to the season. It was sleeting, the taxi-driver was kindly garrulous; there was, as usual, nothing that I could give Benedicta, for she had everything—nothing, that is, of any real value or worth; things such as paintings or books would not have felt to her like presents. It was going to be an unbridled yuletide.

The shops were all lighted up with a ghastly artificial array of colours and forms which signal the triumphs of commerce over religion. Loudspeakers everywhere were playing "Silent Night", pouring the spirit of the Christchild over everything with this amplified crooning of organs and xylophones: into the frosty streets with their purple-nosed crowds of milling hierophants, busy buying tokens of the miracle—poor pink-witted, tallow-scraping socialist mobs. It was cold. It was biting cold. I was angry. The latest jazz hit sawed at the frosty air, with its oft-repeated refrain:

> *She's as sweet as a tenderised steak*
> *And I'll conquer the world for her sake.*

In all this tremendous tintinnabulation Charlock walks, the "self-inflicted man" of Koepgen's fable, wondering what he might buy as an offering to the season. There's something wrong about a philo-sophy which doesn't offer the hope of certain happiness. Despite man's estate (tragic?) there should be at least a near-guarantee of happiness to be dug out of the air around us. In Selfridges the air hovered and lapped us, impregnated with the heat of our bodies and breath. Pressed in sardine fashion on all sides I let myself drift slowly down the carpeted streams. Our predispositions reveal them-selves very accurately in our *moeurs*. Never mind. I bought some ex-pensive gifts and had them elegantly wrapped; then swollen with these acquisitions waddled back to the doors like a woman at term, crushing up my paper as I went. The crowds milled and swirled. "Freed from the economic whip, we will not steer your bloody ship." Nor could I find another taxi. I had to walk almost all the way back to the office where the duty car was waiting for me. At Mount Street Baynes was waiting, he had already packed for me. I looked around to see if anything had been overlooked, gasping a bit, like a goldfish fallen out of its bowl on to the carpet.

But by now, with the falling evening temperatures everything had become stringently real—for heavy creamy snow was falling, showers of white inhaling the white lights of cars, fluttering like con-fetti from an invisible proscenium of heavenly darkness. Speed and visibility got into lock-step; we slithered down Putney and away into the spectral ribbons of main road which led us ever deeper into what now slowly became an enchanted forest—a medieval illustration to Malory. To beguile the time I played over some prints of recent voices which were destined for my collection; it was strange to sit watching the snow while Marchant's somewhat squeaky voice... "The war, my boy, meant all things to all men; full employment, freedom from the wife and kids, a fictitious sense of purpose. Blame your neighbour for your own neurasthenia and punish him. It was all real, necessary and yet a phantom. The reason why everyone loved the war was simple: there was no time to think about the even more pressing problem namely: 'Why am I making a mess of my life?' I had had the time, but not the good sense. I threw myself into this delicious amnesia which only wholesale bloodspilling can give. Thirsty Gods! What hecatombs of oxen. Hurrah!"

It was late when we arrived, hush-hushing down the white avenues towards the strange house, where every light seemed to have been lit and left to burn on in tenantless rooms; who went round and turned off all those lights, and at what time? The lake had frozen iron-stiff and here a great fire of oak-logs sparked and hissed in the centre of it, near the island; several dozens of muffled figures skirred about it on skates. There was even a coloured marquee with fairy lights where some were drinking steaming coloured drinks—presumably hot lemonade, since it was past the drinking hour, and even considerations of Christian charity could not be expected to sway the habits of mind of lazy bureaucrats and publicans. Nevertheless it was a grateful and heart-warming scene in this desolate property to have a few villagers amusing themselves. From time to time would come a pistol crack from the ice, and a fissure would trace itself with soft rapidity, like someone running a stick of charcoal across the whiteness. Shrieks and laughter greeted these warnings. Baynes shook a sage head and muttered something like "It's all very well, sir, but a few minutes' thaw and they'll all be in the drink."

The car drew up, the doors opened. The hall and all its galleries were hung with dusty bunting left over from other festivals; there were a few servants about, engaged on unobtrusive tasks, but not many. Yet from the light and the decorations you would have said that Benedicta expected a great company to descend on us. No such thing. Moreover she had gone up already. No glittering cars disgorging madonnas in evening gowns, no monocles glittering, no sheen of top-hats.

I mounted heart-beat by heart-beat. The bed she lay in was like some fat state barge with its squat carved legs and damascened wings of curtain drawn back and secured with velvet cords. The light fell upon the book she was reading, and which she closed with a snap as I entered the room. The child lay in a yellow cot by the chimney-piece—a small indistinct pink bundle, thumb in mouth. We stared at each other for a long moment. Though her regard was sad, almost humble in its directness, I thought I could detect some new quality in it—a new remoteness? She was like some great traveller who had come back finally after many adventures—come back to find that his experiences overshadowed the present. Sitting at the foot of the bed I put my hand upon hers, wondering if she were ever going to speak, or whether we should just sit like this for ever, gazing at each other. "The snow held us up" I said, and she nodded, still staring into my eyes with her sad abstracted eyes. She had made herself up carelessly that evening, and had not bothered to take the make-up off; the pale powdered face looked almost feverish in contrast to the thin scarlet mouth. "You know" she whispered at last "it's like coming back from the dead. It's so fragile as yet—I hardly recognise the world. So tired." Then she took my hand and placed it upon her forehead saying: "But I am not feverish am I?" She trembled as I embraced her softly and went on. "But you know there is something else to be got over now between us. It's very clear. How patient can you be?" She drew down her frowning brows over those wide-awake eyes and stared keenly, sternly at me. Then she pointed at the cot in the corner. "Have you seen?" To temper the ominous intensity of this mono-logue I crossed the room and stared dutifully at the child. She had turned sideways upon an elbow now, and her concentrated gaze held a strange hungry animal-like quality. She resumed her full voice to say—with a sort of dying fall. "He has come between us now, don't you see? Perhaps for ever. I don't know. I love you. But the whole thing must be thought over from the very beginning."

Over and above the numbness I felt only a sudden rage; like a wild boar I could have turned to rend the world. Benedicta gave a sob, a

237

single sob, and then all at once was smiling again: a smile disinterred from forgotten corners of our common past, full of loyalty and fearlessness. She shook two pellets out of a bottle. They tinkled into a shallow glass which she held out for me without a word. I filled it from the tap in the bathroom. She watched them froth and dissolve before drinking the mixture; then, putting down the glass, she said "The main thing is that I am really back at last." A church bell began to toll from the nearby village, and the clock by the bed chirped. "I must feed it" she said—it seemed to me strange the use of "it". I turned away, muttering something about going downstairs to dine, and then crossed the room with a sudden purposeful swiftness to take up the child. I left her sitting crosslegged in the armchair by the bed, holding "it" to her breast, absorbed as a gipsy.

Downstairs the grizzled Baynes was waiting for me; he had organised my dinner, knocking up a couple of servants from the deeper recesses of the kitchens. I could see he was dying to question me about Benedicta but resisted the impulse like the perfectly trained servant he was. I settled down to this late repast with a sense of anticlimax, but to put a good countenance upon it all—the long solitary table I mean with its coloured candlesticks, the absence of Benedicta—I made some rough notes for a speech I would soon be having to deliver to the Royal Society of Inventors.

Afterwards I betook myself to the log fire in the hall; and while I was sitting there before it, half asleep, I heard the traditional cannonade upon the front-door knocker, followed by the shrill pipe of waits whose voices were raised quaveringly in a painful carol. It was a welcome diversion; I went to the front door and found a small group of village children standing in a snow-marked semicircle outside. Their leader held a Chinese lantern. They were like robins, pink cheeked and rosy. Their infant breath poured out in frosty tresses as they sang. I sent Baynes hot-foot for drinks, cakes and biscuits, and when the first carol ended invited them into the warm hall with its big fire. It was bitterly cold outside, and they were glad to huddle about the blazing logs with small bluish fingers extended to the flame. The teeth of some were a-chatter. But the warm drinks and the sweet cakes soon restored them. I emptied my pockets of small change, pouring it into the woollen cap of their leader, a tough-looking peasant boy of about eleven: blond and blue-eyed. As a parting gesture they offered to sing a final carol right there in the hall and I agreed. They began a ragged but full-throated rendering of "God rest you merry, gentlemen". The house echoed marvellously; and it was only when they were half way through the melody that I saw an unknown figure stalking in military fashion down the long staircase; a tall thin woman with grey hair, clad in a white dressing-gown, which she clutched about her throat with long crooked fingers. Her narrow face was compressed about a mouth set in an expression of malevolent disapproval. "You will wake the child" she repeated in a deep voice. She came to a halt on the first landing. "Who are you?" I said. The waits came to a quavering halt in mid bar. "The nurse, sir."

"What is your name?"

"Mrs. LaFour."

"Can you hear us upstairs?"

She turned back without a word and began to remount the staircase. There was nothing for it but to disband the carol-singers and wish them goodnight.

When I reached my room some time later it was to find pinned to my pillow one of Benedicta's visiting-cards; but there was no message on it. I slept the sleep of utter exhaustion—the kind of sleep that comes only after a prolonged bout of tears; and when I woke next morning everything had changed once more—like the shift of key in a musical score. A new, or else an old, Benedicta was sitting on the foot of the bed, smiling at me. She was clad in her full riding outfit. Every trace of preoccupation had vanished from this smiling reposed face. "Come, shall we ride today? It's so beautiful." The change was breath-taking; for once it was she who leaned down to embrace me. "But of course."

"Don't be long; I'll wait for you downstairs."

I hurried to bathe and dress. Outside the country snowscapes were bathed in a brilliant tranquil light. There was no trace of wind. Occasionally a tall tree let fall a huge package of whiteness which exploded prismatically on the roofs of the house. And now even the house itself seemed suddenly to have woken up, to be full of a purposeful animation. There was a servant actually humming at her dusting; the hall tables were piled with telegrams and packages. This was more like it. The horses were at the door sneezing white spume. Benedicta was giving some last-minute orders to Baynes about lunch. "Julian rang to wish us everything, and so did Nash" she cried happily as she pulled on the close-fitting felt hat with its brilliant jay's feather. She seemed to have restored, with a single smile, a hundred lost familiarities. It was hardly conceivable.

We set off briskly, swinging across the meadows in the snow; though we were upon the path of a traditional ride well known to us, the snow had baffled boundaries and we were forced to work from memorised contours, munching across this abstract whiteness into woods whose trees had become wedding-cakes. And everywhere, as if developed mysteriously from a secret print, we could study the footmarks, trace the movements, of animals which were normally invisible: cuneiform of hare and squirrel and fieldmouse scribbled into the snowcarpet. A whole geodesy of the invisible life which surrounded our own. The shallow ford was frozen, and I dismounted to lead my horse, but with her customary rashness she forced her own mount through revelling in the crunching ice under its hooves. We rode westward towards the Anvil following the long intersecting rides formed naturally by the firebrakes, now outlined and demarcated clearly by the contrasting snow and forest. Once towards the top of the Anvil we turned along the down, and here the going became riskier. A rabbit-warren could have spelt a heavy fall or a broken leg for a horse. But Benedicta defied sweet reason; she turned her flushed face to me and laughed aloud. "Nothing can happen to me any more, now that I have told you the truth, how we must separate. You see, it has freed me to love you again. I am immune from dangers today." And she set herself into a breakneck gallop across the white surface leaning ever closer into the drawn bow of her horse's neck. So we came at last without mishap to the little inn, the Compasses, whose clients, dazed by the bounty of this winter sun in a windless world, were standing about in the snow outside the tap room to drink their brown beer. We tethered at a convenient hitching post and joined them for a few moments to drink hot lime and rum. Benedicta's arm was through mine, pressing softly against me, as we leaned against the fence. "They put me in a huge canvas jacket like a burnous, with long sleeves to wrap around one; it was always when I wanted to write to you. I felt so safe in there. The canvas was heavy—you couldn't poke a needle through. I felt so safe, just like I feel today. Nothing can happen."

"When do we separate? Do you want to divorce me?"

She frowned and reflected for a long moment; then she shook her head. "Not divorce" she said. "I couldn't do that."

"Why?"

"It's hard to explain. I wouldn't like to lose you because of many reasons; the child must have a father, no? And then from the point of view of. . . ." She stopped just in time; perhaps she caught a glimpse of the expression on my face. If she was about to say "the firm", it would have been just enough to make me lose control of myself.

I replaced the glasses on the gnarled counter and paid for the drinks; we remounted and moved off, more slowly now, more soberly. Benedicta's eyes were on her own white hands holding the reins.

"If I stay here until spring you could come at week-ends."

"I suppose so."

"It's only the sleeping business I can't manage; I'm still a little fragile, Felix. Ah but you understand everything—there isn't any need to explain to you. Come, let's gallop again." We broke once more into this breakneck pace, swerving down the long rides, hurling up petals of snow behind us. "I shall leave tomorrow" I called across the few feet which separated us—our labouring horses were neck and neck.

She turned her bright smiling face to me and nodded happily. "Now you understand I have confidence in myself. Tomorrow, then."

The city seemed exhausted and deserted by everyone, abandoned to the snow; not less the rows of empty offices in the Merlin Group's offices. The heating had been turned off or frozen and for a few days I had to content myself with an electric stove trained upon my feet. My secretaries were on leave, as were the servants in the Mount Street house. I had my meals at the club, often staying on as late as I could in the evening, spinning out time with a game of billiards. The late-night ring of footsteps on the iron-bound roads. . . . But yes, Benedicta sometimes rang, full of afterthoughts and moribund solicitudes; one could feel the heavy ground-swell of the resistances licking the sunken rocks—the steep seas of Nash's little pet, the unconscious. He at least was in town, in bed with a cold; I dined with him once or twice, taking care to admonish him when I did. "Theology is the last refuge of the scoundrel." I had read it somewhere among a friend's papers. I also spent some time on the Koepgen scribbles which yielded their linear B after prolonged scrutiny, thunderous aphoristic flights like: "A great work is a successfully communicated state of mind—*cosa mentale*" and "The poet is master of faculties not yet in his freehold possession—his gift is in trust. He is no didact but an enjoiner." Crumbs, I said to myself, crumbs! And we talk about nature as if we were not part of it. I could see the influence here and there of a writer called Pursewarden. Nor could I interest Master Nash very much in such lucubrations. "You see, my good Nash, reality is there all the time but we are not: our appearances are intermittent. The problem is how much can we swallow before closing time?"

O but it was a miserable period . . . I lay choking among my frustrations. "I know it is miserable" said the great man. "But sudden swerves aside are part of the pattern. The recovery will go on steadily, you will see. Do nothing to alarm her."

> *All ye graceful midgets come*
> *Softly foot it bum to bum*

I suppose that in an abstracted sort of way I had begun to hate Benedicta! Even now the idea surprises me; indeed it may not be true. A form perhaps of inverted love, a famished ingrown vegetable love fostered by exhaustion and the sense of perpetual crisis. I had several beautiful photographs of her hugely enlarged and framed— for my bedroom at Mount Street as well as for the office. Thus I was able from time to time to rest a reflective eye upon that long grave face with its confederate eyes. Emotions that refused to maintain any stability of pattern.

I went down for several successive week-ends, heart in mouth,

242

briefcase in hand, soft hat on head—to be greeted by the new composed Benedicta; a quiet, kindly, slightly abstracted woman whom I vaguely recognised. All her thoughts were for the infant prawn-like Mark, a mere series of bone-twigs as yet: but upon whose small thoughtful face I seemed already to see etched the first pull, so to speak, of the sparrow-chested intellectual he would doubtless become. They would send him to Winchester, he would be filled with notions, learn to control his emotions as well as his motions, become a scholar. . . . It was desirable, desirable. Later he could help me on lasers. Dear Mark, Matthew, Luke, John, bless the bed that I lie on. We sat on either side of the fire with the cot between us, discussing neutral topics like elderly folk sunning away a retirement. Benedicta. In the emptiness of my skull I howled the name until the echoes deafened me; but nothing came out of my mouth. It was almost with relief that I returned to my papers of a Monday—to the flat in Mount Street where Vibart and Pulley at least were visitors, where Marchant came to expatiate about the power of light to carry sound-waves— the principle which I was afterwards to adopt for Abel. A single laser beam etc. He covered the grand piano in blue chalk formulae and I had to have it French-polished again. But wait, there was one surprise.

Pulley came into my office on tip-toe, pale to the hairline with wild surmise. "Felix" he whispered, waving *The Times* "unless you did it *he's still alive.*"

For a moment I did not follow his drift; then I followed the shaking finger down the column of Personals until, by godemiche, I struck . . . *a mnemon.* I read out in astonishment: *Lazy dwarf with sponge cogs seeks place in animal factor's poem.* I gave a cry. "No, I didn't do it, Pulley. He must be *alive.*" The word rushed about the room like a startled pigeon. Caradoc! But Pulley was speaking so fast now that he was spitting all over the place. "Not so loud" he cried in anguish. "If it's true it means—O the silly fool—that he's escaped; yet how typical not to be able to resist . . . O Felix." His eyes filled with tears, he wrung his long soapy fingers together. "Why?" I cried, and he answered "If Julian sees this—do you think Julian would ever let him go? No, he'd set to work to find him, to inveigle him back, the silly old bugger." I thought furiously. "Nonsense" I said,

seeing the whole thing in a flash. "We could easily tell Julian. . . ."
And the phone started to ring. We looked at each other like schoolboys caught masturbating. Pulley went through an extraordinary
contortion, pointing to the phone, then to his own lips as they spelt
out a message in dumb show. I nodded. The same idea had come to
me. I picked up the instrument.

Julian's quiet warm voice filled the ear-piece; he spoke in a calm,
thoughtful, amused tone. "I wondered if you had seen *The Times* as
yet? It has one of those oddities of Caradoc's in it today."

"Yes," I said "Pulley and I thought it up as a sort of obituary to an
eccentric man." There was a long pause and then Julian yawned. "O
well, then. That solves the problem. Naturally I was a bit puzzled."
Pulley writhed. I said effusively. "O naturally."

"You see," said Julian dryly "one can be sure of nothing these
days. There were several survivors from the crash; we've heard no
more about them. Our man on the spot was away. And then of course
some of his papers *have* been washed up." I agreed to all this. "Well,"
he went on, his voice taking a sly tinge "I only wanted to ask." He
rang off. We sat on, Pulley and I, discussing this new development in
hushed tones. It was not long before the phone rang again and Nathan
asked if Pulley was with me, as Mr. P. wanted to talk to him. I ran my
fingers across my throat and handed him the instrument. Pulley, all
subservience, sibilated his information into it, the sweat starting on
his forehead as he spoke. Then he put it down and stared thoughtfully at the blotter before him. "He's not convinced," he said
hoarsely "not at all. Wants me to fly out and get at the truth." Then
he flew into a characteristic rage and banging the newspaper with his
palm said: "And this bloody fool is probably sitting in a brothel in
Sydney, thinking he's escaped from the firm. I ask you." He rippled
with moral rage.

"You'll have to go."

"I shall have to I suppose."

Go he did. I drove him up to the airport myself next morning
grateful for a chance to escape from the office. Pulley was dressed as
if for the Pole, his pink stoat's nose aquiver at the chance of having a
holiday from an English winter. Dismay and uncertainty had replaced our original excitement, for enquiries had revealed that the

mnemon had been posted in New York—perhaps before Caradoc had started on his journey. I watched with affection the gangling figure of Pulley trapesing across the tarmac, turning to give one awkward wave before climbing into the bowels of the aircraft. Outside the bar I saw Nash hanging about, waiting for an incoming flight, and we decided to have a coffee together. He looked at my face quizzically and said: "Things are not going too well as yet are they?" I made a face and briefly sketched an ape swinging from a chandelier. "Frankly, Nash, I have almost made up my mind to get a divorce. Nothing else will meet the case." Nash drew in his breath with a groan of dismay. "O Lord" he said "I shouldn't do that. O No." Then he cheered up and added: "As a matter of fact I don't think you could even if you wanted. Felix be patient awhile."

Patient! But it was really my concern for Benedicta which kept me bound hand and foot. I drove back recklessly, half soliciting a crash —always the weak man's way out. But safely back once more I allowed the tranquil little lift to carry me upwards to my office. My fervent secretary looked up and said: "Promotion has been ringing you every few minutes since I came in." Promotion department consisted of three exophthalmic old Etonians, who lived in a perpetual susurrus of private jokes, and an intrepid Bremen Jew called Baum who smoked cigars and looked freshly circumcised each morning. Between them they schemed up ways of marketing Merlin products. Baum's voice was deep and full of forceful enthusiasm: "You remember the idea of having the biggest Impressionist exhibition of all time at London Airport—sponsored by us?" Vaguely I did. I vaguely remembered the memorandum which began "In our age nothing has proven itself so useful to merchandising as the genuine cultural product. Merlin's has found that nothing pays off so well in terms of publicity as the sponsoring of art exhibitions, cultural gatherings, avant-garde films." The latest of these ideas was to sponsor an Impressionist exhibitions of mammoth dimensions at the air terminal—offsetting these cultural trivia with a huge display of Merlin products. "Well, yes, Baum, what about it?" Baum cleared his throat and said: "Well, guess who we've got to open it? I have the telegram of acceptance before me."

Iolanthe! It seemed extremely improbable. But, "her new film opens in London at the same time and she has agreed to come. Isn't it wonderful?"

It was indeed—a wonderful conjunction of commercial and aesthetic interests. Buy a lawn-mower while you sip your culture. "Good" I said. "Very good. Masterly." Baum crooned. "The entry will be free" he said. I waved my paws and barked like a chow. "What did you say Charlock?" Woof, Woof. Iolanthe's new film was called *Simoun, the Diva*. Somewhere, down deep inside, a new and urgent irritation against Julian had begun to materialise. It had its point of departure in a chance aside of Benedicta's, when she said: "And Julian is in full agreement that he should go to Winchester." He was was he? I studied with savage attention that fluent hand which had engraved a few words upon a recent paper of mine. I tried the old graphologist's trick of tracing the writing with a dry nib, trying to feel my way into the personality of the writer; absent yet omnipresent, what sort of a man could this quiet voice represent? And did he simply regard me, like everyone else, as a sort of catspaw to be telephoned whenever he wished to issue an order? Why would he not meet me? It was insulting—or rather it would have been if everyone else had not been in the same boat. And yet . . . that voice could never tell a lie, one felt; it inspired the confidence of an oracle. Julian was good. I tried to brush aside my annoyance as a trivial and unworthy thing. Who knew what pains and sorrows Julian himself had had to endure? And where would I have been had it not been for his far-sightedness? It was thanks to him that my professional career. . . . Nevertheless it came over me by degrees—the idea that I might force the issue, actually waylay him. Face to face I could discuss Benedicta, and the issues which had grown up around us and were threatening my concentration on the tasks vital to the firm. Damn the firm!

When the office closed that evening I took a taxi to the little square in which he lived—there was nothing secret about his address, it was in *Who's Who*. Sepulchral trees, a little snow. The Rolls and the liveried chauffeur at the door raised my hopes of finding him in; but I did not wait to ask the man, who sat stonily at the wheel with the heating purring. I took the lift to the second floor and rang twice. I was let in, already prepared to see Ali, the Turkish butler—a heavy torpid man with the head of a stag-beetle; prepared too to hear the soft plosive jargon he talked, squeezing the words up into a cleft palate.

He was not sure about Julian's movements, and had received no instructions for the evening. I asked if I might wait awhile. I had already phoned Julian's club to ascertain whether he were dining there or not. There was a fair measure of probability that he might come back here, if only to change for dinner—suppose him to be invited out. It was not late.

I examined the fox's earth with the utmost attention, surprised to find how at home I felt in it. It was a sympathetic and unworldly place —a relatively modest bachelor flat with a fine library of classical and medieval books, opulently bound and tooled. A bright fire of coal burned in the grate. The three armchairs were dressed in brilliant scarlet velvet; on an inlaid card-table with its oasis-green baize centre stood a decanter, a pack of cards, a pipe, and a copy of the *Financial Times*. The tips of his slippers peeped out from under one of the chairs. A sage-looking black cat sat upon a low wicker stool gazing into the blaze. It hardly vouchsafed me a glance as I sat down. So this was where Julian lived! He would sit opposite me over there, in a scarlet chair, wearing slippers and cooling his mind with the arid abstractions of the world markets. Perhaps he even wore a skull cap? No, that would have spoiled everything. The cat yawned. "For all I know *you* might be Julian" I told it. It gave me a contemptuous glance and turned back to the fire.

A small upright piano gleamed in the far corner of the room. A bowl of fresh flowers stood upon it, together with some bundles of sheet music. The tall goose-necked alabaster lamps with red parchment shades made a pair, echoing and chiming with the red velvet chairs. Yes, it was atmospherically a delightful room; the good taste was unselfconscious and unemphatic. The pictures were few but choice. Everything hinted at a thoughtful and eclectic spirit. One felt that its owner was something of a scholar as well as a man of affairs.

So I sat, waiting for him, but he did not come. Time ran on. The servant brought me a cocktail. The fire burned on. The cat dozed. Then I noticed, standing on the little escritoire in the corner, a small framed photograph. It had been clipped from the *Illustrated London News*, and it depicted a group of people leaving St. Paul's after some national memorial service or other. The size of the screen was not very fine and the result was a somewhat vague photo; but I noticed Julian's name among those printed in the caption. At last a picture of him! I went carefully along the second row, name by name, until I came to the fifth figure. It gave me something of a start, for the picture was surely that of Jocas. Or so it seemed. I cleaned my spectacles, and taking up a magnifying glass which lay to hand I subjected it to a close and breathless scrutiny. "But it is Jocas" I exclaimed aloud. It was damnably puzzling—there were the huge hands, even though the face was shaded by the brim of a hat. I found the servant standing behind me, gazing over my shoulder at the picture with an expressionless attention. "Is that really Mr. Julian?" I asked, and he turned a glossy and vacant eye upon me, as if he hardly understood. I repeated the question and he nodded slowly. "But surely it's his brother Mr. Jocas Pehlevi; there's some error."

He moved his tongue about in his mouth and pressed some air up into the cavity below his nostrils. He had never seen Jocas, he said; as far as he knew it was Julian all right. I was nonplussed. Of course it could have been a mistaken ascription, a journalistic error. "You are sure?" I said again, and he nodded expressionless as a totem. He shuffled off and left me staring at this singular picture. I finished my cocktail and set the glass down. Then my eye caught sight of another small door in the further wall. It was ajar. I pushed it open and took an inquisitive look into the tiny adjoining room to which it gave access. It was a little work room, with an overflowing desk. But what surprised me was that on the further wall, beautifully framed, was a gigantic picture of Iolanthe, an enlargement from her Greek film. She stood, looking down, hands gravely clasped, on the temple plinth of the Wingless Victory, with all Athens curving away under her to the sea. I had hardly time to take this all in before a clock struck somewhere. I was dying to explore further—I wanted to see the bedroom, have a look at the clothes in the wardrobe and so on. But the noise startled me in burglarish fashion; I turned, and then the telephone began to ring in the hall. I heard Ali answer it with his gasping and grunting delivery—he must be conveying the fact of my presence. And sure enough, he appeared in the door and beckoned me away from my investigations towards the phone. How familiar were the lazy precise kindly tones. "My dear Charlock, fancy you being there. What a disappointment for me." Sometimes it was Felix, sometimes Charlock. "It was another vain attempt to see you" I said lamely.

"My dear fellow." He spoke mildly and yet with a scruple of genuine pleasure in his tone—as if in some obscure way I had actually conferred a compliment on him by coming here unheralded. "It's the weirdest luck" he went on, and the dramatic pointing, so to speak, of his voice, suggested the presence of a cigar between his teeth. "To miss each other once again. Do you know, I had definitely planned to stay in this evening? Then at the last moment Cavendish rang up about an urgent decision which had to be taken about a merger up north—and dammit here I am at the airport, waiting for a plane." He laughed softly. "But is there anything urgent I can do?" So calm, so friendly, so serene did he sound that I felt all of a sudden guilty: as if I had tried to take an unfair advantage of him in hounding him down. My voice faltered in the instrument as I said, "I wanted to discuss Benedicta with you, in very general terms of course." He coughed and said: "Oh that!" with an evident relief, as though the subject were already trivial, or else out of date. "But I know about all your difficulties from Nash—all of them! I was going to tell you how grateful I was—we all are—that you are treating these unfortunate matters with such patience and conscientiousness. It's heroic. And you have even put aside the notion of divorce for the present—for her sake. My dear chap, what can I say? We will make it up to you in any way we can. All our sympathies are with you."

In the scratchy background I could hear a voice from a loudspeaker intoning plane-numbers—the faintest intonation of a muezzin from a tulip-mosque. I could feel that he had half an ear cocked back, waiting for the flight number of his own plane.

"I wonder why you hide from me?" I said at last, with a sort of graceless aggressiveness. Julian gave his quiet surprised laugh; he sounded so fond, almost tender—as if mentally he had put his arm through mine, or around my shoulders. "My dear Felix" he said with loving reproachfulness. "Answer me" I said. "Go on."

"Above all you mustn't exaggerate" he said. "Once or twice I might have found it inconvenient, but for the most part it was sheer coincidence—like tonight for example."

"Would you have come home if you had known I was here?"

"It's too late to say. The fact remains that coincidence kept us apart tonight; how can I say what I *might* have felt? That would be hypothetical merely." I rapped my knuckles on the polished wood. "Verbiage" I said. "You wouldn't have come; perhaps even you *did* know and deliberately sidestepped me." He clicked his tongue in reproof.

"Come now" he said plaintively.

"No, I wouldn't put it past you; the thing is—*why*? I sometimes wonder what you can have weighing on your mind." He gave a small groan—a satirical small sound. "In the age of the detective story one could hardly do less. But I fear you are building up a house of cards. Just imagine me as real, awfully prosaic, but a trifle shy—almost to the point of eccentricity if you wish. Truthfully."

"No" I said. "It won't fit."

"Good Lord, why not?"

As I had been talking I had been sifting through the silver bowl which stood by the telephone, telling over the thick pile of white pasteboard invitations addressed to him—Embassies and Clubs, individuals and societies. I knew that an office secretary came down every morning from the firm to deal with his social correspondence. He had neatly annotated the top left-hand corner of each card in that beautiful secretary-hand of his. On some he had written "Refuse pl" and on others "Accept pl".

"Not too shy" I said—feeling at the same time a trifle ashamed of myself for prowling around his private domain in this way—"not too shy to accept lunch at Buckingham Palace to meet the Persian Trade Mission." He gave another exasperated chuckle and said, without heat: "But Charlock, for the firm's sake I have to, don't you see? I can't afford to do otherwise: besides an invitation from Buck House is really a command, you know that." Yes, I supposed that I knew that: and yet. . . .

"Come" he said in his coaxing, conciliatory tone, as if he were speaking to a child. "Have some confidence in me, in my good intentions towards you. I haven't failed you yet have I? Have I?"

"Quite the contrary" I said, with very real despair.

"And you know how deeply we are all concerned about Benedicta. Believe me, you are not the only one to care for her. Jocas must have told you about this unhappy pattern which repeats itself, no? But it's intermittent, it never lasts for long. You should base your hopes on that, as we all do. As for our meeting—why, better luck to us both next time, that's all I can really say." I grunted. "Ah, there's my plane coming up." A vague burble of sound from a loudspeaker swelled up slowly behind his silence. "I must be off" he said, with a little sigh. "Will you tell Ali to dismiss the car? Thank you. Well, Felix, goodbye for now. ." A faint click, and we were once more cut off.

I went back to the fire to finish my drink and reflect upon the little picture in its silver frame. The cat had disappeared. I heard the man-servant doing something in the kitchen. I sat in bemused fashion, staring into the fire, almost asleep now. Somehow, I thought, I must get a glimpse of Julian's hands, if only to slake my curiosity. At least he could not deny me that! It was strange to feel like a suppliant, like a beggar: and then suddenly again to be overcome by rage or remorse. The moment I heard his voice a wave of sympathy was elicited. I melted. It was baffling this polarity of feelings—and I supposed, to adopt the formulae of Nash, that the whole thing was due to nervous strain, mental weariness which hovered about the central problem of Benedicta. The Victorian word was still the most expressive—brain-fag. Where we cannot establish the aetiology of a disease or of a course of human action—when, for example, the providing brain and the sustaining nerves are out of whack—we can always slap a clinical term on it, give it a name even if the name is meaningless.

I had drunk more than one cocktail from the silver canister before it occurred to me to look at the time; it was not as late as I'd thought. I set out to walk across London to Mount Street. A fresh tormenting wind blew, the parks rustled. In my mood of prevailing despondency I hardly noticed my feet covering the pavements of the capital, be-tween the dark brown houses; slow and regular as breathing. And the half attention I could devote to the life around me cast a curious kind of glow about ordinary realities—making them seem disembodied. In Bond Street the back of a lorry blew down and out fell a hundred gilt chairs. They tumbled out like a river and gave the illusion of dancing with each other on the pavement before subsiding into eighteenth-century curtsies. They had obviously been bound for some Embassy ballroom. Then later, in a narrow street, a woman dropped a big leather purse which exploded on the pavement scattering hundreds of halfpennies. Almost at once the passing crowd, like an ant-file diverted, started to help her gather them up—they had rolled everywhere, even into the centre of the street. Within the space of a breath everyone was transformed into a snail-picker or mushroom gatherer. The woman stood looking vaguely around her, almost tearful, holding her bag open; one by one the kindly helpers filled it with the coin they had gathered. I stood and simply watched. Thence onwards to the dry click of the key in the door, to the ministrations of silent servants, to my tapes and papers. We were still not finished with the Cham, thank goodness. "Modern architecture reflects the dirty vacuum of the suburban mind." Yes, but other voices had to be cleared off the track, vexatious and interfering voices —many of them unidentified; but some of these baffling irruptions were singular enough to be worth preserving. One voice, for example, which said: "When Merlin was dying of GPI he had his Rolls brought out and sat by it in a wheel-chair touching it, as if rubbing cold cream into its glossy velvet skin." Who on earth could that have been?

There remained such a lot to do—so many confusing diversions to be followed up or to be eliminated. In such a chaotic collection, spanning such a long period of time, the problem of ascription had become a formidable one. It was all right where I had captured a distinct voice saying a distinct thing—a voice made recognisable by its familiar timbre—like that of Caradoc. But what of the droning quotations which so frequently supervened; and sometimes even the background noises which gave substance and point to what had actually been recorded? My little dactyls worked loyally enough transcribing all they overheard, but with faulty transmission I was left often with huge sheaves of confusion—speeches one could not faithfully ascribe to one person or another. And yet many of them too good to tear up. It was like some mad accumulator building up its energies to supply a mnemonic museum. . . . Goodness, that was it. Somewhere in the midst of these studies, wallowing in this mountain of white paper, I had the idea which later led to the building-up of Abel, the computer. It was only a germ, then, though in the succeeding months it began to take sharper form. The raw materials of phonology are relatively simple if reduced to an alphabet. But if the actual phoneme—so I thought in my muddled fashion—could be translated, by a conversion table, into vibration . . . why, poor Charlock, in terms of frequency, could sort out the authors of this voice-*fest* and bring scientific order into chaos: not even chaos, just a mis-numbering of the data? It was all horribly vague; I still had much to learn from Marchant of electronics. I might even go so far as to make people seem explicit simply by marking down the tonalities of their ordinary speech. Who knows? A new sort of interpretation of the human being in terms of his vocal chords?

At any rate anything would be better, however factitious, than to surrender all this equivocal but often amusing or instructive babble to the dustbin. We were making a beginning with Caradoc, and for a specific purpose. But even here the identification was becoming questionable. It was mixed up with other things—which might have been his—pronounced in other voices, or in different keys. It was in a way as if his personality (now dead) had begun to diffuse around its edges, become less distinct, less easy to grasp in terms of an individual psychology. He was entering into his own mythology now; and of course our own mistakes of ascription might completely falsify him by adding to his massive incunabula of obiter dicta examples of Koepgen or others. These were the irresolute ideas which crossed my mind as I plugged in and watched the little creature begin to sick out her pages for me on to the expensive carpet—a human ticker-tape from the strongrooms of memory, of destiny.

To what degree is pattern arbitrary? Please help me, little faithful dactyl, with your pretty claws, please help me. I marked slowly and with as much conscientiousness as possible the voices that I knew, using a letter of the alphabet for such of my friends as I could. But often these cursed toys had been left running when I was not there. Both Caradoc and Iolanthe had been shown how to play with them. It was no wonder that there were so many puzzles to be sorted out.

Come, a drink, my boy   an abacus of the   steeplejack
Winch me in a drink,   contemporary moods   your beanstalks
Gaff me a zebib,   (K?)   are the sky
Harpoon me a gin (C)   (K?)

Poets; put your
sperm to work

his death is still fresh   (?)
paint Ah do not touch   my balls have bells Wang Shu
a mystic who likes his breakfast   while your balls have little
in bed would you say? (?)   ad hoc bells, so ting a ling
                                    cherished master as you pass
                                    in your swansdown sampan
                                                 (C)

Fundamentally every woman
wants to give birth to an   One lesson women teach is that
upper-class child, my dear.   it is possible to be superb in
                     (H)   mind without being at all
                                   intelligent. (K)

Little gold ear-rings in the
shape of a guillotine darling;   Eros de-fused will save
they all wore them under the   the human race. (K)
Terror. Look how pretty.
                   (B?)   My ancestors, yogically untrained, died
                                   through the eyes as they say; hence me,
                                   look, a house, a museum, a brothel.
                                                 (?)

So the labyrinth of this intermittent record poured out of the little machine to spread themselves on the carpet, to be gathered and stacked like sheaves; later our three bent heads would try to puzzle them out, to listen to them played back, to dispute their authorship. And some which were only holes in sound. For example, simply a sweet long sigh—the unmistakable sigh of Iolanthe in my dark room. She must have had someone there while I was out? A door opens, a match scratches, someone sees the wooden pattens. Graphos' voice —but in a whisper so that I cannot say for certain it is his: but certainly speaking Greek says "These are your shoes, then?" The silence scratches on for an age; the bed creaks. Later came the equally unmistakable clank of the bath-tap and the sound of running water. Yes, some of the scratched parts could themselves be human sighs, luxurious sighs to correspond with simple acts—a voice whispering "Ah" or else (I am not so sure) "Ah mother". Such faulty transcription defies significance; some of those dreadful crepitations could be the sucking of a breast. My little instrument whirrs on transcribing nothing—nothing in darkness. This is one tape I shall be able to destroy without compunction. Iolanthe!

Sitting among the tall columns of blue cigar smoke I meditate on this broken record of a past which is still not too far away to be revived and recaptured; which can still be compared to itself for example— memory against records. Only the faults in human memory cause the doubt and distortion. Where neither memory nor machine is completely sure you often get this kind of tentative ascription on the page. Palimpsest.

after all nature is big-breasted
indiscreet, undiscriminating, ample,
a spender . . . why not you? why not
you?

(C or K)

you talk of the prodigality
of nature; but the old bitch
in spite of those swollen dugs
is really lean as a bedrail,
all the superfluous fat is
melted off her in her war to
the knife with history.

(C or K)

Zoë Pithou
"the life of the jar"
think of it, for the mind
needs housing-space

(C)

All change for Moribundia!
ah the beautiful anguish of change!

(C?)

I do not usually like the type
but if he is rich he must be
very nice   (H)

a dialogue in whispers, but
the transcription very faulty;
a few phrases, among them:

the present overtaking the past
bit by bit and falsifying it all
the time, breath by breath;
seeing it through the spectrum of
death one supposes. (K)

"But must he die—can't you make
him disappear?"

O God what have I done?

(?)

such salient facts as self-trans-
formation, the pursuit and identification of dead selves, the accom-
modation of the idea of death—
these are the capital preoccupations.
All the rest is tinsel.

(K)

Come in. Lock the door.

(?)

I don't know, I shall never
know. (?)

To wake up with a start at two o'clock in the morning, surrounded by these growing hillocks of paper: to switch off and crawl girning up to bed. Only to echo on, I fear, in the dreams and fevers which crowded the skull of the happy weed. Did I say happy? Ah, Charlock infelix—why ever did you let your fancy stray along these unbeaten paths, lured by the idea of razors which sharpen themselves as they cut, of an electronic Braille vibrating through the sensitive fingertips of blind men? All those hybrid voices filtering through my toys afflicted their creator's sleep. A confused jumble of historical echoes —for once dead everything sleeps in the same continuum: a historical reference from Pausanias or a remark by a modern streetwalker— "a public mouth from which the lipstick has been gnawed"; or a line here and there of poetic aphorism—"poetry which modifies uncertainty awhile". Somewhere walking hand in hand with a girl among the great stored stones of Delphi which seem to yawn at post-Christian relics—the Goth of a yawn.

Or as in the film where the Parthenon by celluloid moonlight seems fashioned in a modern soap; and Io's face faceless with the interior preoccupations of the silent stone women with snail-locks. Stone head with ring? "Once a cut lip which kissing gave back salt and wine, pepper and loot". On airless nights in the desert Benedicta and I climbed into cold showers and then without drying took the car to ride over the coiling dunes, to let the moon dry us out. "Death like hair, growing by inchmeal". Voice of Hippo: "Of course they are starving; the humble always have the biggest wombs." And then Julian's chop-logic. (*I must see his hands.*) I awake with a cry, the telephone is ringing; but by the time I reach it it has gone dead, the caller has rung off. Dozing off again I dream that I enter my office to find a loaded revolver lying on my blotter.

Nevertheless . . . I nearly had him next day at Crockford's; I had discovered that he often dropped in for a flutter. Indeed that very evening he had lost an impressive sum. But I was just too late; he had been spirited away by a phone-call. There was still the butt of a cigar burning in the silver ash tray by an armchair. The manservant showed it to me as one might show someone the bones of a martyr. I watched the cynical smoke curling upwards in the warm air. The tables were buzzing—all these people had seen him, he had been there standing shoulder to shoulder with them, or sitting smiling over a hand, really existing.

Then again I overheard a clerk telephoning some bookings to Nathan; Julian was going to Paris in the Golden Arrow. I noted the numbers of his reservation and with a light heart (and lighter head) I went into the Strand and, somewhat to my own surprise, bought an automatic with six cartridges. I must have looked vaguely furtive, like a monk buying a french letter. Nor was it anything to do with aggressive notions—rather those of self-defence. But the action puzzled me a little. I sat at my desk and cleaned it respectfully, waiting for the taxi which would take me to Victoria. But once again I was bedevilled by traffic holdups. I burst past the ticket-collector and broke into a ragged gallop for my train was sliding smoothly out of the station. Coach six. Coach six. I redoubled my efforts. A window seat, number twenty-six, about the middle. Panting, I glimpsed the six on the side of a dining car and drew level with it. But the machine had gathered speed now and I had to put on another spurt to gain on the coveted carriage. Right down to the end of the platform I held it, gaining only inches.

Yes, I drew slowly abreast of Julian's seat, but just not enough to see his face; *but I did see his hands*! They were not the hands of Jocas, no. Very fine, small, white, Napoleonic fingers, holding a cigar. The hands of a manipulative surgeon, intricate, subtle fingers; but no face, I could not reach the face. I collapsed on a trolley at the end of the platform. Strangely enough I felt elated and a little frightened, perhaps even a shade triumphant. I had seen his hands, at any rate, or rather one of them. I left the automatic in a litter bin outside the station, burying it under some sodden newspapers. Its existence in my pocket was a puzzle which would not yield to analysis; yet once rid of it, the neuralgic pain between the eyes abated. I went down for a shilling wash and brush-up for the sheer curiosity of examining my face in the mirror. I looked amazingly well and quite handsome in an ugly way.

Yes, it was with a distinctly new feeling of relief that I found my way back to the office, to the plush-carpeted cage where I was surrounded with all the paraphernalia of the creative life. (Some new protos had appeared: I pawed them appreciatively.) The secretaries chirped in that white light (which turned fair powdered skins to buckram) excited by the quaint wheels and cogs. Quite suddenly I had lost all interest in Julian, in his identity; my mind had put him aside. I stood at the window, staring out at the beautiful austerities of my winter London, wondering about the symbiosis of plants, and jingling the change in my pockets. I jest of course, for the backdrop of my consciousness was still crammed with the ominous images of the country house where Benedicta walked, with pale concentration, as if waiting for something to explode. She strained to listen to something which was just beyond the reach of human ears. She might even say "Hush" in the middle of a conversation; and once as I walked across the hall towards her I found her eyes fixed upon something which was behind me, something which advanced towards her as I did. She shrank away from me; then, with an effort of will, shook her head as a swimmer does to clear the water from his eyes, and re-emerged, smiling and normal and relieved.

Then one afternoon I arrived to find a long line of hearse-like buses drawn up outside the office, and the whole staff of Merlin's in a ferment. I thought at first it was a funeral, everyone was dressed up in their best black. Extraordinary characters whom I had never seen before in my life poured out the nooks and crannies of the building— all clad with sepulchral respectability; they represented the differing totem-clans of our establishment—the accounts men like casso-waries, the legal men like warthogs or rhinos, the policy-makers like precious owls. Baum, superbly clad and ringed in a fashion which reminded one of a Blue Admiral flirting its wings, was busying himself with the organisation of this tramping crowd, now rushing to the window to assure himself that the hearses were being filled in an orderly manner, now marching up and down the corridors, tapping on doors and calling hoarsely: "Anybody there?" Clearly someone of national importance had turned up his toes. Baum caught sight of me and started: "You'll be late" he cried tapping his sideburns. "What the devil is it?" I cried, and the good Baum lowering his head to an invisible lectern uttered the reproachful words: "The great Exhibition, Mr. Charlock. You mustn't miss that." I had completely forgotten about the affair. I could see Baum running a re-proachful eye up and down my town-clothes. "Come as you are" he said. "There won't be time to change now. I'll tell your chauffeur."

So I set off following this long cortège of apparent mourners across the star-prinkled snow-gashed London, jerked to a halt every-where by traffic blocks (Baum gesticulating furiously), skidding in mush and viscid mud. Had it been a funeral cortège, whom would we have elected corpse? Fortunately there was a well-stocked cocktail bar in the car, and I reinforced my resolution with a couple of strong whiskies, filled now with a sense of resignation. By the time we reached the white billiard table of the airport the snow had thickened and dusk was falling. The white lights of cars crossed and recrossed caressing each other, as if making recognition signals as insects do with their antennae. Some mad draughtsman had drawn black lines and parabolas everywhere on the whiteness, so that the whole place looked like some plausible but tentative geodetic diagram. We settled on the central building like a flock of starlings. But inside all was light and space and warm air.

The exhibition area was roped off by a silk ribbon. Everywhere stood policemen. Baum had told me that the insurance on the pictures was so huge that practically the whole CID would be needed to guard it. It was very well done I suppose. The hessian walls with their treasures confronted a wall of equal length and height which contained specimens of Merlin's choicest products. I could not help chuckling—perhaps too loudly—and was quenched by the flashing eye of Baum. We clotted up in slow fashion to wait for our guests, milling slowly round, ill at ease. No drinks as yet, no smoking. Much pulling down of waistcoats, shooting of cuffs, adjustment of collars and ties. Some slid on the polished floors. I looked down at the notes my chauffeur had handed me to study a list of the guests. Everyone, literally everyone. Now through the swinging snow-silhouetted doors came the Lord Mayor of London, and the senior members of the diplomatic corps. Ye Gods!

And was that an illuminated address he held in scroll fashion upon his bosom? The police teemed like perspiration. Nor were the Worshipful Companies outdone by this social display—for here come the Fishmongers, Skinners, Cordwainers, Tanners, Logrollers, Straphangers, and God knows who else. All pink, all suitably em-baubled, all determined to see justice done to the arts. As for the diplomats, they provided the overture, so to speak—so enormously complacent, so relaxed, so Luciferian in their elegance. They recognised each other in the crowd with little false starts of surprise and mock-cries of astonishment. "Fancy meeting you...." They hugged each other with circumspection like actors who "when they embrace, hold each other's wigs in place". More snow and more lights. I gradually backed away into the crowd, found my way through a curtain into a small bar which was serving the ordinary passengers. Drink in hand I peeped out upon the dark superstitious horde. And Iolanthe? Well, rumours of her impending divorce were in all the papers together with moody pictures. I suppose it must be the same in all fashionable love-affairs conducted in the public eye—when the attraction wears thin you are left with a heap of soapsuds and a film contract. The hum of the company rose up into the glass roofs as if from a hive of bees or: "as sharp-tongued scythes gossiping in the grass". I was feeling unsteady but secure. I yawned.

At last came a swirl of movement outside the great doors; six huge cars settled simultaneously, moth-like, spreading their wings. The police were all expectancy now. A brilliant star-flash of pink light coloured the whole scene—a dense brilliance which gave all out waiting eyes huge shadowed orbits. Cameras began to tattle; the smaller flash of light-bulbs dotted this aurora borealis with harsh white smears. "There she is" cried someone. "Where? Who? There! Who?"

The doors fell back and she advanced slowly in the centre of a semicircle of business-like looking people, perhaps armed guards? A hundred times more beautiful, of course, and set in the pattern of dark-suited men like the corolla of some rare flower. The famous crescent-shaped smile. She walked slowly with soft and hesitant tread, as if unsure of her role, looking about her almost beseechingly. In a twinkling the foyer was brimming with uninvited lookers-on—passengers, desk-employees, hairdressers, pilots. . . . The police started to try and prevent this intrusion. The spacious hall diminished in size until they were all shoulder to shoulder.

Iolanthe advanced with all the shy majesty of a pantomime fairy, certain of her applause and yet still a little diffident about it—I mean the thunderous clapping which swelled up to the roofs. The huge wet false eyelashes set off her features to admiration, giving them shape and grace. Her dress was shot with some sort of bright rayon which made it seem lighted from within. O, she was wired for sense and sound—nor could she escape an expression of alembicated piety as she advanced towards the waiting dignitaries from whom she would unlock the mysteries of Monet, Manet, Pissaro. . . . And this was the girl who had once asked me what a Manet was. ("It says here that she bought a Manet—is it a sort of motor-bike?") I hoped she would tell the Mayor that it was a motor-bike. Vaguely, in a shuffling manner, a line of reception was being formed. I was about to duck back into the bar when Baum appeared and caught me forcibly by the elbow and all but frog-marched me into this forming line, whispering "Please, Mr. Charlock. Please" in an agony of supplication. I hadn't the moral courage to bolt; so found myself elbow to elbow with my fellow slaves in the direct line of march. I closed my eyes for a while to restore my composure and judge how much I might be swaying; but no, I was all right.

The radiance moved inexorably towards us in slow camera-time. It was possible to see how really beautiful she had become—factitious beauty I don't doubt, but very real. The smooth skin had burst from its mask of eggwhite fresh as a chick. Smiling eyes and modelled nose. Moreover she accepted her presentations with a modest distinction which won one as she floated effortlessly down the long line of dignitaries. Kallipygos Io, acting the third caryatid for all she was worth. The cameras traversed lecherously across our numbed faces. I was tempted to close my eyes on the ostrich principle in the hope that she would not see me; but I saw the critical gaze of Baum upon me and refrained. The radiant light was upon me at last and here she was with beautifully manicured fingers extended towards me. "*Xaire* Felix" she said, in a low amused voice, and the little sparks of mischief took possession of the centres of her eyes. Perhaps there was also something a little proudly tremulous there too—she was half pleased and half ashamed of all these trappings of success. I replied hesitantly and in a Pleistocene Age Greek to her greeting. She depressed her cheeks in the faintest suggestion of the old grin and went on, low-voiced, looking about her to judge whether anyone in the line understood what she was saying. "I have been wanting to see you for some time past; I have much to tell you, to ask you." I nodded humbly and said "Very well", which sounded stupid. I could see Baum swelling with pride, however, and this encouraged me to add "As soon as you have time, as you wish." Iolanthe wrinkled her brow briefly and said: "Thank you. Quite soon now." Then she passed slowly along to where the Mayor stood panting and mopping.

She made a speech, brief and wise, and obviously written for her; she did not mention motor-bikes in it. Then with a huge pair of dressmaker's scissors she cut the ribbons. We all poured reverently into the Exhibition behind her. In the heat of battle the mayor had forgotten to deliver his reply to her speech; he stuffed it into his tail-coat and followed manfully. There was nothing further to keep me and I made my way back to the bar for another drink to wait upon her departure—for she might conceivably ask for me again and I didn't want to hurt Baum. Through the curtain I kept a sharpshooter's eye on the proceedings, so intently, indeed, that I hardly heeded a thump on the shoulder from behind. Then, spinning round, I found myself face to face with Mrs. Henniker. "My poy!" The last person in the world I was expecting to see! She extended a hand rough as a motoring glove and pumped mine violently; she spoke with untold vivacity. She had not changed by a day—but yes; to begin with she was dressed in country tweeds and natty brogues, a black pullover and pearls. Neatly smart. Her hair had been cut into roguish curls and dyed reddish. She smelt rather heavily of drink, and there was a slight vagueness of eye and speech which suggested—but this might have been sheer emotion at seeing me again. Her skin was rough and red and windblown. She was carrying several folders and a notebook. She moved up and down on her heels with triumphant delight. To my question about what she might be doing there she jerked her head in the direction of the Exhibition and said: "With her. I am Iolanthe's secretary." Then, draining her glass at a blow: "The minute she could she wired me to come to her. She has been a daughter to me, and I . . ." she broke off to order another round "have been a mother to her." There was no suspecting the deep emotion with which she made me this confidence. "Well I'm damned" I said, and Mrs. Henniker gave a harsh cackle of laughter. "You see?" she said with gleaming eye, raising her glass. "How strange life is?"

We had several more drinks on the strength of this, and it was only when the goddess was leaving that Mrs. Henniker jumped to her feet and exclaimed that duty called. "Can you come to Paris next week? She prefers to meet you there—because of Julian." I jumped.

"Of course I can come to Paris." Mrs. H. shook her red wattles and said "Good, then I'll get in touch with you with all the details. She will have to dress up, you know, and meet you in a café or something. I expect she'll explain everything to you. But she's mobbed wherever she goes. And there's no privacy in the apartment. I'll ring you. Ah my poy, my poy."

I drove back to London with a certain pleasurable perplexity, in the company of Baum who was beside himself with joy at the great success. Full justice had been done both to the painters and also to those superior titillations of the thinking mind like the Merlin lawnmower. "You must have been very moved to see your work bang opposite the great masters" he said. "And she was so beautiful I felt quite afraid. Do you know she gets a million dollars for every film now? A million dollars!" His voice rose in a childish squark of amazement. "She was like a flower, Mr. Charlock." Yes, an open flower filled with synthetic dew. "A dedicated artist" went on Baum impressively. Indeed. Indeed. Full of the *feu sucré*. I was jealous of her success.

It is all very well to be flippant; the truth was that even from the glimpse I had had of the new Iolanthe I had gathered the impression of a maturity and self-possession which made me rather envious. She seemed to me to be very much her own woman leading a life a good deal more coherent than mine. And yet it had been a pretty good mess had it not? I picked up an evening paper at the corner and took it home to dinner, the better to study the pictures of her and of her husband; it was still in the rumour stage, of course, this impending separation, but it remained undenied, which gave it a certain flavour of validity. Well, all this was nothing to do with me. After dinner Julian rang up and startled me—I mean that I had almost forgotten his existence, and the fact of his voice resurrecting thus caused me a real surprise. He talked about the Exhibition, asked me if it had been a success and so on. I described as much of it as I could; and I had the impression that he positively drank in anything I might have to say about Iolanthe. He seemed to linger over anything concerned with her.

Then he modestly cleared his throat and said, almost humbly: "She was your mistress once, wasn't she?" I replied: "No, not this woman. That was quite another girl. She's completely changed, you know." Julian's voice sank a tone. "Yes, I know," he said "I know." There was a long silence; then he said: "Has she asked to see you? Will you be meeting?" But, made cautious by long doubting, I replied: "No. We have nothing to say to each other now, I don't think there is any point." He grunted, and I could hear him light a match. "I see. By the way, I hear that Benedicta hasn't been too well this last week. Nash has gone down to see her." I supposed that meant some more deep sedation. I said nothing. Benedicta rose with my gorge until I was filled with a sensation of nausea.

"In the meantime" said Julian "I want you to spend a few days in Paris." He gave me the details of some negotiations which were going on; I duly noted them down on my blotter. "Very well" I said. "Very well." And that was that; he sounded as if he were speaking from Dublin or Zürich. I returned to my fire and my cigar, full of a certain mild surmise. (To bow or not to bow, that is the question?) Before going to bed I sent a night letter to Mrs. Henniker, asking her to phone me at the office on the morrow.

But it was Iolanthe's voice which came over the wire, heavy with sleep. "Henniker is off today so I thought I'd ring you . . ." she began, and then switched into Greek, in order, I suppose, not to be understood by the casual switchboard operators. "I want to give you a number to ring when you come—I hope you do. I am here for another month at least. I'm so looking forward to it. When do you think you will come? Friday and Saturday I have free." So the appointment was made, aided and abetted by the chance which was to take me to Paris anyway. My spirits rose at the prospect of a short change from snowgirt London—even though it would mean lodging at the Diego which was owned by the company and where everything was free. I know. Everyone hates the Diego—its spaciousness confers an infernal anonymity upon its residents. But then I had some trivial details about patents to discuss: and this was the ideal place to discuss them, for it boasted of elegantly appointed conference rooms smelling of weary leather and Babylonian cigars. Threading and weaving about its great entrance halls with their flamboyant marquetry were grouped all the traditional denizens of the international world of affairs—Arab potentates with black retainers poring over maps of oilfields, gamesome little bankers from the USA moving on hinges, forgotten kings and queens, gangsters, revivalists and fleshy brokers. The never-stopping hum of critical conversations, anguished bids, political lucubrations, arguments, disagreements, hung heavy on the air. All this variegated business fauna pullulated. The Diego buzzed with a million conflicting purposes, schemes and schisms.

I conducted my business with despatch and moved into the fourteenth where I had once lodged as a youth; it was still there, the old Corneille, though it must have changed hands a hundred times since. Still the same high reputation for general seediness and defective plumbing; but modestly priced, and with rooms backing on to insanitary but romantic courtyards, and tree-tufted. Also there was my old room vacant. It was in reality Number Thirteen, but in deference to public superstition it had been renumbered Twelve A. The old telephones creaked and scratched, half transforming the melodious laugh of Iolanthe when at last I reached her. "Listen" she said "you know my problem about being mobbed—she told you? I daren't show my face except over a cop's shoulder. And so I have to dress up a bit to enjoy any sort of privacy." She sounded however as if she enjoyed it. "And this apartment is useless, here I am watched." I groaned. "O God," I said "not you too. Must we then meet heavily veiled or in false beards? And who watches you anyway?" I groaned again. "Julian!" I said with bitter certainty. She laughed very heartily. "Of course not. It's my husband." Out of the window Paris was in the grip of a magnificent early spring thaw, gutters running, trees leafing, birds loafing. The scent of pushing green in the parks, the last melted drops running from the penis of the stone Pan in the public gardens. "Well what, then?"

"I am going to act Solange" she said gaily.

"Solange?" I was startled. "What do you know about Solange?"

"Your little girl" she said. "Everything you told me about her has stayed in my memory like a photograph."

"I told you about Solange?" This was really surprising; Solange had been a little *grisette* with whom I had lived for one brief summer —actually part of the time here, in this room. But when could I have mentioned her to Iolanthe?

"You have forgotten" she said. "You told me all about her, making unfair comparisons with me. I remember being depressed. She was so this, she was so that. Besides I didn't realise that it was all Paris snobbery. In those days everyone simply had to have a love-affair in Paris or risk being ridiculous. But I didn't know that—you took advantage of my ignorance. Nevertheless I listened carefully, always anxious to learn. And I have never forgotten Solange. And what is more, I shall prove it to you. At eleven-thirty. The Café Argent isn't it?" As a matter of fact it used to be the Café Argent all right; then back here for those tender little manoeuvres which by now I had so completely forgotten that I had to make a real effort to recapture the fleeting expressions on the white peaky face of my little Parisienne. "Good God" I said. It seemed an extraordinary thing to bring up; one never knows what lumber one has shed like this—lumber which has been preserved in somebody's memory. Tons of this detritus thrown off by a single life, flushed away one thinks: but no, someone has recorded it—sometimes a chance remark, sometimes a whole case-history. "Very well" I said with resignation. "Come and act her then."

She did it to such good effect that for a moment I did not quite believe it—of course she could not look exactly like Solange: and there were quite a few young women sitting along the *terrasse* even at that time of day—laid up like trinkets in some pedlar's tray. But then Solange! It was only when the waiter brought me a little slip of torn newspaper with a question mark on it, indicating the sender of the missive by a jerk of his head, that Solange burst out of the tomb and into that warm spring sunlight. Solange of the powder-blue skirt badly cut, the dove-grey shoes much worn, the yellowing mackintosh, colour of an uncut manuscript: cheap beads, crocodile handbag, mauve beret. Rising she came towards me with that heavily whitewashed face and over-made up eye, with that flaunting yet diffident walk. (The diffident part was Iolanthe herself.) "*Je suis libre Monsieur.*" Among those shy students, Germans, Swiss and Americans, the little monotonous whining voice, the dire sadness covered by the deliberately pert smile. "Iolanthe," I exclaimed "for goodness' sake—what next?" She burst into a characteristic peal of common laughter as she sank into the wicker chair beside mine,

266

putting her handbag on the table between us. She clapped her hands to summon a waiter and demand a *coupe* in her marvellous tinfoil tones. "Go on," she said "tell me I can't act. *The Times* says I can't act." But the brilliant impersonation of Solange held me spellbound. Of course she was wigged—brown bobbed hair with two points at her dimpled mouth. Certainly she would never be recognised like this. "You see?" she said, clipping her arm through mine as we sat. "So we can be free to talk. Tell me everything that has happened to you." I should have answered perhaps that while much seemed to have happened in fact catastrophically little had. Where to begin anyway? I tried my hand at a brief sketch of my fortunes; there was much that she already knew. She listened carefully, attentively, nodding from time to time as if what I said confirmed her own inward intuitions. "We are in the same boat" she said at last. "Both rich, celebrated and sick."

"Sick, Iolanthe?"

"In my case physically."

"And mine?"

"You've taken the wrong road—I knew you would even then: always in your cards I found it: and then yourself—you always saw real people as sort of illustrations to things—glandular secretions. I felt that you'd never get free, and then later when I heard you had joined Merlin's my heart went down and down. I know what it has cost me to free myself from them. I knew you'd never do it."

"Why should I?" I said sturdily. "It suits my book very well." She looked at me with dismay, bordering on disgust; and then her expression changed. She realised that I wasn't telling the whole truth. "Merlin's made me what I am" I said sententiously, feeling quite sick to hear myself talk such twaddle. Now she began to laugh. Ouf! It seemed as if the whole conversation were going to take a wrong turning. "Come, let's walk" I said. As we passed the Café Dôme she insisted that I entered it to see if there was any message from Solange on the postboard. Sure enough there was, in typically bad French: she had had it planted by Mrs. Henniker. "This is going too far" I said with poor grace. "Now we better go back to the hotel and. . . ." An expression of sadness came into her eyes for a moment and then was swallowed by her smile. Taking my arm once more she fell into step. So in leisurely fashion we crossed the park, quizzing the statues, talking in low voices now, inhabitants of different worlds. "And so you are free, as you call it? What does it mean to you Iolanthe?"

"Everything; I just needed it. But it has cost me a great deal—in fact my company is hovering on the edge of bankruptcy all the time —thanks to Julian of course. He could not bear to see me free."

"Do you know Julian?"

"I saw him once—just a single look we exchanged, a look to last a lifetime. I knew then that he loved me—indeed in a perverse way all the more for crossing him, for breaking free. With my first money I set up my own firm, chose my own parts. Julian has tried to break us because—again perversely—his only way of getting me would be by owning me, having shares in me." She laughed, not bitterly but ruefully. "If you men didn't prey on women where would you be?" she added smiling. "But Julian's expression was so strange that I even tried to learn to draw in order to reproduce it."

"How did you meet?"

"We didn't; our audience research people said that there was one of my fans who was always there, never missed a single film, often saw them over and over again for weeks. They wanted to make a newspaper story of it; but the journalist was told by his proprietor that Julian had had the story stopped. Then they pointed him out to me at a Fair."

For some reason I felt jealous of this.

Across the Luxembourg, the children's play-pit and so on, slowly down, drawn by the inexorable strings of our Athenian memories. There was much to surprise me; it was like coming upon a bundle of letters one had read in cursory fashion and thrust aside into a cupboard corner—and now on re-reading discovered to be full of things which had escaped notice. For example: "It puzzled me afterwards very much to think how much I thought I loved you then. I did love you, but for singular reasons. Ultimately it was your lack of understanding which enabled you to occupy this place in my mind—your very indifference in a queer way. Since you could be objective, cool, and consequently *considerate*." (O dear, this is the mere vermiform appendix of love.)

"At times I thought you quite contemptible as a man, but I never wavered. You don't know, Felix, how little a woman hopes for in life —for an iron ration only: *consideration*. We haven't enough confidence in ourselves to believe that we could ever be loved—that would be butter and jam on the bread. But the bread itself? A woman can be won by simple consideration, she will settle for that when she is desperate. Look, you took my arm in the public street, though all Athens knew I was a street-girl. You dared to be seen with me, opened doors for me. What chivalry, I thought! Everyone will believe us to be engaged. But of course later I realised that it had no special connotation for you—it was pure absent-mindedness and ignorance of the mentality of small capitals." She laughed very merrily; I turned her friendly face round to embrace her, but she groaned with pain, and said her wounds were not yet healed. "You used to talk about going from the unproven to the proven in your work; but later I realised that with each new discovery the so-called proven is falsified. It collapses. The whole thing is only a funk-hole process—necessary because you are weak."

I didn't care about all this, inhaling the warm Jupiterian air, the leaves, the crunching passers-by who walked as if upon a tilting deck, or else were dragged widdershins by huge dogs on heat. Intuition can become a conditioned reflex? "And then" she went on "I heard what you'd done, and I crossed my fingers for you. I half believed that you might decide for independence one day like myself. But when I saw your face the other day I knew that you hadn't made a serious effort. You had the same funny stillborn look you always had; I was tempted to kiss you very hard, very triumphantly, simply because Julian was there in the crowd."

"Julian was there?"

"I *think* it was Julian."

I kicked some pebbles about for a moment wondering if I shouldn't become angry. "I don't much like this sort of curtain-lecture coming from you," I said at last "with its boastful idea that you have done something very special; you who supply a surrogate mob-culture with vulgarised versions of classics watered down by pissy-witted cinéastes. . . ." Iolanthe looked at me with delight. She said: "It isn't the point; even if it had only been a small dressmaker's shop in the Plaka instead of a film company. It means living without deceptions, awkward secrets, living in the round. The real freedom. *My own.*"

I laughed contemptuously. "*Real* freedom?" She nodded briskly. "Inevitably you would ask yourself how real you were; you would think that it isn't just the firm which confers an illusory reality upon you. O I'm not saying the firm is anything but benign, it helps you towards what you want to do, to achieve."

"Then why all this quaker-maid nonsense?"

"I've angered you" she said sadly. "Come let's talk about other things. You know Graphos is dying; now he would have been worth the love of some great-hearted woman if his health had not spoiled his mind. It's typical of the cynicism of fate that he should imagine he loved me, and still does. And I like him too much to deny that he does. After all, he educated me, taught me to see—in spite of his perverse habits and tastes."

We had come to the doors of the old hotel; I took my key and we mounted slowly, arm in arm. She chuckled as she gazed round her. "It's typically your sort of room" she said. She went to the grimy window and stared out into the foliage. It was raining now, quite a storm of rain. "Do you remember the spoiled picnic on the Acropolis when the sky seemed to come down in whole panes of molten glass and our footsteps smoked on the marble?" She kicked off her shoes and lay down beside me, setting a pillow in the nape of her neck, lighting a cigarette. It needed only a lighted candle and an ikon. . . . Ikons, the portfolio of the collective sensibility. I imagined them as I dozed. ("There is no God and no plan: and once you accept that you can start to identify"?) She lay quietly with her eyes half shut. I had penetrated again the cardboard, the outer cerements of the worshipped mummy. Above all, one should not make a mythology out of one's longing.

My hand sought out hers and pressed it; we were half dozing, reconstituting like archaeologists with every drawn breath, a past which had long since foundered. The arcane clicks and whistles of the little owls; mountains of gauche leaves blowing in the parks. The firm was like one of those great works of art which perish from over-elaboration. ("The greatest happiness of the highest few is what nature aims at, the great aristocrat.") The white mice I have cut up, starved, tortured on behalf of science—as Marchant might say; some people one can only convince by drawing blood. I kissed the nape of her neck softly and lapsed into inertia, dozing by her side while she quietly talked on and on in sweet leaden tones. "It's a terrible thing to feel that one has come to the end of one's life-experience—that there is nothing fundamentally new to look forward to: one must expect more and more combinations of the same sort of thing—the thing which has proven one a sort of failure. So then you start on the declining path, living a kind of posthumous life, your blood cool, your pulse steady." She pressed my finger to her slow calm pulse. "And yet it is just the fruitful point at which some big new understanding might jump out on you from behind the bushes and devour you like a lion." Small sighs, small silences, we were like people drugged; without any sexual stirring we had reverted to the prehistoric mode of an ancient intimacy.

"It's a sort of curse, you might say, for I've brought little comfort to anyone; and some I have gravely harmed. Not voluntarily, but simply because I was placed at an axis where all their lives intersected. That Hippolyta—I had to act to deceive her. And others, like that poor Sipple. Whenever I am in Polis I look him up as a sort of expiation, though we never mention my brother."

"What on earth about Sipple?"

She rose yawning and stretching to seat herself at the mirror; she took off her wig and began to comb it softly. "I thought you knew about that boy; he *was* my brother; I was obliged to kill him."

It was like a pistol shot fired in the quiet room. She turned round to me smiling, with an air of patient fidelity. "And poor Sipple has had to bear the odium. He is going blind, you know. He has become a perfume-taster. They dab those little flippers of his with scent and he tells them how to mix their perfumes. He is studying to be received into the Catholic Church, of all things."

"But why, Iolanthe? Why on earth?"

"That's the sad thing—in order not to let my father take it upon himself; he was a very rash, violent little man, and he had vowed to punish Dorcas. To the Virgin, you know. I knew that he would be obliged to do it, if only because of his vow. I could not let him go to

271

the grave with that upon his conscience—a man of sixty-five. So I stepped in to shield him; and Graphos had it all hushed up. I suppose the idea of atonement is a lot of conceit really—who can say?"

"As arrows fit the wounds they make!" She crossed to the bed and placed a lighted cigarette between my lips; so we stayed silently smoking for a long while, staring at each other.

Then she began to speak of her father's death. He at least was unaware of what she had done for his sake. The scene rose so vividly before my eyes—the little house with its cobwebs, its table and three chairs before the fireplace. A dying peasant wrestling with a death by tetanus, closing up slowly like a jacknife. "Have you heard someone scream with their teeth firmly locked together—an inhuman screaming like a mad bear?" And stumbling, knocking over the furniture. He would not submit, fought death every inch of the way. And the rigor setting the body in such strange shapes. He was like a man wrestling with riding boots too small for him. And then the candles smoking; but even dead he wouldn't lie down. Up he came each time they pushed him down like a jack-in-the-box. The piercing lamentations of the villagers. But it was no go, he wouldn't fit. Finally the village butcher had to be summoned to break up his bones like a turkey in order to coffin him properly. But now there was sweat on Iolanthe's brow, and she was walking slowly up and down at the foot of the bed. They tied a ribbon, a green ribbon, round his arm before the barber bled him. There was so much blood in that withered old arm. "He wouldn't give in, you see." Then she paused and went on. "The little house is still there, it's mine, but I daren't go back. I left it just as it was, the key in the hole by the coping of the well—but you remember, don't you? If ever you go that way will you visit it and tell me about it? I'm sufficiently Greek to feel that I might return one day when I am much older—but how? Someone must exorcise it for me. Felix, if you did that I should be grateful. Will you?" She was so earnest and so beseeching that I said yes, in my futile way, yes I would. And of course now it's too late, as it always is.

"Meanwhile I am here." she said with a rueful bitterness "the most beautiful woman in the world they say. O God."

She has gone such a long way away now, dissolved among the shadows of time; only her masks are preserved in the tin cans that

272

crowd the lumber rooms of the bankrupt companies. Iolanthe now is an unidentified wave to sadness which reaches out for me whenever I see a slip of blue Greek sky, or a beautiful late evening breaking over the Plaka. And then the horror and sadness of the way in which she said "Look" in a voice of a frightened child; and ripping open the cheap bodice showed me the bandaged breasts plumped out with their surgical wadding, and taped like hot cross buns. "I haven't completely healed up as yet."

"Cancer?" I exclaimed; but she shook her head and replied: "Not yet at anyrate. It's even more ironic. Last year in Hollywood they brought in a new treatment for falling breasts—injections of liquid paraffin. It was all the rage. But mine went wrong though I am not the only one, Felix."

She sat down at the mirror once more to adjust her disguise, saying tonelessly: "Now I have brought you up to date." Subjects of calendar time trapped in the great capitals of the world. I let Iolanthe sink deep into my reveries; down she went and down like a plumbline, turning and rolling through the subaqueous worlds of memory and desire, dissolving and disappearing from view.

"Come," she said at last "enough of these post-mortems. I have ordered a hire car to wait for us at the office. Let us drive into the country together, have lunch, lie on the grass, forget, pretend."

"Forget" I said, and suddenly remembered Benedicta. "I must just ring the office and see if there is any news of Benedicta; she hasn't been very well of late."

"Benedicta" said Iolanthe. "They say that it is all because she drugs. I heard it ages ago and it may be true. Apparently Julian. . . ."

I felt my scalp tingle with rage; it climbed my spine to burst in the centre of my mind like a black bubble of fury. "I do not want to hear his name any more" I said. "I implore you."

"Very well" she said calmly, and kissed me—the sort of kiss that might soothe a refractory child. I banged Number Thirteen shut behind us as we went downstairs.

We came back in the late evening, and she was careful to adjust her disguise before crossing the pavement to the glass doors of the apartment house. Outside lay the film company's Rolls, with the usual small knot of onlookers hanging about it. Its presence always signified that she was inside and might at any moment emerge to be driven somewhere. It was quite miraculous to see how swiftly the crowd gathered—people seemed to spring from the very pavements: she had only to leave the lift and appear in the soft red light at the end of the corridor for the ferment to begin. Autograph books would flash. It was necessary to clear a track for her. Then as she sat back in the car noses would be pressed grotesquely against the windows; avidly the parched faces would inhale her, drink her up. But little Solange looked like some shabby dressmaker and not a head turned as she unlocked the tall doors and, once safe inside, blew me a kiss and rang for the lift.

I walked for half the night by the river which mirrored the opal-studded floors of the dark heaven powdered by stardust; cold, it was cold. The spring day had foundered back into a subzero night which made me glad of a heavy overcoat. I roamed the deserted bookstalls and the dark ships along the river-front with a sense of confusion and loss; I should have been sobbing, I imagine, but what is one to do if the tears pour inwardly, if the amateur face expresses nothing? All that I deserved was some dirty unknown old woman with a gold tooth and shrunken thighs to drain my semen in an instant, pocket the money and scuttle downstairs again to her lamp-post; but even this seemed merely an act of bravado, an attempt at a self-inflicted wound which hardly penetrated the thick carapace of my narcissism and self-regard. Smelling of dirty underlinen, rubber, and sweat; nor could I assuage the thirsty hounds of introspection which were licking my bones. In a bookshop window I read a phrase from an open volume of Flaubert: "*On ne saura jamais ce qu'il a fallu être triste pour entreprendre de ressusciter Carthage.*" I read it over and over again; perhaps if I had had my wits about me I could also have become a master of corkscrew prose? I walked on and on until my legs would carry me no further; then I took a taxi back to my musty room, to spend the rest of the night sleeplessly doing battle with the giant shapes of a nightmare which paralysed my breathing and my will. My own groans woke me, and I remembered Benedicta saying: "But I suffer from daymares, Felix, *pavor diurnus*, as Nash calls it; it is harder to wake from them." (At midnight the quantity of carbon monoxide in the blood reaches its maximum.) As always when she

274

was talking honestly one had the impression of truth barbed with a ferocious tenderness. Next morning I scribbled a note to Iolanthe promising to visit her again, and pleading that urgent business called me back to London. In some unanalysable fashion our meeting had upset me, had knocked the props from under my self-esteem. It was hard as always to leave Paris—hard, grimy and metallic city where civilisation is always dragging its anchor; harder still to face cold London with the sullen ferocious visages of the young half hidden by hair.

> *the big syringe*
> *the shrunken penis*
> *is all they offer now*
> *to Venus*

No, it won't do; deep in the penetralia of one's self-regard there was an arrow pointing towards something which had remained unrealised and unachieved—though how to formulate it without making a model I knew not. Nor should I let the calculated despair of this realisation drive me towards any violent solutions—violence is for the weak. But then Felix, it is precisely because of your weakness.... Someone said once that Julian was obsessed, not with dying, but with rotting; he could not face the idea of that (was it Iolanthe or Koepgen?). Nor could he submit to having his entrails removed, his body embalmed. He hit upon the notion of having a steel, air-tight coffin built for him by Gantry the famous makers of office safes. I had one in my office which closed with a slight puff. A Gantry with an elaborate combination-system whose code I am always forgetting.

High summer to autumn the year went by, its clock-time not matching the slow accretive growth of the buried decisions I meditated; but they were so inchoate as to have to be disinterred, brushed clean, examined—dug up like the bones of dinosaurs. The flora and fauna belonging to such bones must be imagined, their world visualised. Externally nothing had outwardly changed. Life still held its unhurried glacier-pace. Iolanthe wrote once or twice and I tried to answer, sitting before the blank paper for ages biting a pen. What I most needed to say would not rise to the nib. I gave up the struggle. Banubula, in search of female hormone I suppose, paid me a brief visit and for a few days carried me back to those remote unhurried epochs when we had both time and will to devise, to execute. Also the sacramental whiff of Polis and Athens. Jocas had been shot at by a eunuch and in returning the fire had killed the man; elaborate and exhausting litigation about restitution was still going on. Graphos was much worse; he spent all winter at the Paulhaus now, but the treatment availed him little. Hippo had "gone so white". Well, so had we in a way; both the Count and I found our temples turning. I was sorry to see him go, in spite of his perpetual moaning about not being able to join the firm. ("But why on earth should you *want* to join it?" Banubula stroked his nose. "Well, because of you all; look at you, you are all so happy".)

Benedicta still lay at anchor, not noticeably better or worse; still hovering between white depression and sudden bursts of tender enthusiasm—attacks of almost total lucidity one might have called it. Yet always lying for half the day in the darkened rooms, blinds drawn, candles fuming. "I suddenly realised one day that real people had become shadows—without any substance as egos." It was well expressed, but I was tempted to answer "Except Julian I suppose?" Then self-reproach, of course, and bad dreams in which Julian sat by my bed, a small vampire-snouted man, staring at me with two live coals. I knew of course what all these women lacked—a tablespoon of fresh poet's sperm breathing salt air and seed into them. It can work wonders with a sensitive woman. What we all lacked, it seemed to me —and here I was mentally copying Koepgen with his *ex cathedra* judgements—was the mythological extension of human personality. I remember him saying, in front of a statue of the old king who went on sleeping with his dead wife for months: "And do you dare to imagine that there isn't a real historic personage buried underneath each mythological one?" It was all very well. I went to New York, to Rio, conferring my intellectual bounty on them in well-shaped discourses.

And then, quite unaccountably (or so it seemed, it was so sudden) Pulley walked into the house in Mount Street one evening with an air of rare distraction. He had found the front door ajar as I had been expecting Marchant to come and talk chemicals. A new cadaverous Pulley; without even greeting me he crossed the drawing-room to the sideboard and poured himself a stiff whisky and soda. "Well" I said. He looked at first blush as if he had been beaten up—his forehead was all blue and bruised; moreover his skin was yellow, as if he were just getting over an attack of jaundice. But no, he said, the bruises were due to a fall downstairs and the yellowness due to a bug he had picked up "out there" and for which he had been under treatment by Nash. "Just got back from Zürich this morning to find my digs in an awful mess." He sank into a chair sighing, and giving me a yawning grin with very little grin in it—a funny rictus really.

"Pulley, what have you been up to?"

He shivered a little and said: "They gave me drugs at the Paulhaus, drugs for bugs, old man. And now I don't know what I've told them, at all I don't. I can't remember. It worries me. Did I tell them the truth? I didn't mean to. Anyway, I'm not really sure it was him— Robinson."

"Wait a minute. Stop this babble. Who is Robinson? And where?"

"Sorry" he said with contrition. "Either it was Caradoc or it wasn't Caradoc, and it was only a glimpse. I was sure it was at first; then when I left I suddenly grew doubtful. Maybe it was Robinson after all, the old man. But I'll begin at the beginning. The smell of copra—do you know it? I can't get it out of my nose. Specially rotting copra mixed with a little oil and bilge. Day and night vomiting about in a little boat smelling of singed gym-shoes. I'm not saying it isn't all very beautiful, it is: but I'd prefer to see postcards. The damp in those islands, my boy, the damp winds, damp clouds, steamy jungle. And the diet, chunks of pig and breadfruit inadequately cooked and very badly served on leaves. After about a month I'd had enough. Moreover I'd cleared the few survivors, visited them as from an airline insurance company. There remained a man called Robinson, a de-frocked clergyman they said, who had gone native and retired to a tiny little island miles from anywhere. He had been on the plane, or so the passport people said, and had crawled ashore and disappeared. Presumably he had gone back home again; but the last copra boat had gone ages since and the next wasn't due for a while, so I just had to cool my heels in Pyengo.

"A more godforsaken dump I never hope to see; and if the ladies are kind as they are reputed to be, it's all very well. Only you should

277

smell the local cold cream they use on their bodies. That also takes getting used to. However there was sunshine, there was a sharkless lagoon, and the foodstuffs arrived wrapped in old *Times*, so I made do with it until I could catch the boat for Robinson's little island. Apparently he had quite a tidy copra crop to be collected and some shells. So an occasional visit was on. Anyway there I stuck and waited, slowly getting athlete's foot in my armpits. Nor did such enquiries as I could make offer much hope. In fact the whole thing seemed a waste of time. I didn't sleep very well, the blasted trees make such a noise. Also they said the season would soon be breaking, and I had visions of being stuck altogether. However at last it came, the boat, and the skipper agreed to take me; but he emphasised that Robinson absolutely refused to allow people ashore on any terms whatsoever; the crew were allowed to ship the copra and clear off. There were signs tacked up everywhere saying: 'Strangers forbidden'. I said I would take a chance on it; but I didn't feel too elated as apparently Robinson had a gun and was quite likely to use it. He had once fired at a suffragan bishop who tried to come and draw him back into the fold.

"Well, one has to take risks; and after all that time waiting I felt I really should. The voyage was hell for smell, the sea was oily, everything appeared to be rotting all round us. Three days it took and at last we came to the tiny little island and drew into a rusty iron pier with a crooked crane. The ship tooted to tell Robinson that we had arrived but nobody answered, so the crew just swung off and began to load the copra which was lying around fairly neatly laid out for them; also several big boxes of seashells. I walked up and down for a bit in a hesitant manner, keeping my eyes skinned; but nobody appeared, and the skipper seemed to think that nobody would. It was often like that, he said. He pointed over the hill and said that the village was somewhere over there; and so I started to stroll in the direction he indicated. It was quite pretty and quite green with patches of cultivation here and there; I had been told that the total population of the island was about sixty souls—enough for the harvesting and all that. There was rather an exceptionally large hut standing some way outside the nearest village-shaped cluster and I went towards it, imagining it must be the chief's or Robinson's. All the way along I saw notices tacked to the trees saying: 'Strangers absolutely forbidden. Danger' which didn't sound too reassuring. However on I pressed. As I got nearer to the big hut I saw that there was an old man sitting on the steps, an old man with a mane of white hair. He started when he saw me and gave an inarticulate cry, as if of rage. I waved my hands in a peaceable and pleading manner, like a soldier waving a white flag of truce, and called out in English: 'Is Mr. Robinson here? I have only come for a moment to ask him a question.' My dear Charlock, that was absolutely all. My range was fairly extreme, but I did get a good look at him. He was simply covered in hair, beard to his waist, high-foreheaded sweep of mane backwards, loin-cloth, and rough thonged slippers made of some bark or other. His eyes were small and bloodshot, and at this moment regarded me as a cornered and wounded wild boar might.

"Everything seemed to come together in a confused sort of focus —you know how it is in moments of excitement? And some of the things I saw in that few seconds I didn't take in until afterwards, when I was on the run. For example that he had two small kids at his breasts, *he was giving them suck, old man.* I could even see some of the milk trickling down among the hairs on his breast, white as coconut-milk. It seemed to me that it was Caradoc all right. I mean that at that precise moment it seemed so; later I lost confidence in my judgement. A woman appeared at an upper window, large and rather handsome, and clucked something at him. All this happened in a twinkling. I called his name once in an uncertain sort of way. Then he put down the kids and picked up a gun which was lying beside him and opened fire. A bunch of leaves from above my head fell with a crash on me. There was no time to argue; it was a near miss. I took to my heels with the shells knocking up the stones all around me. Once I thought I had been hit, but it was gravel thrown up by the shots—but it hurt. It must have been a six shot twelve-bore, for he sent all six whistling about my ears, some damn near. I cleared the brow of the hill with thumping heart and galloped down to the pier where they had just finished loading. I took refuge in the deck-house until the ship drew anchor and set off. I feared he might follow me down to the harbour and take a pot shot at me there.

"Well, this whole thing, sort of instant snapshot stuff, had a

279

strange sort of effect on me. It wasn't just the unexpectedness, the fright and so on. I felt as if my mind had been, for one brief second, unfrozen; and even later when it went back into deep freeze again, the experience left something, a nagging something. I'm not much good at expressing these things. Later, of course, when I got very ill I had all sorts of feverish delusions about us all, about the firm. Julian had me flown back to Zürich where they could look after me. But God, the drugs were strong—I'm still woozy from them. And then that old fool, Caradoc or Robinson? Yes, but it *was* Caradoc. It is touching in a way—I saw how clumsily, how shakily he had tried to escape, to leave his body behind so to speak. Why on earth should he do it? The firm is everything to me; it's a livelihood, and a creative way of earning one. And yet, Felix, and yet. . . ."

He gazed at me with sallow concentration from the fireplace, fingering the bruises on his forehead and sucking his teeth. "Another thing I didn't know I'd noticed until after we set sail was the sort of house he was living in there. It wasn't like most of the architecture of the place—it was canted up on piles. You don't remember, do you, how Caradoc used to talk about the theory of Sarasin that the proportions of the Parthenon corresponded in a way to the pile-buildings in Celebes? He used to go on quite a lot about it, and often drew it in the sand for us. No, you've forgotten? Well, anyway, it's this sort of shape if I remember rightly." He took out a coloured pencil and sketched in the following figure on the back of a newspaper.

No, I had never seen it before. "Ah well" said Pulley with resignation. "That was what he had been building for himself. It would prove nothing to anyone else, but to someone who knew Caradoc it would be conclusive. You see, he just could not resist making mnemons and building houses. Try as he would. And he'll always be found out because of it." He paused for a while, finished his drink, and said "I don't know whether I told them all this, I couldn't judge. All that Julian said when he was thanking me was 'Well, the case is closed, then.' But did he mean it, that's the point? Ah! That's the point."

The case is closed. "I don't know" said Pulley. "Perhaps we should act out ourselves more." He strolled about fiddling with things on the tables and mantelpiece. "But I could never dream of trying to get out" he said sadly. "But in your case, Felix, I——"

"Me?" I said with some indignation. "Why pick on me?"

"I wasn't; but somehow I have always wondered about you—from way back at the beginning I mean. Whether you really belonged here, with us."

"Well I'm damned" I said, and the surprise was genuine. It was suddenly borne in upon me that there must, after all, somewhere, be people who didn't belong to the firm. Pulley showed his huge teeth in an infantile grin. "You are one of the few people" he said "one can honestly distrust in this outfit. I would confide anything in you, I think."

"And you feel I should get out somehow?"

"O, I didn't say that exactly. I don't know quite what I feel about anything any more, I'm so damn tired after all this drugging. And I still occasionally get the weeps for nothing at all. So don't ask me leading questions. Besides, Felix, is there really *time* to worry? One minute you are fretting over your income tax, and the next you are staring up from the bottom of a pinewood coffin. Heavens, stay put, old boy, stay put."

"Stay put, you tell me now."

"Well, unless you feel too hampered. Lots of us do. The weak usually resort to acts of senseless violence. I remember old Trabbe—he ran out with a fireman's axe one day and buried it in Julian's car. But they cured him and sent him abroad. And poor Mrs. Trabbe—after she died the servants started wearing her frocks and shoes, surprising everyone and giving pain. O well!" He yawned and stretched. "I must be getting along now. It's been good to see you; we must meet again soon, eh? When things don't feel so damned precarious."

His eyes had a haunted look which somehow I misliked; his walk, too, was the walk of an old man. I accompanied him to the door and suggested that he might like to move in with me for a few weeks, but he shook his head slowly. "Ah thanks" he said. "But no. Cheerio."

I stood at the door and watched him wander off down the street towards the nearest tube station. He did not turn round and wave on the corner as was once his wont.

*   *   *   *   *

I had some difficulty in running Julian to earth—if that is the expression—but at last I found him week-ending somewhere in the country. My call caught him in mid yawn. "Ah good, it's you Charlock" he said. "I was wondering who it might be."

"Julian" I said "I've come to a decision which I want to discuss with you. In itself it may not seem very important, but it is extremly so to me." Julian coughed and said: "Well you know you can always count on me." It sounded not at all sententious. I took a breath and went on. "I have decided to give one of my inventions away to the public—to *give* it away, do you see? Simply, unequivocally donate it." He said nothing, and after a pause I went on. "Recently in playing about with some chemistry work in the lab I tumbled upon something which one might really describe as a boon to the ordinary housewife. It costs nothing, or almost nothing to make. It will completely transform washing-up."

"Well, for goodness sake take out a pat——"

"Ah but listen. This I propose to *give* away. I propose to write a letter to *The Times* describing how anyone can, for the price of a pennyworth of common salt, make this. . . ."

The timbre of Julian's attention seemed to shift and deepen. He sighed, and I heard a match click, followed by a puff. "I'm glad you decided to discuss it with me first before doing anything" he said. "What is the point of it, after all? At a penny halfpenny it would still be a boon—as a Merlin patent. Do you think we are dealing hardly by the public? By comparison with other firms I should have thought. . . ."

"That has nothing to do with it. I simply feel that for once in my life I must make this gesture, *give* something freely, you see; something which is the fruit of my thought, so to speak. Can't you see?"

"I follow what you mean" he said coolly. "But nevertheless I can't

283

quite see the motive. You have given the world so much through the firm, Charlock."

"Not given, Julian. That's the point. Sold."

"There is a pleasing touch of religiosity about your idea" he said dryly. "I commend you." He sounded serious but weary.

"I know it sounds trivial; but for me it represents something momentous, something I haven't been able to imagine for years—an act."

"The married man dreams of divorce" he said oracularly, and I recognised a Greek proverb in translation. "And the scientist thinks of science as a pretty girl with two cunts. . . ." He was wandering, playing for time. Then a little more sharply came: "What am I supposed to do about this idea—agree? How can I, Charlock? Indeed I wonder why you consulted me. You know that you are raising much more than a personal question? It smells of precedent. Indeed whatever I said, I doubt if the firm would agree: and I am not the firm, as you know, only one of the camel-drivers, so to speak, in the general caravan. Anyway thanks for being honest enough to tell me what was in your mind."

"I always felt I could talk to you as man to voice" I said.

"Irony was always your long suit, Charlock. Always."

"Anyway, now you know what I've decided."

Julian cleared his throat softly and let a pause intervene; when he came back to the charge he was dreamy, reflective, unincisive. "I wonder if you have really thought about it—no, it's a pure impulse of generosity on your part."

"On the contrary: the fruit of a long interior debate."

"Hum. Have you considered, for example, your articles of association with the firm? This would cut across our agreement which is valid, if I remember, for some twenty years more at least."

"Twenty years." A shiver ran down my spine. Yes, I knew it all right—but uttered out loud like that it produced a chilling effect.

"It wouldn't work" said Julian at last in a more wide-awake voice. "It would lead to some costly and tedious litigation, that's all. And you'd lose, the firm would win. Contractually you are tied for everything."

"We shall see" I said, but I felt my voice falter. Julian went on

284

suavely: "You know don't you that there is a whole string of charities supported by us in part or in full? Merlin's staff are encouraged to contribute to them—why don't you? You could make over the whole of your salary to them if you wished. Ask Nathan to show you the bound volume with the lists."

"I've seen it." I had. There was a huge vellum tome the thickness of the Bible listing all the charities to which the firm contributed.

"Well" said Julian. "Wouldn't that do?"

"No."

"Why not?" He was almost peevish now.

"We get Income Tax relief on those—it's a company ploy."

"I see! My goodness, you are hard to please."

He puffed away another long silence and then asked: "What is the source of all this unrest, Charlock; where does it come from?"

"I have simply come to a point where I must make a gesture, even the feeblest of free gestures, to continue breathing."

"It must be due to some misconception about the nature of the firm. I feel in all you say a funny kind of moral bias—an implied criticism which cannot be wholly just. Are you just being pharisaical, holier-than-thouish?"

"No, I'm being holier-than-meish for a change."

"What I'm trying to say is that the firm isn't just an extension of moral qualities, a product of a wicked human will, of a greedy mercantile spirit. It goes deeper than that. I mean, it has always existed in one form or another. At least I suppose so."

"What a sophistry! The firm is not the world."

"I'm not so sure. I'm not saying it's an easy thing or a gay thing; but it's a fact of nature, man's nature. One can't blink the firm, Charlock."

"Nature!"

"It must correspond to some deep unexpressed need of the human psyche—for it's always been there. We should take it more coolly. It's not in itself malefic, it is just neutral, a *repoussoir*. It's what we make of it. . . ."

"So the slave is born with his chains, is he?"

"Yes. Some can free themselves, but very few. I couldn't. If you believe in free will or predestination, for example——"

285

"Cut out the homilies" I said.

"Well, who imposed the firm on you, then?"

"I did. Out of ignorance."

"Not really; everything was clear from the beginning; your eyes were wide open."

"Like a three-day kitten."

"I don't see how you can want to back down at this stage."

"Even in prison they get remission for good behaviour."

"But damn it, you might wake up one day and find yourself in charge of the firm, or most of it; Jocas and I won't live for ever, you know."

"God forbid!"

Julian said "Ach!" in an exasperated sort of way and then became mild again. "The firm isn't inflexible" he said, with a faint tinge of reproach. "Despite its size it is a pretty fragile thing, a bundle of long wires stretching out around the world. But it is all based on one slender item—the spinal column of the matter: that is the sanctity of contractual obligation. If you abrogate that you begin to damage the essential fabric of the thing. Naturally it will try to protect itself like any other organism."

"I *must* do this thing, I tell you."

"You will end up by building up a delusional system about being persecuted by the firm—the poor thing does not merit it."

I ground my teeth.

"Anyway," he went on "there is no pressure the firm can bring upon you in the immediate sense; but it would certainly counter any such move as the one you have outlined. It's strange, you still seem to think of it in terms of personalities; but it has long ago outgrown the personalities which created it—Merlin, Jocas, myself: we are already merely ancestors. The firm is self-subsisting now, rolling down its appointed path with a momentum which neither you nor I can alter. Of course he that is not with it is against it, and so on. In other epochs it might have taken other forms. But man rests, unchangeable, unteachable, and the firm is cast in his mould—*your mould, Charlock*! Ask and it shall be answered! Prod the old sow with a stick and it grunts." He paused and his voice sank softly into the tones of a twilit resignation. Under his breath, in a whisper which I could just catch,

286

I heard him say: "And Iolanthe is dying?" He sighed, he was talking to himself. A long silence fell.

"You are still there, Charlock?"

"Yes."

"Well, I think all this must come from your sense of impotence aggravated by success; such feelings always result in rash moral judgements. You have never succeeded in doing the abstract work for which you pined—though that was not our fault. And you have worked up a grudge against the firm in telling yourself that it is caught up in the nets of base matter, is exploring and adapting matter, expropriating matter."

"And the results?"

"My dear, I can do nothing, nobody can. Yes, we can make small adjustments of stress or direction or emphasis. But the wheel turns in spite of one. Come, grow up, Charlock. The firm won't bite, you know."

"I am still waiting to be convinced" I said grimly. "All this is special pleading."

It was, of course; and yet in another way it wasn't. It made sense on one level. nonsense on another. I had not yet succeeded in penetrating to the basic fallacy in these contentions. In a funny way, too, I thought him—Julian personally—innocent of any intention to delude. He believed what he said, and consequently it was true, not for me, but for him. Perhaps even objectively true? My reason was spinning like a top. The vertiginous sense of failure was so intense that it had got mixed up with my breathing. I was suffocated. I heard Julian put down the receiver and walk away a few steps; then in the silence I heard some music begin to play—the opening bars of a Schumann concerto. "As an honourable man," he said "who abhors all exaggeration, I do not know what to tell you."

How many of these ideas would remain waterproof? I wondered. Julian was sighing again. "What about Iolanthe?" I said cruelly. (Marchant said that ideas were simply nags; one rode about on them until one tired of them, then tied them to a tree and fucked them.) "Iolanthe" he repeated slowly, accenting the word wrongly. "What of her?" In my almost drunken state I could not resist a further threat. "A creation of the soap-flakes mind" I said. "Nobody would believe it to see her picture in your flat." Julian smiled invisibly. "An artist" he said, and "A smile to make one rise in one's stirrups."

"I might even leave England," I said "where the national sloth has reached the brain cortex."

Julian coughed. All of a sudden his voice became bony and determined; a sort of cold fury possessed it: "There is only one solution for you—to stop inventing altogether; to retire on your winnings—I will not call them earnings, for without us you would be penniless today. Abandon the game altogether." Then his voice changed again; it sank into a lower register, it became merciful, tender, calm. He whispered almost to himself. "Who can gauge the feeling of a man in love who is forced to sit and look on at the steady deterioration of a fine mind and lovely body? We must celebrate the people who set us on fire."

"Julian" I cried. "Is this your last word?"

"What else?" he said with such world-weariness, such inexpressible sadness, that I felt a lump come into my throat. Yet at the same time gusts of rage and frustration were still there in my mind, I could not still them. "Mountebank! Actor!" I jeered. Yet he did not seem to have heard me—or at any rate the insults produced no recognisable reflection in his tone.

"Graphos" he said "could only love a weeping girl. If she did not weep she must be made to—so he said." All of a sudden I recalled a chance remark of Io's to the effect that only the free man can really be loved by a woman; I wondered which of us she might have in mind? Ah which?

I had said it before I knew the words were out of my mouth— without any premeditation whatsoever. "Julian, for how long has Benedicta been your mistress, and what is the name of the drug?" I heard him draw his breath sharply as if I had run a thorn under his fingernail. "Do you hear me?" I said lurching about drunkenly and laughing coarsely. Silence from his end. It was war now to the very knife, I felt it. Yet the silence prolonged itself into infinity as I stood there. "Julian," I said again "you don't need to tell me; I shall find out from her." There was the dry crisp click of the receiver going down, that was all; and I stood with the sea-shell of emptiness to my ear, mumbling to myself; for somehow these stupid remarks had set fire to my mind, illuminating a whole new area of unmapped action. The key—*of course*—the key to everything was Benedicta! I could do nothing that did not encapsulate her consent, her agreement. Before any problem could be settled I must settle the problem of this wife of mine. "By God" I said to myself as suddenly the fact dawned upon me. "Of course." How unjust I had been to her! I was filled with remorse all of a sudden. I had never really talked to her, explained to her, tried to enlist her support for my plans . . . I must rush to her side to explain everything.

But by the time I reached her Benedicta had already taken one of her characteristic leaps forward into triumphant unreason, eluding more successfully than ever the vain pursuit of her doctors or her lovers.

The slim three and a half litre Lethe lay outside the office—a birthday present from the firm; its glossy black snout pointed down-street like a lance laid in rest. This elegant missile could sway silently through traffic, and climb effortlessly into the hundreds with a faint blue snarl. For the most part it made only the noise of cremated silk —which is to say, no noise whatsoever. Its brief insistent horn copied the note of a trumpeting goose. I tell you the intoxication of driving this deft shooting-star across London soothed away my anxieties. Cool winds came off the river at Hammersmith; cloudy sunshine feathered out the last of the daylight. It would be dark before I arrived. It was dark when I did.

The house presented its usual aspect of tenantless animation—as if the owners had gone out to the pub for a drink leaving all the lights on, the radio on, the fires unguarded. It was the servants' day off no doubt. The lake was still. In the vague enthusiasm of my self-discovery (that I still had the power to conceive of independent actions) I was ill prepared for anything out of the ordinary. I could think about nothing but my own feelings: about how to make them clear to poor Benedicta. So much so that I hardly took in at first the bloody spoor which here and there marked the scarlet staircase-carpet; nor the trail of dummy books which lay anyhow on the landings—an obscure paperchase of empty titles like *Decline and Fall* and *Night Thoughts* and *The Consolations of Philosophy*. Up I went and up: not sufficiently attentive to be alarmed, more puzzled. Yet here

T

and there—it was like following a wounded lion to its lair—I came upon a red pug-mark freshly impressed in the carpet. What could it mean? How on earth could I guess that Benedicta had been at that double toe of hers with a kitchen knife?

Well, the bedroom door was ajar and pushing it softly open I entered, to stand upon the threshold and contemplate the new Benedicta in her latest yet oldest role. I vaguely surmised that her period had surprised her, that was all. But everything was quite different. She was standing on the bed naked, her arms raised in rapture, her face burning with gratitude and adoration; it was clear that the ceiling had burst open to reveal the heavens, clouded and starry, with its vast frieze of angels and demons—figures of some great Renaissance Annunciation. The ceiling had withdrawn, had become the inverted bowl of the heavens. She was talking to the figures—at least her lips were moving. In the heavy pelt of the bed you could not discern the torn foot. She was surrounded by an absolute snowdrift of paper, torn up very small. Most of it was my transcripts I suppose—I recognised the paper I use for dactyl. But there were other things, letters on lined paper. Cupboards hung open with clothes pouring from them. Her dressing table was cluttered with fallen cosmetics. The elegant little leather boxes with trees—her *postiche* and wig boxes—lay about poking their tongue out at us. It was memorably silent. The trance could have been indefinitely prolonged, one felt; the figures in the frieze held up their hands to bless, or to point to breasts, or crowns of thorns. But they were benign, they were on her side, and her tears flowed down her cheeks in gratitude. In the bubble of this enormous concentration there was simply no room for me, nor for my preoccupations. I stood gaping at this tableau until she caught sight of me out of the corner of her eye and turned slowly in a puzzled way—the wonder widening in concentric rings upon her white face, as if I had thrown a stone into a pool. I suppose I must have stammered out something for she stared keenly at me and then put a finger to her lips. A look of sudden panic intervened now with astonishing rapidity and clutching her ears she screamed one: "I've gone deaf." Then just as suddenly dropped her hands, calmed and smiled wickedly.

This called for restraint of some sort, though nothing could be more angelic than the cool sweet smile of the demon. Underneath it, too, far down below the surface one recognised the look of a wounded animal, say a cat which tries to say: "I have a thorn in my foot. Please help." Borne on a clumsy tide of scattered and conflicting emotions I surged awkwardly forward, mumbling, arms outspread in the travesty of an embrace, unsure what the contents of my gesture might be—to embrace, to restrain, to comfort? All three, I suppose. In the corner there was a telephone torn out of the wall which hinted at strength which that slender body did not appear to own. "You see how it is?" she whispered, and slipped from the bed to elude my arms. The operation was more delicate and awkward than I had supposed; like when a swallow flies into a room and one tries to expel it without damaging or frightening the creature. Well, so we walked round, full of an awkward stateliness. Once or twice I almost caught up with her; her attention jumped for a moment from me to other objects in the room. But it was never absent for long, and she continued to elude me in a deft unhurrying fashion. And so out on the landing, with only a pause to topple a small statuette; and down the long staircase, saturated in the loneliness of this dreadful situation. Where the devil was everyone? Normally the house was full of servants. She slipped through doors, shutting them behind her to delay me; as I entered I would see her leaving the room from the far end, still looking at me over her shoulder to make sure I followed, expressionlessly seductive. She was heading steadily across the mansion towards the eastern side—towards, in fact, the old gunroom with its glass cases stocked with weapons. My concern deepened, my pace increased, but she held her distance. Then, as she disappeared into the gunroom she managed to find a key to turn. I was locked out. Under the noise of my impotent banging and cajoling I could hear the sliding doors of the glass cases being opened; then a crackle of paper and carton which instantly translated itself into a vision of Benedicta stripping a cartouche of shells. There were several drawers full of them. I began to sweat; then I remembered that there was a second door, a mere hatch, which led into a tiny bar built into the corner of the room. This was a swing-door, and I rushed for it; but the delay had given her just enough time, and when I barged through it was to see her quietly slipping out from the further end of the room with a gun under her arm.

She had chosen the second ballroom—the huge gilt one—now polished like a skull and empty of everything but its mirror and grand piano. She was standing in the centre of it, waiting for me to appear in the doorway, quite calm and composed. A few streaks of blood only—toes are relatively bloodless—marked her progress across the polished floor. But there she lounged, as if waiting for the machine to flick clay pigeons into the sky. It was no use calling her name. Inevitably, too, I feared at that instant that her target would be myself, framed by the gilt doorway in all my ineffectualness. But if by any chance the idea had not entered her head, I did not wish to provoke it by a sudden move. I stood rooted, expecting to receive the twelve-bore charge in the stomach; but she swung up and away and round, confronting the long chain of mirrors which lined the sombre room. As she let fly she began to recite the Lord's Prayer in a shaky broken voice—a small thread of sound among the explosions. "Our Father which art" (bang) "in heaven hallowed" (bang) "be thy name" (bang). And so forth. She had picked upon a repeating pump-gun, a six-shot. The noise of the smokeless shots was deafening, wit-scattering. I felt dizzy and faint, all my impressions fused together in a dazzle; and yet with the part of one's mind which remains attentive and critical I could not help noticing the voluptuous thwack with which the charge bust into the mirrors, embedding itself deep in the reality of the non-mirror world, shattering her image. A plump sound like someone beating up a swansdown pillow.

The rest doesn't translate so very well. I had picked up, I don't know how or where, a short ashplant—perhaps with some vague instinct of self-defence. I suppose I rushed at her—but it must have been with the toppling sliding motions of someone on ice, for the floor was glossy. Vaguely something in the nature of a football-tackle. I locked my arms round the defiant nakedness and together we stumbled and fell to the ground, the gun pressed between us. Indeed, the last discharge went off as we were falling and its hot breath burned my forehead; the barrel was fiendish hot too. So we rolled over and over until she released it and sent it skittering across the floor. Then to my surprise I began to beat her with my own weapon, but beat her precious hard across the back and buttocks. A sort of voluptuous rage must have possessed me—I was beating Julian, I suppose. And for her part she lay, pale and with an expression of content almost, eyes shut, lips moving in prayer—like someone accepting a well-merited punishment. It was frightening, also sexually exciting in a dim sort of way. But an end was soon put to this disgraceful scene, for by now the room was filling up with people.

The two governesses were upon us, witch-like and purposeful in their rusty black clothes; they hardly spoke as they set about separating and shackling us. Then frightened supers like Baynes, gobbling and swallowing. And lastly fussy Nash with his calamitous concern.

I was sick and feverish and upset—and now very much out of place in all this babble. Nor was the solace of strong drink very much in keeping with so hysterical a mood. I could not sleep in spite of it. I lay awake most of the night, listening to the faint sounds which betokened more purposeful activities than my own in other parts of the house; the telephone ringing, the voice of Nash. "Yes, he's here. I've put him to bed." I laughed grimly to myself and shook my fist at the ceiling. It did not need much imagination to translate the keening of rubber tyres on gravel in the first dawn-light; that would be the limousine with the drawn blinds. Soon Benedicta would be beginning that eternally repeated journey back to the land of the archetypes. "Our Father which art in heaven". By craning my head out of the window I could verify these hypotheses. The child would be in front with the harpies. Benedicta would be carried, heavily veiled, like a statue of the Virgin Mary. I don't say it wasn't all for the best. I don't say it wasn't all for the best. *Om.*

＊　　＊　　＊　　＊　　＊

VI

Human attention is fragile and finite; won't be mastered; can't be bribed; is always changing.... Ah, for one moment of that total vision which might reorder the whole field and make it significant. I suppose from the outside it must have seemed like a progressive melancholia —I mean, resigning from the firm (no reaction to this) and locking myself up in the country in a desperate attempt to abdicate, along the lines suggested by Julian. *Not to invent any more.* Somehow one day one must try and stop being one's own little hero—eh Charlock? You can do it for a year or two at most without faltering. It's all very well, solitude and misanthropy. The beard I grew was patched with white; it gave me a startled look. I had to buy heavier lenses for my glasses. I was drinking a good deal and smoking too much. But it was a pleasure to let my appearance run to seed, to wear torn pullovers and knee-bulged grey bags. Nor was I completely cut off, except from Julian; he was biding his time, I supposed. I spoke to others on the phone, long conversations full of *non sequiturs*, yes, and common-room pleasantries. And all the time, unknown to my conscious me, that bloody old mass of wires I have called Abel was maturing. A certain resignation set in, too, walking about in the snow, hammering out Bach, skating in a deep muse upon the frozen waters of the lake. Well, so be it; if I must occupy myself, what better way? Besides, who would ever understand poor Abel, his foggy calculus of human potentials based upon the first cave-man chirp of the human voice? I was also preparing my revenge on Julian.

You may say that such an instrument could not possibly predict; but the future is only the memory of the past extended into the future. The backside of the moon of memory, if you like. The pre-diction of stars in the sky as yet undiscovered by the lens—that is a fair analogy. From the birth-cry to the death-rattle most lives can be plotted. I shall spare myself the eight lines of maths which resume

297

this statement—crisp pothooks, shell of the cosmic egg. How little one needs to divine the human potentials in a single given life; translate through vibrations back to memory and thence to situation. Something the pundits of the firm will not fathom. When they take Abel apart they will be left with a mute collection of wires, like a human skeleton. Where is the soul of the machine? they will cry. Ah me! An invention as singular, original and definitive as the telescope. *E pur si muovi*, and so on.

The proof was in the pudding; and I had a pitifully small abacus to work with—just the people who had collided with me like rogue stars: just their sayings, visions, and the few facts I knew about them. I took over the big musicians' gallery for my keyboard, mounting the long and complicated panel of my fascia in the manner of some huge cinema organ; behind it was the library with its transmuting system. What is better than reading the stars? Why, listening to them in their transports of love and pain, music of the spheres echoed by diluted animals. It all grew out of my little magnetic boxes—a lot of it scratchy as hell. Sitting there in the tremendous loneliness of the silent house (I had sent most of the servants away) I sat, a lean and bearded man, switching from life to life. It took ages, of course; more than three years before I managed to obtain the first coherent response to my data. In this way I hoped to prosecute the opening moves of my war upon Julian—my persecution of this hidden man. I had thought of other things, but they were schoolboy pranks— messages in invisible ink slowly printing themselves on astonished blotters. But Abel was better. With him I could scry and scan. Much of it was not very palatable—but is truth ever palatable? I discovered much too about myself, about my inadequacy with women. O it was terrible to see the real truth about Benedicta; she was to be pitied, not to be hated. And the quiet Iolanthe's death-bed cry: "How little I have managed to live, and that always in hotels. There never seemed to be enough time, and now. . . ." I should have carried off these women in my teeth to devour them at leisure on a piece of waste ground. But then women cannot help being predatory—to take up with one is to inherit a mink farm.

Mark came, my son—how strange the word sounds! But he sheered away from me, sneaking round corners to avoid encounters.

I saw him, a pale thin little creature with sticking-out ears, walking solemnly to church between those two black harpies, as if between warders. It was clear that they had had their instructions. The boy was doing some sort of preparatory work for an entrance exam though still barely out of kindergarten. I could pick him up on Abel, but dimly. I saw him, *heard* him, sitting at my desk in Merlin's—a pale small-boned young man with a widow's peak. But that lay far ahead as yet, after my own . . . disappearance. This was foggy, with more than a hint of suicide about it. But talking of suicide, since the word has cropped up, I remember Mark's own little effort. I was working very early one morning when I happened to glance out of a window in time to see him walking down towards the lake. The earliness of the hour struck me—it was barely light. He had a slice of bread in his hand and was apparently about to feed the swans. I was about to turn away when something about his walk aroused my curiosity; it was so stiff and stilted, as if he were forcing himself to advance by sheer will-power. A moment later and he has walked right into the icy water, wading slowly outwards. Heavy sleet was falling. I shouted twice but he did not turn. Suddenly the comprehension of what he was doing dawned upon me and I raced for the door. The cold struck one amidships. He was moving steadily into the deeper reaches, already almost up to his neck. In spite of the blazing freeze I plunged after him, gasping with pain. I just reached his head as the water rose to his mouth, and grabbed him. He was blue and contorted with cold, crying and snickering. I half pushed the little creature into my shirt and crawled laboriously back to land with him, myself half fainting from the cold. Through his little blue prawn lips he was saying "They are trying to keep me away from you." Over and over again. I plunged for the downstairs bathroom with its hot taps, in a delirium of cold and anguish; plunging him into the hot water to soothe his numbed limbs. Then I slumped down on the bidet opposite him and wept; I wept my way right back to my solitary childhood, back to the breast, back into the very womb which is the only memory we know about. He wept too, but commiseratingly; and presently I felt his small pale hand touching my head, patting me, consoling me. I did not need to ask who or what was trying to keep him from me. So we sat for an age, staring at each other. Then I towelled his pink frail body back to life, alarmed at his slenderness, his shallow lungs. Our clothes fumed upon the radiators. Waiting for them to dry I said "Would you like to work with me on Abel?" and his eye lit with a frail gleam. He sighed: "They wouldn't let me." "Then they mustn't know, Mark, that is all. You must find times like this, too early or too late for them."

And so it was, he became my famulus, sneaking down before first light to spend two engrossing hours among my lights and wires. It was difficult at first to teach him the first principles of the thing; but later he mastered the whole system and crawled about my organ-loft like a powder-monkey.

"What is Abel really?"

"Well, one day you will want to know about us all, about your past and mine, about your future."

"Will I?"

"Almost certainly. Everyone does. Here look at the programme manual—do you see the different bays marked 'When' 'Who' 'Why' 'Where' and 'If'."

"*If?*" he said with surprise. "Why *If?*"

"It's the most important question of all in a way—it can change all the others: just one tiny grain of *If*."

It was a pleasure too to have someone to talk to; and as we worked I gave him the whole pedigree of Abel, starting with the *Theaetetus* and its block of wax in the human soul eager to imprint itself with every perception, thought, emotion; the whole theory of Platonic memory and all that blubber to which the child listened with wonder and a certain understanding. The only thing was that I had to warn him against the Julian dossier—how to be careful; because when I had finished with Julian I knew he would walk into my trap and come down to find out what there was to know about himself. What man could resist reading a secret report on himself? It was the second panel on the left with an inviting red button. I pushed it open for Mark—in order to make certain that he understood—and to-gether we stared into the barrels of the loaded twelve-bore I had lashed to a stand and wired for action. I would leave this behind me when I left. Mark gazed at it wonderingly, and then at me, his small blue eyes narrowed as he tried to assess the meaning of this present.

But he said nothing. "You won't give me away?" I said, feeling so sure of his love for me. He shook his head proudly.

So we opened up several of the channels and completed the elaborate programmes which would bring them to life—if that is the scientific word. I don't know when I have been so happy. Nor was the business kept a secret; Nash came and had it all explained to him. He looked very strange, declared that he understood, and tiptoed away again. If he did not tap his head significantly before my eyes he perhaps did it before the eyes of others. Marchant also came—but he turned pale and gnawed his lip, whether from jealousy or contempt I do not know. Yes I do, though. I had pitifully little on him and I hadn't really assorted the field with any thoroughness but up in the predicter came the word "plagiarism". I wanted all this guff to filter back slowly to Julian, and it did. But that was only the beginning.

Then unluckily Mark was caught; one of the harpies in a wizard's dressing-gown stood sibilating in the doorway of the gallery. "Mark, you have been *told* over and over *again*." She reached out a hand like a spade. I watched with a sort of recondite insolence, tipping the bottle of lemonade to my lips. Mark allowed himself to be led tamely away, head high, lips white, ears pink—the captive rabbit. It seemed useless to protest, so I did nothing, secure in his confidence. He stepped high and proud, and did not turn his head to say goodbye.

Well: and then what? Why, a whole winter lay before me of ordering and scrying—on a much firmer wicket than John Dee ever was. Fires blazed everywhere, the snow blanketed everything. And now *Julian* was being persecuted. His *own* voice was ringing him up! "Is that Julian?" "Yes." "This is Julian too." It had been pretty largely given out that Abel was some sort of electronic hoax; but truth is relative. It was far less accurate than I would have liked to hope, but nevertheless I found I could use it. After all, the planchette is no good without the hand, the crystal ball without the sorcerer's eye. Yes, I could see backwards and forwards along the tragic ellipse of these segmented lives, to come up now and again with partial fragments of truth. At times my nets were full; at times I had to empty the small fry back into the stream. Goodness, but enough came up to fill Julian with alarm. He tried to ring me several times, and I was delighted by the concealed agitation in his tones. How did I know what I knew? Truth to tell, by the merest divination in the name of Abel. It took hardly any time to convince and disturb him because I fell upon some trivia which proved themselves accurate within days of Julian's voice telling him. Perhaps all this might prove a useful guide to the stock market or the race-course? I made Julian ask Julian this in a slightly bitter tone. But then inexorably I began to edge towards his private life—the field of his emotions and hopes. Ah, I wanted to reduce him slowly, with infinite slowness; already I scented his weakness. He was like a drowning man. At times too I was overcome with remorse to be so brutal, for now he was really suffering. And I brought the whole weight of my tortures to bear upon the sick Iolanthe, upon her silent native death. He had heard enough by now to suspect that the rest might well become true. And then Graphos too: the sad footsteps of Hippo echoing on the lino of some gravid hospital corridor. The ignominy of the acetone breath, the legs gradually filling up, turning gangrenous. So carefully kept, those legs, in grey woollen socks. He had been *warned* not to try and cut his own toenails, for the slightest wound. . . . But Graphos was not used to obeying others. He always knew better.

I had written to Iolanthe, promising to exorcise her house provided she came with me; but the letter arrived too late and she burned it along with many others. All this comes of a strange meeting I was to have with Mrs. Henniker on the Zürich plane. Her face had been hollowed out by suffering, scaled and pared to the bone by the sleepless nights she had spent at the bedside of Io. The tall steel bed against a window full of Alpine stars and tumultuous grass. One candle burning before an ikon—no need to say which. Shaken by a kind of involuntary sobbing which contained no more tears—she had used them all up. At first nobody knew except Julian *of course*. Whenever she was ill she was registered at three different clinics in order to enjoy some peace and anonymity at a fourth. Well, there by candlelight reciting her past and peering with those wild enlarged eyes into the fastnesses of the future, the pinewood coffin. *Tunc.*

It was so slow, the simple declining into the final pens of sleep, without too much pain, too many numbed regrets. Rolling down the green slopes of death, moving faster and ever faster, turning through the slow spirals of consciousness towards the heart of the fire opal. All night long now Mrs. Henniker sat beside the bed, her stone-coloured eye fixed upon the face of the white woman who had become her daughter; all night upright in an uncomfortable steel chair, the whole building silent around her, save for the shuffling shoes of the night-nurse—one for the whole floor. From time to time the patient's eyes would open and wander about the ceiling as if seeking for something. Her lips might move a little, perhaps even tenderly smile. I would have liked to think—I *did* think—that she was picturing both of us crossing to her father's island in the blue fishing-boat. A church, cypresses, sand-coloured jetty, box-dwellings of coloured whitewashes, the pink-toed pigeons crooning. Up and ever up to the abandoned barn where his whole life had been lived, had completed its simple circle. The well overgrown with moss now, the marble well-head grooved by the cable which for centuries had drawn up the sweet water. One loose stone extracted revealed the hiding-place of the key. Let us suppose we entered on tip-toe—entered the smelly gloom of the apple-charmed room full of unbroken cobwebs—the room he died in. Somewhere along the line, at this exact point, everything about my life threatens to become successful; everything takes a turn for the better. A fresh wind fills the sails—so Abel tells me, but always adding the rider "a delusion like so many others, that's all". Then the field goes blank again and the hints about suicide come up. It would not last, you see: could not last.

Well, on and on she sits, Mrs. Henniker with her hanky screwed up in her hand, her red horse-face gleaming with sweat. If I could convey with how much dazzling longing I gazed upon the face of Iolanthe dead—why everything would burst apart, catch fire, disintegrate. The little green book which fell from the bed had no underlining in it to serve as a guide-line to her last thoughts—perhaps she did not have many. Henniker carried it away for me, together with a lock of that famous hair—the sentimental relics which human children so cherish: the evidences of memory which are supposed to endure as long as the last unshed tear. Her eyes, did they fall upon the passage which I was now reading out, my own lips moving stiffly along the lines? "*Vous êtes lié fatalement aux meilleurs souvenirs de ma jeunesse. Savez-vous qu'il y a plus de vingt ans que nous nous connaissons? Tout cela me plonge dans les abîmes de rêverie qui sentent le vieillard. On dit que le présent est trop rapide. Je trouve, moi, que c'est le passé qui nous dévore.*"

Perhaps it was the eyes of Julian rather which traced and retraced these faltering lines written in the hand of the ageing Flaubert; for Julian inevitably was there. He came in silently, unannounced, just after midnight, softly putting his briefcase on the floor. In her confusion Henniker saw only a batlike figure in a black suit and a soft black hat. He motioned her to silence and indicated that she might leave the patient to be guarded by him. Without a word all was understood. With a sigh Henniker crossed to the low divan and plunged into a deep sleep. One thing only she noticed. Iolanthe did not open her eyes at all, but all of a sudden her face quivered and her hand came softly across the white sheet towards Julian's small, childlike hand. So they sat silently with her feverish fingers resting upon his. Of course I asked how he *looked*, but her answers were vague; she had received a dozen conflicting impressions. Terribly tired and old, an ashen face, the crater of an extinct volcano; or else some great quivering bat of pain clinging by his wings to the steel-tubed chair. Or else. . . . But it is useless, useless. Whenever it is really necessary Julian appears, and one knows it: but often only after he has gone.

The night wore on and on into the milky opaqueness of dawn; the white fangs of snowscape glittered in all their fruitless splendour. All nature dozed and even Julian felt his head drooping. It must have been after one of these transitory cat-naps that he woke to feel the full massiveness, the charged weight, of her changed status. Death had made her fingers so heavy, it seemed, that he almost had to prize his own out from under them. Just that. He did not move any more. Mrs. Henniker snored faintly. He continued to stare intently at the white profile she presented to him with such motionless intentness. Even when a drowsy fly settled on the eyeball he could not move.

But they were not to be spared the final indignities which the press reserves for events such as these. Somehow the secret of her whereabouts had leaked out. The clinic was ill-equipped to protect itself against sixty such persecutors, especially at such a time of day. They burst through the swing doors with all the vulgar assurance of the tribe, overwhelming the dazed duty nurse, deaf to all protest. Some even climbed over the balcony from the garden. The candle-lit silence of the room was filled now by their hoarse reverent breathing, the shuffle of their feet, the hiss and splash of their bulbs. Even now Julian did not move; he sat exhausted in his chair. And in some singular way they did not notice him, for not a single glance or question was addressed to him; and in all the photographs which smeared the dailies of the world there was no trace of his presence—the chair seemed to be empty. Why go on? The planned obsolescence of the human body etc. Mrs. Henniker slept right through it and was only woken by a banged door. Julian had gone. "The unlucky thing" he said later "was her loving you; it was completely unsuitable, and anyway you did not care." I cannot answer these charges any more. A fearful horror and exhaustion seizes me. I am guilty of nothing—in fact that's really what I am guilty *not of*. Then later in the gutter-press to read of her grave being robbed. They said that fans had done it—it is true that fans will stop at nothing. At any rate it could hardly have been Julian; nor ordinary robbers, for her jewelry had not been touched. Hair, though; there is a high market value for the hair of a goddess. What she sought was not love but the frail combining of hopes with someone—but how was Henniker to know this? She had choked me with a phrase and I sat there staring at her feeling as if I had swallowed a toad.

It is very still here. *Om*. I said *Om*.

* * * * *

VII

It has been wearing, this brief period of lonely inertia in Athens, waiting for Koepgen to appear. I don't know why I felt I ought to see him before . . . before getting on with it. I kept an eye on the favourite tavern; that too is much the same. One window has fallen in, and the vine had got mildew. The widow is dead, but her son carries on. I have been walking about a good deal at night . . . the brutal velvet Athenian night with its harsh rancorous music and game-smells. I can't record thoughts any more, the spool seems to have run out. The whole bloody thing has begun to seize up in my head like an engine. And then, bang, tonight I ran into him—the pocket Silenus in the monkish gear. A streak of brindle in his hair. But no surprise at seeing me. We sat silently for a while devouring each other with our eyes; I noticed he was rather drunk and hastened to join him in that blessed state. "I knew you'd come." Nodding owlwise and tipping the blue tin can. "You want to hear about me, my story." I did actually. A vague nervous curiosity had possessed me, for in spite of my fairly extensive data upon Koepgen I could hardly get anything out of Abel except fictitious-sounding aphorisms. "The ikon and all that . . your farty fairy-tale." His eyes danced, he leaned his back against the whitewashed wall of the tavern. "My God, Charlock," he said "I am really free. I took ages to earn it, but I stuck it out and got an honest discharge. Free, my lad!"

I raised the wine can and almost let him have it on the crown of his head—so sick was I of the meaningless four-letter. "They've treated me very well" he said. "But that isn't the strangest thing. Yes, I found my ikon at last—and what I took to be some sort of mystical awakening waiting for me turned out to be the most prosaic thing imaginable." He laughed very heartily. "My father's will was gummed into the back of it, together with the deeds for our property in Russia—if ever they decide to give it back to us."

"Where, though?"

"Another fantastic thing—Spinalonga."

"The leper island? The one off Crete?"

"The very same. I got the Church to post me there when Jocas told me and sure enough I found it there. It was the damnedest thing. And it wasn't all. There was a little old man, one of the lepers, who was dying and I was asked to help send him down with all the usual formalities. But he took ages to die; and in his delirium he talked away whole nights. You know, he was English; he told me—what next? He told me he was *Merlin* himself."

"The devil he did."

"It was certainly his name; but how could I tell if he was THE Merlin or just someone of that name? Eh? But he knew a great deal about us all, about Benedicta, about you; and indeed he twice sent you a message through me. I am not lying, Charlock. Wait a second and let me recall." He guzzled some more wine with its bitter twang. Wiped his lips with bread and went on. "He said '*The firm only exists to be escaped from. Tell Charlock.*' What do you make of that? Then on another occasion he said: '*There are two kinds of death open to the living. Tell Charlock.*' " I sat looking incredulously at him, but feeling somehow cheered up in a confused way. We clapped hands for another beaker of the thought-provoker. "In his view he said the firm was something different for each of us; it was something like memory for you—its banked funds too great to be exhausted by promissory notes."

"To the devil with it all."

"I know what is in your mind" said Koepgen seriously. "But you ought to visit the little house before you decide. And you ought to realise that such an act——"

"Shut up, Koepgen" I growled, baring my fangs.

"I know, I apologise. The free should never moralise to the bound. Let's talk of something else. Let me tell you about a stroke of luck I have had; you remember the translations you helped me with? Of my poems? I sent them in anonymously to an agent. They have been accepted without any *piston* whatsoever. Straight off. Like that! I received the contract today. Look!" I took the wad of paper from him and glanced at it. Then I looked at him in slowly dawning horror.

The firm was Vibart's. The contracts were signed by Vibart's partner. Was it possible that the fool did not know? I stared keenly, reverently, tenderly into the eyes of the poor foolish little man and swallowed my Adam's apple a number of times. Should I tell him? "No" cried my *alter felix*. "Not a word."

"Well, we must drink another one on this", and Koepgen echoed my clanking pledge with his own, his eyes full of the tears of fulfilment. We sat until very late, until the violet sky went lilac and started to bleed; until the waiters were snoring on window-sills. Then we clambered down the hill past the Acropolis.

Well, I had made my decision. I would visit Io's house before deciding how and when.

*   *   *   *   *

Nash was always at a loss to account for the depression which welled up in him as his car turned slowly along the axis of the hill, along the double avenue of elms. But the man in the dark suit who sat beside him looked at it all with a studied coldness; Julian had been relatively silent for the first part of the journey down. But in the last few miles he had begun to muse again after his usual fashion. "It isn't beautiful" he said, as if reading Nash's thoughts. "I agree. The grandeur is too Byzantine. It could never be a home for anyone, I suppose." Nash changed gear, shaking his head. A frown anointed his cock-robin's face. "It's not her fault" he said. "She has made a wonderful recovery, you must agree; in spite of so much bad news, the death and so on."

Julian lit a cigar and said: "Presumption of death isn't quite the same thing. Without a body to show for it. You need as much body to die as to live. In the case of Charlock—we will have to wait upon the evidence. At any rate the Mediterranean always gives up its bodies. I think we'll find him, if he is to be found. It's only a matter of waiting awhile." He coughed and settled himself deeper in his seat. They had come down to inspect the curious toy in the musicians' gallery. ("An abacus of the intuition—can you make one?") That and other little matters had to be gone into. Julian went on softly "It's like those legends of the Hesychasts—to die and leave an empty grave. One must beware of Charlock."

"Oh dear, I don't know" said Nash and Julian replied coolly.

"You are not expected to know; you are expected to exist, to be."

"That's the whole trouble."

The lake was of dark and dirty jelly. The swans floated about like white lanterns. The paint had peeled along the benches. Under this lowering sky the skin of wet leaves lagged his tyres. Nash was fastidious as a cat when it came to his car; he could not bear things sticking to his paws. He found a stick to poke at them while Julian stood in the drive, debating heavily. "We will deal with the child first" he said softly. "He may know how the thing is booby-trapped, as obviously it must be. At least we can ask." Nash grunted. He had found a bracelet on the gravel, which he put into his overcoat pocket. The manservant let them in with a silent inclination of the head and they passed together down the long corridors and up the spiral staircase to the room where Julian proposed to interrogate Mark. Nash thumped heavily along behind him, puffing a little on the landings, with a curious air of fugitive derision on his face. "I'll go and see Benedicta, then" he said, and turning left where the landings intersected, marched away towards the bedrooms.

As usual Julian, that master of effect, had chosen a place of interrogation worthy of a practised inquisitor. It was an old cobwebby boxroom with a single uncurtained window looking out across the park. Here an oldfashioned high-backed chair had been placed facing the window—a chair with so tall a back that when Mark did come hesitantly into the room all he could see of Julian was a pair of white hands lying softly, negligently on the arms of the chair. Nothing else. The high back hid even his head. Mark had been marched down the corridors of the east wing by a nurse and introjected into the room at a given signal. He stood now, anxious and pale, with his feeble countenance made whiter than usual by the daylight outside. "Yes, Uncle Julian?" he said when his name was uttered. "Yes?"

Julian put on his slow, sauve reptilian voice, letting the words uncoil by themselves, musingly. "Mark, you helped our dear Felix build Abel, didn't you?"

"Yes."

"Is there a booby-trap of any sort in it: something that might explode and injure someone?"

Mark began to breathe very heavily and his face took on an unwonted expression of determination, of awkward resolution. The man in the tall-backed chair stayed heavily, ominously silent as if he wished to give time for some reaction to these inappropriate emotions to set in.

"I won't tell you. I promised" said the boy at last.

"Then if someone should get hurt you might be to blame?"

"I promised."

"Then if someone should get hurt you might be to blame?"

Mark watched the slow spirals of cigar smoke rise in the eddyless air of the musty room. "I am asking you" said Julian suddenly in a voice so sharp that the boy started. "I am asking you." Mark hung his head. He was hovering on the edge of tears now. Julian resumed his suave impartial voice. "Mark," he said with infinite slowness "you know the story of the Princes in the Tower?" Mark nodded and breathed out his "Yes" into the silent room. "Very well," said Julian "I'm glad you do. It's not a pretty story. Now, Mark, I am going to ask you something else. Is there any safe way of dismantling the trap?"

After a long interior struggle Mark once more delivered himself of his half-choked affirmation. "Good," said Julian "and you know how to do it, don't you?"

"Yes, Uncle Julian."

"And you will help us, won't you? We cannot afford to lose that machine by some clumsy accident."

"There's a switch" said Mark haltingly. "I was shown it."

Julian heaved a great sigh of relief. "Then that settles it" he said. "You will do it for us, won't you? You see, Professor Marchant and I want to have a look at the machine. It's a very beautiful and original work—the best thing Felix ever did. The firm can't afford to lose it. If you would do that this morning, I could come down this week with him and we could put it into motion."

A long, deafening silence fell. Mark stared at the spirals of smoke curving upwards towards the dirty ceiling.

"Very well, Uncle Julian. I'll do it now, if you wish."

"That's my boy" said Julian with relief. "That's a good boy."

"Can I go now?" said Mark.

"Of course you may."

"Goodbye, Uncle Julian."

"Goodbye, Mark, and thank you very much."

* * * * *

Benedicta was still convalescent, still only half up, half out of bed. She was forbidden to move about too much in case the palpitations set in again. Nash sat by the bed full of hopeful optimism. "You are very much better" he said, and reached for his small prescription pad and fountain pen. "We'll have you up and about in a day or two." She watched him carefully as he wrote with small feathery strokes of his pen. Her pale long face was set in a helmet of unkempt blonde hair. She was dressed in greensleeves fashion—a vague smock-gown with a gold rope sash round her slender waist: the attire of a Victorian poetess, one would have said. A small heart-shaped watch ticked on her breast, attached by a brooch in the form of an octopus. She half reclined, surrendering her pulse to Nash, brooding heavily the while.

"Marchant rang me up" she said abstractedly. "About all the tapes by Felix which they found on the beach with his clothes. He has been through them very carefully. The last one is a bit of a puzzle though. He says that there is something recorded which one *could* take for the sound of oars, a squeaky rowlock. But it's all very hazy. Do you think that Felix is really . . . ?"

"We can't think anything" said Nash hastily. "I was discussing it with Julian today. "We must wait. We have all the time in the world now, all the time in the world."

But it was when the dark shade of Julian stood before her, gazing at her from the foot of the bed, that Benedicta recovered some of her wonted animation of look; her eyes stared into his with a sweet burning intensity. His mere presence seemed to ignite her, to return her to the order of coherent things; her indisposition slid from her like a mummy-wrapping. "Julian" she said, and her voice took on a thrilling resonance.

"Mark is going to cooperate" he said in his lazy musing way.

"And that is one point we have cleared. Now then, for the rest, Benedicta: Nash and I both feel that as you have made such a splendid recovery we must take advantage of it. I have spoken to Jocas and he is quite on our side. You must have a decent rest. Go to Polis for a while and leave us to settle up all the details at this end. Will you?"

"If you wish" she said. "If you wish, Julian."

He rested his elbows on the end of the bed and looked down abstractedly at her pale beautiful face. "You could also be useful to us if you wish" he went on slowly. "There is a young German baron, a botanist, travelling about in Turkey with his yacht. He has found a flower which he says could give us something like perfect insect control in a natural way ... I won't bore you with the details. But the firm must try and secure him. You could take the provisional contracts with you when you go, so that Jocas can get to work persuading him. He seems rather doubtful about joining."

"Of course I will" she said with a curious furtive, wolfish look, beginning to bite her nails as she listened.

"But there's no hurry" said Julian. "We have all the time in the world, all the time in the world."

The sound of a distant report, muffled by the heavy walls of the building, was barely loud enough to pierce the hard integument of Julian's abstraction or of hers. She still stared at him with admiration and pity, and he gazed down at her as he had always done—his eyes full of an impenetrable sadness. It was left to Nash to sit up in his chair and say: "Surely that was a shot?"

AUTHOR'S NOTE

By intention this is the first deck of a double-decker novel. Here and there in the text attentive readers may discern the odd echo from *The Alexandria Quartet* and even from *The Black Book*; this is intentional.

NUNQUAM

NUNQUAM

à Claude Vincendon

I

Aut Tunc, aut Nunquam,
"It was then or never...."

Petronius
The Satyricon

Asleep or awake—what difference? Or rather, if there were a difference how would you recognise it? And if it were a recognisable difference would there be anything or anyone to care if you did or not—some angel with a lily-gilding whisper to say: "Well done."? Ay, there's the rub.

My head aches, it isn't only the wound—that is on the mend.

"Guilty in what you didn't know, what you hoped to escape merely by averting your face." Ah!

He wakes, then, this manifestation of myself so vaguely realised that it is hard to believe in him: he wakes in a room whose spare anonymity suggests one of the better-class hotels; no feudal furniture, no curtains smelling of tobacco or cats. Yet the towels in the bathroom are only stencilled over with a capital "p". The Bible beside the bed is chained to the wall with a slender brass chain; owing to some typographical mishap it is quite illegible, the ink has run. Only the title-page can be made out. Well, where am I, then? In what city, what country? It will come back, it always does; but in waking up thus he navigates a long moment of confusion during which he tries to establish himself in the so-called reality which depends, like a poor relation, on memory. The radio is of unknown provenance; it plays light music so characterless that it might be coming from anywhere at all. But where? He cannot tell for the life of him—note the expression: for the life of him! His few clothes have no tabs of identity, and indeed some have no buttons. Ah, that strikes a vague chord! There is a small green diary by the bed, perhaps that might afford a clue? It has the other one's name in it. Felix Ch. But the book seems very much out of date—surely the Coronation was years ago? It seems, too, full of improbable Latin-American itineraries; moreover in the middle a whole span of months is missing, has been torn out. Gone! Vanished months, vanished days—

perhaps these are the very days he is living through now? A man with no shadow, a clock with no face. Something about Greece and Turkey? Had he ever been to Turkey? Perhaps it was the other one. That blow on the head had occluded his vision: the darkness turned violet sometimes and was apt to dance about in his skull. (How she trembled in bed, this astonishing revivalist of a dead love.) But of course he had!

April to October, but where were those vanished weeks, and where was he? I would give anything to know. It doesn't look like spring at all events; from the window the snow meadows tilt away towards tall white-capped mountains; a foreground of pearling sleet upon window sills of warped and painted wood. Some sort of institution, then? (Dactyl, you are rusty and need taking down.) Nothing of all this did you notice until the image in the mirror one day burst into tears. Well, keep on trying. No luck with the soft descriptive music. I must have had a meal for the remains lie there, but they are quite unidentifiable. Last night's dinner? I turn over the remains with my fork. Brains of a hall-porter cooked in Javel, one hundred francs? I press the bell for the maid but nobody comes. Then at last I cry out as I catch sight of the little Judas in the door. The pain of regained identity. Ahhhh! It opens for a second and then slowly closes. This is no hotel. Doctor! Mother! Nurse! Urine!

Someone starts banging, fitfully, on a wall nearby and screaming in a frothy way; thud upon the padded wall, and again thud: and the peculiar reverberation of a rubber chamber-pot upon the floor. I know it now, and the other knows it too—we slide into one identity once more, as slick as smoke. But he feels desperately feverish and he takes my pulse, and his sweat smells of almonds. O all this is quite perfect! Hamlet is himself again. Fragments of forgotten conversations, the whole damned stock-pot of my life memories has come back to me; and with it the new, the surprising turn of events which has given me the illusion of recovering Benedicta (Hippolyta saying: "How sick one is of *les petites savoirs sexuelles*").

I can see no reason why all this should have happened to me, but it has; they go on, these harpies both male and female, tearing their black hearts out. "I received nothing but kindness from him (her) and repaid it with double-dealing though meanwhile unwaveringly loving (her-him). Staunch inside, infirm without, lonely, inconstant, and mad about one woman (man)." These raids on each other's narcissism. And yet, if what she tells me is true? It would be going back to the beginning, to pick up that lost stitch again; going back to the point where the paths diverged. Hark, someone is calling my name—yes, it is my name. Lying beside her I used to reproach myself by saying: "You were supposed to know everything; you arrived equipped to know all, like every human being. But a progressive distortion set in, your visions withered slowly like ageing flowers." Why did they, why have they?

She says that now she is allowed to visit me because neither is observably mad; we are simply mentally mauled by sedatives. "And you, as usual, are pretending." But then if I like to be mad it is my own affair—doctors are scared of schizophrenes because they can read minds, they can plot and plan. They pretend to pretend. Ah, but I care for nothing anymore. Quick, let us make love before another human being is born. More and more people, Benedicta, the world is overflowing; but the quality is going down correspondingly. There is no point in just people—nothing multiplied by nothing is still nothing. Kiss. Eyes of Mark, beautiful grey eyes of your dead son; I hardly dare call him mine as yet. (And what if you are lying to me, that is the question?)

> *Matthew, Mark, Luke and John,*
> *Bless the bed that I lie on,*
> *Ano-Sado-Polymorph*
> *Bless the pillow I slide off,*
> *Giving Sascher-Masch the slip*
> *With his twice-confounded whip.*
> *Let them take me from behind,*
> *But not too very sudden, mind.*
> *Polymorphouse and perverse,*
> *Revelling in the primal curse.*

Serenity, Senility. Serendipity . . . ah my friend, what are you saying?

*   *   *   *   *

13

Of course I am on my guard, watching her like a hawk. A hawk, forsooth? She will feed me on the fragments of field-mice still warm, broken up tenderly bit by bit in those slender fingers. She will teach me to stoop. Of course a lot of this material is dactylised, belonging to lost epochs; they have recovered my little machines for me and returned them to me (give the baby his rattle now!). I recover bits here and there which in the past Abel might well have appreciated. Turn them this way and that, they smell of truth—however provisional it is; as when raising those deep blue, very slightly unfocused eyes she said: "But the sexual act is by its very nature private, even if it takes place on the pavement during the rush hour." When I ask why I have been brought here she adds, on an imperious note: "To begin again, to recover the lost ground. There is much that will be explained to you—a lot by me. For God's sake trust me this time." It is as enigmatic as her way of saying "Help me" in the past. Must I resume the long paperchase once more, Benedicta?

*　*　*　*　*

I suppose that I owe my survival to the last-minute breakdown of Abel, or something of that order. I can't believe that any other consideration would have motivated my capture. Of course nobody knows how to put it right except me and I won't show them under duress. All this is surmise, of course; nobody has said anything. And I am shown every mark of sympathy and consideration: many of my toys have been returned to me, and a place set aside for me to work if the mood is on me. I resist these soft blandishments, of course, though it is hard in a way: time hangs heavy. I admit that I took up an offer to work on the Caradoc transcriptions, largely out of curiosity. The executors want some "order brought into them", whatever that means. Indeed the notion itself is unwise since this type of material, by its very haphazardness, creates its own kind of order. "Attempt to capture the idea quite naked before it strays into the conceptual field like some heavyfooted cow." Thus do I kill time till time kill me.

And now, as I have explained, she has come back, for how long I don't know, or for what reason; but changed, irremediably changed. Yet still the beauty of the domed egg-of-the-highmasted-schooner visage which smiles turn into a stag: still the slant calamitous eyes. Illness, imprisonment, privation—might not all this have brought us close together? I wonder. Why, she even helps me with my papers now. The boy's death hangs over us, between us, the something unspoken that neither knows how to broach. Resilient as I am, that was a thrust right through the heart of my narcissism; and the bare fact does not yet seem to correspond to any known set of words. So I shuffle paper a bit, reflect and allow my moods to carry me where they will. As for the executors, they do not care what I do with the material provided it goes into covers and provides money for the estate. But . . . there are no inheritors to claim it so some committee of cranks will divert it to crank projects: old men smelling of

soap and singed hair. Pelmanism for rodents, birth control for fairies
. . . that sort of thing: everything for which Caradoc, if indeed he
is dead, did not stand. (I hear those growls, I have them recorded.)

And then, from time to time among my own ruminations float
fragments which might almost seem part of another book—my own
book; the idea occurs fitfully to me, has done on and off for years. But
so much other stuff has to be cleared first: the shadows of so many
other minds which darken these muddled texts with their medieval
reflections. Abel would have been able to give them shape and position and relevance; human memory is not yet whole enough to do
so. Was it, for example, of Benedicta that I once said this—or was it
Iolanthe? "Perhaps it is not fair to speak abusively of her, to note
that she never thought anything which she did not *happen* to think.
No effort was involved. Shallow, unimpeded by reflection, her
chatter tinkled over the shallow beds of commonplace and platitude,
pouring from that trash-box of a head. But what beauty! Once in her
arms I felt safe for ever, nothing could happen to me." Prig!

Today is cold again, a Swiss cold. It has all started to become very
clear. The leaves are falling softly and being snatched away across
the meadows like smoke. My God, how long must I stay here, when
will I get out? And to what end if I do? My life is covered in the
heavy ground-mist of an impossible past which I shall never understand. I sleepwalk from day to day now with a hangover fit for a
ghost.

As for these scribblings which emerge from my copying machines,
the dactyls, these are not part of the book I was talking about, no.
Would you like to know my method? It is simple. While I am writing
one book, (the first part might be called *Pulse Rate 103*), I write another about it, then a third about *it,* and so on. A new logic might
emerge from it, who knows? Like those monkeys in the Indian
frescoes (so human, so engaging, like some English critics) who can
dance only with their index fingers up each other's behinds. This
would be *my* way of doing things. Smell of camphor: I must not get
too vivacious when Nash, the doctor, calls. I must remain as he sees
me—an eternal reproach to the death-bed, the dirty linen, the urinals
clearing their throats. Yet vivacity of mind is no sin, saith the
Lord God.

16

As far as Caradoc is concerned what ails me in gathering up this inconsequential chatter is that there are several different books which one could assemble, including some which couldn't have been foreseen by those who knew him; is everyone built on this pattern? —like a club sandwich, I suppose. But here for example is a vein which would be more suitable to Koepgen—perhaps it is the part of Caradoc which *is* Koepgen, or vice versa. I mean *alchemy*, the great night express which jumps the points and hurtles out of the causal field, carrying everything with it. Alchemy with all its paradoxes—I would have logged that as Koepgen's private territory. But no. The vein is there in Caradoc, under the fooling.

I mean, for example: "*Pour bien commencer ces études il faut d'abord supprimer toute curiosité*"; the sort of paradox which is incomprehensible to those afflicted by the powers of ratiocination. Moreover this, if you please, from a man who claimed that the last words of Socrates were: "Please the Gods, may the laughter keep breaking through." Contrast it with the fine white ribbon which runs through the lucubrations of Aristotle—the multiplication tables of thought to set against this type of pregenital jargon. (In between times I have not been idle: on the little hand lathe I have turned a fine set of skeleton keys in order to be able to explore my surroundings a bit.) Is it imperative that the tragic sense should reside after all somewhere in laughter?

*   *   *   *   *

Yet now that I am officially mad and locked away here in the Paul-haus, it would be hard to imagine anywhere more salubrious (guide-book prose!) to spend a long quiet convalescence—here by this melancholy lake which mirrors mostly nothingness because the sky is so low and as toneless as tired fur. The rich meadows hereabouts are full of languid vipers. At eventide the hills resound to the full-breasted thwanking of cowbells. One can visualise the udders swing-ing in time along the line of march to the milking sheds where the rubber nipples with electricity degorge and ease the booming creatures. The steam rises in clouds.

Billiard-rooms, a library, chapels for five denominations, a cinema, a small theatre, golf course—Nash is not wrong in describing it as a sort of country-club. The surgical wing, like the infirmaries, is separate, built at an angle of inclination, giving its back to us, looking out eastward. Operations one side, convalescence the other. Our ill-nesses are graded. A subterranean trolley system plus a dozen or so lifts of various sizes ensure swift and easy communication between the two domains. I am not really under restraint. I am joking; but I am under surveillance, or at least I feel I am. So far I have only been advised not to go to the cinema—doubtless there are good clinical reasons. Apart from the fact that I might see a film of Iolanthe's again I do not care: the cinema is the No play of the Yes-Man, as far as I am concerned. I am for sound against vision—it runs counter to the contemporary trend: I know that, but what can I do? *Konx Ompax* and *Om Mane Padme Hum* are the two switches which operate my brain box: between the voting sherd and the foetal pose of the sage.

There are many individual chalets, too, dotted about upon the steep hillsides, buried out of sight for the most part in dense groves of pine and fir. They are pretty enough when the snow falls and lies; but when not the eternal condensation of moisture forms a light

18

rain or Scotch mist. The further snows loom indifferently from minatory cloud-scapes. One sleeps well. No, I won't pretend that it is anything in particular, either comminatory or depressing or enervating: except for *me*, the eye of the beholder. For I am here against my will, badly shaken, and moreover frightened by this display of disinterested kindness. Yet it is simply what it is—the Paulhaus. Subsoil limestone and conglomerate. Up there, on the further edge of the hill among the pines are the chalets allocated to the staff. Our keepers live up there, and the lights blaze all night where the psychoanalysts chain each other to the walls and thrash each other with their braces in a vain attempt to discover the pain-threshold of affect-stress. Their screams are terrible to hear. In other cells the theologians and mystagogues are bent over their dream anthologies, puzzled by the new type of psychic immaturity which our age has produced—one that is literally impermeable to experience. When he is here Nash lodges with Professor Pfeiffer whose dentures are loose and who has a huge dried black penis on his desk—a veritable Prester John of an organ. Swiss taxidermy at its best. But nobody knows whose it is, or rather was. At any rate it isn't mine.

Here they must discuss poor Charlock in low tones, speaking of his lustreless eye, the *avain* quality of his gaze. "Such a lack of *theme*" Pfeiffer must say. It is his favourite expression. And there opposite him sits Nash in his bow tie, author of *The Aetiology of Onanism*, in three volumes (Random House). Little pissypuss Nash. You wait a bit, my lads. My goodness, though, it was worth the journey, it was worth the fare. Mind you, it is easier to get in than to get out—but that is true of other establishments I have known. . . .

It was not entirely my fault that I awoke with a head like a giant onion—swathed as it was in layer upon layer of surgical dressing. Like the Cosmic Egg itself, and I damned well felt like it. Chips of skull (they said) had to be removed—like a hard-boiled egg at a picnic. No damage to the Pia Mater. Clunk with a couple of pick-helves as I reached for my knife. Then a kind of bloody abstract but rather lovely abdication of everything with darkness hanging like a Japanese print of an extinct volcano. *Angor Animi*—fear of approaching death. It haunted me for a while. But now I have gained a bit of courage, as a mouse does when the cat does not move for a long time. I am just beginning to scuttle about once more . . . the cat must have forgotten me. Actually they must see that I am on the mend; by special dispensation I have been allowed some of my tools back, as I say; along with them some private toys. One, for example, has enabled me to discover the position of the two microphones in my room. Instead of plugging them as a clumsy agent might have done I fill them with the noise of cisterns flushing, taps running, dustbin lids banging—not to mention the wild howls and squeaks of the tapes played backwards; and music too, prodigious wails and farts in the manner of Alban Berg. Poor Pfeiffer, he must shake his shaggy head and imagine he is listening to the Dalai Lama holding a service.

Lately Nash has taken to visiting me regularly about thrice a week—hurried and apologetic harbinger of Freud. Pale with professional concern. "Come Nash, let us be frank for a change. Julian had me captured and brought here so that you can try to break my will with your drugs." He laughs and pouts, shaking his head. "Felix, you only do it to annoy, because you know it teases. Actually he saved you just in time, for all our sakes. Seriously, my dear fellow."

Nature becomes almost transparent to the visionary eye after even a moderate period of sedation. I could see so to speak right into his rib-cage, see his heart warbling out blood, see his timid and orderly soul neatly laid up in dusted ranks like a travel library. A telephone rings somewhere. "Felix" he says tenderly, reproachfully. "I suppose" I said "you must have dreamed of escaping once, when you were very young. Where has it gone, Nash, the impetus? Will you always be the firm's satrap, its druggist?" His eyes fill briefly with tears, for he is a very emotional man and suffers when criticised. "For goodness' sake don't give way to delusional ideas of persecution, I implore you. Everything has turned out right after a very nasty and dangerous passage. When you are rested and well and have seen Julian there is no need why you shouldn't send in your resignation if you wish. There is no obstacle—all that is a comic delusion of yours. We want you with us, of course, but not against your will. . . ." I can't resist acting him a little of a private charade based upon Hamlet's father's ghost—nearly managing to secure the heavy paper-knife which I make to drive into his carotid. I bulge my eyes and wave my ears up and down. But he is fleet enough when danger threatens, is Nash; once round the table and to the door, ready to bolt, panting: "Cut it out for God's sake, Felix. You can't scare me with these antics." But I have, that is what is mildly en-giggling. I throw the paper knife in the air and catch it; then place it betwixt my teeth in pirate fashion. He comes back cautiously into the room. "You want me mad" I say. "And you shall have me so." I comb out my overgrown eyebrows in the mirror and try a stern look or two. He chuckles and continues to talk. "It's lucky you have caught me during my safe period" I say. "If it had been any other woman. . . ."

"D'you know," he says effervescently "I have a patient who makes up natural Mnemons just as Caradoc used to; he was a famous philosopher, and he illustrates the ruins of his dialectical system with them. Free association is the Draconic law, no? *La volupté est la confiture des ours*—how is that?"

"Woof! Woof!"

"Felix, listen to me."

"Ja, Herr Doktor."

"These dreams you are turning in to Pfeiffer—anyone can see they are faked. I ask you, psychoanalysts riding on broomsticks and sliding down moonbeams with fairies . . . a joke is a joke, but this is going too far. Poor Pfeiffer says . . ."

I play a little game with him for a while chasing him round and round the table, but he is nimble and I tire rapidly; I suppose that I am rather ill still, weak in the knees, and of a tearful disposition: and he knows it.

"And Benedicta?" says he.

"Was sent to help me compromise my reason and my feelings."

"Good heavens, Felix: how can you?"

"How did it all happen to me, Nash—to Felix Ch, eh? Perhaps a desire to poke some frivolous and egotistical strumpet, to plough up some sexual ignoramus? Ah, listen to the alpha rhythms of the grey matter." I hold up a finger to bid him listen. He shakes his head and sighs. "Poor darling" he says. "You wrong her and soon you'll know it. Anyway she will be back on Tuesday and you'll see for yourself. In the meantime you see how free you are to walk about, even without her. Even walk into town if you want one afternoon. Treat this like your own country-club, Felix. It won't be long before we have you back in our midst—I've never been more confident of a prognosis. Meanwhile I'll send you plenty of visitors to cheer you up."

I must have given him a woolly look for he coughed and adjusted his bow tie neatly. "Visitors" he added in a lower key, filling out a longish prescription form with deft little Japtype strokes, and adding the magic word in block capitals at the foot of the page. "This for the nurse" he added sportively, waving it as he stood up. "Until next week then, my dear Felix. Julian sends his warmest regards. . . ." He just got through the door in time before the heavy chair burst upon it; a leg fell off, a panel was cracked right across. The German nurse came in clicking like a turkey; a strapping girl with the square walk of the sexually unrealised woman. She had a big bust and an urchin cut. I liked her white smooth apron and her manicured capable hands. Nash had fled down the corridor. I helped her gather up the pieces and redispose the furniture. I asked her if it was time for my enema, but she registered shock and disapproval at this sally. "If not, then will I to the library go," I said and she stood aside to let me pass. As I walked, still puzzled by everything, I told myself: "Benedicta and I come from a long line of muddled sexers, spectres of discontent. What dare I believe about her, or about anyone?"

★   ★   ★   ★   ★

Over the week-end I tested my freedom in tentative fashion by disappearing for the afternoon: no, not into town where I am always followed at a discreet distance by a white ambulance; but into the dangerous ward. Who would ever have thought of looking for one there? I reappeared in my own quarters as mysteriously as a conjurer's rabbit and simply would not tell them where I had been. Would they have believed me? I doubt it. The thing is that I found I was actually picking up the thought-waves of a schizo on one of my little recording devices. He was knocking on the wall at the end of the corridor and singing a bit. I sneaked to the locked door and passed him a wire with a tiny mike on it. (Of course I myself have lots of tinnitus, which is only static in loony terms.) But we hit it off wonderfully well. He didn't really want to get out, he said; he was only troubled by speculations as to the nature of freedom—where did it begin and where end? A man after my own heart, as you see. He turned out to be a wife-murderer; higher spiritual type than the rest of us. Our electronic friendship flowered so quickly that I felt it about time to test my set of keys. The second worked like a charm and I was inside the ward with the red light, shaking hands with my friend. He was a huge fellow but kindly, indeed almost diffident about his powers. The padded ward was just like anywhere else; spotless and obviously well conducted—and with a much more refined class of person than one finds in the rest of the place. Yes, I liked it very much, even the corridor with its sickly saint-like smell: smell of sweaty feet in some Byzantine cloister? And then all the pleasant diversified humours of Borborymi. Woof! Woof! There would be no visitors between tea-time and supper, so we were free to play at nursery games—on all fours, for example, barking in concert at a full moon, trying to turn ourselves into wolf-men.

You see, anxiety is only a state of deadly *heed*, just as melancholia

23

is only a pathological sadness. I might have foundered here, I suppose, had she not appeared; foundered out of sheer exhaustion, out of defiance to Julian's obscure laws. I could have retreated by sheer imitation into a genuine hebephrenia, to follow out the dull spiral of some loony's talk; under the full sail of madness steered this cargo of white-faced gnomes towards the darkness of catatonia. A Ship of Fools, like the very world itself. My friend speaks of freedom without quite being able to visualise its furtherest reaches; yet he is *almost there. Ah! Folie des Gouffres.* But cerebral dysrhythmia will respond to a cortical sedative, even in some cases of cryptogenic epilepsy. . . . You ask Nash! *Om.*

The thing is this: coming round in the operating theatre, under the arcs, surrounded by a ballet of white masks (white niggers, appropriates of a blood sacrifice): bending down to plunge needles into me: I heard, or thought I heard, the quite unmistakable tones of Julian. They spoke, all of them, in quiet relaxed voices, like clubmen over their cigars while I lay there, a roped steer, with wildly rolling eye and flapping ear. I knew that the operation was over by now; I was just waiting to be wheeled away. The figure I mean stood just back from the circle and was obviously neither surgeon nor dresser, though he was masked and gowned like the rest of them. It was this one that said, in the tones of Julian: "I think the X-ray findings followed up by a pneumogram should tell you. . . ." Talk filled the interstices of his phrases like clods raining down upon a coffin-lid. Explanations proliferated into jargon. I felt perfectly well by now, the pain had gone with the tachycardia, leaving only the spearpointed attentive fury of the impotent man. Someone spoke of brainstem sedatives, and then another voice: "Of course for a while he will undergo what will seem like electric charges in the skull—weird haptic sensations." Hence, I suppose, the longish period of surveillance among the odours of guilty perspiration; life among bedridden schizos under insulin torpor therapy, beings whose "Rostral Hegemony" is faulty—to quote the brave words of Nash. Much of this is a blank, of course, punctured by dim visions. I dare say I ran the gamut of D Ward. Petit Mal to Grand Malheur. Bedwetting is common. By day their speech exhibits uninhibited lalling. Welcome, electrically speaking, my new-found friends, possessors of

24

the spike-and-dome discharge! I see the anxiety rising in the Centro-cephalon, the rapid 25 per second high amplitude rhythms of the Grand Mal, the focal seizures rising in the cortex. Last week the Countess Maltessa had an unrehearsed, unsupervised epileptic fit; she died from the inhalation of her own vomit. "It so often happens" Pfeiffer will be saying, shaking his head. "You can't watch everyone all the time."

I do my best to try and remember this ward, but in vain; nor indeed do I remember its inhabitants with their diversified idiosyn-crasies, though of course some of them I have known about, have heard about. But if I met them during my last sojourn here I have retained no memory of the fact. They are all freshly minted—like for example the famous Rackstraw, who was Io's screenwriter, respon-sible for some of her most famous work. I would have been glad to remember him; and yet it is strange for I recognised him instantly from her descriptions of him. She used to visit him very often I recall. He himself had once been a minor actor—and, some say, her lover. In its way it was quite thrilling to see this legendary figure face to face, weighed down by the Laocoön-toils of his melancholia. "Rackstraw I presume?" The hand he tenders is soft and moist; it drops away before shaking to hang listlessly at his side. He looks at one and his lips move, moistening one another. He gives a small cluck on a note of interrogation and puts his head on one side. Watching him, it all comes back to me; how well she described his imaginary life here in this snow-bound parish of the insane.

How he would sit down with such care, such circumspection, at an imaginary table to play a game of imaginary cards. ("Is it less real for him than a so-called real game would be for us? That is what is frightening.") I hear the clear dead husky voice asking the question. Or else when walking slowly up and down as if on castors he smokes an imaginary cigar with real enjoyment; smiles and shakes his head at imaginary conversations. What a great artist Rackstraw has become!

His hair is very fine; he wears it parted in the middle and pasted down at the sides. It is someone else who looks back approvingly at him from the mirror. His ears are paper-thin so that the sunlight passes through them and they turn pink as shells, with all the veins illustrated. He will appear to hear what you say and indeed will often reply with great courtesy, though his answers bear little relation to the subjects which you broach. His pale-blue eye gazes out upon this strange world with a shy fish-like fascination. What a feast of the imagination too are the interminable meals he eats—course after course—cooked for him by the finest chefs, and served wherever he might happen to be. Who could persuade him that in reality he is nourished by a stomach-pump? No, Rackstraw is a sobering figure only when I think that these long nerveless fingers might once have caressed the warm smooth flesh of Iolanthe. (The final problem of intellection is this: you cannot rape yourself mentally for thought creates its own shadow, blocks its own light, inhibits direct vision. The act of intuition or self-illumination can come only through a partner-object—like a host in parasitology.) If one is tempted to kiss, to embrace Rackstraw, it is to see if there is any of Io's pollen still upon him. Can one leave nothing behind, then, that is proof against forgetfulness?

But Ward D is only another laboratory where people are encouraged to live as vastly etiolated versions of themselves—and Rackstraw has taken full advantage of the fact. At certain periods of the moon his old profession seizes him and he fills the ward with his impersonations of forgotten kings and queens, both historical and contemporary; or will play for hours with a doll—a representation of Iolanthe in the role of Cleopatra. At others he may recite in a monotonous singsong voice:

Mr. Vincent	five years
Mr. Wilkie	five years
Emmermet	ten years
Porely	ten years
Imhof	ten years
Dobie	five years

and so forth. At other times he becomes so finely aristocratic that one knows him to be the King of Sweden. He mutters, looking down sideways with a peculiar pitying grimace, lips pursed, long nose quivering with refined passion. He draws hissing breaths and curls back his lips with disgust. He sniffs, raises his eyebrows, bows; walking about with a funny tiptoe walk, lisping to himself. When the evening bell goes and he is told to go to bed he bridles haughtily, but he may mount the bed and stay for a long time on all fours, thinking, "Rackstraw's the name. At your service." His every sense has become an epicure. On the wall of the lavatory near his bed someone has written: *Mourir c'est fleurir un peu.* Then also for brief spells, with the air of someone looking down a well into his past, he will produce the ghastly jauntiness of the remittance man—he is living in the best hotel. "I say some ghastly rotter has pipped me . . . top-whole Sunday . . . the boots doesn't clean suède properly. . . ." He has become the professional sponge of the 'twenties, cadging a living from the ladies.

But the difference between Rackstraw's reality and mine is separated by a hair—at least as things are now. For me too, reality comes in layers suffused by involuntary dreaming. Some mornings I wake to find Baynes standing by my bed with his silver salver in hand, though there is never any letter on it. He says: "Which way up will you have your reality, sir, today?" Yawning, I reply in the very accents of Rackstraw. "O, as it comes, Baynes. But please order me a nice L-shaped loveproof girl of marriageable age, equipped with learner plates. I have in mind some heart-requiting woman to lather my chin; someone with sardonic eyes and dark plumage of Irish hair. Someone with a beautiful steady walk and a thick cluster of damp curls round a clitoris fresh as cress." He salutes and says, "Very good, sir. Right away, sir." But at other times I think I must be dying really because I am beginning to believe in the idea of Benedicta.

I had been about and around for several days when I caught sight of her, sighted along the length of the long corridor with its bow window at the end, standing in the snow in a characteristic distressful way. She had rubbed a small periscope in the frosty glass in order to peer in upon me, her head upon one side. A new unfamiliar look which somehow mixed diffidence and commiseration in one; I gave her the sort of look I felt she merited—O, it was all I could afford: a tired frog's smile: it was a package, a propitiatory bundle of nails, hair, menstrual rags, old dressings—everything that our joint life had brought us. But it contained little enough venom—I felt too bad about it all, too emotionally weak to expend more upon the encounter. And yet there was something in her face at once touching and despairing; her inner life, like mine, was in ruins. It was the fault of neither. So when she tapped with her nail upon the glass I said not a word but unfastened the glass door into the garden and let her in. Of course it was suspicious. We stood, featureless as totems, gazing at each other, but unable to thread any words on the spool. Then with a soft groan she put her arms out—we did not embrace, simply leaned upon one another with an absolute emptiness and exhaustion. Yet the personage in my arms in some subtle way no longer corresponded to any of the old images of Benedicta—images she had printed on my mind. A qualitative difference here—you know how sometimes people return from a long journey, or from a war, completely altered: they do not have to speak, it is written all over them. What was written here? There was no discharge of electrical tension from those slender shoulders—the vibrations of an anxiety overflowing its bounds in the psyche. Her red lips trembled, that was all. "For God's sake be kind to me" was all I said, was all I could think of. She started to cry a little inwardly, then began to *cry*. She crew buckets, but without moving, standing quite still; so did I, too, from sympathy, just watching her—but inside like usual: tears pouring down the inside of my body. "I am coming to you tonight—I have permission. Somehow we must try and alter things between us —even if it seems too late." Only that, and I let her go, a snow demon in her black ski clothes against the deep whiteness of the ground and the clouds. She walked carefully in her own imprints towards the trees and disappeared, never once looking round, and for a moment this whole episode seemed to me a dream. But no, her prints were there in the snow. I swore, I raged inwardly; and when night fell I lay there in the darkness of my room with my eyes open staring right through the ceiling into the snow-sparkling night sky. I have never understood the romantic cult of the night; day, yes— people, noise, motors, lavatories flushing. At night one recites old phone numbers (Gobelins 3310. Is that you, Iolanthe? No, she has gone away, the number has been changed). Recite the names of people one has never met, or would have liked to sleep with if things had been different. Mr. Vincent five years. Mr. Wilkie five years. Yes, the night's for masturbation and death; one's nose comes off in one's handkerchief, an arm drops off like Nelson. . . .

The minutes move like snails; the faintest shadow of a new hope is trying to get born. It will only lead to greater disappointments, more refined despairs, of that I am sure. Yet thinking back—years back, to the beginning—I can still remember something which seemed then to exist in her—*in potentia*, of course. I wrestle to formulate what it was, the thing lying behind the eyes like a wish unburied, like a transparency, a germ. Something like this: what she herself had not recognised as true about herself and which she was all but destroying by running counter clockwise to the part of herself which was my love. (Go on, make it clearer.)

Every fool is somebody's genius, I suppose. Just to have touched again those long, scrupulous yet sinister fingers gave me the sense of having reoriented myself with reference to the real Benedicta; it was because I myself had also changed a skin. Past suicide, past love, past everything—and in the obscurest part of my nature happy in a sad sort of way; climbing down, you might say, rung by rung, heartbeat by heartbeat, into the grave with absolutely nothing to show for my long insistent life of selfish creativeness. Put it another way: what I have left is some strong emotions, but no *feelings*. Shock has deprived me of them, though whether temporarily or so I cannot say. Ah, Felix! The more we know about knowing the less we feel about feeling. That whole night we were to lie like Crusader effigies, just touching but silently awake, hearing each other's thoughts passing. I thought to myself "Faith is only one form of intuition." We must give her time. . . . Are you stuck, then, dactyl? Come let me clear you. . . .

Later she might have been more disposed to try and put it into words: "I've destroyed you and myself. I must tell you how, I must tell you why if I can find out."

To find out, that was the dream—or the nightmare—we would have to face together; following the traces of her history and mine back into the labyrinth of the past. No, not simply looking for excuses, but hunting for the original dilemma—the Minotaur, which itself seemed to connect back always to Merlin's great firm which had swallowed my talents as Benedicta had swallowed my manhood. It is this fascinating piece of research which occupies me to the exclusion of almost everything else now—perhaps you can guess how? With the help of my keys I have vastly extended the boundaries of my freedom; for example, I can now traverse Ward D, and make my way into the central block without being specially remarked by anyone; but more important still I have found the consulting rooms of the psychiatrists and the library of tapes and dossiers which form a part of Nash's patrimony. Up the stairs, then, past the ward with the huge Jewesses (big bottoms and nervous complaints: fruits of inbreeding). Down one floor and along to the right, pausing to say a timely word to Callahan (pushed through a shop window, cut his wrist: interesting crater of a dried-up carbuncle on his jaw) and so along to the duty consulting rooms where the treasure trove lies. The tapes, the typed dossiers, are all grouped in a steel cabinet, according to year—the whole record of Benedicta's illnesses and treatment. . . .

I thought at first that she might find this prying into her past objectionable, but to my surprise she only said: "Thank goodness—now you will trust me because you can double-check me. After so much lying to you . . . I mean involuntary lying because things were the way they were, because Julian came first, his will came first; then the firm. You have already guessed that Julian is far more than just the head of Western Merlin's for me, haven't you?"

"Your brother."

"Yes."

"So much became clear when I discovered that simple fact—why did you never tell me?"

"He forbade me."

"Even when we were married?"

She takes my hand in hers and squeezes it while tears come into her eyes. "There is so much that I must face, must tell you; now that I'm free from Julian I can."

"Free from Julian!" I gasped with utter astonishment at so preposterous a thought. "Is one ever free from Julian?" She sat up and grasped her ankles, bowing her blonde head upon her knees, lost in thought. Then she went on, speaking slowly, with evident stress behind the words: "There was a precise moment for me, as well as one for him. Mine came when the child was shot—like waking from a long nightmare."

30

"I fired that shot."

"No, Felix, we all did in one way and another."

She pressed my hand once more, shaking her head; continued with a kind of scrupulous gravity. "The image of Julian flew into a hundred pieces never to be reassembled again; he had no further power over me."

"And from his side?"

"The death of that girl, Iolanthe."

"How?"

"He described it to me in much the same words, a suddenly waking up with a hole in the centre of his mind."

Yet in Julian's case the emptiness must always have been there; one could imagine him saying something like: "A faulty pituitary foiled my puberty, and even later when the needle restored the balance, something had been lost; I had lived a complete sexual life in my mind so the real thing seemed woefully hollow when at last I caught up with it." Hence the excesses, the perversions which are only the mould that grows upon impotence and its fearful rages against the self.

So lying beside her thus in the darkness I found myself looking back down the long inclines of the past which curved away towards the Golden Horn and the breezes of Marmora; towards the lowering image of the Turkey I had hardly known, yet where my future had been decided for me by a series of events which some might regard as fortuitous. What a long road stretched between these two points in time and space.

Real birds sang all day in the gardens while indoors the mechanical nightingales from Vienna had to be wound up; at certain times one became aware of the beetles ticking away like little clocks behind the damascened hangings, full of dust. The corridors were full of beautifully carved chests made from strange woods—delicately scented sissu, calamander, satinwood, ebony, billian, teak or camphor.

Somewhere among the wandering paths of these old gardens over-grown with weeds and brush-marked by cypresses I saw the pale figure of Benedicta wandering, stiff and upright in her brocade frock, holding the hand of a nurse. How would it be possible to bring her back here again, to my side in this cream-painted sterile room among the snows? It was a puzzle made not the less complicated by the new tenderness and shy dignity which now invested her, and which aroused my worst suspicions; I could not see how a new array of facts alone could clear the air, could exculpate her—or for that matter myself. Ironic for a scientist who cares for facts, no? We sat here side by side on the white bed eating mountain strawberries and staring at each other, trying to decipher the pages of the palimpsest. "You see," she said slowly, staring deeply into my eyes "we have lived through these fearful experiences together, killed our own child, separated, and all without ascribing any particular value to it. It has brought us very close together so that now we can't escape from each other any more. The numbness is wearing off—you are beginning to see that I was in love with you from the very beginning. My appeals for help were genuine; but I was in the power of Julian— a power that dates back to my early childhood. I loved him because I was afraid of him, because of all he had done to me. I was trapped between two loves, one perverse and sterile, the other which promised to open up a real world for me, if only you could see in time how truthful I was—and act on it." Then she bowed her head like a weary doe and whispered: "It's easy to say, I know. Nor is it fair perhaps. You were as much in Julian's power as I was, after all, and he could have had you killed at any moment, I suppose, had he not been in doubt about losing me for ever. He took refuge from me in this strange love for that girl you call Io—and that perhaps saved us from his wrath, his fearful impotent fury which he hides so well under that calm and beautiful voice of his." I said nothing for a long time. In my mind's eye I saw once more those steamy gardens abandoned to desuetude, those chipped and dusty kiosks standing about waiting for guests who never came: the stern sweep of the tombs decorating the beautiful slopes of Eyub. "In the cemetery there—it was your mother's tomb?" Benedicta nodded sadly. "She hardly enters our story. She was ill, you know. In those days syphilis, you couldn't cure it."

It dated back, dated right back. "Nothing could have exceeded the passionate rage and tenderness of Julian for Mother." Here as she lay, after so very long, anchored in the crook of my arm: and talking now softly, rapidly, unemphatically: I saw come up in my mind's eye (beyond the golden head) the sunburnt mountains and peninsulas of Turkey rising in layers towards the High Taurus. "Jocas was the illegitimate one, the changeling; he was never allowed to forget it. He was ugly and hairy. Whenever he spoke my father would get up without a word and open the door into the garden to let him out. And Julian smiled, simply smiled." Though I had never seen Julian I seemed to see very clearly that aquiline smile, the sallow satin skin, the eyes with the thick hoods of a bird of prey. I saw too the landscape of their minds, locked up together in those tumbledown seraglios; a Turkey that had been so much more than Polis with its archaic refinements. Plainland and lake and mountain, blue days closed by the conch. "There was only hate or fear for us to work on after my mother died." Yes, it was not simply themselves she evoked, the tangled pattern of questions and answers their lives evoked; but more, much more, which could only find a frame of reference within the context of this brutal humble land, kneeling down like a camel in the shadow of Ararat snow-crowned. Her inner life lay with Julian, her outer with Jocas; one represented the city, the drawn bowstring of Moslem politenesses, the other the open air, the riding to falcons, the chase. Remote encampments on the rim of deserts mirrored in the clear optic of the sky: to sleep at night under the stars, balanced between the two open eternities of birth and death.

It was much more than the facts which mattered, which had shaped their peculiar destinies, it was also place. I mean I saw very clearly now the tiny cocksure figure of Merlin senior walking the bazaars dressed in his old blazer and yachting cap; high white kid boots and high collars fastened with a jewelled tie-pin: flyswish held negligently in small ringed fingers. Behind him strolled the resplendent kavass—the negro dressed in scarlet and brocade, carrying the drawn scimitar of his office with the blade laid back along his forearm. This was how it all began, with Merlin shopping for the firm, which at that time must have consisted only of a raggle-taggle of sheds and godowns full of skins or poppy or shrouds. Yes, shrouds! The Moslem custom of burying the dead without coffins but wrapped in shrouds had not passed unnoticed by that blue jay's eye. (Was it the little clerk Sacrapant who mentioned this?) Seven shrouds to a corpse, and in the case of the richer and more distinguished families no expense was spared to secure the most gorgeous embroidered fabrics the bazaars could offer. Old Abdul Hamid used to order hundreds of pieces of the choicest weave—China and Damascus silk. These were sent to Mecca to be sprinkled with holy water from the sacred well of Zem Zem. Thus the dead person was secured a certain translation to Jennet, the Moslem Paradise. It was not long before the caravans of Merlin carried these soft bales. But all this was at the very beginning, before Julian could say of the firm: "It has great abstract beauty, the firm, Charlock. We never touch or possess any of the products we manipulate—only the people to a certain extent. The products are merely telegrams, quotations, symbolic matter, that is all. If you cared for chess you could not help caring for Merlin's." He himself loved the game in all its variety. It is easy to see him aboard the white-winged yacht which the firm had given him, anchored upon the mirror of some Greek sound, sitting before the three transparent perspex boards in stony silence; playing three-dimensionally, so to speak. How beautifully those little Turkish warehouses had metastasised, so to speak, forming secondary cancers in the lungs, livers, hearts of the great capitals. In the long silences of Julian one saw the slow curling smoke of his cigar rise upon the moonlit sky.

"But Benedicta, all that rigmarole about them being orphans and all that. . . ."

"My father invented that to get round some complicated Turkish legislation about inheritances, death duties."

"But he said it with such feeling."

"Feeling! Jocas had murder in his heart for many years against Julian. But by repressing his hatred he turned himself into a fine human being; he really did come to love Julian at last. But Julian never loved him, never could, never will. Julian only loved me. Only me."

"And your father?"

"And my father!"

She said it with such a withering emphasis that I instantly divined the hatred between Merlin and Julian. "Julian would not let me love

34

him, forced me to hate him: at the end drove him out. He too had reasons, Julian."

"Drove Merlin out?"

"Yes. As he had driven out my mother."

In the long silence which followed I could hear her shallow breathing; but it was calm now, confident and regular. "Nash always said that real maturity should automatically mean a realised compassion for the world, for people. This Julian never had, only sadness, an enormous sadness. Nor for that matter did my father. He was a bird of prey. What was I to do between them all—with no real human contact to work upon? I dared not show my sympathies for Jocas even, hardly dared to speak to him. You know, Felix, they were all killers by temperament. I never knew who might kill who— even though Julian was away so much, being educated. If they met they met on neutral ground, so to speak, usually some dead spa like Smyrna or Lutraki. All staying at different hotels with their retainers. A sort of armed truce somehow enabled them to survive—it is very Turkish, you see. Formal exchanges of meaningless presents. Then discussions, perhaps in a special train on the Turkish frontier. That was all. Later of course the telephone helped, they did not need to meet, they could be cordial to each other in this way."

"But you were lovers."

"Always. Even afterwards. We found ways."

But I was mentally adding in the data derived from the steel cabinets—or as much of it as I had had time to read. It was not hard to picture them there, the two children, in some deserted corner of the dusty palace among the tarnished mirrors with their chipped gilt frames. The swarthy intent face of Julian, his eyes blazing with almost manic concentration, his lips drawn back from white teeth. Each held a heavy silver candlestick with a full branch of rosy lighted candles. They confronted each other thus, naked, like contestants in some hieratic combat, or like oriental dancers. Perhaps too among the wheeling shadows of the high rooms and curling staircases they must have seemed to anyone who saw them (Merlin himself did once) like gorgeous plumed birds treading out an elaborate mating-dance with all its intricate figures. So they shook the burning wax over one another, thrust and riposte, hissing at its hot tang; they were drenched as if with molten spray. What else was there left to do? They had learned and unlearned everything before puberty—disordering their psyches, forcing them on before they were ripe. Will those who do this not prejudice their sexual and affective adult life: live forever in fantasy acts of sexual excess? Never get free?

Well, who am I to say that? But I could see deeper now into the pattern of their lives which had become so very much a reflection of Turkey—the miasma of old Turkey with its frigid cruelties, its priapic conspiracies. This fitted in well with the small ferocious Calvinist soul of Merlin, bursting at its seams with guilty sadistic impulses. (And him with all the quiet diligence and the family grace of feature!) Here at least he was at home. One saw him during those long winter evenings sitting over his books with some green-turbaned teacher drinking in the charm of the language with all its gobbling sententiousness, its lack of relative pronouns and subordinate clauses. Sitting with the amber mouthpiece of a narguileh in his hand allowing one half of his mind to play with the idea of its cost—silver-hilted amber; (worth perhaps two hundred English pounds?)

Or else up on the bronze foothills (they all shot like angels) following the cautious dogs—himself not the less cautious between the accompanying guns. They walked in an arrowhead formation so that Jocas and Julian and the girl were a trifle ahead of him. Up here, though, in the exultation of the open life of the steppe they were almost united in spirit, almost at one with each other. Disarmed around a campfire at evening they would listen smiling to the ululations of tribal singers, stirred into an exultant tenderness by the magnificence of the night sky and the hills. From this part of their lives single incidents stood out for ever in her memory clear and burnished. Like when the little man was walking alone along an escarpment and was pounced upon by a pair of golden eagles. He must have been near their nest, for they fell whistling out of the sky upon him, wing-span and claws powerful enough to have carried off a full-grown sheep. He heard the whistle and the swish of the huge wings just in time; he had glimpsed their shadows as he ducked. The others rushed to help him—he was defending himself with the unloaded gun, beating the eagles off; but by the time they arrived

36

one of the birds lay breathless on the rock at his feet and the other had gone. He was panting, his rifle was twisted, the stock was cracked. He took a cudgel from a Turk and beat the quivering eagle to death with white face, his teeth showing in a grin. He had deep wounds in his back, his shirt was torn to rags. Then he sat down on a rock and buried his white face in trembling hands. Watching him she understood why she could never bring herself to call him "Father"; he was quite simply terrifying. Julian says laconically: "I can see their nest" and taking a shot gun blazes away at it until it disintegrates. If she closed her eyes and held her breath she could feel the weight of Julian's mind resting upon hers. It was something more than the drugs; he held her by the scruff of the mind so you might say. "He performed an elaborate series of psychic and physical experiments on me—of course in the Levant there is nothing very uncommon or shocking about it." When the telephone came into fashion she learned to ring him up and recite a string of soft cajoling obscenities until. . . . "Of course you can love somebody like that," says Benedicta with her eyes closed, resting her forehead on the cold rail of the bedpost. "Nobody has got more than one way, his own, of showing his love. Too bad if it's uncommon or perverted or what-not. Or perhaps Julian would say 'too good'. I can't say I didn't enjoy being owned by him, engulfed by him—utterly swallowed. In another perverse way it is such a relief to surrender the will utterly. Julian turned me into a sleepwalker for his experiments. He led me up to the point of being able to kill." The white face with the closed eyes looked like some remote statue forgotten in a museum. A long time like that in a fierce muse of concentration, still as a burning-glass.

Was this before or after? Ah, dactyl answer me. No, I do not care. It suffices that it should form part of the central pattern. While Merlin prospered and bought ruined palaces and cypress-groves the children loved and despaired away their youth in sunken gardens guarded by a retinue of impersonal servants, governesses, retainers. Jocas was born to the chase and was always glad to escape to the Asiatic side with his hunting birds and his kites. Julian the tranquil, thoughtful, the vicious, was never without a book, and was already the master of several languages. Yet withal he had in him some of the heavy-souled impersonality of the sleepy Ottoman world where the humid heat lay upon the nerves with the weight of lead. Julian and his sister! Later they were to be separated and his personal hold over her suffered a metamorphosis—he held her through the firm and the needs of the firm, no longer through the body and the personal will. That was how she became the near-witch Benedicta. But during this early time he taught her to fence; naked again, they faced each other on the stone flags and the room rang to the dry clicking of buttoned foils. Then lying in the great bedroom with its mirror ceiling, in each other's arms, as if at the bottom of the ocean they made love, watching each other watch each other. He was soon to meet his peculiar medieval fate—the fate of Abelard; for Merlin knew all. Somewhere inside himself Julian was not really surprised when they all walked in holding candles—Merlin himself dressed in an old-fashioned nightgown and soft Turkish slippers with pointed toes. Julian closed his eyes, pretending to sleep, until they touched his shoulder and led him away. Benedicta slept on, slept on. The tall bald eunuch held the long-shanked dressmaker's scissors reverently, like an instrument of sacrifice, which indeed they were. Also the sterilised needle and the thread to baste the wound and stitch the empty pouch up like a *gigot*. It was not pain that turned Julian into a raging maniac, it was quite simply the indignity. When she told me this I could see suddenly the whole pattern of things lit up by the phosphorescent white light of his anger, translated out of impotence. No, the cruellest thing about impotence is that it is fundamentally a comic predicament. His father had not only punished him but had mocked him as well. A phrase creeps back to mind from some other forgotten context. "They were bound by a complicity of desire and purpose far stronger even than love, perhaps even independent of death." I hardly dare to touch her, to put my hand upon her shoulder when she looks like this. The closed eyes stare on and on into the centre of memory. "All this I will have to be punished for some day I suppose" she said between her teeth. "I was afraid you would find it endearing—another delightful feminine weakness to add to your collection." I had already begun to undress. I said, "I am not going to indulge your sense of guilt any more." I told her to take off her ski pants and sweater and climb in beside me. The sense of familiarity combined with the sense of novelty—new lives for old: a new version of an old model: new wine in old brothels: it held me spellbound. Nor were her kisses any longer contaminated by nervous preoccupations—the stream was flowing clear, undammed at last. "Tell me how you killed him, the husband." Between quickly drawn breaths she said: "Now?" "Yes, Benedicta, now." While she spoke I was making love to her, I was happy.

They had been mounted, had ridden far across the fields and valleys to a marsh where he had been promised game to hunt. By the side of a long narrow causeway ran a group of abandoned clay-cuttings with a rivulet flowing. Beneath the causeway was quicksand, or rather a quagmire. Urging her horse with her spurs she found it no hard matter to press his mount towards the end and softly push it over. He landed in a huge sucking surprised calm, almost disposed to laugh, looking up at her from under the brim of his soft straw hat. The sandy moustache. Two realisations gradually welled up simultaneously in his fuddled mind: namely, he was slowly settling in the black viscous mud, and that she had become suddenly motionless, her eyes staring down at him with an almost expressionless curiosity. But the horse knew and sent forth an almost human wail as it flailed with its legs to free them from the soft imprisonment, the anaconda coils of the mud. Appalling sounds of the sucking farting mud. As for the man he watched himself, so to speak, reflected in the pupil of that blue scientific eye, watched himself sinking down and away, out of time and mind: out of her life and out of his. Surprise held him silent. Only his youthful handsome face, now pale with sweat, held an expression of pained pleading. The treachery was so unexpected: it seemed that he had to revise the whole of their past life, their past relationship in the light of it. It was not only his past which swam before his astonished eyes but his future. He whispered "help" from a parched throat, but his lips barely framed the word. The moustache! But she only sat down upon the parapet, turning her mount loose, and watched the experiment with a holy concentration, forcing herself to memorise the whole thing unflinchingly so that she might recount it to Julian when the time came, when she would have to.

So he settled slowly as the westering sun itself was settling beyond the hills. They stared at each other in bitter silence, almost oblivious

39

of the death-struggles of the horse which blew its muddy bubbles and groaned and rolled its eyes as it slowly heaved its way downwards, suffocating. The mud sounded jocose. Soon he was there buried to the breastbone like some unfinished statue of an equestrian knight. "So that's it" he said, with a wondering croak. "So that's it, Benedicta."

"That's it, my darling."

She lit a cigarette with steady fingers and smoked it fast with shallow inspirations, never taking her eyes off his. But now it was horrible, he had begun to sob; the harsh sniffs broke down the features of his face into all the planes of childhood. He was getting younger as he died, was becoming a child again. And this was hard. A hopeless sympathy welled up in her, battling against the deadly concentration. It was becoming harder to watch with all the promised detachment. He was panting, head on one side, his mouth open. His hands were still free, but his elbows were becoming slowly imprisoned. There might still have been time to throw him a rope and pass it round a tree? She fought the thought, holding it at bay as she watched. It wasn't the fear of death so much, she thought, as the ignominy of her betrayal—that was what lay behind the tears of this adolescent, this infant in the straw hat. But in a little while he decided to spare her feelings, his tears ceased to flow; a lamblike resignation came over his face, for now he knew he was beyond hope. Quickly she cut a slip of reed, cleft it and passed down the lighted cigarette so that he might take a puff. But he brushed it away and with a small sigh turned his face inwards upon himself and floated thickly down in slow motion, with little shudders and no more sound —not even a reproach, a curse, a cry for help. Not a bubble. It was so quickly over. She watched and went on watching until only the hat still floated on the quag. She could hardly tear herself away from the spot now. Muttering to herself, she felt all at once as if she were in a high fever; a fiery exultation possessed her. She had shown herself worthy of Julian. She managed to secure the straw hat—she would carry it back to him like someone carrying the severed head of a criminal. The valley was silent, oppressively silent. She tried to sing as she went, but it only made the silent dusk more eerie. Once or twice she thought she heard the sound of horses' hooves behind her; and she wheeled about to see if there was anyone following—but there was nobody to be seen.

There! Easy to recount, to bring to memory, hard to assimilate. It still stuck in her throat like a bundle of bloody rags she could not swallow.

"And it's no good saying I am sorry; yes, I am, of course. But what really ails me is the wound to my self-esteem, to find myself, my wonderful unique beautiful self guilty of so petty a betrayal. You see what a trap the ego sets you?" She raised a white fist and drummed softly on my breastbone, and then sinking down she fell, mouth to mouth in a suffocating parody of sadness which swallowed itself in the new unhindered sexual paroxysms. "But by far the most absurd and humiliating thing that happened to me was to fall in love with you at first sight. It was unbearable, such a blow to my self-esteem, such a danger to my freedom. And also to you—you were in such danger for such a long time. Poor fool, you wouldn't have believed it; how could I tell you? I did not believe it myself. All that comedy of errors with the little clerk, remember? He was supposed to kill you in the cisterns. Poor man! First your hesitation about signing, then this poor foolish clerk being told to do away with you— he was unfitted for such a task, even though his own life depended upon it. All that excursion you found so funny was a sort of dress rehearsal for the job Sacrapant had been set. Mercifully you hesitated about signing, and this gave me a chance to reach Julian. I persuaded him to countermand the order. 'Leave him to me' I said. 'I will suck him dry. He has lots to offer us as yet. If necessary I will marry him, Julian, until we can dispose of him.' But in all the delay of sign and countersign the suspense became too much for poor Sacrapant, he knew he could never do it, that his time was up."

"So he fell out of the sky?"

"So he fell out of the sky. Kiss me."

"He sacrificed himself for me in a way."

"Not really, there's no such thing. I did."

I began to see a little deeper into the meaning of those first en-counters, those first brushes with the firm. They had already had a chance to see my notebooks which were from their point of view crammed with promises.

"Benedicta, darling, tell me one thing."

But she was asleep now with her blonde head against my breast rocked by our mutual breathing as a seagull is rocked by a calm summer sea. "I see" I whispered to myself, but in fact I saw only relatively. I recalled Jocas talking about the impossibility of ever tracing the real causal relationship between an act and its reason. And in the context of beloved Sacrapant, too, I saw the little man's pale water-rat face in the wallowing waterlight of the great cisterns.

It was here in Turkey that Julian first contracted that thirst for the black sciences which has always coloured the cast of his mind; for here every form of enquiry could be pursued in absolute safety. "The idolaters of Syria and Judaea drew oracles from the heads of children which they had torn from their bodies. They dried the heads and having placed beneath the tongue a golden lamen bearing unknown ciphers they fixed them in the hollows of walls, built up a kind of false body beneath them composed of magical plants fastened together: they lighted a lamp under these fearful idols and proceeded with their consultation. They believed that the heads spoke . . . moreover it is true that blood attracts larvae. The ancients when sacrificing dug a pit which they filled with warm and smoking blood; then from the recesses of the dark night they saw the feeble and pale shadows rising up, creeping, chirping, swarming about the pit. . . . They kindled great fires of laurel, alder and cypress upon altars crowned with asphodel and vervain. The night seemed to grow colder . . ." (Julian silent in a high-backed chair with a book open on his knees). Moreover "if integrally and radically the woman leaves the passive role and enters the active, she abdicates her sex and becomes man, or rather, such a transformation being physically impossible, she attains affirmation by a double negation, placing herself outside both sexes like some sterile and monstrous androgyne."

I was beginning to see him much more clearly, and in ideas like these I thought I caught a glimpse of the *altera* Benedicta, that lovely petrifact which destiny had transformed back into the loved original, the beloved outlaw I had almost forgotten in all this exhausting struggle. As for her mysterious and elusive lover, why should he not aspire to the mastery over age and time that Simon Magus first achieved? "Sometimes appearing pale, withered, broken, like an old man at the point of death: at others the luminous fluid revitalised him, his eyes glittered, his skin became smooth and soft, his body upright. He could be actually seen passing from youth to decrepitude, childhood to age." Nor did there seem to be any perversity in these speculations which swarmed in the young Julian's mind; everything was tinged with the vast oriental passivity of the place. Down below the jetty at Avalon you could still see, if you dived, the weighed sacks with the heads of the women—some forty—done to death like cats by Abdul Hamid in a sudden rage of revulsion against sex. Those that did not sink at once were beaten to death with oars in the green evening; their wails were piteous to hear, the boatmen had tears running down their faces as they worked. And Hamid? Do you remember the description of Sardanapalus the great king? "He entered and saw with surprise the king with his face covered in white lead, and all bejewelled like a woman, combing out purple wool in the company of his concubines and sitting among them with blackened eyes, wearing a woman's dress and having his beard shaved close and his skin rubbed with pumice. His eyelids too were painted. . . ." Then the great pyre he built to end his days; several storeys high it stood: and the conflagration lasted for weeks. Everything, to the smallest of his belongings, went up.

Mind you, only once did she dare to say that she loved him to his face, only once. His look of horror and fury was quite indescribable. He struck her across the face with a book, without contempt yet deliberately. "Hush" he said on a deep resonant note. "Hush, my darling." He was trying to say that it was not love, it was possession, and that her use of the word diminished the truth of the sentiment. Sentiment? No, that is not the word. She endured every kind of physical and sexual humiliation at his hands with the deepest joy, the profoundest pleasure. Julian was born never to weep. It was Jocas who took the scissors and embedded them in the wall of the cellars with their handles protruding. It had been decided that Julian was to go away, to be educated separately; partly it was the strain of the internal hatred between them all that decided the matter. But it was also dictated by the future needs of the firm, the firm that was going to be; for Merlin's quiet calculations were all

43

bearing fruit slowly. His subtleties put many a fruitful project in his way: as when Abdul Hamid had given a concession for the purchase and sale of tobacco *en régie* to a company unwise enough to order Austrian cigarette paper stamped with the Sultan's *tougra* or monogram. Nobody would have noticed this except a man like Merlin. Was the sultan, he asked, content to have his effigy spat upon daily by tens of thousands of cigarette-smokers in the kingdom? It was the same with the postage stamps which bore the monster's head. Were these also to be spittled over by scribes? Within a short space of time he secured both concessions for himself, for the firm.

A kiss is always the same kiss, though the recipient may change from time to time; her kisses were the only thing which had remained young still about her, fresh as spring violets. So many of our gestures are not prompted by psychological impulse but are purely hieratic—a whole wardrobe of prehistoric responses to forgotten situations. (The sex of the embryo is decided at coition; but five whole weeks evolve before the little bud declares itself as vagina or penis.) Io had suffered from a small and useful abnormality in being temporarily sterile: the closure of the lumen of the Fallopian tubes by scar tissue resulting from an early gonorrhoeal infection. . . .

Much of this I could not stand, could not bear hearing, bear knowing. I took refuge in the frivolity of my illness—purely in order to alarm her, to see if she cared. Master Charlock has been naughty this week; he has thrown his porringer on the floor, beat upon the table with his spoon, spilt his soup, roared like a bull, wet his trousers. . . . *Inventeur, Inventaire, Eventreur* . . . . I lie just looking at her, so far from the invincible happiness of possession; all this dirt, all these contaminated circumstances turned my love to vomit for a while. But this will not last; something which will prove to be stronger than the sum of these experiences will forge itself—is already rearing its flat head like a king cobra. If the sex thing remains the way it is I will not falter again.

But even as I lie thinking this, looking into her eyes, the other half of my mind is following her out across the Cilician plains where once she used to be sent to hunt the harmless quail with the women of the little court. They alight in great flocks during the spring when the sesame crop is ripening—from far off they seem to be one huge moving carpet of birds, running along the ground like mice, with a subdued chirping. The women hunt the little creatures with a light net and an *aba*, a strange prehistoric contrivance shaped like a shield, or one side of a huge box-kite; a skeleton of sticks covered in black cotton, but pierced with eyelets. Wearing this over their heads they advance in open order, staring through these huge eyes at the quail, which begin by running away: but soon appear to become mesmerised. They sit down and stare at the advancing shapes, allow themselves passively to be scooped up in the nets and transferred to the wicker hampers. Turning her mouth inwards upon mine I think of Dr. Lebedeff and his *délires archaïques*. Turkish delight, onanism in mirrors.

"It was not only Julian's life which was aberrant," she says clearly, trying to get it all off her chest, "it was the place, too. My father had me sexually broken, as we say in Turkish, by his slaves." Inexpressibly painful to her to retrace her steps over this poisoned ground, yet necessary. There in the night of Turkey I saw Julian as more of a goblin than a youth. The dust-devils racing across the plains, some spinning clockwise some counterclockwise. "You can see from the way they fold their cloaks which are female and which male" say the peasants. In those days to bring rain two men used to flog each other until the blood poured down their backs and the heavens melted. (They pissed on Merlin's eagle-wounds to disinfect them properly before dressing them.)

"Not all our eunuchs were artificially formed. There were some villages on the high plateau which specialised in producing strange but natural androgynes with an empty scrotum like a tobacco pouch; they were bald usually and had high scolding voices." Fragments of other lore have got themselves mixed up with the transcription somewhere here. (A skeleton whitewashed and painted the colour of blood, to present its re-emergence in the world. Or a phrase underlined by Julian in a book, "*Il faut annoncer un autre homme possible*"; you will see from this how deeply he was concerned with his own soul, and for the fate of man. It is not possible to consider him simply as an unprincipled libertine, or an alchemist who went mad under the strain of too much knowledge. No. His concern was with virtue, with truth. Otherwise why should he have said that the most

45

devastating criticism ever made of a human being was in the *Republic*
where the phrase occurs: "Now he was one of those who came from
heaven and in a former life had dwelt in a well-ordered state, but his
virtue was a matter of habit only and he had no philosophy"? I do
not really know him as yet; perhaps I will never know him now.)

Autumn is well on the way with its moist colouring, its rotting
avenues of leaves; but these wards are quite seasonless. Blood-orange
moons over the Alps. But I am miles away still in the heart of Turkey
with Benedicta. There is still so much to comprehend. They have
changed my nurse for a great big sad dun-coloured creature with
eyes like conjugal raisins. In the dangerous wards they are playing
backgammon with little moans of surprise; men and women like
outmoded, damaged pieces of furniture. "Smoking spunk!" cries
Rackstraw with peevish vexation. "What has the dooced boots done
with my suèdes?" There is no answer to the question. Then at times
a touching half-comprehension of his situation comes upon him—in
the mirror on the white wall he will talk to himself thus: "Ah, my
lifelong friend, I have led you up to this point, past so many deceits,
so many suicides. And you are still there. Now what? Something the
blood deposits as it moves about like an old snake. But the reticence
of these ghosts is amazing. Io! Io!" He listens with his head on one
side, then turns away, shaking his head and whispering: "I was sent
here because I loved too much. It was out of proportion. I had to pay
for it with all this boredom." Drawing in breath on the window-
pane with a long yellow finger he will suddenly change mood and
subject and exclaim: "Has anyone seen Johnson lately? I wonder
where he's gone. I last heard he'd been locked up in Virginia Water
for making love to a tree."

Where indeed was Johnson and why did he write so infrequently?
"They may have moved him from Leatherhead to Virginia Water.
He has had a great crisis of *belief*, Johnson. They are studying his
case with care; it is not like me, I am simply here to rest on my
laurels." Rackstraw scratches an ear.

"Pthotquyck" he says suddenly, brightly.

"I beg your pardon?"

"Pthotquyck. It's the Finnish for mushroom."

"I see."

46

"The dooced things get into everything."

From various sources I have managed to piece together the story of his friend Johnson, the great lover. Yes, they are holding him at Virginia Water, in the grip of his fearful but poetical Yggdrasil complex, or so I suppose they must call it. "Things have closed in very much down here," he writes. "The people are kind but not very understanding. Out in the park there are some lovely trees, and next week when I have my first walk I will try and have a couple. Elms!" It was as simple as that—suddenly in the full flower of his sexual maturity Johnson found he loved trees. Other men have had to make do with goats or women or the Dalmatian Cavalry, but Johnson found them all pale into insignificance beside these long-legged green things which were everywhere: he saw them as green consenting adults with diminished responsibility, loitering all round him with intent. They beckoned to him, urged him to come on over; they could hardly do otherwise, for a tree has not much conversation. Perhaps it was due to his long and severe training for the Ministry which had all but tamed him. However it may be, long-suffering policemen on the prowl for more unsavoury misdemeanours used to chase the skinny figure round and round Hyde Park. Johnson showed a surprising turn of speed, running distractedly here and there like a cabbage white, doing up his trousers fervently as he ran.

For several orgiastic weeks he led them a dance, and perhaps they would never have caught him had not the indignant prostitutes organised an ambush for this harmless satyr. He was distracting trade they said, while some people were even complaining that the trees were getting bent, several of them. This was pure jealousy of course. So Johnson, priest and dendrophile, was committed to the doctors for attention. And now Rackstraw is here, brooding on the destiny of his friend. He sighs and says: "And Iolanthe—I wonder if you ever heard of her? She was famous in her day, I made her famous. I wrote them all except one—the one about the lovers in Athens. Films. The whole thing came from her diaries, she wouldn't let me change a word of the dialogue. The young man had died or gone away, I don't know. But she could never see it without weeping. It used to upset me. O I wonder what's happened to Johnson. Pthotquyck!"

47

The woods are full of them, the wards are full of them! Yet they contrive in their disjointed fashion to present a composite picture of a way of life, a homogeneous society almost—even the most alienated. They smell each other's aberrations as dogs smell each other's tail-odours. Even the hauntingly beautiful Venetia, the little girl with two cunts, who has specialised in a crooning echolalia which Rackstraw listens to with delectation—as if to the song of some rare bird.

"Who are you?"
"Who."
"Who are you?"
"Are you."
"Are you Venetia Mann?"
"Mann."
"Are you?"
"Are you."

Rackstraw shakes his head and gives a mirthless laugh. "Priceless" he says. "Priceless."

Ah, but one day we will be restored to the body of the real world—O world of Anabaptists, tax-dodgers and hierophants, O world of mentholised concubines! Yes, my darling wife, with your bright eyes and snowburnt face, we shall leave this place one day, arm in arm. A new life will begin, dining off smoked foreskin in Claridge's, on partridges in Putney. We will leave Rackstraw to play chess with the deaf mute. And Felix will go back to the firm with the same engaging adolescent manner which seems to say: please be nice to me, I have only been educated up to the anal stage. Back to London, back to the vox pop of the banjo-group, back to the young with their unpsychoanalysed hair. Kiss me Benedicta.

But pouring out a drink with shaking hand she says:
"Julian has said that he wants to see us together."
"Well?"
"I'm beginning to feel afraid again."
"The very word is like a knell."
"He says everything is different now."
"It had better be."

Not tonight, though; tonight we are alone, just the two of us, compounding fortune with all her little treacheries. You will tell me once more, lying half asleep, about the locusts—of how the early winds brought them sailing over Anatolia, darkening the light of the sun. How the hunters would see them first, being the longest-sighted: and give tongue. Whistles and gunshots and the winking of heliographs from the ruined watch-towers of the coast. Away across the bronzy stubble and the mauve limestone ranges the marauders came in innocent-looking puffs, coming nearer and nearer until the cauldron overflowered and they were on you. Clouds at first soft, evanescent, tempted to disperse: but no, instead they gathered weight and density, formed into the wings of giant bats, spread out to swallow the pure sky.

The camp went grimly frantic with preparations: as if for an arctic blizzard, for the horny coarse-bodied little insects penetrate everywhere, everything, ubiquitous as smoke or dust itself. Heads wrapped in cloth or duffel, wrists fastened, legs sheathed in puttees or leggings. Then the long wait to determine if the cloud was preceded by an advance guard of wingless green young ones, pouring along the ground with incredible speed, turning the fields to a rippling torrent of scaly green.

Pits were dug, long barriers of tin or wood scooped the advance guard (as far as was possible) into them where kerosene fires smoked and flapped. On they came pouring themselves unhesitatingly into the pits, piling upon the bodies of their burning fellows, until there were tons of them ablaze. The stench deafened creation. But the fliers approached with that ominous deep crackle—first from far away like thorns under a pot: then nearer, more deafening, like a forest fire, the noise of their shearing jaws. The illusion of fire was also given by the speed with which they stripped the forest of every green leaf, hanging in long strings like bees swarming. Shrubs keeled over with the weight of their bodies. The horses kicked and shied at their horny touch; and however many precautions one took one always felt the creatures crawling up one's legs or arms, scratching the bare skin, tickling. In a twinkling the whole visible world was stripped of life, bald as a skull. A winter forest as nude as Xmas under the burning sun. A very particular and utterly silent silence followed such attacks for weeks on end: that and the stench of charred bodies burning like straw.

49

Then camps were broken up, ranks redressed; but exhaustedly, listlessly. Yet there had been no danger. Only it was as if they themselves had been stripped of everything except their eyeballs. In one of the khans a circling vulture dropped a woman's hand into the camp. Well and so back like ants to the skylines, to where the blue gulf carved and recarved itself, smoothing away towards the fitful city.

*   *   *   *   *

Deep sleep was good again though the research ferrets of the unconscious still sniffed around the motives and actions of my silent companion. The past isn't retrievable is it?—too many burnt-out bulbs. Try, Felix, only try!

Now this morning an unexpected envelope with a London postmark—this from Vibart; not a real letter, he explains, but a few pages torn from his desk pad. "I should really have come to see you, Felix, but I'm superstitious about bins. Always have been. Suppose you were glassy, eh? Ugh! Even a real letter might be wasted, then. But a few pages from my desk pad will give you news of me, broadening the old mind as we used to say.

> "*Tell me*
>
> *What strange irrelevance*
> *Dogs the lives of elephants*
> *With trunk before*
> *And tail behind,*
> *With ears of such vast elegance*
> *How they control the state*
> *Of such a massive gait*
> *And still be reasonable and kind*
> *Though almost all behind?*

> "*item*

"It's awkward, isn't it, when the flippant, the effortlessly inconsequent, becomes a tic. We have come a long way together haven't we old man? Without being very much together either; from time to time, like model railways our paths cross at a critical junction. Ting-a-ling!

> "item

"Cogent Memo in Julian's own hand. (He has begun to write very big and sprawly now.) 'From a publishing point of view the only irresistible themes are Quests, Confessions, and Puzzles in that order. Let Vibart govern his judgement by this unshakable truth.' An odd tone to take with me, isn't it? What about all those poems which give us prestige—poems written with a stomach pump? Koepgen's new volume for example. It's all very well for him, Julian, just off to New York again with his star-spangled manner.

"item

"Felix, I am making a very great deal of money. Yesterday my ideal novel came in. It begins 'Smith was a nice big man in good health; but because he had been told as a child that his balls would fly off if he laughed too heartily his face always wore a strange twisted expression. He lived in dreadful anticipation until one day the worst happened . . . (now read on).' I have had to refuse it for other reasons.

"item

"One lives and learns. F.V. the novelist tells me that 'one should know as little as possible about one's characters. The more detail you give the more they sink back into the undifferentiated mass. All you need is one cardinal aspect for each one—a ruling bent, in fact the person's "signature" in the heraldic sense: hunchback money-lender, myopic scholar, deist king. The rest is padding.' And I suppose that the proof of the padding is in the publishing?

"item

"Felix, I'm miserable, how are you? How would F.V. novelise us? I wonder if we might presume ourselves to live in one of his fictions? If only you knew, if only he knew. Pia! The last letters! It is unfair. I can't bring myself to throw them away: yet what purpose would they serve if I kept them? They are fading anyway. Time is very generous in some ways. 'Death comes always by a sort of secret intention, a compact. Like a love affair, one *disposes* towards it, one *inclines*, one intimates the secret need.' I sometimes wish myself in the Paulhaus with you—at times I almost merit it. My dreams, you

52

should see them! What an extraordinary fauna and flora sprouts from the infernal regions.

"item

"And all the time she was staring at me with those candid and un-flinching eyes she knew that she was quietly and confidently betraying me all down the line. She had decided I wasn't a man, I suppose. And with whom? Guess! Yes, with Jocas. I really can't believe it myself as yet. The caption doesn't fit the picture. And yet it's all there, written out in her own fair hand. The riding lessons! Then when we had to go away they both got ill from the separation. How sordid. All those doctor's bills. Damn.

"item

"The fear of solitude is at bottom the fear of the double, the figure which appears one day and always heralds death. The triumph of death over the hero is ineluctable—*le triomphe ignoble du mal remplit le monde d'une immense tristesse*. Would you buy a manuscript with such things in it?

"item

"Pia says: 'What matter? One day my teeth will fall out like rocks out of a hillside. Only the dignity of the mouth—its outline—which once haunted men might linger a little in certain postures. Musculature giving in like an old banjo. Then I shall die—but I *have*; while you are reading this I *am*. The process has started. Let's imagine Pia in a state of infinite dispersion, infinite extension, inhabiting every nook in imaginable space. It will be hard to part with all my jewellery and clothes—even the *toc*. And what of that family of little homeless shoes? How could I do it to them? But I must, I *have*. Yet I cannot bring myself to leave them to anyone, for death is only apparent and mostly by scheming. I would have liked to embrace you once, good and warm—but you would decipher my intention from my kiss. I dare not risk it. Only Jocas knows the date, the time, the minute; I am taking him with me in a funny sort of way, as a fellow-passenger. He will still be on earth of course, and quite unchanged in the physical sense; but in a special sense not. The not-part will have been expropriated. I am trying not to punish him too much. He did

53

me one inestimable service in love—taught me to "listen with the clitoris" as he called it.'

"Well, and then it gets mixed up with my obligatory reading. Listen, 'Love, then, as both teleological and biological trigger'. The weight of these massive ponderations illustrated by Pia's dead gnome's face. Damn them all, the philosophic cut-throats. Mumbo-jumbo, cant and twaddle. In a book on esoteric something or other she has underlined a passage which goes: 'Nothing is hidden, there are no secrets. But you can tell people only what they already know. That is the infuriating thing. And while they may know it, they may not be conscious that they know. Hence the jolt provided by the dry-cell batteries of art. In such a thing all that has been done is to create an area of self-recognition. The reflected light plays upon the observer, he sees, becomes a see-er, a self-seer.' The wisdom of other lands and other time, my lad. What avails it all?

> "Alcibiades,
> Alcibiades!
> Feeling it rise and recede
> Like the Pleiades, bids us
> Take heed.
> 'One gets tired of elderly parties
> Even when they are as wise as Socrátes.'

"item

"So here I am, your old pal Vibart, still walking these rain-benisoned streets, rising morning after morning at cocksparrow-lantern to face the terrible effrontery of a bowl of porridge. I listen to the news before checking latch-key and leaving house. In the tube inhale the twirpy twang of urban English. Life has no sharp edges.

"item

"Lately I have all but managed to see Julian face to face—I've been playing your sly game with him, just to tease him, I mean. I even waited in his flat for a while as you did—of course with no result. I found it much as you told me I would. But those great blow-ups of Iolanthe, they were all slashed as if with a pair of scissors. Someone too had written across one in Greek, 'Αρχείτω βίος! Ιώ! Ιώ!* For the only time in my life my classical education proved of some use —for I recognised the quotation. I don't know why it gave me such a pang. Is it possible that such a man feels?

"item

"I see a lot of Pulley but in the question of Caradoc–Crusoe some new and ambiguous developments have thrown us into a state of in-decision. At any rate Robinson has been expropriated by the Austra-lians and has disappeared. They want his island as a proving-ground for one of your toys, ironically enough: something Marchant has modified and perfected. May one perhaps see the hand of Julian in all this—or perhaps we exaggerate? I'm sick of looking over my shoulder. At any rate that is all we know about Robinson. Mean-while I enclose two little items from the usually so sedate *Informateur* of Zürich which you may find highly suggestive. Could they be . . . ? *Aimable yogi cherche nonne enculable vue mariage.* Box 346 X. Also this: *Young flesh fervently sought by aged but eclectic crosspatch.* Box 450 X.

"item"

I stifled a cry of amused amaze, but my involuntary start must have jolted her out of sleep. She lay with eyes closed, but awake and drowsy. "My goodness" she said at last in a luxurious whisper settling that slender body warmly against mine, revising its posture so that it fitted as nearly as possible into the hollows of my own. "You have begun to believe in me as a possibility at last." It was only our sleepy minds making love, or recovering the part of it which had been so long left unmade. Kiss.

"Caradoc may be alive, do you hear?"

"Of course."

"Did you know it?"

"Not for certain; I sort of felt it in my bones."

"We must try and find out." In my enthusiasm I all but forgot the equivocal nature of the "freedom" Nash had so heartily con-ferred on this patient. Free, yes. To walk along the lakeside at

* Enough of life! Io! Io!

55

twilight, hand in hand with B. if need be; but always following on behind us after a discreet interval came the small white ambulance, keeping its exact distance. This was just in case I should become overtired. Once I amused myself by entering a cinema and leaving at once by another entrance, but it was not long before they caught up with me. The town is small, the streets short. Besides I was, I am, tired; moreover I have no projects, nothing to look forward to, nowhere I would rather be than in this clinical paradise. A philosopher out of work. Benedicta must have been following my thoughts with great accuracy for she said: "No, you won't be followed any more. Let's go and try and find him, if you wish. I know because Julian is here. He telephoned about a meeting. He said so, and you know he never lies." So we sat down to eat together and plan. It was unnerving in its unfamiliarity—I mean the simple act of eating off the same tray. (In the age of chivalry, husband and wife, knight and lady, ate off the same trencher, he feeding her.) Well, I want to keep an exact record of all this; I still don't trust anyone, except sporadically Benedicta herself.

II

The offices of the *Informateur* were easy to find; in an old building smelling of drains and printer's ink. The editor a tiny mollusc in powerful spectacles. The cuttings rather startled him, and he went to files to assure himself that they had indeed appeared in his august journal. It was unusual, it was bizarre. He was a little troubled on the grounds of good taste.

At any rate the offices which handled the advertising were at Geneva, and he thought that current practice would prevent them giving me the address of an advertiser. It was a private matter, after all. I would have to write. This was disheartening; but since the project itself might well prove hopelessly chimerical it wasn't worth being too cast down about it. We sent a couple of telegrams to the box numbers, one from some young flesh signed by Benedicta and one from an "enculable nonne" signed by myself, offering every enticement we could. Then we wandered for a while in the streets, chafing ourselves upon the windows with all their finery, admiring everything. "Buy me something" said Benedicta suddenly. "I want to be given something, anything small and cheap. In bad taste if you like." But I had forgotten my wallet and while she had plenty of money on her it "wouldn't do", for some reason or other, it *wouldn't do*! For some esoteric reason this made me suddenly happy. I felt an absurd disposition to tears almost. She stood me coffee and cream buns in a deserted café with plush seats and barely any light; and suddenly I felt a desire to rid myself of my cocoon of bandages which I did in the lavatory. "Good" she said. "Good. Don't look rueful even if the hair hasn't covered the scars as yet. The move is in the right direction."

"Loving" I said, sinking back into my seat with a sigh, though the word had a strange translated ring to it; it was as if I were trying it out, like a shoe. Benedicta nodded, her blue eyes bright.

59

"Loving" she said, as if she too were trying it out.

Then she added as we rose to walk back up the hill to the Paul-haus: "No more of it for us. We've done it. We've committed it, and need never think of it again. Unless. . . . How sure do you feel of yourself?"

"I don't know. Remember a piece of my brain is missing; suppose it's the piece (like in the old phrenology skulls) which had the fatal word written on it? Then what?"

"Nothing. I've done it, I've had it, I am it."

"My God, is happiness so simple then?"

"When you are committed; when it's a fact."

"Benedicta, what are you planning, what are you dreaming about?"

"For the first time nothing. I'm just content to be, to have escaped Julian, to have persuaded you to try and rediscover me. Let's just let go, shall we, until we see Julian?"

The long walk, the long silence, the plenitude of it, refreshed instead of tiring me.

"This is very absurd."

"I know."

In some vague and unspecified way the wind of destiny seemed to have shifted. A mild sun fumed upon the fir-clad slopes, filling the valleys with a ghostly mist; but now all benign. Even the winding paths, the firmly shuttered look of the buildings, the cars parked in rows along the concrete drive-ins—they had all participated in this subtle shift of emphasis. It only takes a little thing like an outing when you are a loony. . . . No, but there was substance to it. "Come and spend tonight with me up at the chalet. It's all right. Just tell them." Just tell them! I wondered where she discovered this fund of easy insouciant optimism. Nevertheless I returned for a bath and a change of the small dressings and with nervous sang-froid did as I was bid. No objections were raised—though when I think of it what objections could have been raised? It just shows the state of mind I had got myself into.

It was ten minutes' walk over the hill to the chalet with its little chaplet of firs; there were lights on inside, but soft lights suggesting candles. I kicked off my snow and slush and tapped. She was in the little hall already changed into a long dress cut like an abba and made of some heavy damascened material; she was in the act of combing out the new head of curly blonde hair. "It all fell out during the course of my troubles and I inherited a new head from who knows where? My mother perhaps. There's a lot of white in it, Felix." It was quite simply beautiful, much silkier and lightly curling. The face I had so often seen lined with suffering, sulky, anaemic—it had also renewed itself; the so often lacklustre eyes (turning towards grey in candle-light) had a recaptured vivacity. She could tell I liked her this way, better than ever. Someone was moving about the little studio with its warm smells of polished wood, its crude peasant curtains. Baynes was setting a small table for us before the throbbing log fire. It was too much. I reached towards a forbidden whisky, saying, "My God Baynes, is it really you? I thought I dreamed you up." Baynes smiled his wooden smile and said: "I came in once or twice to see you were all right, sir." So he was really here. No dream was old sobersides Baynes, but our very own reality. "Here let me touch you to prove it." It was partly that, and partly an excuse to embrace Baynes without causing him an attack of blushes. Baynes submitted to these proofs of his existence like an elder churchman, modestly benign.

I walked around the little place which had been her self-imposed prison for so long with all the curiosity of a visitor suddenly entering the imperial apartments on St. Helena. The disposition of everything suggested some far-reaching shift of values. The old litter of half-empty medicine bottles, uncut French novels, widowed slippers, clothes tossed in corners—there was no trace of all this. Even with a dozen maids to clear up after her the old Benedicta could leave her thumb-prints on her quarters after half an hour in residence. The telephone rang, but it seemed to be a wrong number. "O I forgot all about it," said Baynes penitently "but a gentleman rang up and left a message for Madam. I wrote it down." Sitting by the fire she took it and read it with a chuckle. "There's your answer" she said. "I told you so."

Baynes had laboriously transcribed it with a few spelling errors, but in sum it said: "Amiable yogi will meet green fruit at Manwick's English Tearoom Geneva Saturday for crumpet and butter. Only place in Europe for crumpet."

I felt the blood rush to my heart. "He's alive." And characteristically the feeling was succeeded by one of vexation for all the amount of missing him I had done. "Damn the old fool" I said. And now a different set of preoccupations raised their heads. Benedicta was putting a disc on the record player. "What is it Felix?"

"I don't want to prejudice him—to make a *gaffe* and lead Julian to him. That's what I was thinking."

"I think Julian has seen him" she said. "So that isn't a problem. In fact I bet you he has been trying to get Julian to take him back into the firm."

"What?"

"Yes. I bet you. And now probably Julian will refuse to do so!"

"Caradoc!"

It was an unheard-of departure after all this elaborate disappearance and fictitious immortality. "How much do you know about it?" Benedicta lit a cigarette and said softly: "Only what I surmise. Julian said nothing when he spoke to me; but once before he puzzled me because he himself seemed not to be quite sure whether it *was* Caradoc or not. Perhaps Caradoc has changed very much; but I was amazed when Julian said something like 'either our own Caradoc or whoever might be impersonating him so perfectly' . . . . Perhaps it was just one of those things which slip out in conversation and mean nothing. Come, let's meet him."

"He can't live without making a mystery of something" I said angrily. "It's his ruling monomania." Benedicta smiled and took my hand pressing me down beside her before the burning logs. "I know" she said. "And yet he has nothing really to hide—not more nor less than any man." What made me angry, I think, was this sudden questioning of Caradoc's reality almost before he had been reclaimed from the grave. Yes, that was it.

"And Geneva!"

"It's not far, just a short drive."

"Do you think we can go?"

"Of course."

She seemed so certain of everything as if something had happened to reassure her; what the basis of this new confidence could be I did not try to imagine. It was good to be here in this way, relaxed within the boundaries of a new understanding that had lost the old fearful vigilance. Outlines of a new maturity of vision? One hardly dared to hope for so much. And yet there we were, effigies of our old selves, sitting in front of the fire and gazing at each other with a curious sense of renewal. "Tonight I want to sleep alone. Can I?" There was no need to ask me, was there? "I want to collect myself a little bit. Count out my loose change, so to speak."

Baynes came and solemnised a little after dinner as was his way before he said goodnight and set up the little silver thermos of coffee which was practically the only relic I could recognise from past habits. "Do you still sleepwalk?" Benedicta smiled. "Not for ages now, perhaps never again. Let's hope, shall we?" I stood up to take my leave but she went on with a restraining hand laid upon mine. "Stay just a second. I want to do something with you here; will you?"

She went into the inner room and emerged with an armful of the little leather postiche-boxes which had been such a feature of her ancient wardrobe. Opening them she tumbled out upon the floor in precious confusion all her wigs—the fine hair of nuns, of Swedish corpses, of Indonesian and Japanese geisha girls, of silk and thrilling nylon. All tumbled together in a heap. Then one by one, combing each softly with her long fingers, disentangling it, she began to put them on the fire. Black smoke and flame rose from this pyre. I did not question, did not exclaim, did not speak. "From now on nothing that isn't my own" she said. "But I wanted to do it with you, somehow. Just to prove."

*   *   *   *   *

It was not a long run, and it was a comfortable one, for Benedicta had unearthed a black sports car with good heating and a turn of rampant speed wherever the surfaces had been cleared. A heavy thaw had set in, the lakeside swam and wallowed in warm mist. The attentive white snarls of white mountain came out and retired again endlessly, like actors taking innumerable curtain calls. She drove with dash, but immaculately. The whole thing was as easy as breathing, or so it seemed to me. Even old Geneva looked its best with its snug Viennese flavoured architecture and its melancholy lake views; thawing ice was chinking along the river where the dark arterial thrust of the waters carved their way towards the southern issues—waters which would soon see Arles and Avignon.

We had lunch at the Quatorze, but were both too excited to eat very much. We walked silently by the water until it was time to turn our steps towards Manwick's Tea Rooms—a relic which had been washed up at the end of the Victorian era and had remained as authentic as any Doge's palace, unchanged, unblushing, uncorrupted. . . . It was the headquarters of the Nannies of Geneva (like Bonington's in Rome). Very old ladies clad in home-weave smocks wielded cake slices. The tables were as heavy as William Morris, so was the cutlery; the walls were papered in something indeterminate which Ruskin would have admired. There was even a complete set of Sherlock Holmes in a yellowed Tauchnitz edition which lined one window embrasure. O the simplicity of everything was momentous. I mean that we saw him directly we entered, sitting at the far end, with his face buried in a book. It was not very crowded. But we were both suffocated with a sort of weird apprehension—we tiptoed towards him as one might toward some rare butterfly, trying to get a closer view without disturbing the rare specimen.

The fact of the matter is that we sat down at his table like a couple of gun-dogs in a point. It seemed to last ages, this little tableau, but it could have been only a second or two before he closed his book and said in his familiar deep voice: "So there you are at last." He must already have caught sight of us entering the place. "Caradoc!" He gave a raucous chuckle and threw back his head in a gesture which was familiarity itself. And yet . . . and yet. There was no doubt that he had changed. To begin with his hair, as plentiful as ever, was now no longer tabby, particoloured; it was white and as fine as the thread of silk. His mouth was mantled by an equally soft and sparse moustache of a mandarin kind. Beard there was none, and his pink rubicund face shone out upon the world like a winter sun. "It's only old age," he said as if to explain "only old age, look you." Yet in another way he had never looked—I was going to say "younger"—but it might be more accurate to say something like "healthier". His skin was firm and unwrinkled, his eyes glittering with amiable malice and hardly crowsfooted. Yes, one did have a moment of doubt about his real identity; but the voice clinched it. "The death and the resurrection" he boomed, ordering crumpets with a capacious gesture, yet taking a precautionary look into a little leather purse while doing so. An aged lady, all politeness, took his order with an approving smile. She had caught his last phrase and doubtless thought he was some friendly religious maniac—Geneva is full of them. The old darned plaid had been replaced with something of much the same style—a sort of evangelical overcoat with heavy cabman collars. He looked like a rather smart music-hall coachman.

"My God, Caradoc! You owe it to us to tell us all, everything." He nodded briskly, as if he had every intention of so doing. But as a preliminary he took a small silver flask of something which looked suspiciously like whisky and tipped a modicum into his teacup; then he produced a tiny tortoiseshell snuffbox and tapped it with a fingernail before whiffing up a grain or two from his extended thumb. "Julian that old bodysnatcher wouldn't believe it was me" he said with a certain pride. "That is what it does for you, escaping. I had three lots of twins straight off in Polynesia—bang off like that, without a moment's effort. The little woman was only a child but she had read the stud-book, she knew racing form. More's the pity,

I've had to leave them all behind because of funds. They would have looked damn rococo in London, I can swear."

"But from the beginning, Caradoc. Why did you cause all this fuss and flurry, cause us such anguish and despair?"

"In one way I had to," he said "to see how it felt. I had to. And the minute I'd done it I knew that it was the best, the most fruitful thing I had ever done. At the same time I knew just as certainly that it wasn't necessary at all—it could have been done another way. But when someone wants jam on their bread it's no good just describing it. They want to taste some. So you've got to provide some. But of course the firm was hard to persuade about this—particularly Julian. I bided my time. I thought in fact my chance would never come. Year after year, my boy, all the time getting more and more successful, piling up less and less reasons to leave my beautiful billet. But when the crash came I realised that I had to try. But aut Tunc aut Nunquam—it was then or never! And mighty successful it was, what I tasted of it, what I learned from it. All that coconut oil, you should feel my breasts. They are like a woman's only prettier." He poured some more tea, spliced it, and plunged into the crumpets until the butter was running off his chin. "After all," he said indistinctly "what is it really to buzz off to a remote isle with a tropical Venus? Nothing very much. Time takes on a wonderful never-quite quality. Infinite extension, lad, causality pulling out like a rubber band. At first of course one misses doctors and dentists and Shakespeare and all that. Of course. I don't deny it. One dreams of cod's roe or roasted shad—many the night I've woken with tears in my voice at a New York restaurant. Waiters always whisked the shad away before I'd eaten it. But it didn't last. Finally a sort of Proserpine feeling came over me. Exhausted by night and droopy by day, living on paw-paw and piggy-wiggy: I was in the lap of the local lotus-eating Gods I was. Never question it."

"Then why come back?"

"That was another jolt from the blue. The whole group of those islands was scooped up by the Aussies. One morning I woke up and found coastguards all over my place and warships poking about. We were bought out for practically nothing. Expropriated! Then they started nosing into my papers because I cut up so very rough, and I was on rather weak ground there. Apparently Robinson had quite a history behind him about which I knew nothing—he was bigamous to the core, old man, and the continent was studded with women crying out for vengeance and alimony. It was a terrible fix. I had to recover my own identity in order to escape from his wives. Then of course I had the inevitable note from Julian telling me not to be a fool. While I had no inclination to knuckle under I was in a squeeze and he knew it. I went through a long period of debate and finally I decided I would come back and rejoin the firm on the old terms. It cost me something to come to the decision, but I did it. And in a funny sort of way I felt relieved at having done it—as if I learned all I needed to learn from the experience out there with little Inky the wife and the funny ten-toed nippers. I bought them a coconut grove with my last cash—in another group—and said a tearful farewell. Landed in England dead broke, dead broke. And now . . . ."

"Everything's all right again" I cried.

"Far from it" said Caradoc ruefully. "Very far from it. I am living for the time being on the charity of old Banubula."

"What?" said Benedicta incredulously.

He gave what in stage directions is sometimes called a "dark laugh" and snuffed once, with a pained hauteur. "I rang up Julian when I arrived but he was awfully evasive though kind: just off on a long trip, you know the sort of thing. I didn't like to talk about reinstatement point blank and he didn't mention it. And I knew that Delambert had been given all my appointments and charges. Well, the upshot of it was that he told me he would like to see me in Geneva to talk things over; and this he duly did a few days ago, but without any result."

"But it's scandalous" I said hotly. Caradoc shook his head quickly and put out a hand as if to intercept the charge in mid air. "O no" he said. "It's not like that. Don't get the impression Julian is out to punish me, to victimise me—nothing like that. He is far above any such considerations. No, it was as if, in a sense, I had missed a step on the ladder, on the moving staircase, and I would have to wait awhile until the turn came round again. It was all to do with the firm, and the destiny of the firm: of us all, I suppose, in a way. It was a most extraordinary interview.

"It took place in a suitably mysterious setting on the lake some way out beyond the United Nations buildings: (by the way, in the course of other matters he said nonchalantly that the firm was hoping to take the building over next year—and I wondered what about the inhabitants, all those people living in the woodwork?) Anyway I was summoned at dusk to meet a small motor-boat. Dead calm oily water, heavy thaw, almost like a late autumn night with a full moon and all those blasted mountains showing their teeth like wolves. It could have been eerie to some I suppose. Nor was it very far along. Just by a landing-stage amid a cluster of tall dark trees there was a rotunda of sorts with a rose arbour, and a table with cold marble chairs surrounding it. He was sitting alone there waiting for me with a great goblet of wine in front of him, opposite in front of what was obviously to be my chair was another equally heartening-looking one with brandy. It was warm; I feared I might get piles sitting on the marble but the sight of the brandy reassured me. 'Well' he said. 'At last. I'm so glad it's over.' Quite a promising beginning wouldn't you say? So thought I.

"I advanced to receive his hesitant cool handshake. Of course as always he was sitting with his back to the moon so that he was all outline, if you see what I mean. His face was in half-shadow. Once or twice I saw a moonflake alight on his crown—white hair or very blond, one couldn't say which. And in a funny sort of way the optical illusion created by the watery moonlight gave the impression that he was altering shape all the time; not very conspicuously, you understand. But it could be seen; it was like a gentle breathing, systole and diastole. But his voice was just the same as always—the pained-lamb voice Pulley used to call it, remember? He questioned me very calmly and quietly about what I had been doing on my island; showed every mark of considerate attention. Also the brandy was excellent. I roughed in my little crusoe, as you might call it. Then he said: 'And you expected to be taken back just like that? You expected the firm to grant you absolution and a hundred lines and take you back?' I mumbled a bit and scraped the gravel with my toe. Then somewhat to my surprise he went on. 'And of course it will. But you will have to wait until it can find a place for you, having abandoned your own so suddenly. The ranks have closed, you know.' "

Caradoc paused.

"Of course I wouldn't want for a decent living outside the firm; I could get something good tomorrow. But . . . I don't know how it is, yet the idea didn't appeal to me very much. All my adult creative life has been spent with the firm. He said it really wasn't a question of money but of order. If he took me back now, before waiting my turn, he could only offer me relatively menial things to do, things which might waste my grey matter and time and in the long run be bad for my credit and standing. 'We have always treated you in the same way, and neither of us can change now' he added, sadly, I thought. 'We have offered you only things which *nobody else could do, nobody living*. So we will have to wait for our reality-jolt as you waited so many years for yours.' I suppose you will think it nonsense but it carried a queer kind of conviction for me. I drank my flowing bowl and gazed sleepily at him. Really, he is a marvellous character Julian, a strange one. I'd like to know him better, to know more about it. He seemed sort of hurt, as if he were nursing some sort of internal grievance against the order of things. I don't know. He surprised me by saying: 'Yes, we must wait for it—who knows till when? Perhaps one of these days you will be asked to build a tomb for Jocas out there in Turkey.''

Jocas! Nobody could have been further from my own thoughts at that moment. "And then what, Caradoc?"

Caradoc performed a rather clumsy mopping up operation with a spruce handkerchief. "Nothing" he said. "Or practically nothing. He spoke a bit about you, with great affection I must add. He said he still had hopes that you would understand the issues better—whatever that meant. Then he said the time was getting on. Right in the background, outside the large house shrouded in big trees, I had heard the continuous noise of car-tyres on gravel and seen the sweeping of headlights as limousine after limousine drew up and disgorged its occupants. There was a steady movement into the lighted hallway of the building; it looked like people going to an opera, for I saw women in evening dress. But Julian wasn't dinner-jacketed; striped shirt and speckled bow tie and dark suit, as I could half guess. He caught the direction of my eye and said: 'It's gambling, Caradoc. For the first time I have started to gamble and lose,

a thing I have never done. It makes one most uncertain. I had become over-confident and always risked very large sums. I had got
used you see, never to losing heavily. But now, I don't know. I dare
not reduce my habits of *play* for fear of altering my *luck*, the basic
psychic predisposition to win which I enjoyed over so many years.
I hope it doesn't mean something serious. I have always avoided
studying the matter of play because I believed in luck but lately I
have been wondering if a computerised study might yield some ideas
which would help me. And yet I feel such a thing would be fatal,
fatal.' He repeated the word with such emphasis that I felt a vague
sort of sympathy and alarm for him. 'I'm stuck in a way' he said, and
then abruptly stood up and said goodnight, keeping himself face
forwards to me as I went down to the landing-stage where the little
boat lay. The driver lit the dash and kicked the engine over. I
turned and looked back across the inky water, just in time to see the
dark indistinct figure of Julian moving away towards the house. He
had his hands folded behind his back, his head bowed. I could see
the glow of a cigar in his fingers. I don't know what I felt—a sort of
confused relief mixed with disappointment and doubt; and also a
kind of confidence in him. I felt he'd have told me more if he could—
if he had known any more than he did. It must sound preposterous
I suppose, but then the simplest things come to sound preposterous. I don't know. Also, he had not touched his wine. How typical
of him to sit there, flower in buttonhole, with a bubble of blood in
front of him."

He lowered his massive head on his breast for a moment and
seemed to brood, though in fact he was smiling a smile of resignation
—or so it seemed, though perhaps I was misled by the new babyish
contours of the familiar face. "So there it is, roughly speaking—that
is the state of play for the moment. I am not unduly worried even
though I realise that it may last for ever—I mean I might never get
back. At my age, you see." He snuffed slowly once more and sat back
in his seat to smile upon us with an unguarded affection as he supplied us with other characteristic details of his earthly life, such as,
for example, that owing to his domestic exuberance he had developed a weakness in the belly wall which forced him to wear a
suspensory which he called a *soutien-Georges.*

Then abruptly turning back to the original matter of his conversation he said: "You might say that not having freed myself completely from the firm and yet not having come back either I was in a sort of limbo. Not a ghost and yet still not quite a man." I put out my hand to touch him—I must confess I went through a moment of doubt as to whether my fingers might not meet through his wrist. "Take my pulse" he said. I tried, but could find no trace of one; yet the flesh was solid flesh. "I suppose you don't cast a shadow either like the traditional *Doppelgänger?*" But he was humming a light air and gazing about him with happy abstraction. "The twentieth of every month is the day of Epicurus. I celebrate mildly, ever so mildly. With old *soutien-Georges* here I cannot go the whole hog. *Je n'ai plus des femmes mais j'ai des idées maîtresses.*" But he was not disconsolate or cast down by having to make the confession. He intoned to a fingerbeat.

> *"Surrender and identify and nod.*
> *That's why you came, remember, little God?"*

This was apparently a free translation from some Epicurean proverb. Then next:

> *"Hail!* Ejaculatio praecox,*
> *No more love among the haycocks;*
> *Yet psyche chloroformed by science*
> *In poems will breathe her last defiance!"*

He paused, attempted to recover some more verses and failed in somewhat uncharacteristic fashion. Then he gave a simulacrum of his ancient roar and gestured at the door. "There he comes, Horatio the Magnificent"; and we saw with surprise and delight another familiar figure weaving its way towards us. It was Banubula.

Yes, it was Banubula all right, but in a somewhat advanced stage of what might have seemed intoxication. He wove towards us, all elegance, gesturing with the silver knob of his walking-stick. He was gloved and circumspectly hatted, not to mention spatted—for he sported his favourite grey spats. Radiant is hardly the word—he smirked his way over to us smiling with his loose lips and moving his eyebrows about. Our greetings were effusive and somewhat confused. The Count turned on Caradoc and said somewhat reproachfully, "I suppose you have told them about me—I suppose they know? How vexatious, I would have liked to boast!" Caradoc shook his burly dogged head. "Not a word" he said gravely. "Not a blasted word. If they do know it's not from me."

"Do you know" said Banubula with breathless coyness "about me?"

"What?"

"That I'm *in* at last, *in the firm*?" He seemed almost on the point of executing a brief dance.

"The firm?"

He gave a whiff of insipid laughter behind his gloves and sibilated. "Yes, the *firm*. Have been now for several months. It's a post after my own heart and I think I may say that I am giving it everything I've got in me."

"Bravo!" we all exclaimed and I banged his rather portly shoulderblade to register my excitement and approval.

"Co-ordinator of industrial disputes, no less. I share the job with my old friend the Duke of Lambitus, who has left the F.O. to come to us. My word, Felix, you have no idea how delicate and yet how all-embracing it is. Everywhere there is a dispute or a falling off of production or simply tension due to a psychological cause—why, we are there, I with my languages and Lambitus with his courteous diplomatic experience."

"It must be devastating."

"It is" said the Count meekly. "It is."

Caradoc grinned at us and dug Banubula boisterously in the ribs. "Tell them about your latest *coup*" he said and Banubula was in no way loth to do so. "But I don't want to bore you with shop. Yet this last case does illustrate the enormous tact and psychological insight we have to bring into play. I'd like to tell you about it, if I may?" Inspired by the raptness of our attention he went on. "Well, just as an example: last year we started having trouble with our German branches in the applied industry sector. It was a queer sort of general malaise, nothing one could really analyse, a lack of heart at the centre of things. And, of course, disputes of one sort or another, mostly idle and foolish disputes for such an orderly and industrious nation.

Julian sent us over as psychological counsellors to study the matter and propose means of dealing with it. Now what really was wrong? Nothing we could see really: to account for the falling off of the statistics I mean. Simply boredom it seemed to us. At any rate it didn't seem something which salary rises could cure. *And this is where psychology comes in.*" The Count pointed a long spatulate finger at his own temple and paused dramatically. His eyes twinkled with keen joy, like summer lightning, like fireflies. "Lambitus finally said: 'The whole thing is this. They are not *enjoying* themselves, they do not know how to. It is our job to find a way, Horatio.' We pondered the matter and at last I hit upon a solution. It may seem simple for such a complex people. Baby Balls, that was it!"

"Baby Balls?" I exclaimed. Banubula nodded and pursued his rigorous *exposé* with raised finger. "You are perhaps too young to remember how the British sense of humour was saved and revived after the first World War? By the Baby Balls organised by the Bright Young Things."

"But what the devil is it?"

"Simply a Ball to which you have to go dressed as a baby, sucking a bottle, and preferably in a pram wheeled by a close friend."

"Well I'm damned."

"It worked Felix" he cried. "You would never have believed it. All those huge German business-men crammed into prams, dressed as babies, sucking on their bottles of milk, and waving clusters of coloured balloons. Nothing exceeded in pity and terror the sight of them entering so determinedly into the fun of the thing. We had thought of everything, you see. We had musical chairs, prizes for bobapple, buns and booby traps, cap-pistols and those streamers which uncurl when you blow them and go *wheee*. . . ."

He mopped his face and laughed shyly adding only the vital words: "All Germany laughed and all Germany went back to work and the needle began to mount again on the production board. Do you see the delicacy of the whole operation, I mean?"

To say that our collective breath was taken away would be an understatement. We sat and gaped our humble admiration. The Count himself seemed transfigured by this simple but subtle success. "D'you know," he went on "we had a special interview with Julian in which he congratulated us and said that he would see to it that we got an O.B.E. each in the Prime Minister's next list." The narration of this great *coup de théâtre* had so moved him that there was a long moment of silence while he applied himself to the delicacies of the establishment, giving himself totally, fervently, to the crumpets, and also to the toasted tea-cake. Caradoc gazed upon him with what one might call tears of admiration welling up behind his eyeballs. After so many years of waiting, of doing menial little jobs unworthy of his manifest genius . . . and at last to find his real bent in the firm. It was wonderful! Benedicta pressed his hand with sympathy and congratulation. Banubula himself was transported—he was quite beside himself, professionally speaking. I mean that there was not the slightest touch of complacence in his manner when he added "And this is only one occasion of many, *many* where we have been of vital use to the firm."

"Tell about the Koro epidemic" said Caradoc who for once seemed generously pleased to let his friend hold the floor.

"Ah that!" said Banubula rolling his fine eyes. "That really did tax us to the hilt. Lambitus was actually ill afterwards and imagined all sorts of things. I wonder if I dare speak of it without indiscretion before. . . ."

He nodded towards Benedicta who acknowledged the delicacy with a smile but spread her white hands in supplication. "Yes, please do. It is fascinating."

Banubula mopped his brow, poked his handkerchief into his sleeve and sat back. "This will amaze you I think" he said. "It certainly took us by surprise. We had not heard of Koro before, which is known as Shook Yong to the Chinese of the Archipelago. In fact the first we heard of it was when Nash, who had been sent out with a group of psychiatrists to stem this epidemic if possible, sent a signal back saying that nothing could be done. It was an S.O.S. if ever there was one. Lambitus and I were at the Savoy Grill when we got orders to move in and set our brains to work on this problem which was threatening to disrupt whole sectors of our work both in Singapore and throughout the whole network of islands where we had enormously important sources of raw materials at work for the firm. By morning's early light then, we were in the air, sometimes holding hands a bit as neither of us liked air-travel and the journey was bumpy: we were on our way to Singapore. May I have this last one?" He took up the last crumpet on the dish and used it lightly at a baton to punctuate his discourse, pausing from time to time to take a small bite from it.

"Now Shook Yong" he said in a faraway fairy-tale voice "and its ravages are hardly known to us occidentals, and when one first hears of it one thinks it rather far-fetched. But it is real, and it creates mass panics. What is it? Well, it is a belief that those who contract this disease experience a sudden feeling of retraction of the male organ into the abdomen; this is accompanied by a hysterical fear that should the retraction be allowed to proceed, and if swift medical aid is not available, the whole penis will simply disappear into the belly with fatal results for the owner." He paused for the inevitable smiles. "I know" he went on gravely. "So it struck me at first. But it spreads like wildfire, whole communities get taken with Shook Yong just as our medieval ancestors, I suppose, contracted dancing or twitching manias. It is real, all too real. Now when a community is so afflicted they experience utter terror and in their anxiety to hold on to their own property they grab and pull it to prevent it vanishing: worse still, they often use instrumental aids such as rubber bands, string, clamps, clothes-pegs and chopsticks, and frequently inflict severe bruising or worse damage on the organ. Now what had caused all this trouble, which spread from Singapore like wildfire and gained the remotest corners of the landmass in next to no time, was a rumour set about (perhaps by the Indians) that Koro was caused by eating the flesh of swine which had recently been vaccinated in an attempt to combat swine fever. At once there was an almost complete standstill in the pork sales in markets, restaurants and so on—but those who thought that they might have been exposed to the disease by accident took fright. So Koro or Shook Yong became an epidemic to be reckoned with.* Everything was done to educate public opinion by press conferences and radio and journalism—but it was all in vain. The Ministry of Health reported that both the public and private hospitals were swamped by mobs of yelling patients holding on to their

* Koro is a real mass neurosis and not an invention of the author's. For a full account of it see *British Medical Journal*, 9 March 1968.

75

organs and calling loudly for medical aid. The scenes were indescribable. Oriental mass panic has to be seen to be believed. Poor
Nash, who had arrived with some severe-looking but orthodox
Freudians, was completely out of his depth, and indeed, when we
found him, quite pale with terror at all the commotion. He was
holding on to his own organ, not, as he explained, because he felt
he had Shook Yong but simply because he feared to lose it in the
general *mêlée*. I don't mind confessing that for a while the whole
problem seemed to me a bit out of our usual range. They hadn't
explained in London the meaning of these deplorable crowd scenes
taking place all over the city. Freud was no help, however much the
disease might have suggested an ordinary anxiety neurosis. You cannot ask a yelling Chinese to lie down on a couch and give you free
associations for the word 'penis' when he is holding fast to his own,
convinced that it is simply melting away. Worst of all, the telephones
were humming from the plantations telling us that the epidemic
had already penetrated into the countryside where the people are
even more susceptible to mass suggestion than in the towns. We
attended conference after conference, Lord Lambitus and I, listening to these grave accounts of a world turned upside down; and both
of us completely perplexed as to what to do to lend nature a hand. As
I gathered that the scourge had already been signalled among the
Buginese and Maassars in Coelebes and West Borneo at other
periods, it seemed to me that the whole thing would sweep over the
subcontinent and perhaps die a natural death in Australia where
they have another attitude to the male organ. But it was very disturbing all the same. It put us on our mettle. Yet there we were in an
unfamiliar world, with the most arbitrary sanitation and precious
little ice for drinks, beating our heads, almost our breasts, so worried
were we.

"And at every conference the case-histories poured in, collected
by devoted and whey-faced doctors. Just to give you a typical one
to illustrate what was happening. A fifteen-year-old boy was rushed
into the emergency ward of the clinic by his shouting and gesticulating parents calling for aid. The boy, they said, had contracted Shook
Yong. The youth was pale and scared and was pulling hard on his
penis to prevent it being swallowed up. He had heard about Shook

Yong in school and that morning had eaten a little pow, which contains some pork, for his breakfast. When he went to the lavatory he saw that his member had shrunk very greatly and concluded that he had contracted the scourge. Yelling, he ran to his parents, who ran yelling with him to the doctor. Here at least he might receive sedatives and reassurance provided he and his parents had reached the stage of evolution when things begin to make sense; mostly however they hadn't. Well, as I say, Lambitus and I were at our wits' end to devise some equitable way of ending this intellectual debauch. The Freudians keeled over one by one and even Nash, who had led the rescue group, was sent to hospital for a while and put under heavy sedation. He had, I believe, become prone to the contagious atmosphere which Koro creates, and had almost begun to believe . . . well, I don't know. Anyway, everyone seemed privately highly delighted in rather a cruel way. But still we could make no advance on the problem. The season was breaking up, the monsoons were heralded. And now Lambitus, who is a man of iron nerve, quite unimaginative, as you have to be in the higher diplomacy, began to show signs of strain. He spent an awful long time in the shower-room every morning examining himself for signs of Koro. I began to suspect him of suspecting. . . . Well, anyway the situation was desperate. I sat night after night swatting giant moths with a bedroom slipper and brooding on the problem.

"Indeed I had reached the point when I had decided that we should return and confess our mission a failure when—how does it happen: Nash would know?—an old memory of my youth came to my rescue. You may know that when I was first engaged to the Countess we went round the world together; she said she wished to see me anew in each continent before deciding whether she would marry me or not—so there was nothing for it. It was a pre-honeymoon in a way, and by no means an unfruitful trip. She was an expert botanist, and I was already then working on my comparative folklore of fertility symbols in east and west. We came to Malaya, among other places, and indeed stayed a month on a plantation. From the recesses of these old memories I suddenly resuscitated Tunc or Tunk—the small fertility God which is responsible for so much of the overpopulation in these parts and whose little effigy in clay one sees on cottage lintels. It came to me with the force of a forgotten dream that we might perhaps invoke the little deity's aid once more to counter the nationwide (so it seemed at the time) retraction of the Malayan penis."

"Do you remember" said Caradoc suddenly "Sipple's account of *his* attack of Koro?—it must have been that. In the Nube, a hundred years ago?"

Of course I did.

"It must have been" said Banubula seriously. "It would have been terrible if such an affliction had spread into England. It could topple a Government—I saw it do so. And we couldn't invoke little Tunc there because nobody believes in him or it. Anyway to resume my account of this strange episode: I woke Lambitus and breathlessly outlined my plan. He was ready to grab at any straw and eagerly backed me up. I obtained some *ex-votos*, some silk drawings unwittingly issued by the British Council, and set myself to think. In half an hour I had roughed out a more modern effigy which, if fabricated in mauve plastic (the national colour, by the way), might have charm and appeal for the afflicted.

"We rang up Julian and flew him home a sample. Of course we had visualised a vast free distribution of this charm, probably sowed broadcast from the air, but as usual Julian's keen mind took hold of the problem and solved it. It would have no value to people unless they had to pay for it, he said, and I quite saw his point. We were to give away only a few thousand through the hospitals but put the rest—some four million at first printing—on the open market in order to forestall some similar kind of effort by the Catholics. Moreover he offered us one per cent which was really very handsome of him, and which has made us both extremely rich men. So was Koro finally brought under control by the kindly intervention of Tunc. I must say I am sentimental about the little God and always carry one on my watch-chain for good luck—though God knows at my age. . . ."

Musing thus the Count produced a new gold watch-chain of great lustre and showed us a copy of the charm. "A pretty emblem, no?" he said modestly.

"But why in European characters?"

"Foreign magic has great *cachet* there. This was the foreign issue given away by the hospital administration. There was also a local version for sales distribution. We were a little worried about religious sensibilities, but everyone was delighted.

```
        T U N C
        U  ⟨⟩  U
        N      N
        C U N T
```

He sighed at the memory of these great adventures and glanced at the pristine gold watch which depended from the chain. "I have a conference" he said. "I must run along. I'll meet you at the plane at six, Caradoc. Without fail, mind, and don't lose that ticket." And so saying he waved us an airy goodbye, only pausing to add over his shoulder, "We'll meet in London I hope."

Caradoc squeezed the pot dry and took up the final teacup. "Isn't it marvellous to see what happens when people really find themselves?" It was, and we said so, somewhat sententiously I fear. Banubula had emerged from his cocoon like the giant Emperor moth he had always been and was now in full wing-spread. "You know," said Caradoc polishing up the butter on his plate with a morsel of tea-cake "that is all that anybody needs. Nothing more, yet nothing less."

And so at last the time came to take leave of him, which we did with reluctance, yet with delight to know that he was still to be numbered among the living. I spoke to him a little bit about his papers and his aphorisms and recordings—and indeed all the trouble Vibart and I had been to, to try and assemble a coherent picture of this venerable corpse. He laughed very heartily and wiped his eye in his sleeve. "One should never do that for the so-called dead" he said. "But it's largely my fault. One should not leave such an incoherent mess behind. I didn't know then that everything must be tidied up before one dies or it just encumbers one's peace of mind when one *is* dead, like I have really been, in a manner of speaking. It was too bad and I am really sorry. We'll order things better next time, for my real death. There won't be a crumb out of place, you'll see. The whole thing will be smooth as an egg, mark me. Not a blow or a harsh word left over—and even tape recordings burn or scrub don't they?" He walked us with his old truculent splayed walk to the car-park and waved us goodbye in the misty evening. I looked back as we turned the corner and gave him a thumbs-up to which he responded. Lighting-up time by now with mist everywhere and foggy damp, and the wobble of blazing tram-cars along the impassive avenues. "I feel sort of light-headed," I said "from surprise I've no doubt."

Benedicta put her hand briefly on my knee and pressed before turning back to the swerves and swings of the lakeside road. "Perhaps you've contracted Koro" she said.

"Perhaps I have."

"You must ask for an amulet from the firm."

"I think I will. You can never be certain in this world; even the innocents like Sipple can get struck down it seems."

The dark was closing in fast and soon I was drowsing in the snug bucket-seat, waking from time to time to glance at the row of lighted dials on the fascia. "Why so fast?" I said suddenly. "Light me a cigarette," said Benedicta "and I'll tell you. Tonight we shall hear from Julian. As it may be a phone-call I suddenly had a guilty conscience and thought we should get back." I lit the cigarette and placed it between her lips. "And how did you know?" I said. "I had a postcard ages ago giving me this date, but it slipped my mind and I only remembered it all of a sudden while Caradoc was talking. If it's too fast for you tell me and I'll slow down."

No, it wasn't too fast: but it wasn't a phone message either. It was a telex to the hospital from Berne, saying: "If Felix feels up to it and if you are free please meet me with a small picnic on the Constaffel, hut five, at around midday on the fifteenth. My holiday is so short that I would like to combine the meeting with a bit of a run on the snow. Will you?"

"The polite request disguises the command" I said. "Shall I decline? And what the devil is the Constaffel?"

"It's where the practice slopes begin up on the mountainside; the

Paulhaus always keeps a camper's hut available there for the use of convalescents."

"Look Benedicta," I said severely "I am not webtoed, and I am not going to scull about in the mountains on skis in my present state of health."

"It's not that at all" she said. "We can go up with the *téléférique* and the hut is about five hundred yards along the cliff-face with a perfectly good path to it. It won't be snowed up in this sort of weather. We could walk, if you'll go, that is. If not let me send him a cable."

I was tempted to give way to an all too characteristic petulance but I reflected and refrained. "Let us do it, then" I said. "Yes, we'll do it. But I warn you that if he appears disguised as the Abominable Snowman I'll hit him with an ice pick and polish him off for good and all."

"I count on you."

They were easily said, these pleasantries, but in the morning lying beside her warm dent, her "form", while she herself was making up her face in the little bathroom next door I found myself wondering what the day would bring, and what new information I would glean from this encounter. I went in to watch her play with this elegant new face, now grown almost childish and somehow serene. She had only half a mouth on which made me feel hungry. "Benedicta, you don't feel apprehensive about this, do you?"

She looked at me suddenly, keenly. "No. Do you?" she said. "Because there's no need to go. As for me I told you I had come to terms with Julian. I'm not scared of anything any longer." I sat down on the *bidet* to wash and reflect. "I used the wrong word. What I dread really is the eternal wrangle with people who don't understand what one is trying to do. I fear he'll just ask for me to come back, everything forgotten, but never to try and run away again. It's what they do to runaway schoolboys at the best schools. Whereas I am not giving any guarantees to anyone. I intend to always leave an open door." Benedicta finished her mouth and eyes without saying anything. Then she went out and I heard her giving Baynes instructions about thermos flasks and sandwiches. So I shrugged my shoulders and had a shower.

81

The day was fine and bright and really ideal for non-skiers; this year there had been very little snow and the press had made great moan about the fact that the season would be blighted because of it.

Rackstraw had seen some reference to the matter in a paper and had kept on about it until I could have strangled him. In the old days he had been, it seems, some sort of ski-champion. Though no longer allowed out he kept a close eye on weather and form. Anyway, this was none of my affair, and about half past ten we set off—she in her elegant Sherpa rig of some sort of mustard-coloured whipcord—towards the *téléférique* which we found quite empty. Operated by remote control, it was an eerie sort of affair, the doors flying open as one stepped upon the landing-ramp and closing behind one with a soft whiff. We had the poor snowfalls and the excited press to thank for the empty car in which we sat, sprawling at ease among our packs and other impedimenta, smoking.

A few moments' waiting and then all of a sudden the cabin gave a soft tremor and began to slide forwards and upwards into the air, more slowly, more deliciously than any glider; and the whole range of snowy nether peaks sprang to attention and stared gravely at us as we ascended towards them, without noise or fuss. Away below us slid the earth with its villages and tracery of roads and railways—a diminishing perspective of toy-like shapes, gradually becoming more and more unreal as they receded from view. The sense of aloneness was inspiriting. Benedicta was delighted and walked from corner to corner of the cabin to exclaim and point, now at the mountains, now at the snowy villages and the dun lakeside, or at other features she thought she could recognise. The world seemed empty. Up and up we soared until we had the impression of grazing the white faces of the mountains with the steel cable of our floating cabin. "I don't know whether Julian is doing the sensible thing" she said "in ski-ing about up here; the surfaces have been flagged here and there for danger and there have been several accidents." The lift came slowly to a halt in all this fervent whiteness, slid up a small ramp and stopped with a scarcely perceptible shock. The doors opened and the cold world enveloped us. But the sunlight was brilliant, dazzling, and the snow squeaked under our boots like a comb in freshly washed hair. Nor was it far along the scarp to where the ski-huts stood; it was from here that the serious performers started their ascent. Benedicta had the key and we opened up the little hut which was aching with damp and cold, but fairly well equipped for camp life. There was a little stove which she soon had buzzing away—it promised us hot coffee or soup to wash down the fare we had brought. We settled ourselves in methodically enough. Then outside in the brilliant sun we smoked and had a drink together and even embarked on a snow man of ambitious size. There had been several bad avalanches that year and I was not surprised when one took place there and then, as if for our personal delectation. A white swoosh and a whole white face of the mountain opposite cracked like plaster, hesitated, and then broke away to fall hundreds of feet into the valley. The boom, as if from heavy artillery, followed upon the spectacle by half a minute almost.

"That was a good one" said Benedicta.

There were some tree stumps and a wooden table under the fir in front of the hut, and we cleared these of snow and set out plates and cutlery thereon. We had all but finished when by chance I happened to look upwards along the crescent-like sweep of the mountain above us. Something seemed to be moving up there—or so it seemed out of the corner of my eye. But no, there was nothing. The unblemished snow lay ungrooved everywhere on the runs. I turned away to the opposite side and saw with a little shock of surprise a lone skier standing among a clump of firs, watching us like a sharpshooter. We stayed for a long moment like this, unmoving, and then the figure, with the sudden movement of a Red Indian sinking his paddle into the river, propelled himself forward and began to ripple down towards us, cutting his grooves of whiteness on the clean snow.

Fast, too, very fast. "Could that be Julian?" I said, and Benedicta following the direction of my pointing finger with eyes screwed up said: "Yes. It must be." So we stood hand in hand watching while the small dark tadpole rushed towards us, growing in size as it came, until we could see that it was a man of about medium height, rather gracefully built in a slender sort of way, and as lissom on his skis as a ballet dancer. When he had reached the little fir about fifty yards off he swerved and braked, throwing up a white fountain of snow; he took off his skis and made his way towards the hut beating the snow from his costume with his heavy mittens. "Hullo" he cried with great naturalness, as if this were not a momentous, a historic meeting, but a casual encounter between friends. "I'm Julian at last" he added. "In the flesh!" But of course in his ski get-up there was nothing very distinct to be seen as yet. Then I noticed that there was blood running from his nose. It had dried and caked on his upper lip and in the slender perfectly shaped moustache. He dabbed it with a handkerchief as he advanced, explaining as he came. "I tend towards an occasional nose-bleed up at this level—but it's well worth it for the fun." His nostrils were crusted with blood, though the flow appeared to have stopped.

We shook hands, gazing at one another, while he made some perfectly conventional remark to Benedicta, perfectly at ease, perfectly insouciant. "At last," I said "we meet." It sounded somehow fatuous. "Felix," he said in that warm caressing voice I knew so well (the voice of Cain) "it's been unpardonable to neglect you so but I waited until we could talk, until you felt well and unharassed by things. You are looking fine, my boy." I gave him a clumsy Sherpa-like bow which conveyed I hoped a hint of irony. "As well as can be expected" said I. He still kept on his heavy mica goggles tinted slightly bronze so that I could not really see his eyes properly; also of course the padded suit and the peaked snowcap successfully muffled all clear outlines of his head and body. All I saw was a very delicately cut aristocratic nose (like a bird of prey's beak), an ordinary mouth with blurred outlines because of the bloody upper lip, and the small feminine hand with which he grasped mine. Benedicta offered to swab his lip with cotton wool and warm water but he refused with thanks saying: "O I'll clean up when I get down to terra a little firma." So we stood, eyeing each other keenly, until Benedicta brought out some drinks and we settled down opposite him at the wooden table to drink gin slings in the sunny whiteness. "Where to begin?" said Julian with a melodious lazy inflexion which was very seducing—the calm voice of the hypnotist. "Where to begin?" It was indeed the question of the moment. "Well, the circle can be broken at any point I suppose. But where?" He paused and added under his breath "Running into airpockets, ideas in flight!"

Then he leaned forward and tapped my hand and said: "Our old quarrel is over, finished; with what more you know now of myself, of Benedicta, you must feel a bit reassured about things, less fearful. I've been planning this meeting for a long time, and indeed looking forward to it, because I knew that I should have to throw myself entirely upon your mercy, to try to win your heart, Felix. Wait!" He held up a hand to prevent my interjection. "It is not what you think, it is not how you think. I wanted to talk to you a bit, not only about the firm but about the general questions it always poses for the people involved in it—like this question of freedom." (As I watched him I saw so clearly in my mind's eye the two grave children; he had tied up Benedicta's mind with his excesses, and then tried to liberate her by teaching her to fence! Fool! Dry click-click of their buttoned foils. Now here he was with his nostrils full of dried blood. Another image intervened, Julian tapping away on an Arab finger-drum while the monkey on its chain chattered and masturbated furiously. And then Benedicta saying to me . . . O centuries later, something like "You were such a surprise it was terrifying; I watched you sleep, off your guard, just to try and verify the feeling. Caught between such tyrants as you and Julian is it a wonder I went mad? With him it was love, but an actor's love—I knew no other.")

But here she was at my side, very composed and smiling, smoking her little cigar and watching us. It was I who was trembling slightly, feeling the palms of my hands grow moist. He was so attractive, this man, that for two pins I could have reached forward and strangled him as he sat there with his poise and his bloody face. "Go on" I said. "Go on."

He made a self-deprecating little gesture with his ungloved hand and sighed. "I am" he said. "I will. But I was just thinking rather ruefully of how much thought and feeling and will I had put into the matter of the firm over all these years—not only running my side of it as best I could, but trying to penetrate also the meaning of it and the meaning of my own life in relation to it. And of course yours, and everybody's. The firm itself, Merlin's firm," he uttered the proper name with a profound, a sad bitterness "what is it exactly? It isn't just a loosely linked association of enterprises co-ordinated under one name; its very size (like a blown-up photo-graph) enables us to see that it is the reflection of something, the copy of something. Though on one plane you might consider it a money-making contrivance, the very terms under which it operates reflect the basic predispositions of the culture of which it is only an offshoot. Of course it is both constricting for some and liberating for others, according to their position vis-à-vis the organism; but they can't escape reflecting the firm, just as the firm can't help reflecting the corpus of what, for want of a better word, we must call our civilisation. O dear, Felix, reality is kindly—but inflexible.

"It doesn't seem possible to break either the mould of the firm or the mould of ourselves as associates or even hirelings (you might think) of the thing. Yet you seem to think it necessary, I suppose because you are a romantic in some ways. And perhaps it might be possible for some, though not in the violent and ill-considered way you seem to think necessary at your present level of understanding. Ah! You will reply that you have played a part in some of our manœuvres and so you can judge—but I wonder if you can? For example, the whole question of that upset in Athens (such a small, such a trivial part of the whole design) was not simply a question of buying the Parthenon—who would want it? The firm manipulates without owning, that is part of its charm. It is the invisible increment which it tries to conquer. A long lease was all we asked for and a say in its management, if you like. My dear chap, in this, our new Middle Ages, investment has become the motor response of all religion; not in God as he was known (he hasn't changed), not in the psychic Fund of Funds which pretends to chime with the ways of universal nature. (That too is balls by the way.) No, for us *money is sperm*, and the investment of it the ritual of propitiation.

"The pattern is only repeating itself; we have placed an unobtrusive hand on much more than the Stock Exchange. Most of the Indian holy places like the Taj and Buddha's tree and so on are in our hands; the Holy Sepulchre in Jerusalem, Herculaneum, Pompeii, Grant's Tomb. The Parthenon held out for a while purely through the muddle of Graphos, the indecision of Graphos. To wipe out the National Debt and balance the Greek budget for the first time ever . . . and all in exchange for a treaty involving a few dead monuments. For us they still offer a fulcrum of operation and a power-yield if looked at from the point of view of our own religion—I use the word in its anthropological sense. We have in fact begun to fit these old things into the corpus of our own contemporary culture where they can be of some use: not just brooding places for sickly poets."

"And the United Nations?" I said.

"That has great value as a relic of the future, like the Rosetta Stone. No less than an Old Master of complete nullity which is overpriced because it happens to be the only one of its period. Do you see? Then let me go a little further. If we are reflections of our culture, and our culture represents something like the total psychic predisposition of man in terms of his destiny, dare we not ask ourselves what makes it come about, what makes it last or decay? At what point does such an animal get born?" He was breathing hard now, as if the effort to enunciate his ideas clearly were a strain. "In a world of brainless drones for the most part this question never gets asked, and it's very few of us who can see that some of the answers anyway lie about in obscure places—like The Book of Changes, for example. Felix it's my belief that you can touch the quiddity, the nub of the idea of a culture only if you realise that it comes out of an act of association of which the primal genetic blueprint in the strictest biological sense is the uniting of the couple, man and woman. In the compact and the seed." Here he seemed to be suddenly overwhelmed by sadness. He faltered, hesitated, and then recovered himself to go on.

"Nature, as you know, is very class-conscious and builds as carefully as a swallow, always in hierarchies; nothing but the best will do. It's difficult in our age where the tail is trying to wag the dog to descry any shape at all in the overall dog.

"Moreover to attempt to analyse or comprehend such matters through chimerical abstractions like capital or labour—why it's like discussing chess in terms of ludo. The problem is not there at all. I first learned this in watching the pattern of Merlin's investments; among them were several singular departures. Of course in his time specie, bullion bars, tallies, shares and so on still had the relative value they do today. But he went after other things as well; for example, he dreamed of owning (not owning of course, but manipulating) six of the largest diamonds in the world—what they call paragons: that's to say a stone with the minimum weight of 100 carats. I remember him reciting their names and weights which he knew by heart. The old 'Koh-i-noor' of course belonged to the Queen and there was nothing he could do about that—she didn't need money! 106 carats that was. Then the 'Star of the South' 125, the Pitt diamond 137, the Austrian 133, the Orloff 195, and last that monster from Borneo, 367 carats. Some of them he actually did own briefly, though of course not all; but his dream was to hold a sort of mortgage on them. He was looking always for an unchanging value or one which would increase on its own.

"No, looked at in this wider context things become vastly richer and more subtle than our polite social reformers would have us believe. Nature is an organism not a system, and will always punish those who try to strap her into a system. She will overturn the apple-cart—a horse with its leading-rein cut, careering over a cliff: that is what is happening today in a way. On the other hand we ants must use our reason as much as possible in order to try to descry the hazy outlines of human destiny in nature as it evolves around us. We are trapped, do you see?

"Nature improvises out of pure joy, always with a miracle in hand; why can't man?—or perhaps he could if he tried. Why do we build these wormcasts around us like civilisations, defensive walled cities, ghettos, currencies? Then another terrifying thought pops into one's head: the very concept of order may never have entered nature's own head. Man has tried to impose his own from fear of the fathomless darkness which lies beyond every idea, every hope? Is it all self-deceit? No Felix, it isn't—but how haltingly one begins to see the 'signatures' of things—the sigil left by the master mason, nature. Yes. Yes. Don't shake your head! They are to be seen. The imprint is there in the matter, in the form things take, in the way societies cohere about a set of basic propositions, form around mysterious points of mind like God or Love. One little misinterpretation of the data and the thing goes sour. Look at our little love-asylum—everyone seeking for somebody with whom they can be thoroughly weak!

"And then all this whine about personal freedom—everyone feels it is his right to worry himself about the matter. They don't see, you don't see, that nothing can be done in this field unless the firm itself becomes free; then and only then could the notion of a personal freedom be assured. And even while the poor fool is waving his arms and talking about freewill he is being subtly grooved by his culture, formed by it—money, fashions, architecture, laws, machines, foods. At what point can he really say that he stands free and clear away from the pattern in which he was cradled and by which he was formed? God! will we never see more than one profile of reality at a time? Yet it has been man's wildest hope one day to turn the statue round and gaze at it face to face. Perhaps this too is a delusion based on faulty conjectures about its sovereign nature."

There was a long pause while he lit a short cigar from the packet which Benedicta had brought with her. "I suppose you might agree that reality is sufficiently implausible to cause people great anxiety?"

"The aphorism refuses to argue, Julian. That is perhaps its strength—or perhaps its weakness. Look both ways before crossing the road."

"Felix" he said, smiling and patting my knee once more. "I can see that you are following me and it makes me glad. But I have more to say about the firm—this tiny microcosm which has formed itself without consulting us and which is not based simply upon human cupidity so much as on a fear of the outer darkness. It would be like taking a stern moral tone with a pigeon for being forced to eat grain to keep alive. And then think of all the different types of society formed by nature from infusoria and fossils up to helpless dinosaurs with a pea for a head. Don't we belong, culturally speaking, to the same canon—woven out of the invisible by powers we don't clearly understand and can only manipulate in certain tiny areas? Think, Felix."

I was thinking; O yes, I was thinking.

"How do cultures come about, how do they vanish? We would give anything to know. Can the firm and its structure perhaps inform us a little—that's the point? Well, to break a chain you must hit a link I suppose—the fragile link upon which the whole structure depends. One such link in man's culture is the fragile link of association of one with another, articles of faith, contracts, marriages, vows

89

and so on. Snap the link and the primordial darkness leaks in, the culture disintegrates, and man becomes the coolie he really is when there is no frame of culture to ennoble him, to interpret himself to himself. A crisis comes about. Then the providers, the secret mole-like makers of the new, go to work to repair the link, or to put in a new one. How easy to break and how laborious to repair! Only a few men in every age are fitted for the grim task, the exhausting task. For them the job in hand is self-evident, but to everyone else it seems a mystery that has got out of hand.

"Then think how puerile is our conception of such men we label with the word genius—it's on the level of Santa Claus! There isn't such an animal. But when a link is broken these rare men address themselves to the problem. What we call genius occurs when a gifted man sees a relation between two or more fields of thought which had up till then been believed to be irreconcilable. He joins the contra-dictory fields in an act of intellectual harmony and the chain begins to hold once more. The so-called genius of the matter is merely the intuitive act of joining irreconcilables. There is nothing new added, how could there be? But these men realise that when you wish to do something new you must go tranquilly ahead in the full knowledge that there can only be new relations, new combinations of the age-old material. The kaleidoscope must be given a jolt, that is all.

"I have always wondered whether the firm could not invent some-thing like a death-predictor; most of our troubles come from the feeling of human transitoriness, of the precarious nature of our hold upon life. But if you knew, for example, that on the 3rd March next year you were going to die it would change your whole attitude to people and things. It would make for resignation, compassion and concentration on the precious instant. It's anxiety over that unknown date which causes so much of the hysteria and consequently panicky judgement and thinking."

"Death" I said. "But the firm itself inflicts death."

Julian nodded quietly. "Merlin deliberately inured us to death—it was part of his code of things. So that from the firm's point of view death itself was only a pastime. One tried to keep one's hand in simply to make sure that one felt nothing about it one way or another. I must confess it meant next to nothing to me: until—well, I should say that I have only once experienced death with its full force and that was not my own but someone else's. I shall tell you more about that anon. But for the moment let me just say that the firm itself, being an organism, feels neither compunction nor conscience nor doubt: it has no guilt—how could it since nature in making indiscriminate use of her raw material has none either? Felix, a culture is based upon an act of association—a kiss or a handshake or a firm or a religion. It communicates itself, flowers, perpetuates itself through a single basic principle, which is sharing. In the genetic twilight of the firm, then, I have had a close look and found it wanting in much. Could we not make a model perhaps, trace out the pathology of memory to follow the broad furrow of the genetic code with its basic structure of the male and female elements? Sex might be the great clue here; certainly the pathology of the imagination was nourished in it, or so I thought. We are still so backward in so many respects—I mean that we so often have to make a model to comprehend a little bit."

In a clean bit of snow at his feet he scratched a few words, but absentmindedly, as if he were doing it for himself rather than for his audience. Like this:

pro CREATION re CREATION.

Then he went on, still half musing. "Such simple acts and such preposterous results! Because every desire wins its reponse. Hence the danger. Nature is so rich that people only have to wish and they quite literally get what they want. As most of us have unpurged desires the child born of the wish is so often a changeling—in fact the last thing one, in fact, wanted. It is too late by then. This so often happens to the mob-wish. Inferior slaves beget inferior masters to parody the awful distortions of the psyches which wish them up. Think of the mob-creations like Nero, Napoleon and Lenin— flowering from the bad dreams of masterless men who desired only to be led to their deaths—and had their wishes answered.

"I was thinking of course of the type of human association which gives rise on the one hand to the sexual compact—you'll say that love is more a seizure like epilepsy than a sober and conscious entry into a bond; but it contains in its genes, if you like to put it that way,

91

the basic male-female dichotomy which mirrors itself in every manifestation of language, science or art even. Whether a cave-culture, city culture, or a religious culture, or even in inventions like tools or wheeled things, chariots or motor-cars. I was forced to consider all this in order to try to understand a little bit what I was doing, sitting in the cockpit of the firm, trying to direct its motions. I didn't hope for much—but I would have liked very much to become a sort of goldsmith of its ideas. Nor is anything I say the usual criticism which one hears all the time of an age of technology. Technology in every age is simply the passive miracle which flows of our attitude to nature, helping the chrysalis to turn itself into the butterfly. It has nothing to do with the worry about raping nature—you can't: because nature will round on you and punish you for transgressions of this sort. But the idea of push and bite, the hand's scope allied to bronze or steel, gave us a new concept, namely 'spade'. In other words technology comes after the Fall and not before it.

"The first man to put one stone upon another may or may not have been aware that he was building a wall but his delight was great when his sheep could shelter from the snow behind it; but when the stones grew too big or too many to lift he was joined by his nearest neighbour, and then he by his; and so gradually you got a wall-culture based on an act of free association—you got the Great Wall of China, if you wish."

"Yes but *free association*" I said peevishly.

"The minute you join in the act you are no longer free, you are bound by the articles of association not less than by the natural obstacles which are posed the minute you start messing about with the natural order of things. Nature did not invent stones to stand up on one another, and will hasten to overturn them. This problem created a secondary one—either stone pruned so accurately that it could stand the ground-swell (the Romans, say) or else some new idea—like sheer weight, or another still, mortar. It is when you are in the act of working on your wall that another idea strikes you, namely if ever one did not have a trust in nature and its basic benevolence one would have none in death, and none in man."

He sat there looking at me, a strange blood-caked goblin of a man in his heavy ski-clothes and with his mica-tinted glance. He seemed to be waiting for me to say something, but I remained obstinately silent. I still wasn't clear in my mind about where he proposed to lead me. At last he himself sighed and rose to take a turn upon the terrace and gaze out across the dazzle of mountains dancing and shimmering with such purity in the light of the slowly westering sun. He spoke again, but it was almost musing once more, almost as if he were refuelling his mind to carry the argument forward upon another plane. "So little time," he said "in which to realise ourselves, one iota of our selves; and life so precarious in this pathetic overcoat of flesh and muscle; and there he goes, man, babbling about freewill with gravity following him about like a salt bitch! The leaden pull of the grave on the one hand and these huge towering structures in stone or paper which he has built to keep out the thought, the unbearable thought of his disappearance. And moreover, each man with different needs, a different rate of acceleration, different physique even. O I forgot, Felix. Koepgen asked for this to be sent to you so I brought it with me." He dug into his breast and produced the slim volume of which Vibart had spoken. I put it carefully away in my pack without stripping it of its cellophane covering. He sat down again, smiling a little, and said: "Koepgen has earned an honourable retirement and he has just realised that many of the infuriating things the firm made him do actually belonged to the plan of self-realisation which he had set himself—he's an alchemist by temperament and has spent his adult life trying to smelt himself out."

"You sent him to Russia to buy mercury."

"Yes, Felix. It must have seemed an arbitrary or even harsh decision. But later on he realised that it was a fruitful one on completely non-material grounds. You probably know that what the sea was for Plato, and indeed for Nash's famous Freudian unconscious, namely the symbol of rebirth—mercury is for the alchemist? It is their primal water! I deliberately did not tell Koepgen this; indeed at times I held my breath because he was on the point of disappearing or resigning. Then one day, just in time, he discovered that what he was doing for the firm on the material plane he was also doing unconsciously on the spiritual. He is glad now that he carried out the task."

"Where is he?"

"On an island. He has discovered that prayer, if rightly orientated, can become an exact science. I am quoting, of course, because all that line of enquiry isn't within my own interests. It's the purest rubbish I believe. But there you are, it makes him happy to think so. Besides, just suppose it were true—prayer-wheels for the lazy. We are making some already for the Tibetans. . . ." He smiled a smile of sad malice and shook his head ruefully, as if at the pure extravagance of human beliefs. Then he looked up and said: "I tried to kill you, Felix, and you tried to kill me—in both cases it was a near thing. But you lost a child, and I have been rendered incapable of making one. In a way this makes us quits."

"Yes."

He had become very pale now, and his nostrils were drawn in. He stared at his ungloved hand as it lay upon his knee with great intensity, as if he had never seen it before. After a long pause, and without looking up, he said quietly: "Benedicta, will you do us the favour of leaving us alone together for a moment? I want to talk to Felix about Iolanthe." Obediently Benedicta rose, lit a cigar, and kissing me lightly on the cheek, walked away across the snow towards the tree where Julian had propped his skis. So we sat immobile as the half-finished snow man on the tree stump. I could see that he was wondering where to begin. He wrote in the snow the word "Io" and then raised his head to look me in the eyes. His whole posture reflected a tremendous contained tension—sometimes if a powerful but delicate dynamo isn't properly anchored to its base its vibrations can make the whole housing ripple and tremble. But his voice was deadly calm, deadly calm. "It's strange the things people have to say about love" he said surprisingly. "About love at first sight, or love at no sight at all, or the love of God or of man. It's a real honeycomb of a sound. But from my point of view, and yours and the firm's, the genetic shadow of the love-child is always there, its silhouette hangs over the love-match. It is generated by the eyes and the mind perhaps less than by the body. The child is implicit in the transaction. When it goes wrong of course you get monsters; changelings, like the umbratiles of Paracelsus or the angels of Swedenborg, are such productions, formed, so to speak, from sperm which has missed its mark or gone bad.

94

"I did not" he went on "choose my own ground for this duel either, the encounter with this weird sort of animal, love. It was chosen for me by Merlin. I saw her, having always believed she did not exist, and the blood rushed to my head—and all the Petrarchian rubbish of our civilisation with it! The anaconda coils of an immense lethargic narcissism wrapped themselves round me! But unlike Dante, unlike that fool Petrarch, I could not ingest the love-object and transform it into self-love. I suppose because I wasn't that other kind of impotent, an artist. No, I was a whole man in every sense but this vital one—this insult to my honour and my very being."

He had swollen now with suppressed rage, and his face had become flushed, feverish-looking, while the fine controlled voice shook slightly. It was deeply moving to have this tiny glimpse of the driving power of Julian—sexlessness, impotence, fury, rage, sexual ferocity. "I received sex and death in one blood-stained package, thrown in my face like the bundle of discarded bones a butcher wraps up for the dog." He paused to master his breathing and then went on. "One minute you are still there, breathing and planning and hoping: the next you are this appalling beautiful toy which will not respond to the controls. Reality rushes in like some fearful bat and circles round the room, knocking over the candles and banging against the white screens. I learned all this from Iolanthe." He looked quickly around him, as if looking for something against which he could dash a clenched fist, or bang his head; and I was reminded of what Mrs. Henniker had told me of the last night of his vigil, of what she had seen in a brief moment between sleep and waking. It must have been the critical moment.

In his confusion he had been completely disoriented. He was hardly aware that he had a tremendous erection—the death-wish of the flesh itself. Little incoherent sounds escaped his lips, little sighs and whimpers. He snatched off the hanging cylinder of transfusion-blood which was hanging over the bed, stripped the needle, and drank it thirstily off, putting the rubber capsule in his mouth like a teat. Never had he known such a thirst. Then, with the same little soundless sobs he went to the mirror of the hanging cupboard and made up his face with her lipstick, staring like a ghoul. He took the candle from in front of the ikon in order to light the spectacle of himself standing here, staring abstractedly at the man called Julian whom he hardly recognised. "Julian" I said, with compassion for his wretchedness. "Steady on." But he was already calm once more, in full control of body and voice. He looked once more at me with a piercing calm and said: "So I come at last to the whole point of the matter. *If the firm could be freed, Felix!* On such a notion we could base a hope however faint of the freedom which you so desperately seek, which I too need. But the only road to freedom of such a kind lies through an aesthetic of some kind. Beauty, from which alone comes congruence and the harmony of dissident parts and which echoes back the great contrivances of nature." He gave a harsh bark of a laugh, as if at the very hopelessness of such an idea. "Beauty, whatever it is, is the only poor yardstick we have; and in my own case Iolanthe's image is the model which suits our book, a universal beauty which has sent her round and round the world in celluloid and which has made her what she is for so many. She has exemplified, projected the wild notion of this inner freedom which we can realise only through the female. She is there like cumulus, she is everywhere like a world-dream—O! a twentieth-century shallow trashy dream, if you wish. But not less real than Helen of Troy. Only on her image can be built, only through her can we realise our mad experiment. It is Iolanthe that we must try to realise."

Now something more astonishing happened. He fell on his knees before me and spread his arms in supplication saying: "Felix, for God's sake help me. *We are building her.*"

"*Building her?*"

"I know. It will seem to you like one of those fantasies which go with General Paralysis of the Insane. It is nothing of the kind. We are building her and her consort, just to see. It is terrible to have to make models to comprehend, but it is all we can do. Rubber, leather, nylon, steel—God knows in the matter of technological contrivance we have everything at our disposal. But *memory*, Felix, for the conditioned responses, she will need a vastly extended memory. She must sensitise to sounds, she must be word perfect in her role— ('Come darling open'). She needs you, she must have you, Felix. Nobody else can do it. We have nobody who could do it for us. You know that for a while we all thought Abel was a typical Felix type of hoax. It was only when the machine made *pi* come out that I woke up with a start and realised that in fact you had made something extraordinarily strange and original, a mnemonic monster."

He sat staring at me with a singular expression of exhaustion and triumph—the sort of relief a lecturer might feel at having completed a triumphant *exposé* of an abstruse theme. "We dismantled it, you know, with the greatest care. Marchant did it. It was perfectly astonishing as an example of technical virtuosity, of technical insolence if you wish. Parts of it you had only sketched out and tied together with string, so to speak. They were only just holding, only just passing a current. But such elegance of thought!"

"I know. I went mad with rage against you and Benedicta and the whole set-up. You see I didn't care if it worked or not; it's when you don't care that sometimes things work out. And really I had need of about fourteen people on the technical side to build such a toy."

"I know you did."

He had by now risen from his knees and dusted himself as meticulously as a cat; he crossed and poured himself a drink with perfectly steady hand. Then he turned to me and said in a low voice, a conspiratorial voice: "I *implore* you, Felix."

But now I was musing, staring at the ground, seeing in my mind's eye the sweating Marchant taking down Abel, probably with earphones like the people who de-fuse mines (after all the staked shot gun must have worried them); calling back in his firm but squeaky voice the name of every nut and bolt he touched. So they had stolen Abel's memory, a thing still so terribly imperfect of execution. (I have had since a number of new notions about how to extend it.) Here they were clearly thinking about a mnemonic contrivance which acted directly on the musculature—a walking memory: what else is man, pray? It was breath-taking as an idea, and also monstrous. "Yes" said Julian, as if he were thought-reading. "It's monstrous all right, but only from one point of view."

"Who would have thought it, Julian?" I said. "Iolanthe as the witch-fulfilment, the which fulfilment—how do you prefer it? How did you reduce it all to size to fit it into the confines of the human skull?"

"We can do almost anything with matter, in the field of imitation; all we can't do is *create* it." He said it with such bitterness that I felt at once that he was thinking of his own castration. And then I looked past him up the hill and saw this other blonde monster Benedicta leaning against a tree and smoking quietly, with her blue eyes raised towards the sunlight which had begun to weaken now, to send blue shadows racing down to the bluer roots of the snowpeaks—and I thought grimly of the long desolating periods of impotent fury I had had to live through because of this man: of the fears and illnesses of Benedicta herself: of a life half lived or at least ill lived (always some cylinders not firing): and thinking the whole damned cartoon-strip through from the beginning I felt a sudden surge of weakness, a lassitude of limb and mind. I took a good swig from the gin bottle and set it carefully back in its place. "So you want me to join forces on the science friction, Julian? I'll have to think it over, you know." But he was already smiling at me in a curiously knowing way, as if he realised how deeply his arguments had pierced my armour, my self-esteem; and also how enticing was the prospect he had sketched in for me. I also had the uncomfortable feeling that he had really gone out of his mind in a queer sort of way. I wanted to say "You are schizoid my lad, that's what you are. But with patience and rest and sedation . . ." but I said nothing. On the other hand, in a confused sort of way I began to wish I had never heard of this toy of his. But here he was, still smiling at me with a funny hangdog tenderness, quite impenitent over the past and still hungry about the future.

"I have good hopes of you" he said softly. "I will ring you up in a day or two. I am making arrangements to take Rackstraw back to England. He has moments, you know, when he becomes quite lucid and recalls quite a lot. I have spared no research into Iolanthe, you know—into her character and her habits. Almost everyone who knew her has had something to tell us, and we've built up a huge library on her, crumb by crumb, to feed into the Abel nervous system, if I can put it like that. I think the elegance of Marchant's adaptation of Abel will please you very much—all sorts of new materials are to hand these days for modelling. My dear Felix, I can't believe you'll refuse me. It would be the crown of your life's work I believe to help me make her so perfectly that nobody would ever believe it wasn't her."

"Why Rackstraw?"

"He was her lover. I want to suck him dry."

"What can he tell you?"

He gave a small impatient gesture.

"The least thing is important for her. Nothing is too trifling to be overlooked." He said this with such childish impish seriousness that I was tempted to laugh. Quite insane! All this would end in catatonia, some delicious twilight-state which would make the doctors croon with joy. O boredom, boredom, Mother of the Arts! But if I didn't do this, what else could I do to escape from it? I was a compulsive inventor, nothing else fulfilled me. I had an irrational rush of hunger and love for this new Benedicta staring into the clouds up there—perhaps she could save me from myself? No. I looked at Julian, and I realised with full force for the first time in my life what the theologians must mean when they speak of being tempted by the devil. The *hubris*, the insolence, to arrogate to oneself the power of the Gods! Vaulting ambition etc. I suddenly wanted to do a pee and be alone with myself for a second. I retired behind the hut for a moment while Julian sat motionless, waiting for me to come back. I did, and sat down. "You are insatiable" I said and he nodded in a thirsty sort of way. The inside of his mouth was very pink, very red, so that in some of his expressions one might descry a touch of vampire. "Iolanthe" he said in a low voice as if she explained everything, the whole earth and the heavens above. "I saw her, you missed her. Now the firm must recreate her. It *must*, do you understand? and you *must help it*."

"And when you have built your Adam and Eve, what then? Will you ask Whipsnade to find a corner for them?"

"I am not going to speak to you as yet about that" he said in a sharp martinet's tone, a soft peremptory flash of fire. "We will face that when and if we succeed in doing what I want done."

"We'll ask Caradoc to build them a pretty little Parthenon to live in I suppose; dependants of the firm with a firmly guaranteed pension scheme and health insurance. . . ." I badly felt the need to insult him, I loved him so much. Badly. He sat quite still and calm but said nothing. I went on truculently, irrationally, "I shall be forced to regard you as a case of intellectual Koro, artificially induced. A *retractio ad absurdum*." He writhed and gritted his teeth with fury but said nothing, always nothing. It would have been pleasant to hit him with something but there was nothing to hand. Such weakness is despicable.

"I think you will" he said at last. "I don't really see what else you can do now you know about it." And all of a sudden he expelled his breath with relief and shrunk down to half his size, as if from exhaustion. He became so pale I thought he would probably faint; he seemed to suddenly feel the cold, his teeth chattered. Then after a minute or so his breathing steadied again and he regained his posture, his norm. He became once more the pleasant conversational man. "As for Caradoc," he said "as you know he is back and *en disponibilité* until the firm finds something worthy of his genius. But even a genius has a few intellectual holes in him and he is no exception; the sense of symbolic logic in architecture escapes him completely. He finds no significance for example in the fact that the diameter of the outer stone circle of Stonehenge is some 100 feet which is about the diameter of the dome of St Paul's."

He stood up again and turned away to stare at the snowrange intently. Then he said, but in a whisper and as if to himself: "One dares not neglect symbolism in either life or art. It is perilous. I threw a lighted torch into Iolanthe's grave!" I was in the presence of someone who had suffered the full onslaught of the European disease, poxier than pox ever was—Love! But of course allied as always to matter for he added in the same breath, "I own all her films now. I play them over and over to myself, in order to regale myself with all that she wanted to be, all that she could not realise of herself. My God, Felix, you must see them."

"So you bought her out at last!" I simply could not resist the bitter note in my voice. He nodded with set jaw. How I hated this mechanical vulture!

"I finally forced her to abdicate" he said, but sadly now, as if the victory were a hollow one. "She abdicated only after her death; and I could do nothing about her life or about mine. Fixed stars!" In a long sad pause he repeated the phrase like an incantation. "Fixed stars!"

Poor Julian! Rich Julian! Vega and Altair!

"Now I must leave you," he said "and find my way down to the bottom of this damned mountain." He gloved his precise small hand and stood up. Together we walked across the snow to where Benedicta was. She watched us quietly advancing towards her, unsmiling, calm. "*Eh bien*" she said at last on a note of interrogation, but there was not much more to be said.

Julian took her hands in his in a somewhat ceremonial fashion. "B., you betrayed us over Count Böcklin, didn't you? Quite deliberately." But there was no rancour in his tone, perhaps just a touch of regret. Benedicta nodded in perfectly composed fashion and kissed him in sisterly wise on the cheek. "I wanted to show myself that I was finally free, Julian." Julian nodded. "That word again" he said reprovingly. "It has a dying fall." B. put her arm through mine. "All too frequently" she agreed. "But not any more, at least for me. You know, if Felix hadn't disappeared and left me alone I would have refused the task when you put it to me. But I was scared, I was scared to death of you." Julian started to put on his skis, tenderly latching up the thongs and testing them with precision on one leg and then the other. "And now you can only pity me I suppose. Don't Benedicta. That might make me turn dangerous again." Strange, agonisingly shy man!

"No" she said. "You are de-fused for us, Julian."

He looked from one to the other for a long moment; then he gave a little nod as if of approval at what he saw. "I shall order you some happiness for a change now that we have crossed the big divide in ourselves. You might even come to love *me* one day, both of you. I doubt, though. Yet the road has opened in front of us. But there is still quite a lot to be done in order to earn it. Felix, I shall ring you up in a couple of days when you have had a chance to reflect."

"No need" I said. "I am your man and you know it."

"What luck," he said in a low voice "what luck for me to have you at my side once more. And so farewell."

He shuffled his way uphill until he gained the edge of the practice slope and then ebbed forward on his skis, propelling himself with his paddles; gathered momentum, curved up small, and glided away like a swallow into the valley. Suddenly with his going we felt that the world had emptied itself; we felt the evening chill upon us as we returned to the hut to pack up and trudge back to the *téléférique*.

"You are signing on again" she said. "Darling, this time I think you should; now I am at your side and you at mine, armed. I'm holding my breath. Do you think some happi. . . . ?"

I kissed her breathless. "Not a word, not a single word. Just go on holding your breath and we'll see what happens."

Sinking down the mountain side in the dark purple cusp of evening was more beautiful than the morning ascent; a somewhat inexplicable sensation of delayed shock had seized me. I repeated in my own mind the words "Well, so Julian actually exists and I have met him in the flesh." The phrase generated a perfectly irrational relief and—indeed why not?—happiness. Also physical relief: I felt done in, exhausted. Why? I don't know. It was as if, during the meeting itself, my mind had been in such a daze that I couldn't fully grasp the fact. I suppose ordinary people might experience this sort of grateful shock-anaesthesia on meeting an admired film-star unexpectedly in a grocer's shop. It was clear for me at any rate. Julian had appeared like some figment of a lost dream flashed, so to speak, on the white screen of the snows. He had disappeared just as dramatically—a dwindling black spot turning back into tadpole and racing away into the huge blue perspectives of the valley. Gone!

Benedicta had burrowed her slender hand into my pocket and was softly pressing mine. "It is fatuous to feel so serene," I said "and possibly dangerous too. Do you know what he is up to? Building a human being, if you please. Moreover one we know. God, I love you, Benedicta. Wait!"

I had a perfectly brilliant idea for a new sort of jump-circuit. It was so rich I feared it might disappear if I didn't make a note of it; yes, but pencil and paper? Fortunately she had a very fine lipstick with her and in her methodical camper's way she had brought a few sheets of toilet-paper against emergencies since she knew there was no lavatory at the huts. Saved! She looked over my shoulder as I blotted and blatched with this clumsy tool. I couldn't stop to explain for fear that the idea might fade. It was my sort of poem to the blue evening, the sliding white mountains, the buzzing prismatic corolla of the sinking sun bouncing off the slopes, the trees, the world, to

Benedicta herself. And how patient she was; probably disappointed that it wasn't a love letter but a set of silly pothooks, equations. (If it worked it might spell the death of the ordinary light-bulb as we know it.) "I love you" I said. "But don't speak for a moment. O I love you desperately, but shut up please."

Ouf! But I felt guilt when it was all duly noted down and stuffed into my pocket. So I wrote on the window a rebus based on the word TUNC with a heart in the middle instead of a you-know-what and the words *Felix amat Benedictam*. In fact such was my euphoria that I missed a step on the ramp and fell headlong into a snowdrift.

"That really is a sign of returning health" said Benedicta approvingly after her first concern about broken limbs was allayed. "With the return of absentmindedness on such a scale we can really prognose a total cure." That is all very well, but in fact I was whacked; I had a bath, got my dressings changed, and was all ready for visiting her at the chalet, but instead I lay down on the bed for a few moments of repose and reflection and fell instantly asleep. It was early morning when I woke to find myself stiff as a lead soldier but wonderfully refreshed. Beside me, scribbled on the temperature chart, was a note from B. which said: "Alarmed, I came to find you. But I like you almost better asleep than awake. You look such a fool, such a contented fool. All the algebra has been drained from your body. You look how one ought to look when one is dead but alas we don't. Anyway I have enjoyed sitting beside you watching you going up and down in a steady purposeful sort of way. In your Chinese book I read the following passage which pleased me. 'Drunk, in a huge green garden, among flowering cherry trees, under a parasol, among diplomats, what a death, Tu Fu, poor poor dear.' So goodnight. (P.S. I want to sleep with you.)"

*   *   *   *   *

But she had gone into town to do some shopping so I spent the morning in the so-called danger ward learning to tie seaman's knots from Professor Plon who was a specialist in the garotte; he had already disposed of a wife and two daughters in exemplary fashion (running bowline?) and was technically not supposed to have any access to rope. But he had found a piece, I don't know how, and was shaping all kinds of elaborate and diverting knots and bows. I finally got it away from him when his attention was diverted, though it was really a pity. He could have emptied that whole ward by lunchtime. But I didn't want poor Rackstraw to go the way of all flesh; though it was almost inconceivable that he should have anything very special to tell us about Iolanthe, it was only fair to let Julian satisfy his curiosity. What else had I been doing but just that? Those elegant debauched hands had roved all over that lovely body, touching it now here, now there, moulding the breasts and stroking the marvellous haunches of the paragon girl, the nonpareil. I felt a sort of sick pang of tenderness when I thought of it. Iolanthe the waif, and Iolanthe the breastless goddess of the silver screen; the sick romance of all our Helens, for whom somebody's Troy always goes up in flames.

Rackstraw himself was enjoying a period of rare lucidity. "I have been invited to go away" he said happily "to a place which is a country house to stay with a man I used to know vaguely—I have forgotten his name, but anyway it wouldn't mean anything to you."

"Julian?" I said.

" 'Pon my soul yes!" said Rackstraw. "You do know him then? He came to see me yesterday and told me about it. It's more like a film-studio than a country house, it's full of inventors. They keep popping out of doors and saying things like 'I've got it, old boy. Look no further. The answer is untreated sewage.' It might prove

104

boring in the long run; but they are going to make a long recording lasting months, perhaps years." Ah the blessed intervals of insulin coma! But he was radiant in a funny etiolated way. He had cleaned his shoes and was fussing over an egg-stain on his waistcoat.

"Rackstraw" I said. "What about Iolanthe?"

"I made the mistake" he said surprisingly "of treating women as grown-ups without believing in the idea; but later I found to my horror that they *were*. It was I who was the child." He shook his head slowly and looked around him. "If only I could have a word from old Johnson. There's no knowing if he will have a happy Christmas or not, down there in Leatherhead. It is very remiss of him. At our age, you know, there aren't very many more shots on the spool." Then he said "Iolanthe!" in a tone of the greatest contempt, and suddenly shuddered with horror as if he had swallowed a toad. "What does that mean?" I said. He looked at me with blazing futile eyes and hissed: "Have you seen the sharks in the Sydney zoo? Then I shall say no more!" If he went on like this I could see that it was going to be a very long and very costly recording. "To be belonged to!" he went on in the same tone of high contempt. "Pah! She killed someone and I found out because she talked in her sleep." He knelt down and patiently undid my shoelaces, then stood up again apparently completely satisfied with his handiwork. "My success with women" he said modestly "was all due to my voice. They could not resist it. When I wanted one I used to put on a special husky croony tone which worked like a charm. I used to call this 'putting a lot of cock into it'. It was infallible. Naturally I took great pleasure in their company."

He walked up and down in his strange tottering fashion but with quite a strut of sexual vanity. Then he stopped and raising his hand in a regal gesture said "Now go! Vanish! Decamp! Vamoose! Buzz off!" So I did, albeit rather reluctantly, for I was intrigued by even this glancing reference to Io. Who knows, perhaps if he sat week after week in the red plush projection room where Julian now spent so much of his time, staring at the films he had helped her to make, something might be evoked in him, some concrete response? And yet to what end? Once dead . . . God, I wondered what sort of toy was in the process of being fabricated; a copy of the human dummy which would pose once more the eternal problem (how real can you get?) without ever being able to answer it. Iolanthe! I had missed her somehow and Julian had never enjoyed the real girl whom Henniker described in the words, "It was her animal fervour, her warmth, her slavishness which won men's hearts, going down to the ugliest client like a humble and devoted dying moon. Later she became tired, and worse still something of a lady: and intelligent, worst of all. She discovered she had a sensibility. This tied men into worse knots, intellectual ones. They were always trying to find metaphors to express things which are best left unexpressed." All right. All right.

I hadn't seen a paper for months, indeed had had no desire to know what was going on in the world. So I was interested to catch myself lifting a copy of *The Times* from a consulting-room desk, to read with my lunch. Nothing very much. I missed Benedicta as I read. Sometimes in some of our expressions, straying into the visual field, so to speak, I saw my son very clearly. Then he dimmed away and she became once more herself. It made me feel shy in a way, and guilty; I had mounted that toy in order to kill Julian and it had recoiled on my head. Bang! I could never have foreseen, even with the help of Abel, that Mark himself might opt out of the whole compact, press the trigger. I had such an ache too when I thought that Benedicta had never mentioned it, never alluded to Mark. I saw now to what extent she had been a prisoner in this fantastic web spun by the firm—a web held firm by the fanatical tenacity of Julian. Well, I read a little bit into the extraordinary fantasy of reality as captured by the so-called press. The world had not changed since my absence, it was the same. Fears of war as usual. They were crying "punish me, punish me". And of course a war was coming. Hurrah! Everybody would be miserable but gay, masochistically gay, and art would flourish on the stinking middens of our history.

I went into the other room to find Benedicta on her knees with half-open trunks all around. "What the hell are you doing?" She said: "Packing." Well, on the one hand it might seem logical enough. "Why?"

Benedicta said: "Nash rang me. You are released, we are both released. Free. Julian is coming to get you tomorrow and drive you back. I'm going by air. Where do you want to live? Mount Street is always there, and also that monster you hate in the country."

"Let me find out a little bit where and how I am working—and at what. Let's go to a hotel first, let's go to Claridge's where the people are so insensitive, shall we?"

"All right I'll book."

III

But you'd have thought that Hitler himself had sent for me if you'd seen the four huge black limousines coming to a halt in the drive of the Paulhaus; Julian travelled like a Black Prince with numerous secretaries, perhaps even gunmen for all I knew. He himself was in the back of the leading car holding the door open for me. He wore an immaculate dark suit and soft black hat turned well down over his eyes—and, of course, characteristically enough, dark glasses. Chauffeurs bustled about with my luggage. "Come into my floating office and admire it" he said indicating a shallow panel full of switches. With childish pride he showed me the radio and telex arrangements, a secretary's folding desk; and there was even a telephone which worked externally. A cocktail cabinet. Everything in fact except a lavatory and a chapel to worship Mammon in. "What splendour" I said to humour him. "Could we call London and given them Benedicta's flight number?" He was delighted to show his mysteries off and in next to no time was talking to Baum over the water. Then he sat back in the comfortable seat of the mammoth and lit a cigar. I watched him with curiosity, still consumed by a feeling of unreality; as much as I could see of him, that is, for the glasses shielded his eyes. "Always the passion for disguise, Julian" I said, somewhat rudely I suppose. "It has always puzzled me." He looked round at me and quickly looked away again. "It shouldn't really" he said. "I have always been terribly . . . shy; but apart from that I have a thing, I suppose Nash would regard it as a complex, about faces. They seem to me quite private things. I do not see why we have to walk about with them sticking out of a hole in the top of our clothes, simply because convention decrees it. I have perhaps overcompensated in one direction; you know that I have had my face made over twice by plastic surgery in order to get it the way I wanted it. It's better than it was but I'm still not completely happy.

It is very boring, for example, always to have the same face—and nowadays thank goodness it's no longer necessary. Here, I shall be quite honest with you and show you my dossier." He groped in a shallow leather wallet and produced some passport photographs which he handed to me one by one, saying "That is how nature made me, this is where art stepped in, and this is the way I look now." I gasped and stared incredulously at him. "But it's three quite different men" I said. "Not really. Look more closely. There is much that cannot be changed." Yes, he was there in each if one peered into the eyes, but in each case the change had been accompanied by a different hair-style. But the differences were more marked than the resemblances. "But of course" he said coolly "this may not be the end of the affair if I begin to get bored with the way I look at present. It's a marvellous feeling of liberty to know that you can change when you wish, even though very superficially."

He put the photographs away carefully and pocketed the wallet. "Now you know all" he said, and lapsed into an indifferent silence as he watched the countryside rolling past us. His hands seemed fatter and coarser than I remembered them to be, and he wore a seal ring. But having disposed of the subject of his disguises he seemed to have nothing more to say. In fact he seemed to doze off, to hibernate inside the dark wings of his overcoat.

We lunched in high mountains on smoked salmon and white wine; Julian had a long talk on his pet telephone to a branch in Holland which manufactured paperclips. "We have two lazy men there I shall have to deal with; one sits all day in a bubble bath of self-esteem, and the other is too scared to move: Jaeger, you perhaps know? A Jewish banker like a very very old very sharp scythe."

I had expected him to make some reference to the sort of work he was expecting of me but he said nothing at all about the Iron Maide, so I contented myself with dipping into unreality again—reading a newspaper I mean. Dear old London! At it again. A new labour party pamphlet which would offer wholesome sex instruction to the under-fours and most probably begin: "Children, did you know that mummy was full of eggs and that daddy had to hatch them, and that is how you are here?" Life, as Koepgen never tired of reminding us, is only being let out on parole for a brief while. *Tous les excès sont bons.* Well, let Julian sleep. But I myself was half asleep when late that night we slanted into Paris in a foul grey rain. "I want" said Julian "to go first to the café where you met her, then to the hotel. I want to see the room you took her to." I protested feebly, but there was nothing for it; a note of such passionate urgency and hunger came into his voice that out of sheer sympathy I felt I had to give in. Sordid rum-whiffing *terrasse* where we sat for a while at the chipped table; strong local colour was supplied by a little whore, a veritable midget, who uncrossed her legs and let loose an effluvium which could be smelt tables away, stables away, could almost be heard. . . . Then to that room where she had told me this and that, and her breasts and so on. Then Henniker with her face flushed with rage, all red and bruised from the crying, protesting about Graphos and the whip. "He taught her to enjoy it, but he couldn't make her love him. No, if she loved anyone sexually it was me. ME. I seduced her, I calmed her, I loved her and was faithful right to the end." What piti-ful wounded stuff we carry around inside us; wounds that gush blood at the slightest touch of memory's lancet. He sat in a chair looking dazed, like some very old tame monkey, gazing round him and yawning; but when I told him about the breasts he put his face in his hands and went very still for a moment. Then he cleared his throat softly and said: "About death there is something curious—a sort of shrinking; if you copy the exact dimensions the effect of your statue or dummy always looks smaller than the remembered original. In the waxworks, for example, everyone seems to have become re-duced in size. Just over life size is the best recipe for copies. Let us go, I have heard enough."

He did not appear for dinner that night and I amused myself by reading Koepgen, ringing up Benedicta and leafing through *Figaro.* Much literary prize-giving and distribution of honorary titles; why don't we? The Epicurus of Letchworth, the great Aubergine of Clermont-Ferrand. Hum!

Next morning Julian decided that he must go to Holland and as I was impatient to see this new-old wife of mine I took a plane, full of a vertiginous excitement and shyness. My impatience led to indis-creet arguments with everyone, officials, porters and lastly with an insolent cabby who had clearly never seen a man in love before, and made no allowances for this desperate illness. (One should be put in an ambulance with a bell; or someone should walk in front of one with a red flag crying: "*Enceinte. Enceinte.*") But at last I arrived to find Benedicta in bed with a cold, so pretty and so woeful that I was tempted to ring up the whole of Harley Street. "You see what happens now when you leave me? I get ill."

"O thank you, thank you."

*　　*　　*　　*　　*

But nevertheless, in spite of the infantile euphoria, I had the most dreadful dreams. "Dreams are but the prose of quotidian life with the poetic quantum added." All right. All right. Cut it out now. They were horrible, and of course they made me wonder if perhaps I had been seduced once more upon the bitter path of. . . . I interrogated her silent form, sleeping so calmly beside me, one hand on her breast: the rise and fall so reassuring, like the spring swell of a marvellous free sea—a Greek sea. And I felt suddenly terribly old and went into the bathroom to examine my old carcase with attention all over again. Bits were falling out—a tooth would have to go: O not another! The hair was coming back quite strong. But an extra magnification of the bloody glasses.

It was amazing that my balls hadn't dropped off after all I'd been through—like Vibart's champion novelist. It seemed to me that I had a very false cringing sort of smile, so I decided to change it all along and because of. . . . But smiling from left to right instead of right to left set the wrong groups of muscles moving. Also the old knowing friendly *kindly* expression in the eyes looked just bleary to me. What despair! I knew exactly how I should look in order to rivet her attention forever. But suppose it got stuck, that smile, from being artificial? Suppose nobody could move it? I would have to go every morning to Harley Street and accept facial massage from some torpid Japanese. Perhaps acupuncture in the dorsal region, huge coloured pins being driven into my inventor's dogged bum? O hell, please not that.

*   *   *   *   *

Marchant rang me the following day and at last I began to think that things were moving along as planned. He asked me to meet him at Poggio's which I duly did, enchanted to see my old stablemate again. But he had changed a good deal; his hair had gone very fine and quite silver and you could see pink scalp through it. He sported a set of new false teeth of fantastic brilliance. His clothes were much the same—the stage uniform of the absentminded professor: baggy grey trousers and a torn tweed coat (acid-stained here and there) with leather patches on the elbows. And a huge college scarf of garish design, bearing his college colours I don't doubt. But he was full of energy and excitement, gesticulating and twitching his face as he spoke like a lively earwig. And yet somehow tired and highly strung; and I noticed that he was drinking rather heavily for such an abstemious man. Anyway "How" he said, giving me the benefit of a Red Indian salute. "How" I replied gravely.

"I had all your news from Julian. Imagine my delight. To hear you were coming to work at Toybrook with me. I have been bored stiff among all those corpses."

"Wait a minute" I said. "First Toybrook. Isn't that a hush-hush plant of some sort?" Marchant nodded and said: "It's where we work on anything which might be on a secret list for the forces; it's a security A factory. I brought you a pass, all neatly made out for you. When will you begin? It's only a very few miles from the country house, if you have your car. You could drive over every day. Why the grimace, Felix?" I sighed. "Bad memories, painful memories. I wonder. I'll ask Benedicta."

"Do. It would be convenient."

"Now what about corpses?"

"A literal fact; working on these models which I must say are beginning to look quite frighteningly like the real thing, we found we knew next to nothing about anatomy. We could have called in great surgeons and all that, but they work on living bodies; we were only imitating and where possible simplifying in glass wool, nylon, jute and so on. In other words the inside of the Iron Maide did not have to be copied provided we mocked out a musculature and a nervous system and allowed her to imitate human behaviour, speech, gesture, mnemonic response. Of course Abel has been invaluable with his memory bank which we have now reduced spectroscopically to the size of a pea virtually—talk about writing the Lord's Prayer on the point of a pin! It's only a matter of detail. She'll have twice the vocabulary of Shakespeare, and all the *souplesse* of a mummy trained for a ballet. Gosh, it is really amazing. Julian is incredible. Do you know when they moved a model of her into Madame Tussaud's he used to go there day after day to watch the crowds filing by her. One day I saw in the paper that this wax model had been damaged and I wondered if he had . . . well, I don't know . . . started kissing it or doing something even more drastic. He hasn't dared as yet to see what they've got. He says he will only come when you authorise him to. You know he is scared, Felix, very scared by this nylon Iolanthe; and she is coming along so well that I'm rather scared too. Suppose we get within three decimal places of a perfect copy? What are we going to do with her? Could she live an independent life as a free dummy, in a three-dimensional world? Eh?"

"What about the sexual stuff—is she designed to poke the other one? Will they be monogamous?"

"All that is feasible; but they will never be able to produce—the whole pelvic oracle is sketched in I'm afraid. But the vagina will please you. And incidentally, another chance remark of yours has borne fruit in a marvellous way. You've probably forgotten. Ejax!"

"Ejax?" I said vaguely. It meant nothing to me. Marchant chuckled and said: "One day when you were drunk you said that for real sexual pleasure the quantity of sperm was important. The heavier the discharge the greater the excitement of the female."

"I said that?"

"Yes, you did."

"Good god! Is it true?"

"Our new sperm-thickening pill called Ejax is having a wild

success—surely you've seen the advertising in all the Tube stations? No? 'Have you taken your Ejax today? If not what will the wifey say?' It's swept the board. And it was so easy chemically to work it out. A very slight provocation of the prostate with an irritant does the trick. So far no side-effects, but by the time these come along we'll have a counterblast to them."

"Marchant," I said "are you happy?" I don't suppose it was the question to put at this time and place. He stared at me angrily for a long moment and then said indignantly:

"Yes."

We went on looking at each other, critically and carefully. "Yes" he said, and again, "Yes, Felix." But it was stagy; he didn't want to be probed on this topic and I realised with a pang of regret the full measure of my tactlessness. Whose happiness is whose business after all? It was also a bit alarming to find that so much of my own was intimately bound up with Benedicta—surely this was a fearful weakness?

"Go on," I said "go on, Marchant boy, and stop me from thinking. I have never heard of such a beautiful project with all the problems it raises. Why it's like having a baby!"

"Exactly" he said, resuming the flush of enthusiasm which I had cut short by my ill-judged intervention. "While society is happily creating a slave-class of analphabetics, '*les visuels*', who have forgotten how to read and who depend on a set of Pavlovian signals for their daily bread and other psychic needs—surely we have the right to build a model which will be at least as 'human' as these so-called human beings? Eh? Whether her limitations of freedom in action will have to be circumscribed for her I cannot get Julian to discuss. He turns a blind eye to the whole matter.

"But if we get what we might—why, we could turn Iolanthe loose one day, kiss her warmly, and say, now you are free—just as if she were being released from Holloway. There is no reason that I can see why she shouldn't hold her own in the world as it is today. Just release her, as a soap-bubble is flicked off a child's soap-pipe. 'Go, my child.' It's not an unfair analogy—babies are born this way; but they arrive helpless and have to be passed through the cultural mincer. Suppose ours arrived at the age of thirty—mentally mature;

with all her experience digested? What is to prevent her taking her place with all the other dummies and pushing a lever for her living, her Pavlovian living? A trap door opens and the soup comes in." He was very drunk indeed in a cold and rational sort of way. His cheeks had a hectic flush. But he wasn't slurring and when he got up to go to the lavatory his walk was quite steady. "Will she have opinions?" I asked and he replied, "That is up to us; we are building the library of her conditioned responses upon the old graph you drew for Abel. Yes, she will feel certain things. But it's for us to decide to a certain extent." He absented himself and I reflected upon this weird assignment with a certain lustful satisfaction. Iolanthe!

"Faustus!"

Marchant, reappearing, said: "On the one hand it might seem complicated, but in fact it's only terribly detailed and intricate. Our responses are not infinite, from a muscular point of view, though of course they are various and numerous. Speech and so on—again it's not infinite; your sound analysis was most useful and adapts perfectly in the new materials. The voice is particularly successful in my view; here, I will play you a test strip." He crossed to where his coat hung and eased out a small tape-recorder with a set of fine earphones. Through them, and clear above the breathing silence of the machine, I heard the real voice of Iolanthe saying softly, dreamily: "Worlds of memory, worlds of desire, echo will set them both on fire. Three two four, three two four. Answer me. Is there anyone in the room who has seen my, has anyone seen my, seen my . . . ? Darling it could only have happened to us." It was a little unnerving —no, I'll go further. The reproduction was so beautiful that I was a bit bloodcurdled by it. On the one hand it was all so remote, Athens, the Nube and all that. But I suddenly felt the wild pang of the Acropolis at dawn with that warm scented little body lying tangled in mine in a sort of holy shipwreck; tasted those pious kisses. "Iolanthe"!

"Isn't it her to the life?"

"It's a funny way to put it, but it's true. I suppose you built up the vocal thing direct from Abel—I had quite a lot to work on."

"Yes, and her films, for example."

"The damnedest thing" I said and for no known reason felt a

disposition to laugh out loud. "Muscles powered by tiny photo-electric mnemonic cells."

"That's it, my boy." Marchant produced sheaves of boring-looking paper and drew out the circuits in very rough specification. "She has five zones of response; her power storage is a new kind of dry cell with a longish life, and is replaceable. We are weaving her from a selection of guts and nylons finer than any fisherman dreamed of, or any violinist for that matter. The hands are extraordinary—utterly beautiful; probably more so than the originals. She travels by the power of light, boyo, light-sensitised cells; becomes a trifle languid at twilight; and fades into sleep at any time you care to name. But of course she isn't done. It'll be weeks before it's all sewed into place and ready to walk down Regent Street."

"Soliciting I suppose?"

"That is for you to decide."

"Why me?"

"Julian seems to think your word is law in these matters. Myself I think he is playing a dangerous game—with your so-called sense of humour. But it's not my affair. I'm playing my part as best I can. But I realise now that I'm a mere interpreter of other men's ideas; you are the real scientist." It sounded pretty strange to me, put that way. I had always believed the direct opposite to be true. "But Julian" I said "is the real brains. None of us would be doing what we are doing had it not been for him." Marchant agreed, wiped his teeth in a napkin and replaced them tenderly. "We've photocopied the daily life of about twenty women to work out the range of situa-tion-responses for Iolanthe. It's really amazing how monotonous the ordinary range of movements, conversations, stock responses, can be. Even with the total range of thought we can conceivably stock her up with it's perfectly adequate for most things that happen to most people. Response-provoking through sound and light. She will move about like some huge abstract dolly playing a perfect part in the world of our time."

"I'm getting to love her already" I said.

"Beware of Julian" said Marchant jokingly. "We've built her a set of sexual organs which . . . but I haven't done the detailed planning yet. Waiting for you to come in with new ideas. But the site of the temple is all there and the foundations of the thing are all sound."

"What temple?"

"Temple of pleasure. I'm too much of a puritan, I avert my face a bit from all that; and Julian supplies no sort of guidance as yet. But if we are to get her as perfect as a real person we can't deprive her entirely of her sexual response, even if it's battery-driven."

It was all very well to joke, but inside I felt rather solemn and indeed a little uneasy. Marchant added an afterthought. "You'll find several old friends down at Toybrook—among them Said, the little one-eyed Christian Arab of your salad days who has been doing the most imaginative and intricate work on the light-sensitisation and the sound. The man who built your ear-trumpet, remember?" Of course I did. An absolutely marvellous artisan in little; the firm was lucky to have such a master craftsman on hand.

"And the corpses will intrigue you, the real ones; it's funny how things tend to call up other things. Involuntarily, so to speak. Just when we were having the first troubles over anatomy and invoking the aid of the Royal College of Surgeons and so on, Julian was faced with another opening for the firm in Turkey: embalming! I know it sounds strange and of course at first we laughed very much in an exasperated sort of way because really we should have thought of it. It is the most ancient of all cultus ploys and we could have launched it years ago. Now, with the help of the two holy churches, East and West, we got everyone into a huddle and, basing ourselves on a profit-sharing scheme, with Rome and Byzantium we launched the whole thing with *éclat*. It was of course preceded with a bombardment of clerical propaganda from the pulpit, specially prepared sermons, telling you that it was wicked for you to leave your nearest and dearest to rot when you could embalm them and stick them on the hall hat-stand as we used to stick wild boar or stags or what not. Also a very nice decoration to very old-fashioned pubs might be Mine Host resurrected in this fashion (if ever so slightly glazed).

"Combined with this we got the avant-garde in Paris interested in it as a sort of beatnik curio with fascinating responses from all. They don't really want to live, the young. They want to be embalmed so that they can impress their friends. Moreover they are prepared to pay for automatic posthumous embalming as one pays for life insurance. The cult went off with a bang; we couldn't meet the demand. It seems to them, I suppose, the only future guarantee that they had actually been alive. And there's always the chance of lending out your mummy for that perfect party where everyone was so 'stoned'. In short we were in business. But . . . on the technological side we ran into trouble with the quality of the embalming.

"In Turkey they were using methods unchanged for hundreds of years. The result was a very friable effort which, if removed from the dry astringent desert air and moved into a more humid climate, deteriorated dreadfully. In fact rotted. Of course we moved 'Chemicals A' over on the job and we are still in the process of wrestling with the formulae for preservatives—it's more difficult than you can imagine. But while the embalmers were using our brains we were using their dead bodies which can be played about with at will, in order to learn what we needed to know for Iolanthe. So you will find a rather strange Embalming Studio (so called) *chez nous*. It's very useful to us for checking; but they are training to conquer the whole Middle and Far East. Nature, beautiful are thy ways!"

"Do you mean to tell me you have been poking about in corpses with a notebook in one hand, Marchant?" By this time he was extremely drunk but not at all shaky; I mean one would have had to know him quite well to divine that he wasn't sober. Also he gave me a funny feeling of being a bit scared. Anyway he gave a great earwig chirp of laughter and said: "My dear chap, all that I know of the human anatomy is based on the dead. I could not play around with the living, and I'm no surgeon, as you know. But the dead have been of enormous help, specially while they are still fresh, while the motor responses are still working. The *rigor mortis* buggers them up from my point of view—at least on the suppleness and response factor. But it is most instructive and delightful to see them taken apart as clockwork is, bit by bit, and then pieced together into the sort of doll we are contemplating.

"In fact one has to stop and ask oneself from time to time 'Who is doing what, exactly?' I'm damned if I know. But anyway right next to us we have this vast embalming studio run by the Americans which provides us with models galore. Of course the American market was already very advanced when all this happened; Europe is terribly backward in some ways." We both cackled with the old-fashioned laughter which nowadays would merit a pistol fired through the skull. "But the Middle East" he said "is going in for this with a vengeance, and Julian has already financed a couple of films based on the subject to orient public opinion towards the notion." He paused. "Always Julian" I said.

"I must go" he said, but he still sat on for a while cupping his brandy in a warming hand and staring at me. Then he continued with remorse, "My God, I've done nothing but talk; I haven't asked you a thing, how you feel, how you are, whether you are keen to take this business on or not. . . . Forgive."

"I'm glad. I would have been incapable of answering any of your questions. I'm newly convalescent and very newly wed, if I dare to believe it, to a re-upholstered ghost called Benedicta. I am just feeling my feet, as they say, but very uncertainly. But whatever the state of things I'll come to Toybrook and look over the set-up with you. Would you like Monday? I'll be there betimes if you think that it would suit?"

Marchant drank off his glass and rose. "Yes" he said. "Monday. I must let you hear a lecture by the top embalmer. You will hardly credit your senses. All good sense mind you. Ahem!"

I took the Tube back, crushed in among my fellow-countrymen who looked on the whole rather nice, after such a long absence from them. But it was like travelling in a parrot's cage, I was all but deafened when I finally crawled up the steps of Claridge's. I walked into the room and said: "Mark, Benedicta, Mark!" She jumped up, radiant. "Thank goodness you said that; I was thinking it. It's the sorest place of our many. So many thorns to be taken out of each other's paws, but Mark. . . ." I sat down: "What brought it on was the discovery that the place where I am working is very near. . . ."

"Yes. I see."

She lit a cigarette and marched up and down for a moment. "We must try and incorporate him, relive him a little bit inside ourselves. It's very selfish in a way, but I fear that if he goes on inside us like a suppurating thing, the memory of a bad act, then things will not grow right between us as they might. Mark still stands at the cross-roads between you and me." She sat down thump in a chair and still smoking furiously gave a gulp which was as much rage and frustration as just tears of regret. I, too, could have beaten my head against a wall and yelled, but not being of that sort of minting I did damn all. I tried as hard as I could to yawn, look natural, that sort of thing. Tried to light a cigarette, burnt my finger, got a fit of coughing. Went off to the lavatory to do a pee and swear quietly at the way things are arranged.

When I came back she was standing in the centre of the room, very composed and with a fine haughty kind of determination in her eye. "We must go back to every place where we have been hurt, or where we have inflicted hurt on each other, and systematically exorcise the memory—what do you think of that?" I jumped at it. "But now" I said. "This very night." And she nodded. "Otherwise it will be no good."

It did not take long to raise a car and alert the housekeeper—nor truth to tell to drive down through the roads which were horribly empuddled and the countryside looking devilish sad. We didn't exchange a single word. I had organised a thermos of coffee and some repellent ham sandwiches. The night was cold. It blew. I suppose the same sort of thing was going on in her—I mean for my part I was rehearsing the whole past of this period in that horrid garish mansion; it was less like a bad dream than an old abandoned tunnel into which one had fallen and been rescued. But now one had to go back and clear it of fallen debris. I thought too with a pang of Iolanthe's island cottage. Ghosts, they need meat too!

Benedicta drove while I fed her with cigarettes; drove in her brilliant fast vein as if anxious to reach the end of the journey as soon as possible. Long white headlight-ribbons winding away over the hills, melting down long avenues littered with a detritus of autumn. Beauty and melancholy of the night country softening away towards winter and the white transforming snow. At last we came slowly cracking down the long winding drive up to the house with its steely lake and horrid toffee-rose towers. O Coleridge where wert thou? A little bit slowed down perhaps by a temporary misgiving; every thing hereabouts spelt Mark, spelt sickness, hag-drawn nights of sleeplessness, Nash, Julian, Abel, Bang. . . . I put my hand inside her velvet coat and touched her breast. "So," she said "here we are, gentlemen of the jury, here we are."

I hammered on the door and rang the interminable bloody bell-rope, while she turned the car and backed it up for shelter under an eave. For a long time nobody. Then the little old gnomish house-keeper came tottering down and tuttering about unaired beds and blown fuses. There was no electric light in the place, and despite all her telephoning she had not been able to get a man in to do the repair. Candles, then, a couple of big silver branches on the great marble table; perhaps more suitable in a way for visiting this great mausoleum of wasted hopes—in the sense of atrophy, I mean. Attrition. I saw her face rosy in the rosy light, so very grave and precious. (Julian had said: "Open your legs, I am going to kiss you," but instead he had shaken the candlesticks and the burning wax sprayed her unmercifully.)

The long desolate galleries grew awake and attentive as they watched us come walk, walking in this warm bubble of candleshine; watched us pass and then slipped back into the anonymity of dark-ness behind us. We went solemnly and without speaking, spending a moment at each of the stations of the cross in meditation. Like visit-ing the picture gallery of a lost life. Here we had married, here lain down in each other's arms in helpless silence, here quarrelled, here shouted deafly at each other, here smoked and mused. Mark had slept here, woken there, played further on. This death newly felt and revived vibrated on the heart like the concussion of some fearful drum.

Abel had gone—there was just a gaping hole in the musician's gallery; my toy of a pet of a monster of a brainstorm of a Thing. I was glad; it had integrated itself elsewhere, been melted down. Here for some reason she kissed me and wept a small tear. And so on through the tower bedrooms and thence down the great staircase to the larger of the two ballrooms. The mirrors had not been replaced though the gunshot-splashed glass had been picked out to leave just the far gilded frames like so many reproaching frowns. Here the silence was immensely real silence, the air stagnant; there was no other resonance except ours in this place. Nobody had ever had a ball here, for a wedding or a birthday. Just she and I and a shot gun and the Lord's Prayer written on the mirrors with number three shot. The gun-room too was now empty except for a few twelves such as cottagers might need to chase rooks out of a tree. But in the little fridge in the buttery the thoughtful gnome had placed a bottle of champagne and two goblets as green as Venice. This too was appropriate.

We took it, tray and all, into the fake library with its tapestry of empty bookcovers; there was a fire laid in the grate which took no time at all to burst into bristling flame. I scouted out cushions from everywhere I could and built a huge oriental divan reminiscent of Turkey in front of it. Here we sat, thinking each other's thoughts and sipping the green champagne while the logs carved out their strange figures and stranger faces. Then of a sudden the telephone rang, which gave us both a tremendous start. We looked at each other in curiosity touched with a certain consternation. Who knew we were there? Julian was in Divonne, gambling. It rang, and rang, beseeching and beseeching. I rose swearing, but she took my arm and said: "No. Just for once let it ring. Don't answer it Felix, I implore you." I said: "Don't be superstitious B." But she was adamant. "I just know we must not answer it." On it rang and on; I sat down again. We couldn't talk or think any more for the noise of the damned instrument. Then it choked off. "Now we shall never know what it was, or who it was" I said with regret. But she sighed a great sigh of relief and said: "Thank Goodness no. Yet that one conversation might have made us change direction all over again— have put us back on a fatal course."

So we lay down at last and fell asleep by the warm fire, like hibernating squirrels, too drowsy to make love even. It must have been nearly dawn when I woke in the chill to revamp the fire and to scout out our coffee and sandwiches. Benedicta was yawning and combing her hair, quite refreshed. I went to test the water in a nearby bathroom but found no hot; boilers unstoked for ages, I suppose. Benedicta was saying: "There's that old cottage in the grounds which was revamped, do you recall? Why couldn't we live there for a while and acclimatise? I would like to live more alone with you. We could have a little boat on the lake. Felix, answer." But I was struck dumb by the brilliance of the idea. It was a very pleasant little wooden chalet, not too small; I had once started to build a studio in it. It had originally been built to keep a housekeeper in, but proved too far from the house. So there it was, yet another place lying empty. "If I remember right the sanitation and kitchen were done over."

"Brilliant. Let's go and see it."

This we did cutting swathes of dew across the meadows. A tiny brook, a meadow, an abandoned mill. A small jetty for a boat. . . . How the devil had I never thought of it before? "Darling, you are speaking directly to the romantic bourgeois in my soul. The secret of a happy life is to reduce the scale of things, circumscribe them; a girl doesn't need to fill up more than the circumference of one's arms. I have never liked big women anyway." Yes, it was there, the cottage, but I had to force a kitchen window to get in. It was quite dry and warm because of all the timber I suppose, and spotlessly clean. A pleasant studio looking out through a weeping willow on to the misty waters of the lake. "It's ideal." Was it too much to hope for a few happy years here without the nagging frontal brain intervening to muck everything up with its bloody hysterias? One hardly dared to formulate the sort of hopes it offered, this queer scroggy chalet, looking in a vague sort of way as if it had been influenced by Caradoc's Parthenon of Celebes.

"Don't you feel we should at least try here?" she said. "It hasn't the terrible gloom of the big house with all its memories—the horrid backlash of the past. But it's only across the meadow—we could go there from time to time like one goes to visit a friend in the cemetery." I said "Yes."

With a certain amount of awe, though. What had poor Felix done to deserve all this? Invent Ejax by mistake?

"Yes. Agreed!"

*   *   *   *   *

"You say you've never been to Toybrook" said Marchant with a certain happy condescension. "I can hardly believe it." No, I was sure I hadn't. "They were working upon an obscure nerve-gas and documented me once when I was doing Abel, but that is all I know. Central nervous system." He chuckled in a specious professorial way, like a don who is delighted to take you to lunch at the Athenaeum because you aren't a member. He settled the car rug round him and fiddled with the heating—I detected indications of old age and badly lagged pipes. The afternoon was mild and clammy. "As a matter of fact," he said "I opened this morning's paper and got quite a start. I thought I was looking at Toybrook but in fact what I was looking at. . . ." He fumbled among his cases and bundles and produced a paper which he opened and spread before me, stabbing with a lean nicotined finger. The caption was one word, a familiar one: Belsen! We laughed very heartily about this—a long terrain of old-fashioned potting sheds with the two funnels, like a liner or a soap-factory. All indistinct and furry.

"Come," I said "didn't Caradoc build it? It can't be less than a Parthenon of some sort in that case."

"It's very beautiful," he admitted sitting back and settling the rug around him "really very beautiful. And also marvellous from our own point of view. There are no labs like it in Europe, nowhere. The nearest comparison is Germany, but even then I think we have the edge of them. No, Toybrook is quite something. Sound like an invention of Enid Blyton doesn't it? Do you know those children's books of hers?"

"Of course. I read them in the Tube."

"Then?"

"Well, I'm curious to see what you've got and to find out where you want to go." Marchant looked at me curiously, humorously.

He said: "We want to get as real as we can." Silence. "You mean fundamentally you want to give yourself the illusion of actually controlling reality? How real can one conceive, I mean?" Marchant gave a chuckle. "Felix, Felix" he said reprovingly, putting his hand on my knee. "The old weakness is peeping out. You want to intrude metaphysical considerations into empirical science. It's no go. You are tapping on a door which does not exist. The wall is solid."

"It's quite a consideration if the things you make get up off the operating table and start being MORE real than you? You will surely be forced to reassess your . . . dirty word . . . culture?" Marchant shook his head vigorously. "We must move step by step, not in your quanta-like jumps—you can do nothing scientifically if you get the typical clusters; it's like seizing up your engine by over-heating, hence the Paulhaus." I watched the wonderful socialist country rolling by with all its marvellous advertising. "Ejax makes a man of you." Why not a woman, I wondered? It damn soon would. Hair down to the waist and a costume from Napoleon's Grande Armée. Perhaps there was a future for poor Felix in all this?

"*Bon*" he said, with a growing sense of familiarity. It was not simply the firm—it was the particular smell of self-satisfaction it unleashed. "And Julian?" I said. Once more Marchant gave a small earwig chuckle. "Gambling," he said "all the time. But now he has started losing and this is not in nature—at least not in his. I love Julian, you know, now that I have really got to know him. He is humility itself—humble as the Pope. Self-effacing. Tender. Felix, what a man!"

"What a man" I echoed piously, and indeed the funny thing was that I felt it; I felt a strange sort of reverence for this . . . mummy. I don't know if that is the right word. But to have so much under-standing humanity as Julian had and to manage to live apart, to play no direct part in its strange or deformed operations—why really it was something to doff the hat to. "All that Planck stuff is fruitful from a theoretically viable point of view; but from our point of view it is a matter of scale, in our empirical test-tube business the three dimensions are all one can cope with." He was pursuing the argu-ment like a sort of granny. He cleared his throat while I lit a cigarette. 'Our only problem down in Toybrook is a simple one, namely does it work ninety-nine times out of a hundred? If it does it is real." I coughed slightly and scanned off the scenery a bit. We were travelling mighty fast with a chauffeur who, for all I knew, might have been a dummy invented by Marchant. Then I said: "And the hundredth? Is there no room in your system for the miracle? That trifling shift of temperature or wrong mixture of chemical salts . . . it's so easy to go wrong. What exactly would be the miracle for you, Marchant?" Chuckle. "Well," he said "something like Iolanthe. She can for the moment be exactly controlled. Or so we hope. So we hope."

But reassuringly enough Toybrook was not in the least like Belsen —quite the contrary; despite the two stout brick towers exuding a lick of white smoke from the ovens in the experimental section. Toybrook was laid out with great dignity in two long complexes enfilading a piece of wild woodland, so that there was no laboratory or theatre without its fine green view. Moreover in the woodland there were several families of wild stags which appeared and disappeared dramatically among the trees, mating and battling in full view of the scientists; sometimes even coming shyly down to put a wet muzzle on the plate glass of the aquarium-like laboratories. It was both elegant and very peaceful—the chemists' studios with their long rows of microscopes glinting, their scales and pulleys and grapnels. A long pendulum hung slowly swinging in the hall. They had everything, these boys, even a wind tunnel and a cyclotron. Marchant was in high good humour as he showed me round, stopping here or there to present me to a colleague. Thence to the elegant theatre where the progress reports were read and recorded audio-visually for whatever posterity a scientist might believe in or hope for.

In the darkness Marchant flicked a couple of switches and a bald man appeared on close-circuit image. "That is old Hariot" he said while the celebrated man read haltingly against a blackboard upon which someone had written in violet chalk: "Does perhaps the rate of blood-sedimentation dictate the oxygen intake?" A vexing question, I should have thought. Anyway Hariot went on: "As you know, oxygen pushes carbon dioxide out of the blood and vice versa; as far as the circulation is concerned, about five litres of blood a minute are pumped by the heart of an ordinary resting adult. The distribution is not uniform; I mean that brain and kidneys get disproportionately large amounts compared to their relative size. As far as the brain is concerned, a decrease of ten per cent oxygen will give the first signs of confusion; decrease it by twenty per cent and you get the equivalent of four or five strong cocktails, say; around forty per cent you would expect to get coma. If the total supply is cut you get unconsciousness in a few seconds; and after four to five minutes the damage to the brain may be irreversible."

I said: "I suppose you had to mug all this stuff up for your dollies?" And Marchant nodded as he faded down on Hariot and came up with an image of rubber hands occupying the whole screen, poking about in the entrails of something or someone. However it was Hariot's flat voice again which continued the exposition with: "From the umbilical cord of twenty-five newborn children an appropriate test-length was clamped before first cry; blood samples were drawn anaerobically with special all-glass syringes from the umbilical vein and umbilical arteries. Coagulation and glycolysis were inhibited by heparin and potassium oxalate and sodium fluoride. . . ." Marchant chuckled approvingly. "You can call for any damn thing under the sun" he said, consulting a panel of data. Other images wallowed up, once more of rubber fingers moving about in a uterus as if performing some obscure rite of divination. "This particular demonstration monkey was merely anaesthetised, its abdomen opened and copious amounts of Bouin's fixative solution poured into it, over and around the uterus *in situ*. At the end of three to seven minutes all uterine ligaments with their contained blood vessels were clamped and the specimen removed . . . ."

"Ugh" I said. "I think I must be getting home to the wife and kids if this goes on." He laughed and tried another lucky dip on the dial to produce this time a strange surrealist picture of three men in white coats gathered round a seal which had been lashed firmly to a board and suspended above a water tank. The poor animal was terrified and struggled with all its might, rolling bloodshot eyes and moaning through its long silky moustaches. One of the men was holding a stethoscope to its body and saying something grave about lactic acid levels. Then the pulley swung and down the whole contraption fell out of sight. Crank!

"Enough" said Marchant. "It was only to give you an idea of the data-processing side of the thing."

In the mathematical section there were a hundred small hanging mobiles gyrating slowly in the sluggish air of the studios; a tiny planetarium, mock-earth, and God only knows what else. To Marchant's annoyance however the experimental embalmers had taken the day off and locked up the studio. "It's most vexatious" he said. "They have probably gone up to town for more dead. It isn't all that easy to get them, and one cannot run a Burke and Hare body-snatching organisation from such a respectable address as this." Why not, I wondered, surely old Julian could provide? (Cut out the flippancy, Charlock.) At any rate there was nothing for it now but to proceed to business and visit his own section, which would later become mine as well. It had no name as yet, just Experimental Studio B.

He had doubtless been keeping this special treat for the last, deeming it the most exciting, which of course it was. He unlocked two sets of doors and locked them again behind us with a stealthy gesture that reminded me of the Rackstraw ward in the Paulhaus. A high, bright, airy studio almost as tall as a hangar for cub aircraft came to light; white silk curtains moved softly in the breeze. Silence!

The bed she lay in was a long white surgeon's operating table with gleaming leverage members in tubular steel. She lay so still, like the experimental aircraft she was, so to speak, (still on the secret list): covered completely in a sheet of soft parachute silk, which stretched down to the floor on both sides. But her silhouette gave the illusion of completeness—a whole, undismembered body of a corpse, woman, doll or whatever. "You said she was still in bits" I said and Marchant tittered with pleasure. "They are not completely joined up as yet for action, but I want to give you the illusion of how she's going to be by showing her to you bit by bit, so you don't see the joins. The power isn't in yet, but I get some traction off another unit which enables us to check the whole flexion patterns of our fine plastic musculature. I plug her into a g-circuit." He performed some obscure evolutions in the corner, switched on powerful theatre lights above the body, and beckoned me over with a shy grin, lifting as he did so the corner of the silk to reveal the face. It was extraordinary to find myself gazing down upon the dead face of Iolanthe—so truthful a copy of the reality that I started with surprise even though I had been expecting something like this. But what really took me away was the perfection of that fresh and dewy skin. "Feel it" said Marchant. I put my finger to her cheek; "She's warm." Marchant laughed; "Of course she is, she's breathing, look now." The lips parted softly and a tiny furrow of preoccupation appeared on the serene brow. In her dream some small perplexity had surfaced here. It was skin, though, it was human flesh. Here she was, simply lying anaesthetised upon an operating table. "Iolanthe!" I whispered and the lips parted as if to answer me, but she said nothing. Marchant watched my confused excitement with a happy air of complacence. "Whisper again and she will wake" he said, and in an incoherent uncomprehending sort of way I said: "Darling, wake up, it's Felix." For a moment nothing, and then the whole face seemed to draw a waking breath. The lids fluttered and very slowly opened. "Damn" said Marchant. "Said has taken out the eyes again for restitching. I forgot, sorry." But I was staring entranced through the eyesockets of the model into her skull with its intricate nest of coils and wires in different-coloured threads, finer than the finest cotton. Marchant passed his palm over the eyelids to close them, as one does with the dead; I felt rather sick in an elated sort of way. "The eyes are over there" he said, indicating a small white glass bowl in which the eyes of the goddess floated in some sort of mucus—gum arabic? They lay there like oysters—unrecognisable now as the most famous eyes in the world, simply because they were detached from context.

Ah Osiris, we must gather up the loaves and fishes; O Humpty Dumpty we must put you together again. But Marchant was irritated by this trifling misadventure and drew the sheet back over the face. He went on to a demonstration of the thigh and ankle flexion—a perfect beautiful leg was revealed, of positively Botticellian elegance, and again warm, palpably real, a breathing leg so to speak. "Of course most of the fun has been in playing with the surfaces, the decoration, since we were ordered to reproduce from a known model. But her skin, boy, is just as beautiful as the real stuff and rather longer lasting. I must say that nylon pencil you invented has been a godsend." So I had invented a nylon pencil—what the devil can that have been? "Once again you've forgotten" he said. "It was just a hint you threw out once which we took up. My dear boy, look." He took a fine scalpel and cut a long incision in the thigh, spreading the wound with a clamp. No blood, of course, nor sawdust as in an oldfashioned gollywog but a beautifully coiled nest of vivid plastic cones and wires, packed tight as caviar. "Now look" he says and takes a thick metal pencil which he draws along the lips of the wound. It closes instantly leaving no trace of the gash in the warm thigh. "For running repairs—what would we have done without it? So swift, so easy. You can open it, her, up anywhere in an instant and reseal the wound. Good old Felix" he added with an incandescent admiration.

"Good old Felix" I echoed. We know not what we do, Bolsover, we know not what we do. I sank into an armchair and began to smoke like Vesuvius. "Mother of God, Marchant, what a treat she is. Will you give me the specifications please?"

"Of course" he said, rubbing his hands. "I don't think there will be much you don't understand; most of the data comes from your old scrying board—only of course very much reduced and in finer-web materials." I shook my head doubtfully. I had never worked on this scale before—through a jeweller's eyepiece or a microscope, so to speak. I stared into the mental sky of science and muttered "*E pur si muove*." That was the damnedest thing of all. Marchant stared at me with schoolboy glee and said: "Yes, you can't put your telescope to your blind eye on this lot; we are getting as near as dammit to the target objective."

He was acclimatised, I could see; but despite all he had told me about the project I found this experience to be quite a shock. Nor was it all. "Come and look" he said "at the vagina, the real treasure." He made some artful disposition of the shroud and revealed the downy sex of Iolanthe. "Stick your finger in there and feel—a self-lubricating mucous surface imitated to the life." I felt an awful cringe of misgiving as I did so, albeit reluctantly. He cackled happily and slapped my back. "You don't like it, do you? It seems an intolerable affront to her privacy and her beauty? I know, I know. I couldn't do it for weeks, she had become so real to me. But I had to. I had to take myself in hand and remind myself that I was a scientist after all—a man rather than a mouse." I felt shaken by a sort of remorse; it was silly to feel like this about the private parts of a dummy. Yet, so deeply buried are these motor complexes derived from the education of the tribe, that they come to the surface in quite involuntary fashion. Poor Iolanthe, lying there asleep and in pieces, to be fingered over by mousemen! I felt as if I had insulted her dignity. Marchant knew perfectly well the feeling. He had already felt that way himself, and steeled himself against it. I mopped my brow and thanked him. "But why does Julian want this sort of thing copied?" I asked in an outraged and aggrieved fashion. "Does he expect them to reproduce?" Marchant shrugged. "I don't know; they won't ever be anything but simulacra of fertility. Not only that, they can neither eat nor excrete. But he won't say what he has in mind. What will she do for an *état civil* my lad? No good asking me." He burst into a small cackle of helpless laughter and sat down in a chair to wipe his spectacles. "Phew!" I said.

The dossier on the figure was almost as thick as the Bible, though rather more intelligible for someone of my outlook. I riffled it and put it in my briefcase abruptly. I had a sudden feeling that I wanted to go away and be alone with myself, with my brief, with my dossier —and singularly enough with Benedicta. Marchant seemed a little disappointed that I had nothing much more to say at this stage. He eyed me keenly and said, "You are in on this thing Felix, aren't you?" I smiled and nodded. "You aren't" he went on "going to let theoretical considerations intrude on the work, are you?" It was as if he were pleading for Iolanthe's life—the life of that marvellous mummy lying so silently under her silken shroud of grey. "No" I said. "I'm in it all right."

He heaved a sigh of relief, as we went out to the car. I was to be driven home and dropped—the great *déménagement* to the cottage from Claridge's was only a day or so old. But I was glad when the chauffeur produced an afternoon paper for Marchant as it kept him busy, inveterate punter that he was. A headline said MOBS SOB AS DALI LAYS EGG. Good. Good. "I want to watch when you replace the eyes, remember." But I was thinking to myself about memory—is everything recorded in it from the first birth-cry to the death-rattle? Why not? Or does it simply wear out like an old disc?

In Abel's system the sound unit, the πὸγον, gave you a clue to the basic predispositions of character which was then modified by experiences, environment etc. . . . Yes, that side of the thing was all right. "My God, it's begun to snow" said Marchant, and so it had; the sky fell out of its frame, turned into a great flocculent pane of melting confetti and came down over us locking up visibility; we nosed down the country roads between spectral hedges and sculptured gateposts—griffins in wigs on the front gates of Drue Manor. Plastic elves in white cauls on the lawns of suburban houses. Ah to be a quiet man, living sagely with a little plastic wife, following out the serpentine meanderings of my inner self . . . why hasn't God made me a quietist? *Nigaud, va.*

I made them keep the headlights on to enable me to grope my way across the meadow and skirt the disappeared lake; it was all crackly underfoot. When I looked round the snow had swallowed them up. Like a blind man I clutched my way up the steps of the chalet and at last found the latch. Ah, the warmth inside, the blazing fire of thorn and oak, the smells, and Benedicta pyjama-clad asleep before the fire with Osmosis the cat on her stomach. "One side of your face is all burning, bottom as well" I said. "Better turn over." But she preferred to wake. "Caradoc has been ringing you this afternoon. He seemed to be rather drunk. I told him to record himself and go to hell, which he duly did." But either he had been more than just drunk or else his sound track had got itself mixed with other stuff for it was a mighty incoherent display of temperament beginning with a poem of which I could only make out the lines:

> *Fornication's pedalled jam*
> *Which has brought me where I am*

and ending with a request for a Christmas Box of fifty pounds. "I am at the Metrofat Hotel in Brighton with a young lady who is all warm breast of Christmas Turkey; greetings of the season to one and all. Did you see my little thing in *The Times*? 'Grand génie, légèrement bombé mais valide, cherche organiste.' Had no replies yet."

"Well," I said "he sounds all right." I poured a drink and resumed my inward brooding upon Iolanthe. I told Benedicta a bit about the marvels of the dummy—it, her?—and how it had given me quite a turn to see the faithfulness of the copy. She looked at me curiously, seriously, and said nothing. "I wonder if I could raise Julian!" I said. "I would like to have a talk with him about her. He hasn't seen her as yet himself. I wonder if he knows what's in store if she really works down to the last rivet."

"Try the Casino in Divonne. Anyway he always leaves his number wherever he goes."

The night switchboard at Merlin's took not much more than half an hour to trace him. That characteristic voice, full of the illustrious melancholy of a dispossessed potentate . . . . "What is it Julian—you sound so sad?" He sighed ruefully. "Yes. I am losing so heavily. It gets more and more mysterious. I wonder what I have done to shift the axis, so to speak, of my luck? It was always in perfect working order. I lost at Divonne and am continuing to lose down here in Nice, where it is snowing if you please." He paused and in the background I could hear the yelping of croupiers. "Consult Nash" I said and he sighed again. "It would be useless. He could tell me why I played but not why after always winning I have started losing—why the bung-hole has dropped out my luck. I have done everything, changed my game more than once. Damn it all."

There was another long pause; of course Julian had always been of a melancholy and introspective cast of mind, but he had never given himself, his views, so freely to anyone. "It's your fault for taking Abel apart" I said. "He might have suggested an answer." You can't hear a smile on the telephone but I did—a world-weary sad smile. "It was another gamble. I had to try to suck you dry in case you never came back, to ensure the perpetuity of the firm!" A fine light irony played about the phrase. "Like Rackstraw" I said and he nodded invisibly. "The vulture always waits" said Julian. I heard the puff puff of his cigar. I stayed silent, feeling that perhaps there was something he wanted to get off his chest before listening to whatever I myself wanted to say to him. But he said nothing, and an operator asked if we were still talking: actually we were. All his loneliness and despondency were leaking down the wire like a low-tension current: also a certain anxiety. I felt he was glad to have even this mechanical contact with someone.

"Felix" he said hesitantly, as if he were feeling slowly, blindly

N–E*   137

along the Ariadne-thread of an idea he wanted to express. "How lucky you are not to be a gambler. We constitute a different tribe, you know, belong to a different totem. I realised tonight that I am only really at home in a casino; I really have no *foyer*, no hearth of my own, except here. When I go from here I don't go anywhere in particular. A hotel isn't a home; and my so-called home is only a hotel. Now be a good boy, don't quote Freud. The matter is much more fundamental than that."

Pause for breath. "When you see all these pale, exhausted faces in the light of dawn, after their fruitless love-affair with the wheel or the dice or the pack: this sterile love affair, because even the winners express a haggard lost feeling—why, you realise that masturbation isn't the real clue. The gambler is really dicing with death, as the popular saying goes. Just as all dancers are simply persuaders to the act, so gambling is a sort of questioning, an act of divination. How weary of it we all are, yet it is the only situation which enables us to feel vicariously alive, this side of death."

I said nothing; the sorrow in his voice was absolutely overwhelming. He went on very slowly, like an exhausted climber reaching for handholds, languid for lack of oxygen. "But then what is the question that the gambler put to himself by the act of gambling? What does he hope that the dice will tell him? Well, think of the strange symbolic pilgrimage he is forced to make to the casino when he can find one—as characteristic as that made by other men to a brothel. He enters, reveals his identity by producing a passport or other document; he fills in a *carte d'admission*. Then he passes in front of the '*physionomiste*', a 'scanner' who subjects his face, hands and body to a close scrutiny. This is as intensive as a police check though he does not touch you. My various faces must be on record somewhere in somebody's mind. A scar, a tattoo mark, a blemish—that is what they look for, this race of 'scanners'.

"Once past this barrier he is admitted to the temple of the supreme Game which he craves; and here everything speaks to him of the past, of a vanished epoch. An old-fashioned anachronistic décor, whole surfaces of dusty unspringing carpets such as one would find only in abandoned Edwardian hotels or in late spa hotels at Vichy, Pau, Baden. The fuzzy chandeliers, broken-down *salons de luxe* festering away in their desuetude. Even the costumes of the croupiers and often the gambler's own partake of this strange out-of-dateness. It is as if everything had become stuck fast like an atrophied limb—death in aspic. The formulae too are all part of this strange marvellous stereotype, as superannuated as a half-forgotten liturgy. It smells like a page or two of Huysmans. Yes, but all this is deliberate; this atmosphere is anxiously preserved, conserved, watched over. And the premises themselves should if possible smell airless and ever so slightly dusty. You do not want fresh air in a casino. The ritual forbids it. The air must rest, tideless, scentless, and only just breathable. The gambler feels at home then like a fish in water of the right temperature. His nostrils breathe this warm welcoming balsam. He knows what he *must* do, he simply *must*."

In this slow near-soliloquy I felt once more all the rancour and despair of his inner loneliness welling up in him—though why for the first time he should choose to allow me to be a party to it I could not tell. Somewhere a bell rang and voices buzzed to the tune of the big wheel. Julian appeared to be listening to it all with half an ear even as he was talking to me. So much of it I remembered myself, too, from my one brief flirtation with the law of probability—is there such a thing? Poking the cat with my foot I shared Julian's curious muse in silence for a moment.

Yes, he was right: the weight of the ritual, the entering, the form-filling. . . . Then the decision between *les Salles Privées* and the *cuisine*. . . . On which front to attack the demon of hazard, he whom Poincaré called "the real mathematician of genius"? Ah, those long interior debates on the thirty-seven slots in the wheel (alchemy?), eighteen red and eighteen black with the somehow inevitable white zero. A sort of Tarot of probability instead of a calculus . . . (perhaps Abel?). But behind the silence of Julian I heard a voice calling, as if from a cloud, "*Vingt-et-un rouge, impair et passe.*" And I saw the lean face of the arbiter, the *chef de partie*, sitting up there on his throne, his baby-chair, overlooking the celestial game, impervious to human feelings of gain or loss, a sort of God. And then I thought, too, of all the gambler's fevers and follies. In that expensive and beautifully cut suit of his, in the breast pocket, he carried a typical talisman, a rabbit's paw.

139

"Change your talisman" I said. "Why not get a fox's paw, or the dried paw of a great lizard, or a human hand?"

"Fatal" he replied drily. "You know it."

Julian was a heavy staker in the *Salles Privées* and richly merited the French slang word for the breed, *flambeur*, inflamer: the flame of pure desire, the mathematical desire to *know*. Not to *be*, but to *know*. And of course he had always won. The croupiers had always passed him his mound of golden ordure which for him symbolised so much more than a unit of value. Negligently but voluptuously he must have fingered it always, before throwing it back into the melting-pot —for only with gold can one make gold, whatever the wizards may tell you. I remembered too that when numbers run in a series they are said in gambler's slang to be *en chaleur*, on heat.

"None of this can have anything to do with what you wanted to talk to me about," he said "and I apologise. I was in rather a reflective mood this evening. What did you want to tell me about, Felix?"

"Iolanthe. I went to see her with Marchant today, and I'm still a little groggy with surprise. It is the most astonishingly life-like thing I've ever seen. And if everything he tells me is true it will be rather unique. But I haven't read the specifications in detail yet. I'll do that this week. But there were one or two things which struck me about her, it."

"I'm delighted that you are excited" he said, and sounded almost moved himself. "But" I went on "I felt that I wanted to go over some of the points with you in case we hadn't fully understood your idea—I suppose, for example, the male will be much the same?"

"Same what?"

"Fair without, false within. I mean I found myself wondering why we were copying the outside with such fidelity when the inside is an artificially arranged thing with simply a stress, strain, flexion index."

"It's not entirely true—what about the brainbox?"

"But they will never eat, excrete or fornicate. . . ."

"We are perhaps asking for too much at this stage. Let's go step by step. I wasn't hoping for reality so much as for the perfect illusion which is probably more real than reality itself is for most people; hence my choice of the screen-star symbol. As for fornicating, I suppose they can go through the motions, though it will be without result, sterile; but they *will* try to illustrate an aesthetic of Beauty, which is always in the eye of the beholder as 'The Duchess' tells us. Eh?"

"Eunuchs!"

"If you wish; but did Aphrodite eat and excrete? I am not enough of a classical scholar to quibble about it. After all these are only serious toys, Felix, *serious toys*."

"But Marchant insists they are so perfectly adapted from the point of view of responses that they could, according to him, be turned loose in the real world without danger of being discovered for what they are."

"Why not, Felix? They will probably be more real than most of the people we know. But of course I have no intention of setting them free; first of all, Iolanthe's face is world-famous. We mustn't run the risk of their getting damaged. No, I thought of them living in seclusion quietly somewhere where we could work-study them; they are far the most advanced things of their kind, after all?"

"Hum. And who will the male doll be based on; we only have legs and the outline of a pelvis as yet. Eh?"

He yawned briefly and then went on in the same even tone. "You can guess how much I would have liked to aspire to the role myself—but it would be too Pharaonic, a sort of embalmer's picnic. So I have stepped down in favour of Rackstraw."

"*Rackstraw?*"

"We will confer a vicarious immortality on him; he will end as a museum piece in some colony of waxworks. But of course I mean Rackstraw as he was once, not as he is now. Once again, we have all the information we need about him. Any objections?"

"No. But the whole thing seems bizarre."

"In one sense I suppose it is; but then Felix, it's only a gambler's idea. I remember you once insisting that habit grooves the sensibility, that even movements repeated endlessly generate comprehension, just as an engine generates traction, or sticks rubbed together, fire. What I wonder is this: will perhaps this creature of human habits one day, simply by acting as a human being, REALISE she is a dummy?" The capital word was practically hissed into the telephone.

"As much, I mean, as the original realised she was Iolanthe? It's a gamble, and like all prototypes our models may prove too clumsy for us to practise divination on or by them. But then if one does not live on hopes in this life what else is there to live on?"

"I see."

"Good night Felix" he said. "Wish me a run of luck will you? I am in mortal need of it."

The line went dead. I sat for a long moment before hanging up from my end. Benedicta was laying out our dinner before the fire, ladling out soup into the bright earthenware pots which looked Italian. I was in a state of unusual and rather violent excitement—though I honestly don't know why. Of course in part it was all the implications of this extraordinary project; but I had seen others, far more theoretical, where the issues were much more in doubt. And of course, with one half of my mind, I could not help thinking of it as a bit infantile. Was it though? At any rate, whatever the cause, I ate in very perfunctory fashion while I dipped here and there into my brief—the dossier.. It was all as beautifully and methodically laid out as the specifications for a new aircraft. The only question was: would it fly, how would it handle etc. etc.?

"Benedicta," I said "I must go out for a walk. I simply must." She looked at me with surprise. "In this weather? It would be fool-hardy, Felix." But I was already groping for a heavy sweater and the stout ski-gear I had acquired in Switzerland. Seeing I was serious she sprang up at once and joined me. "I'm coming with you; I am not going to risk letting you fall into the lake or break your head against a tree. It's all too new this, Felix, to be risked." I felt a bit of a swine, but was really extremely glad to have her beside me as a sort of thinking generator. It had stopped snowing, everything was hushed back into whiteness—apocalyptic flocks of solid cumulus which had filled out the world and blotted out the edges of things. No moon, but an infinity of white radiance which turned the sky into an upturned inkwell. We found a stout storm lantern in the kitchen for want of a torch, and let ourselves off the dry balcony as gingerly as swimmers entering the sea splashlessly. The forest had still some edges left which were a help in judging our general direction—as if someone had spilled Indian ink over a lace shawl. Within

142

a few yards we divined rather than felt that we were upon the ice of the frozen lake. The snow was so dry it screeched underfoot. Somewhere in the sky wild geese cranked out to one another.

We made our way slowly across the lake to the little island in the centre, now piled up like a wedding-cake of whiteness. At the far end of the lake itself a solitary figure, a gamekeeper, moved about in the greyness absorbed in a task which could only be gradually identified as we approached him. With a crowbar and hammer he was knocking holes in the ice and pushing something down them— to feed fish perhaps? We called out a greeting but he was completely absorbed and did not hear us. We skirted the little islet—and gained the further shore, lengthening our stride at the feel of terra firma. "Science is only half the apple," I told myself aloud "just as Eve is only half Adam." Blundering along thus the mechanised philosopher could hardly help falling over the odd tree trunk, or banging his head on a branch or two. But gradually we became accustomed to the light and were able to move about with as much certainty as one might have done by day.

A distinct violet shimmer in the light where it caressed the shoulders of the little hills. On a branch one old and perished-with-cold-looking owl, fluffed out in his mink like some run-down actor. (The margin of error in the case of such a talking mummy was, of course, enormous.) "There is little that I can guarantee about her once she is buttoned up and launched. I can't even say for certain that she will be good, for example, or bad; only that she is more likely to be clever than stupid." So we struggled on down the avenues of shrouded elms, along the firebrakes which once we used to ride down, and over the frozen gudgeon. Gradually the warmth came to our bodies despite wet boots and wetter trouser-bottoms. Sometimes she looked at me for a moment without speaking. So we passed the little crooked pub called The Faun which was locked and barred at this hour; a bedroom window glowed like a jewel. Our boots rang musically on the frozen tarmac of the road as we traversed the hamlet. Then from one of the dark barn-like houses we were surprised to see a deep red flame spring up, and spit out a great gush of brilliant sparks; it spurted and subsided, spurted and subsided, and we heard the massy ring of the blacksmith's hammer on the anvil, and the wheeze of his bellows. In the shadow of his smithy, bobbing his shadow about on the roof, moved the huge creature, stripped to the waist and sweating profusely. We stood to watch him for a moment but he worked on methodically without giving us a glance. Perhaps he did not even know we were there.

On we went, up into the white night, and it was only when we reached the old crown of Chorley with the famous "view" from its summit that Benedicta said: "By the way, I meant to tell you before. I have completely surrendered, made away, all my share in the firm. I now own nothing but what I stand up in, so to speak. I am a public charge. All that stands between me and starvation is your salary. Do you mind?"

We stood up there gazing at each other smiling—like a couple of explorers on an ice floe, oblivious of everything but the extraordinary pleasure we were deriving from the new sensation of harmony, of comprehension and trust. "How marvellous" I said. "Is that what Julian meant about you having betrayed him?" Benedicta nodded: "Only partly, though. He was also thinking of the young German Baron; I was supposed to make him sign on the firm's strength, but I did the opposite and the firm didn't get him. It was the first time I had deliberately set my face against Julian—he didn't like it; but so long as he needs you he can do nothing."

★   ★   ★   ★   ★

"O! O! O!" Marchant was humming under his breath as he worked on Iolanthe. "You great big beautiful doll! I'm so very glad I found you. Let me get my arms around you." A low current was discharging itself through her throat and she stirred slightly in her sleep, turning her head from side to side, then yawning and smiling. Marchant still adhered to his superstitious convention of keeping her covered while she was in pieces; so that we were working on different sections at the same time. We would see her whole, so to speak, only when she came to be launched; by that decisive stage it would be hard to make rectifications without totally dismantling the power box with all its hair-fine infratopes—it would be as if we were forced to begin again at the beginning. God knows how long she had cost already, probably years of amazingly detailed work. I had a great reunion with Said, who was very smart in hefty British tweeds and who had assumed the habits and the dignity of the uniform with his usual equanimity. It was good to feel that all that infinite patience and delicacy was really making its mark on a world which could reward him as I had never been able to when I began work with him in the Greek capital.

"Now" said Marchant "try her for kisses, Felix, just in case she ever needs one, or feels that way. Eh?" He gave her a scientific kiss on the lips and pronounced himself satisfied by their marvellous springiness, better than the real thing. "And the mucus imitation is wonderful—like fresh dew. And look!" Iolanthe sighed and pouted like a child in her sleep, seeking another kiss. Adorable! "Your turn" he said, so I tried her out. "I say, this is wildly exciting" I said. "It's so damned . . . well!" Marchant burst out laughing. "Art imitating nature" he said. "But what about this?—come over here. I just geared up Adam's penis yesterday for a simulated orgasm. Man, it's perfect. Shades of my prep school!" On another table he uncovered, with a proprietorial air, the thigh and pelvis arrangement of the male dummy. "Now watch" he said and began to rub the penis, which rose strongly, darkening as it became tumescent, to discharge its mock-semen. "Talk about Ejax" said Marchant in high delight, wiping his hands on a towel. "Once again, it's a much heavier orgasm than Dad was ever able to manage. We could perhaps rent him out, Felix, and make a little dough. Why shouldn't somebody love him a little, bring a little light into his male life, eh? He should have as much chance as you or I?" Gutta-percha, plastic, rubber, nylon . . . .

"And to have done away with those two time-wasting and boring activities, eating and excreting, surely they will be grateful to us for having done it." I scratched my head. "Suppose she becomes too inhibited by half—I mean what does she do at mealtimes?" Marchant replied tartly: "Exactly what any other actress does—takes out a cigarette and says, 'Darling, I think I'll just have a glass of water.' She will go through all the motions without actually eating. She is not forbidden tobacco, by the way. My dear chap, she is fully fashioned this girl. Easy to be with, easy to love. . . ." He was humming again, in high good humour. What a strange thing the human body is—I was feeling that warm hand with its lazy fingers moving slightly under mine. Strange foliage of toes and fingers, elaborate patterning of muscle, striped and streaky.

So the great work moved slowly forward towards launching day; it was arranged that Iolanthe should imagine herself to be waking in hospital after an operation, recovering from the anaesthetic. Once dressed she would be moved into a small villa which had been furnished for her with her own possessions—Julian had acquired them all, furs, and ballgowns, and shoes and wigs. In other words, to give her reaction-index and memory a chance to function normally, we would provide ideal test-conditions in ideal surroundings. All around her would be the familiar furniture of her "real" life—her books and folios of film photos, her cherished watercolours by famous artists (careful investment: all film stars buy Braque). . . . There would, then, on the purely superficial plane, be very little to distinguish between Iolanthe dead and Iolanthe living. Except of course. . . . The dummy would be living the "real" life of the screen goddess.

But if we were working, so was Julian in his tortuous way; he had returned from his gambling bender both poorer and richer—for the fever had left him abruptly as it so often did for months at a time. It was like an underground river this illness, appearing and disappearing, now above ground now below—never constant. But he spent long evenings now in the little projection theatre he had built for himself, playing through the films of Iolanthe in a quiet deliberate muse; beside him sat Rackstraw mumbling and nodding with flickering attention, and on the other side the strange graven image which was Mrs. Henniker. There they sat, the three of them, fixed by the silver dazzle into silhouettes of hungry attention. Mrs. Henniker was going to take up her old post as companion-secretary to Iolanthe as soon as she "awoke". As for Rackstraw, there was little enough to be squeezed out of him. At times he seemed to have glimmers of recognition, but then his attention would slip, and he would mumble incoherently before subsiding into sleep, the softly nodding drowse of old age. Yet in some way, and for some particular purpose, Julian held this little group together for a whole winter— though really I could not understand for what reason. At least, Henniker had a role to play, but what about Rackstraw? Julian must clearly have had something fairly clear in mind which prompted these sudden periods of self-dedication to what might have seemed a futile activity. There was also in the case of Julian a curious intermittent play, an alternating current, so to say, between intellectual boldness and cowardice. Perhaps the word is too strong—but when you think that the Iolanthe we were building was his particular obsession: why did he never come and see her? He used on the contrary to ring up Marchant and myself and discuss the various stages of our work with a kind of voluptuary's nostalgia. But when I said: "Why not come and see tomorrow what you think of her?" he replied at once. "No, Felix. Not until she is word-perfect, until she is complete." I sensed a tremor of something like fear in the words; but of course it was always accompanied by that wonderful self-deprecating charm. "You see I have never met her, I shall have to be introduced."

As for Io, she was getting so real as almost to be a pet. Machinery has this peculiar tug on the crude affections of the human race; why else do men christen their cars and sailing-boats? I must confess that the first time we hooked up the memory-reproduction complex I had the most extraordinary thrill, almost sexual, in hearing that marvellous rather husky voice saying (as if she had a hangover): "And I told Henniker it wouldn't do, it simply wouldn't do; Felix, love is all in compartments, otherwise it wouldn't be a universal disease. It's silly that we only have one word for it. And the ones we have are very inadequate to deal with its variety—like esteem, affection, tenderness, sympathy. It isn't classified as yet in any language." I sat down with a bump on my chair and Marchant thrust a glistening sweaty face up against mine, exulting: "Do you think one could improve on her? Now tell me honestly." I could only shake my head wonderingly. It really was quite devastating the extent of the dummy's habituation to the ordinary terms of what we might call the human condition—if you can just simply imagine an object called "self" operating with a frame of memory, habit, impulse, inhibition and so on. It looked as if in another month or so she might be safely placed in the orbit of an ordinary life—held in harness as all of us are, purely by the routines of the daily round. Feeding on the rarefied air of inner space, correcting by willpower the gravitational pull of the passions—which to so many modern scientists seem little better than a bundle of assorted death-wishes. But of course inevitably the unlegislated-for quality made its appearance—for an example, we hadn't really thought of "charm" as an ingredient when we specified her; but her charm was devastating—and surely it is the one thing you would expect her *makers* to remember from the original actress? So that, on the one hand, while we really knew all about her, she continued to surprise us during the long period which passed between her being in pieces, and being united. The day I mean when she woke up completely, yawned, knuckled her eyes and said: "Where am I? What time is it?" And then as she gradually took in her surroundings and the men in white coats around her, added: "Is it all right—that old appendix?"

At the moment she was still a set of intermittent responses; her eyes were in, but had to be left a week or more to "set" properly so that she might use them. So that she still slept all day, and still kept her eyes closed when she spoke, the sound welling sleepily out of that beautifully formed humorous mouth. We had even forgotten (how is this possible: please tell me?), we had forgotten that she would know all about us, even our names. Or let me put it this way: we knew with one part of our minds, but not with such conviction that it didn't give us a tremendous start to hear her use them. It was even stranger when, fetching back a memory from the very beginning of our Athens days, she spoke to me in Greek. "They say I shall never have a child, but I am glad. Would you like to have a child, Felix?" And it was here that *my* memory was faulty while her artificial one worked perfectly; I had forgotten what my answer was on that particular occasion. She was full of small surprises like these. But we still had to select a date for an awakening.

IV

Perhaps the most cogent reason for our habit of walking down the corridor into the embalming studio was that we wished to compare what we were building with what they were preserving with such care. There was not much trade in their business—somehow embalming had not really caught on, even among publishers. Nevertheless that mere trickle of corpses provided Cyrus P. Goytz with a theatre of operations in which he could train staff. He was an endearing man with a face like a spade and a swarthy skin which occasionally flushed in a dull way when a pupil made a mistake. He was clad in black to lecture, which he did with his hands clasped in front of his stomach. A big smooth minatory-looking man, dressed in such heavy materials that he looked not unlike one of his own products—drained of all blood, like a kosher dish, and not as if he had just been warmly sacrificed on the altars of gluttony. He wore a very obviously short-cut wig which gave his face a curious expression of transience—again like his subjects, who apparently began to melt after about a month. But he was a pet Goytz, the soul of patience, and (so they said) the best embalmer in the universe. On New Year's Eve, at staff parties, he had been known to take out a glass eye and show it to everyone on the palm of his hand. In the evenings he played the violin to timid little Mrs. Goytz (who looked like a taxidermic waterfowl) in a semi-detached at Sidcup. He was spearheading the firm's embalming attack on the Middle East.

But this was not all; it was really his homely philosophy which gave us so much pleasure; he was so full of a benign desire to spread light and goodwill, dispel the clouds of gloom—or whatever misgivings his students might have about an avocation so, well . . . unusual. "Contrary to what many might assume," he might say, taking up his penguin-like stance with hands joined in front "a corpse can prove a friendly, even a companionable thing—while it is

153

relatively fresh, I mean." This sort of thing Marchant used to treasure, and whisper it into Iolanthe's ear as we knelt beside her, working on the eyes. The embalmers, by the way, worked to music—mostly the strains of *In a Monastery Garden* played in a reverent sort of way by a Palm Court Orchestra. Goytz kept it low so that the sound of his voice was not drowned as he instructed his students in the use of the trocar or the siphon pump which drained the bodies on the slabs. He was such a kindly man that he could even pretend to take a mild teasing from Marchant—as when the latter suggested that the appropriate motto for his little parlour should be "The More the Messier or the Nausea the Better".

His specimens, though, had rather a different feeling about them; they were vulnerable, you see, the decay could be contained but only for a while. They had not that noble abstract quality of Iolanthe, lying there asleep under her silk sheet. You could smash her, but she wouldn't rot away, or melt under the coating of resin poured over her in her coffin—I am thinking of Egyptian kings and queens. All this of course Goytz knew and perhaps at times he smelt a little condescension in our tones, in our way of questioning him about his work. At any rate he once or twice uttered a phrase about our work which might have seemed barbed—as when he said: "And when she wakes up and asks you imploringly: 'Is there any hope for a little happiness for me?' what will you reply?" Marchant chuckled. "Nothing, of course; for she knows the answer, just like every human being knows the answer to the questions he or she poses. The question contains the answer in capsule form."

Mr. Goytz smiled briefly and said: "You see I have no such problem with my children; they have entered into the Great Silence, borne on the wings of their nearest and dearest. For them there are no problems. But for us, of course, they are numerous; we must dress them as if for a fancy-dress ball. And darned quick. Come in by the way, we have a few most unusual specimens this week." He turned on his heel and led us through a curtain into the main studio where three or four corpses were laid out on trestles—the "cooling-boards" where they are trimmed and coiffed before the make-up goes on. All but one were covered, or half covered, in sheets so that there was a superficial resemblance to the other studio across the way where we ourselves worked. But the resemblance was a very superficial one; and ended when we saw the venous system being pumped out into a bucket. The pump hissed, the pink blood tinkled. (Rather like having the oil changed on your car I suppose.) A young man devoutly pumped and pumped. The body was much mutilated by a street accident, and a second youth kept the wounds free with a sponge. Goytz touched the cheeks with a quick white hand, as if to judge their springiness, and seemed satisfied with the rate of progress. He consulted a watch. "You got an hour I guess" he told his acolytes who did not so much as look up from their work. They had expressionless faces and square Jewish heads. Goytz inspected with some care the bucket which was half-full of the pumped blood of the subject and said, in his lecture-room voice: "One of the characteristic features of carbon monoxide poisoning is the bright cherry-red colour of the blood, and a greatly delayed coagulation time. One must not, of course, confuse it with the similar blood-coloration in drowned subjects."

So we moved from slab to slab while Goytz talked pleasantly and discursively about corpses and their habits, of the different ways of enbalming them through the ages, of the methods used to secure anatomical subjects for study—and a hundred other fascinating sidelights on his art, which showed us plainly that we were in the presence of a master of the trade; but more, an enthusiast. He knew all the names and dates of embalming history off by heart. And he spoke of his own particular hero, William Hunter, the Scot, with a reverence that was almost tearful. "It was this great man" he said "who not only gave the world a method of embalming which advanced the whole technique a hundredfold, but also listed the chemicals he used in so doing. He was the first to use the femoral artery as his point of penetration for his mixture of oil of turpentine, oil of lavender, rosemary and vermilion; this he allowed to diffuse through the body tissues for several hours before he started to open the cavities and remove the viscera for cleaning and soaking in essential oils and wines. These were then of course replaced and covered with preservative powders like camphor and resin and magnesium sulphate as well as potassium compounds. The powder was also packed tight in the cavities like mouth, nose, ears, anus; and finally the whole

body was placed on a bed of plaster of Paris and allowed to remai
there for about four years. In this way he dehydrated the subject an
prevented the decomposition which comes about with bacteria
growth." All this seemed to move Goytz very much.

"And here" he said "is an Eastern Potentate who died of a
embolism on his arrival in this country as an Ambassador to you
Queen. He is quite fresh and will come up very nicely indeed, ye
very nicely indeed. He will give them all a thrill by his naturalnes
back there in Abyssinia."

The sheet turned back revealed a dark hairy man with enormou
clenched hands which Goytz soothed out flat at once, tenderl
elongating the crude fingers. He was anxious that no trace of a
apparent arthritis deformans should remain when he had complete
what he was pleased to call his final "composition" of the subject.
thought, as I saw him, how the fingers of our Io did not need to b
kneaded into softness; her hand lay in yours like a snowflake of softness. Goytz was forced to knead and rub at his subjects, to massage
them, rub them down with rollers—all to squeeze the blood out o
them before he could start work on the outside. In this case the
corpse was a huge dark simian brute of a man, part Negro, but whos
face strongly suggested that of Jocas Pehlevi, the half-brother o
whatever of Julian. Something about the swarthiness contrasting
with the bright blushing warmth of the skin in which the beard
grew, black as the bristles of a wart-hog. The same tips of gold in the
teeth which were very slightly revealed by a retracted lip. But of
course no ear-ring. The abundant hair and nails would outlast the
great part of the final decay of this "potentate". He was clad only in a
blue underpant. His toenails were huge, broken, and very dirty, as
if he had always shovelled coal with them. Goytz again gave the
flesh of the corpse a quick almost affectionate run-over, patting it
here and there with some of the complacence of a woman rubbing
cold cream into her face. In a sense I could see that his subjects had
become a sort of extension of himself; it was his own flesh that he
patted, smoothed, stroked, like some great painter his canvas. "He'll
be no trouble" he asserted. "We shall compose him something
lovely. Eosin" he added somewhat cryptically.

I remembered. Of course: one of the interesting properties of eosin is its capacity to fluoresce when exposed to ultra-violet light; to some extent even in bright sunlight it can do the same. But the best is when a shaded ultra-violet bulb is used—the so-called "black light". It was the use of eosin which enabled Goytz to obtain what he called his "internal cosmetic effect"; his subjects looked lit from within, they glowed with an illusion of warmth and life. We were also taking advantage of it, but our skins were finer, more supple, and at least a thousand times more durable than his. But I could see his weakness for swarthy subjects because of this luminous dye which removed the residual greyness caused by the kosher treatment of the body, the draining out of its blood. At points then our preoccupations chimed; at others they diverged. For example he had been always far more preoccupied by the question of odour than we had been, though in an opposite sense: we had to invent smells which were indistinguishable from the real animal smells of the human body. But he had had to disguise, first of all the smell of decay, and then the smells of all the powerful agents he was using in order to preserve the illusion of life, or the quasi-life of his subject; an abbreviated life in time? No, but heavens! Surely both were dead in the technical sense? Well, Iolanthe was a little less dead because of a perfect memory which *she could use*: it was her radar. So that dying . . . was a case of loss of memory, both mental and physical? "The first thing" said Goytz with the air of a hunter giving a colleague a tip "is to select your drainage points with the full knowledge that here and there you may discover a clot or other blockage to free movement which will have to be sucked out by the trocar syringe. But it's not very hard.

"The intercapillary pressure of the blood during life is very low, and movement of the blood itself can be accomplished only by the squeeze-action of the muscles against the veins. This squeeze we imitate when it comes to voiding the body of blood. But the first really important thing is to select your drainage points and then raise and open the veins you have chosen. In them you place the largest possible drainage tube to facilitate the movement of the blood." He illustrated this for us with the unerring skill of a seasoned darts player scoring an "outer". The harmless simian arms of the "potentate" lay there; Goytz drew on rubber gloves ("always guard against infection" he said under his breath) and made a couple of magisterial incisions on the inside of the forearm, some way below the elbow; then, with an experience obviously born of long practice, he took an elevator and raised a dark vein, passing the instrument through it, so that it was indeed raised above the surface and ready to be tapped. This he repeated with a kindly absorption on the other arm, saying to Marchant in abstracted tones, "You see, all we know is thanks to the great anatomists; you may laugh, but Leonardo prepared specimens this way." But something went wrong, the wounds began to bleed. "It's nothing" he said. "You will see." He called over some students and with them proceeded to tug the arms of his subject above his head, pulling them as far as they would go, and in such a fashion as to squeeze the maximum amount of blood out of them; meanwhile the arms were being sponged from fingertip to shoulder by the students. It was in a sense a kind of Japanese massage that the "potentate" was receiving. "Poor drainage" said Goytz "has been universally recognised as the cause of embalming failure. We use surface manipulation, vibration, even a roller-stretcher—anything to get the blood moving. After all, in terms of quantity, you can calculate that there is about seven pounds of liquid blood per hundred of body-weight; now with the best will in the world and the most up-to-date equipment (taking one gallon of blood per one single hundred and fifty pound body) we should expect to remove perhaps one half of the total quantity, certainly not more: that is to say, two quarts of blood from this hundred and fifty pound fellow here." He tapped the potentate lightly on the forehead, demonstrating with kindliness; now he was like some champion fisherman, standing beside a huge white shark almost taller than himself, and talking modestly about the means he had employed to take it.

"But" he went on in cautionary vein "continuous and *uncontrolled* drainage is one of the common causes for the situation in which the body is firm and clear and, on the face of it, well preserved when embalmed . . . yet" he raised a finger to the ceiling and paused dramatically "becomes soft and begins to decompose a few hours later. That is the tragedy! In other words, the embalmer's work is really an art based on a calculated judgement of a given situation. Both under-embalming and over-embalming result from inaccurately judged drainage-control. With over-embalming you get wrinkling, leatherising and dehydration in low-resistance areas; with under-embalming you risk premature decomposition areas of high resistance. Scylla and Charybdis, my friends, that is what you might call it! Ah!" He sighed again.

When he was in this vein—which Marchant called his "Sermon on the Mount" vein—he was irresistible, and we did everything we could to encourage him to continue. Indeed the subject was so dear to him that his features took on a rosy tinge, almost eosin-tinted with the enthusiasm he felt for "composing" his subjects. But he was also a modest man and feared to bore a non-professional audience, and so from time to time he paused, smiled vaguely and self-deprecatingly round, and gave a little sigh of apology. "Don't stop, man" said Marchant. "This is fascinating; we are learning from you, Goytz. Don't stop now!" The Compleat Embalmer simpered and said: "Very well. Let me then just run over the main points in regard to this Eastern Potentate. I think we will have to consider some of the main factors of cavity-embalming with him— attacking the main points of putrefaction with a trocar."

He snapped a finger and one of his acolytes held up for our inspection a heavy metal syringe with a sharp nozzle, looking for all the world like some article of gardening equipment; Goytz smiled. "I know" he said. "It has been often said. Yet it is the most invaluable piece of embalming equipment there is." (The sort of thing one sees old ladies using to spray soapy water on their roses.) Goytz took it in a cherishing fashion and presented it at his subject in a manner obviously perfected by long practice. "I will just outline what must be done!" he said. "First we must penetrate at the intersection of the fifth intercostal space and the mid-axillary line; press down until with a slight puff you enter the stomach. Next we must tackle the caecum which is slightly more complicated. Direct the point one-fourth of the distance from the right anterior-superior iliac spine to the pubic symphysis; a tiny bit tricky here, you must keep the point well up near the abdominal wall until within about four inches of the right anterior-superior iliac spine, then dip the point two inches and press softly forward and . . . with a puff you are in the colon." His smile was beatific, his audience rapt. He paused to blow his nose in a tissue.

"Now" he said "there remains the urinary bladder and, most difficult of all, the right atrium of the heart." He issued his instruction for these two delicate operations with burning enthusiasm, though his voice was modulated and serene. He took a pencil from one of his students and marked the places as he spoke cn the skin of his subject. The "potentate" said nothing, though he also appeared to be listening attentively to Goytz. "Onwards until it touches the pubic bone; you will feel the slight jolt. Withdraw about half an inch and dip the point slightly and you will find yourself in the bladder. Now as for the atrium, the target is a small one; you must imagine a line drawn from the left anterior-superior iliac spine to the lobe of the right ear; keep your point firmly up against the anterior wall of the cavity until you pierce the diaphragm. Then dip down and you are in the heart." He sighed again and looked around him benignly, apologetically.

"You see, Marchant" he went on. "And you also have had to take such simple matters into consideration: the combined weight of the viscera in the average adult is around fifteen or twenty pounds, and since this material is so highly putrefactive a considerable amount of fluid is required to disinfect and preserve it. We generally reckon upon between twenty-four and thirty-two ounces of concentrated cavity-fluid as a mean dose. But of course cases vary. Sometimes you get blow-back from intestinal gases, specially if the subject is not too fresh, or if it has succumbed to a disease which has filled a member with some putrefactive fluid. But one can judge usually after a bit of experience." At this moment the "potentate" gave out a noise, a strange rumbling of the stomach, for all the world as if he were hungry. Goytz smiled and raised a finger, saying: "Hark at that! The formation of gases. You must learn how to interpret the sound." There was a slight hiss from the anus of the "potentate", like the noise made by a torn balloon at an Xmas party. "That is normal" said Goytz. "But if things have gone too far we are frequently obliged to make an incision and snip the gut here and there with scissors in order to avoid it. It is a messy system and is better avoided if possible. But in this craft one is always up against unknown factors like freshness or serious illness; and sometimes we have to take emergency steps and use aspiration to void the chief cavities. A six-inch incision, for example, through the ventral wall, along the median lines of the abdomen between the umbilicus and the xiphoid process of the sternum. . . . Then clip-clip and void by aspiration; then the viscera are quickly covered with fluid, embalming powder or hardening compound. But of course the trouble with the holes you make is that they have to be sealed. Yet here we may take courage; to stitch up an embalming subject is less delicate than the stitching up of somebody alive who has been operated on. A simple sailmaker's stitch will draw the lips together; and then you may coat it with a wax sealer as a final operation." He paused in order to give emphasis to what must have been a staple lecture-room joke. Then he said benignly, "Your body is as good as new." There was a slight ripple of sycophantic laughter from his little group. One of them made an involuntary gesture of the hands as if were about to applaud, as one does at the end of a concert. Goytz nodded his thanks at the youth and went on to demonstrate the various types of suture he would use according to nature and size of the incisions made. It was of course fascinating for Marchant, who had been laying life-lines so to speak, made of almost invisible thread, through the photoelectric body of Iolanthe. How crude, compared with our work, it all seemed. Nevertheless there was an affinity of attitude. It lay in our attitude to Beauty!

There was a long pause for breath, during which Goytz paused, as if hovering on the edge of a final peroration: but in fact he was drawing strength to deal with the trickiest part of his art, gazing down with quiet attention at the face of the "potentate". He placed a finger reflectively on the mouth of the personage and gently eased the lip back to reveal a white wolf's tooth before replacing it with care. Then he turned back to us and continued.

"Now the great painter Sargent once said that the hardest thing to get right in portraiture was the mouth of his sitters. One would have thought that it was the eyes, which are so mobile and so full of variety and expression. But in fact he was right. The position of the mouth is absolutely the thing which must be right or else the whole expression goes wrong. The eyes may smile, the eyes may blaze, but if the mouth is wrong, everything is wrong, and your subject will instantly be criticised by his beloved ones as unnatural. Now if this was true for one of the greatest portraitists the world has ever known it is much truer still for the embalmer.

"The mouth position is the most delicate of all, and is also the weakest part of the physical structure—for in death the jaw often falls, the musculature tenses or yields, the lips shrink. Here some swift action has to be taken. We must rub in our embalming cream and massage well before proceeding to the 'set' of the mouth. But in very many cases one has to do what we have called an 'invisible mend'; technically speaking there are two sutures of great import- ance, that of the musculature and that of the mandible itself. The first is really a septum suture. A full curved needle is passed through the muscle tissue at the base of the lower gum, at the septum. The needle is kept as close to the jawbone as possible and the stitch should be quite wide. The needle is then directed upward between the upper lip and gum and brought out through the left nostril. It is then pushed through the septum of the nose into the right nostril and back down between the upper lip and gum. The loose ends are then softly pulled together to coax the jaw into position. When the operator stands at the head of the table he can hold the mandible in position with the little finger and tie the knot with the remaining fingers. But a bow knot is advisable here, as it leaves a little play for any future adjustments one might be called upon to make.

"Of course in this domain, too, the rule of chance obtains, and very small factors play a large role; dentures, for example, or heavily retracted gums which death will shrink out of shape all too quickly; decomposition, ulceration . . . many imponderables with which only the skilled embalmer can cope and still remain true to his vision of reality—if I may make so bold as to call it that, for he tries to get as near to life as possible. He is an artist trying to reform the effects of death in a subject, particularly those of the *rigor mortis* and associated conditions. But sometimes too, in subjects which have suffered a long illness, his kind of beauty treatment is up against many of the problems faced by beautificians who have to compensate for a lifetime of sadness or selfishness or stupidity showing upon the faces of their patients.

"I'm thinking, for example, of the *facies hippocratica,* so called because first described by the greatest little doctor of All Time, Hippocrates. All literatures both before and after have drawn attention to the fact that the faces of those about to pass on tend to have a sort of stamp of death about them. Of course it is almost infinitely variable according to the causes of the death, but sufficiently consistent to have been noted down. It is not just folklore, my friends, though each embalmer may cite you different characteristics of the condition. I myself would cite a sharp pinched quality of the nostrils, and a general semblance of skin-shrinkage around the temples. But of course each case is modified by circumstances; those who die in peace will not show the same signs as those who die in high emotion, shrieking, or suicides who have blown their brains out. It takes all kinds to make a world."

He smiled round at us in kindly and abstracted fashion, and then turned back to reflect upon the problems which his "potentate" would pose to the class. "In his case," he said "we can congratulate ourselves on his freshness but on little else—for there is a problem or two connected with his mouth. I have asked for some photographs of him in life. His lower jaw must have protruded a good deal and I think we will have to consider a mandible suture—inserting the needle straight down between the lower lip and gum and bringing it out at the point of the chin; then reinserting the needle into the same hole but pushing it upwards behind the mandible, in order to bring it out through the floor of the mouth just beneath the tip of the tongue. The actual decision of course depends on our documentation.

"By that," he went on "I mean that if he has no friends and relations to mourn him here and to complain about the likeness; if he simply has to be casketed and package-shipped to Abyssinia: why then I might in the interest of pure speed resort to a more primitive method known as 'tack-and-thread'. This is much swifter. You take a long slim carpet-tack and a tack-hammer such as picture-framers use; you drive the tack into the mandible, between the roots of the teeth. Then you drive a second into the maxilla. Then a strong piece of cord attached to the two tacks will draw the mandible into position and hold it. But the method is not foolproof, and often not profes-

sionally attractive. On the other hand I have to take into consideration other factors. For example, his own folks back home may want
him gilded from head to foot, not just painted like a photographic
likeness hand-tinted by however expert a hand. We must first
secure the cavities while we are waiting for a word from his Embassy."
He smiled, pulling off his gloves, and prepared the air for yet another
lecture-room jest. "You see," he said "often the dead are just as
choosy as the living." This too was acknowledged with rapturous
respect.

"And now it's past my work time" said Goytz. "So I will invite
you into my study for a cup of tea." He led us as he always did into
his smart white office, the walls of which were covered with charts
and graphs showing the progress of the embalming campaign. There
were advertising leaflets everywhere. A trolley with freshly made tea
on it stood by the desk, and this he dispensed with care. "At the
moment it may seem very slack," he said "but the build-up is impressive. I reckon within ten years everyone in this country will
have taken to the idea of embalming; already the advance sales to
the young with our special bonus have soared into millions. It's
become a bit of a fad, if you like, specially since that pop group
launched that song 'My mummy is a mummy', but nevertheless the
advances have been *paid for* on these policies, and they will have to
be honoured. There is no time to be lost. We shall soon need hundreds of embalmers working through the length and breadth of the
land. I have warned Julian that a special effort will be needed. Of
course in my case I am concentrating on Turkey and the Middle
East where totally different methods both publicitywise and science-
wise will be necessary; we can do a cheaper job, use cheaper fluids
and cruder methods. More bright colours and less representational
art if you follow.

"But that too is virtually pre-sold, thanks to the brilliant campaign
that the firm organised with the clergy. We offered free embalming
to the Byzantine church, and after our second Greek Archbishop
there was a stampede. The lying-in-state of the Archbishop of Belgrade was for the first time prolonged for weeks thanks to our up-to-
date methods. Normally in those lands of the Noonday Sun the
decomposition sets in all too swiftly and after three days or less even

. . . why you can't get near enough to show your reverence. Then came the Catholics; they don't like to be left behind, and they smelt the political power behind the drive. At once they issued a special Bull authorising the embalming of everyone. It averted dangerous riots. But the last and most positive victory of all was over the Communists when we pointed out that Lenin had used our own patented cavity-fluid! Fancy! After the first suspicious hesitation Toto the dictator of Bulgaria signed a full policy, and he is next on our list.

"So you see by the time I send out four or five fully trained embalmers to the Middle East we shall have captured the whole market to a point where it only remains to sweep up Mecca and we're home. Then . . . gazing even further away to the Lands of the Lotus we might envisage Persia and India playing their little part. . . ." Goytz was in a sort of dream as he sipped his tea and waved vaguely at these vast horizons. Marchant rubbed his hands in high delight. "Yes," he said "you are right. Nothing will stop the march of science." And he gave forth a characteristic titter; Goytz, still in his creative muse, smiled upon us from behind his desk. "How long" he said "before the reign of Real Beauty begins?" This was rather a harpoon for Marchant who put on a somewhat schoolmistress' expression and said with a touch of tartness, "Our own Iolanthe won't be long now, Goytz. Another month or two at the most." The embalmer raised a hand in kindly benediction, and then a faint cloud passed over his serene countenance. "For me" he said "the only trouble is that Julian's brother is not pulling his weight; something is wrong. He is ill perhaps. But at any rate he has disappointed us rather, because he won't play any part in our scheme, or so it appears. And Julian is vexed with him. That's all I know of the matter." Suddenly I recalled with a start Julian saying something about Caradoc building Jocas a tomb . . . when was it? But the tea party went on with decorum until the duty cars arrived and we all went home for the night. Goytz shook hands with both of us and charitably invited us to come back whenever we wished.

That evening I was sitting by the fire reading a book when the telephone rang and the quiet voice of Julian sounded—a voice which was perhaps just a shade less languid than usual, yet nevertheless controlled and modulated. He was phoning from Paris, he said, and added: "And particularly to thank you my dear Felix, for thinking up so charming a gesture; you will have guessed how much it meant to me to hear her voice. . . ."

"Whose voice?"

"Why Iolanthe's" he said in puzzled tones. "It was only a few words, of course. But what a thrill for me after so long. Thank you."

"But wait," I said. "She couldn't possibly have talked to you Julian; the magazines aren't dated and placed yet. She is still asleep, my dear. Yes, she can say a few words all right but she couldn't get up or lift the phone as yet. Has Marchant been playing you some recorded stuff to try it out? I wonder."

"I assure you," he said, almost pleading "there was no mistake. She said: 'We have never met, have we Julian? It is as if I had missed a vital part of my real life.'" His voice shook a little. "Then she went on: 'Now the doctors will remedy that together with a lot of other things, and when I am well I will ask you to come to me.' It was terrifying in a way, but so very real. . . ."

I was on my feet by now, full of a very real perplexity. "I'll check back," I said "and let you know."

The thing was how, and in which order? I rang Marchant and cleared him from suspicion. He was as mystified as I was. Then, on a sudden impulse, I phoned to the studio itself—though on the face of it this was an absurd thing to do; for I myself had locked up that evening after drawing the covers carefully over Iolanthe. And here was a funny thing. The phone returned an engaged signal, which clearly showed that the receiver was at least off. I listened to the monotonous bleating tone and my thoughts began to race. And then, even as I listened, there came the decisive click and silence which could come only from the replacing of the receiver. Click, followed by the engaged tone again.

"Now what the devil?" I said. Benedicta looked up to see me rushing myself into an overcoat and scarf. "I must just go to the studio and check" I said. "Come with me, only hurry, darling; you can drive me if you wish."

*   *   *   *   *

166

Light powdery snow drifted across our headlights, a shadowy distracted moon wandered in the sky; B. drove at full tilt, a cigarette burning between her lips. The car had been well christened when the makers chose the name "Spear" for it. I chewed the inside of my lips, chewed my ragged thoughts. I felt an extraordinary despondency arise in me. It was too early for things to start going wrong, before we had even got our model on to its feet. It was partly fear, I think, of finding some mechanical defect in our dolly which might cost us months' more intricate work—but also: fear of an unknown factor which hinted crudely at a sort of physical autonomy for which we had not yet made room *in our minds*. How *free* was the final Iolanthe to be? Freer than a chimp, one supposes . . . yes, infinitely; but free enough to pick up a phone and charm Julian? "You are looking scared" said Benedicta quietly. "Is it my driving? I'll slow down." I shook my head. "No. No. I was debating a little matter of freewill, of conditioned reflexes . . . . Drive faster in fact. Much faster. One is only scared when something happens which one can't explain to oneself. She could not, for example, have done what Julian says she did, namely, lift the telephone and talk to him. At this stage, at any rate."

"I'm dying to see this dummy."

"You have been very patient, Benedicta; why you have never even asked me, darling. Of course you shall. Now."

"I knew my voice would shake with jealous rage and you would suddenly look at me in astonished fashion. To be deprived of the female right to be jealous by the logic of things—that is the unkindest thing that could happen to a woman." She laughed.

"Are we jealous of Iolanthe, then?" I said.

Some hefty branches torn from a tree by the wind lay astride the main road and we swerved to a halt, nonplussed for a moment, for there seemed no alternative way forward. Fortunately the wood was not quite so heavy as it looked and I was able to shift it enough to clear a fairway for the car. Panting, I sank back at last beside her, revelling in the warm gushes of air from the heater as we raced on again towards our destination. "Who could have done it then?" she asked. "Could he have imagined it in his sleep?" There was nothing to be said as yet, until I had seen Iolanthe with my own eyes. Of course when she woke such an act would be part of her enormous repertoire of "autonomous" acts. Ring anyone up and say anything, in fact. "Did you say she could not eat or excrete?" I placed another lighted cigarette between her teeth and explained. "She won't know it. We built her the reflex movement and the functional pattern which go with them; only she doesn't have to trundle a disagreeable bundle of faecal matter around with her. She will feel the same punctual need as you do, and like you will sit down on the bidet and run the taps. But unlike you she only imagines the act of defecation, though she has all the same enjoyment—why she even gives the little shudder that we men find so endearing. But she is full of labour-saving devices like that. O God, Benedicta, she is marvellous; you will have quite a surprise, truthfully you will. Maybe feel a little scared as well—I confess that at first blush I was quite taken back, awed."

We swerved at long last into the driveway to find the whole complex of buildings in darkness, which of course was what we would have expected. There was a bright green light in the lodge which housed the two security guards whose duty it was to make two late night patrols through the studios and labs. The tagged keys to our studio hung on a nail behind the grizzled head of Naysmith who lumbered to his flat marine's feet to welcome me. "Is there anything wrong?" he asked catching, I suppose, a touch of urgency from the expression on my face. "Not exactly. It may be me. But I thought I'd come back and check over my section. There's a little matter of a phone-call I have not cleared up as yet. By the way, Naysmith, come with me and bring some fingerprint snuff would you? I'd like to see if our inside phone has any prints on it. The last lot should be mine or Marchant's."

Benedicta was waiting for us in her lamb furred overcoat and boots; and together we cut across the main pathways and walked the hundred yards or so towards the studios. We entered, turning up the white lights of the theatre of operations as we advanced; I was relieved to find everything as I had left it. Though why I should have imagined or looked for a hypothetical disorder I know not. "That phone over there, Naysmith. Give it the gold dust treatment will you and see what you find?" Obediently the security man dusted his goldish powder over the instrument, puffing it softly from an atomiser. Then he took out a large magnifying glass from his professional kit and ran it over the suspect instrument, grunting as he did so. "There's nothing *at all* on the damn thing" he said at last stretching his back straight with relief and turning to me in a mild perplexity. "It's been wiped clear by someone." For a moment this too seemed strange, but then I was determined not to invent mysteries where none existed. The air was kept at a specially moist heat to be kind to Iolanthe's skin, which had been woven from pure Mel, a derivative of nylon. I explained briefly to Naysmith and he seemed satisfied enough with this explanation as indeed I was myself. I could think of no other; an invisible skin of moisture particles formed upon the bakelite receiver and washed out any fingerprints. And Iolanthe? Well, she had not moved at all under her sheet; poor dear, she was still in pieces though nearing the final joining together. There was quite a lot of juice roaming about inside her because we had plugged her in to a low-power induction current to keep her body at a satisfactory temperature. And it was this factor which suddenly presented me with a solution—or the sketch of one. Benedicta stood at the door, looking very pale and extraordinarily youthful all of a sudden. She was afraid of what lay beneath the sheet! I didn't want to unveil the head until Naysmith had taken himself off—a twinge of proprietorial jealousy I suppose? But this the good man did in a few moments and now was my chance to show off my beauty to Benedicta. I took her cold hand in mine and together we crossed the room to the operating table.

"I mustn't forget to show you the weaver team that made the skin for her; you'd think you were in a Japanese watercolour in their studio—finer than the petals of any flower you might conceive." I turned back the sheet and we gazed down upon the still serene

N–F*   169

features of the screen goddess. I could feel that she was terrified, Benedicta. And when, at this juncture, the telephone suddenly shrilled we both nearly jumped out of our skins and into each other's arms. I picked it up with trembling fingers and was relieved to find that it was only Marchant. "I've thought of an explanation" said he. "She's still on the feeder isn't she? Well there's a fairly big build-up of juice, enough to enable her to pass a thought or a phrase along a wire without using the phone. It doesn't sound very plausible, but I think that must be it."

"It will have to be" I said. "There isn't any other solution." Marchant sucked his teeth cheerfully and went on. "If you switch on and pin her on to feedback she might even answer the question herself." But I wasn't keen to start fooling round at this time of night. "It'll keep" I said. "Until she walks in beauty like the night." There was a gasp and stirring sound; I turned to see Benedicta gazing fixedly at the face which had suddenly altered its expression. And then, even as we looked, the two sapphire bright eyes opened and gazed fixedly, unwinkingly at Benedicta. B. moved back a few paces with obvious fear. "It wants to speak" she whispered. "Poor thing. Poor thing." She was about to faint but I caught her. In the little lavatory next door she was violently sick.

"Leave me a moment" she said, between spasms of nausea. "She wants to tell you something. Please go back." But I waited until she could accompany me back; I wanted her to get over her shock and come to accept Iolanthe for what she was—a modest enough copy of reality, not a creation. I hung about obstinately, not saying a word, until she shook herself at last and said: "There! It's done with." She washed her face and dried it on the little white napkin behind the door; then slipped her arm through mine. "What an experience!"

Iolanthe's head had hardly moved, but her features tenderly sketched in a shoal of transient feelings, impulses bathed in memory or desire, which flowed through the magazine of the coded mind on the wings of electricity. For such low-voltage feeding it was remarkable to find her "live" at all. Yet she was. Her blue eyes gazed into the white glare of the theatre lamps with a sort of abstract curiosity; then, attracted perhaps by the glimpse of our shadows moving upon the general whiteness, lowered their gaze and came to rest at last, in troubled and loving confusion, upon my own face. You could have sworn she recognised it—the little mischievous pucker of the mouth came, as if she were about to utter her sardonic greeting in Greek, "*Xāire Felix mou*". And yet also timid, abashed, a *gamine* who fears she may be reproached. But of course with a current so far below optimum the threads had got jumbled as they do in an ordinary delirium—in high fever for example—and what she said she uttered in the back of her throat and not too clearly at that. The tone of course was low contralto, not very like her ordinary one because of the fallen levels. "The deep inside wish to be level with the grave, Julian; you are worn out with the sin of wishing you had died in childbirth—how well we understand! Now that I have come back from this great illness I shall bring you some comfort, you will see."

"Christ!" Benedicta vibrated with a mixture of fascination and horror. "She's jumbling" I said; and I ran my hand softly and tenderly through the hair of Iolanthe in a gesture which I knew would elicit the response she must have so often made in life. She arched her head slowly, flexing it on the lovely stem of her neck, and breathed in deeply, voluptuously; then she expelled her breath slowly, uxoriously through her mouth and gave me a sleepy smile. "Kiss. Kiss" she said. "Felix." And pursed her red smiling mouth for a kiss which I gave her while Benedicta looked on in a kind of scanda-lised amusement mixed with loathing.

We kissed and she brushed my ear with her lips murmuring: "Precious. But life could have been full of so much hope, only we're cripples, cripples. I spoke to Julian." Well, if there was enough juice for all this there might be enough for her to get back on to the mnemonic register without an additional charge, and actually answer a "real" question. "How did you do it?" I asked. She closed her eyes, appearing not to have heard, not to have understood; then she opened them again and the tiny dimple appeared in her cheek. "The Arab doctor is kind; he got me Julian. Just for a minute. It's so tiring." So that was the answer! Said had obtained the call and placed the receiver to her ear and mouth. Switched on the power. Ah, my schizoid goddess, you are falling asleep again. She couldn't help it; her long lashes declined softly and she subsided quietly once more into nescience pillowed on the sea-rhythms of the current.

Receding, receding into the tideless sleep of scientific time; her bloodstream was a wavelength only in her tissues, its force measured now upon a small dial with a face no larger than a lady's wristwatch. A little nodding blue bulb of pilot-flame winked on all through the night. Such silence and such beauty!

"Well, we've solved the mystery" I said. "Let's go home. I am beginning to feel tired."

"Kiss me just once" said Benedicta. "I want to feel how it must have felt to her . . . to it. No, you don't kiss very well. Inattentive. Your mind's always elsewhere, you are woolgathering. You should plunge it in like a spear." But I was tucking back the white sheets round my dolly, drawing the transparent curtains once more. It was very late, and for some reason I felt very excited and nervous—a relief-reaction I suppose to find everything as it should be. Naysmith had left an evening paper and in this mood of slight disorientation, anxiety-powered I suppose, the most banal headlines took on a tinge of almost sinister ambiguity. "Attendants steal fittings" "Birds lodge in soil" "Work-providers for landless". Amen. Amen. I locked up with method, whistling under my breath. Then with a sigh I clicked the studio door behind me. "Now," I said "when I tell you I am working late at the office, you'll know who I am kissing. Would it be possible to become jealous of a model? I suppose so; one can about a child or a dog, and in cases of great mental cruelty brought before the Californian courts you even find inanimate objects playing a perfectly satisfactory role. A man who went to bed with his golf clubs for example. Extreme mental cruelty. Benedicta when you read cases like that and then think of me don't use bad language, will you promise?" But Benedicta would not rise to my nervous banter; she remained pale and abstracted, her hand clasped hard in mine as we found our way across the grass to the asphalt carpark. She sensed that it was mere diversionary babble, that all of a sudden this trifling incident had upset me, had made me feel hesitant, unsure of myself. Yet I could not formulate any special reason why. There was nothing really wrong, nothing at all.

She drove slowly on the way back, and indeed took a longer way round, through Croley, Addhead and Byre, which must have added some forty miles on the clock. I wondered why for a while. Of course. Then I remembered the road all but blocked with fallen branches. I was glad anyway of the long detour; I always think better out of doors than in, and best of all when I am travelling as a passenger in a fast car. But it was mighty late when at last we came back to the cottage, sharing the last puffs of the last cigarette. It had stopped snowing. A large limousine lay at the stile across the fields with its headlights blazing. It was the office Rolls that Julian always used. Indeed his chauffeur sat inside at the wheel. We pulled in alongside him and he saluted when he recognised us. "He is waiting up for you, sir. Mr. Baynes let him in and made him a snack to eat. I am to pick him up within the next hour or so, so I'm keeping the car warmed up to run him down to Southampton."

We docked the little Spear and cut a glittering path across the field to where the cottage stood, with its one warmly-lit window. The latch was off the door and it opened with a slight touch to reveal a blazing fire and the figure of Julian sitting in a high-backed chair holding a dossier on his knee; the little silver pencil raised in his small neat hand was poised over some abstruse calculation. He looked completely different once more—perhaps it was the clothes, for this time he was dressed in morning dress with a high stock, for all the world as if he had just come from a wedding or Ascot. A grey topper and gloves lay in the window sill, together with a copy of the *Finance World*. The man appeared to be eternally surprising, unpredictable.

He had chosen, too, a highly dramatic point of vantage in the room—over against the old fireplace and directly under a brilliant lamp with a dull blood-coloured vellum shade. The result was bright light upon the crown of his head and on his knee, but a subdued swarthy reflection upon the skin of his face making it seem deeply sunburnt. With this great contrast of tone one could not but find his hair very white, or at least much whiter than usual. Yet the warm tone shed by the vellum'd light gave him all the benefit of a whole skiwinter of snowburn. "Ah," he said, and recrossed his legs in their polished shoes "I took the liberty of calling in on my way to Jamaica. I hope it is all right? Baynes has looked after me like a child." He indicated with his chin a tray with sandwiches and some champagne in a pail. But he did not stand up. Benedicta slipped across the room

173

to embrace him in perfunctory fashion while I busied myself in pulling off my stormcoat and slipping my feet back into my lined slippers.

Baynes must long since have gone to bed; so while foraging for a cigarette I implored Benedicta to put some coffee on the hob. "You were right, Julian" I said, and all of a sudden I recognised my own relief by the tone in which I uttered the words. "But you gave me the devil of a start. What you suggested was impossible at this stage without outside aid, and when I rang Marchant he swore that he hadn't taken a hand in it. All kinds of gross scientific short-circuits flashed into my mind. But of course we had both forgotten Said—he provided the number and arranged the call. Phew!" I sank down in front of the fire, and a silence fell—the deep rich silence of the countryside; I could feel him drinking it in with nostalgia, his head cocked like a gun-dog. "How still it is here" he said, in a wondering sort of way. "Somehow much stiller than the big house—there were always noises there. It's the small rooms I expect." Benedicta came with coffee on a tray; she had already changed into her pyjamas and combed out her hair. We sat down before the fire, stirring it into flame, and pouring ourselves mugs of the steaming stuff.

Julian stared hard into the fire over our shoulders. He seemed very calm, very much at peace—and yet with the sort of peace which suggested the resignation of old age rather than the inner resolution of, say, conflicting anxieties. "You said she would be ready next month, didn't you? We must start of course insinuating her into our lives a little, no? She is after all, from her own point of view, taking up a long life from the point at which she left it off. One wouldn't want her to have the cold comfort of being some scientific orphan." I was very touched by a curious sort of plangency in his tone, rising and falling like the rosined note of a viol; it had an accent of rather naïf sympathy. Even his face looked somehow juvenile and unlined in the firelight as he spoke. "Wouldn't you say, I mean?" he ended a trifle lamely, but with the same unemphatic wistfulness which I found somehow touching. "I only hope" I said "that you don't identify too closely with the model we've made, and mistake it for the actual subject! It wouldn't be too difficult as a matter of fact—she's so damn true to life, if I may use such an expression. Indeed Marchant and I have both found ourselves thinking of her as if she were real and not merely a man-made doll, however word-perfect." He nodded once or twice as I spoke. "I know," he said softly "I know." And his lips moved as if he were whispering some *sotto voce* admonitions to his inner self. I suddenly said impulsively: "Julian, how did it come to you to . . . think of having her copied, made?" He looked at me now with such a reproachful sadness, such a concentration of unanswering pain, that the superfluousness of my question became all too clear. Damn! "One does the obvious thing in given circumstances" he said at last. "It never occurred to me that anything else was possible." He was right. What question was there to be answered which could not be so within the terms of the experience we had both undergone with Merlin's? The apprenticeship I myself had served, for example. No, the fantastic was also the real. It was all as clear as daylight, as the saying goes.

He lowered his head for a moment and hooded his dark eyes like some bird of prey, and watching him there in the reflection of the vellum shade I could not help reflecting that the whole power behind his mental drive, and indeed that for the firm itself (they had become co-equal) rested really upon impotence; the slowly spreading stain of a self-conscious ignominy, a shame, and all the spleen which flowed from it. Nothing much more than that—as if that wasn't enough! But it was something at least to be able to formulate it, to indicate the region in which it lay. It threw into relief so much that I had wondered about, so much that I had been quite unable to explain to myself before. Indeed the article of value about which we were all fighting, brandishing each his sterile and desexualised penis, was the eternal anal one—the big tepid biblical turd of our culture which lay under the vine-shoots of modern history, waiting to be. . . . ("The Moldavian penis is all back and no sides" writes Tinbergen, while Umlaut adds the rider, "And not seldom glazed like the common eggplant". Where would we be without the studies of these northern savants?) The enormous cupidity of impotence!

"You have been lucky in a way," said Julian slowly while my attention had been wandering "in that you came to us fresh from the outside. What you had to fight—or felt you had to fight—was something quite apart from yourself. But if, as in my case, your adversary

175

is more than half yourself . . . ? What then? I found myself trying to do two different things at the same time which were mutually contradictory—trying to harness and direct the firm's drive, and at the same time to enlarge the limits of my own personal freedom within it. I *belonged* to Merlin, you see; you never did. And yet I feel a greater need for freedom than you ever could. And then, other things which nail me down—family, race, environment . . . all these things held me spellbound and still do. Benedicta, don't cry." Unaccountably Benedicta had given a brief sob before bowing her head upon her knees; but it was only the noise of a child troubled in sleep by some fugitive day-memory of a quarrel over a toy.

"Her death *halted* Me" said Julian with a meek softness of tone which carried a sort of weird hidden intonation in it—the provisional hint perhaps of a madness which one had come increasingly to feel was not so far away? No, this is too strong. "This week" he went on wearily "has been a week of great misgivings, all due to Nash, who has suddenly appeared on the scene with all kinds of new questions to ask about her. None of which I am able to answer, though I am quite as much up in the lingo, and anal-oral theology, as you are. Nash, incidentally, wants to have her destroyed."

"Destroyed!"

" 'She will do us no good' he says. 'Indeed she carries buried fatally in her construction the thumbprints—the Freudian thumbprints of her makers.' So he says. In other words, she can't as I suggested stand for an aesthetic object related to our culture because you have deprived her of the very organs upon which it is based. I am repeating only what he said. Where is the *merde* that sank a thousand ships? That is what he asks. In fact he has been trying in his clumsy way to analyse why I should have decided to have her created, and specially in the image of the only person. . . ." He broke off and stared into the fire, following with restless intentness the shifting flames as they patterned themselves upon the wall. "They are satisfied with so little," he went on "these psychologists, and the most trifling analogy offers them an apparent explanation to something. As when Nash analyses why I should choose her, above all women, as my prime symbol—the money goddess, the goddess of the many. It smells too easy, doesn't it? And analysis is often along a very shallow trench; it isn't very far down to the Palaeolithic levels either. But on Nash plods, with his free association. The screen itself is a sterile thing in essence—bed-sheet or winding-sheet, or both; but lightly dusted over with alchemical silver the better to capture the projected image so dear to the collective unconscious— the youthful mother-image with its incestuous emphasis. . . . On the one hand one would have the right to burst out laughing, no? Yet on the other . . . ah! Felix.

"Yes, this week of misgiving has been chock full of questions about Iolanthe; it would have been better if you yourself had been there to answer them, however provisionally. I tried my best to get Nash to see her as simply a small observation-post upon the field of automation—nothing much more. But that does not quite satisfy him. It was a mistake in the beginning to talk to him about culture or aesthetics—unconsciously we were all trying to disguise the base metal of our search in a number of pretty ways. Yes. To the psycho-analyst it is dirt. By the way, have you ever seen a gold brick? I happen to have one with me; I am taking it off to Jamaica. Let me show you."

It couldn't well have been more incongruous the juxtaposition of tailcoat, top hat, and the small brown paper parcel which lay under them, tied up with string. A middle-class enough looking parcel which he undid with an air of dogged, modest triumph and then set the little greenish loaf with its deeply indented seal squarely upon the carpet between us. It sat there glinting saturninely in the firelight.

Julian said: "Freud says that all happiness is the deferred fulfil-ment of a prehistoric wish, and then he adds: 'That is why wealth brings so little happiness; money is not an infantile wish.'" He sat down, musing deeply for a moment; then he got down softly upon one knee and began to do up the little green loaf in its brown paper, tying the string carefully round it. Having secured it he replaced it once more upon the window-sill, in the folds of his overcoat, under the topper. "I have been studying the demonic of our capitalistic system through the eyes of Luther—a chastening experience in some ways. He saw the final coming to power in this world of Satan as a capitalistic emblem. For him the entire structure of the Kingdom of Satan is essentially capitalistic—we are the devil's own real property, he says: and his deepest condemnation of our system is in his phrase 'Money is the word of the Devil, through which he creates all things in exactly the way God once created the True Word.' In his devastating theology capitalism manifests itself as the ape of God, the *simia dei*. It is hard to look objectively at oneself in the shaving-mirror once one has adventured with this maniac through the 'Madensack' of the real shared world—this extended worm-bag of a place out of which squirm all our cultural and gnomic patterns, the stinking end-gut of a world whose convulsions are simply due to the putrefying explosions of faecal gas in the intestines of time." He paused, musing and shaking his head. "And then gold itself, as Spengler points out, is not really a colour, for colours are natural things. No, that metallic greenish gleam is of a satanic unearthliness; yet it has an explicit mystical value in the iconography of our Churches." He relit his cigar with a silver lighter.

"And then from gold to money is only a very short jump, but a jump which spans the shallow trench of our whole culture and offers us some sort of rationale for the megalopolitan men we are and our ways; *our ways*! For money is the beating heart of the New Word, and the power of money to bear *interest*, its basic *raison d'être*, has created the big city around it. Money is the dynamo, throwing out its waves of impulse in the interest principle. And without this volatility principle of Satan's gold there would have been no cities. The archaeologists will tell you that they have noted the completest rupture of the life-style of man once he had founded his first cities. The intrusion of *interest-bearing* capital is the key to this almost total reorganisation of man, the transvaluation of all his rural values. From the threshing-floor to the square of a cathedral city is but a small jump, but without interest-bearing capital it could never have been made. The economy of the city is based wholly upon economic surplus—it is a settlement of men who for their sustenance depend on the production of agricultural labour which is not their own; it is the *surplus* produce of the country which constitutes the subsistence of the town. But Nash will hasten to tell you that for the unconscious the sector of the surplus is also the sector of the sacred—hence the towering cathedral-city with its incrustation of precious gems and sculptures and rites; its whole economy becomes devoted

178

to sacred ends. It becomes the 'divine household', the house of God."

He put back his head and gave a sudden short bark of a laugh, full of a sardonic sadness. He looked so strange, Julian, bowed under the weight of these speculations; he looked at once ageless and very old. "I've had difficulty in convincing Nash that our science is still so very backward that for comfort's sake we still feel the need to build ourselves working models of things—whether trains, turbines, or angels! In aesthetics as against technics, of course, a whole new flock of ideas come chattering in like starlings. We are at the very beginning of a phase—one can feel that; but one wishes that the bedrock were newer, fresher, contained fewer archaic features. No? The old death-figure is there side by side with creative Eros, longing to pull us back into the mire, to bury us in the stinking morasses of history where so many, innocent and guilty, have already foundered. As far as Iolanthe is concerned I freely confess that I am at a disadvantage as compared with you; you knew her, you knew the original, you have something real to compare her with. But I have only a set of data, like outworn microscope slides, with which to compare her; her films, her life—I have assembled the whole dossier. But when I meet her it will be a momentously new experience—I feel so sure of that. Yes."

Suddenly he seemed to be almost pleading, like a schoolboy, his hands pressed between his knees, his eyes searching mine for a trace of reassurance. I felt it was in some way unhealthy to become so intense about a dummy—the whole thing filled me with unease, though it would have been hard to explain to myself why. Nothing could have been saner than his glance, nothing more unflinching than his grasp on language when it came to trying to disentangle all these interlocking concepts. Julian sat for a long moment staring into the fire and then continued. "I am probably ready for her in this new form. I have always behaved as much like an immortal as I could—the negative capability, you might say, of deprivation. Like a Jap prince or a Dalai Lama I have been forced to develop in captivity, all by myself. But if I haven't been evil I have been a keen student of evil—in alchemical terms, if you like, I was prone to the white path by nature; but I trod the black in order to divine its secrets. Some few I managed to appropriate for myself—but pitifully few. I wanted like everyone else to assuage the aches and pains of humanity. What an ambition."

"I wonder, Julian" I said, gently caressing the nape of Benedicta's neck. "I see you rather as enjoying it as pure experience, for its own pure sake." He gave a soundless little chuckle and half admitted the truth of the charge. "Perhaps. But then that *is* the black path. It admits of no compromise, one has to become it, to tread it; but there is no obligation to remain fixed there, like a joker in a pack. One can extricate oneself—albeit after a long struggle against the prince of darkness, or whatever you might call the luciferian principle. The struggle of course makes one unbelievably rich; if you keep your reason, you emerge from the encounter with a formidable body of psychic equipment at your disposal. Not that that does much good to anyone in the long run. . . ." He yawned deftly, compactly, like a cat, before resuming. "I must be on the high seas tomorrow. Look, Felix, you do understand why I have been having these long sessions with Nash? I wanted to plumb as far as possible the unconscious intentions behind my desire to make a neo-Aphrodite—one who cannot eat, excrete, or make love. In terms of her own values—and I use the phrase because I know that you have endowed her with a built-in contemporary memory which can give an account of any contingency. Total memory, seen of course from our own vantage point in time. But suppose her to be free—suppose the world were in charge of a dozen models as perfect as she is—various other factors would obviously come into play. What, for example, would be their attitude to money? What sort of city could such creatures come to found and finally to symbolise? Eh? It's worth a thought. Then, what would happiness represent for her since she is free from the whole Freudian weight of everything that makes us 'un'; could you arrange for her, ideally, to have the free play of a natural lubricity, an eroticised function which ideally need never rest? No, because she isn't fertile—that's the answer isn't it? And yet she is word-perfect, she walks in beauty like the night. Felix . . . could such a thing . . . could Iolanthe in her dummy form *love*? And what form would such an aberration take? I suppose when we have Adam we will be able to see a little more clearly into this abyss. I am so looking forward to seeing her, knowing her in natural surroundings—pardon the phrase. This free woman, free from the suppurating weight of our human mother-fixation. She can neither love nor hate. What a marvellous consort she might make for someone. Does she know good from evil? There is no such question; does anyone? We are impelled to act before we think. No, let me finish. . . .

"Action, whatever they tell you, in almost every case precedes reflection; what we recognise as right and wrong action is almost always the fruit of a retrospective judgement. God, what a host of ontological problems she could raise . . . could she, for example, realise she is a dummy as much as, say, you realise that you are Felix? We don't really know, do we, until we ask her? And even then, one slip on the keyboard might give one totally unknown factors to consider. At what point could she invent, could she be original, supposing she slipped among the mnemonic signatures?"

He had begun to walk slowly up and down the room with a kind of burning, I could say "incandescent" concentration upon this conversation to which I myself did not wish to add a word. I was an artificer, I was simply there to wait and see at which angle the thing went off; and then to correct its trajectory whenever possible like a good mathematical papa. No, this isn't quite true; it would be truer to say that when one is dealing with inventions it is safer to go step by step, and not lose oneself among theoretical considerations before the actual model can start ticking over.

"Julian" I said. "Give yourself time; you will soon be able to call on her in her own snug villa, take tea with her, converse on any subject under the sun; listen to her as she plays jazz to you, cherish her in every way. We can promise you a degree of the real which you will find quite fascinating, quite disturbing. I wouldn't myself have believed that our craftsmen at Merlin's could have been capable of such fine workmanship. Indeed she's so damn near perfect that Marchant suggested that we built a small fleet of them—our 'love-machines' he called them; we could turn them out on the streets and live on their immoral earnings. From the customer's point of view they would be virtually indistinguishable from the real article—better dressed and better bred, perhaps, that is all. And from a legal point of view our position would be quite unassailable. They would, after all, be dummies: nothing more."

He smiled and shook his head: "I wish you wouldn't use that word" he said softly. "It always suggests something old and primitive and creaking, studded with levers and buttons. Not something sophisticated, something of our decade. By the way, when she is launched will there be any way of controlling her?" It was my turn to stretch my aching legs, and prop B.'s head with a pillow. "That's the whole point, Julian. Once launched there is no stop-go button or rewind or playback; she is as irrevocably launched as a baby when you hit it on the bottom and force it to utter the birth-cry. I had to confer full human autonomy on Iolanthe, don't you see? Otherwise our whole experiment would have been diminished; I could not have given her the mnemonic range if we had had to allow for cutting out the current every ten days, rewiring, recharging—as if she were a model train or yacht, run by remote control. We simply leaped over all these considerations; and when she rises from her bed of sickness and roams abroad in the world there will be no calling her back! We'll have to take her as she is, for better or for worse, in sickness or in health, in fair weather or foul. But that is how you wanted her, isn't it?"

"God, of course!" he cried softly but passionately. "I wanted her absolute in every way." I heard the words with a pang, so charged were they with love, with desolation, with hunger. "She's breakable, of course, and ultimately wear-outable I suppose, but probably less than you or I. She will outlive us all, I dare swear, if she isn't smashed or run over by a car. The organisation is pretty delicate but the substitutes we've used for bone and cartilage and vein-paths is a hundred times more durable and dependable than what God gave us poor folk. And of course she won't age, relatively speaking; her hair and skin will keep their gloss longer than yours or mine."

Benedicta said suddenly, without opening her eyes, "Julian, I'm afraid of this thing."

"Of course. You must be" said Julian, his voice full of a vague reassurance. "Nothing like it has ever been done."

"What good can come of it?" said Benedicta. "What will you do with her—she cannot breed, she's just a set of responses floating about like a box-kite, answering to every magnetic wind. Will you just sit and watch her?"

"In holy wonder," said Julian greedily "and with scientific care."

"Benedicta, there hasn't ever been one" I said mildly.

She lay there still, my wife, her head supported by the cushion, her eyes closed, but with an expression of intense concentration on her face—as if she were fighting off a painful migraine.

"No" she said at last, almost below her breath, with a tone of firm decision. "It won't do. Something will certainly go wrong."

Julian looked at his watch and whistled softly. "My goodness it's getting late and I haven't yet come to the real subject of my visit to you two; of course I was worried about that phone-call but really there was something else on my mind. It concerns my brother Jocas in Polis."

"Jocas."

The wind rose suddenly and skirled round the house. I had not thought of Jocas for ages now; and the memory of him, and of Turkey, had faded like an old photograph. Or perhaps it was simply that in this rain- and snow-swept countryside it was hard to evoke the bronze-stubbled headlands where the sturdy little countryman rode to his falcons, calling out in that high ululating muezzin's voice of his as he urged his favourite bird in to the stoop. Jocas existed now like a sort of coloured illustration, an illuminated capital, say, in some yellow old Arabic text; yet he was after all in Merlin terms all of Africa, all of the Mediterranean. "First of all Jocas believes he is dying, and perhaps he isn't wrong, although the information comes to him from his Armenian astrologer—a very acute man I must admit, who has seldom been at fault. Well, anyway, there he is, for what it's worth. He has several months ahead of him, he believes, in which to prepare himself, and is apparently doing it in customary Merlin style, in the high style, that is to say. In my own case, this new turn of events has sort of blunted the edge of the lifetime of enmity I have borne him—I can confess it freely only now. It had ebbed away now, the hate, leaving only respect and regret for the man."

"Julian!" cried Benedicta sharply, opening her eyes and staring angrily at him. "I don't like you in the mock-humble mood. It is false. You cannot stop being a demon now just because Jocas is dying, just because you will get your way at last. You have been at each other's throats ever since you were born."

183

Julian paled, his dark eyes flashed briefly like precious stones before hooding themselves once more under their heavy lids, to give his whole face an expression of massive and contemptuous repose— like an Inca mask, I thought. He paused for a long moment and then went on in a quiet voice, ignoring her and addressing himself to me, as if he were seeking a sympathy or comprehension which I was more likely to accord him than she. "I shall leave myself out of the picture, then, and simply sketch in the details of the matter for you, supposing that the business of his death is a fact, and actually takes place a few months from now. It will raise of course the question of his replacement in the Eastern field; and I have no doubt, Felix, that the senior boardroom will be extremely keen to have you take over the responsibility from him. It doesn't surprise you, does it? Of course the decision is yours and hers, Benedicta's. That is the first point."

"My God" I said with a mixture of wonder and distaste, never having visualised myself as occupying any position of administrative power in this octopus of a firm. "As I say," went on Julian, a trifle sardonically "all that is contingent upon the movement of a few planets across the natal chart of Jocas. When and if it does happen you will have to think about it. But for the moment all Jocas wants is to see you again; he wants you to visit him briefly. I leave the question of timing to you. Obviously you won't want to abandon our experiment before it is complete, I mean Iolanthe. But once she breathes, once she walks, you might feel like taking Benedicta for a short visit to Turkey. Or perhaps before. It's how you feel."

The thought itself was full of the meretricious dapple of unfamiliar sunlight—seen through the long grey corridors of an eternal English winter; one forgot the damp, one forgot the scorching winds on the uplands, the miasmic stenches of the great capital at evening. . . . No, all that remained was this travel-poster sunlight with its enticing glint. Benedicta looked once more sunk in thought. "The timing is up to you," said Julian again softly "but I shouldn't leave it too long. As a matter of fact we are sending out a small party of people at the end of the month—we've chartered a plane. You know some if not all of them: Caradoc, Vibart and Goytz, for example."

"Caradoc! Why?"

"He's coming back to us again on the circular staircase. Jocas has been on for some time about building himself, indeed all of us, a mausoleum—if that's the word. He wants to unite the remains of my mother and . . . father." A funny little contortion travelled over his features as he uttered the word. It was as if the word itself cost him something to bring out. He repeated it in a whisper. "My *Father*" as if to secure a firmer purchase on it; to possess it more thoroughly. "I think perhaps Caradoc is the man to talk to him about it; I have no views one way or the other. As far as parents are concerned I am hardly aware of having had any; my father was something quite different—he was simply Merlin. I owe him everything good and bad that has happened to me in my life. I am not a sentimentalist like Jocas—more particularly now he is growing old, and feeling, I suppose, his childlessness. Anyway, that is roughly the picture as he has sketched it for me. O and by the way, according to the soothsayer I myself don't outlive him by very long. As if I cared. . . ." His weariness, his sadness rang out clearly in the silence of the little room, and the phrase hung fire, remained unfinished. "When I was young, and could not sleep at night, Benedicta was sent to read or recite to me to calm my spirits. I can still remember one of the poems you recited—perhaps you have forgotten?" In his soft negligent tones, so fluent and at the same time so full of charm, he repeated the lines:

> "*Merlin, they say, an English prophet born,*
> *When he was young and govern'd by his mother,*
> *Took great delight to laugh such fools to scorn,*
> *As thought, by nature we might know a brother.*
>
> *His mother chid him oft, till on a day,*
> *They stood, and saw a corse to burial carried,*
> *The father tears his beard, doth weep and pray;*
> *The mother was the woman he had married.*
>
> *Merlin laughs out aloud instead of crying;*
> *His mother chides him for that childish fashion;*
> *Says, Men must mourn the dead, themselves are dying,*
> *Good manners doth make answer unto passion. . . .*"

He hesitated for a moment, hunting in his memory for the next line; but Benedicta took up the strain and finished the poem in a voice which seemed charged with a queer mixture of pride and sorrow.

> " 'This man no part hath in the child he sorrows,
> His father was the monk that sings before him:
> See then how nature of adoption borrows,
> Truth covets in me, that I should restore him.
> True fathers singing, supposed fathers crying,
> I think make women laugh, that lie a-dying.' "*

Julian smiled and said: "Thank you. That's it. And it's a fitting note on which to wish you an apologetic goodnight. Felix, make your own decisions about Jocas. I shall be away anyway if you decide to go now. And another thing, could you give Rackstraw a glimpse of your handiwork—I fear he is really completely useless for my purposes, he's too far gone? I would really like him out of the way before the others come into the picture. And so good night to you. My God, it's nearly morning."

He had slipped into his coat and muffled himself up in his white scarf; the brown paper parcel with its trophy was tucked under his arm. He hesitated at the door for a moment, as if he were hunting among all his available expressions for one which might seem perfectly suitable to this leavetaking. "Don't worry" he said at last, lamely, to Benedicta, and to me, "Until very soon."

Thus he outlined himself for a second upon the spectral snowscape and then was gone, softly closing the door behind him. An effortless disappearance as always.

There was a long silence; Benedicta stood drooping with fatigue and staring into the fire. "He is no Greek" she said at last, grimly. "Our Julian does not know the word *hubris*; he thinks you can give life as easily as you can take it—and you are following him blindly, perhaps into a trap, my poor foolish Felix."

"Come" I said. "He is transformed since we gave him back the hope of an Iolanthe. He's a new person!"

"You don't know him" she said. "His form of ambition is so abso-

* Fulke Greville.

lute that he could crush anyone in his path without a thought. I have been his victim once. I could tell you a strange enough tale of his alchemical experiments on me, his powers over matter—a long sad tale of false pregnancies, mock-miscarriages, even the birth of a changeling with the head of a . . . thing! Murder, too, if you wish. But it was all sanctified by the fact that these were scientific experiments conducted not from evil motives but purely in the name of alchemical curiosity; rather like your scientific self-justifications for the torture and vivisection of animals and so on. He has abandoned all that now—or so he says."

"I don't know what you are getting at."

"I am only saying that whatever his final intentions are he is masking them from us; he is using you as usual."

"Of course. What is wrong about it? I am doing a job for him—but a job after my own heart as well."

Suddenly she turned round and put her arms round me. There were tears in her eyes as she said: "Well, I am so happy to have escaped him, to have freed myself. I can't tell you the relief. I should be the one to put red roses on Iolanthe's tomb every day as a thank-offering. Free!"

Nevertheless that night, for the first time for ages, I surprised her sleepwalking; rather, I woke to find her standing at the window, having drawn back the curtains. I thought she was watching the wonderful snowfall of the early morning, but when I moved to her side and put my arm round her slender shoulders I saw with surprise that her eyes were shut. And yet, not entirely, for she felt my touch and turned her sleeping face to mine in order to say: "I think we must really go and see Jocas. I think Julian is right. We should go and see Jocas as soon as possible."

"Wake" I said shaking her. She came to abruptly and shook herself. "What have I been saying?" I kissed her and said, "That we should go and visit Jocas. It was exactly what I was thinking. But you were sleepwalking, an ominous sign."

"Fatigue," she said "nothing more. Kiss me."

V

Some ten days later, having made my arrangements with Marchant and Said to keep Iolanthe "feeding": that is to say "charging": and to fill in the time by working on the male dummy Adam until my return . . . having done all this, I drove a patient Benedicta down to Southampton, our point of embarkation for the journey to Turkey. A freezing rain fell upon a muted landscape of rime-stiffened hills and clay-pits—the winter at its beastliest. Perhaps it was a trifle wicked to allow the heart to lift with every thought of a spring-pierced Mediterranean, with its oranges glowing on far-away islands and its lofty March seas . . . but lift it did. Only she was thoughtful while I whistled to myself cheerfully to drown the skirling of the tyres upon the black wet roads. Moreover it was impossible not to feel that this would turn out to be some sort of holiday—despite, I mean, the sobering news of Jocas and his death-oriented preoccupations. A holiday feeling was in the air, and it was accentuated when we at last ran Caradoc to earth in a dockside pub on Pier 3 to which, for some mysterious reason, we had been directed. We were not going by sea, were we? I would have preferred the old Orient Express with its long romantic rumble across the heart of Europe. But we were in the hands of the firm's travel people. Everything had been arranged, as usual.

As for Caradoc, he looked both flushed and incoherent, as much with pleasure as with alcohol; but it was quite appalling the physical state he was in—his clothes dirty and torn, his new shaggy beard ungroomed. "I know" he said, taking in our consternation. "Don't look now; I've been camping in Woodhenge and Stonehenge—damn disagreeable month I can tell you, living like an ape under a bush. But the firm is sending me down a couple of suitcases of decent clothes and shaving kit. I'll soon be worthy of your respect." He made a hermetic gesture which the barman instantly translated into three double whiskies. "I'm back in the firm" he said suddenly, jubilantly, laughing a harsh ho-ho. "Once more into the breach, dear souls. For the moment I'm being forced to work in the grave-yard section it seems, laying out cemeteries, designing mausolea and all that; but Julian says if I'm a good boy I can work my way back through public conveniences and council-houses towards some real architecture. For the moment it's a sun-oriented mausoleum—once more Jocas has called for a funeral monument! It may be my last really free job—but who am I to worry? Two more Mnemons in today's paper, have you seen?" He was beside himself with self-congratulation.

"And now to cap it all," he added, jerking a thumb "look what the firm has hired. Just look." The mystery of our presence in the dock-area was at last explained by the old grey flying-boat which lay at anchor in the swell, snubbing the light craft surrounding it, and presumably waiting for its passengers and crew. My misgivings were only to be allayed when we finally did go aboard by tender and found out just how spacious and comfortable it was with its two decks, its bars and conference room where we were to dine and pass most of our time. It was a good choice, really, but as a craft she was slow, slow as the devil; moreover I gathered we would have to touch down almost everywhere to refuel—Marseille, Naples, Bari, Athens. . . . Ah, but that was something else in its favour for we could stop overnight anywhere. Perhaps in Athens we could look in on the Countess Hippolyta, Ariadne? I conferred with Caradoc and des-patched a telegram warning her of our threatened descent upon Naos, her country house.

What was not easy was the take-off, however; we leeched up and down the sound trying to get up sufficient speed to free ourselves, to get airborne, but in vain. We were stuck to the water as if to a flypaper; the great engines groaned and screamed, the spars shud-dered, the hull vibrated under the thwacking of waves. But at long last, after a run which seemed to last an eternity she suddenly broke free, tore herself loose from the shackles of the water and swayed up into the free air, turning in a long slow curve over the land with its toy houses and gardens and infantile piers and railway stations—turning her prow towards the tall blue spring sky which waited for us somewhere off Corsica. And all at once the noise diminished and speech became possible; from everywhere stewards appeared with drinks and sandwiches. A few light pantomime clouds puffed around us in glorious Cinerama giving us the illusion of speed and mastery. Our spirits rose.

There was so much room that each of us had a choice of different corners if we wanted to read or work or doze. Vibart, for example, he had gone off to the far end of the saloon to sit alone, briefcase on knee, gazing out of the window. We had hardly had a chance to exchange a nod. He had arrived at the last minute in an office car, and had been forced to gallop down to the tender and crawl aboard with scarcely enough time to exchange a wave with his friends and colleagues. But he looked sad and somehow withdrawn in his dark city clothes and broad-brimmed Homburg. Goytz on the contrary looked splendrous but completely relaxed. One might imagine him to be perhaps a great violinist on his way to fulfil an engagement abroad. He had a mysterious leather box which, though somewhat like a gun-case in shape, could easily have housed a master's Stradivarius. Spectacles on nose he benignly if sleepily leafed his way through what looked like a large seed catalogue—though the illustrations were of corpses in various states of prize-winning splendour. But if Vibart looked unhappy and withdrawn how much more so did Baum, the firm's overseas sales representative? He looked as if he were listening intently to his own inner economy and trying to ascertain whether he was going to be sick or not. I went to pass the time of day with him, for he was very sensitive, very Jewish, and quick to imagine that neglect by a senior might be a slight. I found though that his preoccupations, though unusual, had nothing to do with air-sickness. "I am worried about England" he said broodingly, gazing down at as much of it as swam into visibility through the low cloud. "I am worried about the young, Mr. Felix. They are all studying economics. They are all taking degrees in it—you can get them anywhere now. Now you know and I know that economics isn't really a subject at all. But the mental evolutions necessary to study it can easily fix one at the anal stage for the rest of one's life. And people fixed at the anal stage are a danger to humanity, Mr. Felix. Is it not so?" It was. It was.

I agreed seriously with him; his brooding concern for the national fate was so well grounded and so sincere. I wondered if Goytz was fixed at the anal stage . . . and Nash? Or Julian, trotting about with that golden turd in the brown paper parcel? I patted Baum's shoulder in silent sympathy and signalled the steward for another reviver. Benedicta slept, so innocently, so discreetly. If I had to be murdered, I thought, by somebody I would like it to be by somebody like her. Caradoc's voice poured in upon me, raised half a tone against the massive thrum of the great engines as they pushed us across the skies of France. "I haven't wasted my exile one bit" he said exultantly. "Although this trip to Stonehenge nearly killed me with cold. I went down with Pulley and a sextant to take some readings and do some drawings. You know my old interest in deducing a common set of principles for all our architectural constructions? It still stands up, and wherever I touch the matter I get verifications, whether the Parthenon or the Celebes—whether ancient or modern, whether Canberra or Woodhenge. It's as if city-builders had a built-in gyrocompass which pushed them to build in respect to certain cosmic factors like sun, moon and pole."

He sipped his drink and adopted a pleased and somewhat glassy expression as he divagated about megaliths aligned to the sun as early as 1800 B.C.; about early Pole Stars like Vega and Betelgeuse and their influence upon the orientation of cities and temples. "Why," he said regally "Pulley and I even discovered a magnetic field at Stonehenge—a certain place near the centre which gave off enough juice to demagnetise a watch, or make a compass squeal with pain. It's reminiscent of the spot at Epidaurus where the acoustic wave is at its highest and clearest. I hadn't got anything to leave as a marker but my drawings have it. I don't know yet what such a thing might prove. And by the way the same goes for St. Paul's Cathedral—there's a magnetic spot in the main aisle, about where they've sunk that black hexagonal stone. Again I'm not surprised as perhaps I should be. St. Paul's is of course more an engineering feat than any of the other cathedrals and naturally much less aesthetically beautiful. It was built by a great artificer in conscious pursuit of mathematical principles; it was not a dream of godhead full of poetry or frozen music or what not. No, it belonged to its age; it was a fitting symbol for a mercantile country in an age dedicated to reason, hovering on the edge of the Encyclopaedia and the Industrial Revolution. It is no accident that the business part of the city, the moneyed part, grouped itself round this great symbol of the stock and share. Nor is it an accident that it should in some ways feel strongly reminiscent of a railway station—say Euston or Waterloo. It stands as a symbol for the succeeding ages which produced both. But after St. Paul's where do we go? The Dome's rise is like the South Sea Bubble. The Mercantile dream has been shattered. And now the mob has too much pocket money we can expect nothing so much as a long age of bloodshed expressed by the concrete block. It is hard nowadays to distinguish a barracks from a prison or a block of dwellings—indeed I'd go so far as to say it was impossible. They belong to the same strain of thought—Mobego I call it after our old friend Sipple. I wonder if we'll see him in Turkey? It is quite impossible to predict what might come out of it, though one can almost be sure that some sort of universal death by boredom and conformity is being hinted at. And I won't live to see what happens after the blood bath. . . ." He mooned on, slowly drumming himself into innocent slumber with his tongue rocked by the soft drubbing and jolting of the huge plane in the aircurrents of the French mountain-ranges.

I wondered what Julian might make of these considerations. Obviously he would have seen the results of Caradoc's work.

As Benedicta still slept with the new *Vogue* on knee I started to make my way across to Vibart in order to exchange a word with him, but I was waylaid once more by the pensive Baum who motioned me to sit down with the obvious intention of opening his heart to me. I hoped we would not have to dwell any longer on the English nation and its habits, as I had long since given up worrying about it; fortunately not, it was now the turn of the Jews. "I am wondering" said Baum *sotto voce*, looking round to see if we might be overheard "if there isn't a touch of anti-Semitism entering the firm from somewhere. Lately I have been troubled." When Baum was troubled he had a very troubled look indeed. "From where?" I said, longing to break free from what threatened to be a curtain lecture.

"From Count Banubula" he said surprisingly enough, suddenly staring me in the eye in a challenging manner. "Banubula?" I said with genuine puzzlement. Baum nodded with compressed lips and went on slowly, with emphasis. "Yesterday I overheard something in the senior boardroom which made me pause, Mr. Felix. He was there addressing a very large group of salesmen. I don't know what the meeting was about or where they were selling but what he was saying was this: I made a note." Always meticulous, Baum produced a pocket diary with a note in shorthand. He cleared his throat and read in a vague imitation of Banubula's aristocratic drawl the following: " 'Now the foreskin, as everybody knows, is part of the poetic patrimony of man; whether firmly but gracefully retracted or in utter repose it has been the subject for the greatest painters and sculptors the world has known. Reflect on Michelangelo, his enormous range. . . .' " Baum put the book away with pursed lips and said, "That was all I heard because they closed the door, but I was very struck. I wondered if all those salesmen were Jews and whether he was. . . ." I drained my drink and took the dear fellow by the forearm. "Listen," I said, "for Godsake listen Baum. Michelangelo was a Jew. Everybody was a Jew: Gilles de Rais, Petrarch, Lloyd George, Marx and Spender, Baldwin, and Faber and Faber. This much we know for certain. BUT THEY HAVE ALL KEPT THEIR FORESKINS. What you don't know is that Banubula himself is a Jew. So am I."

"He is not. He is Lettish" said Baum obstinately.

"I assure you he is. Ask anyone." Baum looked mollified but in some deeper way unconvinced. He said: "Now that this work of his is so delicate that it is on the Top Secret list one doesn't quite know what he is doing. I hesitate to accuse the firm of course; but with a Lett one never knows where one is." He looked overwrought. I took my leave of him in lingering loving fashion, smoothing out his sleeve and assuring him that everything would be all right. "Above all resist the impulse to become anti-Lettish" I said, and he nodded his acquiescence, though his face still wore a twisted and gloomy expression. He buried himself in his papers with a sigh.

Nor did Vibart seem the less gloomy as he sat looking sideways and down across the clouds to where somewhere slabs of blue sky were beginning to fabricate themselves. "Ah Felix" he said moodily. "Come and sit down; you never answered my letter." I admitted the fact. "It was hard to know what to say; I was sorry. One couldn't just be awkwardly flippant—and flippancy has been our small change up until I ran away, got banged on the head, and wound up in the Paulhaus munching sedatives."

"I had to tell someone" he said. "And I was hoping that you would stay mad and locked up with the information. But it didn't work."

"Heard about Jocas?"

"Of course."

"Are you coming to see him? Or are you on some other mission and just using the firm's transport?" Vibart peered sideways at me and shot me a quizzical twisted look. He said nothing for a long time; then he replied with considerable hesitation. "I deliberately made an excuse to come, a publisher's excuse. But I wanted really to see him once more in the flesh."

"But you know him, have met him."

Vibart sighed. "I knew him without really recognising him as the man who had completely altered my life. I suppose it is a common enough experience—and always a surprising one. But what puzzles me is that in getting me my job with the firm he knew full well that I would be transferring myself to London and taking her with me. Why did he, then, feeling as he did and she did? Why not let me moulder away for another four-year spell in the Consular, rising by slow degrees to a Chancery and some trite Councillorship in Ankara or Polis? When I suddenly heard the truth I closed my eyes and tried to remember this benign little man's face. 'So *that* was *him*,' I said to myself 'all the time *that* was *him*.' All right, it's not good grammar; but the surprise hit me between the eyes. And death was the result. It's so very astonishing that I don't believe it yet. But I want just to look at him for once—my only link with Pia now on earth, Felix. My Goodness, what a sublime trickster life is, what a double-dealer."

His eyes had filled with tears, but he conjured them away manfully by blowing his nose in a handkerchief and shaking his head. He stamped on the floor and cursed, and then all of a sudden turned quite gay. I recognised this feeling: after one has talked out a problem there is no longer the weight of it upon the heart; one can get almost gay, though the situation remains as desperate or as disagreeable as ever. "Now" he said, putting away his handkerchief with an air of decision and clearing his lungs. "Now then. That's enough of that." Poor Vibart and his lovely wife; I felt rather ashamed to have the figure of the reclaimed Benedicta lying asleep in one of the seats back there. But then death . . . ? We were all crawling about like ants on the Great Bed of Ware, choked with our so-called problems; and with this extraordinary unknown staring us in the face. "To hell with death" said Vibart robustly, as if he had read my mind. "It is merely a provisional solution for people who won't take the full psychic charge."

"What on earth's that?"

"To live for ever, of course. Immortality is built-in my dear boy; it's like a button nobody dares to touch because the label has come off it and nobody knows what might happen if one dared to press it. The button of the unknown."

"You are romancing, Vibart."

"Yes: but then no. I am serious." He shot another look at me, pensive and thoughtful, and settled himself deeper in his seat. "The thing is," he said "that things turn into their opposite. For example this man wounded me to the heart, and naturally I hated him—hated him long and with concentrated fury. But after some time the hate began to turn into a perverse kind of affection. I hated him for what he had done, yes; but in the end I was also feeling affectionate, almost grateful for the fact that he had made me suffer so much. Do you see? It was something that was missing from my repertoire, a most valuable experience which I might never have had without him. So now I am ambivalent—love-hate. But I am also consumed with curiosity just to see this chap—this demigod who could hold the future and the happiness of a fellow human being in the palm of his hand. Could administer such advanced lessons in suffering and self-abnegation to others—for I presume that in sending me to the firm in England he knew that I would take her away from him. Did he think more of the firm than of *her*? And was the inner knowledge of this what decided her fate, made her commit suicide, eh?"

What could one add or subtract? These long and furiously debated questions had obviously gnawed him almost away; they were responsible for the new grey-blond hair, thick and dusty, which had given his features a rare glow of refinement. They were equally responsible for his present slimness—for people who don't sleep well usually get thin. He had never, in fact, looked handsomer or in better physical trim; the weary, well-cut features had lost the last suspicion of chubbiness, had become mature, had settled into the final shape which the death-mask alone could now perpetuate. Vibart was complete. (I found myself thinking rather along the lines of a dummy-builder, occupied with the stresses and strains of false bone and ligament, nylon skin.)

"You know" he said "that *we* had a child very late in the day? No? Well we did, or rather perhaps *they* did. At any rate it was too late in the day for Pia for the result was a Mongol—a horrible little thing with flippers. Thank God, it died after a very short time—but there again I am not sure: did it fall or was it pushed? I think Pia did away with it in pure disgust, and I am glad that she did, if she did. And so on. And so on in endless *mélopée*. Ouf! my dear Felix, here I am chewing your ear down to a stub when you yourself have really been through it. I came to share your distrust and terror of the firm after I had been in it awhile, after I had watched your antics, your long battle in and around the idea of a personal freedom which must not be qualified by this Merlin octopus. I too wanted to react against all this moral breast-feeding and might well have run away like you did, in order to hide myself away and start something un-contaminated, something really my own. But I decided that we were looking at it from the wrong point of view. I mean that in thinking of the Firm as a sort of Kafka-like construct exercising pressure on us from without we were wrong; the real pressure was interior, it was in ourselves, this pressure of the unconscious lying within our consciousness like a smashed harp. It is this which we should try and master and turn to some use in the fabrication of . . . well, beauty."

"Lumme!" I said. "Beauty? Define please."

"In the deepest sense Beauty is what is or seems fully congruent with the designs and desires of Nature." We both burst out laughing, like people discovering each other for the nth time in the same maze —instead of finding each other outside the exit, I mean.

"Enough of this" I said and he bowed an apology, his eyes full of laughing exasperation. "Anyway, now it's too late" he went on. "So we must put a firm face on it; here, have a look at this outline will you? Some spy in the industry has unmasked all the activities of the firm in the drug business. Fortunately for us the manuscript was sent to me; they—he must have been unaware that my house was a Merlin subsidiary. So it gave me a chance to look at it and to muse; how much of this do we want out, and what can be done about it if we don't? That is why I am here; the Polis end of the drug business is shrouded in mystery, simply because business methods are so different; abacus-propelled, old man. So I want Jocas to see and judge. That's my excuse anyway."

He absented himself for a while and I took a look through his drug dossier which was written in rather a jaunty journalistic vein which reminded me vaguely of Marchant's minutes—though the paper could hardly have been by him. . . . "Resin of cannabis is collected in various ways including, in Turkey, running through the fields naked to catch it on the bare skin . . . . Cigarettes are dosed with the dried tops, the shoots, or the flower-pistils powdered . . . . As for qat, you must chew leaves or branches of the plant, but smoke while you chew and drink water copiously. In Ethiopia it is mixed in a paste with honey or else dried into a curry powder for use with food. In Arabia the leaf is rolled and smoked. But these are only some of the humbler drugs in which Merlin's has come to deal. The firm has also a virtual corner in Mexican Morning Glory seed— *ololiuqui*. But if the oriental end of the firm handles products which give it rather an old-fashioned air, the London end is fully aware of contemporary standards and demands. The pharmaceutical subsidiaries of Merlin have gone further than any other such organisations. Befotenin, for example, is a drug first found in the skin-glands of toads (the Bufo vulgaris) and also in the leaves of the mimosacea of the Orinoco. This is already finding new medical uses as a hallucinatory snuff, though it is still on the secret list of the firm. Merlin subsidiaries are also working on a protein fraction obtained from the blood serum of schizophrenes which has been named taraxein; injections of this substance induce apparent schizophrenia in monkeys. But most disturbing of all the new secret drugs is Ditran—

which is calculated to be very much more powerful than LSD or Mescalin. . . ."

Here at last I came upon some marginalia in the characteristic handwriting of Marchant. "Ref Ditran. A single dose of 15 mg. rocks the world, old man; for extreme cases in the Paulhaus they supply multiple doses of 30 mg. intramuscularly. God, you should hear them scream! It is so painful and so terrifying that the cures are often instantaneous as Lourdes and often much more general. The author is also slightly out about LSD. When the syndrome gets out of hand chlorpromazine can save the day with 20 to 50 mg. intramuscular doses repeated every thirty minutes—unless the heart gives out."

Vibart was back from his wash and brush up. "Well I see nothing wrong about all this." He lit a cigar and said: "I don't know. It's a question of degree. For example we have launched (under the counter, so to speak) a new cocktail with immense adolescent appeal —equal parts of vodka and *Amanita muscaria* juice—the hallucinogenic mushroom, no less. It's called a Catherine Wheel, after Catherine the Great I suppose who used to mushroom herself insensible in between love-affairs. For my part I just don't know how much of all this should go out or not. We shall see what Jocas thinks, and then what Julian says." He read in a sententious voice a phrase which went: " 'Since earliest times a change of consciousness has been accredited with great healing power; this was recognised since the Eleusinian Mysteries and long before them.' " Then he snapped the MS shut and thrust it back into his glossy briefcase. "We shall see" he said.

Night was falling over the dark sea, the clouds were straining away westward. We had lost altitude and gained the last frail blueness of the evening; softly we came down with an occasional rubbery bump, as if an air bladder had been as often smacked with the flat of the hand, until we were moving along almost in the water. Under us a fresh spring sea tilted and coiled back on itself, it's simply lazy gesturing suggesting all the promise of sunshine which could not long be deferred. The lights went on and turned the outer world to lavender and then to dark purple. We were running along a heavily indented coastline with an occasional mountain pushing its snout into the empty sky. Somewhere a moon was rising. In another hour or so we should be skating and strumming across the Bay of Naples, where the captain had elected to stay the night and refuel. But it was not worth going ashore as his plan was to start on the next leg of the flight a good hour before dawn, to gain as much light as possible for the Greek touch-down which he seemed to regard as rather more chancy than the Naples halt. None of this was our affair; we dined early and slept in our comfortable bunks.

Athens when at last it came was something quite other—at least for me; poised in its violet hollows like some bluish fruit upon the bare branches of night. The day had been brilliantly calm with here and there a mountain in the deep distance showing its profiles of snow, and a sea calmly pedalling away to a ruled horizon. But of course it was not only the old and often-relished beauty of the site, it was really the thronging associations. I suppose that Athens will always be for me what Polis must be for Benedicta—a place as much cherished for the sufferings it inflicted on one as for the joys. I had spent part of my youth here, after all, that confused and rapturous period when everything seems possible and nothing attainable. Here I had lived for a while with Iolanthe—not the semi-mythical star whom we were trying to recreate out of the pulp of rubbers and resins; but a typical prostitute of a small capital, resolute, gay, and beautiful. (I repeated her name to myself in the Greek way, reclaiming the original image of her, while I pressed Benedicta's arm with all the recollected tenderness I felt for this other shadow-woman whom I had not recognised as a goddess when I actually owned her. Was I later to start almost to love her retrospectively, so to speak? And perhaps this is always the way? The amputated limb which aches in winter? I don't know.)

We moved now in a great fat bubble of violet and green sunlight, sinking softly down into the darkening bowl to where the city lay atrembling. The night was darkling up over Salamis way. The outlines were turning to blue chalk, or the sheeny blue of carbon paper. But always the little white abstract dice of the Acropolis held, like a spread sail, the last of the white light as the whole of the rest of the world foundered into darkness. Hymettus turned on its slow turntable showing us its shaven nape. We were just in time. We circled the city and its central symbol in time to see what was to be seen.

Ants waved to us from under the plinth of the Parthenon and Caradoc waved back in a frenzy of amiability—to what purpose I could not discover since nothing could be seen of us save smudges of white. Nevertheless. Meanwhile my eye had taken a swift reading, basing itself upon the plinth, and was racing through the streets to find the little hotel where, in Number Seven, so much of my life had passed. But I was not quick enough; by the time I got my bearing right the street had slid into another and the buildings formed fours, obscuring the site I was hunting for. By now of course we had come down low for our landing, but must perforce carry out a long loop which would take us several miles out to sea, thus enabling us to run landwards into Phaleron and touch down upon its placid waters. Everything went calmly, smoothly; a naval tender full of chattering Greek customs officials carried us joyfully towards the shore, making us feel that we had been anxiously awaited and that our arrival had thrown everyone into ecstasy. It was simply the national sense of hospitality manifesting itself; later on land we started to have trouble with an elderly official but all at once Hippolyta's chauffeur appeared. "Grigorie" we all cried and there was much embracing and dashing away of happy tears. Overcome by our bad Greek and obvious affection for the venerable Grigori the customs people passed us through with bows and smiles. We were in. There were two cars, and after a short confabulation we decided on our various objectives. Caradoc, Benedicta and myself were to go to Naos and stay with the Countess while Vibart elected to spend the night in Athens with the other members of the party.

Caradoc was strangely subdued as we set off; Benedicta peeled a mandarin which a child had handed her; I thought, for no known reason, of the sunken rose-garden with its nodding yellow tea-roses, and of the draughts of music which flowed out into it on those still summer nights when we would sit so late by the cool air which hovered around the hushing lily-pond. It would be too cold to dine out as yet. It was an age since I had seen Ariadne. I asked Grigori how the Countess Hippolyta had been keeping and he shot me a glance in the mirror. "Since Mr. Graphos died," he said "she hardly goes out any more. She is gardening very much and has built a little church for St. Barbara on the property." He paused, racking his brains for something else to tell me, but obviously there was not much. Or perhaps he did not wish to speak too freely before the others. Grigori was a northerner and had rather a fanatical sense of rank and the general proprieties. Chauffeurs should be reluctant to discuss their mistresses, even with old friends. So!

It was dark now, but the house was ablaze with light as we crossed the garden, leaving such luggage as we had to Grigori. She came to the door, she must have heard the engines of the car—Hippolyta, I mean. She stood rather shyly holding it open and gazing short-sightedly into the darkness from which, one by one, her friends—her lifelong friends—would emerge. The greetings were long and tender. Back in the firelight in the huge room with its medieval vaulting one could see how thin she had become.

"Welcome to Naos" she said softly. "O strangers to the Greeks." A quotation doubtless, and perhaps a soft reproof for so long a neglect. "But still out of season" she added, leading us in to divest ourselves of our coats. Yes, the rose-gardens, the green citrons, the oleanders would have to wait until the spring became more generous with its sunlight. But the big awkward country house was gay with light. Fires blazed hospitably in the long vaulted rooms with their oil-paintings of three generations of Hippolytas echoing each other. Degenerate trophies of the past—she had once called them that. The vaulted monastic rooms echoed with our voices. We had a chance to really look at each other. Ariadne, though very much the Countess still, and though transformed by age and experience—as we all had been—registered no really critical change for the worse. She had become thinner, yes, but this only emphasised the new frail boyish-ness of her figure, the slenderness of her arms. But nothing could submerge the dark mischievous Athenian eyes, with their swift sympathies and swifter touches of mirthfulness. The naïveté, the candour, these were there still; and from time to time touched by a kind of lofty sadness. Watching her smiling, and thinking about her love for Graphos the politician, and what it had done to her life: and then of his death—I searched in my mind for a word which might do justice to this new maturity. She had the fruitful, sad yet happy look one sees on the faces of young widows. "Undamaged" I cried aloud, at last; and she gave a tiny shrug.

"I mean you are still living a life" I went on.

Now she laughed out loud and said: "Get thee to a nunnery, Felix, and see how it feels. The boredom! Ouf!"

The servants brought in trays of drinks and olives now, and we pledged each other in the firelight. Once Ariadne had hated Benedicta, but now this feeling appeared to have given place to a warmer one. At any rate she held B.'s hands and shook them until the bracelet of ancient coins on her wrist clicked. Then she said in her frank way: "Once I remember hating you; it was because I was jealous of Felix and sorry for him and you were hurting him. But it didn't go really deep with me. Do you think we could be friends now? Shall we try?" Benedicta, with a word, put an arm round her waist, and together the two slender women walked the long length of the room in sisterly comradeship, saying nothing. I was delighted.

The companionable silence was broken only by a vast and somewhat typical hiccough from Caradoc. "Alcohol provokes the fruitful detonations from which ideas flow. But my digestion is not what it was, I must beware." Ariadne smiled down upon him benignly. "An echo from the past" she said. "For when did whisky never detonate you?"

"I am old, my locks are white" he replied gravely.

But she clapped her hands softly together, saying "No; it is just that we have all changed places, haven't we? The pack has been shuffled. Everyone will be going round counter-clockwise now. I expect the good to get badder and bad to get gooder; except in the exceptional cases—where one or other have got up enough momentum to stop the pendulum. Then if bad, they will achieve greatness by becoming horrible, unspeakable. If good they will become angels. What do you say to that?" In the calm of the great country house such propositions did not sound what they perhaps were—a trifle sententious.

"All change for the worse" said Caradoc testily. "Why since last we met I have been dead in Polynesia. I have been a bigamist, a trigamist, and heaven knows what else. I have been unrepentantly happy, Ariadne, and still am. I am just in the right mood to build Jocas the mausoleum he wants."

"Good Lord" she said. "Has he started all over again, poor darling

Jocas? There's an echo for you. Do you remember the last time?" She laughed and replenished Caradoc's drink. He too gave his histrionic lion's roar and slapped a knee. "Damn him, yes" he said. "He wanted nothing less than the Parthenon. At least he wanted the Niki temple—I just had to add a few rooms to that for members of the Merlin triple and he would have been quite happy. The ass!"

I remembered in a vague and indeterminate fashion the movement and bustle—and not less the mystery—of this long ago period. I had first met Caradoc here, in this house, and had subsequently spent a night in a brothel called the Blue Danube with him—a brothel run by Mrs. Henniker of all people, and where Iolanthe herself had worked for a while before being swept away on the wings of good fortune into the world of the film.

"I simply never got to the bottom of that business" I said. "Nobody would explain anything."

"Nobody could; or rather everybody thought something quite different. We were misled by Julian and also by Graphos. I only pieced it together slowly over the years. I don't think even Benedicta knew what was going on; all she knew was that you were in some sort of danger in Polis—you were then regarded as quite expendable, since the firm had complete possession of your notebooks. Yes, but here in Athens something else was going on; first of all a tug-of-war between Julian and Jocas, all over this blasted temple. Julian, as you know, had set his heart on getting control of the Parthenon for the firm. Now of course it's a *fait accompli*, everyone is used to it, but then . . . where would he find a politician daring enough or crooked enough to sign a secret protocol vesting the Parthenon and the hill it stands on in Merlin's? Of course Graphos was the obvious choice, but he demanded a very heavy price, partly out of patriotism and partly out of personal greed. On the one hand Merlin's must wipe out the National Debt, on the other rig an election to get him in as Prime Minister and keep him in until he had invested a personal fortune in Switzerland. They all told me lies: Graphos said he was saving the Parthenon from Julian, not selling it behind my back. Jocas, getting wind of this, wanted to walk off with the temple of Niki. That would have given the show away, so he had to be stopped. Julian did it somehow. But then came another complication. You remember a small, rather despicable figure called Sipple, the ex-clown? Caradoc does. He admired him extravagantly I remember. Well Sipple got wind of the protocol from some indiscretion of Caradoc and rang me up, hinting at blackmail. Silly fool . . . one word would of course have ruined Graphos. So Sipple had to be neutralised and sent away. We did that, and we were lucky to be aided by a personal scandal which made the little spy anxious to leave Athens and hide away somewhere. There, that is my story, at any rate. How right and how wrong I don't know. I still don't know."

"It was all my fault" said Caradoc.

I thought vividly of the boy with his throat cut lying on his side in Sipple's bed; of the birds beginning to chirp and preen as the dawn came up over the Salamis sealine; I saw Sipple standing there in his braces with traces of clown's makeup still on his face, round the eyes. I thought of Iolanthe who had committed the murder. It was unbelievable really. Unbelievable.

"It's all like a dream" I said.

"So much is. Time plays such strange tricks. Do you remember the old brothel, the Blue Danube, Caradoc?"

"Of course" he said robustly. "How could I ever forget what it taught me from the great book of life?"

"Well," said Ariadne "the other day I was driving along the corniche and I suddenly thought of you; I was passing the place in the car and I decided to stop and look at it. But my dear, *it had gone*. There was nothing but an empty sand dune where this quite considerable villa had once stood. I could hardly believe my eyes. I stopped the car and started to search like a lunatic. I knew the spot like the back of my hand. No good. There was nothing there. Yes, by dint of poking about in the sand I uncovered a few pieces of plaster and the tracing of what might have been a bit of foundation . . . yes, but an archaeologist would not have dated it as different from the old pieces of the Themistoclean wall one sees down towards Phaleron. *Gone!* The windows, the doors, the cupboards, the beds . . . all vanished. Even the *house* had vanished. What do you make of that? I wondered if there weren't gaps like that in the middle of our memory, vanished people and events. I felt so awful that I had to lean against a wall. I was very nearly sick when I thought of you and Felix moving from room to room there. I suddenly thought of you as if you were dead. So long ago, all of it." She repeated the phrase in Greek in her low musical voice, and then added under her breath, "And death behaves in such an arbitrary fashion, striking when you are not looking, not expecting."

"I refuse to be sad" said Caradoc. "May my dying breath be a giddy oath, that's all I can say." Benedicta patted his hand reassuringly as if to comfort him.

Ariadne turned to me and in a lower register said: "I saw a good deal of Julian, of all people; he was in Switzerland when I was. To my surprise he decided to manifest and was most attentive in his strange way. You are building him some sort of echo of her— Iolanthe—aren't you? He told me and I felt suddenly alarmed. Not for the fact but from his way of speaking about it. What has come over Julian? He seems to have lost his devil, to have become somehow subdued. For example he said in a sweet resigned sort of way: 'Obviously Felix will betray me when he can' and I wondered whether he was serious or not. As for what you are building, any Greek would warn you against *hubris*—tempting the wrath of the Gods. . . ."

"The Gods are all dead, or gone on holiday" I said gloomily. "They've left their looms and spindles behind for us to use as we see fit. Has Julian really changed so much?"

"Yes. A sort of resignation. 'The firm has given and the firm has taken away; blessed be the name of the firm.' " She intoned softly but mockingly with her arms crossed on her breast. "No Felix. Some new element has entered the picture. Julian has become so *human*!" I don't know why, but the remark seemed to me to be one of the most sinister I had ever heard. It was ridiculous, of course, but a sort of shiver ran down my neck. I looked over at Benedicta and saw, or thought I saw, that she herself had turned quite white; but it may only have been her hair, the candlelight. "Human" I said, turning the word over like a playing-card and gazing at its face, so to speak. Spades or hearts, which? There was a silence broken only by Caradoc's champing of celery. He was not paying the least attention to what was said.

Ariadne went on. "He told me a great deal of his last long wait by her bed all that night when she was dying—the last night. How he felt so crazy with grief and surprise, so unhinged that he found himself doing strange thing like making up his lips in the mirror with her lipstick. It terrified him but he felt compelled to do it. And then the lines of Heine kept going through his mind, his lips moved, he kept repeating them to himself in a whisper, over and over again, quite involuntarily. Do you know them, remember them? The Faustus ones?

> "*Du hast mich beschworen aus dem Grab*
> *Durch deinen Zauberwillen*
> *Belebtest mich mit Wollustglut—*
> *Jetzt kannst du die Glut nicht stillen.*
>
> *Press deinen Mund an meinen Mund;*
> *Der Menschen Odem ist göttlich!*
> *Ich trinke deine Seele aus,*
> *Die Toten sind unersättlich.*
>
> *You conjured me from my grave*
> *By your bewitching will,*
> *Revived me for this passionate love,*
> *A passion that you'll never still.*
>
> *Press your cold mouth on my cold mouth;*
> *Man's breath's by the Gods created.*
> *I drink your essence, I drink up your soul,*
> *For the dead can never be sated.*"

A silence fell once more, in which the tenebrous and perverted verses of the returned Helen talking to her Faust echoed on impressively in the mind, vibrated on the heart; lighting up with their fitful shadow play the figure of Julian crouched there batlike in a clinic chair, watching a fly moving upon a dead eyeball. A picture to inspire both pity and despair. Ariadne went on in a low voice: "It was clear that only some sort of vampire would do for him—nothing less."

Benedicta pressed her hands to her cheeks and said: "I know, Ariadne. I know only too well. But he has had reason enough to become what he is; I tell myself always that it should still be possible to love him despite it all. But I don't know whether I can myself any more. I don't know whether I can. And who else will? It's all so unlucky, so meaningless."

A draught blew in from a window and the candles wagged and danced on the long refectory table; we were quite startled, as if in some intangible way it was the breath of Julian which had entered the room, attracted perhaps by the verses or by the mention of his name. "An unquiet ghost" she said in Greek, and shivering drew her shawl about her shoulders. The impression of some such silent visitation was slightly heightened when, in a little while, the telephone began to peal in the depths of the house, insistent as a child calling. Ariadne went out into the hall to answer it while we took our cigars and coffee back to the warm firelight in the outer room. We sat down, each absorbed in the thoughts set in motion by the verses of Heine and the mood they evoked. Presently Hippolyta came back and said: "The firm is calling you from London; they've traced you here. Shall I say you are out or in bed?"

"Why?" said I, "I'll see what they want."

I went out into the hall where the little phone booth stood; it had been converted from a satin-lined sedan chair. Inevitably the line was poor and the voices were criss-crossed with whirrs and clicks—it was like talking across the reverberations of some giant sea-shell. But yes, it was Nathan, waiting patiently for me. "It's Mr. Marchant, sir. He has been asking for you rather urgently. Hold on while I put you through to him."

Marchant sounded testy, as if he had been called out of bed in the middle of the night; and yet relieved. "I wouldn't have bothered you," he said "only Julian told me I should try and make contact and tell you that we've had rather a nasty accident on our hands here."

"Iolanthe!" I cried, my heart beating faster from sheer anxiety. "What has happened to her?"

"No. No" said Marchant. "It's the man, Adam. He's a total wreck, a write-off I fear; but he's gone and killed poor old Rack-straw, of all people. Completely unexpected."

It could not well have sounded more astonishing, more improbable. "But how? Where?"

Marchant sighed with exasperation and said: "You know we had orders to let old Rackstraw into the lab to acclimatise himself to Iolanthe, and to test any reactions he might have. It was Julian's idea; I wasn't keen on it but he said he'd discussed it with you and that you had seen no reason why not. Well, anyway, we drew a blank from the point of view of reactions. The old boy simply stared at our girl-friend for ages without moving a muscle; I think he would have gone on for ever had he not been led away by Henniker. Incidentally the effect on her was terrific; I have never seen anyone cry so hard and so long and so passionately. She kept saying 'My God, she's so real' over and over again and going into paroxysms, leaning against the wall. She is hardly calm as yet and they've been visiting us in the lab every day for a few hours. The old boy just hissed and croaked and wagged his eyebrows; but really they'd drawn a blank with him. He kept asking about the whereabouts of a chap called Johnson, that was all. Then yesterday we got so used to him standing there motionless that when I went to lunch Said forgot to lock up; or rather he just went out of the lab for a second overlooking the fact that Rackstraw was still there. The next thing is he heard a crash and smelt a roasting smell. He rushed back to find Rackstraw rolling all over the floor like a centipede with this Adam creature wrapped round his neck; it was what you'd call a muscular reflex with a vengeance. I don't know what he could have been trying to do but he was badly burnt and concussed and covered with Ejax into the bargain. Well, Said gave the alarm, and of course we had some difficulty over the current, the dummy had become live. But anyway they finally turned everything off and disentangled Rackstraw who was led away to hospital. The next thing we heard in the middle of the night was that he had died of heart-failure. It's being hushed up, the whole episode, and presented as a normal death—heaven knows it was about time; he'd long overstayed his welcome, the old man. But Julian said that you ought to be told. There is a bit of electrical damage to the big feeder but that can be repaired. Otherwise we are moving along; you will have to make a much stronger temperature control stat. or else she will overheat, and then she's likely to write free verse: I suppose as any normal person might do in a delirium. It all happened yesterday. She lost optimum temperature control and committed a poem. Felix, are you there still?"

"Yes. I was thinking of Rackstraw. Poor old thing. Is the dummy completely smashed, irrecoverable?" Marchant thought for a moment. "Yes" he said, but doubtfully. "But the funny thing is that Julian has told us to stop work on it and get on with Io. I had a funny sort of feeling that in a way he was almost jealous of the mate. He said 'We don't really *need* a male dummy do we?' He said it in a funny sort of voice, too, kind of complacent and rather pleased—unless of course I am romancing, which I don't think. Indeed when I spoke of trying to recover the outline drawings of Adam with a view to rebuilding he looked extremely peeved and told me sharply to lay off and consign the plans to the wastepaper basket. So there. The funeral was yesterday afternoon. I don't believe anybody went except Julian. I didn't, though I am sorry for the old sod. Anyway, I have told you all and done my duty. There is nothing else to report unless you would like to hear the fever-verses that Iolanthe produced yesterday. First verses from beyond the grave, my boy, and not half bad. I thought of sending them to a paper."

"Have you got them on you?"

"Just a sec. Yes, I have."

"Read them, then."

It was a strange feeling to hear these dissociated ramblings which had been produced by a simple temperature rise; was it an illusion or did they make a strange kind of sense, perhaps "poetic" sense—since poetry isn't a stock report on experience, or written for a seed catalogue. (So I have been told.)

> *Just supposing because*
> *death is never too fervent*
> *though water suffer little damage*
> *and women have a descriptive function*
> *simple conjectures about loving*
> *in adolescence sweet and turbid*
> *brief caption on the love-box merely,*
> *will announce her engagement to spring*

or winter or one of its forms, yes,
its memory kicks back and throbs
if bivouacked on Windermere
made one with the ferny forms.
All and none of these functions
would be valid, a cause for surprise
when reality is so taut and gnomic,
digestible and without unction,
all and none, I say, all and none.
just supposing because, now
surely every allowance should be made for such things?

"Bravo" I said, but in a confused puzzled sort of way. The line went dead. The roaring in the sea-shell stopped.

Somewhat to my surprise they had all taken themselves off to bed save Ariadne who was waiting up for me; she sat, lost in thought, and gazing into the fire. I poured myself another drink and joined her—extremely depressed by the story of poor Rackstraw. I had got quite fond of him, of using him as a sort of touchstone for my own sanity in the Paulhaus where, at a certain time, I even placed Benedicta among the disorderly figments of my own waking dreams. Fancy to find when I woke that she was really there, in my arms! Not just a daymare. "Thinking?" I said and she: "Yes. A lot of muddled and inconsequent thoughts—what a jumble. Thinking about you all with an affectionate concern—it's allowable in a friend, no?"

"Concern, Ariadne?"

"Yes. For example this new Benedicta—she's suddenly normal, sensible, in full possession of herself; won't you find her diminished, less interesting than the other?"

I groaned. "My God, you aren't wishing me another long spell of misery with her are you?"

"But the whole mystery must have gone."

"Thank God it has, if its only manifestation is in hysteria. Besides, she's exactly how I wanted her, always imagined her. I almost invented her. It was written on the package so to speak; if the contents were different there was many a good reason. We now know the reason. But when I fell for her I saw the possible person embedded in the witch. I fell for the blueprint of what she might be. It was a terrific gamble, but I've won, don't you see? Ariadne, you've always thought of me as one of nature's mother-fixated cuckolds who revelled in his suffering; but it doesn't go very deep, my masochism. You must have misjudged the issue."

She looked at me with smiling relief tinged with doubt. "And you don't hate Julian any more?"

"How can I now I can see him in close-up? His life has been such a calamity, and the type of genius he was given was a catastrophic gift for someone condemned to impotence."

She put her hand on my cheek and I kissed it. "You are an ass" I said. "I'm sorry" she replied, and then went on. "Strange how we ascribe fixed qualities to ourselves—and really we are only what others think of us: a collection of others' impressions merely."

We sat a long time in silence now, smoking and pondering. Vague thoughts passed through my mind like shoals of fish. I thought of the effect that her love for Graphos had had on her life. Then of a sudden a fragment of my intuition stirred and an original thought made its appearance which was disturbing and upsetting. It was: "Ariadne has outlived the death of Graphos now, it has melted, with all the luxurious pain and emptiness it conferred. She is now in mortal danger of relinquishing her hold on life, of dying from pure *ennui*." I took her hand as if to hold her back, as if to prevent her slipping downstream. And as if to confirm and echo this dispiriting thought she said: "We can't believe it, can we? That we are all condemned, that it's only a matter of time? Death is something we accept as part and parcel of others. Why do we never get used to it in regard to ourselves? O the boredom of waiting! One has the impulse to race towards it, get it over." There! I had no consolations to offer; neither love nor opium ever really meet the case. For a pure scientist and an impure man—how to steer a safe course between the inconsequent and the outrageous?

We said goodnight; Ariadne spent all her mornings in bed reading, and would not be awake when the cars came for us at nine. She opened a window to purge the room of its cigarette smoke. The smell of lemons came in out of the darkness like a friendly animal. We did not know when we would meet again—if ever.

We had been put in the room with the ikons and the heavy old-fashioned beds; the sheets were of coarse island linen. Prison-bars on the windows. By the light of a single guttering candle Benedicta slept, her pale blonde head on her arm; so utterly motionless was she that she might have been dead. I climbed in beside her. She was naked and deliciously warm. She turned in her drowsing and asked me about the telephone call, and I told her of the death of Rackstraw and the destruction of the model. This awakened her. She stared at the ceiling for a long moment, and then at me. Then she said: "There! You see?" as if the mishap proved something, as if she had foreseen it. "But I wish to God it had been the dummy of Iolanthe. That would have solved something."

I was outraged. "Darling," I said "take pity on me. You aren't developing a jealousy of my poor dummy, are you?"

"In a perverse way yes. I expect you will want to sleep with it out of curiosity one day— to see how real it is, to compare it with me perhaps." My breath was taken away by this scandalous statement. "With Iolanthe?" I said in tones of mortal injury. "And why not?" she went on, talking to herself almost. "It must stir up all the most perverse instincts. Wait, vampirism. I know exactly what Nash would say."

Ah! so did I, so did I. And not merely the matter but the manner as well—oblique regard of the cuttlefish, fussy voice and so on. And the ideas all neatly laundered and folded by courtesy of Freud. (Now *him* I love for his modesty, his hesitancy, his lack of a dog-matic theology; it is what poor Nash has done to him that I con-demn, avaunt, conspue.) Anyway I had a long dream colloquy with him in which I manfully defended my dear dolly against the pene-trating criticism of this marvellous but as yet incomplete science. Ah, the infantile theory with its congeries of undigested impulses jump-ing about in the mud like fish leaping from the subconscious water. Who was I, poor Felix, to deny the double fantasy—both of birth and of coprophilia: the faecal matter which the infant will one day knead into cakes, and then from cakes, into sugar dollies and statues of bronze and stone? Yes, but dead dollies these. Ah, there we were —poor Iolanthe for ever dead, for ever part of the *merde*, that cosmic element which makes up the *Weltanschauung* of the groping analyst;

element in which the poor fellow struggles waist high, holding his nose, and yet convinced on the basis of the evidence that what he is slithering about in is really gold. GOLD, remark you—the cement of a basic material value which binds together the shabby cultural brickwork of the times. The citizen's toy and talisman, the giver's gift and the receiver's wafer. . . . Gold, bread, excitement and increment pouring from the limited company of the dreaming big intestine. And then, via the same nexus of associated ideas direct from the chamber-pot to Aphrodite, the austere and terrible and mindless, her sex tolling like a bell. What a vision of judgement for a simpleton like Felix . . . I heard Marchant singing at his work!

> *O, O, O,*
> *You great big beautiful doll.*

Benedicta stirred in her sleep, dreaming no doubt of the scarlet Turkish slippers she had promised herself, of the slices of holy muslin out of which she would make a ballgown. Softly breathing as she circumnavigated those vast and shadowy fields of sleep—the other reality which is a mirror image of our own. A living corpse like myself suffering only from the *beta* decay of the world within us. (The wish to die together is the image of the wish to lie together.)

And then all the shaggier motives which wake and howl like ravening mastiffs after dark. Through them I could align my faecal image of the ideal Aphrodite with everything that woke and stirred in the bestiaries of necrophilia, in the huge syllabaries of vampirism. Sliding, sliding the good ship Venus through the conundrum of the *anus mundi*, plop into the ocean where time has run wild: to circle the huge constipated Sargasso of the reason and melt at last into the *symbolon tes gennesiois*, the symbol of rebirth which Plato knew was the sea, cloaca of the archetypal heart. ("The grave so longed for is really the mother's bed." "All right, Nash, I take your point.")

And then of course a natural and completely ineradicable sadism is always inflamed by the thought of communion with a dead body— partly because of the helplessness of the latter: it cannot defend itself: "lie down, dead dolly, and come across": and also partly, but much more important is the idea (so firmly implanted) that the dead

216

mistress cannot be wearied by excessive caresses. In death there is no satiety. Yet beyond the foetal pose and the faecal death the mystery of decomposition offers the promise of renewal, of a new life for dolly. Grave Aphrodite, formed from the manure out of which we are all constructed, has coaxed the gift of fertility—for manure also nourishes; death is defied by a change of code, of form. The smoking midden is also of this world, of this culture, of our time—indeed of all time. The compost generates another life, another echo, to defy with its heat the fateful laws of decomposition, of dissolution.

"You groaned, my darling, in your sleep."

"A nightmare; I dreamed we were at the World's Fair and I bought you a pretty sugar doll. And you ate it, crunch, and the paint ran all over your tongue, turning it scarlet. And when we kissed my lips grew bloody too."

Somewhere a dog barked, and the wind lightly shuffled the sleeping trees; listening hard I thought I could perhaps discern the sound of the sea. I rose mechanically and lit a candle under one of the little ikons in the niche; other eyes in other corners woke and winked. Then I got back into bed and took her in my arms. The pretty seizures of the love act brought us once more to comfort, to wholeness and at last to sleep—a sleep so innocent that it seemed we had invented it for ourselves, as the only fitting form of self-expression.

Tomorrow would be Turkey. Tomorrow would be Turkey.

* * * * *

So we embarked on the next long leg of our journey, skimming over the taut and toothy ranges of the northern chain of mountains—much higher now, and a good deal snowier; although we in our heated cabin were blissfully warm and were made welcome by innocent morning clouds, soft cirrus. No boundaries to this airy world save the very last peaks stretching out their necks like upward flying geese. Then at long last, clearing them, we moved down once more to a lower octave over an evening sea which played quietly, half asleep. Water and sky here divided the lavender dusk, parted and shared its clouds, and presaged a spring nightfall.

Here somewhereabouts scouts came out of the sky to salute us—grim visages staring out of the fighter-planes like Mongolian dummies; faces like medieval armoured knights' of the Japanese Middle Ages. Yes, but they were all smiling and beckoning, and they wished us softly down until we landed in a dense whacking of waves and great spools of white foam, almost under the heroic bridge itself. Through this thick water we taxied like mad, hunting for a windless lea which might let us moor safely.

We had taken it all in, however: there had been time and light enough: the huge thickets of spars moving in soft unison, the beetle-grooves carved by the tankers and small brigantines upon the blue skin of the gulf. It was sunset, too, and blowing fresh and keen from Marmara. And my goodness, how sinister it all felt to me as I sat smoking and gazing down upon the long walls once more—the long irregular buckler of hide or mud-daubed osier such as savages might run up about a stockade. From a great height they looked absurdly flimsy but as we scaled down out of the sky the whole mass began to take up a denser stance, obdurate and threatening: and softly the tulips rose like the horns of shy snails, to take the colours of the sinking sun upon their pale skins. Benedicta, leaning at my side, stared down with me; her nostrils dilated a little, and with an expression of mingled horror and anticipation, of nostalgia and regret, upon her pale face. We were swimming together once more into the great tapestry of Polis—and at a certain moment, quite precisely, everything spun round as if on a jeweller's turntable, to present its profile: fused into the single dimension of an old shadow-play manipulated by the fingers of some great invisible shadow-master.

The journey had been tiring; everyone had been grumpy, out of sorts, in some way or another. Vibart buried himself in his papers, was off-hand with me and non-committal. I had the feeling that he was angry with himself for confessing as much as he had to me on the day before—I know not why. Caradoc too was in a scolding mood, and only the promise of a glass of authentic *raki* or *mastika* seemed to give him a hope. I think in a way all our thoughts had begun to turn one way, to quest out towards that long bare headland where, among the jumble of forts and kiosks and shattered palaces—the fabled Avalon of old Merlin's dream—somewhere out there Jocas, the brother, was waiting for us. I suppose that Benedicta must have read my thoughts for she said softly, echoing in a strange way the recent thoughts of Ariadne: "We tend to forget it, but people do have this awful tendency to die."

"Come. Come" said Caradoc peevishly. "You will never console me in this way. Cut out all this nonsense."

It was natural that in this developing gloom, this heavy preoccupation with what waited for us, I should take refuge in Baum: for he had business of his own, he was not heading for Avalon as the rest of us were. The town itself was his objective. Yet even he was depressed in a smaller way, though of course his behaviour was exemplary. I was soon to learn the reason. It was our good friend Banubula who was causing him anguish. "You see," he said "I am disquieted because the Count has begun to hunger for the power to initiate. So long as he was quietly working for the firm his role was a fulfilling and useful one. But now . . . you see Mr. Marchant has played this dirty trick on him and he has taken it seriously. And the awful thing is that it has *become* serious. The thing is launched. You must never joke in the hearing of the firm, Mr. Felix, because the firm takes everything deadly seriously."

"What dirty joke, Baum?"

"Fresh sperm" said Baum moodily, poking his ear with a long spatulate fingernail, as if to clear it. "Fresh sperm!"

"What is that all about?" I asked, perplexed.

"Mr. Marchant was very drunk and he said that the latest findings of the chemical section showed quite clearly that the only really nourishing skin-tonic for women was fresh male sperm. This is all very well, Mr. Felix, but he went on to add that there was really nothing to stop the firm marketing the stuff if only it could be collected on a large enough scale; and of course if one paid for it well enough one would be able to get as much as one wanted from private producers—just like any other commodity in our modern civilisation. From donor to factory, at controlled temperatures, presented (according to Mr. Marchant) hardly more complicated a problem than picking lavender and taking it to the perfumery. This was very wicked of him; he should have known how gullible the Count is. But he should also have known that the firm takes everything very seriously indeed. Just what Mr. Marchant envisaged I have no idea— I suspect he had none himself when he made the joke; it was simply to tease his friend. On the face of it the idea is mad—thousands upon thousands of people making this sort of contribution to a factory which fills up phials with it and markets the product. On the other hand, as Marchant said, conserved sperm was already used in artificial insemination, why not in skin-food? I was of course horrified when Count Banubula told me this; but what is worse the whole thing was set out as a memorandum and discussed by the chemistry board, and *passed*. I could hardly believe my ears when I heard. Not only that, a subsidiary called Lovecraft Products had been set up, and a subscription list for willing donors has been opened. Moreover it shows every sign of sweeping the continent. Can you imagine it, hundreds of thousands of males all over the world selling their . . . product? And yet the chemical group say that they can sort and grade it, keep it in a temperate emulsion form, and distribute it to all who seek beauty through skin-tonics. I must admit I was sharp with the Count when I saw what had happened. But he produced a number of disingenuous arguments in which is immediately recognised the drunken hand of Mr. Marchant. Why, he said, was it any worse than the sale of Chinese or Malayan hair by the women of underprivileged nations? Why should the overprivileged nations be denied the right to part with their surplus—assuming it was a surplus? At any rate, whatever my own reservations, the scheme has gone ahead so fast that I fear it will get out of hand; so many donors have joined that new factories have been opened and the whole project has had to be twice re-financed by the Germans and Americans. Meanwhile, too, all the letterpress and the advertising devised by the Count and Lord Lambitus I find distasteful to a degree. Look."

He whipped out his briefcase and groped about in it, to extract at last a thick batch of letterpress which bore the unmistakable imprint of Banubula's innocent genius. I was surprised that Marchant was the author of the jest which the firm had so swiftly turned to profit. It was the sort of thing Caradoc might have done, but not Marchant. Yet here it was.

Nor was it hard to see and to sympathise with poor Baum's misgivings, for he was in the advertising and promotion department, charged to dish out all these pamphlets and advertisements to a weary world. They were designed both to attract new donors ("Why not give your all for Lovecraft and be in the swim? You can make a fortune if you work at it. Study our bonus scheme. Moreover it's work you can do at home in your own time. Why not have fun with the firm? Take life in hand and double your income" etc. etc.); and also to appeal to a gullible beautician's market ("The safest natural skin-food, so kind to the thirsty pores") . . . but why go on? I could see that Banubula's literary side had been quite carried away by the whole scheme.

Baum had been scanning my face as I read in order to gloat sympathetically on my expressions of horror. "You see?" he said, as I handed back all the gaudy letterpress. I did. "Moreover" he went on "I have been sent out here to try to sound out the Turks, to get them interested in the scheme as possible donors. Of course everything has its market value, Mr. Felix—I would be the first to admit that. But there are dangers here, we might make a mistake. The Turks are Moslems and deeply religious—suppose we started a holy war without meaning to, eh? I prefer simpler, more material ideas; I like to know where I stand. Now when Lord Lambitus proposed marketing whips in gold *lamé* I saw the possibilities instantly. But this could prove to be . . . well, grotesque! I am supposed to meet the religious leaders tomorrow to outline the scheme. I am much afraid of what might happen. How, for example, will all this stuff translate into Turkish, eh? One doesn't know. I don't want to die with a spear through me just for encouraging Turks to . . . well, market their product through Merlin's. Yet on the other hand it's my duty to obey orders." He sighed heavily. I wondered whether he was wearing a bullet-proof waistcoat.

There was no time, however, for long-drawn-out commiserations for by now the officials had come aboard, clucking like hens, and stamped our passports. Long strings of coloured lights had demarcated the outlines of the bay; the nether sky was still molten but cooling fast, like the steel lid of a furnace. Out of the nearby darkness a large white pinnace whiffled once, and then, at a signal from a man in uniform, began to sidle towards us sideways—like a smart cat.

Our belongings sorted and our various destinations decided upon, we crawled aboard her—Benedicta, Caradoc and I. The others had other duties and would spend the damp Turkish night in the magnolia-scented gloom of the Pera. But Vibart? "I thought you were coming with us?" But he had made one of those inexplicable volte-face. "So did I" he said. "And now suddenly I'm not. I'm not even sure I shall come and see Jocas—I don't seem to need to any more. It came over me just as we hit the water." He looked suddenly elated, his smile had grown younger, more self-confident. "I shall walk about Polis tonight and think myself over" he said, and with a brief nod joined the others in the pilot's launch. I was curious enough to want to question him further, but Benedicta pulled softly at my sleeve and I desisted.

The wind was fresh as we came out of the sea, but the sturdy little pinnace rode sharp at fifteen knots. In the comfortable little cabin with its smart leather-upholstered seats we found a small insect-like man dressed in white who turned out to be the doctor who was looking after Jocas. He spoke only French, and he smoked very slowly and thoughtfully as he spoke. He held the white bone cigarette holder in a tiny clawlike hand which suggested that of a mantis. But what he had to say to us disabused us immediately of any notions we might have had about astrology and destiny and suchlike. Unless of course the progress chart could accurately trace the course of a long-drawn out metastasis. It was our old friend, the contemporary scourge. On the other hand he said: "He is weak, but in very good courage, in spite of knowing the truth. But the place is in an awful mess and needs clearing out. He has got rid of many of the servants and has more or less moved in with his birds. *C'est gênant* from the medical point of view—washing him and so on." We were silent now for the rest of the journey. B. looked at her fingers. Caradoc contented himself with a heavy sigh from time to time. The little doctor sat watching us and smoking and reflecting. The journey seemed to last an age. But finally our nose sank into still water, we throttled down and softly ebbed along a dark landing stage where a figure from the past—the old eunuch of my first visit—stood holding a lantern high above his head and giving the Islamic greeting to the darkness. Mouth, forehead and shoulder, mouth, forehead and shoulder. But even when we stepped ashore he gave no intimate signs of recognition—perhaps because Benedicta had her head done up in a scarf. He did not at any rate recognise me. We huddled ashore in the humid darkness to the slapping and slobbering of water along the wooden piers. A sense of desolation invaded me, I do not know exactly why. One felt that everything here had run down, gone to seed—but how one could feel such a thing when one was surrounded by darkness I really cannot imagine. Perhaps the little doctor's few brief words had prepared us for such a thing. At any rate, leaving our baggage we followed the majordomo with his hissing white light, the doctor leading us. The paths had been marked out with little kerosene lamps which faltered here and there in the wind; but they gave hardly any light, and were simply markers upon which to orient ourselves. Uprooted trees and creepers and bushes lay about beside the path, and once a couple of starved-looking mongrels emerged from the dark to sniff at us and retire. I thought of the fine pack of hunting dogs with their lustrous fur which had been Jocas' pride in the old days; they would have simply wolfed mongrels like these, or driven them into the sea.

The air of desuetude must have been largely imagined, then, for we could take in few details until we reached the cypress glades with their kiosks. The eunuch was talking now to the doctor, with a soft high clucking voice; it appeared that a once elaborate electrical lighting scheme which illuminated everything, had recently foundered owing to a faulty generator, and that nobody had bothered to have it repaired. He wagged his huge bald head in resigned disapproval. "You will see" said the doctor.

There was more light in the two villas with their cracked windows and starred mirrors—but the smell of kerosene was everywhere. The flagged floors were full of chicken bones and unswept feathers. We were asked if we would eat first—indeed in the old salon a table had been clumsily laid with a dirty tablecloth (of the finest Irish linen), several branches of dribbling candles and a solitary bunch of dusty artificial grapes in a cracked plate of alabaster. Here the stink of the birds warred with the kerosene. The walls showed cracks. The door jambs heaved and creaked—the sea salt had been at them. There was a swallow's nest in one corner of the room.

But it was to Jocas that we were going, and he had apparently moved out lock, stock and barrel into the old shot tower—on the eastern ramparts of what had once been a fort with a high keep overlooking the gulf. Here in the old days he had spent his time delecting in a huge marine telescope pitched on a low tripod. Sitting in a deck chair, pausing only to eat an olive from time to time, Jocas could follow the whole movement of the shipping in the gulf below. But to gain access to this martello one had to walk along a crazy broken parapet built along the sea-face of the headland; a ruined staircase which Benedicta as a girl had come to know as "The Battlements of Elsinore".

On this stone ramp we embarked in single file. I could hear the squinch of my rubber soles on the stone. Hereabouts too an occasional lemon-yellow lizard darted for cover—they are always first to emerge with the spring sunlight. But the climb was steep. Smell of thyme. So at last we crossed a walled courtyard, skirting an uncoped well disguised by tall thistles, and then climbed on to a balcony and opened a huge door.

It couldn't have been much smaller than a good-sized parish church, the room in which Jocas had taken up residence; but the height of it was such that the upper shadows pressed upon the lighted areas like a whole sky of darkness. One expected to see stars upon that black damascened darkness. For the rest it was a robbers' cave from some old fairy tale. A huge fire of thorns blazed in one corner. Branches of candles and small oil lamps picked out and punctuated the foreground where the figures of men and boys worked and moved. Wait. We stood upon the threshold and gazed into this cave with its dark flapping shadows, expectantly, hesitantly. We had come at an inconvenient moment. An enormous Victorian hip bath was being filled with steaming water by a small boy while two other shapes were carrying a shrunken form from the bed towards it—the figure you'd say of a large white frog, legs spread apart. The bed itself was enormous and hung about with a dark red velvet baldaquin whose ropes bore the unmistakable signs, even in that erratic light, of greasy hands. The curtains were drawn back. Jocas therefore advanced towards us, carried by four arms, helpless as a child, but cheerfully smiling; the smiling languor of the small infant longing for the surcease of hot water. It had a powerful resonance this sudden glimpse—like some sombre oil painting of the Spanish school. Moreover there was enough light here on the ground to take in the dirty deal tables, the flagged floor covered in droppings of bats and birds, the smashed windows.

Our natural instinct at this unwitting intrusion was to draw back in some confusion, but the white figure waved at us with cheerful languor and cried: "At last you come. Very good." His tone, his mien, transformed the tableau suddenly into something different, say a friendly rag in a boys' dormitory, something which might end in a pillow fight. But he was shrunken and much withered, had lost the sturdiness of his buttocks and thighs. Yet his face was still agleam with intelligence and the little gold caps on his canines glittered as he smiled upon us. "Don't go" he said. "I will soon be washed." The two expressionless figures carrying this pale frog deposed their burden with slow carefulness in the tub. Jocas sighed to feel the water rise up round his waist. He leaned his head back against the high rim of the bath and then extended a pale hand for us to touch. There was a kind of lucid and rather moving simplicity about the gesture; his helplessness was as disarming as his smile.

His magnificent head of hair, now plentifully touched with white, was combed loosely back; it fell in a straight shock almost to his shoulders. Benedicta knelt down to kiss his cheek and then turned aside to order the rumpled bed while Caradoc and I stood looking down at him. His servants sponged him softly and rhythmically. "Well this is a fine business" said Caradoc harshly, disguising his affection and concern in a habitual gruffness. The doctor made some professional movements among the bottles and pans which were laid out on one of the long white tables in the corner. What a jumble of spoons and forks, of half-eaten dishes, and broken fragments of meat for the birds. The birds! They would account for that heavy rotting fragrance in the vaulted air of the room. They were ranged like trophies along the end wall, the darkest corner of the room, all but invisible, but one could hear the tinkle of their bells as they stirred and sighed. His belongings stood about in isolation, as if they had lost context. It was a trifle surrealist, the old horn gramophone with its records (Jocas loved military marches and had quite a collection). There was a tall cupboard whose doors hung open. A few articles of attire were hanging up in it; but for the most part his belongings occupied the other wall, and were hung on nails. A fez, a deerstalker, binoculars. An old-fashioned typewriter lay on the floor beside a flowered chamber-pot. Thigh boots. Two gaunt armchairs, of the style called Voltaire, stood beside the bed with a strip of tattered carpeting between them. Everything looked quite haphazard, the result of a series of hasty afterthoughts.

But now they were finished with him and carefully lifted him from the bath. He let them with the same air of weary innocence, smiling, but delightfully unashamed of his nakedness. They laid him out upon one of the white deal tables to dry him—and I was reminded at once of the white "cooling-tables" of the embalmers. He hissed in with pleasure at the harsh touch of the towels and in a whisper urged the men to curry him harder and yet harder, like a horse; until at last his pale flesh took on the faintest warmth of tone. Then they produced an old-fashioned night-shirt and slipped it over his head. Now it was the doctor's turn; first an enema and then various injections. The little man whistled softly, abstractedly as he worked on his patient. Jocas had a whole lot of new and very beautiful expressions on his face—a whole new repertoire it seemed born of the illness, no doubt, and all the considerations which it raised. Had he thought very much about death, I wondered?

But once in bed lying back like an emperor under a Byzantine covering, pressed into puffed pillows, he became suddenly completely himself. I mean one would not have thought him ill at all. He held Benedicta's hand in his own confiding childlike grip and spoke in a new calm voice, smiling. "I wanted just to take leave" he said, and I realised that he was planning to die in the time-honoured, traditional eastern fashion. Here death itself had a ceremonial value and form; in the East there always seemed to be time to gather all one's relations together and take a formal leave of them. To distribute alms to the poor and order the family estate. We used to die like that once in England, a hundred or so years ago. Now somehow people are rushed into the ground unceremoniously, like criminals thrown into quicklime. Jocas was doing it in the old style. I caught sight of his scarlet slippers (*les babouches*); there was an ink-spot on one. Under the bed, as if hastily thrust aside there was a bit of railway line and a model train lying on its side. In the far corner under the window stood a huge and beautifully coloured box-kite with a long tail. Of course! One could lie in bed and fly a kite through the window.

He said suddenly: "But they must be hungry. They must eat."

It took some time to penetrate the heavy Turkish skulls of the servants, but at last the message got through and several heavy silvery trays made their appearance with two huge loaves of village bread, some olives, tinned meat, and a rank black wine. Caradoc carved all this into the semblance of helpings and we all fell to, suddenly ravenous.

The fire was built up with wood-shavings until it bellowed and bristled, throwing our shadows about the room. The small dark eyes of Jocas watched us with a benign affection—the expression on the face of a mother watching her children eat. I took my doorstep-sandwich and sat on the edge of the bed to share a friendly smile with him; he sighed with deep satisfaction as he watched us dispose ourselves around his bed. Like a child arranging his toys upon the counterpane. And I saw also that this whole visit of ours was part of a design, a deeply considered design. His architect was there to consult about a funerary monument; the embalming team were already on the spot. Jocas was good at mind reading, and followed my thoughts clearly, like somebody reading print. "Yes" he said. "It is like that. I had at first difficulty in my ideas because Julian could not understand; but now he's united with me. He has agreed with me. The need to have all our unhappy family—Merlins—under one roof, in one ground." He spread his hands in the direction of Caradoc who was munching. Then from under his pillow he produced a piece of parchment and handed it to me. It was in Greek. "Permission of the Orthodox Church to remove the body of the old man; Koepgen will bring it. He is still alive there in Spinalonga working, happy. I saw him last week." He chuckled softly. "Then what else? Yes, I wish myself to be golded, or do you say gilded? All gold. I have a firman for the whole headland, Caradoc." But this sort of talk made Caradoc extremely uneasy and shy; it seemed to him rather ill-mannered to talk so openly about death. "It's bad form" he said severely and munched his bread. Moreover he was very superstitious, had no intention of dying himself, and didn't want to hear about such matters. I watched the new vivid imperial face of Jocas and racked my brains to think of the prototype; at last click, up came the Ravenna mosaics, together with a whole lot of half-forgotten debris about Justinian and Theodora, that brave soul. I felt the long heavy night of the Turkish soul exemplified in its old half-dead capital— the Venice of the East. "And Julian will give me a service in St. Paul's." It is impossible to describe the smiling childish joy with which he uttered the words. His eyes sparkled with cupidity. "St. Paul's!" He crooned the words almost. He had begun to make everything sound extremely attractive—death should be like that. It was the ancient Greeks who couldn't take the idea.

He took a long drink from a glass at his bedside and subsided again into sighing happiness. "Though I have never seen it," he said "Julian once had a photograph faked to appear as if I was there at a memorial service. It was politically necessary, Amin Pasha. Here everyone thought I was in London specially for him; but it was a fake, I was here. Julian did it. Ah Julian! Only now I have come to understand him a little bit. He will never love me, but now he doesn't care. And he fears death very much. O yes."

The little doctor coughed. It was time for him to take his leave. He shook us each by the hand and said goodnight, placing a hand briefly upon Jocas' forehead and nodding, as if to say that he was satisfied with his patient. The bald old eunuch recovered his lamp from the outer darkness and led him slowly away. They had put some knobs of frankincense on the fire and the air had become rich and fragrant. The servants had retired, though one remained on call. He sat on an uncomfortable-looking kitchen chair in the shadows by the birds; appeared to sleep, head on breast. But Jocas was not done with us; he still radiated energy, and it reminded me of the Jocas I had first encountered, the tough and tireless countryman, hunter, swimmer. We sat around him on the bed—the stiff brocaded counterpane of some Byzance weave, the candles, the frail oil-lamps . . . all that. And the past sat heavily on us, too.

"Felix," he said, still holding the white hand of Benedicta in his "I followed with so much interest all your attempts to destroy us, to sabotage the firm, to escape from us. It was all in my heart, and it was so very interesting, so very passionately interesting to me. You see, I could understand you, but Julian not really. For Julian the firm perfectly expresses something, perhaps his impotence? Eh? I am not clever like him, and because I am not clever I was always in danger from him. O but I love him so." An air of rapturous infantility took possession of him. He licked his red lips and went on slowly, picking and choosing his words from his limited knowledge of English as one might pick flowers at random in a field. But he could express himself well, and here and there tumbled upon a mistake which itself was a felicity. "But you I sympathised," he said "and for why? Because I myself had the great search for the freeing of my soul, Felix. I too made a great calculation. But I had no courage to do it because I was afraid of Julian. He was so clever, he could simply kill me." He thrust out a hand to arrest my interpretation of the remark. "I was not afraid of the death. But I did not wish to join everything else in Julian's conscience; you see he pretends he has none. You must not have with the firm. But he has. Julian has seen much weeping." He swallowed and looked sad for a moment. One saw that he really did love this enigmatic figure, it was not simply oriental exuberance. One detected too the kind of pity

229

that the simple, uncomplicated and healthy man can have for the cripple. Julian had never shot, flown a bird or a kite; yes, but he had made love I suppose. I caught a glimpse of Benedicta's white serene face. She sat to me in profile, still holding Jocas' hand and gazing at him with an air of admiring confidence. He had sunk back among the pillows and closed his eyes—not out of weariness but in order to recover the thread of his argument.

"In the old days," he said "at the very beginning when the firm was a small thing, a [he inserted the Greek word for a newly born infant] . . . in those days every one of our transactions had to be done on trust, on an exchange of salt mostly. Arabia and so on. People could *not write*, Felix. All was human memory. Even quite late our whole accounting was with the oldfashioned abacus which you still see in Greek grocery shops today. The only factor that made for our security was mutual trust. When I thought about freedom and remembered the old days I thought very heavily—elephant-heavily—around this quite small but precise condition. All our money was deployed around the sea of the east, and while here and there was some little scraps of paper signed with thumbs, the most was in risk of trust. We had to *believe* in such a thing as an exchange of salt with a sheik. It was the only strong thing, the only plank. Now then all this paper came, all this contract business came. The whole firm became so big, so complicated. The salt had lost its savour, doesn't it say somewhere in the Bible? I thought. I thought. When Julian told me that the whole of the contracts of the firm had been photographed on film and that one little house held them all I had an extraordinary idea . . . I thought one night very late, while I was talking to myself. I thought: suppose we destroyed all contracts—the whole of the written thing. What would happen?"

He looked terribly excited, swallowed twice heavily, and then joined his hands on his breast. I suddenly felt myself face to face with one of those tremendously simple, but at the same time critical, veins of thought which belonged to what Marchant and I (in the case of Iolanthe) had labelled the contingency vector; it was the "supposing scale" and I imagine it represented in rough mechanical terms that sector of the human consciousness where the full horror of the idea of freewill comes to be understood or felt. It is this terrifying idea which causes people to throw themselves off cliffs (just to see what will happen): or to play Russian roulette with a pistol they just happened to find on a shelf. . . . If is the key of If. And then I thought of the little library which housed the total contractual commitments of the firm on microfilm. There had been a good deal of newspaper ballyhoo when Merlin's went on to microfilm; its contract department had by then grown to the size of the Bodleian. Now all the paper had gone. A special little funerary monument—not by Caradoc this time—had been erected to house the film in a London suburb. An ungainly little building, something between a Roman villa and the old Euston station. I recalled Caradoc's fury at this awkward neo-Egyptian monster of a creation with it four stout elephant columns. Above it was a small flat where the egregious Shadbolt lived (the same old chap who had drawn up Benedicta's marriage contract with me). He was now Registrar of Contracts. Well, it was not unlike a small and hideous crematorium. But I interrupted this train of thought to concentrate rather more deeply on what Jocas was trying to tell me. "What would happen?" he repeated again, dramatically, but in a lower register. "Either the whole thing, the whole construction would dissolve." He threw his eyes back into his skull, showing the whites, which is the Turkish way of illustrating total catastrophe. "Or else . . . *nothing* at all. Without the bonds of the paper and the signatures *trust* might come back, the idea of obligation to one's word, one's spoken bond, one's salt." I realised that I was in the presence of a great, but completely insane idealist. Trust indeed! But he went on headlong.

"Now I am so happy to know that you will try this freedom yourself—you will do this thing when once you are the head of the firm. Zeno has seen it all very clearly. He sees you give a last supper with twelve people in the big house. That same night you will completely burn every contract and announce it to the world. Very exciting. It will be a big fire. One old man will be burnt in it. But it will be the crown of your career. Only what happens after, if the firm continues or if it dissolves, Zeno cannot see clearly and he is too honest to pretend all this."

He gave a little chuckle and added, "Of course Julian doesn't believe in these nonsenses, perhaps you don't either. But she does,

Benedicta does. She has lived long enough in Turkey to know how sometimes strange things are real."

"Who is Zeno?" I asked purely to avoid taking up a definitive position vis-à-vis all these shadowy postulates. It seemed that he was an old Greek clerk who worked in the counting house in the city; subject to visions. Genus epileptoid, I had no doubt. It was as if the great aborted dream of Byzance lived on in the weaker psychic specimens of Polis, troubling their sleep with its tenebrous floating visions of a future which chance had aborted. I suddenly seemed to hear the disagreeable yelping of the barking dervishes ringing in my ears; how they flopped about the floor of the mosque yelping and foaming just like the schizos in the Paulhaus. Or else fell about like toads, beating up the dust and screaming. It was all part and parcel of the same type of phenomenon I have no doubt.

Beside the bed lay a stout oldfashioned family Bible encrusted with coloured wax from the candles. From between its leaves Jocas produced a small piece of paper written over in a very fine Greek hand; there was a drawing of a table-plan. From the red thumbprint (the attested signature with date) I recognised it as a witnessed prophecy —the sort of thing that idiots and hysterical soothsayers produce on saints' days. But the writing was crafty and very beautiful, the hand of an educated man. I took it and put it away to study at leisure— cursing the infernal rustiness of my Greek. "He does not know the people," said Jocas "but he described them and I put the name in with a pencil. You shall see. Anyway." He made a vague gesture and sank back, drooping a little from fatigue at last. I wondered whether we should leave him.

Benedicta seemed disposed to stay awhile as yet, and he for his part seemed to derive comfort from the touch of her hand on his. But Caradoc provided a slight diversion by picking up a lantern and saying that he must attend to the calls of nature; and I took the chance of joining him to get a breath of air. We climbed out upon the unwalled shelf, the balcony above the sea, and made our slow way along the paths which led to the headland of which Jocas had spoken. A cloudy sky obscured the nascent moonlight; far below us the ocean gulped. Somewhere in the obscurity below us ships moved, their lights glimmering frail as fireflies. But clouds were rolling in slowly towards the shore and a heavy dew had fallen. At last we came out upon the site of this proposed building—perhaps it was an old threshing-floor, built up belvedere-like over the sea. Despite the general darkness one could feel the dominance of the position, could divine the splendour of the surrounding views in fine weather. But Caradoc was morose; he set down the lantern to attend to his business, and then came and sat beside me on a boulder, shaking his head and growling a bit. "What is it?" I said. "Don't you think you can do it? I said this to annoy him, and the remark was quite successful. "Do it?" he snarled. "Of course I can do it. That's not what's worrying me. The problem is Jocas. He has got ancient Greece on the brain, and has been pining for the bloody Parthenon for half a lifetime now —he will never pass my drawings; not of the sort of thing I have in mind. Not in a month of Sundays. He does not realise the first thing about building; his idea would be something between a cassata ice cream and a Georgian rotunda. He doesn't realise that a real piece of building must be responsive to the emanations of the ground upon which it stands. To a certain extent the available materials create limitations and point out clues. In the Celebes, for example, bamboo, fern, leaves, lianas, they all dictate the weight and form of the construction—but they also echo the soul-form of the man who inhabits them. For those islanders the notion of life and death are dream-like, unsubstantial, poetical; their culture is born in a butterfly's soul. Just as Tokio is all mouse-culture, a mouse-capital. We must build with this sense of congruence to place. The Parthenon would be a joke propped up here on this Turkish headland. Why? Because the soul-form of the Greeks was different, their metaphysical attitude to things was sensual, relatively indifferent to death and time. And their sense of plastic was really related to plane surfaces decorated on the flat, not to volume. All their stuff is radiantly human because the scale is small, nothing larger than life size. Their sunny philosophy domesticated not only life, but also death, one has the feeling that even the huge Gods were home-made, perhaps formed by the hands of children in a cookery class. No morality either to shock and frighten. Innocence, a gem-like trance. All the ominous or minatory elements in their history were imported from death-saturated lands like Egypt, like this here bloody Turkey?" He flashed me a glance of righteous indignation from under his shaggy prophetic brows. "Just sit here and listen to Turkey, listen to what it says" he went on. "It's a heavy death-propelled wavelength, the daze of some old alligator slumbering in the mud. It has all the solemnity the heavy somnolence of Egypt, the one country above all which specialised in death; if Turkey ever showed flower in a cultural way it will echo Egypt, not Greece. That is why all this embalming business of Goytz is a stroke of genius. Some cultures are so death-weighted that they store up their dead, they are an-cestor-obsessed like the Chinese. *That* is the call-sign of this gloomy old land. Consequently if one tunes in and tries to set it to an archi-tecture one is almost driven to echo the grave ponderous style of an Egypt; the bright blue and white of Greece would never work. But how to tell Jocas that?"

I changed the conversation abruptly. "That well over there" I said gravely. (I was surprised to find myself a trifle drunk.) "That well already houses the genius of your mausoleum. Jocas has imported a snow white python from the island of Crete; and he has planted an almond tree for it to climb. Prophecies will spring from this tomb, Caradoc." I invented all this of course in order to scare him. I knew he was particularly frightened of snakes. It had the desired effect. He secured his lantern and said irritably, "Why didn't you say so before? We might have sat on the damn thing."

When we got back to the house it was to find most of the lights turned low and Jocas asleep with a smile on his face; Benedicta had disappeared. The attendant drowsed on his upright chair. We made our uneven way back to the villa where we had been allocated rooms. Caradoc holding his lantern high examined the cracked plaster cherubs, the broken marble fireplaces, the litter on the dirty flags, with a sustained curiosity. I found a candlestick and lit it. Benedicta had been given a room to herself on the balcony side of the house. I had been allocated a sort of uncomfortable box-room. Though I was weary I found it difficult to sleep, I suppose because of the atrocious but heady black wine we had been sluicing. So I wrote a little letter to Benedicta—something to read when she woke up alone in bed. "Dear Benedicta, the whole point—why will you never grasp it? The whole point is that time gives birth to space, but space gives

234

death to time. (The ancient liver mantic was an attempt to read forward into time—and it might have worked for them.) That is the only reason for my loving you—because you simply cannot grasp the meaning of causality in the new terms. I would add an equation or two but I am rather drunk and the light is bad. So I will content myself by warning you gravely about the perils of such homely ignorance. It saps the will and rots the cortex. Squinch. Felix." I suppose it lacked warmth; and it certainly wasn't what I intended to say when I took out my pencil. I pondered, and at last traced the missing component. My postscript read: "I would be quite willing to dismantle and abolish Iolanthe if you asked me to do so."

An uneasy night of shallow dreams, bird noises, howling of dogs; but then I dozed off and slept quite a way into the morning. It was a dark and gloomy day with huge shaggy clouds hanging motionless over everything; the gulf was the colour of gunmetal. Beside my bed I found the response to my letter of the night before. "It's my job now to see that you do what you feel you must. Anything else would be fatal to both of us. I must say you are an awful fool, which is consoling in a hopeless sort of way. Meet me at Eyub at four."

I was startled to find that it was already ten o'clock; she had taken the launch into Polis, in order to spend the day wandering about its streets and mosques. Meanwhile the returning boat brought the little doctor with it. Jocas was wide awake and alert in his birdlike way. "She wants you to meet her in Polis" he said. I said I knew. From the only bathroom came the sound of prodigious swishing— as if a herd of elephants were hosing each other down. "It is Caradoc taking a bath" said Jocas solemnly, and then added (for all the world as if he had mind-read the whole of our conversation of last night): "I have told him that I do not wish to see any plans. He is free to design what he pleases. He has the money and the site. I will trust him to make a most characteristic thing for the family." I whistled with surprise and pleasure. Presently Caradoc, hale and ruddy after his ablutions, emerged from the depths. He was looking happy for a change, indeed radiant. "Did you hear?" he boomed. "Jocas is going to trust me all the way." This seemed to call for a celebration and despite the earliness of the hour and the slight trace of hangover I coyly accepted a glass of fiery *raki*.

235

I left the company gathered about the huge bed and (grateful for an old umbrella I had brought) found my way down through the gardens to where the white launch lay at the landing stage, waiting with steam up to take me into town. The sea was black and calm, luminous and bituminous all at once; we rustled across it at full speed. I studied with interest (perhaps amusement, so foolish am I) the prophecy of Zeno and the elaborate table-plan he had drawn for this classical last supper of mine. What the devil was it all about? It reminded me a little of the Banubula Tunc talisman—twelve places of which three were empty. But the pencilled names were those of my friends—Vibart, Pulley, Marchant, Banubula, Nash, etc. etc. There were empty places, too, at this table and I wondered a little about them. It seemed that neither Julian nor Jocas was to be of the party; and perhaps one of the missing places might belong to Iolanthe? I don't know. It was all pretty vague as these things so often are; and of course there was no precise date for the thing— there never is! However I felt charitably disposed towards occultism on Tuesdays, and I pocketed it with a sigh, and turned to regale myself with the black water and the livid marks we were making in it. And the sombre city came up like a long succession of "states": I am groping for the image of an etching evolving through a number of different stages, slowly as the elaborations of detail are multiplied. I wondered what Benedicta might be doing; I closed my eyes and tried to imagine where she was—perhaps sitting on a block of masonry by her mother's grave in Eyub or else (more likely) sitting in the little garden by the mosque where Sacrapant fell, drinking a benedictine and smoking a gold-tipped cigarette. There was time to kill. In this gloomy sodden-looking weather I found my way across the arcades of the grand bazaar to the little restaurant where once (how many centuries ago?) I had dined with Vibart and his wife, and listened to his histrionic dissertations on good books and bad. Pia, I had almost forgotten how she looked; I had a recollection of brilliant eyes, watchful, amused. For the life of me I could not associate her with Jocas—but there it was. And following out this train of thought I bumped into Vibart himself just as he was about to seat himself at a table. "Join me" he said, and all of sudden it was a new version of my old friend which presented itself to my vision; no more was he morose and cast down. He radiated rather a recovered composure, a temperamental calm. He saw me looking at him and smiled. "It's come out, the equation" he said at last, turning his handsome smiling head sideways to examine himself in the mirror. "I spent all last night walking about until I found the missing collar-stud. I've solved it, man. It's the smallest thing imaginable but it has been teasing my reason for so long now that it was a great relief to catch it by the tail. I was right to do it for myself and not ask poor Jocas foolish questions. It has to do with the quality of my loving, the subtle thing that didn't click between Pia and me. It came from the fact that I loved her not as a man loves a a woman, but as a woman loves a man. In a subtle sort of way my attitude qualified my masculinity in the exchange. I wonder if you see? It is so clear to me. I'd turned the flow of affect or whatever upside down; and she was too much a woman to love except as a woman. It's such a relief, I feel like singing."

"I can see Nash," I said "bicycling like mad towards you and muttering things about the 'homosexual component'."

"Yes, it would seem from my diagnosis that I am a common or garden bugger at heart. What do you know?"

He burst out laughing. Thunder crackled and a brief skirl of rain fell. "Just like last time we were here, isn't it."

"What a weird light; the whole damn city so subaqueous and *sfumato*. How is Jocas?"

I gave him an account of the patient to which he listened thoughtfully, patiently, nodding from time to time as if what I had to say confirmed his inner convictions. (The strictest style in classical painting limited its palette to yellow, red, black and white. Why? This singular fact has never been satisfactorily explained. Must ask Caradoc what he thinks about it.)

"I bet you" he said, falling to work with knife and fork "that Benedicta hasn't gone up to Eyub with all this uncertain weather; bet you she's hiding in Gatti's eating ice cream or something. Anyway it's on the way so we shall see. And by the way there's a telegram for you from Marchant which they gave me down in town. Take."

It was a simple and brief message to tell me that our model was "critical"—a word we used to denote the final stages before she woke up. That meant in about a fortnight's time. I felt my pulse quicken at the thought that we were so near launching day. Perhaps mingled with the feeling was a small touch of misgiving; this parody of a much loved person, how would it stand the test of scrutiny by those who had known her?

There was time before my rendezvous with Benedicta, and we elected to dawdle away an hour or so in the Grand Bazaar where I surrendered completely to the long stride of Vibart and the longer memory he had for everything in it. It was delightful to hear him talk now, with nostalgia and affection for the past—no longer hatred and shock. As for the Bazaar—despite its size he knew every flagstone, every stall; and despite gaps and changes brought by the times there was enough for him even to evoke what was absent as we rambled about it. The circumference of the place cannot be less than a mile, while about five covered arcades radiate from its hub, the so-called Bezistan. It is really a walled and gated city within the city, and it claims to contain 7,777 shops. Mystic numbers? Vibart walked about it all with a sense of ownership, like a man showing one round his private picture gallery. He had, I think, come to realise how intensely happy those long years in Turkey had been for him, and indeed how formative; yet he had spent the whole time grumbling about books he could not write. The little square Bezistan, so clearly Byzantine in feel, is less than fifty yards long; square and squat, it spiders this stone cobweb. The one-headed Byzantine eagle over the Bookseller Gate places the building as tenth century, after which time the eagle became two-headed. The gates are called after the quarters which they serve, each characterised by a product —Goldsmiths, Embroidered Belt Makers, Shoemakers, Metal Chasers. . . .

I could see now that Vibart was living in the romantic schoolboy glow of the mysterious East. These empty rainy stalls once held damascened armour, silver-hilted pistols, inlaid rifles, musical instruments, gems of every water, seals and terra-cottas and coins. Even what wasn't there he was able to describe with complete fidelity in this new youthful voice. I think too that in a way he was talking to Pia in his mind, remembering for her, to so speak. I fell silent and let him go, as one lets a hound off the lead.

"And to think" he said "that in a few days we'll be back in bonny Blighty facing up once more to all the contingencies which face the creative man—buggery, gin, and menopause Catholicism. Well, I shall take it all calmly from now on. To each his well-deserved slice of sincere dog. To each his cinema picture—the best way of trivialising reality."

But despite the characteristic grumbling tone and matter of his discourse one felt his calm elation. Nor was he wrong about Benedicta for she was indeed at Gatti's, sitting at the end of the terrace in a brown study with a cassata before her. In her absentmindedness—or was it due to old memories, old hauntings?—she had adopted a style of sitting with one gloved hand in her lap. One glove off always—that seemed once so characteristic of her; the glove hid a ring Julian had given her, a ring which came from the tomb of a dead Pharaoh. But with the new dispensation she had thrown it away thus symbolically marking the new freedom which she claimed to have won.

Catching a glimpse of her sitting this way, her blonde head turned away to scan the nebulous city with its turrets and minarets, I suddenly thought of what Vibart had been saying about Pia and realised not only how much I loved her but also why; and by the same token why she must love me, why she would never break free again. It was one of those cursed paradoxes of love which hit one like an iron bar. I sat down with a bump in the chair next to her and said to myself: "Of course, we are most united in the death of Mark, our son. The child we unwittingly murdered. At bottom what brings this hallowed sadness to our loving is a sort of criminal complicity in an evil deed." I longed at that moment to embrace her, to comfort her, to protect her. But this train of thought would not do. Instead we listened to Vibart in full exposition while she let me hold her ungloved hand in mine. (Bookstores near the Mosque of Bayezid in the old Chartopratis or paper-market; here in an old Byzantine portico resided a turbaned and gowned old gentleman who sat at a table with reed pen and colour box, with gold leaf and burnisher, filling page after page of parchment with exquisite illuminated script. Left over from a forgotten age in which his art was as necessary as it was graceful. Now all he got in the way of commissions were a few petitions from government clerks or illiterate farmers. For the jewellery and the silks you must try Mahmoud Pasha Kapou. . . .)

"Astonishing how much you've remembered and how much I've forgotten" said Benedicta; to which Vibart replied with a certain smugness, "Isn't it, though?"

Clouds furled back to admit a streak of sunlight; we were joined by a relaxed and almost gay Baum. "So they didn't put essence of powdered rat in your soup?" He shook his relieved head and sighed. "To my intense astonishment I found them most receptive to this new idea; the religious leaders heard my exposition in complete silence. Am I to assume that there are passages in the Koran which sanction solitary practices—unless I misunderstood the interpreter I think that is the case? What impressed them was the insistence on the modern world with its change of viewpoint. After all Turkey abolished the fez out of a desire to make itself a modern state, and then the Latin alphabet replacing the Arabic . . . I rubbed it all in. And when I had finished they practically gave me a standing ovation, if I may use the phrase without indelicacy, and rushed to fill in membership forms at once. Moreover from every minaret and pulpit in the city the news will go out and true believers will flock to the standard. I am so relieved." He smiled all over his face.

Our rendezvous with the pinnace was for dusk, so we idled away the afternoon in the shelter of Gatti's awnings while Baum and Vibart completed several small purchases in the immediate environs. Once again we were favoured by a calm sea. It was dusk by the time we landed once more at the jetty and straggled our way up to the house, to the bed, the lamps and candlesticks; to Jocas who was completing his toilet, but in a very good mood. "Everything has gone well" he said. "All our plans agree. Even Caradoc is happy and when has he ever been happy?"

Caradoc was enthroned in a Voltaire and was playing with coloured bricks, absorbed as a child; it was indeed a child's toy—this architectural kit. And I could see that having sat for an hour or two on the site by daylight had fired his fancy and given him the itch to begin his task. The evening passed very pleasantly indeed; we almost forgot the plight of Jocas he was in such a good humour, and so lively. But at last when dinner was brought in he said: "So you will go tomorrow will you? Yes, I think it is best. Now that I have seen you all I am quite content to say goodbye."

It was the end of an epoch I suppose, but it did not feel very momentous so natural were the talk and banter in the fire-light.

It is retrospectively that one marks up and weighs the value of experiences. Looking back—as a matter of fact looking down—over Polis as the huge lumbering aeroplane swam in widening gyres, gaining height over the capital, I was touched by a nostalgia which I had not felt on terra firma. Benedicta too I suppose felt it, and per-haps more sharply than I. Yet she said nothing. Dawn was breaking over the forest of tilting masts and spars, the long walls turned briefly poppy-coloured before the lengthening rays of sunlight made them revert to bronze, then to umber. I had a feeling that I should not come back for a very long time, if ever; and I was also glad in a per-verse sort of way that the pilot had decided to overfly Greece on the return flight. The melancholy and solitude of Ariadne had saddened me; it was so absolute that one could think of no consolations worth the offering—you cannot console anyone against reality.

"Thinking?"

"Yes. Thinking and cross-thinking; all the map references are criss-crossed. I was thinking of Jocas, of you as a child, of Ariadne in Athens. And I was thinking of that absurd prophecy of Zeno." I took it out of my pocket to study once more. The idea of destroying the firm's entire contract system had begun to tease the edges of my mind; of course it was preposterous, but then everything was. What was more preposterous than returning to England to set Pygmalion's image walking?

"I saw Sipple" said Vibart. "He's blind now and pale and ghostly as a mouse. He is head of the embalming section which Goytz has started up. He does everything by touch, like a mouse nibbling at cheese. He was at work on a small corpse, a boy, silently, happily. It terrified me. I buzzed off hastily."

He looked round carefully to see that Goytz was sleeping tran-quilly, and had not heard the remark. Goytz was so easily offended when his craft was mentioned in flippant tones. "He's become like one of those pink transparent eyeless lizards which live in caves in

241

total darkness. Opaque, completely opaque. You can see the sunlight shining right through him, Sipple."

I had forgotten until now that the clown was still with us, in the land of the living, the land of the dying. A steward brought drinks. Benedicta had fallen into a doze now with her head on my shoulder. Soon we would be booming across the high spurs of Albania, bound for England, home and Iolanthe.

VI

I have the impression that if anyone had seen us that evening as we wheeled our trophy of love across the crisp green lawns, down the winding gravel paths, through the woods, until we could settle her into the little villa—if anyone had, he would have been tempted to smile at the solemnity and concern written upon our visages. As for her—why she was breathing softly but regularly under her parachute silk shroud; you could see that faint rise and fall of her breast as she lay stretched out on the long steel trolley. She was gradually coming out of the anaesthetic, so to speak. The last threads had been snipped which attached her to the machines that had been feeding slumbering life into her all these long months; the life which, in due course, she would be free to turn to her own uses, to the exploitation of good or evil. "Today she wakes, today she walks" Marchant had chanted with schoolboy enthusiasm which masked, I think, a concern nearly bordering upon hysteria. He had worked harder than any of us on the model. When first her breasts began to rise and fall, her lips to move into the soundless shapes of words, his surprising reaction had been to burst into peal upon peal of laughter, high girlish laughter. And he was still poised on the edge of a triumphant giggle whenever she gave the smallest sign of responding to the demands made upon her by the life-currents into which she was entering. His pink scalp shone through his thin silvery hair; his silver-rimmed spectacles, which gave him a slightly White Rabbit look, steamed over all too easily with emotion. He had to wipe them in his apron. It alarmed me, this laughter, I must say.

I confess that I too felt a nudge of concern and perhaps even horror as she began to take her cues—sorry, *it*. She was moving like a planet into camera range, telescope range. . . .

She licked her lips slowly, tentatively, and her small red tongue flickered over them like that of some marvellous copperhead. Then she sighed once, twice, but it was a very small boredom as yet. We had allowed ourselves a quarter of an hour to dress her and conduct her to the little villa where she might wake in surroundings appropriately familiar to her intricate memory-codes. After all, we wanted her to feel at home, to be happy, just like everybody else. So here we were, wheeling her away across country with Marchant dressed in the elaborate white intern's coat and Mrs. Henniker tricked out as a nurse. Myself, I was still a civilian, so to speak. Marchant was going to play the doctor who by a brilliant operation had saved her life. As for Mrs. Henniker, she was ashen pale, her hair was glued to her scalp with perspiration. But she was behaving very nobly. I had given her a long talking-to about this excessive emotion. There was no need for it, after all, and there was a risk that the experiment, so delicate in its various contingencies, might be spoiled unless she kept a straight face, so to speak. "Above all nothing must be said in the presence of the dummy to suggest to her that she *is* one, that she is not real. She must not be made to doubt her own reality— because that might lead to some sort of memory collapse; whatever doubts she may eventually have must come out of her own memory-fund and its natural reaction-increment." Easy to say, of course, but the thing was that she was so damn real that it was difficult not to think of her as a "person" . . . already! And she not walking and talking as yet—the acid test of her mock-humanity! Yes, she could even read, and by her bed lay the familiar bundles of film papers and weeklies which she would nose through like a dog, quizzing the fashions as she picked her front teeth with a slow fingernail. Yet, she was typical, as contemporary as a mere man could make her.

Julian was there at this briefing, if I can call it that, sitting very still with his hands in his lap, listening intently, looking somehow diminished, somehow like a schoolboy. He too had been showing signs of strain from all this cruel anticipation—symptoms more suited to a young bridegroom than to a grown man playing games with a dummy. Yet there it was: changing his clothes several times a day, studying himself with sombre attention in mirrors, fussing over the freshness of the carnation in his buttonhole. I could see that he was going to choose his clothes for the first meeting with the

Ur-Iolanthe with great care, for all the world as if it mattered. Yet perhaps after all it did to him. (She would hold out long phthisic fingers towards his, smiling, saying nothing.)

We had chosen the evening as the best time for her to start; it enabled us to see if our settings were right, by her reaction to night-fall and bedtime and so on. Iolanthe used to wake punctually at six every morning, and was usually in bed by eleven at the latest every night. Henniker had promised to re-enact her usual role of nurse-secretary and friend with all the fidelity she could command, and I presumed that she would soon get over her initial worry and take everything naturally; she would familiarise herself with the new Iolanthe in the long run. It was just a question of the initial awakening. If the dummy was as "real" as we expected its memory-reaction code would instantly throw up the whole of Henniker's history to-gether with "her own" past—every damned thing. Yes, from the simple point of view of memory, she would simply be coming back to life after a critical illness—the gap created by the real Iolanthe's death would be filled in the memory of the false one by vague in-timations of an illness, an operation, an absence. Her life hence-forth (though we had not made out any elaborate schema to cover the range and scope of her activities: how could we?)—but her life henceforth would be a sort of long convalescence. At least so we thought. She was not "coded" or "programmed" forwards. She was, so to speak, free.

The little villa in the woods was unobtrusively surrounded by a tall wire fence and entered through a gate. It was very pretty, set upon a deeply wooded knoll. The garden was a riot of wild and tame flowers; behind ran a brook and beside it lay an apple-orchard. It was if anything prettier and more comfortable than the house in the woods which I myself occupied with Benedicta. Inside this elegant little place Henniker had arranged all the possessions (they were astonishingly few for such a rich woman) of Iolanthe senior; laid them all out in familiar dispositions to re-engage memory, yet also haphazardly to suggest perhaps that she (who had lived out of suitcases for half her life) was simply on location for some film or other. But it was beautiful, it was peaceful, the little house. A fire sparkled in the dining-room with its new novels and *bibelots*; the

247

Renoir hung upon the wall. On the small upright piano stood the sheet music of a film-score and a volume of Chopin's Études. *Eh bien,* the sheets had been aired. On the bedside table were two novels she had been reading when she, the real one, had suddenly lapsed into death. (Some underlinings in one.) Everything in fact conspired to produce a normal setting and atmosphere for this softly breathing Other, lying under her aeroplane silk. I touched her fingers. They separated easily, flexibly. They were warm.

Marchant had timed it all very accurately. We unpacked her body softly and slipped on the blue silk nightgown while Henniker brushed out her hair with long strokes (she sighing luxuriously the while). Then we lifted her to bed. She smelt the newly-ironed freshness of the sheets with appreciation, wrinkling up a newly-minted nose. There were also the faint wisps of odour from the lighted joss-sticks which burned in a small Chinese vase. It was time; there was nothing to do but wait. Marchant hung over his watch like a demented crystal-gazer, his lips counting silently, a smile upon his face. "A minute" he whispered. And then *"Ahhh"* with a long delicious inspiration the lady woke; the two eyes, bluer than any stone, inspected first the clean white ceiling, and then travelled slowly down to take in our own surrounding faces; recognition dawned, together with that famous mischievous smile which was so warm that it had always suggested a marvellous intimate complicity, even when projected on a screen. The slightly husky and melodious voice said: "Is it over? Have I come back, then?" While she addressed the question to Marchant her long slender arm came out and touched me, grasped my fingers, giving them a tender squeeze of recognition as she whispered in Greek "Hullo, Felix." Marchant was bobbing and ducking his affirmative and vaguely going through a repertoire of Chinese gestures, shaking hands with myself, as if to congratulate himself for this feat—this living and breathing feat of science, with her china-blue eye and scarlet, rather ravenous mouth. "It's all over" he said. "A great success; but you must rest for a while, quite a long while." She yawned as naturally as a cat and whispered "I feel wonderful Felix. Doctor, may I go to the loo?" She had not as yet recognised the blenching Henniker, but now as she turned back the sheet in order to stand up she did, and gave a sharp delighted cry like a bird.

"But it's you—I didn't see!" In some curious way the very natural-ness of this embrace seemed to allay the emotion and anxiety of the older woman. Perhaps a sense of verisimilitude, of the reality of the flesh and blood, the gesture, released her from a very natural fear—I don't know. But all at once she looked unafraid again. "I'll come with you" she said, and accompanied Iolanthe to the bathroom, smoothing her hair with her hand as she sat on the lavatory and gave her little mechanical shiver of pleasure. "Is it really all over?" she asked Henniker. "Are you sure?"

Henniker reassured her gravely and then escorted her back to bed, puffing up the pillows behind her head and smoothing the sheets with her hard scaly hand. Yes, she had ceased to tremble now. Marchant played the doctor damned awkwardly, swinging a stetho-scope in his hand. "Well" he said. "It has all been a great success." She turned her smile on him and expressed her gratitude by taking his hand in hers. "I am so grateful" she said gravely. "I had given myself up for lost, in a way." We studied her gravely, amazed at what we had done, and wondering a little if she would keep up this extraordinary performance of an understudy who had so thoroughly mastered an intricate part. I could well understand Marchant's unease, his desire to get away. It was like the first impact of falling in love—one paradoxically wants to get away, to be alone, in order to ruminate upon the feeling. His love was scientific, that was all. Dolly worked! Iolanthe was saying dreamily: "When you come out of the anaesthetic it's with a soft bump that you land in the middle of consciousness—like those lovely flying dreams one has when one is a child." Marchant stood on one leg and then the other. Finally he took his leave promising to call on her in the morning. "Henny," said Io, yawning profoundly "O Henny dear, can I eat something? Something small, a boiled egg?"

"Of course, darling."

Henniker retired to the kitchen and left us staring at each other with amusement, yes, affectionate amusement. It was a very unreal feeling indeed. "I must just see" she said at last "what they have managed to do about my breasts—that was what really worried me and brought on the other, I think." She got out of bed with a swift lithe gesture and turned her back to me to enable me to help her divest herself of her blue nightgown. Naked she walked towards the full-length mirror at the other end of the room. She gave a little crooning cry of relief as she caught sight of the beautiful new breasts the doctors had given her, cupping them in her palms, head on one side like a parrot. Then she leaned forward and stared intently into her own eyes as if to make some critical assessment of her own looks; then, sighing, turned to me as naked as sunrise and put her arms round me to kiss me lingeringly on the lips. It was the old affectionate, concerned kiss of Io, quite unbearably real yet utterly without any new sexual connotation. It was as sister to brother, not as lover to lover; but I was thrilled to have a chance to put my arms about her, to test the smooth flexion of her muscles, to stroke the pearly haunches of my darling, proud as any sculptor to have confided such a thing to nature. She giggled as she got back first into her nightgown and then into her bed. "You look so serious" she said. "Still the same old Felix, thank goodness. How is Benedicta?" she added with a faint frown of concentration as if she were trying to summon up an image of her face. "Happy at last" I said. "And me too. Everything has changed." She shot me a cool and rather quizzical look, as if she were in doubt as to whether I was being ironical, or pulling her leg. Then she said "If it's true, then I'm glad. It was about time, I must say, that you had a decent break."

Henniker came back with the long-legged bed-tray on which lay her boiled egg, some nursery bread and butter, and a glass of milk. I watched with anxiety, for all this she would eat only in her imagination; the plate, the glass, would seem to her quite empty, though all she had done was to cut the food up and mess it about a bit. But ideally the reflex hand-to-mouth action would satisfy her sense of participation in a natural ritual; one could hardly have denied her that. (I was reminded of the slow imaginary meals of Rackstraw in the Paulhaus.) She did her act and leaned back pushing the tray away and wiping her lips. "Gosh, I'm full" she said, and then "Felix, is there an evening paper? I want to see what plays are on." I found one and she consulted the theatre pages with attention, her lips moving. "I don't know a single one of them" she said, and then looked at the date. "How long have I been here, Felix?" I parried this with talk about long sedation and memory lapses and so on. She wrinkled her brow and wandered through the headlines of the paper before abruptly putting it aside.

"By the way," I said "Old Rackstraw is dead." She looked at me with wide-eyed regret for a moment and then turned away to fold up her napkin. "It's probably for the best" she said in a low voice. "He was so ill it was to be expected I suppose. And yet everyone who dies takes a whole epoch with them. Racky was a saint to me, an absolute saint. Sometimes quite recently when I thought how contemptuously I had let him sleep with my body—not my me, my *you*, so to speak—I felt shocked and disgusted with myself. In a way I owe him everything; he made my name with his scripts. Felix, do you ever think of, do you ever remember, Athens?" The words came over with a kind of wild pang, saturated with a sort of forlorn reserve. "Ah yes, Iolanthe, of course I do." She smiled and shaking out her hair said: "I tried to reconstruct us in a film at one time, you and me. It didn't work. Racky was doing the writing and couldn't get it."

"I'm not surprised" I said. "But then why?"

"Because. I do things backwards. Experiences don't register with me while they are happening. But afterwards, suddenly in a flash I see their meaning, I relive them and experience them properly. That is what happened to me with you. One day by a Hollywood swimming pool the heavens opened and I suddenly realised that it had been a valid and fruitful experience—us two. We might even have christened the thing love. Ah, that word!"

"I took it as it came, with perfect male egoism."

"I know; I suppose you thought we were just . . . what was your pet expression? Yes, 'just rubbing narcissisms together and making use of each other's bodies as mirrors'. Cruel Felix, it wasn't like that; why you got quite ill when I left. Well then, I got quite ill too, but retrospectively, by that Hollywood pool, and within the space of a second; people wondered why I suddenly burst out crying. Really it is absurd. Then later I tried to build a film about us in Athens in order to cauterise the memory a bit; but that didn't work. So I just had to let it dwindle away with the years. How absurd. Yes, the film got made, but it was rotten."

She had spilt egg on her nightgown. It was so natural, so babyish.

251

I wiped her with my handkerchief, clicking my tongue reprovingly the while like a nanny. "Now Iolanthe, please be a good girl, won't you, and obey Dr. Marchant to the letter? No originality, no tricks, no bright ideas. You have got to take it easily for some weeks at least."

"But of course, my dear. But will you come and see me often, just to talk? Bring Benedicta if you wish." She hesitated. "No, don't bring Benedicta. I haven't got rid of my dislike for her as yet. It would make me shy."

"Come. Come."

"I know. Sorry! But still. . . ."

I stood up and removed the tray from the bed. "I'll tell you more about Racky" she said, settling herself more comfortably in the bed. "I'll tell you anything, everything. Now I feel at ease. Now my career is finished, the company bought out. I feel a new sort of relief. I have a little time in hand to do the things I want. See Bali properly, read Proust, learn to play the tarot. . . ."

I didn't want to ask her but I had to. "Tell me, do you feel the capacity for happiness inside you? Happiness!"

She considered. "Yes" she whispered as I stooped to kiss her forehead. "Yes, I do. But Felix everything will feel indeterminate until I meet Julian, the author of all my professional misfortunes."

"How so?"

"I'm exaggerating of course, but he hangs over me like a cloud, always invisible. Have you ever seen him up close?"

"Yes, but only recently."

"How is he? Describe."

"He is coming to see you tomorrow."

She sat bolt upright in bed, clasping her knees, and said "Good. At last." Then she clapped her hands and laughed. Henniker came in to draw the curtains and remake the bed and I took the opportunity to take my leave. I was glad to. This first encounter make me feel weak; my knees felt as if they would buckle under me. I stumbled out into the garden with a feeling of suffocation and relief. On the way to the car I had a moment of faintness and was forced to lean against a tree for a moment and unloosen my collar.

On the way back home, at a deserted part of the road over the moors, I came upon the black Rolls laid almost endways across the road in a fashion that suggested an ambush or a hold-up. As I hooted I recognised Julian's car; his chauffeur replied with a warning ripple of horn like a wild goose sounding. What the hell? Julian was in the back of the car. I got out and opened his door; he was dressed as if he had come from some official reception. A black Homburg lay behind him on the rack, and in his hands he held a pair of gloves. The funny thing was that he was sitting with his head turned away from me, stiffly, hieratically. I had the impression that he may have been trying to avoid showing the tears in his eyes. Probably false—it was just a fleeting thought. But he swallowed and said: "Felix—for goodness' sake—*how is she?*" The intensity of the question was such as to bring on my shakes. I climbed in beside him and told him—I fear with growing incoherence—all about her awakening, her naturalness. "We've done the impossible, Julian. They talk of portraits taken from the life; but this is liver than any portrait. Liver than life. It's bloody well *her*." I was shivering and my teeth began to chatter. "Have you any whisky Julian? I'm shaken to the backbone. I feel as if I am getting 'flu." He pressed a button and the little bar slid out of the wall with its bottles and bowl of ice cubes. The telephone rang but he switched it off with an impatient gesture. I drank deeply, deeply. It was nectar. He watched me narrowly, curiously, as if I *myself* were a dummy, astonishing him by my lifelikeness. "Julian, you wanted this creature and we've produced her, it, for you. I wish you the *densest* happiness in the words of Benjamin Franklin. Her sex is more in the breach than the observance, though technically she could make love, Julian." It was extremely tactless. He struck me across the mouth with his gloves. I didn't react, feeling I had deserved it.

"You are babbling" he said contemptuously.

"I know. It's pure hysteria. But I tell you Julian that on the present showing the damned thing is as real as you or I."

"That is what I'd hoped." Now his little white fingers were drumming, drumming upon the leather arm-rest. "How much does she recall?" he said. "Did she mention me at all?" I laughed. "You still don't realise, Julian; she remembers all that Iolanthe did and more perhaps; we won't know for a while until she has a chance to develop her thoughts. So far though. . . ." His eyes looked queer, vitreous; he hooded them with his heavy lids as he turned them on me, sitting there with his brooding vulpine air. He sighed. "When shall we meet, then?" he asked in a low resigned voice, as if he might be asking the date of an execution. I finished my drink. "Tomorrow, at tea-time. I told her you would be there." I got out and banged the door on him. He put down the window to say: "Felix, please be there; remember we have never met. This is the first time."

My nerves reformed by the whisky, I got back into the car, and felt a sudden wave of elation mingle with my exhaustion. I don't know when I have driven quite so fast or taken so many risks. I was in a hurry to get back to Benedicta, for better or for worse, in slickness or in stealth. . . .

It was so natural—Benedicta before the fire reading, with a sleeping kitten beside her, it was so familiar and so *reliably real* that I was suddenly afflicted by almost the same sense of unreality I had had in talking to Iolanthe. The comparison of two juxtaposed realities like these gave me the queer feeling that might overwhelm a man who looks in the mirror and sees that he has two heads, two reflections. But she didn't ask, she didn't question; I simply slumped down beside her, put my head on my arms and went straight to sleep. It was dinner time when she woke me. Baynes had unobtrusively set out a tray in the corner of the room on a table which we moved into the firelight. By now of course I was as ravenous as a pregnant horse and bursting with euphoria. She looked at me quizzically from time to time. "I can see it's gone well" she said at last.

"It's not quite believable yet." That was all I could say. We embraced. I exploded the champagne, laughing softly to myself like a privileged madman. "Eternity is in love with the productions of Time" says Will Blake. "You have nothing to fear Benedicta; drink my dear, let us toast reality awhile."

*　　*　　*　　*　　*

It could have had its funny side, too, the meeting between Julian and Io—I suppose—to an objective observer. I mean that he for his part had dressed most carefully, his hair was neat, his nails newly manicured; moreover he had developed a new and stealthy walk for the occasion, a sort of soliloquy glide out of *Hamlet*. He was at pains perhaps to disguise his fear? Whereas now I had more or less got on top of my own anxiety—the primitive terror that all human beings feel when faced by dummies of whatever kind, representations of hallowed reality: an Aurignacian-complex, as Nash might have called it. I was indeed swaggering a little in my new-found relief. Like a young man introducing a particularly pretty fiancée. I smiled upon my *patron* indulgently as I led him across the green lawns and down the long gravel paths, Julian snaking slowly behind me, rippling along. He had brought a small bunch of Parma violets with him as an offering. But suddenly he threw them away and swore. I think he was saying to himself, "My God! Here I am thinking of her as if she were *real*, instead of just an expensive contemporary construct." I chuckled. "You will get used to her, to it, very quickly Julian. You'll see."

Henniker was in the room when we arrived. She pointed; apparently Iolanthe was in the lavatory. Julian seated himself with the air of someone taking up a strategic position, choosing a chair in the far corner of the room. At that moment Iolanthe entered and catching sight of him stood stock still smiling her soft hesitant smile with all its shyness welling up through the superficial assurance. "Julian at last" she said. "Well!" And walking across to him took both his hands in hers and stood staring down into his eyes with a candour and puzzlement which made him turn quite white. "At last we meet" she said. "At last, Julian!" He cleared his throat as if to make some response, but no words came. She turned triumphantly aside

255

and got back into bed with the help of Henniker. "Henny, let us have tea, shall we?" she said in rather grandiose tones, and the older woman nodded and moved towards the door. Then Julian from the depths of a recovered composure said: "I don't know where to begin, Iolanthe; or even if there is a place to begin, for I think you know everything by now. At any rate every bit as much as I know. Isn't it so?" She frowned and licked her lips. "Not entirely," she said "though I have made some provisional guesses. But now you own me don't you? I wonder what you plan to do with me? I am quite defenceless, Julian. I am just one of your properties now." His nostrils dilated.

His upper lip had gone bluish—like someone in danger of a heart attack. Iolanthe continued in a dreamy voice, almost as if she were talking to herself, recapitulating a private history to fix it more clearly in her own mind. "Yes, you were always there behind us, sapping us, sniping at us from behind the high walls of the company. How cleverly you disposed of Graphos too when you found he was my lover; I mean of course his career. He was very ill of course, that wasn't your fault. And I kept expecting you to appear so that I could perhaps do a deal with you, plead with you, trade my body, even to save my little company, save my career. Nothing. You never did. Sometimes I thought I knew why really; I worked out reasons from what people told me about you—feminine reasons. Were they wrong I wonder Julian?"

The artless blue eyes, inquisitive and chiding, rested fixed on his face. He stirred uncomfortably and said:

"No. You know all the reasons. I don't need to explain at this stage Iolanthe, do I? You haunted me just as much."

He spoke gently enough, but at the same time I felt a sort of fury rising in him; after all, here he was being ticked off by a *dummy* for defections of behaviour towards an all too real (though now dead) Iolanthe! It was very confusing this double image. Moreover he could not lean forward and tapping her wrist say: "That's enough now; do you realise that you are just a clever and valuable little dummy, fabricated by the experts of the firm? You are simply steel and gutta-percha and plastic and nylon, that's all. So kindly hold your tongue." He couldn't do that, so he just sat still looking stubborn, while she went on in the voice of reminiscence. "Yes, when the production company failed, when Graphos died and when my career collapsed and I got ill, I expected some word from you—after all so much of this had been your deliberate design against me. I was puzzled, thought I might find some sympathy, some understanding of my plight. But no, you were out to smash me and take me prisoner. And now you have, Julian. But for a long time I dreamed about you: about how you would appear one day, all of a sudden, without warning. Yes, sitting just where you are now, dressed as you are, and a little tonguetied for the first time in your life by a woman's *love*. You see, part of my fantasy was to imagine that you loved me. Now I know I was right. You do. Poor Julian! I do understand, but when Graphos went out the mechanism rusted, broke, and now I have an empty space where the thing used to live." She gave a short and sad little laugh. "I grew tonguetied."

"Tonguetied" he repeated ruefully, seeming somehow put out of countenance. They looked at each other steadily, but with an extraordinary air of mutual understanding. Then she said: "But not any more somehow" and a renewed cheerfulness flowed into her. "I have half recovered from that period and perhaps so have you. Now there seems to be something else before us—I don't know how to put it, perhaps a friendship? At any rate something unlike anything I have ever known before. Julian, do you feel it too?"

He nodded coldly, critically. His face betrayed no emotion whatsoever at this somewhat extraordinary speech. Then she added calmly, with an air of simplicity, a Q.E.D. air, which was completely disarming, "I don't think I can do without you any more, Julian. It's more than flesh and blood can stand." It was terribly moving, the way she said this.

"Of course," he said softly, greedily. "It's the loneliness. No, you won't have any more of that, I promise you."

She extended her long languid waxen hands and he got up to take them and carry them to his lips with swift precision, yet without any trace of deep feeling. I could see however that the strain of his first interview with Iolanthe was beginning to tell on him as it had on me; he was being slowly flooded by the same unreasonable sensation of gradual suffocation. Just like me. We of course were both conscious

that we were talking to an experimental dummy; but she, unconscious as yet of her own unreality, was at ease and as perfectly sincere (if I can use the word) as . . . well, as only a dummy could be.
What am I saying? It was an extraordinary paradox, for we were
literally worn out by having to act a part while she was fresh as a
daisy. One wanted to laugh and cry at the same time—how well I
understood Julian's desire to be gone! "Now there will be time," said
Iolanthe coolly "all the time in the world, to take a leisurely look at
everything I have missed in my rush through life. Later maybe you
may help me to rebuild my career once more; unless you think I
am too old to act any more."

He shook his head decidedly and said, "First things first; when
you are quite well we shall see."

"But I feel so well already" she said.

"Nevertheless."

At this point Henniker produced the tea and I could see the proconsular eye of Julian fixed upon Iolanthe to admire the excellence
of her tea-time deportment. His alarm had subsided somewhat, the
temperature of his anxiety had dropped a little. Then she added:
"In a way we were well-matched enemies . . . parricide against
infanticide . . . no, that is not the way to say it."

"What a memory you have got" he said bitterly, and she nodded,
taking an imaginary sip of China tea. "Mine is as long as my life,"
she said "but yours is as long as the firm's, Julian."

I was in bliss. A dummy that could forge repartee like this . . .
better, cleverer than a real woman; because less arbitrary, less *real*,
less feminine. And yet, on the other hand, the little note of bitterness
in her voice was very human, very feminine. If she were absolutely
identical with Iolanthe surely she *was* Iolanthe? Obviously we must
spend a bit of time to work out the differences between the real and
the invented; but if there were none? Julian was talking again, softly,
indifferently it seemed: "Well, you would not join the firm so how
could I reach you—for I am more the firm than I am myself in a
manner of speaking; what could I bring to you or offer to you that
did not bear the fingerprints of Merlin's? But you refused all my
offers, you evaded me." He paused to take out a cigar and crackle it
in his fingers; but then he replaced it in his cigar-case with an air of

258

irresolution. Her lip curled as she said with a tinge of contempt, "But now? I am broken and bridled am I not? The firm has swallowed my little company. I am your captive at last, Julian, amn't I?"

At this a sudden little flash lit up both pairs of eyes, a sudden spark of fury, of antagonism, of sexual fury. I had not seen this look on Julian's face before. Then she drawled with her most mischievous air, "I could come to you tonight, Julian, if you wished. Just tell me where and when!" He went deathly white at the insult but he eyed her contemptuously, his eyes glittering like those of a basilisk. He said nothing, and it was obvious that he was not going to say anything. "Just tell me" she repeated, and I thought she took a sort of savage delight in provoking his male pride thus; surely she knew the sad story of Julian—the fate of Abelard? Nevertheless she stayed there staring at him with the same expression of provocation on her face outfacing his silence, trying to discountenance him. He was absolutely still. But now I saved the day by putting in a word or two. "Now. Now. You are under Dr. Marchant's orders Iolanthe. Don't forget it please." It broke the spiteful spell. She pouted adorably and said "I was only teasing, Felix; just to see how far one could go with Julian." But she began to pick at the tassels of the bedcover with long painted nails. I did not particularly care for the note of insolence in her voice: I thought it might be a good moment to make our exit. I announced that I must leave as I had an appointment and Julian immediately elected to come with me; yet he seemed without visible emotion, visible relief. I kissed the warm cheek of my angel, and gave her fine fingers a squeeze. "Until tomorrow" I said, confiding her to the faithful ministrations of Henniker who stood at the foot of the bed smiling tenderly at her; the older woman was by now quite cured of her original fright and dismay. But she had overcome it in the simple fact of *believing* in the new Iolanthe—of *believing her to be real*! By some simple *déclic* of the mind she had abolished the knowledge of Iolanthe's dummyhood and replaced it with a fully conscious belief and acceptance of her as a real woman.

We walked slowly along the gravel paths towards the carpark; Julian was sunk deep in thought, gazing down at his feet. "I suppose you have a set of experiments to subject her to?" he said at last quietly. "Yes. For the time being we are recording her night and day to study the general patterning of the memory-increment apparatus. I propose later to set her back into the Iolanthe picture by letting her meet a few of the people Io knew in real life—people like Dombey, her agent—just to see how capably she works."

"I abolished the mate, you know" said Julian quietly. "I wonder whether it was right or wrong. You say she could make love this creature?" I said I saw no reason why not, she had the organs. "Of course, when she speaks about love and so on, you have to make a sort of mental correction in realising that the words are simply coded into a machine by an echo-master, and in the final analysis simply come out of a metal box."

"I know," he said "it's weird. But she is so word-perfect that one wonders if she couldn't live happily with a member of the human species, as a wife, I mean." The chauffeur opened the door of the car for him but he still stood, shaken to the bottom of his soul by this interview and the possibilities it promised. "We must be careful not to feel too much affection for it" I said. It was easily said, I know. "But *you* are half in love with her already" said Julian, smiling up at me suddenly, and of course he was speaking the truth—I was mad about my own invention, like every inventor is. O yes I was. He went on slowly, thoughtfully. "And what sort of future do you envisage for her, for it? Will she ever be allowed out into the world?"

"Nothing very definite was worked out for her—we didn't know how real she might turn out to seem; she might have been vastly more limited both physically and mentally than she is. The whole operation was done on spec, Julian, you know that. Now I think we must really submit her to extensive testing before letting her increase the range of her activities; we must think about her a bit as one does about a handicapped person, which of course she is, because she is only a machine, a love-machine." I don't know why I used that stupid phrase, it simply popped out. "I see" he said, frowning at the ground. "We can begin by bringing the world to her for a while; then if she satisfies every requirement, if she is fool-proof, we can gradually insinuate her into quotidian reality, so to speak; in the end we might accord her an autonomous life of her own, like any other taxpayer, lover, wife or dog."

He hoisted himself slowly into the car, still sleepy with thought. "I will see her every day with you until I get over that extraordinary feeling of panic" he said; and then very suddenly: "Felix, if we wanted to abolish her it would be an easy matter wouldn't it?" I jumped as if he had stuck a pin in me. "Abolish her?" I cried sharply, and he smiled. "I'm sorry; but one must think of every possible contingency mustn't one?"

"Not that one" I said. "Never that Julian."

"Well, I am in your hands."

Slowly the car wound its way down the leafy roads. I betook myself to the studio to study the schemata that Marchant had worked out for the daily life of Iolanthe in these initial stages. A masseur who did not know she was not real had turned in a most interesting report on her body which made me swell with pride. That at least showed no particular anomalies in the disposition of the muscle schemes; he had found her musculature if anything too firm. He wondered if some predisposition to sclerosis might not be envisaged! No, in every way so far she seemed to be of a mechanical perfection that eluded all criticism. Every word she uttered was also being monitored, and playing through this library of speeches one could find nothing disoriented, nothing out of key. She had a fully grown organ of memory to fall back on as she lived her real life. Marchant had scribbled a note or two about his visits to the patient. She had proved very docile and co-operative. "*Too* damn real for my liking" he added sardonically. "I keep almost forgetting she is an It."

So we embarked thoughtfully and I hope skilfully upon this experiment; but it was hard to shed the feeling of unreality which crept over us as we watched the perfected mimicry of her gestures, heard this highly articulate woman talking, arguing, even singing. It was a good ten days before we let her out of bed, but finally there seemed little reason to deny her the right to walk about her house and garden. Julian was away for part of this time, and I had to visit Geneva for a week. We took it in shifts to attend her levees. Nor did Benedicta react in any particular manner to my absorption in the life of this model—I had not really expected her to; yet her little speech in Athens had filled me with a certain misgiving. I felt that, like the rest of us, she would get used to Iolanthe, conquer an initial repulsion and panic, and come to accept her for what she was—an experiment. But I told her quite candidly what Iolanthe had said about disliking her, and asked her if she would mind waiting a while before risking a meeting with her. In the meantime the daily life of Iolanthe herself was being gradually filled in at the edges by designedly quotidian events. For example, we got hold of her agent and invited him down to see her; now, *despite* the fact that he was fully briefed about the doll, the impact of Iolanthe was so marked and so faithful to the original which he had loved that he passed out cold upon the carpet and had to be revived. He *was* revived, of course, but he was badly shaken. Naturally we explained this away as relief to find her recovered from her illness. We tried as far as possible never to let her doubt the reality of herself—to make her self-conscious in the true sense of the word.

But gradually, inevitably, she began to feel a sense of constraint; after all, she was being pretty closely watched and monitored, and up to now had not been allowed to go beyond the garden fence. The excuse we gave was of course medical. But the minute a patient begins to feel better he or she is tempted to throw good advice to the winds. This aspect of things was a trifle preoccupying; but Henniker was always unobtrusively there to follow her movements. She reported the fact that Iolanthe had asked if she might go down to the village, and had shown some pique when told that Marchant had forbidden it. Later she tackled Marchant himself about it, and I must say I thought the reasons he gave sounded somewhat shallow if not downright shifty. "We are fighting a losing battle" I said. "She has got through all her tests so quickly, I don't see how we can keep her locked up much longer without arousing her suspicions. Indeed it might be a good idea to start letting her out a bit, though of course someone will always have to be with her; she's too valuable to lose, or to let get damaged."

Julian asked to see her alone during this time, and spent many long hours in the house talking to her; I could hear him pacing up and down slowly in her room. Once I heard his normally low voice raised as if in anger; another time I had the illusion that she was shedding tears. But there was nothing much to be done. When I was in Geneva I opened a weekly paper and found a picture of the gambling rooms at Gunters—baccarat in progress; and there to my surprise stood Julian in his dinner jacket, shoulder to shoulder with a bewigged Iolanthe who was watching the play with great interest. As soon as I got back I rang up Julian and he confirmed that he had taken her out for an evening, with Marchant's consent. "I can tell you something new" he said. "She has the devil's own *luck*, computer luck you could call it. We made a packet. Felix, I want to thank you; I feel extremely happy. When do you think she can be declared absolutely autonomous, absolutely free?" I could not really think up an answer to this question. "It raises one of those bogies, Julian, and I think you've heard enough chop-logic about freedom, specially from me. How free will she be? How will her freedom compare with our own imaginary freedom? Goodness, I can't answer you; the whole thing is still in the realms of pure experiment. But why should you ask? Are you in danger of falling in love with my little toy, are you going to ask for her hand in marriage?" Once again I had slipped tactlessly; I felt rather than heard him grinding his teeth, and in a low voice, almost a whisper, he uttered an obscenity. "I'm sorry," I added vaguely "but the question just set me off on a long train of thought. Her precarious freedom against ours . . . but we mustn't start taking her too seriously, Julian." I had the impression that he gave a little groan. The line went dead. And that was all.

But after that gambling outing she seemed to show an increased impatience with constraint, and I began to fear that she might take the law into her own hands. She said to Marchant, "In the long run you can't deny me my freedom forever. I have the right to start to rethink out my career, to rebuild it if I decide I would like to." Then she discovered that one of her teeth had been given a small filling which she could not remember having had placed by her dentist. It was just a passing cloud, so to speak, and she was easily persuaded that her memory had slipped. But she was right; when we had another look at the dentist's jaw diagram we discovered out mistake. "How could I have forgotten," she said "I who live in such terror of dentists? Ah well, my memory must be failing—it's old age, darling Felix, that is what it is."

Ten days later I braked the car violently in the middle of the village; there was Iolanthe walking nonchalantly out of the door of the Gold Swan, lighting up a cigarette. She burst out laughing as she saw my alarmed face. "I couldn't resist" she said. "I gave Henny the slip and trotted down for a whisky." Like the real Iolanthe, who had had so much trouble from her public, she had taken to a brown wig which completely transformed her face. In this way no fans would pester her. I didn't know what to say; it seemed ridiculous to chide her. After all there was nothing intrinsically dangerous or harmful in what she had done—it was just an agreeable escapade for her. But it made me think. I had a long confabulation with Marchant. We wondered perhaps whether it might be time to move her into a large hotel, say, where there would be plenty of movement, plenty of life around her. Or whether we should buy her a dog—no, but like the real Iolanthe she wasn't keen on dogs because of the infernal quarantine restrictions in Britain. Well then, what?

"Felix," she said "I've had a strange feeling growing up inside me that I must change everything—make a break for liberty." This is what I had been fearing; but she went on in a low infinitely touching tone: "The awful thing is that the inevitable has happened—I always knew it would." She paused, and her beautiful eyes filled with tears. She put her hand on my arm and said, "My dear friend, the worst that could happen—I have fallen in love with Julian. That is what frightens me so much. I was always ferociously independent, as you know. I feel now that I mustn't sink any deeper into this adoration. I must, so to speak, negotiate from a position of strength. But he won't help to set me free; he wants me bound and gagged, and at his mercy."

She walked slowly up and down the room with her hands in her armpits, thinking. On the table lay a fat bundle of five-pound notes and a specimen signature-card form such as bank managers present when one opens an account. She caught my gaze upon it and smiled. "I was going to open an account but I've changed my mind. It's better to have the cash in hand. Funny thing is that when I'm with Julian, when he bets for me, I turn tremendously lucky. Did he tell you? We won a fortune." She groped for her slippers and sat down in a chair, frowning and preoccupied. "You see," she said at last "I must envisage some way of remaining myself, of not being engulfed; I've played snakes and ladders with the firm long enough—and at the moment I am snaked out, so to speak, sent to the very bottom of the board. But I can't stay there; so long as I have health enough and will enough I must try and climb. Unfortunately this is not what Julian wants. It makes him angry. Do you know he even insulted me? He called me 'the parody of a woman', said I wasn't real, that I had a heart of steel wool . . . . That sort of thing has never been in Julian's repertoire has it? Well, it just goes to show that we are both under some strain. Felix, something's got to change to make it all right between us." O! God!

Naturally all this talk made me feel ineffectual and distracted, for I could not image any practical changes in her "life" which might meet with these inherited feelings—feelings which belonged to the dead woman whose mind and body he had had foisted upon her in so Faustian a fashion. "But what?" I said vaguely, noting with another part of my mind that her signature was perfect—I mean that it was unmistakably Iolanthe's handwriting. No professional forger could have produced such a perfect copy. "Let's not do *anything* impetuous" I said in the feebly admonishing tone which would be bound, I knew, to irritate her, to fill her with impatience "until you are quite clear of Dr. Marchant. Then we'll really go over the whole position. By that time perhaps Julian will have thought of something; he may invite you away on the yacht, he may take you to the villa in Ischia or Baalbek. Don't be too impatient and hasty, that is all I beg."

It was all too easily said, and secretly I rather echoed in my heart the impatient sign that she gave now as she sat, looking into my eyes like some distraught jungle-cat—a cheetah, perhaps. Nor did I see really why she should not be allowed to travel about a bit provided she always came back. Of course it would mean that she was out of the range of our monitors, and it was Marchant's expressed intention to do some depth-findings in the memory-code of the doll's "mind"—laborious and perhaps as unfruitful (for the most part) as Nash's depth-analysis which kept people nailed to the horsehair sofa for years on end. She was talking again. "I have been very shaken these last weeks by the fact that Julian is so exactly what I knew, dreamed, felt, he would be. It gives me a strange feeling of unreality—as if he were an artificial man, constructed by my own mind, by my dreams or something. . . . When he speaks I feel I am listening to someone who is word-perfect reciting a part. It is very queer. But Felix, what a strange mind he has; what extraordinary passions—yet all locked up in steel strong-boxes inside his mind. He attracts and scares me at the same time." Naturally this did not surprise me; I knew enough about him at first and second hand to gauge the impact of a character like his upon her. The real Iolanthe would not have been any different, of this I was sure. Were they not as alike as two signatures, the dummy and the dead memory?

"He has offered to let me see all my old film successes again—there's a projection room apparently in the labs. But that also scares me a little bit; at the moment the mirror seems to console me on the score of beauty—perhaps I should say still flatter? But I don't really know if I am past it all, films, or whether there might be just a glimmer of chance about recovering my position. Have you any ideas on the subject?" I had none, naturally enough. If she were sufficiently lifelike to live in Claridge's, surely she could act in front of the camera? What I *couldn't* say was: "That would raise a capital problem for us—you see, you were once a world-famous screen star, your face was known to the whole world. But you *died*! It would take some explaining if you reappeared and competed for the crown all over again. You see, darling, it would put us in the jam of having to find an excuse for your being here. If we told the world you were a dummy you would find out the truth yourself and it would destroy your confidence in yourself, and in the esteem of the world. In fact, you might very well commit suicide or take to drugs—or adopt any other conventional form of self-abasement. In some ways, Io, you are all too human, despite the fine firm construction of you; you are still as affectively mentally fragile as any human counterpart." All this I said in my own mind. "What are you mumbling about?" said Iolanthe peevishly. "Reciting the creed?" I blinked bashfully and stood up. It wasn't far off the mark.

As a matter of fact a muddled series of quotations had been bubbling about in my mind, among which was "I am the resurrection and the life, saith the Lord God." Where that came from I have no idea, I am not well up in Holy Writ. And then again a line—"freedom, freedom, prison of the free"— from the best of our modern poets.* But none of this provided a coherent frame of reference upon which we could base a discussion of her preoccupations. I had a feeling that everything was beginning to slip a bit; the feeling of ineffectuality grew and grew. I finished my drink and said that perhaps I ought to be going. "So you can't think of anything?" she said with a touch of grimness. "If of course I am seriously ill and likely to die soon, and if you are simply keeping the truth from me. . . ." It might have offered a way out but in my naïve way I omitted to take the chance. "Far from it," I said "you are healthier than you have ever been."

I took my leave, kissing her softly upon her impatient forehead; and I was glad to do so, in order to think things over a bit in the quietness of the cottage.

In view of this steady development towards some attempt to claim a margin of freedom for herself, I was not unduly surprised to find her sitting in the garden one morning in a bathing costume, half asleep in a deck chair, and radiating a high good humour. She chuckled with pleasure as she said: "Henniker is not on speaking terms with me. She is *furious*, Felix, and swears she will report me to you and Dr. Marchant. I ask you, *report*; I was astonished by the choice of a word, it belongs to prisons or girls' schools. And all just because I spent half the day in London without telling her. I knew she wouldn't let me go—why should I tell her? And whose permission should I have sought? Yours?" As a matter of fact, yes; she should have told somebody. But I said nothing. She looked at me quizzically, uncertain whether to scold me or to remain aggrieved, defensive. "I had to see this new film of Escroz. He is one of my oldest friends. So I went. The bus service is very convenient. And I was back by seven. I've sent him a telegram to tell him I am well again. I'd like to see him if he could get down here." I made a mental note of this; Escroz had been at the funeral of the real Iolanthe, and may not have realised that she was once more in the land of the living so to speak. "How was it?" I said, more to conceal my sense of misgiving than anything else. "Not too strong," she said "but

* Lawrence Durrell.

267

some lovely camera work as usual. He's marvellous on atmosphere."

I coughed. "I've had a word with Dr. Marchant," I said "and we were wondering whether you would not be happier in a hotel like Claridge's or the Dorchester, with a bit of life and movement around you; you could finish all your tests there for a while and at least get about, shop, and so on." She was suddenly contrite. She put a hand on my arm. "I'm not trying to be a trouble, Felix," she said. "It's just that everything is going so slowly and my health seems wonderful; and I have been made a bit impatient by these meetings with Julian. He is coming back from New York on Saturday. That's all. A very nominal freedom would satisfy me and cure my boredom for the present; later of course I shall decide what I will and won't do, naturally." I did not quite know whether to like or dislike the tone of this last sentence. "You were always an impatient soul" I said, and she nodded humbly. Then she produced something which, considering the terms of reference, sounded out of character. "Last night I hardly slept a wink, and had to take a sleeping tablet or two. I hope it isn't a return of the old migraine I had in Athens long ago. What a *supplice*." Of course it *was* part of the old memory-code coming back, and from that point of view unexceptionable; nevertheless it hinted at strain of some kind. She had taken a very strong dose of M.I.S.T.[2] I presumed the taking was an imaginary act, for the tablet could not by any conceivable manner of means have had any effect on her body as it was then constituted. "Did you sleep at last?" She nodded. "But I had palpitations and nausea and so on."

Beside her on the lawn lay a long gunny sack full of her fan-mail. (I had a whole department busy writing nothing else; they were part of our verisimilitude-team, as we called them, filling in and reviving the quotidian life of the Ur-Iolanthe.) The letters were of course all fabrications; any answers that she wrote back to these imaginary fans came straight back to us for analysis. Henniker spent a part of every evening taking letters destined for fans and sending out signed photographs and so on. All this part of her life worked impeccably so far, it seemed. A mountain of glossy screen-stills lay neatly stacked on the rack above her writing desk with its many pictures of leading men in silver frames. There was one empty photograph-frame among them which I knew was going to be destined for a picture of Julian (she had asked for one and he had promised to have one sent to her). But which Julian—that was rather the point? Yes, which?

*　　*　　*　　*　　*

You will appreciate that I am simply recording all this matter of fact as I can for the record—both personal and scientific, I suppose. I don't remember being particularly surprised by the *dénouement* when it started to work out—I mean the sudden fugue and disappearance of Iolanthe; but just about the same time other events started to impact themselves so that when I think back upon this period I see a succession of juxtaposed images rather than a straight chronology of events. But the whole thing led up in a steady series of small surprises to St. Paul's. Benedicta is sitting beside me following the recording; from time to time I switch off to debate a date or an event with her. It's taken a hell of a while, and in this summary I am of course dealing with quite a long extent of serial time. Since Iolanthe disappeared, of course, all our monitoring preoccupations were so much wasted machine-food. Marchant and I, Julian and Benedicta, we seemed to spend all our time on the phone; and every time it rang it was something to do with her, some polite hint, or a tip-off from a friend.

But her disappearance was very quietly and confidently planned; Henniker woke up at early light to find herself pinioned to the bed with a length of stout cord. Skilfully, too, for she could not free herself and had to wait for Marchant's regular morning visit. Iolanthe was walking about the room chuckling in a rather sinister, disoriented way, and packing two of her pigskin suitcases with the most indispensable articles of wear. Clothes, wigs, personal notepaper, etc. etc. She was deaf to the protestations of Henniker who by now was almost beside herself with fury and anxiety. She tried to get her to say where she was going, but the busy figure would not even turn its head, let alone answer. She packed with miraculous speed and despatch, still making this queer crepitation. Henniker gritted her teeth and renewed her appeals. She wondered whether to scream for help—but who would have heard her at such an hour and in such a place? Useless! Once the task was complete Iolanthe drew the curtains and looked out, as if expecting someone, and the thought did cross Henniker's mind that perhaps Julian might be abducting her. The clock struck. Quickly, like a master cracksman after a night's work on a safe, Iolanthe made herself a cup of tea and drank it in imaginary fashion. She came and stood before the pinioned figure of her profoundest human friend, slowly sipping and staring down into her eyes, saying nothing, sunk apparently in the profoundest reflection. Then there came the sound of a car. Iolanthe was shaken by little sobs, tiny youthful little sobs, so separate, so painful. Nor could Henniker now restrain her own tears. "Iolanthe, don't leave me." But the mechanical maenad was already humping the two large suitcases to the door, and thence down the garden path to the car. Later we found that she had simply ordered the village taxi to come for her and take her into the town where she caught the morning train to London. That was that. It may well be imagined that this event threw us all into a frightful disarray. Marchant first flew into the most terrible rage and threw equipment about, and then sat down on a stool and cried. It was curious what we had come to feel for this creation; one felt a little as if one's heart were broken.

Julian appeared looking as if he were fresh from hell. An urgent conference was held; it was first necessary to try and work out the places she might visit, the people she might call on. But this was a task of the greatest complexity; Iolanthe was a citizen of the world. Besides, nothing could have prevented her from taking a plane to Paris or Rio—she even had Iolanthe's old passport. It was necessary to invoke the aid of the police but on what terms? Could we ask them to watch the ports and air terminals by saying that she was wanted for some crime—larceny perhaps? An excuse must be found so that the law could weigh in and help us trace her. "She must be brought back alive and undamaged" Marchant kept repeating, somewhat absurdly I thought. Alive! The police when we finally alerted them were kindly, understanding and very efficient; and we did have a collection of pictures of Io in her various wigs. But it took a long time to try and formulate a story which might not seem too preposterous; somehow one didn't dare to talk about a dummy which was at large. Yet there was hope; between the firm itself and the police force we managed to throw out a fairly effective net into which, with any luck, she might stray.

Somewhere in the real world, freed from the dead sanctions of science, strayed the new Iolanthe, perfectly equipped to mix into the background of people and events without raising the smallest suspicion that she was not as others were. But it was a blow, and there was no disguising it; moreover until we were sure of her whereabouts, or indeed of her fate, we had no stomach for anything else; we had concentrated so deeply upon her that all other work of the firm seemed suddenly stale, profitless.

She went to see her agent who reported the fact at once to Julian; but though we tried we could not trace her. However it proved that she had been in the London area and was still travelling about incognito in a wig—apparently fully aware that if her fans recognised her she risked being compromised with us. She was clever and agile. We could not watch all the cinemas and all the theatres, but we managed to keep an eye on some of them, and in particular those where likely films or plays were being put on. She was signalled as coming out of the Duchess one night; but if it were she, she slipped through the net once more. Other sightings were reported from various parts of the country now, as if she were moving about fairly quickly. Harrogate was a likely one—she had always liked Harrogate. But again we were too late. One day she even walked into the firm, though nobody saw her, and left a note on Julian's desk.

He seemed disinclined to let anyone see it, and we did not press him; but it contained no news of her whereabouts. It was simply about their relationship—so much he vouchsafed in a low voice. I must say that since her disappearance Julian seemed to have aged very much; he walked with a stoop, his hair seemed whiter, and his suave swarthy features appeared more deeply lined; this touched something profound in Benedicta, and her sympathy for his . . .

well, his plight . . . made her demonstrate a new warmth and affection for which he seemed deeply grateful.

Ipswich, Harrow, Pinewood: these visitations were all characterised by the same deftness, the same unerring choice of time; the same cool disappearance. There seemed nothing to be done. Perhaps we would never find her again; she had so perfectly integrated with reality, one supposed, that there was hardly any need. Was there nothing to be done, was there nothing which might lure her back? Julian! He had been told to write to her, but she gave no address, so he was constrained to imagine that she meant him to put a notice in *The Times* which he dutifully did, imploring her to come back to him. But she contented herself with ringing him up once from Dover to say that she was going to Paris. That she was very happy. That she missed him, and all of us. That she would come and see us all after she had experienced a number of unspecified events which were of great importance to her. She visited a producer in Paris for a moment, and telephoned to Nury the film star, who thought she was a madwoman impersonating the other Iolanthe. By the time we heard of this she had vanished again.

Then one evening, one dark and rainy evening I found myself in Chatham, in a dockside street, walking back from some appointment or other in the harbourmaster's office. A sordid drizzly evening with the bluish street lamps casting a greasy glow in the darkness like disembodied heads. I was picking my way through the slime and wet of the broken pavements when the swing doors of a pub flew open and a woman walked out on the arm of a young sailor; in the bar of light thrown by the open door I saw them turn, and I was at once struck by some small singularity of pose in the way the woman turned her head. "Iolanthe!" I gasped with delight, with ecstasy I might say; for when she turned her head I saw that it was indeed she. But she screwed up her face into a vile simian expression and pretended not to recognise me. I advanced towards her in my usual naïve and ineffectual way—feeling tolerably sure that when she recognised me she would at least greet me. What to do? Somehow I must try and capture her, make her see reason; perhaps if we had a talk. . . . I took off my dark hat so that she might recognise me the more easily. But still she wore this common expression, and then in broad cockney she said: "What the 'ell do you want, sonny? I don't know you." The impersonation was so good that for a moment I almost doubted; she had blacked out a front tooth which gave her whole face a gap-toothed lopsided look. I hesitated and made as if to put my hand upon her arm; whereupon she cried again in this baroque cockney accent, "Lemme go, will yer?" And the young sailor turned all gallant and stepped in between us to deliver a blow which hit me between the eyes and knocked me flying. They walked on unhurriedly, arm in arm; at the end of the street she paused under a street lamp to look back and give a coarse little laugh. Then they turned the corner and disappeared from view. I scrambled together all the papers which had flown out of my briefcase on to the pavement, and nursing my jaw followed them. But by the time I reached the corner they had vanished. I did not tell Julian about this unsuccessful encounter, I don't know why; but yes I do. In the afternoon paper of the following day I came across an item which reported the discovery of the body of a young sailor in Chatham; there was nothing very unusual about it except that it was standing up in a doorway. But these things happen almost everywhere, and all the time.

Then late at night Julian suddenly appeared at the cottage, holding in his hand the buff telegraph form which announced the death of Jocas. We sat for a long time in complete silence, staring in the fire. I don't know what hopeless regrets, what formless memories, stirred in the mind of Julian, but for me it was as if we were looking down the long curving vistas of the Turkish capital towards the origins of Merlin's—towards the blue waters of the gulf, the masts, the walls, the coloured kites floating and tugging against the sky. I was reminded of someone saying something about each death marking a whole epoch in one's life. Was it Benedicta or Hippolyta? So Jocas had gone! The thought had a heavy resonance; even when one had forgotten his existence or had passed months without consciously thinking about him, he had always somehow been there, a swarthy presence that represented the weird complex of colours and sounds which made up the patchwork quilt of the Eastern Mediterranean. An old benign spider, sitting at the centre of the Merlin web. How pale Julian looked, and suddenly how vulnerable! "Zeno was out in his prediction, but only by a couple of months" he said with a kind of melancholy zealous calm. "Things are changing around us" he added. "And all this business about Iolanthe—that has been a blow, I don't deny."

"Has she written again?"

He shook his head slowly and said softly, "Neither has she phoned me. Goodness knows what has become of her." Benedicta said suddenly, surprisingly, "She has been here, you know. I was away yesterday, and Baynes says that she came in and said she would wait for me to come home. He went up to the house to try and tell someone, to try and phone to Felix; but when he came back she had vanished. She may have got into a sudden panic at the sound of a car, as it seems that Nash drove up to the house about that time."

"But how can you be sure it was she?" Benedicta crossed the room to the cocktail cabinet and extracted from it a woman's handbag—a rather *chic* new handbag; she turned it out before us on the carpet, and among the visiting cards and other trivia which identified the visitant was something which gave us all a start. It was a small pearl-handled revolver. I thought at first it was a stage prop, but no. It was a real weapon and was fully loaded. We looked at each other with surprise, perhaps with consternation. "What on earth could that mean?" said Julian at last. "Who could she be afraid of?" But I had another idea. "Who could she hate enough to . . . ?" For the first time we felt that Iolanthe was starting to behave right out of character. It was late when we went to bed that night, all of us very preoccupied by these mysteries.

VII

Boom-treacle . . . Boom-treacle . . . . The big bell was punctuating the ruminations of the organ which succeeded in weaving an almost tangible curtain of sound across the great doors of the western face. *Om mane padme boom.* The spendthrift monotony of the Gothic soul trying to realise itself, to anchor itself in the infinity of darkness created by the ample dome. Clock of ages cleft for me, let me in thy tick reside. The cars and buses had disgorged their freight of workers—practically the whole of Merlin's London staff had turned up. In my own case I had had a drink or two—I must admit it— which gave me, according to Benedicta, an air of melancholy sincerity. It was not perhaps the time or place to feel gay, with the thoughts of Jocas on the edges of the mind. So few of us had seen him. But I could now, and very clearly. I wondered what thoughts hovered like dragonflies above the now placid surface of Benedicta's mind. This was what he had wanted, and here we all were full of the fragile self-deluding hope that somewhere he might be listening to us, perhaps smiling under the mask of gold. Here in this old petrifact which crowned London town. The organ growled and prowled about among the shadows, about the narrow fallopia of the naves, dull and repetitive as the Saturnalia of Macrobius. Long long ago, somewhere in Polis Benedicta recited to me some children's verses about the sound of bells—a touching onomatopoeia which came back now to me under the hammer strokes of the heavy clapper. The small bells in Turkey exclaim *Evlen dirralim* over and over again, while the big ones intone on a slower note *Soordan, Boordan, Boolaloum.*

What was he dreaming about, old Jocas? Surely not about this rainswept London where the fat blue pigeons ruffled and crooned about the statue of Queen Anne? No, but of the islands of Polis, of Marmara threaded through by its fishy migrations, of Smyrna, of

277

the famous wharves stacked high with merchandise. Of the slow plains with their black herds of goats and horses and fat-tailed sheep. In fields and arbours where the jackals come out by moonlight to scavenge the muscat grapes; or in glass-penned coffee houses suspended over flowing water where the hubble-bubbles clear their throats in rose water. . . . Something like that I suppose. Well, here I was at last in St. Paul's reflecting on the vehemence of great art and regretting that Caradoc had missed his plane and stayed behind in Turkey.

I had bought a shilling guide to the monument and put it inside a prayer-book, fearing a long sermon. Thus in the intervals of standing up and sitting down I was able to inform myself (I imitated Caradoc's voice in my mind) that the nave is narrow (forty-one feet), while the exterior length of the church (without the steps) is five hundred and fifteen feet, and the height of the church to the top of the Dome approaches three hundred feet. Doubtless all this was of the utmost esoteric significance, if only I could grasp it. A hundred feet above our heads was the Whispering Gallery, and above it again the gamboge cartoons of Paul basking in the white light of twenty-four windows of clear untinted glass. Characteristically in this house of Paul, this Paulhaus of ours, there was no Lady Chapel. Well, Felix whispered an irreverent prayer, touching elbows with his pale girl in black: "O Lord, deliver us from the primacy of the Mobego whose genetic silhouette is the Firm, and its closed system. Suffer us to wander like rational men in the fair psyche-haunted fields of Epicurus, inhabiting our own fair bodies. If you can't do this, Lord, you should say so clearly and resign."

Somewhere about now the terrible thing began to happen. Julian was quite a way up front flanked by numb-looking members of the senior boardroom. Though the service was in progress the broad side aisles of the church were still full of Dutch and German tourists, buying postcards and making the sort of noise that people only manage to make when they are trying to be respectfully quiet. How everything echoed, every scrape of shoe or thwack of hassock! I was in my usual bemused dream when Benedicta prodded me with her elbow and said in a shocked whisper, "Look over there. Isn't that her?" At the far end of the aisle a tall girl was just turning away from the postcard stall having purchased some sort of souvenir; she was hemmed in by the press of tourists which clogged all movement, and for a moment she disappeared from view so that I could not get a clear look at her. Then, as the shuffling crowd moved forward she reappeared once more and I saw that it was indeed she, my one and only Iolanthe; yet somehow subtly transformed. She looked flushed, as if she had been drinking, or had had some strange inner revelation. Her wig wasn't quite snug, and looked badly in need of cleaning, as indeed did her whole person. The heels of her shoes were worn down to stumps. A torn raincoat. There was a small gash in her left calf which had been mended with a piece of surgical tape. She limped.

For a long moment I stood frozen into a statue of surprise, and then I started out in her direction; and as I did so I saw another figure detach itself from the front pews and start to glide towards her, as cautiously as a child trying to catch a rare butterfly. Julian had seen her! We were still quite a way off when all of a sudden she turned her eyes (they seemed to blaze with a fierce and somewhat distraught glare) upon the congregation. It was her turn to feel surprised—for the whole of Merlin's was there! How common she looked now, like some down-at-heel whore; her features had gone drawn and ugly. But recognition was swift. She started so sharply that she dropped her handbag. In a flash she retrieved it and tried to struggle back into the crowd, to regain the west door; it was pure panic, for we were moving with relative freedom while she was clogged in the mass of visitors. Baffled in her attempt to penetrate the solid mass and thus gain the street, she suddenly changed her tack, and tried to lose herself in the crowd ahead of her—the crowd which was trickling forward into the church. Here there was less resistance and she was able to get herself pushed and shoved forward. But we were now close behind her, and her desperation was obvious from the way she looked this way and that, hunting for an escape route. "Iolanthe" I hissed in a bloodcurdling stage-whisper but she did not turn round; she simply burrowed more deeply into the sheltering crowd. Julian was ahead of me, crouching like a wrestler as he pushed and shoved his way towards her. We were both expelled at the end of the aisle, like cartridges from a gun, by the sheer press of human bodies. And here to our dismay we lost her to view. A moment of despair held us motionless and then Julian gave a little cry and said: "Up there Felix." She had darted up the spiral stairway in the south side. We could hear her panting as we started after her. Everything began to get blurred in my mind now; what, after all, were we going to do, pinion her? I don't believe Julian had really thought about it; he just wanted to grab hold of her and never let her go . . . . We heard the footsteps running across the gallery of the south triforium. We galloped after her, panting, dishevelled, incoherent—and so up into the famous Whispering Gallery which my guide had just told me was a hundred feet from the floor of the church; if you stand where we now stood, glaring hungrily at her, panting, pale as hunters, you can hear with perfect clarity the whisper of someone opposite you 107 feet away. . . . But she had come here to hide, not to whisper; nevertheless she was whispering now, talking to herself under her breath in the most affecting way. I heard: "O please God don't let them get me. Don't let them take me back. I'll do anything, anything." It was bloodcurdling this little whisper. She did not address a word to us as we stood there trying to catch our breath. It was to herself she was whispering; and in the midst of the whispered appeals came little clicks like sobs out of focus, and little clucks like a tiny chick. There was no need for us to concert our plan—the design of the gallery made it automatic. Julian went one way round, while I took the other; there was, at last, no escape for poor Iolanthe. But now her rage and despair had once more transformed her features into those of some sick demon let loose from the lower floors of the Inferno. Now at last she began to gabble and click and whistle at us, to deride us, to defy us. Never have I heard on the lips of a woman such obscenities as she uttered now. Julian was faster than I, and she spat and spat again into his white face as he approached her with the expression of a sleepwalker. Indeed, we both felt caught up in some waking nightmare so unreal did it seem. Below the leather-bound booming and crooning made an almost solid sea of sound, washing back and forth; above the bright white light illuminated the cartoons in *grisaille* which pointed up the main events in the life of Paul. And here we were on this echoing catwalk, holding on to the low golden balustrade in order to grapple with a raging steel maenad. "Iolanthe!" I cried in despair as I approached.

Julian had reached her now and they began to reel and struggle like drunkards. And now, just as I came up, the horrible thing happened. She gave a sudden leap like a high-tined stag over the balustrade; in a flash Julian had caught at her frock and held it, himself hanging over the rail. For what seemed a hundred years they hung thus like some human snail, and then the cloth began to tear. Julian made a desperate grab to increase his purchase, but in vain. They fell together into the echoing nave; in a wild and shattering moment of vision I saw them flatten out like arrows as they fell. But the scream I uttered deafened me to the noise of the crash as they hit the marble floor with its black brooding hexagonal stone. Hardly knowing what I was doing I lurched back across the gallery and down the spiral stairway. Like the rings made by a stone in water the impact of their fall had deflected the crowd. From the corner of my eye I thought I had seen something small and white fly from Julian's body as it hit the floor; strange how in moments of utter panic some small observation gets registered with the utmost fidelity. I could not see the body of Julian, there was a crowd round it; but I crossed to the pew and verified that the white object had indeed skimmed there. I picked it up. It was the little white rabbit's paw he always carried on him—the gambler's mascot.

But if I could not get to Julian Iolanthe presented no such problem; she had, so to speak, cleared her own space. At this moment, this very moment, she was slowly turning on her axis and making a low humming sound. Sometimes when a motor bike falls on its side with its engine still running it turns in an arc in just this manner. I felt the tears rise in my eyes. Everyone was there, the confusion was raging like a cataract: Baum, Marchant, Benedicta, Banubula— all shaken out of their wits, white with surprise and horror. But it was really Iolanthe who had broken my heart, as I had hers. And the danger now was that she was "live", could electrocute someone. I suppose I should have used a thermal lance, but all we could raise was a boy scout's sheath knife. "Felix, for Godsake *careful!*" shouted Marchant above the din of voices, but somehow I didn't care. I crawled into the magic circle she was tracing with that lovely

281

body of hers, and plunged my knife into her throat. I knew just where, in order to stop the whole works. And that is the story of the Fall, and how I slew my darling more in sorrow than in anger, more in sickness than in health. Iolanthe! Benedicta cried, "Felix. Don't cry like that", in a voice of anguish; but what's a poor inventor to do?

*   *   *   *   *

The days pass.

"I, Felix Charlock, bound in mind and body!" You will see now why I had to bring all this up to date, in order to straighten the record—for now the whole responsibility of the firm has fallen on my shoulders. These last weeks have been full of boardroom conferences, votes of confidence, resolutions, and so on. I have not hesitated to shoulder the burden for the vanished Julian and Jocas. Outwardly nothing much has changed—or else I went through everything in a sort of dream. Baum fed the press some story of an advertising firm with a dummy, and successfully accounted for the accident, which satisfied the law. When Julian's will was proved we found that he had agreed to let his body be taken to Polis to share the family mausoleum—probably the only concession he had ever made in his life to Jocas.

For the rest, we have come to a great decision, Benedicta and I; it will not be hard to guess that the prophecy of Zeno has been occupying me, preoccupying me very much. Indeed I now feel it less as a prophecy than as a sort of command, from myself to myself, so to speak. I have hardly had to mention it to my wife, she knows full well what I am planning. The microfilm archives which house all our contracts—I have had a careful look at the small building. Fortunately all the stock is on nitro-cellulose film, so highly inflammable that a single time-pencil should be enough to set it off. This is a relief—I feared that we had transferred it to some new acetate which might be hard to dispose of. Marchant is in full agreement with me. The job is an easy one. It should burn fine in the archive vaults with their 118 degrees controlled temperature. I feel tremendously calm and composed, very much master of myself.

We are already in the big house and preparing for Christmas; I have chosen Xmas Eve for the send-up. I have explained carefully to our guests that the fire will be lit while they are at dinner. The first reactions should come in within a day or so. The only one who has shown alarm is Baum who said "Either everything will disintegrate, the Firm will begin to dissolve; or else nothing, Mr. Felix, absolutely nothing. People will be afraid to take advantage of the fact that they have no contractual written obligations. They might stay put from funk or. . . ." So it will be either/or once again; it will be now or never.

I have been working all day and am enormously weary. Benedicta has had fires lit in the big ballroom where once she shattered all the mirrors. It has been transformed now into rather an elegant room. It is full of flowers. There is some fine black jazz playing and we have been dancing, dancing in complete happiness and accord. And we will keep on this way, dancing and dancing, even though Rome burn.

THE END

POSTFACE

Dear C.-M. V.,

Well, here it is, the second volume I promised you. As always I have tried to move from the preposterous to the sublime! It was you who said once that all my novels were inquests with open verdicts. This was true. But in this one I have tried to play about with the notion of culture—what is it? The provenance of the ideas will be familiar to you. It's a sort of novel-libretto based on the preface to *The Decline of the West*. Freud is there too, very much there. I remember too that you remarked once about Spengler "He's not pessimistic at all. He is a realist, that is all." Well in its way this novel in two parts tries to take a culture-reading merely. Of course the poetic game is to try and put a lid on a box with no sides. But when you go on deck, for example, to find that the ship is out of sight of land you are pleased to see a map in the chart-room with a flag in it, stuck there by an invisible hand. It marks your position. By intention this is such a flag.

For the rest, the form presents no singularities. A two-part novel of an oldfashioned sort; perhaps you might say an Ur-novel. Nor do the epigraphs present any mystery. It's always now or never—since we are human and enjoy the fatality of choice. Indeed the moment of choice is always now. For the rest, the fabled two is the human couple, but it is also the basic brick out of which our culture is constructed—mathematics, measure, motion, poetry. And so cheers,

ever thine

LD

P.S. To Ur is human to forgive divine.